MAD WORLD

A MYSTIC BEACH FANTASY ROCKSTAR ROMANCE

AISLINN ARCHER

MYSTIC BEACH PRESS

Contents

Content Warning

A content review for these books, and others in the series, is available on the author's website at AislinnArcher.com. Some of the content of these stories may be disturbing to some readers. If you have any concerns about whether you might find the content of this work disturbing, please take a few moments to check the content review on the website and do not read if you think you might find any of the content disturbing. The recommended reading age for this work is 18 or older.

For Mom,
who keeps reading my books
even after promising not to.

Prologue
Dream Girl

Rhys
Six months ago

S he smiles sweetly at me, and it's like the sun just came out from behind a cloud. Warm and summer-clear, blue skies. Blue like her eyes.

Well, no — her eyes aren't summer-sky blue. They're darker, like when the heat and humidity boils up and there's a storm on the horizon. But I love storms, too. They're exhilarating. Clear skies for jumping out of a plane or climbing a rock face, but there's nothing like a late afternoon thunderstorm to energize a session on my kit. The rumble of thunder in the distance mirrored in my floor tom, the crash of lighting replicated in a cymbal, the boom of a close strike in my kick drum...

"Rhys! For feck's sake! Stop kicking the feckin' bunk! I'm feckin' tryin' to sleep here!"

"Sorry, Kier!"

Oops.

But it's not the first time I've woken up Kieran or one of my other aMUSEd bandmates by drumming in my sleep. At six-foot-four, I barely fit in the bunks on our tour bus, so there isn't a lot of leeway for my perpetually tapping feet before I'm kicking the partition between the bunks instead of my kick drum.

We've been on the road for a year, touring the world with our third album, and I think everybody's patience for close quarters is wearing thin.

It's kind of like sharing a single bedroom with your five brothers, including the cranky egocentric quarterback. That would be Declan, our lead singer. Kier — we're kind of like twins, only totally different, since he's quiet, and a guitar player. And Irish. And I'm not any of those things, in spite of my hair color. Dave, our bassist, is the brainy brother. (Really — he's Declan's actual brother.) Hunter, he's like the king of the misfits — that one guy in the group of guys who don't fit in who manages actually to make that work for him. I think maybe it's the guitar. And then there's Alex... Well, he's more of a mom than a brother. He tries to keep us in line, and then smacks us on the back of the head when we get out of it. OK — that's mostly me. My attention span isn't great, so I tend to lose track of where the line even is.

Where was I?

Oh, right. Life on a tour bus.

It's actually pretty fun most of the time. Playing a new city every night, crowds cheering the moment we hit the stage, losing myself in the beat while the crowd moves in time. And, after the show, meeting all the fans. Girls mostly. I mean, usually I prefer to stumble across a sweet, pretty waitress when we stop for a meal, but Kier decided he hates wingman duty, so I've been defaulting to groupies. Well, I had been. Lately...

Did I mention I've been dreaming about the same girl for months now? Sweet, smart... and those eyes... just magical. Really — how can any real-life girl hold a candle to that? So, no — I haven't been indulging myself in the groupies either. It's been me and my right hand for longer than I care to remember, and that's less fun on a tour bus than you might think.

If only there was...

Is that Hunt playing guitar? He hasn't written a new song in years. I like this one, whoever's playing it. But Kier's trying to sleep, so...

Wow, all of a sudden I'm sleepy again.

But seriously, if only there was a better way for guys to...

Four hours later

"**G**uys! Guys! I've got it! This is going to change every-thing!"

There's a round of inhales and slow exhales, and then a lot of silence. Declan rolls his eyes.

"What's going to change everything this time, Rhys?" Alex asks, with exaggerated patience.

"The Cock Sock!"

There's some moaning, which seems almost appropriate, until Dave just gets up from the table and walks back toward his bunk.

"No? You're not even going to ask me what it does?"

"Well, you've already pitched us on the Rhys sock-puppet, so I'm guessing this a sock, for your cock," Hunter says, continuing tuning his guitar from his spot on the couch.

"Yes! Exactly!"

The guys exchange a look.

"You don't get it?"

"Get what, Rhys? The Red Hot Chili Peppers have already done the sock-as-sole-clothing-item thing. Us doing it would be unoriginal, not to mention likely illegal in most venues."

"No! No, it's not sock as clothing! It's new-and-improved sock-as-masturbatory aid!"

Now the moaning has turned into groaning.

"Does no one get this? This is a breakthrough for lonely guys!"

"Guys have been jacking off into their socks since socks were invented, Rhys! You didn't invent that!" Alex says.

"No — I've invented a better sock! One that is designed for the purpose — lined with fabric that's designed to mimic the feel of a tongue, or a girl's hand, or—"

"We get the picture," Alex says.

"You could choose your color, size and preferred texture, and you could put it in the microwave or the dryer to warm it up. And it would be designed to be easy to clean, resistant to stains..."

"That's actually not a bad idea," Declan says. "Not that I'd ever need it, what with so many lovely ladies so eager to get as much of me as they can," he adds, hands on his forward-thrust hips, as if he needed to emphasize... the point.

Alex snickers at him skeptically, shaking his head. But Declan said my idea is a good idea!

"See! I told you! It'll be a hit! I should take it on that 'Big Fish Finds' show!"

"Rhys — you've got enough money in the bank to finance something like that if you wanted to," Alex points out. "You don't need a reality show to make it happen. You could even hire people to do it all for you."

"No! That's the fun part! I want to figure it all out myself, but with some marketing experts to make sure it'll go viral."

"Your name on it will make it go viral, Rhys. You're famous!" Kier points out. "And you're welcome to steal my spotlight any-time."

"And if you really want it to go viral, just ask one of Hunt's girlfriends to endorse it on her influencer accounts," Declan suggests.

Hunter just glares at him. No idea what that's about. They're *his* girlfriends...

"I think I'll give the 'Big Fish Finds' thing a shot first."

"Uhh... Rhys — I'm not sure they're exactly going to jump at the chance to put a sex toy on their broadcast TV show," Alex says. "They're kind of PG-rated with that stuff."

"But it's a sock!"

"Yeah — a sock for your cock. We got that part. Are you sure you do?" Declan asks. "Because *that's* the part they're going to have a problem with."

Hmm... Not as enthusiastic a response from the guys as I'd hoped. Maybe with all the fangirls trying to get backstage every night, they're not my target market. I mean, if I wanted, I could probably get off at our next refueling stop and find a girl who'd be happy to... But, no — I'm not taking anyone back to my bunk or hotel room. Because I can't stop thinking about my dream-girl...

Yeah — also not thinking of her in the context of me jacking off. She's too special for that. More than pretty enough, with that blonde hair and those stormy-sky eyes. Just... special. She's special. I can just tell. I wish I could figure out who she is. I feel like I've seen her before somewhere. Maybe it was just in my dreams. She's my dream-girl, that's for sure.

Chapter 1

Drumming Song

Rhys
Present

"Hi, there."

The boy looks at me out of the corner of his eye, but his gaze darts away before I can make eye contact. He reaches for my snare but pulls his fingers back at the last second, as if he's thought better of it.

"Tommy! There you are! Mommy's been looking for you!"

A tall blonde woman approaches from the side of the stage, snatching the boy up the moment he raises his arms toward her, even though he's really too big to be carried around.

"You have to stay with Mommy tonight, buddy. We're close to the water, so we have to follow the rules — like when we go to the beach. OK?"

She doesn't wait for him to respond, doesn't check his expression to see if he's even acknowledged her words. Which he hasn't. He's still staring at my snare.

"Sorry. We got distracted by his little sister, and he ran off. We try to keep an eye on him, but he can be sneaky when he sees something he likes." She nods at my kit.

"Here, bud — here's your contraption," she says, handing him a Lego... well, "contraption" is pretty much the word for it: bricks blended with gears, axles, elastic bands... It looks like fun, though. I should get myself some of those...

"No problem. I already loved drums when I was his age, so I know how that feels. I don't think you could have dragged me away."

She gives me a gentle smile and a nod before turning around and merging back into the small crowd on the deck, filled with friends of my bandmate Declan and his girlf— no, wife! They snuck off and got married today. Again. Go figure. All these years, I thought Declan was afraid of commitment, and it turned out he'd had a wife since even before I met him. I'm not sure how that works with all the girls he's been with since we got famous, but that's between him and Callie, and they seem really happy now. Declan's not even being much of a dick anymore. It's kind of weird, actually. Good weird, though.

It seems love is in the air here in Mystic Beach. We'd been performing here at this bar for the first time when Dave instantly fell head over heels for our temporary sound engineer, Piper. And he's already managed to knock her up, with a little bass player on the way. Not soon enough to replace him on tour if he decides to stop going on the road with us, which would kind of suck. But then I guess if the kid was old enough to tour with us, they'd be old enough that Dave wouldn't be so reluctant to leave this place to go on tour. They seem to like this baby idea, though, so I'm happy for them.

Hunter and his girlfriend, Brighid, got together earlier this summer, too, after years of saying they were just friends. They got engaged here in this very spot like a month ago.

If you'd asked me ten years ago who Brighid would end up marrying, I'd have said it was even odds whether it was Hunt or Mace Mason, who back then existed in a rockstar stratosphere we'd barely brushed our fingers against, even while standing on our tippytoes. And at 6-foot-4, that's pretty high up there.

I saw Mace kiss Brighid once. Backstage at one of our shows, when we were opening for his band, Telltale Signs. They weren't making out or anything, but you don't usually kiss a girl on the top of her head when you just met her the night before — not unless there's something there. Something more than sex.

I don't think I've ever kissed a girl on the top of her head. I've had lots of girls in my bed, though. Just not *the one*. Even if I've been dreaming about her for months now.

She's blonde — not like the woman just now, with her golden-blonde waves, or Brighid, with her light blonde hair, but a more neutral shade, and almost straight — with what Mom always called "stormy sky" eyes, and more petite. Not little, like Piper, though. No, my dream-girl is the perfect height. How tall? No idea. But however tall she is, it's perfect, just like she is. The only thing wrong with her is I have no idea who she is.

I've been waiting weeks to play this song in front of an audience. It's the one we usually open our shows with, and my adrenaline is already on an upswing. It doesn't matter that there's just a few dozen people in the audience — I'm already antsy, bouncing on the balls of my feet as I tap my sticks lightly on my legs.

Hunt captured it in this song — that creative energy that licks through my veins like flame... like my blood is gasoline and the drumsticks ignite a spark that sets the world on fire the moment they hit my snare.

And then there's that moment when all six of us are in our spots on the stage — doesn't matter whether it's a little stage like this one at the Pirate's Cove (weird name, because I have yet to see a pirate here, and not even one parrot) or someplace like Madison Square Garden — Declan puts his hand on his mic, and Hunt straps on that green guitar his mom gave him, Dave drops his right hand down to rest his fingers on those thick bass strings, Alex finishes pushing all of the eight million buttons that make his keyboards sound right and Kieran pulls himself inside his shell, which then lights up the stage like the brightest spotlight we've ever had on us as he hits those first notes and the song blazes out and through all of us.

That's when it happens, when the sticks make that snapping sound I've loved since I was a kid no older than that one earlier tonight, regimenting the chaos of the world around me within the space between the beats. My feet match the heartbeat of the earth beneath them, which it seems sometimes like I'm the only one who can hear. Right now, it's got seven beats to it, but sometimes it's more, or less. That doesn't matter either — or, rather, it's all that matters.

The guys don't always get it when I tell them the song needs to be faster or slower to match that heartbeat. But we always find a place where they meet, like that lowest common denominator thing from math. School and I were not friends, especially before Mom got me put on meds that let me focus a little better. But math — I live in a world of math. Fractions of this, multiples of that, parts divided into even smaller parts, numbers running through my brain from the moment I get up until the moment I finally fall asleep, usually with my arms full of that wonderful soreness after a day of beating on my kit and my legs still tapping out the beat on the double pedals that aren't even beneath them anymore.

My brain is like a metronome. If you threw it into a tornado and let it keep time for the universe. I keep perfect time with every song. The guys rely on me for that, and that's like my mission in life, keeping the song on track, letting Dave know where to put his beats, guiding Dec and Hunt and Kier so they put their parts together in the right way to make each song work, cuing Alex's flourishes underneath and over the top of it all.

Because when the song is the thing I'm focused on, all the chaos, all the distraction, all the excess energy... it just falls away, and I become the song. Dave's the spine, but I'm the feet that keep us moving, onward and forward, relentless and inevitable, until we reach that spot we stop, for just a moment, and then it starts all over again, on my count. And right now... now, I'm the song. Hunt wrote it, but it's part of me and I'm part of it now, floating through the air with the sound waves until my toes barely anchor me to the ground. It stretches me to my limits, until I feel like I encompass not just the song, but the universe — every star in the sky, every electron moving through the wires, every molecule of air, every ray of light, every dancer moving on the floor to the beat that I create.

But she's not moving. She's frozen there, watching... watching me. And I'm watching her. Can't take my eyes off her. Not now, not any more than I can in my dreams. She's too far away to see what color her eyes are, but that's OK. I know already. Those stormy-sky eyes I've seen nearly every night for months now. And I'm lost in them... My feet on auto-pilot, my arms flailing to reach toms and snare, high hat and cymbals, unguided, because the only thing I comprehend, the only language I speak right now is her.

And then, suddenly, like I've been shoved, I'm careening out into the space over the dance floor, peering down at her from above, where she stands next to the blonde woman from before — taller, broader, brown eyes lit up like amber in the sun as they move across the space between my dream girl and me... or rather my body, which I look back to see is, somehow, keeping the rhythm, the same as usual. My mind... my mind is filled with another song, a melody, as elusive as *she*'s been in my waking hours... but now...

I look back down to find *her* looking up at me, with those storm-blue eyes, taking me in as if I wasn't some shapeless, translucent version of myself, like a cloud I might fall through on the way back to earth after jumping out of a perfectly good airplane, as Hunter always calls it. But she sees me. No — not just sees me, like she realizes I'm there, floating above her. She *sees* me. And I'm not sure anyone's ever done that before.

Too often they see giant red-haired Rhys, freakishly tall and with hair you wouldn't miss in a crowd, no matter how tall I was. Or Rhys the nutty inventor with his off-the-wall ideas that never amount to shit, except when things literally blow up, as they sometimes do. Or Rhys the rockstar, the crazy adrena-line-junkie who does backflips off his drum riser to drain excess energy before a show and can't pass up a climbing wall, because it's the only time, aside from when I'm one with the beat of a song, when my focus is absolute and my mind clear.

Except now. Now it's crystal clear, like a drop of rain falling from the sky, pure arctic ice, the tone of a bell or the fact that this woman... she *sees* me.

And then, suddenly, it's like a rubber band snaps. The blonde woman, the one from earlier, she touches her hand to my dream girl's arm, and she blinks, my girl, no longer seeing me flying above her, and suddenly I'm rocketed back into my head, peer-ing out of the eyes in my skull and not the ones in my mind. And she's gone. Where'd she go? Did she leave? Did I dream her up when I was awake this time? Or did I just long so much for her to be real that my brain, high on beats, conjured her up out of thin air?

I feel a tap to the back of my head, and I expect to find Alex has somehow reached over from his spot behind his keyboards to snap me back into reality, but there's no one there. Alex stands amidst his "cockpit," looking at me curiously, like I've done something unexpected.

I'm not sure what that would be, because I'm still keeping the beat, and the only thing unexpected about me tonight is that I saw a girl with stormy-sky eyes look at me and truly *see* me. And now nothing's ever going to be the same.

CHAPTER 2
MEET VIRGINIA

Lyric

"Lyric... Lyric. Lyric? Lyric!"

The urgency in Rory's voice finally cuts through the fog in my head, my limbs going loose like a marionette with its strings cut.

"What?"

I shake my head, hard, trying to send the lingering bits of cloudy mind flying off into the ether.

"The song's over. I was going to head backstage for my interview... I wanted to make sure you had Tommy and Aria before I..."

She glances over at my kids, who — astonishingly — are occupying themselves at the table next to her, Tommy with his gears and Aria with illustrating one of her poems.

"No — no. I've got them. Of course. Go do your thing. Thanks for helping watch them."

"No thanks needed with my godkids. You know that, Lyr. But... are you sure you're OK? You seemed a little... scattered? Almost..."

It's not like Rory to beat around the bush, nor to scramble for the word with the right shade of meaning. Words are her medium, as surely as they're mine. At least for my part-time work.

"Almost what?"

"I..."

"Spit it out, Rory."

"Fine. Possessed. Like you weren't even in there."

I give her a look. I'm one of the few people who has some clue what Rory's real talent is, and it's not writing or reporting. She's not claircognizant like Brighid is, but she reads people with an adeptness that's beyond body language. She's an empath, in the supernatural sense of the word. And I don't have to be an empath myself to read the concern in her words.

"It was nothing."

"That's not a denial," she says, calling me on dodging her unspoken question.

"We can talk about it later." If I can put her off, maybe I can digest what just happened before I have to put words to it myself.

Rory backs off, but the look of concern doesn't recede. Instead, it refocuses, after a glance up at the stage.

"Sure. Later. But are you sure you don't want to come backstage with me? Meet the band?"

Leave it to Rory to make an offer I have a hard time refusing. She knows how much I love aMUSEd's music. She also knows how much I love musicians. But then she knows better than anyone why I'm not open to meeting guys — even if they are musicians. Especially if they're musicians...

"I can't. The kids..." It's an excuse, and she knows it.

"I'm sure Callie would be happy to watch them for ten minutes, so you can meet the rest of the band," she suggests. "Or Piper. You've already let her watch them."

"With David. And he's part of your interview."

"So? She and Callie can do it together. Give them some sister-in-law time..."

"I don't know, Rory... maybe I should just take the kids home. It's getting past their bedtimes. And you know how Tommy is when his schedule isn't followed."

"It's not that late. Come on — live a little! Meet the rest of the band. You already know Declan, David and Hunter... Complete the set!" She's teasing me now, but it's been long enough since she's been in a teasing mood that it starts to win me over. She's due to live a little herself, after what she's been through. Maybe we can both just pretend things are normal, for just a little while...

"Fine. But only if Piper and Callie are willing to watch the kids. They're too much for one person, as we already learned tonight."

"I'll go get them now. I'll be right back."

I brush my hand down Aria's dark blonde hair, smoothing it back from her face.

"That's beautiful, Aria! I love the colors!"

"Thanks, Mommy! It's what I saw in my 'magination!"

"It's like a sunset!"

Aria nods enthusiastically, her focus on adding even more shades of red and orange to her abstract drawing.

My hand moves automatically to smooth Tommy's wild hair into some semblance of a normal style, but I stop myself. He doesn't like being touched — especially his hair. Hence why it's so hard to get it looking like it's seen a brush in the last month. He'll need a haircut soon, but I'm not even close to ready to tackle that.

He sticks two fingers in his mouth while he spins the gears in his Lego creation with the other hand, faster and faster.

"That's an amazing contraption, Tommy!" Callie tells him as she and Piper arrive at our table.

"And your drawing is pretty, Aria," Piper chimes in with a shy smile.

"It's a poem, too, Auntie Piper! See — all the colors and clouds!"

I was a little leery of letting Aria call Piper and David "auntie" and "uncle," but the kids already had an Auntie Rory, Auntie Callie and Auntie Bridge, and with two of my closest friends settling down with members of aMUSEd, in the end it just seemed easier. Especially with Piper expecting and David planning to make his home here in Mystic Beach with her and their baby, it all just seemed like a wave washing over my life, and I've learned how pointless it is to fight life when things happen like that.

It's been harder to accept the constant fretting by everyone and their brother over my lack of self-care... my mother, all the aunties and otherwise. Except for Mom, not one of them has kids (yet), and not one of them has ever had the challenge of trying to raise two kids — one of whom is autistic and non-verbal — alone. And that's before we get to my other complication...

"We've got them, Lyric," Callie says pointedly. "Go meet the rest of the band."

I sigh, giving in before Callie can say anything about how much I love the band or musicians. I am *so* not in the market...

Rory grabs my hand and drags me back toward the dressing room. This'll be fine. Just some lighthearted fun, a flashback to my life ten years ago, a carefree moment of indulgence for the me before I had a job, a husband, kids...

"They're expecting me," Rory tells the venue security guard standing by the door. As long as I've known her, she has been a force to be reckoned with, and I'm unsurprised when her matter-of-fact confidence in our welcome in these rockstars' dressing room is met with simple acceptance. The man nods and opens the door for her, allowing us to enter—

Chaos.

Complete and utter chaos.

"Chug! Chug! Chug!" five members of the band chant — even mild-mannered David — as a bottle of champagne is upended in front of my nose. My brain takes a second to make sense of what I'm seeing, mostly because what I'm looking at is upside-down from its normal orientation — head below feet, red ringlets dripping down toward the floor, away from a chin that is just as awash in frothy liquid as the hair.

I look up to see how he's even suspended like that, finding knees bent around an exposed pipe in the ceiling.

"Ladies! Fáilte! Welcome, that is!" a voice says from behind the spectacle, an Irish lilt at top volume so as to be heard above the band and the music being pumped through the dressing room speakers. A head of hair twice as long and half as red peeks out around the spectacle. "We're celebrating Declan's secret nuptials. Please — join us! Champagne? A fine stout? A nice Irish whiskey? A fruity beverage in a brilliant shade of pink? We can we do you for?"

"I... I... I..." I stammer, until Rory comes to the rescue.

"We're fine, thanks. I'm ready to do the interview, if you all are..."

She nods vaguely at what I now recognize as aMUSEd's drummer, Rhys "The Madman" Madigan, living up to his nickname. Her eyebrow arches in that way she has, always seeming older than 27, more judgmental than she should, but considering what she's been through... her responsibilities... A wave of guilt hits me, and I stuff it down, along with all those other feelings, picturing a block of ice.

"What's wrong, dream-girl?"

The ice melts in an instant in the heat of the brown irises in front of me.

Dream-girl?

I stand there, staring at this upside-down rockstar whose mild frown comes across to my mind as a gentle smile instead, due to his head-over-heels position.

Rory clears her throat.

"This is my friend Lyric. I hope you don't mind if she joins us."

"Hi, Lyric," David says quietly.

"Mistress of ceremonies!" Declan declares enthusiastically. "Without whom we would not be here tonight!"

"You're definitely welcome, Lady," Hunter says respectfully. We've met a few times about his and Brighid's impending hand-fasting, and she's been teaching him a few things about ritual and such, including that my role in her circle entitles me to... well, a title.

"Lady? She's nobility?" Kieran asks.

"No..." I object, not wanting to explain further.

"Priestess of Brighid," Hunter clarifies.

"Ah — like our own Brighid." Kieran nods, obviously having encountered the idea before.

"So she's a witch?" Rhys asks, curling up with his abs to grab the pipe with his hands and then dropping down onto his feet with the grace of an acrobat. A few drops of champagne trickle down his bare chest. Not that I was looking. "Or is she only half of one, like Brighid? You know — there's a lot of witches here. Is there a quota?"

Clearly my friends and I have been a topic of discussion among the band members. That's the last thing I want to be — especially where the W-word is being bandied about so openly by some very famous men. As comfortable as I am in my identity as a priestess and witch, I've got a job to worry about, and not everyone is as open-minded as these worldly rockstars apparently are.

"What are you all doing to poor Lyric?" Brighid asks indignantly from behind me, grabbing up a nearby towel and tossing it in Rhys' face. "I swear — you're as incorrigible a bunch of gossips as the ladies at Kara's yarn shop! Leave the poor woman alone! Rory's here to interview *you*, not to have you interrogate her friend!"

"Sorry," "Apologies," the guys chorus, seeming oddly instantly chastened for a bunch of grown men. Brighid's not always as mild-mannered as she comes off at first, but it's strange seeing these entitled celebrities so easily cowed by her, even though she's known them for more than a decade.

"Lyric — you know Hunter and Declan, of course. And David now, too," she says, gesturing to each of them in turn. "The Irishman with more knowledge of Herself than he should admit — that's Kieran. And, that's Alex on the sofa," she adds, gesturing to the band's keyboard player.

"Why am I last?" Rhys objects. "I saw her first!"

Everyone looks at him, varying degrees of confusion on their faces. I try to recall any moment I've been face-to-face with Rhys Madigan before tonight. And there's nothing, despite how familiar his face is to me.

"I met Lyric when I was 17," Declan says, frowning. "What are you talking about, Rhys?"

Rhys frowns — right-side up this time. He looks a little lost.

"Nevermind," he says, glancing at Alex before pulling a clean T-shirt over his head. At a glance, it looks like an AC/DC concert shirt, but when I look closer, it actually says, "AD/HD — Highway to... Squirrel!" Hmm...

"Anyway... If you all are ready?" Rory prompts after an uncomfortable moment of silence.

"Have a seat," Alex says, taking charge with a gesture at the chairs across from the sofa.

It's time to go.

I've gotten used to it enough now that my expression doesn't change. What happened earlier tonight was very new, worth at least an expression of shock. But this... old hat now. It's just Vivienne offering a little motherly advice.

Aww... Let the girl stay, look at the man-candy!

That's Annie, but it could as easily be Frank. Neither of whose opinion I'm inclined to listen to right now.

Lyric's a respectful girl. She won't ogle the boys.

Boys? I'm not sure Vivienne knows what goes on in my head all the time, if she thinks I'm thinking of these guys as mere boys, or that there isn't a part of me that might enjoy a few minutes of ogling at least one of them. But she's right. It's time to go.

"I'll let you all get to work," I say. "There are two kids out there who are very much up past their bedtimes, and I really should get them home."

"No! You can't leave!"

Rhys' objection reminds me of Aria on the verge of a temper tantrum, which only serves to reinforce my need to leave and get back to my kids.

"Ow!" Rhys adds as Alex smacks him on the back of the head.

"The lady needs to go, Rhys. Use your manners."

Brighid has said before how much Alex reminds her of a mom with a bunch of kids who drive her crazy, and I can see now why she said it. But I can't say I like his model of parenting...

Go...

"It was very nice to meet you all — those of you I hadn't already. Enjoy your time in Mystic Beach!" I add, since I know at least half of them will be going back to New York at some point soon.

"Nice to meet you, too," several of the guys reply, mixed in with a couple bidding me goodnight.

"Sweet dreams," Rhys says, oddly intent. It's... disconcerting, maybe? Distracting, definitely.

"You OK?" Rory mouths at me.

I reply with a nod and a smile that I'm sure doesn't reach my eyes, turning quickly and moving to reclaim my kids, with thanks again to Callie and Piper.

"Lyric? Is everything alright?" Callie asks. She knows me almost as well as Rory does, and has known me much longer.

"Just tired, Cal," I tell her. "Time to get these guys to bed, and then myself."

"Get some rest, OK?" she says, frowning in concern. Exactly what I don't want to be dealing with right now.

Chapter 3

Ghost Dance

Lyric

Loading Aria and Tommy back in my car gives me a reassuring sense of normalcy, and an hour later, they're tucked into bed, two bedtime stories read — a dragon tale for Aria and a chapter in his new astronomy book for Tommy.

It's past my own usual bedtime at this point, and gods know I could use the sleep. But I've got to make more headway on the final planning for the music department fundraiser or there will be no new instruments for the kids when school starts. I shoot off a couple more emails to likely sponsors among the local business community, requesting donations in support of the event itself or auction items. I give a grant request to a local non-profit a final review before submitting it. It's a desperation move, considering the usual grant award period isn't for two more months. But maybe they'll take pity on me and find some funding early.

A giant yawn catches me.

"So much for working on my fellowship application tonight."

It'll have to wait until morning. Time is ticking down if I want to be considered for this coming year, but I've got so much else I need to do — starting with the kids' final weeks of summer vacation... Polishing my poems and the application are way down on my list of priorities.

And that's before I consider what happened tonight...

"Mother Goddess Brighid."

It's half appeal and half protest.

I've served the Irish goddess of poetry since I was 16. I've solemnized dozens of marriages in her name. I've experienced any number of supernatural occurrences, and that was before these most recent "visitations." But never before have I had happen what happened tonight as I stood on that dance floor and watched aMUSEd play, my eyes drawn to the passionate performance by the tall, red-haired drummer.

Brighid — my friend, not the goddess — had described Rhys Madigan to me once, having known him since they were in college: "He's tall and rangy, built kind of like Stewart Copeland of The Police, but even taller and with even more muscles now that he does rock-climbing — Rhys, not Stewart. And that hair — like Jamie on 'Outlander' — loose, rich red curls down to his shoulders..."

Brighid loves Hunter, whose blonde hair is nearly as long as hers now. But she has an admitted weakness for redheads, so Rhys and Kieran, with his red-gold hair, both elicit sighs from her from time to time, even though I doubt she'd admit that part. (Certainly not in front of Hunter.)

Oh, and she had one more thing to say about Rhys: "Take all of that, and add the personality of Dug the dog from 'Up.'"

Oh, boy...

The thing is, Dug comes off as being kind of stupid, because that ridiculous voice simulation collar sounds the way it does. But as I can tell you from the million times I've watched the movie with the kids, Dug is actually the smartest of that entire pack of dogs. Probably smarter than most of the humans, too. He's also incredibly loyal, devoted to his friends. Yeah, he's easily distracted — reminding me, aptly, of Rhys' shirt tonight. But Dug has a happy-go-lucky streak most golden retrievers would envy — and that's a characteristic I could certainly use a heaping helping of in my life.

No, not like that. I'm decidedly not in the market for a boyfriend — especially not a rockstar one who lives hours away. And a drummer? That's a big no.

Thank the gods Siobhan's little tequila party game for Callie never got around to asking everyone whether they'd fantasized about Rhys... I'd have lied my head off, priestess or not. I'd been fantasizing about Rhys Madigan since my 20s. I'd even admitted it to...

Adam...

No. No more drummers. Too close to home. Even selecting the percussion instruments I hope the fundraiser will pay for has been hard.

It's just more proof that I'm going to finish this life in solo mode. It's not that bad… I barely have energy for everything else I need to do. No time or energy for boyfriends. Except the battery-operated variety. I've barely got time or energy for that, either. Even that form of "self-care" has fallen by the wayside of late.

There's a light touch on the back of my head… No — light doesn't describe it. Ethereal. But real. I've felt it before, so many times in the last sixteen years.

"I know — I'm a poor priestess to others if I can't take care of myself properly," I say to the air around me. "But would you mind explaining to me what that craziness tonight was all about?"

A feeling of determination, almost smug, washes over me. Not me, I know — nor Vivienne, nor any of my other new "friends" from the last few years. This is bigger. You learn to identify the presence of a goddess when She comes so often to you, like She does to me, and to Brighid, and…

It was needed. You have opened your ears to words that needed to be heard. You must also now open your eyes to see the road in front of you.

"What does that mean?"

Silence, both in my ears and in my mind.

I didn't really expect an answer. But it would have been nice.

I've never even traveled out of body in my sleep. But looking back at tonight, I know that's exactly what it must feel like, only… it wasn't so much that I wasn't in my body as it was that I wasn't the one driving the bus, steering the ship, doing the decision-making.

One moment I was watching aMUSEd on stage, sitting next to Tommy and Aria at our table, Rory standing next to us, and the next, I was standing on Rory's other side, watching everything unfold from a spot a few feet above my actual eyes, which were fixed on my longtime crush as he kicked, smacked, snapped and tapped on that massive drum kit. And then those beautiful, warm brown eyes of his, fixed on me — the physical me, which I was no longer in control of.

I watched, pushed aside from my own body, as the red-haired drummer and the blonde mother/teacher/musician/poet/priestess were fixed in each other's gazes, locked together. And then I glanced up — *we* glanced up, both my physical body and this sense of self oriented above that body — to see a warm cloud of light, shifting in all the colors of the sunset... Reds, yellows, oranges and purples, like a watercolor wash across the late afternoon sky, presaging the real sunset so soon to come.

A sense of connection. Warmth. Welcome. Delight. Ebullient energy wafting over my head, coalescing like a warm hug, but one that sets my skin to tingling. No — not just my skin... All of me, inside and out, body and soul. Excitement. Something new.

Then a sense of satisfaction, both then and there, and now here. Herself. For I know now that She'd shoved me aside from my own body, taken the wheel, if just briefly.

It happens. Priests and priestesses of older gods historically, and even today, sometimes give over control of their physical bodies to become vessels of the gods they serve. Usually, it's intentional, but not always. When They need something done, a suitable vessel is found. But never before have I been that vessel. And what was the purpose behind this—

Well, Rory had it right, as usual...

Possession.

There's no other word for it. Literal truth.

Honestly, I don't mind. I'd have volunteered if I'd been asked in advance. And that's another question I'd like answered — not just why, but why no warning?

But the only answer I get, for now, is that same sense of smug satisfaction, of a thing that needed to be done having been done.

A trace of a hand down my hair. Benediction.

Fine. Keep your secrets. I am Your priestess and I am here to serve. But maybe a little warning next time?

I shut off my laptop and get ready for bed, taking pains, as always, to lie down in the middle of the queen-sized bed. I learned early on in my mourning that sleeping on "my side" of the bed just led to waking up in the middle of the night with the feeling that something — someone — was missing. And that just complicated the rest of what happened...

They say the veil between the worlds of the living and the dead is thinnest around Samhain — Halloween to most people. And that's true, at least in my experience. But that veil is thin all the time, for me. At least since he passed.

No, I don't see dead people.

I hear them.

Whether I want to or not. Except one.

How ironic is it that the one person whose death impacted me the most is the one I can't hear? I don't know if Adam passed on so quickly and easily that he's now beyond my reach, or if there's some kind of metaphysical Catch 22 that means I can't hear him. But it's a frustration that just makes the ache worse... wanting to hear his voice and knowing I can't, no matter how many others now speak to me.

In the days after Adam first passed, when I lay in our bed alone, if I didn't get right to sleep, the silence of my half-empty bed was quickly filled with the murmuring of others lost and not yet ready to move on. It was like trying to sleep with the television on. After a week, I resorted to Brighid's special sleep tea and an extra daily meditation session to quiet the voices, exert some control over this new ability I'd never thought I'd have, let alone acquire at 29.

With that done, the voices manageable at least, I realized they'd waited until I was half-asleep for a reason — my waking mind shut them out, ignored them. Like many witches, I'd always been taught to ignore the dead when and if their spirits tried to get my attention. Mom said it was something her high priestess had warned her about when she was first initiated: acknowledge them, and they pester you to do things for them, or just to listen, because most people can't perceive them. She never had. I never had. Until I lost someone myself. And then they came to me, not caring that all I wanted was some restful sleep.

Most recently, it was Callie's beloved grandmother, Nonna, my next-door neighbor for much of my life. I'd called her Nonna, too, which seemed only fair when she was the closest thing I'd had to a grandmother, since Mom was estranged from her parents and my father... well, I never knew him.

Nonna had been an herbalist of a sort, steeped in European magic that thrived in the garden and in the kitchen. And when Callie pulled away from everyone after her parents were killed when she was 17, Nonna had been happy to share her knowledge with me — the second-generation witch who was but a garden gate away. And Nonna had come to me recently, years after she'd passed, her voice stronger in my mind than any of the others, asking for a favor. I'd done as she asked, out of love and loyalty, and in hopes that she was right that Callie needed a push to find happiness with Declan once again.

And she was right. It worked. I'd renewed their vows earlier today and celebrated their reunion with their friends tonight, culminating in a performance by one of my all-time favorite bands, along with a supernatural experience even I didn't understand, and then meeting, in the most unlikely of ways, the man I'd had a crush on since before I met my husband. No wonder my mind refuses to settle tonight. Maybe I need a cup of Brighid's tea. But I'd really rather not get up again...

I sigh and close my eyes, wishing that, for once, the voice in my head was the one I long most to hear. So many others these days — for a moment or a day, a few longer, like Nonna. But not his. Not Adam's. He's truly gone. And sleeping in the middle of the bed doesn't change that he's gone. But it reminds me that my life has changed, that I need to keep focused on the present and keep the past locked away, as surely as the nominal guest bedroom in our house has been since the day he died.

Now, it's time for sleep, I tell myself firmly, pulling my mind into a meditative state, and, finally, I drift away...

Soon.

CHAPTER 4
PICK UP THE PIECES

Rhys

"Are you confident at this point that you've exhausted the national paparazzi and social media interest in the band being here in Mystic Beach? I know they've been a bit of a nuisance since the incident with Holly Harwood," the reporter asks.

"We're sorry if they've inconvenienced anyone in Mystic Beach," Alex says. "We'd hoped to stay under the radar while we were here recording, but the universe seems to have had other plans."

"Things have settled down with Brighid and me, for the most part," Hunter adds. "And thanks for the part you played in getting them away from her and her shop that first day."

"No thanks needed. Brighid's become a friend, and I don't like seeing people harassed by self-proclaimed members of my profession, celebrity-adjacent or not," she says. "You don't think the news that Declan's married will stir things up again, especially after the photo scandal?"

Declan shrugs.

"I'm not worried about it. Any of it. Things will settle down again."

"And what about this sudden drop-off in the number of single members of the band? First Hunter, then David and now Declan."

"How did you know about David?" Alex asks her, looking concerned.

"Rory is Piper's sister-in-law. Kind-of," David interjects.

Judging from everyone's expressions as that news sinks in, I wasn't the only one not in on that secret.

"And you didn't think to tell me a member of the media knew about you and Piper, about the pregnancy?" our manager, Billy, asks David pointedly.

"Rory can be trusted with a secret. Believe me," David says, exchanging a look with her.

"I wasn't going to mention David and Piper in the story," Rory assures us. "I'd rather that wasn't public knowledge, truth be told. I don't want to add any unneeded stress for Piper while she's pregnant."

"And that makes two of us," David says.

"And then some," Alex says. "But, to answer your question... aMUSEd has been on the road for the better part of two years, which is the second extensive tour we've had in the last five years. None of us are college kids anymore. It was overdue for at least a few of us to settle down."

"As you know, Callie and I have a history, so while this might seem sudden from the outside, it's really not," Declan says.

"And Brighid and I have been friends since we were young kids growing up here in Mystic Beach," Hunter adds. "I've just finally gotten to a point in dealing with what happened with my parents that I allowed myself to consider that maybe I might be worthy of a relationship with her, or anyone, really."

"How's that coming, Hunter? You've become a bit of a role model for those dealing with childhood trauma."

"I've been working with a therapist who specializes in trauma therapy — specifically, complex PTSD, which often results from prolonged or repeated exposure to traumatic events, like what I experienced," Hunter says. "She's been wonderful, and we both feel like I'm making good progress. And I've got both Brighid and my bandmates offering me all the support I could ask for, as well as our fans. I'm really grateful for all of it, and I'm hopeful that I'm establishing some healthy patterns for my life going forward."

"With you and Brighid engaged, that leaves Alex, Kieran and Rhys as the eligible bachelors in the band. Are you three, as Alex suggested, looking to settle down with someone special?"

"I'm always open to finding that someone special," Alex says. "But I think we've already snapped up more than our fair share of Mystic Beach's single female population." He chuckles, but there's an edge to it.

Kier, meanwhile, looks like he'd rather be anywhere else than in this room with a reporter asking about his personal life. He's my closest friend, but he's never even told *me* much about his past. I decided long ago that it didn't matter. We have fun hanging out, and we've always had complementary taste in women, so we made good wingmen for each other, back when that was what both of us wanted. But Kier's been dodging the groupies for months now — no explanation given to me, or to anyone, other than he's just not in the mood.

"Kieran?" she asks, and I make the sudden decision to throw myself between my friend and his nightmare of being in the media spotlight.

"He's too busy tuning his guitars to worry about girls," I tell her. I can almost feel Kier sigh in relief. "But *I'm* giving some thought to following in Hunter's footsteps with a dating show." I'm pulling that out of my ass, thinking on my feet, and the guys all look suitably alarmed. "It looked like fun, right up until the blackmail part," I say. "But I'm also looking to get on 'Big Fish Finds' with a new product I'm developing. I really think reality TV is a place I can shine."

"Oh? What's this product? Can you give us a preview, or are you keeping it secret until it's patented?"

"Well, I'm working on a—"

"I really think you should keep that to yourself for now, Rhys," Alex interrupts. "You don't want to spoil your reveal once you get on the show!"

Yeah. He's right. Probably better to keep the Cock Sock on the QT until the show airs.

"Understandable," she says, seeming satisfied. "What about the album? How's recording going?"

"We're making some real progress now," Declan says. "We took some time to relax, get our minds cleared, and the songs have really been flowing. We've got a few that are kind of a new sound for us — a little lighter, a little retro, with a hint of folk to them, even some ballads. Dave's got a song recorded already and a couple others written, and I've got a half-dozen written and ready to record. Hunter's back on the horse with one of his own, and Alex even has one we're recording right now."

"And then there's my song..." I add.

"No!"

It's five voices, all denying me my song once again. I've been pitching this six-minute drum solo for the entire time the band has been together, and I can't get any of them to take me seriously. It's frustrating, because I know the fans would love it, and it would play really well in front of a live audience.

Rory raises an eyebrow over the reaction from my bandmates but doesn't ask about my song. Disappointing, but at least she's no longer asking Kier personal questions. That's the important thing. My mind wanders as she continues to ask the guys about their songs, their favorite things about Mystic Beach, plans for the next tour... It travels back to what happened tonight during our performance, which seemed weird at the time, but made total sense once the reporter arrived in our dressing room and introduced her friend... Lyric.

It's perfect isn't it? Her name. Just her. She looks just like she did in my dreams, with those stormy blue eyes and blonde hair. I just wish she'd stuck around so I could talk to her. Because I'm just realizing that I don't really know anything about her.

"Well, thank you all for your time. The story will be in this week's issue," Rory says, getting up and offering her hand to each of us in turn. When she gets to me, she frowns slightly, giving me a hard look.

"What?"

"You need to be more careful," she says.

"You sound like my mom," I tell her, hoping she'll find my smile charming. I've seen Hunter do this, schmoozing with reporters, especially the female ones. I can pull it off, too, right?

She frowns again.

Apparently not.

"Rhys — don't be rude to the lady. She's about to write a story on us!" Alex says.

"What? How was that rude? My mom tells me that that all the time. And I love my mom."

"She's not old enough to be your mother, nor is she saying anything that's out-of-order, considering she walked in here with you hanging from the ceiling."

"Right. Sorry."

"Not really what I meant," she says under her breath. Then what *did* she mean?

"Goodnight, all! David — I'll see you later."

Dave gives her a nod, while the rest of us turn to look at him.

"What?" he says after she's left the room. "She stays in — in Piper's brother's apartment sometimes, when she's going through his... effects."

"His effects?" Kier asks. "Piper's brother died?"

David sighs, exchanging a look with Alex and Hunter, who I guess were already aware of this.

"Accident at sea, about a year ago," Dave says. "Her foster-brother, actually. They — he and Rory — were serious, probably getting married."

"Hence her being Piper's 'sort-of' sister-in-law..." Alex says, as if the entire world makes sense now that he's got the other half of the pertinent information.

"Yeah."

"And her seeing you later?"

"Piper and her foster brother lived in the same building. And Rory's still working on getting his affairs in order."

"A year later?"

"He had a lot of business dealings, some of which no one else was aware of. So it's taking her a while to unravel it all, especially with a full-time job. She ends up at his place very late a lot of the time, taking care of his business interests."

"I feel very lucky right now," Declan says, his eyes drifting to the doorway where we can see Rory talking to Callie.

"And Lyric's her friend? Rory's?" I ask Dave.

"Yeah. She helps Lyric out a lot, on top of being a reporter and handing the business stuff. She's the kids' godmother."

"Wait. What kids?"

Lyric has kids? Does that mean she also has a husband? My heart cracks a little under the weight of my disappointment.

"You really missed that exchange during my speech?" Declan says, clearly offended that I wasn't pay attention the entire time.

"I heard 'again.'"

"Of course..." Declan rolls his eyes.

"So my attention span is both short *and* selective! Sue me!"

"Lyric was irked because I was cursing in front of her kids."

I vaguely remember that now. I just didn't see the woman or the kids.

Wait... kids... The little boy!

All of that whole scene earlier escaped my mind, blown away by everything that happened afterward.

The tall blonde woman who came to get the little boy — that was Rory!

"A boy, like yea high, with blonde hair and Legos?"

"Yeah — that sounds like Tommy," Declan says. "Not sure about the Legos."

"Oh, that's definitely Tommy," David says. "You can't separate that kid from his Legos, unless it's to give him some gears instead."

"How do *you* know?" I demand.

It's starting to seem like everyone knows Lyric except me.

"Piper pitched in with babysitting the kids a couple times, and I went with her, trying out the parenting thing." He shrugs. "They're awesome kids."

"Tommy and..."

"Aria," Piper says quietly from the doorway, toting a bin of cables with her iPad perched on top. "She's a poet, like her mother."

"Lyric is a poet?"

Of course she is... Brighid Weaver is a weaver, and Lyric is a poet.

"Sometimes," Piper says.

I give her the hairy eyeball, waiting for the rest of the explanation. Piper seems nervous, and Dave pulls her into his arms. Piper doesn't always like rooms full of people, I've found out. Especially when she's not working. When she's working, she's a different person, not shy at all. I get it, but it's so different from how I am that I don't always know how to deal with her. More gently, apparently.

"She's a music teacher, Rhys. And she writes poetry," David finishes.

Lyric the poet and musician...

All the pieces of the dreams I've had these last few months are starting to come together, like a giant puzzle with no picture on the box.

But a mom? A wife? How do these pieces even go in my puzzle?

"Her husband? Where's he?"

"Dead," Piper says plainly, apparently accustomed to the topic after her own experience. Yeah, I should be more gentle with her. "Three years ago."

Whoa. OK. She's a widow. A single parent.

My dreams — and this puzzle — just got very complicated.

Four hours later

I run through the song — my song — for the twentieth time tonight. You'd think I'd be exhausted after the wedding reception, the performance, the fun in the dressing room, the interview, but I'm wired. I tossed and turned in my bed for half an hour before I gave up and came down to the studio to burn off some energy.

After going through my epic drum solo twice, I gave up on the studio kit. It's fine for what we've recorded so far, but I need *my* kit for this. So I pulled the kit, piece by piece, out from the storage room to the studio's live room, then began setting it up.

It's 3 a.m. now, and I'm glad the studio is soundproofed, because Kier and Alex crashed hours ago, and I'm still not sleepy.

In fact, I'm frustrated. No one at the party would tell me where Lyric lives or works, or give me her phone number.

"You have to let *her* give you her info, dude," Hunter said. "It's not cool otherwise. I mean — didn't we just go through this with Declan?"

Yeah, we did. And he drove us all nuts trying to find Callie, scrounging the internet, the newspaper archives...

Wait.

Newspaper.

Rory.

Maybe Rory will tell me how to find her! And I know where Rory works, because she interviewed us for her newspaper!

I hit up the internet answer machine and find out that Aurora Carmichael works for the Mystic Beacon newspaper. I type the office address into my phone.

I'm typing the last digits when a hint of a melody starts to hit my brain. That song! The wisp of melody I heard before... Not a drum solo! But then it finally hits me — a wave of exhaustion, now that I'm no longer fending off sleep with frustration. Time for bed.

But, yeah. This feels right. I'll go find Rory tomorrow and beg her to tell me where to find Lyric. Or at least to give me her number. And then I'll go from there.

I'm not sure "I've been seeing you in my dreams for months now" is going to fly as an opening line. Not with a widow. A girl at a bar, maybe. But not Lyric...

But I have been. Seeing her in my dreams, I mean. Why, I don't know. But there's no way it doesn't mean something. And I'm going to find out exactly what it means.

Starting tomorrow. Right now, sleep... and maybe, if I'm lucky, another dream... of Lyric...

CHAPTER 5
RUNNING DOWN A DREAM

Rhys

"Rory? There's a really tall red-haired guy here to see you," the geeky-looking guy says over the phone.

"Oh, god..." I hear her say, both over the phone and over the balcony above.

I don't think she's got me confused with a deity, but I could be wrong. Maybe.

"I'll be down in a second," she adds.

"She'll be down in a second," he repeats.

"Hey — are you Native American?" I ask him.

"Inuit," he says.

"Like an Eskimo?"

"Yeah."

"Oh. Is it OK to use that word? I don't want to offend anybody."

"It's fine. We embrace it in the part of Alaska I'm from, even if some people are moving away from using it."

"Oh. Cool! I asked because I'm actually part Native American myself."

He does a double-take, his eyes focusing on my hair.

"Sure..." he says, hesitantly.

Rory starts walking down the stairs and the guy gives me a nervous smile, like he's not sure I'm fully sane. *I'm* a little offended by *that*, actually. Mom told me I'm part Ojibwe, and Mom never lies. He passes Rory on the way back up the stairs, exchanging a look. Well, it's not the first time that's happened when people are around me. It won't be the last.

"Hello, Rhys. What can I do for you?" Rory asks, giving a little sigh, as if she's afraid of what I'll say.

"I need Lyric's phone number."

"No."

She says it flat-out. Like it's not even in the realm of possibility. Kind of like the guys and my song. That's disappointing.

"Why not?"

"Because Lyric should be the one to give it to you if she wants you to have it," she says.

"And how will she know she wants me to have it if I can't talk to her?"

Rory frowns and sighs again.

"Come with me," she finally says, heading through the office to a closed door, which she then opens and gestures me inside.

"Have a seat," she says, pointing at a conference table surrounded with chairs. I pull one out and sit. She takes the one next to me. And I wait. For like the first time ever. I've got a lot on the line here. I can wait.

She watches me, appraising. I let her. I've got nothing to hide. I'm an open book. Even if I wanted to keep secrets from people, I'm kind of constitutionally inclined to spill them. I *have* managed not to tell anyone that Declan and Callie got married the first time when they were 17, though. So I've kept their secret, for like twenty hours now. Go me!

"Rhys — why do you want Lyric's number?"

"She's my dream-girl."

Rory scoffs.

"You don't know her! You met her for like 30 seconds!"

"Yeah. But I knew her before that. Kind of."

"What are you talking about?"

OK. I know I said I was an open book, but Lyric being in my dreams — it feels kind of personal, intimate, like something maybe I should tell Lyric before anyone else. And I don't want to give that up. Not unless I have to.

"It's hard to explain. And I'm not sure you'd believe me if I did. But I need you to trust me. It's important to me, to get the chance to talk to her, really get to know her."

Rory tilts her head, assessing. I had occupational therapists look at me like this when I was a kid. Usually right before they recommended yet another planner or to-do list technique to help deal with my "executive function" issues so I could remember to both do and turn in my homework. This examination feels about as likely to help me as those did.

"OK," she says, finally. "I'm not giving you her phone number. She'll have to do that. But I'll tell you where you can find her."

Wait. What now?

"You don't like me. Why are you helping me?" I ask, truly bewildered.

"It's not that I don't like you, Rhys. But I'm the newspaper's music reporter, so I know a bit more about aMUSEd than the average person. And I know you've got a history of doing some pretty crazy things."

"Like what? I don't think I—"

"Jumping out of airplanes?"

"Lots of people skydive."

"With your drums?"

"No snares were harmed in the filming of that solo."

"Diving with sharks."

"Sharks get a bad rap."

"Without a cage."

"A really unfair bad rap."

"Getting set on fire."

"I worked with a stunt coordinator for two weeks. I had on a fireproof suit and flame-retardant gel. Not so much as a red mark on me. And you have to admit it looked cool in the video, right?"

She frowns at me. Maybe not.

"BASE jumping. Off a skyscraper."

"I had a wing suit and a parachute."

"Climbing sheer cliffs?"

"Lots of people climb. Falls are rare."

Her expression shifts, her eyes sad.

"Did you lose someone?" I ask, wondering if that's why she seems to consider climbing so dangerous.

She blinks, hard, then frowns.

"After a fashion," she says.

"I won't ask if you don't want to tell me."

She tilts her head again, looking closely at me, then nods.

"What else have I done that concerns you?"

"Hanging from the ceiling by your knees wasn't a reassuring moment... And that's before we get to the champagne."

"We were celebrating! Come on!"

"What about all the girls... the waitresses?"

"Haven't tipped a waitress for anything other than food in nearly a year. Haven't tipped a waitress *with* anything other than a generous amount of cash in nearly that long." She rolls her eyes at me. "You really do pay attention to the music press, don't you?"

"Part of my job, but I've always loved music. It was something Lyric and I had in common, that and..."

"Losing a loved-one. I'm sorry."

She frowns.

"I'm not going to ask how you know that about me. Actually, I meant my grandmother, who left me her house here right before Lyric and I met. But I guess you know about Rónan the same way you know about Lyric."

"Brighid wasn't wrong about band members and gossip. Well, no — not gossip. That's tacky. We just asked Dave about the connection between you and Piper, and he kind of had to tell us. Was he not supposed to?"

"No. It's fine. David is family now, one of us, and he has every right to tell his band family that Piper lost her brother. I hope you all will treat her like family, too, especially now that you know about Rónan."

"We always would have. She's going to have Dave's kid. Even if he stops touring with us, she's still part of the family. We'd always take care of her."

"That's really reassuring."

Her shoulders relax a fraction, like a little bit of weight has dropped off of them. As much as she has going on in her life, maybe it lightens her load a little, knowing that we consider Piper part of our family, too. I like that. I like that I gave her that.

"And that confirms my decision to tell you how to find Lyric. But — and I want you to listen to me really closely about this — you have to promise me you'll be more careful. OK?"

"You said that last night. But careful how? Like not skydiving ever again? Are you witchy like Brighid is? Predicting my death in a skydiving accident?"

"Oh god no," Rory says, shaking her head. "I try to leave that tarot, crystals and magic stuff to Brighid's circle. What I meant — what I meant when I said it last night — was that Lyric's still really fragile. It's been three years since Adam was killed. And she couldn't deal with it. Couldn't even be in their house for the longest time. That's why they ended up living with me."

"She and the kids lived with you?"

"For more than a year. Then... Well, something happened, and she didn't feel safe there anymore, not with the kids. And I don't blame her. So, she moved back into her mother's old house, where they'd lived when Adam was alive."

"She lives with her mother?"

"No. Her mom's kind of a retro, hippie type, and once Lyric went off to college in Baltimore, Iris took off in an RV, exploring the country, kind of a nomad. She does a lot of Renaissance faires, Highland games, music festivals, that kind of thing — she sells her art, takes a turn as a wandering minstrel, does Reiki healing, reads tarot, that kind of stuff. And once or twice a year, she shows up back here to spend some time with Lyric and her family. It's been a while since she's been back, though. She and Lyric were at odds over Lyric taking on too much, which I think everyone agrees is a problem — except Lyric herself."

"Lyric looked tired last night."

"She always looks tired. I'm sure I do, too, these days. But I do what I can to help her with the kids."

"Tommy and Aria."

I can tell I've surprised her.

"Band full of gossips is right!" Rory says, shaking her head.

"It didn't do me a lot of good. Their names, that her husband had passed and that she's a music teacher and poet was all I could get out of them. That's why I'm here."

"That you bothered learning their names says something about you, Rhys," she says. "But they're also another reason I need you to be careful. Those are my godchildren, and I will take down, with prejudice, anyone who hurts them, or Lyric."

There's a fierceness to her words that takes me aback. I'm not sure what Aurora Carmichael's vengeance would be against someone who harmed her family, but I know I don't want to be that person, because I suspect they wouldn't live a long or happy life.

"Understood."

"There's more... a lot more. But I'm not going to spill all of Lyric's life story or give you a 'how to win her over' playbook. You'll have to do that the hard way. And, no matter her inclinations otherwise, I expect she's going to make it really hard, so be prepared. I wouldn't have told you any of this if I didn't have a good feeling about you and that you might be good for her. But you need to understand that this is a very complicated situation you're walking into."

"I can see that. And I still want to get to know her."

"Alright. Listen — I've got some things going on, with work, with... other things, so I'm not going to be around as much as I usually am, which isn't nearly enough. And I want to take this timing of you showing up here like this as the universe finally stepping up to be helpful for once — both to me, and to Lyric and the kids. She'll deny it, but she needs help, and if you can take some of the weight off her, it'll do her a world of good."

"What's she need help with?"

"You name it," Rory says, scoffing. "But, right now, the big thing is the fundraiser for the music department at the school. She's organizing it single-handed this year, because the teacher who usually helps her is out on maternity leave. They'd planned to try to replace all the school band instruments and even expand, upgrade their stage and the equipment. But as busy as everyone is at the end of the summer around here, Lyric's having a hard time with getting donations for the auction, on top of organizing the food, the music, advertising..."

"I could buy the instruments, the equipment, and donate them. I've got plenty of money. She can just cancel the fundraiser."

"That's not how it works, Rhys — the fundraiser gets the whole community involved, instills pride in the students and their parents, sets the scene for the music department for the coming school year... It's really important that it happen and that it's successful, both to the department and to Lyric personally. She's got so much invested in this."

"She just needs help to make it happen."

"Yeah. And I... I've helped where I can, but right now... I've got things going on, and I just can't."

"Then I'll do it. I'll help her."

"Good. That's what I needed to hear. And you can start right now. She's over at the school — just her and the custodial staff, working on the staging, rearranging the music classroom for tours, making up programs and posters..."

"I'll go over there right now and see what I can do to help."

"Thanks, Rhys. And good luck. I think you're going to need it."

CHAPTER 6

CAREFUL

Lyric

"**I** don't know... what do you think? Does it make more sense over there, by the stage?"

Donnie shrugs at me. I'm not sure he cares whether the silent auction table goes by the stage or the doors, or in the restroom down the hall.

This is the fun part of being the sole person in charge of this event. I'm the only one who can make the decisions. And, yes, I was being sarcastic about it being fun. I'd like nothing more right now than to have someone to bounce ideas off of, maybe even take a few of these responsibilities off my shoulders.

I made every menu choice with the caterer. I picked a theme for the décor and the programs and the advertising. (Rory did help there, getting her awesome graphic designers to create an ad, and doing a trade on ads in the paper and online for a mention in the event program.) I was already in charge of organizing the music for the evening — our regular accompanist on keyboard, some of the more advanced students whose parents were willing to let them come rehearse together a few times during the summer, a former student with realistic ambitions of becoming a singer-songwriter and, out of pure desperation to fill out the program, a piece or two from me.

"I'm looking for Lyric?" I hear a man say from down the hall. That's one thing about an empty school building — good or bad, it echoes.

I can see Donnie's second-in-command, Phil, through the cafetorium doors, gesturing in my direction.

Did I forget an auction item drop-off? I wouldn't be surprised. If I didn't have everything written down in my phone, complete with reminders, I dread the mess this would all be. As it is, I got here fifteen minutes late today because Tommy spilled iced tea on his favorite shirt and I had to find another orange shirt in the laundry before he'd agree to put any shirt on at all. I wasn't going to leave him half-naked for Callie to watch, even if it was just for a couple of hours.

"Let's put them in a line down the back, on both sides of the doors. We can add a couple on the corners if we end up with more items. Thanks, Donnie," I add, giving him a weary smile.

The squeaking coming down the hall is what every teacher recognizes as the trademark sound of sneakers, which is a little surprising, since most of the auction item donors I'm waiting on now are Realtors and gallery owners — the domains of high heels and dress shoes, even while most of the rest of the locals are wearing sandals and flip-flops.

My back to the doors, I help Donnie shift one of the tables to establish the line for the others.

"Lyric?" a deep voice says from behind me.

"Sorry I wasn't out front to meet you..." I offer over my shoulder. "I know you all are incredibly busy right now, and I appreciate..."

I turn to find myself face-to-face with a rockstar, not a Realtor. My cheeks flame as bright as his hair, and I stand there, my jaw working up and down but no sounds coming out.

What else do you expect from someone who is surprised in their place of work by the incarnation of their earliest adult fantasies? And, yes, I mean "adult" in both senses of the word. If anything, with that thought, I blush even harder.

"Hi."

There. I said a word.

"Hi."

See — he's only got one word, too. Maybe it's not just me.

"Mrs. Larson, if you're happy with this one, Phil and I will start moving the others in."

I blink, coming out of my Rhys Madigan-induced trance.

"That's fine, Donnie. Thanks."

He heads out into the hallway, giving Rhys a nod, which Rhys returns.

"Uh... You're not here to drop off an auction item, clearly," I tell him. "Sorry about that. I thought maybe I'd forgotten a drop-off appointment."

"No. At least not one with me," he says, an amused (no pun intended) smile on his face. "But I'd be happy to donate something if you still need anything."

"Oh. Well, that would be great! We'd be happy to have anything you want to donate. A signed poster? Drum head? Maybe some concert tickets, if you're feeling really generous?"

"Yeah. I can do that," he says, nodding.

We stand and stare at each other for a minute. It gets uncomfortable.

"So, is there anything else—"

"You're probably wondering—" we say over top of each other. We both stop and laugh.

"I'll go first," he says. "You're probably wondering why I'm here. I mean, how I found you. Or why I was looking. Or... yeah."

He exhales, like a musical top winding down with a final few notes before it falls over.

Well, I wasn't. Wondering, I mean. I was too awestruck that he was here to wonder why. But now that he's mentioned it...

"Yeah." Eloquent, aren't I?

"'Yeah' what?"

"Yeah, I am wondering."

"Which one?"

"Well, all of them, really."

"Oh. OK. Um. It's kind of a long story."

"Do you want to come sit down?"

I look around me at the empty space and realize there's not a single chair in the room right now.

"Better idea — come down to my classroom, and we can talk."

"That would be awesome!"

Such enthusiasm, just for walking down a hallway at an elementary school.

He follows me down one hallway and then a second, then inside the door.

"Oh, wow! This is both just as cool as I remembered music class being and way cooler!" he says.

"How so?"

"You've got more stuff! And not just desks or a carpet to sit on, but beanbag chairs? Bouncy-ball chairs?"

"Well, the latest learning models show that some kids learn better when they're not forced to sit in one spot, or in something hard and constrained like a desk. So I've tried to get a few different options for the kids to try, so they can figure out what works best for them."

"I'd have loved that when I was a kid! I hated sitting in a desk. I kept getting in trouble for tapping on the edge of the desk."

"Drumming?"

"Well, not really — not when I was this age. But, kind of, yeah."

"These days, I'd hand you a fidget and see if that didn't let you get that energy out, without bothering the other students."

"Fidget?"

"Yeah. You haven't heard about all the little spinners and things they have now?" I pull one out of my desk drawer and hand it to him. It's just a couple metal rings attached to a central post they flip and spin around — the perfect size to hold in a palm or add to a keychain. "They became a huge fad. Which is a shame, because they're really useful for neurodivergent kids, to help them focus, and a lot of schools banned them because they became a distraction for the neurotypical kids."

"Mom always said I was 'neurospicy,'" he says, trying out the fidget.

I laugh.

"That's perfect."

"Yeah, you are..."

Huh?

The non-sequitur reminds me why we came down here.

I turn and sit on a corner of my desk, offering Rhys my desk chair, since it's the only normal-sized seating in the room, let alone something that will accommodate someone his size. He shrugs and drags one of yoga balls over, sitting on top of it.

"Comfy," he says, giving a few tentative bounces, while still fiddling with the fidget.

I can't help smiling. There's a childlike quality about Rhys Madigan that makes me want to forget all my adult responsibilities and just play. But I've got so much to do and so little time to do it.

"So... Why are you here?"

"I want to help."

"You want to help...?"

"You. With your fundraiser thing."

"Well, like I said, I'm thrilled to take anything you want to donate for the auctions."

"No — I mean I want to help you with the fundraiser."

"As in the event."

"Yeah."

"How'd you even hear about it?"

Rhys Madigan showing up at school with this specific task in mind, the day after we met for all of about a minute, exactly when I was working on the fundraiser?

"Your friend Rory told me you might need some help."

Rory. Of course. I swear — her and my mother. OK — and Callie and Brighid... All of them fretting about me taking on too much. Maybe they're right, but I don't have a lot of choice. If I don't do it, who will?

And for Rory to enlist Rhys Madigan, of all people, to help me? She and I are going to have a talk very soon. And by talk, I mean me giving her a piece of my mind.

"It's nice of you to offer, Rhys... Can I call you Rhys?"

"Rhys, Drummer Boy, Bae — you can call me whatever you want." he says, waggling his eyebrows at me.

OK. Now that took a turn.

Eww... Annie's voice says in my head.

I've heard a lot of pickup lines, but that had to have been one of the worst! Frank adds.

I silence the peanut galley as I consider how to respond.

Would Rory have sent Rhys over to my place of work so he could hit on me? That doesn't sound like her. More likely he bamboozled her with his rockstar charm and made her think he was sincere about wanting to help me out, when all he really wanted was my phone number. At least she didn't give it to him, I have to assume, since he showed up in person, without calling first.

"Listen, Mr. Madigan..."

"Ouch."

I ignore the wounded expression on his face.

"I'm not sure what you hoped would happen when you came over here today, but this is my place of work, and this fundraiser is very important to me and my students. I've got precious little time to get things sorted out, and precious little energy to do it with. I can't afford to waste it catering to some entitled rockstar who thinks all he has to do to get into my pants is hang a few streamers."

"Whoa! Wait a minute! That's not why I'm here!" he says, getting up off the ball.

"If you *really* want to help — if that's *all* you really want, you can drop off any donations for the auction in the school office. They'll make sure I get them. We appreciate your generosity. But I'm afraid I have to get back to work, so I'll have to ask you to leave. Please."

"Hold on, Lyric..." he says, his tone pleading.

"That's Mrs. Larson to you! And I can ask Donnie and Phil to show you out, if you can't find your own way."

He starts to say something but stops, shaking his head. Then he turns and walks out the door.

"Make sure to sign out in the office on your way out!" I call out after him.

I sit down, deflated. What was Rory thinking, sending Rhys Madigan over here?

Probably that you could use some up-close-and-personal time with a hot rockstar. And she was right, even if his pickup lines suck. You think that size thing is true?

Annie!

She snickers at me.

"Goddess bless. What a mess," I say to myself.

"What was that, Mrs. Larson?" Donnie asks from the doorway. "I thought I heard someone shouting."

"Nothing, Donnie. It was nothing. You can go back to what you were doing. Thanks."

And now I can get back to what I should have been doing, which isn't entertaining rockstars.

I dunno. I still think you should entertain *that one. Naked.*

Annie!

R ory isn't picking up her phone. That's not unheard-of, but I don't think it's because she's in a meeting or an interview.

Lyric: *I cannot believe you sent Rhys Madigan over to school to "help" me! What were you thinking? Tell me you didn't give me him my number. He didn't make it five minutes before he hit on me! I don't want him sending me sexts.*

No reply.

She's got read receipts turned off on her phone, for security reasons, after all the things we've been through. So I can't tell if she's even seen the text.

Well, at least she knows Rhys' plan didn't work.

And now I can't believe I'm saying that.

That warm feeling I used to get when thinking about my favorite drummer... gone. That giddy excitement of finally meeting him? Now transformed into a sour taste in my mouth.

Lyric: *What the Hel is wrong with Rhys Madigan? Does he think every woman he meets is just going to spread her legs for him if he asks?*

Callie: *Do I want to know what happened?*

Lyric: *Probably. LOL But yuck. He came to school under the guise of helping with the fundraiser and then hit on me. Told me to call him 'Bae.' Just yuck.*

Callie: *Well, Declan always says that Rhys has no filter. And he's... well, he's kind of odd. I mean, he had us all saying 'Flibbertigibbets' instead of dropping F-bombs. It may not have been as bad as*

*it seemed. You've got to cut him a little bit of slack,
at least from what Brighid's said about him.*

And now I remember how Rhys' and my conversation started, with the discussion of him being "neurospicy." Whether
it's ADHD or autism, or any number of other neurodivergent
behaviors, I've had enough training to know that some people
don't handle social cues as well as others. Could that be all this
was? A filterless Rhys with what I have to assume is likely a
hyperactivity disorder, saying something out of turn? Something
that would have been rude from someone else, but wasn't meant
the way I took it?

The problem is that, even if it was, I'm not in a position to
be dealing with a guy — *any* guy — who might be looking for a
short-term fling, or even a one-night-stand. I've got the kids as
my top priority, and a rockstar who's constantly leaving on tour
isn't a suitable potential father-figure...

And that thought stops me cold.

I got hit on today by the guy I once fantasized about. But I'm
no longer 20. Not even close. And I may not be in a committed
relationship, but I loved my husband, and I'm not looking to
replace him — in my life or my kids' lives.

So, regardless of what Rhys' intentions were, it's obviously
best if I steer clear of him entirely.

Lyric: *I don't think so. I'm good with my life as it is.
And I've got too much to do right now to be dealing
with any of this. I'll be home in an hour. Thanks
again for watching the kids.*

Callie: *No problem. You know that. But maybe Rhys
really did just want to help. I think maybe you
should consider giving him another chance.*

Sometimes, I think Callie forgets that I'm no longer that
20-year-old who married her and Declan the first time. She's
happily child-free, at least for now, and she's freshly reunited

with the love of her life, too. Everything is sunshine and roses for her. She has no idea what my life is really like, even if she's on the bandwagon that I try to do too much.

I really don't know anyone who might understand. Except maybe Mom, and she's in... Florida? Georgia? Somewhere in the Southeast, anyway. And if I call her, complaining about some guy hitting on me, she's going to end up on another one of her "momologues" about me doing too much and how much lighter the load would be if I'd just find a nice guy, or girl. It's weird how often she ends up on that topic, considering that she raised me by herself from Day One. But I guess perspectives change over time, or at least when her grandkids are involved.

Regardless, I don't have the time or energy for that conversation. I've got a fundraiser to finish organizing. And now, thanks to Rhys Madigan, I'm a good half-hour behind.

A second chance? No way.

CHAPTER 7
GIVE ME ONE GOOD REASON

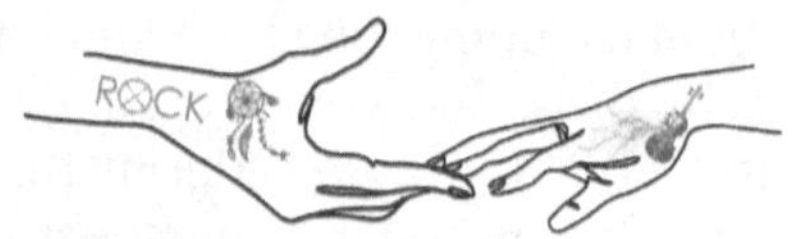

Rhys

"Alex?"

"Hmm?"

"You know how women think, right?"

"Uh... I guess. I mean, they're not a lot different from men in most ways, and they're all unique. Why?"

"I think I flibbertigibbeted up."

Alex's lips twitch.

"What'd you do this time?"

"I told her she could call me 'bae.'"

"Stop right there," he says, holding a hand up in front of my face and everything.

Yeah, I flibbertigibbeted up. Flibbertigibbets!

"Exactly which woman did you tell to call you 'bae.'?"

"Lyric."

"The girl from last night? The one you had no idea how to find?"

"Well, I was up playing most of the night, and I had an idea."

"That's never a good thing, Rhys."

"Well, the idea was to track down her reporter friend and ask her for Lyric's number."

"And Rory gave it to you?"

"No."

"See — bad ideas come from late hours, too little sleep and too many drumbeats in your head."

"No! I mean, no, she didn't give me Lyric's number, but she told me where to find her, and she even asked me to help her!"

"Well, that's unexpected..." Alex looks thoughtful.

"Yeah. Kind of blew my mind. Somebody asking me to help someone they care about, trusting me with that!"

"But then you fucked up."

"I think I really did. We were having a nice conversation in her classroom — she has these cool bouncy-ball seats, and these fidget things she said they give the kids who are neurospicy like me..."

"Neurospicy?"

"Mom calls me that. Because of my ADHD."

"Ah. OK. So she knows about dealing with people who have ADHD."

"And other stuff, too. But, yeah. She even gave me one of her fidgets." I show him the little piece of metal I haven't let go of since she pressed it into my hand.

"So you were having this nice conversation, and..."

"She asked if she could call me Rhys, and I told her, yeah, she could call me whatever she wanted, and I remembered that girls call their boyfriends 'bae' so I said she could call me 'bae.' Because I'd really like to be her boyfriend."

"Geez..."

"What?"

"Rhys — I know you're used to your 'relationships' lasting an hour or two at most, but most women are looking for something a little longer-term, and that usually means slow-playing the getting-to-know-you part of the relationship. You just went from zero to sixty on the girl!"

"Oh."

"And you did that to a widow with kids."

"Oh..."

I smack myself on the forehead.

"Rory told me I had to be more careful."

"Yeah, I heard her. She didn't seem impressed by your acrobatics."

"No — it wasn't that. She was warning me to be more careful with Lyric. She said she's still fragile..."

"After losing her husband."

"Yeah." I rub my hand over my face. "I blew this. I totally blew it. She's never going to want to see me again."

I throw myself down on the sofa, my arm over my eyes.

Alex sits down on the coffee table next to me.

"You giving up that easily?"

"What else can I do?"

"The same thing Hunter did with Brighid, and David did with Piper, and Declan did with Callie: You fight for her, if you really want to be with her."

He's right about that. Hunt, Dave and Dec all could have given up when things got tough with their women. They didn't. And they're all happy now. I'm not going to pretend everything is perfect for all of them, but you look at them and you can see the love.

I'd never even thought about that kind of relationship before, but now I'm surrounded by them, and that and seeing Lyric in my dreams for all these months? That's not a coincidence. I'm not sure I believe in a higher power, or fate, or the magical waters of Mystic Beach (which have yet to yield a single mermaid sighting!) or whatever Brighid would say was behind it all. But I knew the moment I saw Lyric with my waking eyes, the moment I knew she was real, that I had to get to know her. And then Rory told me just a little about her, and I wanted to help her. Not just so I could get to know her, but to really help her, because I want her life to be easier, you know? And I still want that. But then I had to go and flibbertigibbet things up and end up making her life harder. Rory's going to be pissed. Unless I can fix it. I can fix it, right?

"Can I fix this?" I ask Alex.

"Maybe," he says. "Kind of depends on how much she liked you before you fucked it up."

"I thought maybe she did. She seemed a little... starstruck, maybe? You know — like the teenage girls at our meet-and-greets? At least at first..."

"Well, it sounds like the starstruck part wore off when she realized you were hitting on her."

"I wasn't hitting on her!"

"Well, you kind of were. And not very skillfully at that."

"So how do I do it *carefully*?" Rory's warning rings in my ears.

"Well, you can start by just trying to honestly help her. What was it Rory said you should help her with?"

"A fundraiser she's organizing for the music department at the school where she teaches. She was setting up tables and stuff today, organizing auction stuff."

"So you showed up at her work, offered to help and then hit on her."

"Not on purpose! But, yeah."

"Then you need a do-over, a chance to prove to her that you really want to help her, not just get into her pants."

"No pants. Got it."

Alex chuckles.

"Do you want to write this down?"

"I'll just forget to look at the place I wrote it down."

"True. You realize if you're going to help her with this fundraiser, you're going to have to be a little more organized yourself, right?"

Oh, flibbertigibbets.

Yeah, this is the kind of thing Rory was warning me about. Forget no more skydiving. It's worse than that. I'm going to have to get a planner or something.

"Your phone is your friend," Alex says. "There's an app for everything."

"Is there an app to get a girl to give you a do-over?"

"Probably not. But I've got an idea that might help, even if she doesn't want to give you that second chance. Just make sure you don't waste it. I doubt you'll get a third."

The next morning

"Carla Frostberg. How may I help you?"

"Ms. Frostberg — or is it Mrs.?"

"Doctor, actually. But Carla's fine."

"Carla — my name is Rhys Madigan. I'm not sure if you've heard of me, but I'm the drummer for a band called aMUSEd—"

"Oh my god."

It's very strange how many people have been saying that lately when I introduce myself. I'm going to get a god complex pretty soon.

"Carla? Are you still there?"

"Yes. Sorry. I'm listening."

"Anyway — as you may have heard, my band's in town, working on our next album, and it came to my attention, through a media contact of ours, Aurora Carmichael..."

"Yes, I know Rory quite well."

"Well, she brought it to my attention that you were scheduled to hold a fundraiser for the school's music department in the next few weeks, and I'd very much like to offer some assistance with that."

"Oh! That would be amazing! Were you wanting to donate a signed drum head or cymbal, or some concert tickets for the live auction?"

"Well, I had something bigger in mind. I have a number of items of signed memorabilia I can donate, including some concert-used instruments, and I'd like to also donate a full kit from my signature collection — two, actually, so one can go to the music department itself and one for auction."

"That's an incredibly generous offer, Mr. Madigan."

"Rhys, please."

"Rhys. Again, that's incredibly generous. I'm happy to put you in touch with our event organizer, Mrs. Larson, to get the details."

"I'd also like to make a monetary donation to help with the cost of putting on the event."

"You want to underwrite the event itself?"

"Yes, assuming you still need that kind of support."

"I believe we do. I'll let Mrs. Larson know you're interested in underwriting as well. This is really..." Carla gasps a little, clearly taken aback. Good. Hopefully, she'll be cooperative with my request. "It's just so incredibly generous."

"I do have one condition that I'm afraid will have to be met."

"Oh? What's that?"

"I need to be personally involved in organizing the fundraiser event itself."

"Why would you want to do that?"

Uh... I look up at Alex, desperate for help. This was his idea, after all. He gestures for me to mute the microphone.

"Tell them you have a personal ethic of being hands-on with your philanthropy, and that the label would like to ensure that anything that reflects on your image or the band's is actually being handled personally."

"I'm not sure I can remember all of that."

"Hand me the phone."

I hand him the phone. He takes it off mute.

"Hello?"

"Yes? Mr. Madigan?"

"This is Mr. Madigan's public-relations assistant... uh... Alexander," he rolls his eyes at me and shrugs. "I've got the stipulations from the label right here in front of me... One second." He pauses and taps his toes a few times, makes as if he's shuffling papers. "Yes... The label would like to ensure that anything that reflects on Mr. Madigan's image or the band's image is actually being handled personally, by Mr. Madigan. Additionally, Mr. Madigan's personal ethic of philanthropy is to be hands-on. It's very important to him, so I'm afraid we must insist that he be involved."

"Well, it's a very generous donation. I'm sure we can accommodate Mr. Madigan's request. I'll have Mrs. Larson get in touch with him to coordinate. We're very grateful for his support."

"He's very interested in this particular cause," Alex tells her. He hands the phone back to me.

"Yes — very interested. Passionately," I add. "I'm really looking forward to helping make the event a success."

"Well, thank you again, Mr. Madigan. Someone will be in touch." The line clicks.

"Yes!" I yell, reaching over to Alex for a high-five.

"Ow! Not so hard, Rhys!"

"Sorry! I was excited!"

"With good reason. Now you just have to make it count with your girl."

Suddenly, I'm a lot less excited. I'm not sure how Lyric is going to react to being told she has to work with me on the fundraiser, but I suspect it won't be with an ode to my ingenuity.

Lyric

"He did what?"

"He offered a substantial donation of signed memorabilia, concert-used instruments and a signed signature drum kit, plus one for the school, as well as offering to cover the remaining underwriting costs for the event itself," Carla says.

"Wow."

"Yeah. It was too generous of a donation to refuse. The auctions alone are likely to outraise last year's event total, if my quick bit of research is at all accurate. He had just one demand..."

"Which was...?"

"That he be permitted to help with the hands-on parts of organizing the event."

"He didn't."

"He did. I thought it was a little weird, with him being who he is — I mean, how does he even find the time? — but he had some PR assistant who said the label was demanding it, and I wasn't going to argue, with that kind of donation on the line. I figured you could have him hang streamers or something. He *is* very tall. Probably wouldn't even need a ladder."

"So he's now helping me organize this as we get down to the wire for everything. Rhys Madigan."

"Yeah. I have to admit I'm a little envious. He's seriously cute."

"Yeah, cute's the word," I grumble.

"Is there a problem?"

"No. No problem." Yeah. I lie. Because how would I explain why there is actually a problem without sounding either ungrateful or like I've lost my marbles?

"He gave me his personal cell number to call so you can arrange things with him."

"Of course."

CHAPTER 8

SWEET CHILD O' MINE

Lyric

"**M**r. Madigan, this is Mrs. Larson from Mystic Beach Elementary School."

"Please, Lyric, call me Rhys," he pleads.

I pause, waiting for the rest of the request.

"I'm so sorry about yesterday," he says when I don't say anything. "I... Well, I'm the first to admit I tend to stick my foot in my mouth pretty often, and then I usually manage to find room for the other one, too. But I can promise you I didn't mean to come off as rude as I did yesterday. It's just... That neurospicy thing..."

"Your brain didn't realize how your words would be perceived."

"Yeah. That."

"Why do you want to help with the fundraiser? Really? Be honest with me."

"I like you. I want to get to know you better. But I also saw how tired you looked, and I wanted to help. And Rory told me I could help by helping you with the fundraiser."

"Let's get one thing straight right now: I'm not interested in a relationship, casual or otherwise. I need you to understand that. If you help with the event, you're there to help with the event. That's it."

I can hear him sigh over the phone. I knew this wasn't about helping the school. But he's backed me into a corner. I don't have a real choice about accepting his help, not if I want the amazing windfall in auction donations and funding he's promised. But if I can keep this professional, cordial, maybe I can make it work. Maybe I can even lighten my load, at least a little. And it'll make dealing with his bandmates less of an issue going forward, since they've established themselves in my friends' lives.

"Rhys? Are you still there?"

"I am. And thank you for calling me Rhys."

He sounds so relieved that I almost feel bad for him. That childlike, golden retriever part of his personality is hard to hold a grudge against. It's the entitled rockstar I need to keep at arm's length.

"We have to work together on this. You left me with no choice in that. But there's no reason we can't be friendly while we're doing the work. As long as you understand that friendly is as far as this goes between us."

"I hear you," he says. "I'll be more careful from here on. That I can promise."

"Then I thank you for your donations and your willingness to help."

"What can I do?"

"Well, if you're available, I can meet you at the school in two hours so we can divide up these tasks and start knocking them out. Oh — and Rhys..."

"Yes?"

"You'll have to pass a background check if you want to help at any points when kids are in the building."

"Already done. I had our security team send over background documents right after I talked to Carla."

"OK. I'll see you in two hours."

Two hours later

“**A**ria, open that door for Mommy, please.”

I lug a big cardboard box through the door, holding it open while Tommy passes through behind me.

This is not going to plan. None of the aunties were available to babysit today, and I couldn't afford to lose any more time. Ordinarily, I'd have no qualms about bringing the kids to school with me. Tommy's autism makes him a natural at solo play. The challenge is getting him out of "Tommy world" and interacting with the rest of the world. And Aria is happy as a clam with a pad of paper and some crayons. They'll both watch videos or play games on my tablet or phone, but they're not fixated on them. The bottom line is that I can usually get a couple hours of work done before I have to stop and actively parent. In my classroom or working with other members of school staff is no different. School is a kid-friendly place, and the staff all know my kids.

But Rhys Madigan? Rhys Madigan, rockstar, who skydives and hangs from ceilings with champagne bottles and asks a woman he's barely met to call him "bae"? Totally different circumstances. Even if I was in a place where I wanted a boyfriend, I'd date the guy for a good long while before I introduced him to my kids. I wouldn't want them to get attached to someone who might be gone from their lives tomorrow. I wouldn't want to risk Tommy feeling rejected if some guy decided he wasn't up to the task of helping to parent a kid with autism. Not everyone is eager to understand a kid like Tommy, even if they're willing to become a stepparent. So I'd be damn sure of any boyfriend I'd introduce to the kids.

Rhys Madigan is not my boyfriend. But it's pretty clear he thinks he wants to be. Maybe just for a night or a week. But I've set boundaries for this situation, and I just hope Rhys will be able to stay within those lines. Because if he doesn't, I run the risk of my kids getting hurt, and I cannot allow that to happen. I won't allow it to happen. You think a mama bear is dangerous when she's protecting her cubs? You ain't seen a mama witch protecting hers...

"Can I help you with that?"

Rhys emerges from the office, a visitor badge with his photo on it stuck to his shirt.

I want to tell him no. That I'm self-sufficient and don't need his big, strong, manly, rock-climbing drummer arms to relieve my load. But who are we kidding? This box is heavy, and I've got Tommy's bag slung over my shoulder, my purse...

"Yes. Please."

He grabs the box like it weighs nothing and tucks it under one long arm.

Well, that's humbling.

"Where to?"

"My classroom."

We walk down the hallway in silence, Tommy and Aria on either side of me, and Rhys at my back with the box. Aria looks up at me, a question burning through her patience. She manages to wait until we get inside the classroom.

"Where do you want it?" Rhys asks.

"On that table back there. Thanks."

Tommy holds out his hand for his bag, and I give it to him. He plunks down in the beanbag chair and starts fiddling with his latest contraption.

"Mommy? Who's that tall man?" Aria half-whispers. Well, what passes as a whisper for a 7-year-old.

Rhys puts the box down and turns around, smiling at her.

"This is Mr. Rhys," I tell her, having made the decision before we left him to not add Rhys to the list of uncles that it seems like the entire band has started to become. I need the distance of that language choice, even if no one else does.

"Rhys, this is my daughter, Aria..."

"Like the song!" Aria emphasizes. "Not the sword-girl."

Aria's had enough people ask her about dragons and swords that she preemptively eliminates any confusion.

"No — like the music of an opera. Of course," Rhys says, as if there was no other possible explanation. "It's a very beautiful name!"

He offers her his hand, and she takes it, shakes it enthusiastically.

"Do you know a lot about music, Mr. Rhys? Like Mommy?"

"I know a bit. I'm not a music teacher like your mom, but I am a musician."

"What do you play?"

"The drums, mostly. I have a band, and I play drums in my band."

"Are you any good?"

I cringe at the directness of a kid her age, but I can't help smiling when Rhys chuckles.

"I'm not the best ever, but I'm pretty good. People seem to like our music," he says.

"Oh. You're not as good as 'MUSEd, then. They're the best."

Rhys looks at me, questioning.

Aria never saw Rhys during the wedding reception, buried as he was behind his kit and as engrossed in her writing and drawing as she was.

"Aria, Mr. Rhys' band *is* aMUSEd. When we saw them the other day at Auntie Callie's party, Mr. Rhys was playing drums."

"Oh! Cool. Tommy loves the drums, Mr. Rhys. Can you teach him?"

"Aria!" I interrupt, both alarmed at the idea of incorporating Rhys into our lives and reminding Aria of the family rule that's been in place for most of her life. "Mr. Rhys is very busy. And Tommy has other things he needs to learn."

"I know — to talk."

"Aria... We've talked about this before... There's nothing wrong with your brother not talking. We just need to help him communicate however he feels most comfortable. OK?"

"Sorry, Mommy."

"And?"

"Sorry, Tommy."

He glances up at her and then goes right back to his contraption.

"Aria, why don't you unpack your drawing supplies while Mr. Rhys and I start working?"

"OK."

Rhys approaches me and speaks quietly.

"Tommy's autistic."

"Yes. And non-verbal. We're working on his communication skills. It's easy to fall into the idea that he needs to learn to talk, but it's an ableist idea they're trying to get away from. He attends a special school about twenty minutes from Mystic Beach, and we do therapy during the summer."

Rhys just nods.

"Tommy, this is Mr. Rhys."

Tommy glances up again, his eyes roving over me but pausing a second on Rhys.

"We've met," Rhys says. "Hi, Tommy," he adds with a smile.

Tommy goes back to his Legos.

"You've met?"

"He escaped from Rory the other night, for just a minute. He found me — well, my kit. He does seem to love the drums."

There's no denying that, but there's no accepting the import of it either. I can't.

"Are you named after the candy, Mr. Rhys?" Aria asks suddenly, breaking the tension.

Grateful, I chuckle, because it never occurred to me to get the two mixed up. I've known how to spell Rhys since I was 20.

"No, Aria. I used to think so, but my mom says I'm not. My name is spelled R-H-Y-S. It's from Wales. They like to spell words with Y's there."

"Oh. Cool," she says.

"So — shall we get to work?" I ask him.

He grabs the yoga ball again and settles in as comfortably as he did yesterday. Before things got weird, anyway.

"I've got very little time left to finish a long list of tasks. Mrs. Tielmann was handling these details, but she got put on bed rest, and now she's on leave. So it's all been up to me. The big stuff — the caterer, the music, the advertising, staff — that's all been handled. Now, it's making sure the auction items are in, that the donors are credited in the program, arranging and decorating the cafetorium..."

"Cafetorium?"

"That room we were in yesterday — it doubles as a cafeteria and an auditorium."

"I just assumed it was an auditorium."

"It's pretty common in schools now. The lunch tables fold up into seating, or they can be moved out to open up the room or add regular chairs. Right now, they've been removed so that we can have an open room for the event. We'll have tables along the back wall for the auction items, with food tables along the sides for small-plates stuff while everyone mingles and browses the auction items. And the music will be on the stage, happening sporadically through the event."

"Like a standing-room-only concert."

"Yes."

"Sounds like you've got it mostly figured out. What can I do to help?"

"Carla suggested I have you hang streamers," I deadpan.

Rhys gives me a questioning look, then cracks up.

"Because I'm so tall!"

A smile leaks through on my face. Then I start laughing, too.

"It does reduce the liability concerns if you don't need a ladder."

He chuckles again, his eyes tracing over my face.

"You have an amazing smile."

And I shut down. I need to keep this to the business at hand. Letting down my guard with Rhys even for a moment gets us here. So I ignore his pushing up against those lines I so firmly drew.

"Realistically, the steamers are going up at the top of the walls, so not even you are tall enough for that. I'll probably just ask Donnie to do it."

"That's OK. Get me a ladder. I'm comfortable with heights. I'm actually more comfortable up high than I am on the ground."

"Of course you are..."

"Of course? Is that another joke about my height?"

Uh... I'm not admitting that I know a lot more about Rhys than the average person should. I don't want to unintentionally encourage him.

"Rory mentioned that you skydive."

Total lie. I still haven't heard back from Rory. Why do I find myself lying so much where Rhys is involved? Mostly keeping my guard up, I guess. And it's not like he's going to know I'm lying.

"She did? She didn't seem too comfortable with the idea of my skydiving."

"Mommy, what's skydiving?"

Suddenly, I'm reminded that we're having this conversation in front of my kids. I've learned the hard way that Tommy's silence, his extreme introversion, doesn't necessarily mean that he's not paying attention to what's going on around him, or taking in what's being said. But he doesn't usually actively eavesdrop. Aria, on the other hand...

"Aria — what did we say about eavesdropping?"

"That it's rude."

"And?"

"That I shouldn't do it." She looks down at her hands and away from me.

"And?"

"Sorry, Mommy. Sorry, Mr. Rhys."

She picks up her crayon again.

"Is it OK if I tell her?" Rhys asks.

I can't see the harm if he does, so I nod.

"Aria, skydiving is when you put a big parachute on and jump out of an airplane way up in the sky. And then you fall down, nice and slow, and land on your feet."

"You don't smash into the ground?"

"No. The parachute makes you fall super-slow, and if you practice how to land, you can land right on your feet, just like you'd only jumped off your bed."

"Mommy says not to jump on the bed. It's bad for the mattress. And you could get hurt."

I blush. Now I feel like an overprotective parent. Mom always said not to jump on the mattress because she'd worked hard and saved up for us to have nice mattresses that would last forever. In fact, Aria's mattress is the same one I had as a kid. Tommy's sleeping on the one my mom used. As for getting hurt... We've had one major run-in with the kids having an accident, and that was enough.

"Well, your mommy is right. Mommies always are," Rhys says.

Hmm... Sounds like Rhys has a good relationship with his mother, respectful. Not what I expected from the adrenaline-junkie rockstar...

"But these days we have trampoline parks to have that kind of fun. It's easier on the mattresses," he says, giving me a wink.

But I cringe, because he's opened up a can of worms in a way no parent would ever do, mentioning the trampoline park so casually... Ugh.

"Can we go to the trampoline park, Mommy?" Aria asks. "We haven't been all summer!"

I sigh and roll my eyes. I knew it was coming. Even worse, Tommy's now looking at me, making eye-contact, which is his version of seconding his sister's request. And when he bothers to do that... I'm looking at a full-on meltdown if I say no.

"We've been very busy this summer, Aria. We haven't really had time. And we've been to the beach, to the amusement park, to see the ponies — lots of fun things."

"But I want to go to the trampoline park!"

Tommy's eyes are pleading with me. And once again, meaning to or not, Rhys Madigan has backed me into a corner.

"We'll talk about it later, after Mr. Rhys and I get done with what we're doing. OK?"

"Alright..." Aria drones, disappointed. Tommy frowns but returns to disassembling his contraption to begin a new one. I just got very, very lucky. Somehow.

Rhys steps closer and speaks in an undertone.

"Oh, man — I'm so sorry. I didn't even think about whether mentioning it was a good idea."

"You don't have kids, or you'd know that all too well. Never mention the existence of something a kid wants or wants to do, unless you're prepared to give it to them or endure begging and/or temper tantrums. We got lucky. I think they're on their best behavior because you're a new person. At home, Tommy would probably be on the floor, kicking and screaming right now."

"Can I make it up to you?"

"What? You don't have to do anything. No harm done. I'll just have to find some time to take them in the next few days."

"You've already got too much on your plate."

"That's what you're here to help with, right?" Even though we haven't gotten any actual work accomplished yet...

"Right. But... Can I take you — the three of you — to the trampoline park? My treat. I'll even help watch the kids."

"That's not necessary. And, honestly, considering yesterday, I'm not really comfortable with it."

"Please? It's the least I can do after that and getting their hopes up just now."

I think about the number of times I've had to try to watch two kids at the trampoline park, and how many times in the past I've dragged Rory or Brighid with me, and how much fun the kids had with another adult there to watch them and even jump a little... I'm already dreading taking them alone again. And everyone else is so busy...

"I'll think about it."

"OK."

That's it? No pressure? No bargaining or trying to bribe me with more donations? I'm starting to realize that my idea of who Rhys is isn't the full picture of the man. I've made assumptions about him, based on my second- or third-hand knowledge and on a few brief (and messy) interactions. I don't know him at all. I know Brighid adores him, though, like a goofy younger brother, so he can't be all bad. But if there's more to him than that, I'm going to have to get to know him better to see it, see how all the puzzle pieces fit. Part of me wants to do that, and as soon as I realize that, I realize my barriers against this man are already starting to break down. I'm in so much trouble...

"So... Let's look at my to-do list and see what you can easily take over..."

CHAPTER 9
TAKING CARE OF BUSINESS

Rhys

So far so good. I came close to flibbertigibbeting things up again, mentioning the trampoline park. But I think I fixed it. Maybe even made a little inroads with Lyric, who still seems very determined to keep me at arm's length. Fingers crossed that she'll let me take them.

But now I have to do the really hard stuff: being helpful with a million tiny details that I have no idea how to handle, in a town I'm only barely familiar with. And...

"So, if you take this half of the list and go check in with the donor businesses, pick up whatever's ready, remind the others gently that we're nearing our deadline, then I can take the other half and make phone calls to them, set up times to pick up their donations when I've got someone to watch the kids..."

Sounds entirely reasonable. And yet totally out of the realm of possibility for me.

"Uh... One problem: I don't have a car."

"You don't have a car."

She blinks.

"No. I mean — yes, I have a car. I just don't have one here. We flew down from New York. And we've been using Brighid's car to lug gear and when Hunt needs to go somewhere. And Declan uses Callie's car. Piper doesn't even have a car... Actually, I'm not sure she even knows how to drive, because I've never seen her... And we called a Lyft to take Hunter to the hospital when he yelled at a goddess and punched the house—"

"Hunter yelled at a goddess?"

"Yeah — yours, I guess. I mean, that's the only one I've heard anyone mention. Brighid — like our Brighid, but, you know, a goddess."

"There are a lot of goddesses in the world, Rhys. But chances are good that it was Herself."

She smirks at me.

"No wonder..." she says.

"No wonder what?"

"No wonder things went as haywire as they did before Hunter made it up to her... and to Herself, presumably."

"Why do you call her that? Herself?"

"That's a better question for Brighid or, better yet, Kieran. It's a common expression in Irish, referring to someone as 'himself' or 'herself,' especially if they're an important someone."

"And she's important."

"She's a goddess, Rhys. And, to a lot of people, just as beloved as a saint. It's a matter of respect."

She looks up at a noise in the hallway.

"Hi, Donnie! Did you need me?"

"Just needed to check on where you wanted the food tables set."

"Give me about ten minutes and I'll be right there."

Donnie nods and heads back up the hall.

Lyric seems oddly nervous.

"Something wrong?"

"No. It's nothing."

I don't quite believe her, but I don't want to offend her by implying that it's a lie. Careful, Rory said. Probably not about whatever this is. But it never hurts for me to remind myself to be more careful. Maybe I'll actually learn to do it, somehow.

"Where were we?"

"My lack of a car."

"Yeah... Kind of hard for you to pick up auction items with no transportation."

"I'll ask Brighid to borrow her car. She lives in walking distance from her shop. Hunt's in walking distance from the studio. She'll be fine without it for a couple hours."

"A couple hours today, and for the next week? Remember — she's also finalizing wedding details..."

I did actually forget that. I'm kind of just waiting for Hunter to tell me one day that I need to be somewhere in an hour because the wedding is happening...

"Right. Well, let me ask about today, and I'll try to think of another solution for the rest of the week, even if I have to rent a car."

"Don't do that. I can just take the whole list and work on it myself."

"And what's left for me to help you with?"

"Right now? Not a lot. I've got to oversee things like table placement, the program — which we can't finalize until I've got all the donations."

"So until we do that, everything is still on you."

"Well, yeah. But I can handle it."

"Nope."

"Nope?" Uh-oh. Outrage. "You think I can't handle this on my own?"

Danger. Danger, Rhys Madigan!

"Whoa! No! Not what I meant. Sorry — feet in mouth, remember?"

She takes a breath, lets it back out.

"What did you mean?"

"I meant that I'm not going to let you handle it on your own. I'm sure you could, even if you fall over when you're done, but—"

"Mommy? Are you going to fall over?"

I cringe. I did it again.

"I'm sure your mommy will be fine, Aria. She's a smart lady. Too smart not to let people help her."

Lyric glares at me, but it's a gentle glare — I can say that, because people glare at me a lot, and I know when they're really mad. She's just irked. And maybe a little touched that I care. Yeah. I'm sure that's it.

"Fine. I'll let you figure it out."

"Can you help me figure out how to remember who I've checked with and who I haven't?"

She gives me a look.

"You don't keep notes on your phone?"

"No. Mostly I use it for checking social media when the guys mess up and go viral in ways that make their girls angry."

That makes her laugh.

"No calendar? No to-do list? No reminders?"

"I tried all that planner stuff in school. I forgot to use the planner half the time. These days, I kind of just wait for people to tell me I need to be somewhere, and then I go there." I shrug.

"How about this — I'll share my to-do list to your phone, and then we can divide the list up and you can just check off your parts as you do them. That way, we'll both know what needs to be done and what's been taken care of."

"Sounds like a plan. You just have to show me how to do that." And then I have to remember. Somehow.

"**H**i. I'm—"

"Oh. My. God! Rhys Madigan!"

I smile at the girl behind the desk. Yet another who seems to think I'm a higher power...

"That's me. Listen — I'm helping out with the fundraiser for the music department at Mystic Beach Elementary, and I was supposed to stop by and pick up a donation?"

"But you're Rhys Madigan!"

"Yes. Hi. About the donation..."

"Will you sign an autograph for me?"

"Sure."

She shoves a piece of letterhead at me, then a pen.

"What's your name?"

"Sarah. With an H."

"Alright." I sign my standard autograph inscription and slide the pen and paper back to her.

"Now, about that don—"

"Could I take a selfie with you?"

I'm starting to appreciate Gryffin and his guys right now, because it's been a while since I've been totally at the mercy of our fans when I'm actually trying to get something accomplished. And I'm trying really hard to stay focused on what I'm supposed to be doing here.

"Sure. Just give me like ten minutes before you post it, OK?"

She's already standing next to me, pulling my arm around her. I smile, let her take a couple shots with her phone and then step back.

"About that donation?"

"Let me check. I'll be right back. Don't go anywhere!"

I tap my fingers on the desk while I wait. When I look up, Sarah's still gone, but three women are standing in the hallway where Sarah went, staring at me. They're kind of trying to hide it, but they've got even less subtlety going for them than I do.

"Selfies?"

One of them jumps up and down, the other two smiling and striding right at me. By the time I've done selfies with all of them, three more people are waiting in the wings.

This is going to be a long day.

"**T**hanks for all your help, Sarah!" I wave. "And thank Martha for her donation! I'll get it straight to Mrs. Larson."

I'll have to do that, because this one stop has taken so long that I'm due to meet up with Lyric and compare notes on our progress. I have a sneaking suspicion that she's going to be a little disappointed in me. Especially when I tell her I forgot how to check off the completed item on my new to-do list.

Ugh.

CHAPTER 10

WE CAN WORK IT OUT

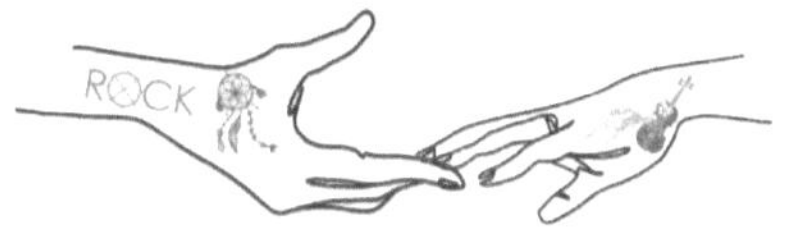

Lyric

"How'd it go?"

Rhys hands me a modest-sized gift basket.

"From Starfish Realty, as promised."

"Awesome! Did you mark them off the list?"

For a pretty big guy, Rhys kind of shrinks in on himself, tapping the toe of one shoe on the floor. I'm going to take that as a no.

"I couldn't remember how you did it."

"It's fine. I'll show you again."

I demonstrate on his phone as Rhys looks over my shoulder. It gives me a little bit of an idea what it must be like to have an attention deficit, because having him so close... it's definitely distracting. This close, I smell hints of spice and... Nonna's lessons on herbs supply their names — cardamom, pepper, juniper, sage...

Rhys clears his throat, and I realize I've paused in my demonstration.

Laughter echoing in my head...

Finding it hard to focus? He's a hottie, for sure. And I don't even like redheads.

Pull it together, Lyric, I tell myself.

"See — just tap the circle. Then you can tap here to add a note, write down what they gave you. 'Golf-themed gift basket.' There."

He stands up straight and steps back a step, and I breathe a sigh of relief.

"OK. I'll try to remember for the next one."

"That's fine. You'll get the hang of it. And then you'll be able to make your own lists whenever you want to."

"Cool."

"Now — what else do we need to mark off? Do you want me to have Donnie come help you unload Brighid's car?"

"That's all of it."

I frown, confused.

"You've been gone for two hours..."

"I know," he says, his expression sheepish. "But I got distracted by all the yarn in Brighid's shop when I went to pick up the car, and then I got lost trying to follow the directions you gave me, until I remembered that GPS works for cars and not just hiking a trail to get to a rock... And then I finally got there, but Sarah wanted an autograph, and then a selfie, and then her friends, and then..."

"OK. I get it." I sigh. "So you got one marked off the list."

"I'm really sorry. I'll go out right now and work on the next one. Unless you'd rather someone else helped you. I can see if Kier can do it. Not as many people recognize him. And he's better with this organizational stuff."

"No!" It's an instinctive reaction to watching Rhys try to give up and back out of helping me. And I'm not sure exactly why. He looks a little taken aback by it. And so am I. "This is my fault — I should have realized that sending a celebrity to do a simple errand wouldn't be... well, simple. Of course people are going to want your time. And you're not familiar with the town..."

"Maybe I can take over with the tables and things so you can go out."

"No — I got the tables sorted out while you were gone."

He looks disappointed.

"I could watch the kids."

"Uh... no."

"Why not? We're getting along."

This has already left Rhys feeling like he isn't capable of doing a simple errand. I don't want to tell him I don't trust him with my kids. But I barely managed to get myself to leave them with Piper and David. If Brighid hadn't told me Piper had lots and lots of experience with kids and that David was incredibly responsible,

I wouldn't have even let *them* stay with the kids. Not even with Callie needing me pretty urgently at that point.

"Why don't we try this... We'll go together. The kids can stay in the car with you while I collect the donations. That way, you're not gathering a fangirl train that slows you down, and if something happens with the kids, you just text me and I'm right there to handle it."

Rhys smiles, looking relieved.

"Best of both worlds!"

"Yeah."

"Thanks," he says.

"For what?"

"For letting me help."

That's the moment I finally believe that Rhys really is here for the right reasons. He really does want to help.

"Let's get Brighid's car back to her, and we'll go from there."

"T hanks again, Bonnie! I'll make sure the shop is credited in the program. And I'll see you at the fundraiser!"

I let the door close behind me and walk back to the car. Rhys leaps up and opens the back door, taking the basket and setting it down next to the others.

"Here."

I hand him a stick of candy.

"For me? Thanks."

I close the door and get back in the driver's seat.

"How's it going, kids?"

"Mr. Rhys told me a story about a lady who saved a spider, and to thank her, it taught her how to weave a magical web that kept bad dreams away."

I look over at Rhys, who smiles.

"My mom used to tell me that story when I was a kid," he says. He pulls his shirt sleeve up, showing me the dreamcatcher tattoo I already knew he had. Only I never knew there was a story attached. A tattoo of a story his mother told him as a kid? Rhys seems to really love his mom. I didn't know that, either.

I unwrap and hand a second candy stick to Aria.

"How you doing, buddy?" I ask Tommy. He glances up at Rhys and then goes right back to his gears.

"He doesn't get one?" Rhys asks, gesturing with his candy.

"He doesn't like hard candy. He's picky about a lot of things, especially food."

"Oh," Rhys says. "You sure, Tommy? I think this one is grape."

He offers Tommy the candy. Tommy grunts, pushing Rhys' hand away.

"Sorry about that," I say quietly, "but I warned you. And since he doesn't talk, I can't reprimand him for telling you no in the only way he'll use."

"No — it's fine. You were right, and you did warn me. I'll listen next time." He looks back at Tommy. "Sorry, bud. I'll listen better next time."

Well, huh... I think it's the first time that anyone's ever apologized to Tommy for not listening. Except me and... I shake my head, getting myself back on track.

"Who's ready for some dinner?"

I don't wait for Tommy's vote. It's his usual dinner time. It's more likely he'll start getting cranky if we don't eat soon.

"Me!" Aria says, waving her hand.

"Me, too!" Rhys says, mimicking the gesture.

"I can drop you off at the studio if you need to get back. Or at Callie's. We're just going to the little family restaurant down the street. Nothing fancy."

"Hey — I'm not Declan! I'm good with burgers and fries most of the time."

"Are you sure? I'd normally just head home and pull something out of the freezer. But since we're out and the kids are hungry..."

"It's fine. I'd enjoy it, actually."

"Alright, then. Off to the Coastal Kitchen!"

Rhys

Aria is coloring a paper hat, while Tommy is playing Angry Birds on Lyric's tablet.

"Raspberry tea?" the waitress asks. Lyric gestures to Tommy.

"And a milk," the waitress says, putting the cup down in front of Aria.

"A peach milkshake," she says, setting that in front of Lyric, who only ordered it after I insisted she treat herself. She'd have drooled over it on the menu and then ordered a glass of water if I hadn't.

"And a Dogfish SeaQuench Ale."

For all that I'm not the foodie that Declan has turned out to be, I try to taste the local brews when I'm traveling. Dogfish isn't the little local micro-brewery it once was, but I'm taking advantage of being near its origins. Lime, salt and malt. It's beachy. Perfect when I'm sitting on a deck a couple blocks from the ocean, with the tang of salt air on the breeze.

I'm not as passionate about the ocean as Dave is, but I think I had a past life as a beach bum, because ever since we got here, I've been feeling like I belong here. Amusement parks, a bayside bar (even if it seems like the pirates headed to the Caribbean for the summer), a studio to record in... I haven't made it out kite-surfing yet, but that's next on my list. Right now, I want nothing more than to enjoy some downtime with my dream-girl. Even if I can't tell her that. Yet.

"So, we've knocked out about a third of the list..."

Lyric's all business, at least when she's not doing something with her kids.

"Did you mark them off on your phone?" she asks.

"All except the last one." I pull out my phone and do that now. "There."

"At this rate, we should be able to get the rest of them done this week, leaving plenty of time for the program and decorating. And then I just need to get in the final rehearsals for the musical performances."

"Does that mean you have time for a little break tomorrow? Maybe take the kids for that outing?"

See — I'm getting this subtle-around-kids thing down.

Lyric frowns. I can tell she wants to say no. But something... something is making her consider it. Can I hope it's something more than wanting to avoid a meltdown — from me or the kids?

"I'll behave. I promise."

I'm learning all kinds of new skills this week. Patience and not blurting out every thought in my head are two of them, though I can't promise how long that will last. I'm trying really hard, though.

"Please."

She looks at me with those stormy blue eyes of hers, and I do my best to mimic those puppy-dog eyes that Hunter does so successfully with Brighid. I call it "the smolder."

Lyric rolls her eyes and sighs.

"Fine. But just for an hour or two. Then we've got to get back to work on the donations pickups. OK?"

"Perfect." I take a long sip of my beer, and for once, I find myself not tapping on the table, not bouncing my legs. The world feels full of peace and promise. Is it just relaxing on vacation at the beach? Or is it that I'm having dinner with my dream-girl?

"Grilled cheese, with a side of macaroni-and-cheese, and an extra side of fries."

That's Tommy's meal. All yellow-orange-brown. Mom would have been pushing a plate of broccoli on me, but Lyric already showed me that she knows her kids very well.

"Kids' fish-and-chips with applesauce." For Aria, who is now wearing a very brightly crayon-colored paper hat.

"Citrus Sunrise Salad with grilled tuna." I couldn't talk Lyric into getting her "burgers and fries." I'm not sure if she's doing that girl thing of eating a salad because she thinks she can't eat "real food" in front of a guy or if that's what she really wanted. But at least she got the tuna and that milkshake. She's delightfully curvy, and I wouldn't want her thinking I don't like her just like she is. Brighid dealt with that for a lot of her life, before I first met her and again more recently. Lyric isn't quite as curvy or as tall, but I think she's perfect. I'm not sure who told women guys don't like curvy girls, but they didn't consult me or Hunt.

"Double crabby burger with beach fries and steamed broccoli."

Lyric smirks at me.

"What?"

"You got the most over-the-top burger on the menu, with tricked-out fries, and then you ordered steamed broccoli to go with it."

"Mom reminds me to eat my vegetables every time she calls. 'Are you eating your veggies?' 'Are you taking your meds?' 'Are you getting enough sleep?' 'Did you check your parachute?' She's got a laundry list of stuff she always asks me."

Lyric chuckles.

"I'm going to be a terrible nag when Aria is out on her own..." she says quietly.

"Not Tommy?"

Her lips purse, and she glances up at him. A french fry in his hands, he raises it up to his nose, sniffing it, then nods. And then he begins picking it apart, dropping small bits back onto his plate.

"I'm hoping he can get into a career training program at some point. He loves mechanical stuff. Maybe he can learn to assemble things. But everything else will depend on how much we can improve his communication skills. At his current levels, he couldn't really live alone, and I'm not sure I'd be willing to risk trying. He'll likely be living with me my entire life, and with Aria after that."

She looks up, catching the expression on my face, and then looks away.

"Oh."

I'm not sure what else to say. Lyric's just told me that she'll spend every single day of her life parenting. My mom's not even retired yet, but she cut back on fostering a few years ago, preparing for retirement, taking actual vacations now that she doesn't have a kid in the house 24/7. Most days, she gets to just be herself, do things she likes. Lyric... Does she ever do that? Will she ever?

And suddenly I realize why it is she looks so tired.

Kite-surfing? The freedom to do that, to do all the other things I do that scare a lot of "normal" people — it's a luxury. It's a luxury Lyric doesn't have. And... for some reason, it's one I feel driven to give her, even if she doesn't want to use it for kite-surfing.

"Your food's getting cold," she says.

She's eaten a third of her salad. At least she has no issue digging in.

"Right. I've never had a crabby burger before, let alone a double..." I take a bite. "Oh, my god. That's amazing."

"Eastern Shore specialty. Crab dip on a burger. Creamy, cheesy, burgery, with crab spice, on a pretzel bun."

"Why didn't you get one?"

"Too much. I'd never finish it."

"Have a bite." I hold the burger out to her. She shakes her head. "Come on! Just a bite. Enjoy life."

She frowns but pulls the burger closer to her face, taking a big bite.

"There you go." She chews. "Good?"

"Amazing," she says, moaning just a little in her enjoyment.

The sound hits my ears and drives straight to my dick.

I'm in public, in a restaurant, with two kids, a single mom — a widow — and my dick is hard. Awesome.

I try to put it out of my mind, but that's one of those things about my neurospicy brain — something as distracting as a hard-on doesn't fly fleetingly out of my head like the tasks and appointments do. No, instead it sticks to my brain cells like glue. Total hyperfocus. To where I can't focus on anything else. See — this is where the cock-sock would come in handy. A quick trip to the men's room, an empty stall and I could get my head back on straight. As it stands, I take another bite of this insanely delicious burger, focusing on that as best I can, only for my brain to remind me that Lyric's lips touched this exact spot, which sends me back into thoughts of that moan of hers, and... flibbertigibbets!

I put the burger down, making sure my napkin is camouflaging my difficulty. I reach for my glass of water, choke down a swallow, glance over at Lyric to make sure she hasn't realized what she's doing to me, see her smile, and then, dazzled, lose my remaining focus just long enough to drop the glass.

On the up side, I just doused myself with ice-water. On the down side, it will take a while for that to offer me any help with my dick situation.

"Flibbertigibbets!"

I duck under the table, as best as I can at my height, and use my napkin to mop up the spilled water, grabbing the glass and setting it back on the table.

"Oh, no! Are you OK?" Lyric asks, ducking down to help me.

"I've got it," another voice says from the other side, and the waitress is now down on her knees, too, wiping up the spill with a towel. I stand up, only to find her staring right into my crotch, half-hard dick and all.

Lyric's attention, thankfully, is back on the kids.

"I'm going to go dry off. I'll be right back," I tell her.

"We'll be here," she says, sounding concerned.

I hustle off to the men's room, hoping that no one notices my situation. I stop in front of the sink, staring at myself in the mirror. The damage isn't too bad. And it's just water. It'll dry soon enough. I grab a handful of paper towels and mop up what hasn't already soaked in. By the time I'm done, I've gotten hold of myself again, and the last remnants of my hard-on are fading. Thank god.

I open the door to head back to the table, only to run — almost literally — into the waitress.

"Everything OK now?" she asks.

"Yeah. It's just water. Sorry about that."

"No problem. Just water, like you said."

She smiles, and then her eyes slide downward.

"If you need any more *help*, here's my number," she says, tucking a piece of paper in my hand.

Oh, god... A year ago, I'd have gotten her to take her break and come out to the bus with me. But now, today? The idea doesn't appeal to me in the least. If there is any excess bloodflow in my dick at this point, that takes care of it.

I smile stiffly at her, tuck the paper in my pocket so I can get rid of it later, and head back to the table.

The look Lyric gives me is inscrutable. Tell me she didn't see that.

"Sorry about that." I'm apologizing for the mess — whether it's the spilled water or the waitress hitting on me. I just hope she doesn't hold either of those things against me.

I dig back into my burger, trying to let go of my worry over what Lyric is thinking.

Tommy's fries are now a big pile of potato pieces, and it strikes me how little of them he's actually eaten.

"Does he like eating fries or just dissembling them?" I ask Lyric.

She gives me a smile just as stiff as the one I gave the waitress.

"He doesn't like the dark spots. He won't eat them. So he tears them out of each one."

Oh. I see.

Lyric's expression has only gotten tighter.

"I didn't mean that to come off as critical. Really."

I smile and put my hand over hers on the table, trying to reassure her. She jerks her hand away.

"It's fine."

Oh, flibbertigibbets... I've done it again. Not nearly careful enough. Will she even still let me take her and the kids to the trampoline park?

We finish the meal in silence, and I know it's not looking good for me. When the check comes, Lyric offers to pay, and I emphatically refuse, paying the whole check and leaving a too-generous tip for the waitress, whose number I leave on the table to make sure she understands I won't be calling.

We pile the kids back into Lyric's car. Buckled in, Aria now has on headphones, plugged into her mom's phone, listening to music. Tommy has on his own set of headphones, plugged into the tablet.

"Back to the studio? Or did you have somewhere else you wanted to be?" she asks pointedly, nodding back at the door to the restaurant.

OK, then... So she did see that.

"I have nowhere I'd rather be than right here," I tell her just as pointedly, imploring her to understand what I'm telling her. Otherwise, I'm going to have to go back into Rhys default mode and lose the filter. And we know how well that usually goes...

"You sure?" she asks.

I glance back at the kids in the back seat.

"Listen — I think you saw something happen in there that wasn't what it looked like."

"You mean you taking what I assume was the waitress' phone number? A day after you were hitting on me? I don't know why

I was surprised. But it's none of my business. I already told you I'm not interested in any kind of relationship with you. You can 'date' all the waitresses you want. It's no skin off my nose."

She even crooks her fingers to make the little air quotes. It's cute, and I want to smile, but the import of what she said isn't lost on me.

"I'm not 'dating' anyone right now, Lyric. Yes, she handed me her phone number. I stuck it in my pocket. It was instinct. But I left it on the table with the check. You can go look if you don't believe me."

She's quiet for a moment.

"Like I said — not my business who you date or whose number you take. This is just you helping me with the fundraiser, right?"

Careful.

I don't know what the right answer to that question is. But I opt for honesty.

"I am here because I want to help you, Lyric. Anything else takes a back seat to that. Including my dick."

Lyric's eyes flick up to the rear view mirror, checking that the kids aren't overhearing this.

"Good. Because I haven't changed my mind."

"Fine. Have you changed your mind about tomorrow?"

Her eyes widen as she remembers our plans with the kids tomorrow. And she sits there quietly, thinking. And I sit there quietly, watching her. Which is a miracle in and of itself. After a minute or two elapses, my toes start wiggling. I glance at the clock. It's nearly time for my evening meds. And the tension is ramping up my nervous tics.

"No. We can take the kids — for an hour or two," she emphasizes. "Then we have to get back to the fundraiser. Deal?"

"Deal."

I wipe my hands on my legs, trying to resist the temptation to start drumming. I did it earlier, when she was inside the shops, picking up the donations. Tommy's eyes were glued to me the entire time. But she didn't react well to Aria suggesting I teach him to drum, so I didn't mention it when she came back. I'm not sure what she has against drumming, but since it's pretty much half my life, I'm hoping it's something she'll get over.

In the meantime...

"I need to get the kids home, do some lesson-plan prep. Back to the studio?" she asks.

"That's fine. Thanks."

Five minutes later, she pulls into the studio driveway.

"I can pick you up right here, tomorrow morning at ten. Does that work for you?"

She's still kind of stiff with me, but at least she agreed to go. Hopefully, a couple hours of jumping up and down like maniacs will break the ice again.

"That's perfect. I'll see you then."

She nods, and I get out of the car, watching her drive off toward home.

Well, on the negative side, I pissed her off at least twice today without meaning to. On the plus side, though, I think at least one of those times was because she was jealous. And, in my book, that's progress.

Chapter 11
Rock a Little

Lyric

Both kids freshly bathed and in their pajamas, I put on "Up" and get them settled in front of the TV, while I pull out my lesson planning materials and sit down at the kitchen table to try to finalize what's due in tomorrow.

Halfway into my final review of my plan, I get a text from Jennie's mom to confirm her piano lesson for tomorrow afternoon. It'll be tight, going to the trampoline park, getting lunch, working on the donation pickups with Rhys for another couple hours, and then rushing home in time to get the kids settled in their rooms so I can focus on Jennie's lesson. But I've done more in a single day before, and I'll pull it off tomorrow, too, I'm sure.

Aria conks out on the sofa before the movie is over, while I find Tommy lying on the floor, his contraption in one hand, spinning away, and two fingers of the other in his mouth.

"Alright, buddy — let's go get in bed. We've got another big day tomorrow."

He picks himself up off the floor and heads up the stairs. By the time I've got a still-sleeping Aria tucked in, he's quietly turning the pages in his astronomy book. I read it with him for a few minutes, then turn off the light as he settles down under the covers.

When I told Rhys I'd pick him up at ten, I gave myself plenty of time, just in case things go haywire with getting the kids out of the house. It's a fifty-fifty shot either way. But that should mean I can stay up a while and get some writing done.

When I get back downstairs, though, it's not my pen and paper that call me. Instead, I open the door off the kitchen and turn on the low-power ceiling light.

The piano it gently illuminates was my wedding present from Adam. He'd scrimped and saved from his irregular income and bargained with a friend of a friend to get this old baby grand for me and then have it repaired and tuned. It was in this room, waiting for me, when we got home from the wedding reception.

"Now you can start giving lessons," he said. "Or just play whatever song sets your heart on fire."

He knew me so well... knew that music and words are life to me. Knew that poetry and lyrics are both under Brighid's purview. It's a realm of inspiration — the fire of inspiration. Hunter wrote about it, and "Fire in the Head" became aMUSEd's first big single, with my friend — his muse, Brighid — channeling our goddess to bring him that song.

The goddess — She comes to me most often in poetry, rather than lyrics or song, and it's been a while since I've come in this room without a student as my focus. My hand trails unconsciously over the smooth wood of the instrument hanging on the wall nearby, but it's the piano it settles on, and I sit down. I take a deep breath and let the spirit guide me, my fingers tracing over the keys in a pattern I know as well as the ridges in my palm or the flecks of gold in his green eyes, but not pressing them down.

Play it.

No.

It's beautiful.

It is. But I won't play it, Vivienne. Don't ask me to.

Silent disapproval.

I get up from the piano bench and pick up the instrument I usually seek out in this room. A moment and a few taps later, the backing track starts, pulling me into the music with it as I pull the bow across the strings, weaving in time with this wistful song that offers me solace when no other song will do. It's one of my mother's favorites, a throwback to even before her youth, but now made my own as I follow the airy melody and the story of nature, contained and free... or nearly free, rather...

A song about a beautiful bird who doesn't ever leave her cage.

Apt.

I ignore the uninvited commentary.

What I always loved about this song — other than the use of the violin in a rock song — was the energy of the descriptions of nature and the passage of time: rain in the winter, storm-blown leaves, the turning of the planet painted in sunsets and clouds. I've always loved storms. The energy of lightning and thunder feeds straight into my bones, the wind and rain blowing through me, leaving me feeling cleansed and energized, full of potential.

Or they did. Until the storm that came after Adam's funeral. The one that broke off a huge tree limb that just missed the house. A few inches in any direction... I shudder just thinking about it, even now.

A week later, the kids and I moved in with Rory, into her grandmother's old house, just enough different in architecture from mine and with just enough company that it didn't remind me at every moment that Adam was gone. And I leased our house — the house I'd grown up in, that Adam and I had spent our honeymoon in, that the kids had spent their entire lives in — to a family of strangers. The piano went into storage, the practice room upstairs locked with a key only I had. I knocked a bit off the rent to make up for it. But I couldn't face clearing it out. So I didn't.

And the kids and I... we moved on. Aria was young enough that she barely remembers her dad. Tommy... well, I got a lot of sad, questioning looks for a while, but he seemed to understand when I told him Daddy couldn't come back to us, that he'd been hurt too badly and had moved on to the Summerlands to wait for us to come to him someday, when the Fates said it was our time.

Which it nearly *was* a couple years later, about a year ago, when someone came after Rory, and the kids and I got caught in the crossfire.

So we got out of the way.

I felt bad about it, leaving her to face that. But she understood. In fact, she insisted I get her godchildren someplace safe. We just got lucky that the tenants had found a house they wanted to buy when their lease ended. And Rory wasn't facing things alone, either. Not then. She had Rónan at her side then. Later... Later, she learned firsthand what I'd been through in losing Adam. I wouldn't have wished it on my worst enemy, let alone my best friend. But it was common ground that brought us back together. Only instead of immersing herself in kids and work, like I had, she took on Rónan's burdens, on top of her own.

So, it's a little hypocritical when she nags me about taking care of myself, getting more sleep, letting others shoulder some of the weight...

And then foists a rockstar on me...

I let the bow fall.

She should have known better. But she's been distracted for weeks over some story she's working on, so maybe she just didn't think it through past Rhys offering to help and knowing I had a lot to do. Maybe.

And now she's not responding to my texts.

I put the violin away and turn off the light, shutting the door behind me.

And I call Rory. It goes straight to voicemail.

"Rory — it's Lyric. Listen — if I was too harsh about Rhys, I'm sorry. He's trying to help. He's not great at it, but I think he's being more of a help than a hindrance now. So, there's that. Just... Next time, ask me first, OK? Love you."

I check the locks on the front and back doors, shut off the lights and head into my bedroom, getting ready for bed. While I'm brushing my teeth, my phone beeps for an incoming text.

> Rory: *Love you, too. Wouldn't have sent him if I didn't. I've got some stuff to deal with. Won't be around much for a while. Don't panic if you don't hear from me. Investigative journalism. Deep cover. LOL Give my godkids a kiss from Auntie Rory and tell them I'll see them soon. And let the rockstar help!*

Neither one of them is giving me a lot of choice in the matter. But I'd be lying to myself, too, if I didn't admit that half the reason I don't want Rhys around is that he makes it really hard to keep my walls up. It wasn't just the hair and the rockstar status that had me crushing on him at 20. It was his zest for life, on display on stage and off, his inability to hide who he was inside, and his passion for his drumming, for aMUSEd's music, for life. I didn't need Rory's empathic gift to see who Rhys Madigan was, and 20-year-old me longed to have someone like him in my life. One day, I hoped, I would...

And I did. And then I lost him.

So I don't think it's overreacting to tell Rhys — just like I'd tell any other man who expressed interest in me — that I'm not open to a relationship. Maybe it's demanding too much to ask Rhys to respect that, knowing of him what I did, and what I do now. Impulsivity, fixation on what's shiny and new — it's a hallmark of ADHD. He can't help that. But he can take no for an answer. No one gets a pass on that. I can just keep being firm with him about it, and it'll sink in soon, I'm sure.

CHAPTER 12

JUMP START

Rhys
The next morning

"Good morning, beautiful!" I say as I get in Lyric's car.

"Rhys, please... We talked about this," she says.

"I was talking to Aria."

"Oh."

"And hello to you, too, buddy!" I continue, addressing Tommy, who looks up at me and tilts his head, like I'm something interesting. Cool.

"And to your mommy, too! I'm glad you decided to come with us today. I think you're going to have a lot of fun."

Her brow furls just a little. I'm not sure if it's because she doesn't believe me about having fun or if it's because she's still digesting that I said hello to the kids first. But she's going to have a blast today. I'm going to make sure of it.

"Do you like the trampoline park, Mr. Rhys?" Aria asks as we pull out of the studio's driveway.

"I *love* the trampoline park, Aria. Especially when they have climbing walls, and I checked online, and this one does!"

"It does!" Aria confirms. "But Mommy doesn't like us climbing them since Tommy got hurt."

I look over at Lyric, who glances at me and then focuses back on the road.

"Tommy got hurt on a climbing wall?"

Lyric sighs.

"No. He got hurt spinning on the stool at the snack bar."

"And you won't let them climb because of that?"

Weird, but OK...

"I was watching Aria on the climbing wall when he got hurt. They had her all rigged up, with a spotter, so she was perfectly safe. And Tommy was sitting right next to me..."

"And he got hurt."

"He was spinning on the stool, and his foot got caught on the footrest."

"Because he wasn't paying attention and it didn't occur to him that he was at risk of getting hurt."

"Yes. And, honestly, it didn't occur to me, either. And I'm not autistic. But I know to watch him closely when we're at the park, because he's run in front of the swings before and gotten wiped out by one of the kids swinging. But a stool? Sitting right next to me? It didn't occur to me. So I wasn't watching, and he got hurt."

"How badly?"

"Spiral fractures of his femur and tibia. It required surgery, and he was in a cast up to his hip for three months."

"Ouch."

"Yeah. And a challenge for everyone involved, because he didn't really understand that he had to be in the cast and had to be careful while it healed."

"That couldn't have been fun. Right, buddy?"

I look back at Tommy again and find him looking at me. Then he looks away, back down at his Legos.

"Maybe it seems like an overreaction, not letting them climb..."

"No. Not really. You've only got one set of eyes. Two kids, one parent — it has to be a challenge."

"I just don't let them do anything where I can't keep my eyes on both of them at the same time."

"Good thing there's two of us to watch them today." I smile at her, hoping she'll realize that it takes some of the pressure off of her.

"Does that mean we can climb the wall today?" Aria asks.

"It's your mommy's decision, Aria, but I'm happy to watch you climb while she watches Tommy. Maybe Tommy can climb, too."

"I'm not sure he wants to," Lyric says.

"Well, if he does, I can climb with him, help him figure out where to put his hands and feet. I've done it with other kids who weren't sure about trying it."

Her expression is thoughtful.

"Maybe," she finally says.

A little while later, we reach the trampoline park, which is even bigger than I'd realized.

"You've got to have something for the kids do to on a rainy day during the summer. Movies and books and video games don't burn off the same kind of energy as a day on the beach," Lyric explains.

"Oh, I know."

"Oh. Of course you do."

"Yup. I'd have loved to have had a place like this when I was a kid. Mostly it was me on the playground, until I got too big for the playground. Then it was my bike, skateboarding. And, once I went off to college in Virginia — rock-climbing, skydiving, whatever I could try that would give me those moments of total focus."

"Not adrenaline?"

"Not really. It's not all about the adrenaline. It's about the moments when my brain finally goes quiet."

"Like it does when you're drumming?"

"Yeah." I look at her, curious. "How'd you know that? Most people think I love the noisiness of drumming, the movement and the chaos."

"Most people aren't musicians."

"No. They're not."

I look at her with new appreciation. Not that I didn't appreciate her before. But this is insight that most people don't have. Especially about "The Madman." I'm not sure anyone but my mom has ever really gotten this aspect of my love for my kit. Lyric seems to get it, though, even if she still jumps to conclusions about me sometimes.

"So — what's first?"

There's an array of options here, from jumping surfaces to foam pits, obstacle courses, inflatables, gymnastics apparatus and jungle gyms.

"Obstacle course!" Aria screams, jumping up and down.

I look at the first of the obstacle courses, dubious. It looks like Aria is the only one of us small enough to fit under the maximum height requirement for this one.

"How tall are you, Aria?"

She looks at her mom.

"She's four-foot-one, last time I measured her."

I lead Aria over to the larger obstacle course and nudge her up against the height guide.

"I fit, Mommy!"

She jumps up and down, clearly ready to burn off some energy.

"What's the maximum height?" I ask the attendant.

"There isn't one. We have bachelor and bachelorette parties here sometimes. This one's for anyone four feet or taller. Just watch out for the smaller kids," he advises me, looking up to the top of my head. *Yeah, dude, I'm way up here.*

"Let's do it!"

"I'm not sure Tommy..."

But Tommy's already handed her his Legos and is climbing into the padded entrance cube. Aria follows eagerly.

"Come on!" I tell Lyric.

"I usually just watch, in case he gets stuck."

"He won't. And you can help him even better if you're in there with him."

She hesitates.

"Come on, Mommy!" Aria begs.

"Fine," Lyric says, almost disgruntled. I try to hide my smile.

"Hold on, kids. We're right behind you."

Lyric steps to the side and grabs a locker, sticking her purse, Tommy's bag and the kids' shoes inside. I pull mine off and stick them inside the locker, too, holding the door open for her to stick hers in there as well.

"Oh! Can you stick these in your purse? I'll need them later, but with all that climbing..." I gesture at the obstacle course, handing her my meds. She takes them and nods, then fishes around in her purse. When she's done, I close the locker door and pull out the key.

Lyric pulls her hair up into a messy bun and secures it with an elastic ribbon. She holds her hand out and takes the locker key, sliding the coiled wristband over her hand.

"Last one to the end buys lunch!" she yells, diving in after the kids. Aria squeals. Tommy giggles. And I smile. Told her she'd have fun! Almost as much as I'm having watching her.

An hour or so later, we've explored nearly every area of the trampoline park, with Tommy only showing a little reluctance to try climbing across the monkey bars. I boost him up and give him a little support. His upper body strength isn't great, but a regular outing like this would help with that. With a little help from me, he's got the hang of it after just a few rungs. Lyric watches Aria as she takes on the balance beam like she was born to it.

"Lunch?" Lyric suggests when they're done.

"I want to climb the wall!" Aria says, clearly reading her mom's body language that suggests she's ready to leave.

Lyric looks at me a little helplessly. I know I'm the one who started Aria on this today. But we've all had so much fun. We can do this.

"I'll watch her like a hawk. And the safety equipment will do its job," I promise her. "You just keep your eye on Tommy, and it'll be fine."

Lyric sighs and gives a nod.

Aria takes off at full speed, joining the short line of people waiting to climb. I step up behind her. Once again, she's tall enough to try the full-size basic climbing wall, so they start strapping her into a harness and helmet.

The attendant looks back and me and does a double-take.

"You're Rhys Madigan!"

"That's me!"

"Dude! I saw that video of you doing Sleepwalker last year. That was fire!"

"Thanks, man. I was so glad I got a few days during our Vegas run that I could get out there and climb."

"How do you stay in shape for climbing, as much as you guys tour?"

"We've got a gym built into our equipment trailer, and I had them add a portable climbing wall during the U.S. leg last tour. Hunt does it with me sometimes."

"Lucky! I work here just to afford time at the climbing gym. Hey — you should stop by while you're here. It's just down the road a mile or so!"

"Sounds awesome! I'll see what I can do."

I don't tell him that the gym at the studio has a climbing wall. It's not a challenging one, but it's been great to have just down the hall from my bedroom. I could definitely use a more challenging workout. And the wall here isn't it.

"Sorry," I say, excusing myself from the conversation. "I told her mom I'd watch her. She's a little nervous about them climbing."

"Didn't know you had kids, man..."

I start to correct him, but Aria is grabbing her first handholds on the wall, and my attention is glued to her. Her belayer has her rope in hand, so I study Aria's approach. She misses a few obvious holds, but her long legs and arms allow her to reach ones farther out and up.

"You've got it. Aria. Stretch!" I encourage her as she nears the top of the wall.

She pushes off with one foot, grabbing hold of the next handhold, and misses.

The belayer catches her weight and lowers her gentle down to the mat below.

She sits down, pouting. The staff help her get her helmet and harness off, but she's cooperating reluctantly.

"Aria, come on! Your turn is over! You can try again another time!" Lyric calls.

Aria gets up slowly, still pouting.

"I fell down, Mr. Rhys," she says, dejected.

"I saw. But you got way high up there, and you picked some more challenging spots for your hands and feet. That's the most important thing about learning to climb. Even if you fall — and everyone falls, and they fall a lot at first — when you do fall, you learned something new for next time. You learned what didn't work or what might work if you tried things just a little different next time. That's way more important than just climbing up to the top! It's all about learning so you can do better."

"Just like with music!"

"Exactly! How'd you know that?"

"That's what Mommy says — that making mistakes is how you learn."

I give a look back at Lyric.

"Your mommy is a very smart lady and a really good teacher."

Lyric smiles, almost shyly, and Aria runs back over to her.

I get geared up for my turn on the advanced wall, which is still an easy climb for me, since this is more of a kids' place than a real climbing gym. A few people have gathered around, watching, by the time I pick my first holds, but as I make the climb, everything fades away. It's just me and the wall, me and gravity wrestling for control. I think that's one of the biggest reasons I got into climbing — when I started shooting up as a kid, I was awkward, never feeling like I had full control of my body. Add in the ADHD, and I was kind of a klutz. But as soon as I started climbing, the challenge became about taking control over even the smallest movements of my body, making it do what I wanted it to do. So, gangly Rhys turned into strong, capable Rhys. And I loved that. The confidence it gave me was incredible. And I never looked back.

Until now. Until Aurora Carmichael told me to be careful with her friend. And now I'm second-guessing myself every five minutes. Because Lyric was important to me when she was my nameless dream-girl. And she only got more important once I knew who she was. Now that I'm getting to know her, getting to know her kids... it's actually a little terrifying, the idea of screwing things up with her. And we're not even dating. Yet. *Yet.* I'm going to persuade her to give me a chance. I just have to go slow, be carefu—

And I miss my hold at the top of the wall and fall free.

The belayer catches me after a second, with 220 pounds of mostly muscle hitting him harder than he expects.

"Sorry — got distracted," I tell him when I'm back on the ground.

"No problem, man. You were doing great right until that last hold. Probably the fastest climb on that wall all year."

"And I wasn't even trying."

He gives me an understanding smile as I start stripping off the climbing gear.

"See, Aria — even experienced climbers fall sometimes."

"But why'd you fall, Mr. Rhys? You were doing so good!"

"'Well,' Aria," her mom corrects. "We use 'well' when we talk about doing things. Good is an…"

"An adjective. I remember now."

"I always forget that one, too, Aria," I tell her. "And I fell because I got distracted."

"By what?"

"Just thinking about something other than climbing. That's why you have to focus when you're doing it. To do it well, you have to focus. And if you don't, you can make mistakes. I have a hard time focusing sometimes, just not usually when I'm climbing."

"So what were you thinking about Mr. Rhys?"

I give Lyric a glance, and she looks away after a second, having clearly read my mind. These witches and their mind-reading. Brighid does it a lot.

"Is Tommy ready for his turn?" I ask, hoping it'll distract Aria from the fact that I didn't answer her question.

"I don't know, Rhys," Lyric says. "After watching you and Aria fall, I'm not sure he'll want to try."

"What do you say, buddy? You want to give it a try? I'll be right there with you to help."

Tommy glances over at the wall and then back at me. He spins the wheel on his contraption and looks pensive, then hands it to his mom.

"I think that's a yes," I say. "You want to give it a try?" I ask her. She shakes her head.

"I'll just watch this time."

I take it as a good sign that she says "this time." It makes it sound like she might want to do this again with me. Maybe a date at the climbing gym might be possible down the road?

I take Tommy back over to the line and gesture at the guy I talked to earlier once he's got the next person in their gear.

"You think I could climb alongside him, give him some encouragement? He's autistic."

"Yeah, man. We do that a lot. We even have a sensory session once a week, just for kids with sensory issues. A lot of them do side-by-sides. We're already rigged for that."

"Awesome."

I drop down next to Tommy and point up at the wall.

"You and I are going to climb together this time, buddy. You'll put your hands and feet on these colored spots, and then pull yourself up. And I'll help you figure out where to put your hand or foot next, then you pull up again. OK?"

He glances sideways at me and then back at the wall. That's all the response I get.

I help them get him into his harness. But he balks at the helmet.

"He doesn't like things on his head," Lyric calls from behind us.

"He can go without. A lot of the sensory kids just do a little bouldering until they get up a few feet. He's probably not going very high the first time anyway."

"Let's see."

I gear up again next to him, skipping the helmet myself this time, with a top line to the top of the shorter basic climbing wall.

Then it's our turn.

"OK, Tommy — start by putting your left foot here." I point to an easy foothold for him. He sets his foot there. "And your right hand here." I put his hand on a hold. "Now, put your other foot here. And push up so you can grab here."

With the natural skills of most kids, he pulls himself up, looking over at me with a glance that bounces right off.

"That's awesome, Tommy! Keep going, and I'll be right over here next to you."

I take a couple steps up the wall until I'm just above him. He grabs for another hold and pulls himself up. He scrambles to reach the next one but comes up short on his reach. Before I can advise him, he pushes off with his feet, making the same kind of grab his sister missed, and pulls his feet in to grab purchase below him.

"That was great, buddy! Keep going!"

I climb slowly alongside him, watching as he analyzes each next step, each possible route. It's like watching him assemble one of his contraptions. He's thinking through the mechanics of it, comparing his options, picking the one he thinks fits best. And he's got an instinct for it, it seems.

Soon, he's reached the top of the wall.

That's when things get hairy.

With no handholds ahead of him, he starts to look wildly around, whining a little, sounding in distress.

"Tommy — I'm right here. You're fine. You did it! And it's time to go down." He looks down, trying to see past his own body, but he can't see his feet at this angle without pulling away from the wall. It's clear he's close to panicking.

"Tommy — we're going to make a big jump, OK? You and me. We're going to let go of the wall and push away, and then we're going to slowly drop back to the ground on these ropes."

I look down to make sure the belayers are ready for us. Me more so than Tommy. They both nod.

"OK, buddy. They're ready for us to jump. Just push away from the wall and let go with your feet and your hands. I'll count to three and then we'll jump. One. Two. Three! Jump!"

As soon as I see him push away, I jump back off the wall myself, and we glide gently to the floor.

Tommy looks a little lost when his feet hit the ground, and he just stands there. But I bound across the space between us, offering him a high-five. He's clearly done that before, because he smacks my hand after a second, then starts shifting side to side, humming to himself. It's the first time I've seen him do that, and I'm not sure if it's a good thing or not. But it's also the first time I've heard him make more than a momentary sound. Maybe it's a good thing?

I unhook myself from my gear and then help Tommy with his, and we return to his mom after a nod of thanks to the staff.

"Tommy, that was incredible! I'm so proud of you!" Lyric says, wrapping him in a hug that he doesn't seem fully happy about.

"You did even better than me!" Aria says. I expect her to be jealous, but she seems genuinely happy for her brother. It's nice to see.

Lyric's looking at me with tears in her eyes, beaming a smile, and I'm pulled right back into the last dream I had about her, with her smiling at me like this. It beats the high of a cheering crowd any day. Impulse says to grab her up in my arms, kiss her. *Don't.*

I guess my subconscious mind agrees with Alex about slow-playing things with Lyric. I want to tell it to go take a flying leap, but it's probably right. Oh, well. Progress is progress. One slow, careful step at a time.

"Lunch?" I suggest instead.

"That sounds perfect," Lyric says, and I grab those words and pull them close. I want to hear her say those words again, and often.

CHAPTER 13
WHITE BIRD

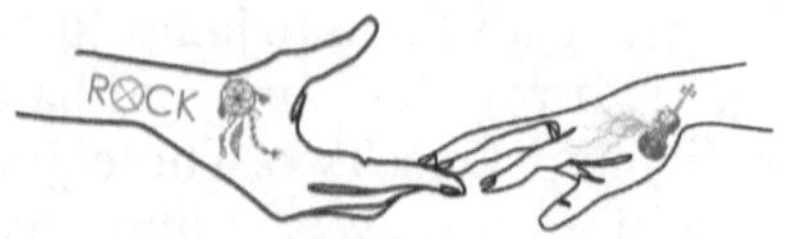

Lyric

I give Tommy most of my fries to disassemble. Rhys insisting I take a bite of his burger the other night whetted my appetite, so I ordered one for myself at the fast-casual restaurant next door to the trampoline park. It's not as good as the other one, but it's been a while since I've had one, and it hits the spot. And I indulge in a vanilla shake, too.

We all get one, except Tommy, who gets his usual lemonade. He also gets another grilled cheese, Aria a hotdog, Rhys a bacon cheeseburger *and* a bacon cheesedog. The guy's six-foot-four, mostly muscle and hyperactive. He'll burn it off in an hour, if today's activity didn't already.

He doesn't comment on Tommy's fry habit this time. I guess I've gotten inured to it. Yeah, it's wasteful, but if I ordered my burger and decided I didn't want the bun, that would be waste-ful, too. It's just one of those quirks of his you have to accept.

And accept it Rhys does, it seems.

All in all, it's been an amazing morning, and I'm kind of sad that we have to go back to business mode and start working on the fundraiser again.

"Thanks for taking us out today," I tell him after we get in the car again. He let me pay for lunch, so I feel a little better about things. "It was a lot of fun."

"It was! I'm glad you came with me. I'd probably have come on my own if you hadn't, and that wouldn't have been nearly as fun."

I can't tell if he's being serious or not, but I think maybe he is, and, you know... I like it. I feel so relaxed right now. If I didn't have so much to do, I'd happily head home and just chill out with a book or a movie.

I'm so enamored of the idea that I don't even consider driving straight to school to get back to work. Instead, I find myself pulling up at my house. Only there's already a car in the driveway, and a familiar little trailer behind it. I open my door but stay in the car, confused.

"Why are we at Declan's house?" Rhys asks, also confused, but about something else.

"That's Auntie Callie's house, Mr. Rhys," Aria corrects. "Uncle Declan just lives there, too. On account of they got married."

"OK. But why are we here? Are they watching the kids this afternoon? I thought Declan said he was doing vocals today..."

"That's probably true," I tell him. "But we're not at their house. We're at *my* house."

I point at the house I'm parked in front of.

"And so is..."

"Grandma!" Aria yells, unbuckling her seatbelt and jumping out of the car. She races up the driveway and into the arms of my mother — who, last I heard, was several hundred miles away and headed for Florida.

I unbuckle Tommy from his seat, and he jumps out and heads straight for Mom, too, though at a slower pace.

"You live next door to Declan and Callie?" Rhys asks, still a step behind in the conversation.

"I've lived next door to Callie — well, her grandmother — for nearly my entire life. I grew up in this house. And Callie came to visit her grandmother in the summer sometimes. That's how we became friends. It's how I met Declan, before I married them the first time."

"And now you live next door to each other. And Declan."

"Is that a good thing or a bad thing? You seem... undecided."

"No! It's good! It's just... I annoy Declan sometimes. I'm not sure how he'd feel about me being next door."

"Well, it's not like you live here," I tell him with a chuckle. "You're just visiting."

He's quiet, thoughtful, and I wonder what's going through his head. It seems unlike him to have a thought and not voice it.

"And I get to meet your mom?" he finally asks.

"It would be hard to avoid it, since she's parked in my driveway and you don't have a car."

"Me just walking away would be kind of awkward."

"Yeah. So come meet her."

Rhys and I get out of the car and walk up to the group hug that now has my mother squashed between two enthusiastic grandkids.

"Well, this is a surprise!" I tell her. "I thought you were headed for Florida next."

"I decided to skip that festival. Something about my wonderful grandchildren was calling me. I figured I was needed here." She pops a kiss on each of their heads before giving me a significant look that shifts to Rhys, where he stands next to me.

"Mom, this is Rhys Madigan. He's helping out with the fundraiser this year," I tell her. "Rhys, this is my mother, Iris Monroe."

"Happy to meet you, Mrs. Monroe," Rhys says.

"It's Ms. I never married," Mom corrects. "But call me Iris, please. Everyone does. Even Lyric does sometimes, when she thinks I'm not listening..." She gives me a look of amusement.

And... at least looking away guiltily gives me a chance to peek at Rhys...

"Iris," he agrees.

"Shall we?" I suggest, gesturing toward the house.

We all head up the walk, but Mom lingers behind the kids until she's next to me.

"He looks familiar," she says quietly.

I know what she's getting at, but I play dumb.

"Hmm..." Non-committal. But not a denial.

"Didn't you use to have his picture on your dorm room wall? When you were in college? I remember that lovely red hair..."

I glare at her as unobtrusively as possible. Because those two things go together so naturally. She purses her lips and holds in a laugh.

I chance a glance behind me to see if Rhys overheard the exchange.

He's looking over my head at the kids, who are holding open the front door. But his expression is full of delight, almost mirthful. It kind of reminds me of the expression on the comedy mask in the original aMUSEd logo. Not that I'm so much of a fan that

I'd know that. Nope. And there's no way I'm admitting it in front of him.

I roll my eyes. I normally love it when Mom visits, but her timing is terrible, coinciding as it does with Rhys' involvement with the fundraiser. Fine. *And* today's extracurriculars. I can't pretend that was work-related. Not really.

"Mom, I'm happy to see you, but I'm afraid Rhys and I have some work to do on the fundraiser."

"That's fine! You two go out and do your thing. I've got the kids."

I'm tempted to say yes, but I have one question first.

"Mom? Where are you planning to sleep? You know how bad your back was after you slept on the couch last time you visited."

"Oh, I've got it all sorted out. Callie said her apartment is still vacant, for now, and it's furnished."

"Callie?"

"I was waiting for you to get home. I ran into her when she left for work."

"Oh. OK." Then another question occurs to me. "How long did you drive today, Mom?"

"Oh, a few hours…"

"Just a few hours? Weren't you in Georgia?"

"South Carolina."

"Unless you bespelled your car to drive a hundred and fifty miles an hour, without being seen by the cops or having an accident, that was more than 'a few hours,' Mom."

I frown at her. She shrugs.

"Give or take six hours or so…"

I shake my head.

"You are going to go over to the apartment and get some sleep. I'll ask Callie to bring you up dinner."

"But I want to spend time with my grandkids!"

"Tomorrow. You can have them for the whole day tomorrow, if you want."

"Fine," she says with a resigned sigh. "Give Grandma a hug, my lovelies!" she adds, opening her arms to the kids, who both run into them and get a solid squeeze. "I'll see you in the morning," she says, stifling a yawn.

Uh-huh.

"It was lovely to meet you, Rhys," she says, using a tentative handshake to pull him into a hug, too. "Thank you for helping out our girl."

"Our"? She's practically sending out wedding invitations.

I give Frank a mental elbow.

"My pleasure. Truly," he says, giving me a glance.

Oh, Rhys Madigan, you are going to be the death of me...

Mom gives us a wave as she pulls out of the driveway, pulling off the maneuver in the narrow street with incredible deftness, despite the trailer. She's an old hand at maneuvering that thing, after all these years spending most of her time living in it and moving it from one place to the next.

"OK. Now, before we get any more unexpected surprises..."

"Is there such a thing as an expected surprise?" Rhys asks.

"Good question... But it'll have to wait. We've got just enough time to get today's stops checked off our lists before my student gets here."

"Student?"

"I teach individual students in my free time," I explain. "I've got a piano lesson to give today."

"On top of everything else?"

My sigh is weary, a little annoyed, too. Because I'm tired, and I'm tired of everyone implying that I'm doing too much when I'm only doing what I have to.

He's not wrong, dear, says a voice only I can hear — Vivienne. *You can't take care of your children if you don't take care of yourself. I learned that lesson too late. You've got to find some balance!*

"You don't *have* any free time that I can see," Rhys says. And I snap.

"Just drop it! Please! It may be a novel idea to you, rockstar, with your rockstar money, but teachers don't make much. Music teachers even less, because they've cut music from so many schools these days. And I don't have a second person bringing in a paycheck every week to help make ends meet. If Mom hadn't just given me the house..." I sigh. "I do what I need to to make ends meet for me and the kids. So do me a favor and stop making me feel like I'm doing something wrong!"

There's a sudden crash as the screen door on the front porch slams in the wind. The sound startles me, but it's my outburst that's shocked everyone in the room. Aria and Tommy are both staring at me, their eyes big. And who can blame them? They should never have had to hear that kind of thing. I hope it doesn't stick with them. I hope.

"I'm sorry," I say to all three of them. "I'm just... I'm just tired. And I lost my temper."

"It's OK, Mommy," Aria says, giving me a hug. "I lose my temper sometimes, too. And you said, 'Sorry.' That means it's all fixed."

Well, it's rarely that easy, but having her let me off the hook so easily takes away a little of the guilt.

"Aria, you and Tommy should go use the bathroom before we get in the car again."

The kids each head for one of the two bathrooms in the house.

I let my eyes fall closed, for just a second, shutting out the world.

Only there's one person in this world whose spirit is louder than any mechanical noise, song or shout. And he won't let me shut him out with the rest.

"It's fine, Lyric," Rhys says quietly. "I get it — I really do. I just want to help." His arms reach around me from behind, giving me a gentle hug. There's no sense of him trying to cop a feel. It's just... supportive, reassuring. And I have to keep myself from falling back against him. I can't give him mixed signals, give him hope.

I feel more arms around me and look down to see both Tommy and Aria joining in the hug. And for some reason, it doesn't feel weird that there's another adult involved. It just feels... good.

"Let's go get this done," I tell them.

We got most of the remaining list done. One more day, maybe two, and that task will be one I can check off my list. I'd hoped to get some more of the event planning done today, but that'll have to wait.

Jennie's mom pulled up in the driveway five minutes after we got back from the fundraiser errands. I didn't have time to drop Rhys off back at the studio, so he came with. And when I suggested he grab a Lyft to go home, he said he'd stay so we could work on the planning. And I let him. It'll give us a head start on work I'd expected to put off until tomorrow.

"Very good, Jenny! But watch closely..."

I demonstrate the passage she's just played, but I use a different fingering than she'd tried. I'd showed her this when I assigned the piece last week, but kids forget.

"Try it again."

She runs through it another time, a little slower than I did, but with the correct fingering this time, and she no longer stumbles.

"That's it! Now practice it this week again, plus the new one I showed you. Half an hour! Every day!"

Jennie's old enough for a half-hour of practice. My younger students aim for fifteen minutes. But she can handle it. Hopefully, she'll reverse the practiced-in mistake.

I've already tucked away her mother's check in my lesson box, so I just wave to her as they walk back to their car.

On a whim, I pick up my violin and start playing the song about the bird in the cage. Maybe it's Mom showing up today that reminds me of it. The first time I heard it, Mom was watching an old episode of "Knight Rider." You know — David Hasselhoff with the talking car? Maybe not. It seems a little silly now, especially now that I'm old enough to have kids of my own, but it was one of Mom's favorite shows when she had me, and she used to watch recordings of it while she did her crafts.

But there are a couple episodes about a singer the main character needs to protect, and she and Hasselhoff sing on a cover of this song — a duet called "White Bird."

It may be a big part of the reason why I picked the violin when Mom asked me what instrument I wanted to learn in third grade. I'd already had piano lessons. Why not violin? With her love of that song, Mom wasn't going to argue.

I don't think I realized at 8 that a violin isn't commonly used in rock music. It's possible that a song originally recorded in 1968 sounded way cooler in the middle of a once-popular TV show. Or maybe the little girl who drew hearts and music notes all over her notebooks was swept up in the romantic subplot of the episodes. Regardless, "White Bird" settled into my soul, and it's the song I usually play when I'm alone.

The song starts with the violin right from the top, and I'm lost in it within moments. I sway heavily with the beat, almost a dance, moving in time not just with the sound of my violin but the twin vocals, male and female, that I can hear in my head... in my soul. A gently driving percussion and the caress of a guitar under it all. I wind my way around the room, around the piano, my eyes closed. I know this room well enough to safely navigate it with senses other than vision. I reach the halfway point in the song, and a break fills the room with the sound of rich Spanish-style guitar. Soon, the strings will blend back in and the soar in a solo of their own. I ready for that emotional peak of the song, moving my feet in time with the guitar, until they unexpectedly bump into...

Rhys.

Rhys Madigan, who I'd somehow forgotten was even here, is sitting on the piano bench with my acoustic guitar, playing the guitar solo to this song. A song that basically no one born after the mid-1970s is likely to have ever heard. It's not like it's one that lingers on the classic rock stations' playlists, let alone the streaming channels.

"Keep going," Rhys urges me, reproducing the rich, percussive melody with a beauty that catches me.

He plays guitar? He plays guitar like this? And he's a drummer.

"Come on! It's not the same without the violin."

I close my eyes again, regaining my composure, and pick up the trail of his solo just in time for the back-and-forth between the two instruments. For a few measures, it's a duel — no, a tango. Two dancers weaving together on a shared axis, the playful interplay, the passion-infused tension between partners. Then they join together again, flowing around each other, as naturally as the turn from day to night and back again, as the whisper of wind in the autumn, as the flight of a caged bird flying free at last.

As the last notes from my violin, the guitar, fade away, my eyes pop open again, and I find myself looking right into Rhys' eyes. A luminous shade of brown I don't even have a word for. Imagine me — at a loss for words! But there's a sense of connection between us that overwhelms rational thought. And a building tension.

And I turn away, breaking both, and put the violin away.

"That was... Wow," he says.

I turn and look back at him. He seems almost... overwhelmed.

"How do you even know that song?" I ask him. "No one knows that song."

"My mom loved 'Knight Rider.' She used to put it on when she had paperwork to do and needed to keep us kids occupied. It was actually pretty perfect for a 10-year-old boy with a short attention span and a taste for action and adventure. But all that aside, I always loved that song."

"Me, too."

"You watched it when you were a 10-year-old boy with an attention disorder?" he asks, smirking at me.

I chuckle.

"No — my mom loves the show. She still watches it when she's working on her crafts. That's actually one of her favorite songs."

"Which explains why you learned it."

"Well, it's become one of my favorites, too."

There's a moment of silence, neither one of us seeming to know what to say.

"Perfect," he finally says.

I don't ask him what he means. I'm too afraid that I already know.

"Mommy, I'm hungry!" Aria calls from the living room.

Saved by the grumbling tummy.

Chapter 14

Cows with Guns

Lyric

R hys ignores my subtle hints that he head back to the studio.

OK, maybe subtle hints aren't the best communication option with Rhys. That's probably my fault. But on some level, maybe I didn't really want him to leave.

Before I can even get my head wrapped around dinner, my phone beeps with a text.

Patty: *You may want to keep Monday evening clear on your schedule.*

Patty's one of the secretaries at school, and she's usually the first to hear any rumors about anything.

Lyric: *Why?*

Patty: *Call me.*

"Problem?" Rhys asks.

"I'm not sure. I think I have to make a call."

"Go ahead. I've got the kids," he says. He's handled them when they were in the car for a few minutes. He can handle them when we're home and I'm on a quick call. I head into my bedroom.

"It's just a rumor," Patty says, "but the rumor is the new school board members who were elected in June are on a tear about 'inappropriate class content.' And they've pulled a bunch of lesson plans for the coming year to scrutinize whether the class content has become too 'woke.'"

"'Woke'? I thought the board was leaning more progressive these days."

"They were, but apparently some of these candidates snuck in under the radar by talking about 'supporting parents and families,' rather than openly saying in their campaigns that they wanted to start banning books and stuff. *That* they saved for their base."

"For gods' sake." I'm always careful with what I say in front of my work friends, but Patty can't tell from a call where an apostrophe is placed. So that mild swear won't out me as a polytheist.

"Really," she says, agreeing with the sentiment, regardless of where the apostrophe is.

"But why are you calling me? I'm not teaching history or biology. What can they find objectionable in my music curriculum?"

"I don't know. But rumor is you may be on their list."

"Maybe they're just doing spot checks," I suggest. "Or maybe they meant Mrs. *Carson*? She's been using that news program with her fifth-graders, and those people hate anything that involves 'mainstream media.'"

"Carson/Larson. Maybe that's it. It's like a game of 'Telephone' around here sometimes. But I wanted to give you a heads-up in case the rumor was true."

"Yeah. Thanks, Patty. Have a good night."

"You, too. See you tomorrow. Hey — wait!" she says just as I get set to hit the button to end the call.

"Yeah?"

"Is that hot drummer going to be with you tomorrow? I don't want to be wearing my summer casuals if he is."

I sigh and roll my eyes at the phone, since she can't see me.

"I'm really not sure. He's mostly been helping me out with the auction donations."

I'm not sure why I lie to her. It certainly isn't because I'm trying to keep Rhys to myself. Nope.

"Oh, I bet he is. Carrying around all that heavy stuff with those drummer muscles of his…"

"Bye, Patty."

Great. Now I have to add going back over my lesson plans with a fine-toothed comb to my never-ending to-do list. And actually do it before Monday. And find somebody to stay with the kids during the meeting. Mom's likely to be back on the road by then, if her past patterns hold. Rory's off the grid, apparently. The band's heavy into recording vocals, according to Rhys, so that means no Piper, which also means no David. And they're Declan's vocals. Callie will be busy with the restaurant, Siobhan with her clientele. Brighid is in the final stages of her wedding planning, and I already feel bad about how much time she's taken away from that to help me out. I'm pretty much out of options. Except…

I walk back into the living room, expecting to find Rhys and the kids there, or in the kitchen. But they're not. I start to check outside, but then I hear… music? And — surprise! — it's coming from my music room.

I open the door to find Rhys sitting on the floor, both kids in front of him, both enraptured as he sings along with the acoustic guitar. And I'm instantly transfixed. I knew he sings backup vocals for the band, but… His voice is lovely, a rich baritone that I can pick out in the band's harmonies now that I've heard it in isolation.

Wait… what's he singing?

I make it about thirty seconds further into the song before I realize he's singing about an armed bovine revolution. To my kids.

"Well, that was just wonderful!" I exclaim over the music, my voice tight. "Let's thank Mr. Rhys for singing such a… such an *interesting* song for us."

"Mommy, why's your voice weird?" Aria asks.

"I'm just surprised," I tell her. You tell a lot of white lies when you have kids… "I didn't know Mr. Rhys could sing like that."

"I sing. I play at lot of instruments, too," he says brightly. "I like trying new things." Of course he does. Until he gets bored. Note to self. "Sometimes the new things stick. And 'Cows with Guns' is cool, like straight out of a Western. It's one of the first songs I learned how to play on guitar."

"Right." I pause. "Kids — let's go wash up so we can get dinner going, OK?"

Aria races past me, with Tommy and his contraption right behind her.

"'Cows with Guns'? Have you lost your mind? How would that ever be an appropriate song to sing to kids?"

He looks puzzled.

"The video's a cartoon! With cartoon cows!"

"It's about an armed cow revolt, with Uzis! It has 'pissing' and 'groin' in just the section you just sang! That is not kid-friendly."

"What? People pee! They have groins! And cows can't really use automatic weapons — they don't have opposable thumbs." He shrugs, like he thinks I'm being unreasonable. I'm not unreasonable! I'm a mom!

"It's not appropriate. End of discussion."

His face falls.

"So I shouldn't show them the video?" he asks.

"No!"

"It's just... I kinda promised them I would..."

"No!"

I shake my head. I can't leave him alone with my kids for ten minutes before he has a colossal lapse in judgment. How could I ever trust him to watch them during the school board meeting? What was I thinking?

"OK," he says. "You're the mom." He shrugs again.

"Yes. I am."

"So, am I invited to dinner?" he asks, making puppy-dog eyes at me.

And, as mad as I am about inappropriate cow songs, I melt, my outrage floating away like rain off a duck's back. What is it about Rhys Madigan that makes it so impossible to stay mad at him?

"Fine. But you have to help cook."

There. I've set expectations, shared responsibilities and re-solved a potential conflict all at once. All my best teacher and parenting skills in action.

Now, if I can just figure out what we're having for dinner...

"**I**f all else fails, pasta plus sauce plus protein plus veggies makes an easy and nutritious meal," Rhys says, like he's quoting someone. "Mom always told me that. And like everything Mom says, it's true."

I have to give him that much. In the space of five minutes, we went from me blanking on what to pull together for dinner to having a plan, as Rhys pulled out dried macaroni, jarred tomato sauce, frozen broccoli and a package of chicken breasts, and declared it a recipe. Even better, with Callie's secret easy cheese sauce recipe, I turned Tommy's portion of the macaroni into mac-and-cheese and then fried up homemade chicken fingers in the air fryer Brighid got me for Yule last year.

Rhys and I sit quietly, eating our food, our earlier disagreement put behind us.

Tommy eats carefully around the three microscopic broccoli florets we snuck into his mac-and-cheese.

"Told you," I say quietly to Rhys.

"That you did. It was still worth a shot. I loved broccoli with cheese sauce when I was a kid. Still do." He pitches his voice toward Tommy now. "And it makes Mom happy when I eat my veggies."

Aria instantly spears each of the pieces of broccoli in her pasta, stuffing them one after another in her mouth. Then she beams at me, her mouth still stuffed with them.

"I ate all my veggies, Mom!" she mumbles, her mouth full of food.

"Aria, what did we say about talking with our mouths full of food?"

"Not to," she mumbles at me again. I roll my eyes.

"Well, you did ask her while she still had a mouthful of food!" Rhys says.

He's got a point.

"Thank you for eating your veggies, Aria."

I stab a piece of chicken with my fork and get it halfway to my mouth when Rhys elbows me in the side. I turn my attention to him, only to find his attention on Tommy, who is holding a broccoli floret up to his nose. He sniffs, looking suspicious, then takes a tentative bite of the tiniest piece.

He frowns and puts the broccoli down.

"Told you," I whisper to Rhys.

"Yeah. But at least we got him to try it."

He's got a point there, too. It's progress.

"So, are we wrapping up the auction items pick-ups tomorrow?" he asks.

"Yes. And it should be pretty quick. My mom is going to take the kids for the day, get in some grandma time."

"Woohoo! Grandma!" Aria shouts.

I want to feel a little insulted, but the kids don't get to see my mom very often, so I get the excitement.

"We'll pack bags for both of you before you go to bed, so figure out what you want to have with you, because Grandma says she wants the whole day."

"Yay!" Aria cheers again.

"So it's just you and me tomorrow?" Rhys asks, sounding as cheerful about the circumstances as Aria does.

"Yes..."

"Woohoo!" Rhys cheers.

I frown at him.

"I love the kids," he says, and my heart sputters a little, hearing him say those words. "I'd just like a little time where it's just us," he says.

It's not anything Adam never said. And realizing that both reassures and terrifies me.

"Besides, I've got a car here now, so I can drive us!"

"Oh. OK."

"I need to check in with the guys at the studio in the morning. So I'll pick you up at one?"

We don't have a lot of items left to pick up. One is early enough. Especially if I do the stuff I don't get done tonight after Mom picks up the kids in the morning.

"That will be fine."

"Awesome!" he says, smiling at me, looking genuinely pleased.

I'm no longer sure what I've gotten myself into with Rhys, and the uncertainty looms over the rest of my evening, even after Rhys thanks me for a great day and heads back to the studio for the night via Lyft.

With the kids in bed, I withdraw to my altar, which takes up half of the little sunroom off the master bedroom. A section of screened porch that was long ago enclosed, it's offered a private retreat for me since Adam and I first took over the house. During the day, it's full of sunlight, and the windows open to let the sea breeze in when it's warm. A set of shelves holds a variety of books on mythology, ritual, history, herbs, poetry, as well as an array of crystals, essential oils, tarot decks and other divinatory devices.

At the far end of the room, a wooden trunk contains some of the tools I use for more elaborate ritual, while just a few things rest on the lid of the trunk, which serves as my altar.

I don't light the small oil lamp. It's not my flame-tending night, and I'm not feeling so off-kilter that I need a more tangible representation of Her presence. Instead, I look deep into the eyes of the statue of the goddess Brighid that takes center stage on my altar, losing myself in their aged-bronze depths.

"What am I to do with him?" I ask. "He's alternately delightful and infuriating. Utterly irreverent. But in the most innocuous of ways. And he wants to get to know me... But I don't have room in my life for him, and he's leaving as soon as their album is done... That should say it all. But somehow, it doesn't. Why did it have to be Rhys Madigan, and why now, when I have so much that needs my attention?"

There's no reply. There isn't always. And that's OK. Sometimes She makes you figure things out on your own. I just wish there was an easy, obvious answer here.

She's been my primary refuge since I lost Adam, a steady presence full of warmth and support. But sometimes, when needed, She delivers a solid kick to the posterior.

Hunter found that out the hard way, demanding of Her a "fix" for what was broken in his life. He broke his hand moments later, leading to a series of events that brought him and my friend Brighid back together, and for good this time. Brighid — not the goddess — confessed that to me not long after they became an official couple, though she never told me what Rhys now has, about Hunter yelling at Herself. Brighid and I — we're two of the three priestesses of Herself in her little informal circle. She knew I'd believe the tale and understand its import. And I did. It also made me miss the presence of our third.

Amber withdrew from the world after the accident at her shop, and she's only started to emerge again in the last couple months, reopening the shop with her friend Cam's help. He's a sweetie. Way too handsome for his own good, but also very gay, so the fact that they're living together isn't awkward for them. And it means she's had a trained physical therapist caring for her. I just wish she had a trauma therapist caring for her, too. She won't even talk to Brighid, who is certified in pastoral counseling. So Brighid and I wait and watch and worry over her, hoping she'll find healing with time, for both her physical and emotional injuries.

I kind of wish I had my own Cam, to take care of what I can't, to pamper me a little, force me to take care of myself.

I look into those bronze eyes again, and I realize where I've seen eyes that color before. They're the exact color of Rhys Madigan's eyes. Aged bronze.

With that thought, I see them flash green — verdant fire, the color of Her eyes when She makes Her presence known to me directly. And I realize she's given me the answer I sought. It was in me all along.

Self-care. Attention. And a delightfully distracting rockstar with bronze-colored eyes.

It's an invitation to indulge, to prioritize myself. Well, to prioritize myself more than I have been, at least. And to let Rhys lead me on this little adventure, however long as it lasts.

Chapter 15
It's Raining Moms

Rhys
The next morning

"**S**o she pulls up right next to your house — I mean, Callie's house..." I'm telling Declan as we walk out of the studio and head upstairs. He's working on vocals. I just came in to watch. Sometimes Declan does weird things in the iso booth, like space out and then walk right out the back door and into the ocean. He didn't do anything weird today, though. Oh, well... Maybe next time.

"Next door? Rhys, you know Callie and Lyric lived next door to each other as teenagers, right?"

"I do *now*!" I tell him. "And then Lyric tells me the woman parked in the driveway — hers, not Callie's... Not *yours*, I mean... But then I don't even know if you consider it your house or Callie's or both of yours, or maybe she still thinks of it as her grandmother's, because it was her grandmother's first..."

"Rhys!" Declan snaps at me. "What's your point? Who was the woman?"

"Lyric's mom!"

"So you met her mom?"

"Yeah. She's cool. And she seemed to like me. And — get this — I wasn't supposed to hear it, but I've got really good hearing because I wear my earplugs when I'm at shows, when I don't already have my in-ears in, of course..."

"Rhys!"

"Yeah. Anyway... Lyric's mom said that Lyric used to have my picture on her wall when she was in college! Me! On her wall!"

"Well, that's an interesting development," Declan says. "Did you ask her whether there were any other pictures on her wall? Mine, maybe?"

"Well, no, because I wasn't supposed to be eavesdropping," I tell him. "Mom always told me eavesdropping is rude."

"And your mother needs to do a better job of practicing what she preaches," a familiar voice says from the doorway between the kitchen and the living room.

"Mom!"

"Kieran let me in before he went back in his room," she explains. "I told him I'd just wait up here until you all were done working."

"It's raining moms!" Declan jokes. "Good to see you, Ms. M! Always a delight."

Mom looks at him skeptically, like she's searching for some sarcasm under the words.

"And marriage seems to have done wonders for you, Declan," she finally says. "Congratulations!"

"Mom, what are you doing here?" I ask, grabbing her up in a bear hug and twirling her around a few times.

"Just missed my boy," she says. "And I thought maybe I was overdue for a little beach vacation."

"I'll send you on a beach vacation anytime you want, Mom! Billy can book you for an inclusive resort in the Bahamas! No — Fiji!"

"Are you trying to get rid of me?" she asks. But I can tell she's only half serious.

"No! I'm happy to see you! I just didn't want you thinking you had to come see me to get a vacation. I've got tons of money now, you know."

"I know, Rhys. We've talked about this."

"And you don't need my money, and it's rude to discuss money in public."

"Exactly!"

"But I'd still like to send you on a real vacation."

"Maybe when we're done with our visit," she says, nodding wisely. Mom is nothing if not wise.

"Do you want to come hear what we're recording?" I ask her. "Piper — that's Dave's girl and our engineer — she's got the track we're working on mostly finished. Declan's doing his vocals now. We just took a break so Piper could go puke."

Mom looks concerned.

"She's pregnant," I explain.

"Ah. I'll have to offer her and David my congratulations and my sympathy when we get down there. And then maybe lunch with your old mom?"

We took a break earlier than expected, due to Piper's condition. So I've got time to take Mom to lunch and still pick up Lyric on time. Cool. But Mom? Old? I lean back to look at her. She's not short. Maybe five-foot-six, but it's still a long way down. Maybe a little longer than it was the last time I saw her. Hmm… and there's a few more strands of silver in her brown curls.

"You're not old. But you *do* look a little older than you did," I tell her.

"Rhys! You don't ever tell a woman — *especially* your mother — that she looks older than… well, than anything. Hello, Ms. Madigan!" Alex says to her as he comes in from the bedrooms down the hall. He pulls her into a hug, band-mom to mom. "You look amazing," he says.

"Thank you, Alex! And thanks for keeping an eye on my boy."

"I do my best. He doesn't always cooperate. In fact, he's been curiously absent for most of this week." Alex gives me a suspicious look.

"I'm helping!" I tell him.

"Helping what?" Declan asks as he emerges from the kitchen.

"My dream-girl."

Declan hands Mom a glass of iced tea, with a cute little lemon twist on the rim. He does these things now that the big secret of his culinary training is out. I kind of feel like we've been shortchanged, since he could have been cooking for the six of us this entire time, instead of just letting Alex do it when he feels like it.

"Thank you," Mom says before looking at me with the same kind of suspicion in her eyes as Alex had. The suspicious mom-quotient for this house has official been filled. Maybe too well. "What's this about a dream-girl?"

I don't want to spill too much before I get the chance to talk to Lyric about this. But this is my mom…

"Let's go sit outside," she suggests, "talk mom to son."

Following behind her, I stick my tongue out at Alex on my way out the sliding glass doors to the deck. Mr. Nosey Band-Mom will have to wait until I'm ready to talk, for once.

"Wow — what a gorgeous view!" Mom says, settling down in a chair at the table on the deck. I take the one next to her. "What a wonderful place to be working! And the town is just darling, with all the little shops and restaurants."

"One of them is Callie's, Declan's wife's…"

"I know. It was in the news."

Right.

"Is that why you're here? Because we keep making the news?"

"No," she says. "I'm here because I missed my boy and it seemed like a good time to catch up and relax a little, too."

"Oh. That's cool. You said you saw the town?"

"I did when I checked into my hotel," she says. "It's right on the boardwalk. I could have walked here, right down the beach, but there's that section of private beach between here and the town beach," she says.

"Hunt just ignores those signs. I keep telling him—"

"Rules are rules for a reason," she joins in. That's fine. She's the one who said it.

"Now, tell me about this 'dream-girl' of yours…"

All of a sudden I'm tongue-tied. That never happens to me.

"She must be some girl if she's rendered *you* speechless," Mom says, giving me a gentle smile. "Let's start with the easy parts. What's her name?"

"Lyric."

"What a lovely name!"

"It's perfect, just like her. Except she told me she doesn't want to date me."

"That had to be disappointing."

"Big-time, Mom. But I offered to help her with this fundraiser she's doing for her school…"

"She's a teacher?"

"A music teacher. She's raising money for the music department, and I was going to just give it to her, but her friend told me Lyric really just needed help with the fundraiser itself, so I offered to do that. But then she thought I was hitting on her, and she kicked me out. So I made a big donation and told them I wanted to work on the fundraiser as part of that deal. So now she's letting me help."

"And this was all your idea?"

"Well, no — requiring that she let me help, that was Alex's idea."

"Remind me to talk to Alex."

"About what?"

"Nevermind. So you're helping this girl out, hoping that she'll let you date her once she gets to know you?"

"Kind of. I mean, I wanted to help her — she's tired, Mom. Really tired. Like you were that Christmas when we had Benji and Marcus and Poppy all come into the house in the week before Christmas, and my birthday, and so you had to work, take care of the kids and get everyone Christmas presents at the last minute."

"I remember. You're right. I was really tired. So why is this Lyric of yours tired, Rhys?"

"Well, she's a teacher, like I said, and she's getting ready for school to start, and she's doing this fundraiser, and then she's got two kids..."

"She's a mom? Divorced?"

"No. She was married. But... he died."

"Oh! That's terrible. Maybe it's just too soon for her to feel like dating?"

"It's been three years, Mom. How much longer could she want to wait?"

She reaches out and pats my hand.

"For some people, forever is how long they wait. They don't want another relationship after they lost someone. That's a hard thing, Rhys. Even if they do want another relationship, some-times it's many years before they get there."

"I won't be here in many years, Mom. The time has to be now."

"Rhys, if you're not thinking in terms of being here for her in even a few years, *you're* the one who's not ready for a relation-ship."

Ouch.

"But Mom! She's the one. I know it. She's been in my dreams!"

Mom frowns, and I realize this is going to sound nuts even to her. And she's been dealing with my off-the-wall ideas nearly my entire life.

But, "Explain, please," is all she says, sitting back to listen.

"I've been dreaming about her for months."

"About this girl specifically?"

"The woman I've been seeing in my dreams looks exactly like her, Mom. Exactly. Not like they're related or the same type, but exactly like her. It *is* her. So when I met her the other night..."

"You didn't tell her you'd dreamed about her, did you?"

"No. I've been waiting for the right time, when I know she'll hear me out and not think I'm crazy or hitting on her with some fake story."

"You don't lie. But she has no way of knowing that."

Mom always taught me that it was better to tell the truth and get in trouble on the spot, rather than lie and not only probably eventually get found out, but to then have the person you'd lied to mad at you and no longer willing to trust you. So, no, I never lie. I flibbertigibbet up a lot, saying or doing the wrong thing, but I own it when I do. People mostly forgive me. Mostly.

"What's she do in these dreams?"

She hesitates, like she's just thought of some things that might be in my dreams that she might not want to know about.

"Not anything like that!" I reassure her. "It's just little moments, like having her look at me and smile — she's got an amazing smile — and holding her hand. That kind of stuff."

"And you think these dreams are telling you you're meant to be together?"

I nod, hesitantly at first, then more vigorously.

I know how this sounds. But I trust Mom to take me seriously.

"OK, then," she says. I guess she did take me seriously. "You've got some hurdles in front of you. What resources do you have?"

This is another old habit of ours — Mom helping me figure my way through a challenge.

"Her best friend is the one who told me to go help her."

"That's a big positive. What else?"

"She likes me. I mean — she seems to like me as a person, now that she's gotten to know me a little. And... her kids like me. I even got her son to do the climbing wall at the trampoline park! You should have seen him, Mom! It was awesome! I mean, he didn't say anything, because he doesn't talk, but he was so into it!"

"He doesn't talk?"

"He's autistic."

"Ah..." she says, as if I've given her the answer to a puzzle.

"What?"

"She isn't just a widow, Rhys. She's the mother of two young kids, one of whom can't fully fend for himself, regardless of his age. Of course she's reluctant to get involved with someone. Anyone she dates has to show promise as a potential step-parent. Have you considered that?"

"Yeah. I mean, I know that I'd have to help out with the kids if we were dating."

"It's much more than that, Rhys. Parenting is 24/7. Single-parenting is even harder, which is why she's exhausted, I'm sure. Add in a special-needs child..."

She gives me a look full of empathy. And that's when I realize — she was the single mom of a special-needs kid. She knows almost exactly what Lyric is dealing with. Except Lyric also lost her husband.

Yeah. This going to be hard.

"You tell me, Rhys — are you willing to consider giving up being on the road? Would you be able to put those kids first, just like she does? Because if you're not, you need to stop pursuing her. It's not fair to her without that kind of commitment. Does your dream-girl mean that much to you? After so short a time of knowing her? Are you willing to put her and her kids first?"

It's almost the same question Rory asked me. My mind goes quiet, for just a moment. And in the silence...

You can do this.

"I think I am."

Mom nods her wise Mom nod.

"Then I think I'd like to meet this dream-girl of yours, as soon as you're ready. She sounds very special."

"Oh, she is, Mom. She really is."

"Good. Now, let's hear what you've been recording, and then you can use some of that big pile of money you mentioned and take your mom out to lunch."

"It's not a big pile, Mom. I can't go dive into it like I'm a cartoon duck! But wouldn't that be cool? Maybe I should build a vault and fill it with cash, just so I can do that. No! Even better — I'll open it to the public, so everyone can do that for real! I can charge admission, and all the money goes right into the vault!"

"I'm not sure people want to be reminded how much money you have and they don't, Rhys. Let alone pay you to play in it..."

"Oh... I hadn't thought of that. Oh, well. I can still send you to Fiji. You know, Declan and Callie are going on a honeymoon. Maybe they can join you in Fiji. That would be fun!"

"I'm sure they just want to be alone on their honeymoon, Rhys. Most newlyweds do."

"Well, the truth is they've been married since they were 17..." I hear the words come out of my mouth, and I panic. "Oops. I never said that. If Declan asks, I never even mentioned him ever being 17. OK?"

"Certainly, Rhys," she agrees with an affectionate smile.

Cool! Mom's here to visit, and she wants to meet Lyric, and she's not going to rat me out to Declan that I told the secret I swore to him and Callie that I'd keep. In hindsight, maybe that wasn't a good idea.

CHAPTER 16

DREAMER'S CHANT

Lyric

Rhys pulls up to my house at exactly one in the afternoon, exactly as promised. Only I can't believe what I'm seeing.

He's the picture-perfect image of an '80s rockstar — tight T-shirt showing off his drumming- and climbing-honed body, classic black Wayfarer sunglasses on, cocky smile, arm dangling casually from the open window, his hair flowing in the breeze from the open T-top of the classic black Firebird he's driving.

My jaw drops. I can't help it.

How did he manage this? Less than a day after we talked about our mothers' mutual love of "Knight Rider," which featured a Firebird that looked... well, exactly like this one. I've never even seen a car like this in person. I kind of assumed they'd stopped making them.

"Did you rent this just for me? And where on the entire peninsula did you find one to rent?" I ask as soon as I've recovered enough to speak.

"This is *my* car," he says.

"Your actual *personal* car that you *own?*"

"Yes. I had it brought down from New York a couple days ago. Pretty cool coincidence, huh?"

My skepticism must be obvious.

He shrugs.

"I missed my car, and I needed some local wheels. The Lyft drivers are starting to talk about the rockstars who are too poor to have their own cars. Not to mention, it's rude to make out with your girl in front of strangers, even if you're in the back seat and the stranger is being paid to drive."

That snaps me out of any remaining reverie over his dramatic arrival. I roll my eyes at him. I'm definitely *not* his girl, and there will be no making-out in this car either.

"Not happening, Drummer Boy... Nice wheels, though..."

He reaches over and opens the passenger-side door for me. Those long arms come in handy at times. I slide in, closing the door after me.

I turn to tell him where our first stop will be, but the interior of the car catches my attention before I get the words out.

"*This* is your car?"

It's a perfect replica of the KITT car interior from the TV show.

"Yup. Bought it ten years ago with my signing bonus from our first album, had someone replicate the details. After I got my mom a new washer and dryer, it was the first thing I got with my 'rockstar money,' as you called it the other day."

"Sorry about that." I still feel a little humiliated at having lost my temper like that.

"Forget it. You were right. I have no idea what it's like to struggle to make ends meet. But I watched Mom do it early on. I have total respect for what you do to take care of your kids."

His expression tells me he's totally in earnest, and that sets me at ease.

"I know I was very lucky," he says. "I don't think I realized how lucky. I still think Brighid might have done her witchy thing to make sure Hunt made it big, after he was mostly homeless for a while. I told him to buy her a llama with his bonus money, to thank her."

"A llama?"

"She did all that cool yarn stuff. That was what I associated with her, and the fact that she was in love with Hunter... Well, and..."

He stops suddenly, clearly thinking hard about whatever he was about to say.

"And...?" I prompt after a minute.

"Uh... And that was what I associated with her. So, I figured she might want her own llama to make yarn from scratch."

"Llamas can be mean. They spit," I tell him.

"Really? Hunt said that when I suggested it. He said alpacas were better. But he didn't send her an alpaca either." He shrugs. "How did you know llamas spit?"

"I've chaperoned a few trips to petting zoos over the years. I actually got spat on once. Cranky llama."

"He should be ashamed, being mean to a wonderful person like you." Again, his eyes say he's being earnest, not like he's flattering me so he can get in my pants. Which is good, since he's not.

"I think it was just that llama, maybe. I've seen llamas at the zoo, too. But none of them ever have ever spat at me."

"That sounds like fun."

"What? Not getting spat on?"

"Well, yeah, but I meant the zoo."

"We've got a zoo nearby. It's a small zoo, but the kids love to go whenever I get the chance to take them."

"Cool. You ready to go?"

"Yes..." I'm a little leery of what happens when we start moving, though.

"What?" he asks.

"Nothing." I hesitate, feeling very silly. "I mean... Does it talk? It doesn't drive itself, does it?"

He chuckles.

"Not yet. I've got a request in to retrofit it with a self-driving mode, but they're not ready for that yet. And, yes, it does talk."

He clicks a button on the steering wheel.

"Play Rhys' Special Mix."

"Playing Rhys' Special Mix," the car replies, sounding like the original KITT. A Led Zeppelin tune starts playing. Rhys reaches over and turns it down a little.

"And the navigation system uses the original voice, too."

"But it's not..."

"No, it's not self-aware or anything. I wish," he adds with a chuckle. "Now — where are we headed?"

I give him the address, which he repeats to the car's navigation system. I'm relieved to see that Rhys drives carefully, safely, his attention focused on the road and his surroundings, with just the occasional glance at me. KITT could drive up to two hundred miles an hour or something. But Rhys keeps things to a sedate thirty-five, just like the signs say.

"So what are we picking up?" he asks when we're about halfway there.

"Another basket. This one's probably my favorite, though."

"Why's that?"

"You'll see."

We pull up at the shop a few minutes later, and I can see that the window display already has Rhys' attention. It's full of handmade rugs and clothing, bags, hats, décor items — even a hammock. And, mixed in with the other items are an array of musical instruments: pan pipes, ocarinas, flutes, traditional percussion instruments from a wide array of indigenous cultures.

"What *is* this place?" he asks, his voice full of wonder.

"It's a fair-trade shop. All the goods are sourced from locally owned small businesses in their countries of origin, certified to be sustainably created in safe working conditions, with an eye toward ensuring a livelihood for the people who make them. No sweatshops, no slave-labor. Fair wages, and often giving employees a stake in the business' success."

"That's very cool."

"Yeah. It is."

Rhys spots a display of musical instruments and heads straight for it. I chuckle. His almost childlike delight in trying all of the various instruments shines from him like a light. It lifts my mood, almost like a bit of weight falling away from my shoulders. In fact, I feel lighter right now, in this moment, than I have in... well, a long time. My morning included a review of my lesson plans, reaching the conclusion that there's nothing in them that any reasonable person would find objectionable. If the rumors are true, and if I'm one of the teachers called to account, it'll just be a cursory random check, I'm sure. So that's a weight off my mind. Mom has the kids, and she's really good with them and will call if there are any issues, so I have no worries there. And now, watching Rhys... I take a deep breath and let his joy infect me, too. I head over to join him, but I don't make it that far.

"Lyric? How wonderful to see you!" a voice says from behind me. "I'm so sorry I couldn't just bring our donation over to you. I know you've got to be swamped."

"Hi, Marian! A little. But it's really no trouble. I've got a few other pickups to make today."

"And you have help, I see," she says, nodding toward Rhys.

"I do."

"He's cute," she says quietly, "if you can call a guy that big cute."

"Rhys? I want you to come meet someone," I call out to him.

He turns, and the warm smile on his face practically makes me melt.

"Marian Shepherd, this is Rhys Madigan, drummer for aMUSEd. Rhys, this is Marian, who owns the shop with her husband, who is..." I look around, expecting to see René around somewhere.

"He's off on a buying trip," Marian says. "I'm holding down the fort for a couple weeks."

"Your shop is really cool!" Rhys says. "I love all these instruments. I don't usually see them in the music shops I get to."

"They're all handmade by local craftspersons in their countries of origin. Well, and this one, too. I have a few Native American drums and flutes."

"You do? I'm part Ojibwe," he tells her.

She frowns for a split second, then smiles indulgently as she takes in that red hair of his.

"Of course," she says tightly.

I'm not sure how to smooth over the faux pas. Marian, who's a member of the local Nanticoke Indian tribe, gets told all the time when people meet her that they're part Native American, too. She's mentioned it at a few of her cultural presentations at school. So many people have those old family stories. And they're rarely true. Marian has said it's off-putting to many native peoples that so many with no connection to their cultures are so eager to claim one.

I can't bring myself to correct Rhys in front of her, especially when it's possible that he does, somewhere in his family tree, have some Native American ancestors. Unlikely, given that screaming red hair of his. But possible.

I give her a small smile, trying to convey that no offense was meant. She smiles patiently back at me. As she's said, this does happen to her all the time.

Rhys spots a large drum in the corner next to the instruments, and heads straight for it.

"Sorry about that," I tell her quietly. "I don't know what his background is. I'm not sure *he* does."

"It's fine. You know how it is," she says. "Now, about that auction basket..."

She leads me back toward the storeroom and returns with a huge handmade basket full of instruments, cushioned by a handmade rug, little Mayan dolls tucked in here and there.

"Oh, Marian — this is wonderful! It's incredibly generous of you, and it fits perfectly with the theme of the event!"

"I thought so. And people love the instruments, even if they don't already play." She looks over at Rhys, who's gently caressing the head of the big drum. "You said he's a drummer?"

"Yeah. You haven't heard of aMUSEd?"

"You know I mostly listen to indigenous music," she says. "Most of the stuff on the charts these days..." She shakes her head in distaste. "It's all Autotune and computer-analyzed for appeal. I prefer something more genuine."

"Well, aMUSEd is just that, even if they manage to land on the charts on a regular basis. They're actually in town to record their next album."

"Oh! Well, that's exciting."

"How much is this?" Rhys asks, still running his fingers over the drum.

Marian looks surprised.

"Well, I mostly got it for an interactive display piece," she says. "It's an authentic Ojibwe drum, made from elk skin, with hand-painted decoration from their traditional tales."

"Is it for sale?" he asks intently.

"Well, yes, I suppose. I can order another one for display if you really want it. But it's a little expensive. With our usual overhead, it's about fifteen hundred."

"I'll take it," he says.

Her jaw drops.

Mine does at little, too. I know the money is no concern for him. But his fixation on the instrument suggests something deeper is going on here. And it's got me curious.

"And this," he says, reaching over the drum to the art on the wall.

"Also authentic Ojibwe — Anishinaabe," Marian says. "The dreamcatcher is from one of the traditional Anishinaabeg stories, though most of the ones you see nowadays are poor imitations made after they became a fad."

"Yeah," he says. "I'll take that, too."

His expression is thoughtful. And for someone who, in my experience at least, is so forthcoming with his tiniest transient thought, his silent contemplation is all the more intriguing.

Five minutes later, we've loaded the basket into the trunk of his car, and the drum, beater and dreamcatcher on the back seat, along with a plush wool llama. "For Brighid," he said. "It's overdue."

Despite that sweet gesture, Rhys' expression remains muted, his demeanor restrained.

"Where to next?" he finally asks, giving me a smile.

"Another real estate office, just down the street."

And we head off to complete the rest of our list, my mind full of questions and my heart softening even more toward aMUSEd's "madman."

CHAPTER 17
DON'T WANNA FALL IN LOVE

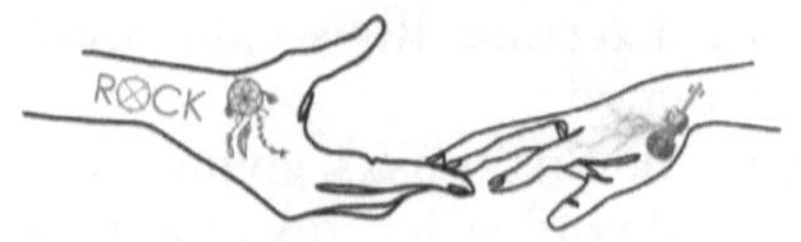

Rhys
Three hours later

"That was an amazing dinner! Thank you!" Lyric says, and her smile finally overwhelms her tired eyes. It makes me glad to see it.

"You're welcome. I wanted to try more of the local seafood, and you were right — this place is awesome!"

"I'm glad you liked it. It's great that we got the last few items picked up so quickly. Now we can celebrate a job well done. Thank you so much for your help!"

That sounds kind of like a dismissal. She's not thinking she's getting rid of me that easy, is she?

"So what's next? You said something about streamers?"

She hesitates.

"Are you sure you want to keep helping with the fundraiser? You've done plenty already. Underwriting, the auction donations and helping me pick up the others..."

She's giving me an out, letting me off the hook, in case... in case what?

In case you've already gotten bored with her and the kids, rockstar.

I look behind me to see who said that, but there's no one there. Some kind of weird ventriloquism? I check out the rest of the diners, and no one's paying us any attention. It's nice for a change. I could get used to this.

But I haven't answered her question.

"There's nothing I'd rather be doing." I put my hand over hers where it lies on the table. This time, she doesn't pull away. Score! Well, not like *score* score. But it's a small win. "Really."

She looks away shyly. The shift in her reactions to me gives me hope. She's not throwing herself at me, but she's not giving me reproving looks, either.

"Well, if you're really sure... We have to finish up the decorations for the event, put out all the baskets with their descriptions and the bidding sheets, finish setting up the stage..."

"That's a lot of stuff. Including something I'm an expert at! Good thing you have help!" I squeeze her hand. She blushes.

"So when do we start?"

"We can start right now, if you have the time. Mom's got the kids for a few more hours. We can take these items straight to the cafetorium and then get the others out of my classroom, to start."

The little bit of melancholy that's been dogging me since I found that drum starts to fade. I've got time to think about that stuff later. Right now, I want to enjoy this time with Lyric.

"Sounds like a plan!"

An hour later, we've got all the auction items moved into the cafetorium — what a weird word — and placed on the auction display tables, including the items I had Billy send over. Lyric has printed descriptions and a bid sheet to go with each of them. And as I place the last clipboard by the basket we got at the fair-trade shop, I feel the same sense of accomplishment I do after a gig. Maybe even better, because Lyric and I did it together.

"That's the last one," I tell her. "Did we check them all off?"

"Yup! And now we can move on to the stage setup, if that's what interests you..."

"Sure. What do you need?"

"Well," she says with a smile, "someone graciously donated not one but two amazingly large drum kits, of which one now needs to be put together."

I smile back at her.

"Sounds like a job for a drummer!"

"Indeed it does. So, have at it!" she says, gesturing at the stage before heading up the side steps.

I follow her, wondering where the kits are. She pulls back the curtain to reveal a large number of boxes. Oh, boy. I haven't set up a kit from scratch since they shipped me the demo version of this signature kit for my approval. This is going to be fun!

"**H**and me that cymbal there, please," I ask Lyric, pointing to one of the three remaining cymbals in the kit from my central place on the drum throne.

Yeah, it's a lot. But I use all of these drums, cymbals, high-hat, cowbell... Well, it goes on for a while. This is actually just the base model of the kit. It still has more pieces to it than the average drummer uses.

Lyric reaches over one of the toms on the far side of the kit and stretches her arm out to me, but the cymbal's heavy and the distance is big, and she overbalances. The tom slides out of its place, and she falls forward.

My arms instinctively reach for her, snatching her out of the air before she hits the floor and turning her, cradling her. She's not petite like Piper is, nor is she as voluptuous as Brighid, and I've picked up Brighid before, even though she told me not to. Lyric, she falls right into my arms, like it's the most natural thing in the world. I find myself staring down into those stormy blue eyes. My hand traces down her cheek, enjoying the feel of her skin under my fingers. She looks a little dazed, but I know she didn't hit her head.

Kiss her.

Oh, flibbertigibbets. Why not?

I lean down and press my lips to hers, soft at first, leaving her room to object. She doesn't. I open my mouth to capture her lips with mine, kissing her harder, more urgently. She grabs hold of the back of my head, pulling me harder against her, and I pull her closer in my arms, sliding my hand up her back. It catches the hem of her shirt and slides underneath, giving me a handful of bare back that feels so good that I moan.

"Uh-hmm."

That's not Lyric. And it's not me. It's not even that weird head-voice I keep hearing lately. Is this what Brighid hears when she's got her magical ears going? Is it even her ears?

"Uh-hmm."

That sound again.

Lyric suddenly pushes me away. Hard. She scrambles to stand up, and I lift her up onto her feet.

"Donnie!" she says to the maintenance man I'd seen here before. "I didn't realize you were still here. I thought all the regular staff had gone home."

"I'm just doing my last rounds before I head home, Mrs. Larson. We had some work to do in Mr. Johnson's science lab. But I heard a noise. Thought I'd better check it out."

"Oh. Well, that's fine. I just dropped a cymbal. We're almost done here. I can lock up behind us."

"Yes, ma'am," he says.

The look he gives us is... curious. A little too curious. I don't like it.

Me, either.

What the flibbertigibbets?

"Goodnight, folks," Donnie says, turning and walking back to the school entrance.

"Oh, my gods!" Lyric exclaims, wringing her hands. Not the usual response women have to me kissing them. That's concerning, too.

"You OK?"

She stares at me, like she can't believe I'm asking that.

"You kissed me!"

"And you kissed me back."

She gives me a look but doesn't argue the point. Good.

"And Donnie... Donnie saw it. Saw us kissing." There, that's better. "And your hand..."

"That wasn't on purpose! I promise!"

Again with the look.

"Doesn't matter — it's what it looked like."

"I imagine it looked like two consenting adults enjoying a passionate kiss."

"Rhys! Oh, my gods! You don't get it. I could lose my job over this!"

"Over a kiss? Admittedly, it was a very sexy kiss, and I'd like to explore where things would have gone if we hadn't gotten interrupted..."

"Rhys! It's a violation of the conduct code to engage in any behavior like that on school grounds! They could fire me if Donnie tells... well, anyone... what he just saw! If he tells Patty, it'll be all over the school district in a matter of hours."

"It was just a kiss, Lyric. It's not like we were flibbertigibbeting on the floor. No reasonable person is going to..."

"Flibbertigibbeting?" she asks.

Oh.

"Mom suggested I use the F-word less. So I changed it up."

"You sound like Mary Poppins if she was pissed off at Bert!"

She can't help it. A smile steals across her face.

"The real question is whether *you're* pissed off at *me*."

She looks at me, looks into my eyes, searching for something, and I want to hope she'll find it and lean in and kiss me again. But she shakes her head.

"No. Two consenting adults, like you said." She groans. "'Indulge,' She said. 'Self-care. Balance. Follow adventure where it leads you!' And I listened! Why did I listen? Because She's a goddess! And She never steers me wrong, and now I've got Rhys Madigan's taste on my tongue and no job. Probably."

I'm not sure what any of this means, except the taste part, and I'd like to taste more of her... her lips, her breasts, her back, her—

Hey! Pay attention to Lyric!

Who is still wringing her hands and is now mumbling disapprovingly to herself.

"I'm not sure what any of that means," I tell her.

She doesn't explain. She just starts pacing back and forth behind the kit. I swivel on the drum throne to follow her. She continues to mumble to herself, the tone chastising. I don't like it.

But I let her do it, unsure what the right thing to do is here. I mean, if she's right, and getting reported for kissing me in the school tonight is going to get her fired, there's nothing I can do about that. Well, I can try giving them another big donation, but somehow I doubt her bosses will be as cooperative as they were about my last demand. And Alex masterminded that plot. I don't think I'm up to strong-arming an entire school district.

I reach down and pick up the cymbal she dropped when she fell, the cause of all of this. Not that I regret all of it. But upsetting Lyric... that I regret.

"Is it damaged?" she asks, finally stopping the pacing.

I give it a good look.

"No. No dings, dents or nicks, even on the edge." I place it on the stand and secure it there. "I think it slid down off my foot."

"Are you OK?" she asks, concerned.

"Would I have kissed you if I hadn't been?"

"I honestly don't know."

"Actually, that's a good point. I've been wanting to do that for months now. I probably would have even if it had chopped off a couple toes."

"Rhys," she says urgently. I like my name on her lips. I'm tempted to focus on that. "That can't happen again."

"Why not? Consenting adults, remember?"

"Yeah. But I can't keep consenting. This is all a mess. You're leaving soon and I'm not ready for a relationship, and I can't bring someone into my kids' lives who's going to be gone in a month or so. And that was before we got caught making out in the cafetorium."

There's that word again.

"First — your kids love me." She winces. OK, we'll come back to that. "Second, you have no idea whether Donnie is going to say a word. I doubt it's the first time someone has kissed their significant other in this building."

"You are not my significant other!"

I ignore the objection. Another thing to deal with later.

"Worst case, we just tell them I was giving you mouth-to-mouth after your fall."

It's a lie. But it might save Lyric's job. If I practice, I could pull it off. Maybe.

"Gods above and below! No one is going to buy that. As soon as I realized he was there, I got back up. If I'd needed mouth-to-mouth, I'd have been too out of it to get up, let alone that fast."

"I'm very persuasive." I hope.

"No kidding. Otherwise, we wouldn't be here right now."

I grab her hands and pull her closer to me, so I can look into her eyes and let her look into mine to see that I really mean what I'm about to say.

"I won't pretend to know what the future is going to look like. But I can tell you that Hunt, Dave and Declan are all planning on living here full-time when we're not on tour. Dave's even building a house! And they've already talked to the label about shorter tour legs, fewer days on the road. Hunt even said something about buying a jet for the band to use so we can come home more."

Home. I just used that word to mean Mystic Beach, not New York.

Yes!

"You're talking about wanting a committed relationship."

"Yeah, I guess. I..." I want to tell her, but this doesn't feel like the right moment. I hedge. What? It's not a lie. "I feel like I'm supposed to be here, with you. And the kids. And I know I came on too strong at first, and I know we're just getting to know each other, but I'd like the chance to really do that, to see where this new adventure leads us both." She blinks at me. "That's all I'm asking for — that chance. I think the time we have left here, recording, however long that is, gives us that."

I sigh, knowing there's a chance this won't work. But I'm going to be honest with her, just like Mom taught me.

"Even if things don't go that way for us, I want to be there for you, be your friend. We've got so many people in our lives now who are planning forever together. We're going to be in each other's lives as long as aMUSEd is still a band, which I expect will be a long time. So, I want us to be friends. I want to help you out, help the kids out, just like all of your other friends. And, right now, I have the time to do that. So, I'd like you to let me be the friend you need right now. And beyond that... we'll just walk down this path the universe has laid out in front of us and see where it takes us. Please."

Tears are welling in her eyes, and I hate the idea that I'm making her cry.

"You're right," she says after a minute. "We've got too many people in our lives who will tie us together. We'd end up as some kind of friends. But that — that's all I can offer you right now, Rhys. Especially after tonight. Because I'm not sure if I'm going to have a job come Monday..."

She rolls her eyes and groans.

"Monday..." she repeats.

"What about Monday?" I ask.

She sighs. Her shoulders droop. I don't like it.

"There's a school board meeting. And the rumor is I may be one of the teachers whose lesson plan for this school year might not meet with board approval."

"You're a *music* teacher."

"Yeah. It's probably just a rumor. But I spent hours going over my lesson plans to make sure they were up to scrutiny, just in case."

"On top of everything else you have going on."

"Yeah. But *now* I have to worry that I'll be called onto the carpet by the board on Monday for an entirely different reason."

"He won't say anything."

"I can hope, I guess."

"Anything you need — anything — you just ask me. OK? I can give a testimonial, take the blame for what happened. I kissed you first, after all. I can offer them a big donation if they cut you some slack."

"Rhys — you have to stop trying to use your money and fame to get people to do what you want."

"I'm not like that! It wasn't even my idea the first time."

"Whose was it?" She frowns.

I feel kind of bad throwing Alex under the bus, but he'll survive if Lyric gets angry. It's not like she can hurl lighting bolts at him, right?

"Alex."

"Band-mom Alex?"

"Yeah. He has a thing for meddling in our romantic lives."

"Brighid mentioned that." She sighs. "OK, you are forgiven for following bad advice."

"It worked!"

"It almost backfired on you, Drummer Boy. And it wasn't *you* — because I realize now that you'd never do that on your own."

"You know that about me already?" I smile. I like that idea, that she knows me.

"I'm starting to. And I want to know this new friend of mine better — without any trickery or ulterior motives. Cards on the table. Siobhan says that all the time. I just never expected to need to use it." She frowns slightly and raises her hand up to my cheek. "Just be yourself, Rhys. Well — don't sing cow-revolt songs to my kids. That part you can keep hidden. But, otherwise, if we're going to be friends, I'd like to get to know the real you."

"Same. And I meant it about helping with anything you need. Let me take some weight off you for a little while. Even if that's just with the fundraiser. But whatever you need, you just ask."

She tilts her head, looking closely at me.

"What are you doing Monday night?"

Ooh... could she mean...?

"I hope I'll be on a date."

"Oh, you will, Drummer Boy. With my kids. You're going to babysit."

Oh.

And I have to do it without cartoon cows.

Oh, boy...

CHAPTER 18

LOVELY, LOVE MY FAMILY

Lyric

I spend most of the drive home questioning my decision to kiss Rhys Madigan. I pay a lot less attention to the road than I should, since I keep glancing over at him.

In the moment, going so quickly from falling to being in Rhys' arms, I didn't stop to think when he kissed me. And then... Well, I did stop and think. For a microsecond. And all I could think was that She'd encouraged me to let Rhys distract me, to let him lead, to give myself a break and let someone take care of me for a change. And I wanted that. *Really* wanted that. I still do.

So, my pulse pounding from his kiss much as it was from the sudden fall, I gave myself permission to enjoy it, and then I gave into instinct, need. I mean — it was Rhys Madigan! And it's been so long since someone kissed me. But that's the thing that should have stopped me, even before Donnie interrupted us. I still feel like Adam's wife. No one other than Adam has kissed me in more than a decade. I feel... disloyal? Maybe. Torn? Definitely.

And that's before we get to maybe losing my job, Rhys definitely leaving to go on tour at some point in the near future, the uncomfortable situation we'd be in if we dated and broke up, but all of our mutual friends are married... And the kids...

"Mommy! Mommy!" Aria yells as she runs through the front door, Tommy and my mother close behind. I catch her mid-air as she hurls herself at me. Mom skills!

"Grandma took us to the beach! And we had hotdogs and french fries and frozen custard! And we got to go to the bookstore and pick out a new book! I got a book about mermaids!"

"That's great! And what did Tommy get?"

Tommy walks up to me and shows me a pop-up book on bridges.

"That's amazing, Tommy! Look at all those girders and bolts!"

"They were both perfect angels all day," Mom says. "Did you get everything done that you needed to?" she asks, giving Rhys a significant look where he sits on the sofa.

"Almost." Rhys and I exchange a glance that I hope doesn't look as guilty as I feel. "Except for two final rehearsals next week and a few more tweaks to the decorations, we're basically done." It's true. And, blast it, I'm overdue for a break. "So, I'm going to take the day off tomorrow."

I don't miss the looks of surprise on everyone's faces.

"How about a trip to the zoo tomorrow?" I ask the kids.

"Yay!" Aria cheers.

Tommy smiles. It's a rare moment that he expresses his feelings that clearly, except when he's frustrated. But he loves the zoo and the little playground next door, which has a bunch of gears to play with.

"You two go get on your pajamas and brush your teeth, and then we'll have a story before bed, if you get ready fast enough, OK?"

They're both up the stairs in a flash.

"How was it really, Mom?" I ask her.

"It was fine. Really," she says. "Tommy dropped his ice cream and had a little meltdown. But that was fixed as soon as we got a new one. They even gave it to him for free."

That's one of the things I love about this town — it's full of small businesses with heart. A real community.

"Aria got tumbled around in the surf a little. She's a little overconfident about her mermaid skills," she warns.

It's not exactly news to me. I've had to pull her back in to shore several times already this summer. It's not that she's not a strong swimmer, but while she's playing in the surf, she forgets to watch out for the riptides that create the tidal pools Tommy loves to play in. One second I'm helping him build a sandcastle and the next I'm having to make sure she doesn't get swept out to sea. I wouldn't trust anyone other than Mom to watch the two of them at the beach without some help. Mom taught me to swim, and she was a lifeguard for years and is still in amazing shape. Better than I am, really. But her warning is all the more impactful because of that.

"Message received. Now… I have one more favor to ask where your grandchildren are concerned…"

"Oh?"

"What are your plans? Are you headed back to Florida?"

"Louisiana next, actually," she says. "But that's not for a couple more weeks. I thought I'd stick around a while, enjoy the end of the season."

"So you can watch the kids on Monday night? I've got a meeting."

This will let Rhys off the hook.

"No can do. Sorry, honey. I already have plans that night."

I try not to goggle at her. Iris Monroe? Plans? That she won't drop in an instant? For her grandkids? Even her being here was a deviation from the plan. That's how she operates.

"Care to elaborate?"

"I," she says, "have a date."

Now I do goggle at her. Mom never dates when she's home. I think she's exhausted the entire population of eligible women — and no few of the men — in her age range. To my knowledge, her last local date was the girlfriend she had for a few years when I was in my teens.

"Vacation romance. Well, the beginnings of a friendship," she explains. "We'll see how it goes as we get to know each other."

"Does this have anything to do with you sticking around for a while?" Now, that would be more on par for Mom.

"Maybe… Partly," she admits. And that's all I'm getting out of her. She likes to keep her romantic life private. It's mine she wants out for public consumption. Hers mostly.

"OK, then. I guess that means I'm calling in that favor, Rhys. You're on babysitting duty on Monday night."

Mom's eyes get big as she looks back and forth between us. I'm careful to keep my expression neural. I can smell a mom on the hunt for juicy details.

Rhys' eyes are big, too, as the reality seems to hit him.

"You want to change your mind?" I wait for him to back out.

But he shakes his head.

"You tell me what time, and I'll be here."

"Alrighty then," Mom says. "On that note, I'm going to go get some well-earned rest. If those kids don't sleep like logs tonight, I'll be astonished."

She gives me a quick hug and a peck on the cheek. For Rhys, she has a speculative look.

"Goodnight, all!"

And off she goes.

Seconds later, the kids come racing back down the stairs, ready for their bedtime stories.

But first, one more hurdle.

"Kids — I have a work meeting on Monday night. Mr. Rhys has offered to hang out with you two while Mommy's gone. Would that be OK with you?"

"Yay! Mr. Rhys is cool!" Aria says.

"I'll take that as a yes," Rhys replies.

Tommy is looking at Rhys, his eyes big and adoring, and I stifle the instinct that says the kids are already getting too attached to someone who spends most of his life on the road. But then maybe I am, too. It's harder to stifle that thought.

"That's a go, then," I confirm for Rhys' benefit. "Five on Monday. I'll order a pizza, and nuggets for Tommy."

"I can cook," Rhys says.

"I'm sure you can. But you're probably going to want your attention on the kids."

"Right."

"And now it's time for stories!"

To both of our surprise, Tommy hands his book to Rhys and climbs up on the sofa next to him.

"Can Mr. Rhys read our stories, Mommy?" Aria asks. "Tommy wants him to."

"I'm sure Mr. Rhys is tired and ready to go back home, Aria." I smile apologetically.

"No — that's cool. I'd like that," he says.

Aria climbs up on Rhys's other side, handing him her book, too.

"You sure?"

"Yeah. Definitely," he says. "Go chill out. Take a break. You've more than earned one. I've got this."

"Alright. I'll be right in the next room if you need anything, and when you're done."

"Cool."

I walk slowly down the hall to my bedroom, not fully willing to trust what's just happened. When I get to the bedroom door, I resist the urge to look back out at the tranquil domestic scene I know is there. It's too much to hope for, and simultaneously too much to take. I feel like I'm in a no-man's land between possibilities, with no idea which way to turn — and I'm afraid it's becoming a minefield.

CHAPTER 19

LET'S GO TO BED

Lyric

My eyes flutter open, a tremendous sense of peace and satisfaction washing over me. I smile, stretch and turn over, snuggling back into the comforter.

And then reality invades as the time displayed on my phone on the bedside charger sinks in.

It's 9 a.m.

And I'm asleep in my own bed, by myself.

No — it's not like that!

I just can't remember the last time I wasn't either awake before both kids or awakened by one or the other of them crawling into bed with me.

And the silence is deafening.

No — alarming.

Everyone learns this when they have kids: It's not the sounds of crashing or crying that you should fear. It's silence. Silence where it doesn't belong. Such as a house with two kids younger than 12 at 9 a.m. on a Saturday morning. Because the odds of not one, but two kids oversleeping or even just deciding to play quietly in their own rooms are... well, they're not good.

I throw off the comforter and race up the stairs to Tommy's room. Empty. Back down the hall to Aria's room. Empty.

Sheer panic.

The TV's not on. I'd hear it. So they're not in the living room.

I run back down the stairs and grab my phone off the charger.

My teacher training kicks in. The first thing to do when a child goes missing from home is to check places they commonly go, probably within easy walking distance.

I overslept.

The kids were hungry.

Where would they go if they were hungry?

Auntie Callie's!

Callie had even started encouraging the kids to help her cook.

I dial Callie's phone.

"Answer! Please answer! Come on, Callie!"

"Hello?" she mumbles sleepily.

"Callie? Are the kids with you?"

"What? No!" she replies, clearly starting to wake up. "I just got up and walked into the kitchen. Haven't even had my morning beverage yet. They aren't there?"

"No! Oh, my gods!"

"OK — don't panic. I'll have Declan call 911, and I'll come over and help you look."

"Mommy!"

"Was that Aria?" Callie asks.

I look up, and my 7-year-old daughter is indeed standing right in front of me, in the doorway to my bedroom.

"Yes," I tell Callie. "I'll call you back. Hold off on calling 911."

I hang up, take a deep breath, trying to collect myself.

"Aria, where's your brother?"

"In the kitchen, Mommy! He's making waffles!"

"What do you mean, he's making waffles?"

"We're making you breakfast in bed, Mommy! Now, lie down so we can bring you your food!"

I've heard about this phenomenon before — the kids get ambitious and decide to make their parents breakfast in bed. That usually means one of two things: play-dough waffles and a big juice spill on the kitchen table, or some inedible concoction that the kids have decided resembles some recipe they've seen mom make, and a giant mess left from their creative kitchen endeavors. And I'm still nervous about Tommy being in the kitchen...

"I think I'd better come help," I tell Aria.

"No!" she tells me adamantly, pushing me back onto the bed and straddling me, pinning me down. She lands on my diaphragm hard enough that my legs reflexively pull up, my feet perched on the edge of the bed. The result is that I'm now staring at the ceiling, my sleep shirt bunched up under my butt, while I'm trapped under 65 pounds of child. "We're serving you breakfast in bed! So you have to... Stay. In. The. Bed!"

"Aria, honey — let me up! We can't leave your brother alone in the kitchen."

"But he's not alone!"

And that's not Aria's voice telling me that...

I struggle to look around my daughter, despite Aria's weight on my torso, only to find a red-haired rockstar standing in my bedroom doorway, halfheartedly trying not to look at my butt in my very not-sexy plain white cotton hipsters.

"Oh my gods!" My cheeks go red.

"You forgot I was here, didn't you?" Rhys says, smirking at me.

"Aria — get off of Mommy, please. I need to at least sit up."

And pull a very not-long sleep shirt back over my butt. How mortifying is this?

"You can slide right back under the covers, because the kids made you breakfast in bed," Rhys says, gesturing to the comforter.

I decide compliance would work in my favor, since being under the covers would at least hide my naked legs and near-naked ass. What was I thinking last night, wearing my usual sleep shirt to bed when Rhys was in the house, asleep on the sofa? I've got yoga pants I could have put on.

I wasn't thinking. That's the answer to that. I walked back into the living room twenty minutes after I left Rhys and the kids with their books, only to find all three of them asleep in a pile on the sofa. I carefully picked up Aria and carried her up to bed, then Tommy. By then I was beyond exhausted, and once I had the kids in bed, I couldn't bring myself to wake up a sweetly sleeping Rhys to send him back home... or back to the studio, at least. I just threw a blanket over him and left a spare pillow beside him in case he woke up during the night.

So here we are, with me not quite half naked on top of my bed and an undeniably hot rockstar standing in my bedroom door, trying not to stare at my ass. So what do I do? I slide under the covers, just like he said.

It's only then that I look back at Rhys and realize that he isn't fully dressed himself.

"Are those SpongeBob boxers?"

"Yup."

"That's what I thought."

"Mr. Rhys has SpongeBob underwear, Mommy!" Aria pipes up.

I'm not sure how to feel about my 7-year-old daughter taking note of a rockstar's undergarments. Better than form-fitting boxer-briefs or tighty-whiteys, I suppose, if he's going to be running around my house in a state of undress. And, if I'm honest, I can't imagine sleeping in jeans would have been comfortable if he woke up in the middle of the night. With a T-shirt on, he's at least as dressed as he would be on the beach, too. So I can't really object. But SpongeBob?

"I see that, Aria." I decline further comment. "Now where is your brother?"

"If you're tucked back in and ready to break your fast, we'll answer that question," Rhys says with a smile.

I look at him, uncertain. All of this is... overwhelming. But I nod.

Now that I'm not panicking over missing kids or worrying about Rhys Madigan seeing me in my underwear... or seeing him in his... my other senses kick in, and I can smell... Is that waffles? For real?

Tommy comes around the corner, carefully carrying the breakfast tray that was buried in the back of the pantry, having gone unused since the last time one of the kids was sick.

On top of the tray is a glass of apple juice, a plate of waffles and scrambled eggs, a bottle of syrup, a paper napkin and silverware, and a single red tea rose in a glass that matches the one with the apple juice.

I take the tray as Tommy reaches the bed, sliding it over my legs. I hand Tommy the one other thing on the tray — his Lego contraption.

"Thank you, buddy! This looks wonderful!"

"I poured the juice, Mommy! No spills! And Tommy made the waffles!"

I glance over at Rhys, not wanting to call Aria out for fibbing.

"No — he really did make them!" Rhys says, nodding enthusiastically.

I look back down at the plate and recognize the distinctive shape of frozen waffles.

"We had a little lesson on using the toaster. After a series of experiments that proved your toaster creates charcoal with the dial to the far right and mushy lukewarm waffles at the far left, we concluded just to the left of center yields the perfect combination of warm and lightly toasted."

"And Tommy cooked these?"

"That batch, yeah. With supervision. Now, enjoy your break-fast while it's still warm. The kids and I are going to go get some more toaster practice in and fix ourselves some breakfast. Take your time. Relax. I've got them."

Aria puckers up, asking for a kiss, and I overcome my surprise at today's turn of events long enough to give her one.

"Thank you, honey. You and your brother did a great job!"

Aria bounds out of the bedroom, followed closely by Tommy, who's so focused on his Legos that I half expect him to walk into the wall.

"You really taught him to use the toaster?" I ask Rhys, who lingers in the doorway.

"Yeah." He shrugs. "My mom taught me when I was 8. He's plenty old enough. I mean — I hope that's OK..." he adds, suddenly seeming unsure of himself. "I just thought it might help take some of the pressure off of you, let you sleep in once in a while."

"It's fine. Callie had been talking about teaching him."

"We talked about making sure the waffles popped up high enough to take out without burning his fingers, and about un-plugging it when he's done. I'm going to let him practice again for the next batch, make sure he remembers."

"You said your mom taught you when you were 8?"

"Yeah. She was a single mom, too. She said she wanted to teach me to be self-sufficient, but I think she really just wanted me to let her sleep in. And I never burned down the house, even with my short attention span! So I figured it was safe and might be some help for you."

"It is. Thank you. And thanks for breakfast."

"I made the eggs. I figured that was a little over their heads," he adds with a chuckle.

"Yeah. Thank you for that, too." I smile at him, the relaxed feeling I woke up with starting to reassert itself now that I'm not panicked over the whereabouts of my kids.

"Oh! I need to let Callie know the kids are OK."

"She knows — Aria said we were allowed to go into Nonna's garden to pick a flower if we didn't take too many or bother Callie and Declan by being too noisy. But Declan was already out in the garden doing his pre-run warmup while Callie slept in. I told him we were making you breakfast in bed. I'm sure he's told Callie by now."

Oh. My. Gods.

What is Callie going to be thinking? Rhys bringing my kids over in the morning, dressed in his underwear? Brighid talked about how gossipy the band is. Rhys in his underwear is a detail Declan would never leave out. And making me breakfast in bed?

"I'll let you eat," Rhys says, heading back toward the kitchen, oblivious to my impending mortification.

I grab my phone, risking cold eggs to correct the assumption I'm sure has already been made.

Lyric: *It's not what it looks like.*

Callie: *I bet... >;-D*

Lyric: *No. Really. He fell asleep on the sofa. I slept in my bed. Alone.*

Callie: *OK.*

Lyric: *I'm serious!*

Callie: *Gotcha. I have to say... Until I looked out my kitchen window, I didn't picture him as a boxer man.*

I have no idea how to respond to that. So I put down my phone and start eating some really good scrambled eggs and perfectly toasted waffles... that my son made. I shake my head, marveling at that.

Rhys may have gotten a better look at my ass than anyone has in years, and I really wish that mortifying moment hadn't happened, but would I trade a do-over of that moment for Tommy making himself waffles right now? Not a chance.

CHAPTER 20

I BELIEVE

Rhys

I watch carefully as Tommy pushes up the lever on the toaster before he grabs a toasted waffle and puts it on the plate, followed by a second. Then the other two for his sister. He's got the toaster mastered. Cool. Maybe it'll give Lyric some peace of mind, as well as a little extra sleep.

I can't help myself. My mind flashes back to walking into her bedroom, finding myself looking at those luscious legs of hers and that curvaceous ass, in those sweet little white panties.

Lyric's so wholesome, so girl-next-door... except the witch part. But I'm fine with her being the witch next-door.

When the band first got to Mystic Beach, Dave had disappeared out on the beach, and we thought maybe he'd finally found himself a mermaid, which would have been perfect for him, as much as he loves the water. And, honestly, I loved that idea, too. I've got some seriously fond memories of seeing the mermaids at a stop along the way when Mom took me to Disney World when I was a kid. But that whole story Kier told us, about Irish mermaids capturing human mates and keeping them under the sea — it sounded a little less appealing than having one come onto shore with legs and all... I mean — can you even drum underwater? I've done it while skydiving, but the acoustics under the ocean have to be a problem, right? Not to mention that water's bad for wood, and my drum shells are made out of wood. Rusty cymbals? No thanks.

So, Dave found himself a cute little sound engineer instead of a mermaid, and now it turns out my dream-girl is a witch. This town seems to be full of them, so I guess the odds were good. And I already know and like Brighid, so it's not like I'm worried about ending up in Lyric's cauldron as dinner or something. Actually, come to think of it, I didn't see a cauldron in Lyric's kitchen. The closest thing was the slow-cooker in the pantry with the breakfast tray, and I definitely won't fit in there.

"Mr. Rhys?" Aria asks as she puts some butter on her waffles. It seems neither of the kids likes syrup on their waffles. I'm not sure Lyric does either, but I figured I'd hedge my bets since there was a bottle of real maple syrup in the kitchen.

"Yes, Aria?" I take a drink.

"Are you Mommy's boyfriend now?"

I choke on my juice.

Uh-oh...

"Uh..."

"It's OK if you are," she says. "I've got a boyfriend. His name is Noah."

"Like the guy with the boat and all the animals?"

"Yeah! I had to ask Mommy to tell me the story, because Noah said there was a story about his name but recess ended before he could tell me the story! And then Mommy 'splained that it was a Christian story from the Bible, which is why I didn't know it, since we're Pagan."

"Oh. I didn't think about that. We had all kinds of kids in my house when I was a kid, so my mom told us all kinds of stories from lots of religions. And I think the Noah story was actually Jewish first. They have the same god, though."

"Mommy tells me stories about lots of gods, just not the Christian one, 'less I ask. She told me I can ask her about anything."

"That makes sense."

"But I'm not 'llowed to talk about the other gods with my teachers or friends."

"Why not?"

"Mommy said some people don't think they're real, or that they're bad, and that might get her in trouble."

Huh. Kind of a heavy thing to drop on a kid. I wonder what that's about.

"My favorite story is about Brighid and her nineteen priest-esses keeping the fire lit. Mommy lets me help her sometimes when she does it. And when she's done, it's Brighid's turn."

"Your Mommy's friend Brighid?"

"No, silly! The goddess! On the twentieth day, the goddess keeps the flame lit!"

"Oh. Of course."

Of course.

"Auntie Bridge does her turn before ours," she says before taking a big bite of her waffle. "So, are you?"

"Am I what?"

"Mommy's boyfriend?"

"I'd like to be," I tell her. "But that's something your mommy will have to decide."

And she's made it clear she needs more time to ease into the idea. I can't push the issue.

"OK. Cool. I'll go ask her!"

Aria jumps up from the table, and I make it across the kitchen just in time to snatch her up under her arms and plunk her back down in her chair.

"Whoa, kiddo! It's not a good time for that. Mommy's eating her breakfast, and you and your brother should eat yours, too!"

"What about you, Mr. Rhys? Do you want Tommy to make you some waffles, too?"

Tommy's busy spinning gears with one hand and munching on a waffle — no butter — with the other. I have no idea what he's made of this conversation. But he doesn't jump up and make me waffles.

"That's OK, Aria. I can do it. And I'll talk to your mommy later about being her boyfriend. That's kind of a grown-up conver-sation anyway, since we're grown-ups."

"Oh. OK."

I set a couple more waffles in the toaster and press the lever down. Watching the kids eat breakfast, I realize that Mom was right, as usual. This is all a lot more complicated than whether Lyric wants to be my girlfriend, whether she's even ready to date again. Being with her is more complicated than reading bedtime stories or making waffles. Lyric's not just a widow — she's a single mom, to two kids, one autistic. The fact that she slept late just because the kids didn't wake her up underscores the story those shadows under her eyes tell the world. She's beautiful, but all it takes is one glance at her to recognize that she's exhausted. And that's during the summer. What will it be like for her when school starts again?

And that reminds me of a bigger issue standing between the two of us, one she already noted... I'm supposed to head back to New York soon, and then out on tour. Even if Lyric wants to hang out with me now, what kind of future do we have with her job, the kids in school and me out on the road? Hunt and Dave have talked about slowing down our touring schedule, but Dave's also talked about us maybe getting a touring bassist so he doesn't have to leave Piper and the baby. Even if he and Hunt bring the girls on the road, babies and all, it's not the same thing, because Lyric's kids aren't babies. They have school and friends, doctors, routines...

Thinking about it like that, I'm not sure how we could ever make things work between us.

And that hurts. The idea of leaving Lyric — it hurts.

Is this how Declan felt all these years when he and Callie were apart? Then no wonder the dude was so cranky.

There's got to be some kind of solution to this problem, something that's not obvious. I just have to think of one, get creative. But that's OK. I'm good at thinking outside the box. It's a lot harder for me to think *inside* the box, actually. And when I put my mind to something, I usually figure out a way. Let's just hope this situation isn't one that blows up in my face, literally or otherwise.

Lyric

I finish off my breakfast. Pretty good for scrambled eggs and frozen waffles from the toaster — made all the more enjoyable knowing that my kid made them.

Might be a good time to get dressed, before the hunk returns.

I want to tell Frank off, shoo him back out of my head and preferably back to his living haunt in one of Rehoboth's gay bars, but he's right. About me getting dressed and about Rhys being a hunk. So, instead, I scramble out of bed, grabbing a pair of yoga pants and sliding them on quickly as possible. Only I get one leg twisted and have to stop to straighten it out so I can get my foot through. There.

"Hey, I'm sor— oops!"

Too late. I'm bent over, pulling the pants legs up my legs, my butt hanging out toward the door, as Rhys walks through the doorway. Why didn't I just close the door first? I am obviously not thinking clearly right now, and the key factor there seems to be that there's a rockstar in my house — who turns halfway around, eyes into the door frame. I yank my pants up the rest of the way, tugging my sleep shirt down over them. There.

"It's fine. I'm dressed now."

"OK. I... uh... I wanted to apologize if the... uh... the Sponge-Bob thing was a problem," he says. He's wearing his jeans once again, and I'll admit that I'm a little disappointed.

"It's not a big deal. I wouldn't have expected you to sleep all night in jeans. And the kids didn't see anything shocking. I probably should have just woken you up so you could go home before I went to bed. I'm afraid we don't have the extra bedroom set up for guests right now. I know the sofa couldn't have been comfortable at your size. In case you haven't noticed, you're kind of tall."

"It's been mentioned before." He smiles. "Brighid once told me she'd make a good chinrest for me. She's almost too tall for that — I checked."

"Yeah, she's taller than I am."

"Let's see," he says, crossing the room and pulling my back against his chest. It's so unexpected that I don't resist. My instinct, somehow, is to lean back into his hold. I catch myself before it gets weird. Mostly.

Sure enough, there's a chin on top of my head.

"Perfect fit," he says, exhaling softly into my hair.

Oh, gods — my hair! I've been surprised by him twice this morning while not fully dressed, and at no point did I consider what my hair looked like.

I pull away, turning to face him while I hurriedly smooth down my hair.

"It's fine. Pretty," he says, even though I didn't ask. "Almost as pretty as your eyes…"

He's staring into them with those warm brown pools of his, and once again I'm caught.

"Mommy! Are we still going to the zoo today?" Aria yells from down the hall.

It breaks the tension between Rhys and me, and I walk past him to the doorway, finding her standing at the bottom of the steps.

"That's the plan. But you and your brother have to get dressed first! Hair brushed and teeth brushed, and dishes in the sink!"

"I'll go take care of the dishes," Rhys volunteers.

"You don't have to do that! You've done more than enough, fixing breakfast, helping with the kids… It was delicious, by the way. Best breakfast I've had in a long time."

"Well, the kids helped. I mostly just supervised and made eggs."

"Still… thank you."

"You're welcome," he says, his smile warm. "I'll go straighten up the kitchen if you want to get the kids ready to go out."

"You don't—"

"I know I don't have to. I *want* to," he says.

"OK. Thank you. I'll get the kids going."

Mommy, can Mr. Rhys come with us to the zoo?" Aria asks as the three of us come back downstairs.

"I'm sure Mr. Rhys has other things he needs to be doing today, Aria."

"Actually, I don't. I've got plenty of free time right now. I've already done my drum tracks for Alex's song. I usually go first in the studio—"

"To set the rhythm the rest of the band plays to."

Rhys looks surprised.

"You know about recording? I mean, I know you teach music at school, but most people have never been in a studio, let alone understand multitrack recording."

I'm torn. How much do I tell him?

"I've done a little work in the studio. And I've known a lot of musicians, including a drummer. So I've got a passing familiarity."

"Oh! That's cool! I should have known, with that amazing piano in the other room, and you giving lessons. Did you play keyboards for someone?"

"Violin, actually. I was a soloist when I was a teenager, into my 20s. I double-majored in music and elementary education."

"Wow. OK. Smart girl. And violin — fancy. I hadn't seen anyone play violin since college. I was terrible at it when I tried. One of the few instruments I can't play. Actually, speaking of majors — that's something we have in common. I was a—"

"A music major — I know."

"Brighid told you? I mean, she was there..."

"No, actually..."

And now I've backed myself into a corner, where I'm all but required to admit an embarrassing truth.

"Then how?"

"How do I know you were a music major?"

"Yeah... I mean, I'm a professional musician, so maybe it's not a big leap..."

"I'm a fan." The words come out in a rush, like they're eager to eat all the oxygen in the room. It certainly feels like I'm holding my breath now.

"A fan. Of the band." His expression is full of surprise.

"Yeah."

"That's kind of detailed knowledge..."

He looks a little freaked-out.

"Fine," I say, rolling my eyes. "You were my favorite. I've been a fan of aMUSEd since right after you joined the band, and you were my favorite. So I paid attention."

Rhys' face lights up.

"You're a fan. Of mine."

"Don't let it go to your head, rockstar. I was 20. And that was a long time ago."

His smile falters, and instantly I regret saying it.

But then his eyes light up again.

"But you still remembered. It's been a decade, and you still remembered my major."

His smile is a little smug, a little teasing, and I find myself smiling back at him.

"I have a fangirl!"

I grumble in embarrassment, opting not to point out to Rhys that he's got thousands — probably tens of thousands — of women who'd be happy to be called his fangirl. Am I? The 20-year-old me is having a hard time believing Rhys Madigan was walking around my house in his underwear. A T-shirt and his underwear, but still... The 32-year-old me? The mom? I don't have the time or energy to be anyone's fangirl.

As if to prove my point, Aria gets bored with the grownups talking and interrupts with a dose of reality.

"Mommy! You have to get dressed! You're still in your 'jamas!"

"You're absolutely right! I'll go get on my going-to-the-zoo outfit!"

"You have a going-to-the-zoo outfit?" Rhys asks.

"Otherwise known as my mermaid T-shirt and a pair of shorts, with comfy shoes."

"Mommy wears her mermaid shirt when we go to the zoo so everyone knows she's half fish! Just like me!"

Aria does a twirl in front of Rhys, her hands out to the side to show off her mermaid-scale top and matching leggings.

"Wow! You really are a mermaid!" Rhys says to her, full of enthusiasm.

"Nope! Half a mermaid. Actually, Mommy says I'm a quarter mermaid, since she's half mermaid. That's math. But I have to wait 'til next year to learn factions."

"Fractions," I correct.

"Mommy's half a mermaid?" Rhys asks her.

"Yup. Because Grandma's a mermaid!"

"Was. Was a mermaid, Aria. Grandma's retired now."

Now Rhys looks truly confused.

"When my mother was in her early 20s, she was a professional mermaid at one of those places in Florida where the 'mermaids' have the little air hoses and perform underwater for tourists," I explain. "Here—" I point to one of the photos in a cluster on the wall. "That's my mom. See — there's her air supply hose."

"Wow. OK."

He looks stunned.

"What is it? What's wrong?"

"I... My mom took me to a place like that when I was a kid, and I was fascinated by the mermaids. I never even noticed they were breathing through hoses."

"The best of them do it so the audience never sees. Mom was good enough to do that. It's just this photo that shows it. The illusion was seamless when she was doing her act."

"Illusion..."

"Yeah." Suddenly I realize why he seems so out of sorts. "Did you think they were real? All this time? Real mermaids?"

He shakes his head, but not in the negative.

"I honestly thought..."

"It's a convincing illusion, especially for a kid. I'm sure a lot of people never realized."

"Do you believe in mermaids? Real mermaids?" he asks with a note of desperation.

But I can answer this.

"You're asking a witch whether she believes in mermaids?" I chuckle.

Rhys smiles. It doesn't quite reach his eyes.

"Rhys — I see, hear, experience things on a daily basis that most people would never accept as real. Mermaids? I've never met one — a real one — but there's no way all the legends are just about manatees seen by delusional sailors. There's something out there. I'm not sure what, but there's something. I'm sure of that."

"So it's not ridiculous that I believe in mermaids?"

"I don't think so, no. I mean, a lot of people do. Probably as many as believe in witches. Maybe more. And you don't doubt that I'm real, right?"

His hand reaches up to rub across my cheek.

"You feel pretty real to me," he says.

My breath catches.

"Mommy! 'Jamas!" Aria sighs impatiently.

I pull away from Rhys.

"Right. I'll go get dressed. You three OK for a few minutes?"

"We're good," Rhys says. And it seems like he means it, in more ways than one.

CHAPTER 21
ZOO STATION

Lyric

"**O**h, my god! Bison! And prairie dogs!"

That's Rhys, not my kids. I think they're almost as excited to visit the zoo as he is. Almost.

I'm not sure why he's so excited. The zoo is small. Some of the animals I loved when Adam first brought me here on our second date are long gone, though others have arrived to replace them. And I'm sure Rhys, in his travels all over the world, has seen all of these animals and many more. Heck — he went to college near D.C., and the National Zoo is right there!

But Rhys is practically bouncing with enthusiasm for our little zoo. Maybe it was being in the car for the better part of an hour to get here. I know the kids are usually ready to run around as soon as they get out of the car. We've only just stopped at the entrance to get a map. And he's already this excited. Wow.

We walk up to the two-toed sloth habitat. They've got a hanging bar that invites the kids to see if they can hold on to it like the sloths do to tree branches. Tommy won't usually do it, but it's a favorite spot for Aria.

"Look Mr. Rhys! I'm hanging upside-down like a sloth!"

I step back and take a picture of her with my phone, like I always do.

"Let me try!" Rhys says when she hops down again.

An instant later, he's hanging upside down, by his knees and hands, his smiling face nearly down to the ground, with those long arms of his.

It's too cute. I take another photo.

"Mommy? How do the baby sloths get around?" Aria asks. "Their claws are too little for a big branch like that."

"Well, I think they hold onto their mommies until they're big enough to move around on their own."

"Let's try it!" Rhys says, still hanging upside-down. I'm getting dizzy just looking at him.

He lets go with one hand and gestures Aria to hop on. She's up in an instant, draped over Rhys' chest. He's still only holding on with one hand. Wow, he's strong.

"Come on, Tommy!" he says.

"Oh, that's too much, Rhys! You're going to fall and somebody's going to get hurt! Brighid said she's not healing any more broken bones, and I think that goes for you and Hunter both."

"It's fine! My hiking pack weighs more than these two put together. Come on, Tommy. Hop on!"

Tommy glances back at me, as if asking permission.

"Tommy doesn't usually like to climb here," I tell him.

But then Tommy pulls himself up across Rhys' stomach, behind Aria.

"There you go, buddy!" Rhys says triumphantly, finally grabbing hold of the bar with his other hand again. "Hurry up! Get the picture!" he tells me.

I snap another photo. And a few more for good measure. And still Rhys is hanging on to the bar with both of my kids laid over his torso. He swings a little from side to side, and the kids giggle.

The other families approaching the sloth exhibit are staring. I don't blame them.

"Hey, kids — let's let other people have their turn," I tell my brood.

"We can come back later if you want," Rhys stage-whispers to them. "But we've got to mind your mom."

Tommy's already down on his feet again when Aria goes, "Aww..." But she climbs down off Rhys, too.

"You want to try?" he asks me, still hanging from the pole.

"I get dizzy if I hang upside-down."

"You wouldn't be upside down. Hop on! Let someone else take a photo."

I can't tell if Rhys realizes how risqué that might look, or whether this is just his usual enthusiasm and he wants to include me. I also know I weigh more than both my kids put together.

"Maybe later," I say diplomatically.

Rhys drops his hands to the rubbery cushioned floor below, completely upside-down now. Then he lets go with his knees and does a handstand next to the bar. The passersby goggle at him. I do a little, too. Then he drops back onto his feet, coming up smiling.

"That was awesome, Mr. Rhys! Can you teach me to do that?"

Rhys looks at me, asking permission. I shrug.

"Sure. But later, when we have a better place to do it. Right now, let's go see those prairie dogs!"

Aria, knowing exactly where she's going, takes off at full speed, dragging Rhys behind her. Tommy and I follow at a more reasonable speed. We visit the bison, prairie dogs, red wolves, Andean bears and river otters, then double back around to see my current favorite — the lynx.

I love big cats. There was a black panther here when Adam and I first visited, and she was an instant favorite for me. But she headed off to Kansas to make baby panthers, and now we have a lynx.

"Lyric! Look! Alpacas!" Rhys shouts from up ahead.

I knew the alpacas were here, of course, but Rhys is so excited to see them that he's literally bouncing up and down.

The contrast between this Rhys and the one who kissed me so passionately last night strikes me. For all that he seems to be an open book, there are definitely different sides to him. As we move on to the lynx exhibit, I watch him move in a very different way — so graceful, despite his height. Yes, there's a controlled, catlike grace to him in his quieter moments. Callie has often likened Declan to a panther, with his prowling around the stage during aMUSEd's shows. Rhys is famous for his "Madman" energy behind his drum kit. But here, now, this Rhys is almost tiger-like. And I'm drawn to it.

"Lyric! Look! Capybaras!" he shouts, bouncing on the balls of his feet, with his hands braced on the fence.

OK, scratch that. Rhys is definitely more *Tigger*-like than tiger-like. At least when he's excited. But he was right last night — my kids visibly adore this Tigger-like creature inhabiting a rockstar's body. And I'd be lying to myself if I said that — and the glimpses of the sensual adult male who also inhabits that body — aren't a combination that appeals to both the mom and the woman inside me.

We agreed we'd try this friends thing first. But he's not making it easy.

Rhys
A few hours later

"It was the best day ever, Mom!"

"Ever?" she asks, winding some of Callie's excellent pasta around the tines of her fork. "That's a lot of days to beat."

"I know, right? First the kids and I cooked her breakfast in bed."

"Wait... You were there for breakfast. While she was in bed."

"Yeah." Wait. "Oh! No. No no no. I didn't sleep with her! I slept on the sofa. Actually, the kids and I fell asleep during their bedtime stories, and she just let me stay there. So, when I woke up, the kids and I made her breakfast in bed. Her bed. Where she slept. Alone."

"I was going to say... That would be a little fast, considering what we talked about the other day."

"I know. And I'm trying to take things slow with her. Her daughter asked me if I was her mommy's boyfriend, and I told her that Lyric had to decide that. When she's ready."

"It sounds like the kids really like having you around."

"Yeah! See!" I pull out my phone and show her the photo Lyric took of me and the kids hanging on the bar at the sloth habitat.

"They're very cute kids."

"Yeah — and super-smart. Aria's already wanting to learn fractions, and Tommy picked out a book on bridges when their grandma took them to the bookstore the other day."

"Their grandmother lives here? I thought you said she was alone, except for her friends."

"Well, she is, most of the time. Her mom travels a lot, does big craft shows and fairs and stuff. But she came for a visit. And she's nice. She hugged me and everything."

"She does sound nice, then. And you're being respectful of Lyric's boundaries?"

I look away.

"Rhys..." Mom says, with that warning tone she gets when she thinks I might have flibbertigibbeted up.

"Fine. I kissed her. But she kissed me back! And if the guy hadn't come in the cafetorium right then, I think she'd have kissed me some more. Isn't that a weird word? Cafetorium. Cafetorium."

"Yes. But you find cafetoriums in schools, Rhys. You didn't kiss her while she was working, did you?"

"She fell down, Mom! She fell, and I caught her, and... Well, I couldn't resist. And she didn't, either — resist I mean. She kissed me back! And I told her Donnie won't tell anyone, so she doesn't have to worry about getting in trouble for making out with me at school."

"I don't know Donnie, but I'm not sure that's true, Rhys. You've got to be more careful."

"That's what her friend said. That I needed to be more careful if I was going to be with Lyric."

I sigh.

What with all the witches around here, I'm not sure Rory isn't one of them, even though she said she isn't. Because she sure saw this coming. But I'll have to try even harder to be careful from now on, for sure.

"Do you all have any more performances planned soon?" Mom asks, changing the subject. She does that when she wants what we just talked about to stick in my head. Kind of like a bookmark. "I'd like to hear some of that new music live."

"I think the week after next? I'd have to check with Billy."

"Well, do that. I was thinking about extending my stay by a week or so, and I definitely want to hear you before I go, if I can."

"Will do, Mom." I grab her hand on the table and squeeze it. "I'm really glad you could come visit."

"Me, too. This vacation is starting to seem like it's exactly what I needed. So, what are your plans for the next few days? Are you back in the studio?"

"Tomorrow, for the whole day. Declan put his finishing touches on his latest, finally. He's such a perfectionist! But he's ready for me to lay down my drum tracks. And then... Oh! Monday — Lyric asked me to watch the kids while she goes to a meeting, because her mom was busy."

Mom seems surprised.

"That's a big responsibility, Rhys. And it's a very big thing for her to trust you with when she hasn't known you for very long."

"I know. But she ran out of other options, and she's seen how good I am with the kids. And it's just for a couple hours. I can do it."

"I know you can. You helped me with the fosters often enough before you went off to college. But Lyric doesn't know that, right? That you helped with kids before?"

"I didn't tell her. I told Aria that we had lots of kids in the house when I was young, but I didn't tell her mom."

"It's up to you if and when you want to tell people you're adopted, Rhys. You know that."

"I do. I told Hunter the first day we met. It just kind of slipped out. I just..."

Yeah. There's that mood again.

"You know you can tell me anything, Rhys."

"Well, Lyric took me to this shop the other day, and they had all these instruments and—"

"How's your dinner, guys?"

Callie pops up over Mom's shoulder, smiling widely.

"It's amazing, dear!" Mom says. "You are really an extraordinary chef! These flavor combinations you come up with... Very impressive."

"It's great, Callie," I tell her. "Thanks."

"Sit down and tell me all about your honeymoon plans!" Mom suggests. "Rhys said you might be going to Fiji?"

"Well... I guess I can take a few minutes, get off my feet," Callie says, taking the chair between us.

That's OK. I can talk to Mom about that other stuff later.

CHAPTER 22
UNDER A STORMY SKY

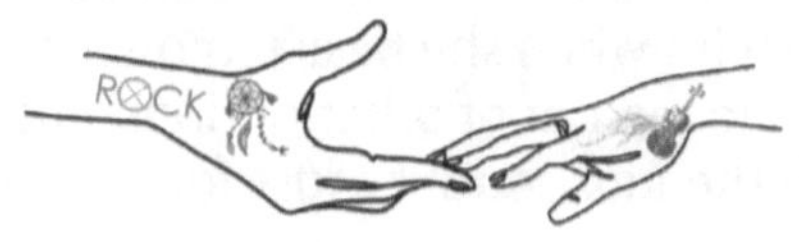

Lyric

It's ten a.m., and I'm pacing around my living room. I've got a lesson to give in an hour, but I've been waiting all morning for someone from the district office to call and tell me that I need to be at tonight's board meeting. So far, nothing. I hope that means Patty was right that it was just a rumor. But my nerves are on edge. There's a storm front moving in, too, and it's not making things better.

I went over my lesson plan one more time, so I know I'm ready to discuss it, if need be.

The kids are watching a Disney movie they actually both love. Once it's over, I've got some summer bridge workbook pages for them to work on.

I've confirmed the caterer, auctioneer and the volunteers for Friday. I've confirmed rehearsals on Tuesday and Thursday, with an email out to all of the parents and our accompanist. I'll have Rhys to help me tomorrow with the remaining decorations and final stage prep. And he's set to be here at five, so I can leave for the meeting. If I'm leaving for the meeting.

My phone beeps.

Patty: *Not a rumor. You are on the list. No details as to why. Carson is also on the list, along with a few others. Most of them are middle-school and high-school. No clear common denominator, except no math teachers on the list. ;-D*

Patty: *Too soon? Sorry. Just trying to lighten the mood. Good luck!*

Lyric: *Thanks! Here's hoping I don't need it.*

I will not panic. I will not panic. I will not panic.
"Aaaahhh!"
The kids both look over at me. I smile reassuringly.
That scream — it wasn't panic. It was being startled. Because my phone, still sitting in my hand, is ringing.
It's the district office. OK. *Now* I'm starting to panic.
"Hello?"
"Mrs. Larson? This is Connie over at the district office. The board is doing a review of lesson plans for the coming school year, and they've requested you come to tonight's board meeting to discuss your submitted plans with them. Are you able to do that?"
Keep it together, Lyric.
"O.K. Yes, I can do that. Can you tell me their specific concerns?"
"It's a routine review of lesson plans across the district," Connie says. "Yours was one of several dozen they wanted to discuss in person."
"Is there a problem with my lesson plan?"
"The board members will have to talk to you about that. I'm just calling to notify you that they've requested you be there to talk to them tonight. Can I confirm that for them?"
"Yes. Yes, I'll be there."
"Great. I'll let them know. Have a good day!"
"You, too."
Why do I suspect that her day is going to be better than mine?

At 4 p.m., I'm dressed in my most professional clothes, with a subtle amount of makeup on, instead of my usual mascara and lip color alone. I was careful to pick low-key, natural tones. Truthfully, I'd have rather gone with my usual barely-there look, but this sends a subtle message that I'm taking whatever this witch-hunt is seriously and...

Yeah.

Probably better if I, as an actual witch, don't flippantly call what may just be a routine review a witch-hunt. Especially when I live in daily fear that these same people will find out I'm a witch.

I'm nervous, OK?

So, I'm wearing a subtle, professional amount of makeup, so the board knows I'm taking whatever this is seriously, but that I'm not a streetwalker. Not that there's anything wrong with sex-work. Some of my closest friends are sex-workers. No. That's not true. If there are any sex-workers in the area, I have no idea where or who they are. But I totally respect their decision to do that work, unless it's not their decision. Consent is vital.

And I'm rambling. Oh, yeah, that's going to impress the board members...

"Kids, I'm going to go meditate for a little bit. If you need me, you have permission to come get me. OK?"

Tommy's glance is as good as agreement.

"Yes, Mommy. Are you OK?" Aria asks, little witch in the making. Rory's non-witchiness aside, I suspect Aria may be walking in her auntie's footsteps where the gift of empathy goes, or maybe...

"Yes, honey. I just need to go talk to Herself for a little bit."

"OK, Mommy. Have fun!"

I chuckle. Only a kid would think of meditation or ritual in those terms. It gives me hope that I'm passing down the traditions in a way that she finds accessible. If she decides she's not interested later, that's OK. But just like Christians pass down their Sunday church-going, their Easter and Christmas traditions to their kids, I have Aria help me tend the flame sometimes when it's my turn, and we open presents on the winter solstice, put out our "Brighid's cloak" for Imbolc, do our (usually early) egg hunt on Ostara, bake bread and make corn dollies for the autumnal equinox, and remember our ancestors around Halloween (usually before the trick-or-treating).

That's the hard one these days — Samhain. Aria doesn't remember much about her dad, but I try to tell them stories about him as things come up. At Samhain, Aria likes to talk *to* her dad. I've told her he's in the Summerlands now, waiting for his next life to begin. But she insists he can hear her. And maybe he can. But if he's hearing me, he's not talking back, and goddess knows I have enough of the dead speaking to me these days. More than.

Thanks, hon. We love you, too.

"I can hear the sarcasm, Frank, even if you're invisible."

It's nice to be heard.

"I know, Vivienne. And I hope you find your closure soon."

She's never told me what she's waiting for, why she's still here. But she's got a soft spot for the kids, and I suspect her own children are involved, whoever they are.

That weirdness with David and Siobhan at Callie and Declan's wedding... Whoa. Even with the dead talking to me, I never expected to end up in the middle of that. Very few people come back from the dead. And Siobhan wove her magic into... part of a complex working that is far beyond me. If the only fallout for her from that is that she and David are uncomfortable around each other, at least for a while, then I'll consider her lucky. I haven't told either of them that I know what happened. At least that part of it. The rest... Nope. Don't want to know.

Nonna's been quiet for weeks now, and I'm sure that has to do with Declan and Callie getting their happily-ever-after. I'm glad I could help her with that. Now, I hope she's found her peace at least, found her way to her own beloved husband again.

I miss Adam. And that makes me feel guilty about kissing Rhys.

Oh, gods. Could that be the real reason they're calling me before the board?

No. They're calling in a bunch of people. I don't think we've all been kissing rockstars — or anyone else — on school grounds.

Shh...

It's subtle, quiet, but direct. And my mind instinctively follows the instruction.

I didn't even make it to my altar. I'm still standing in the doorway to the little room.

But now... I go sit down in front of the altar, automatically falling into the slow, rhythmic breathing of my meditation routine, my eyes closed.

Good...

All will be well, child. You can't see all the pieces yet, but they're coming. Have faith. Be patient. Especially with him.

I don't ask who She's referring to. Rhys' image comes into my mind so clearly. The look on his face as he touched my cheek the other night, reassuring me, those eyes of his looking at me so earnestly, reverently.

With him looking at me like that, I can almost believe that it will be alright.

"The pizza and nuggets should be here any second. I got half cheese and half deluxe, since I wasn't sure what you like. But I know you're not a vegetarian, so I figured that was safe. I've already started their favorite movie for them. Their pajamas are laid out on their beds, just in case I run late. As long as their teeth are brushed, they can just put those on and jump into bed. And you probably won't even need to do that."

I stop to take a breath.

"I really have no idea how long this is going to run. They usually wait until after the main business of the meeting is done before they deal with personnel and student issues. I'll get back as soon as I can. If it seems like I'll be later than eight, I'll text you to let you know."

"I've got it, Lyric. Really. We're cool. You can just focus on the meeting. I've got the kids."

That loose screen door on the front porch catches in the wind and slams closed again, and I jump.

"There's a storm coming through. If the power goes out, there's a flashlight in the pantry, where you found the breakfast tray. And both of the kids have one on their bedside tables. They all have a hand-crank for power, so if they start to fade, just wind them up again. Tommy's afraid of storms. I usually keep him with me, in my bedroom or on the sofa, just to reassure him. Aria loves storms, so you may have to keep her away from windows and doors if there's lightning."

"Lyric."

"Make sure to lock the door after me, and after the food comes. It's a small town. There's no violent crime. But, just to be safe."

"Lyric."

"If there's an emergency and you can't reach me for any reason, my mother's number is on the fridge, along with Poison Control, the power company's emergency number, and Rory's, Callie's and Brighid's cell numbers. But don't call Rory. She said something about the swamp and being off the grid."

"Lyric!"

"What?"

"I've got it. We'll be fine. I'll protect those kids with my life, if it comes to it, but it won't. So, you can go off to your meeting now and know that they're safe. OK?"

"OK."

"Good."

I pick up my purse and toss it over my shoulder, grab my keys, and look back at the kids on the sofa.

"It's fine," Rhys says quietly. "It'll all be fine."

And he brushes a kiss across my forehead.

It's sweet, innocent. Not at all like the way he kissed me the other night. Not a single thing to object to as far as him crossing the line from friend to...

"It'll be fine."

He squeezes my hand.

And I walk out the door, waiting until I hear it lock behind me before I get in my car and head off to meet my fate.

CHAPTER 23

RIDERS ON THE STORM

Lyric

I check my watch.

It's a quarter to eight. I sigh, and then I text Rhys — making sure for the third time that my phone is on silent.

> Lyric: *They're running late. Feel free to tell the kids to brush their teeth and get into the pajamas. I'm sure they'll happily accept bedtime stories, but you're not obligated if you're not feeling it. I'll text you when I'm headed home.*

> Rhys: *We're doing great. Aria's already mastered the triangle base for a headstand. And Tommy's added about twenty gears to his contraption. It's pretty amazing. I want one of those things!*

> Rhys: *It'll be fine. I just know it. You've got this.*

I put my phone away again.

"M rs. Larson? The board will see you now."

"Right."

They seem to be going alphabetically, so I'm about halfway down the list of a few dozen teachers. Mrs. Carson went early on, coming back out of the room shaking her head, her lips pursed. I silently implored her to tell me something, anything, about what happened, but she just shook her head more emphatically and left.

Not a good sign.

The board is meeting in their chambers, rather than out on their dais in the meeting room. And there's no one in here but the board members, a couple staff members and me.

"Please have a seat, Mrs. Larson," the board president, Mr. Manetti, says.

I take the obvious empty seat, setting my purse down on the floor by my feet.

There's a minute of silence, while papers are shuffled around. One of the staff hands me a copy of my own lesson plan, which I had in my purse anyway. But I take it.

"Mrs. Larson, the board has undertaken a routine — and I emphasize the word 'routine' — review of this year's lesson plans. Some of our members—" He looks down the table toward some unfamiliar faces. "They have concerns about some of the content of a variety of the courses we've reviewed. One of them was yours."

No one invites me to speak, but I do.

"I confess that I'm a little baffled as to why my music class lessons for this year would be of concern to anyone."

"It's the theme of your winter concert, Mrs. — It is Mrs., isn't it?" one of the board members in question — a middle-aged man with a beer belly and mean eyes — asks. I nod, wondering why it's so important to him that he get my honorific correct. "Yes, Mrs. Larson — the theme of the winter concert is of concern to myself and a number of my fellow board members." A few other heads nod in agreement.

"Can you tell me what your concerns are? The class content is the same as what I've taught for the last five years, with the exception of the specific songs and theme, which we change each year."

"And your theme this year... 'Soundtracks of Childhood — A Disney Movie Sampler' — whose idea was that?"

"Well, mine. Everyone knows the songs already, so it makes it easy for the kids to learn early in the year. And it has universal appeal — the kids all love these movies, and their parents love them. Everyone loves them."

"I would beg to differ with you on that, Mrs. Larson. Perhaps you are unaware, but the Walt Disney Corporation has taken on itself to advance a number of political and social views that are highly objectionable to an increasing number of morally-centered families."

Morally-centered? Is that what they're calling it now?

"I really don't keep abreast of politics, Mr. ... Galworth." That is a lie. I don't know any witch who doesn't keep at least a loose eye on this stuff. It's self-defense. You do that when you're a misunderstood minority. Like the people he's saying Disney's sided with. But it's best if I declare myself apolitical, considering the tone of this inquiry.

"Well, then we can perhaps forgive you for being unaware of the serious concerns of a vast number of families over the insertion of liberal politics into what has traditionally been family-friendly entertainment. It's been a slow incursion, really, until recently. But it's gone too far."

He seems to expect me to respond.

"I understand your views, sir. But these aren't even very recent films I'm drawing from. The newest one is 'Frozen.'"

"The concern over the company remains — especially as prominent as the name is in the title of the concert. And we do also have some concerns over individual songs."

"May I ask which songs?"

"Well, this first one, 'Circle of Life'? You're aware who the composer of that song is?"

"Yes. It's Elton John. A very popular performer for decades."

"And an openly gay man."

"Yes."

"You don't find that of concern? To be teaching our children to play music written on that glitter-spangled piano?"

Can you spangle things with glitter? I thought that was stars. But I keep my mouth shut about that.

"The song is beloved to a large number of people, Mr. Galworth. I don't think many of them think in terms of the sexual orientation—" the objecting board contingent all wince at my use of the term, but I keep going "— of the composer. It's an uplifting song, from a widely praised film."

"Yes, well... We also had some concerns about the beginning of the song..."

"The Zulu chant?"

"Yes, exactly. Don't you feel it is of more importance that our children be learning to read and write English at this age? Why are you encouraging them to learn this African language?"

My mouth opens. And closes. And opens again. I take a deep breath.

"I'm not sure I'd call it 'encouraging' them to learn Zulu, sir. It's part of the song, and I'd like the children to sing the words correctly, rather than mumble them, as so many people do. That's a part of learning music — learning songs accurately."

"Then why not start the song after that?"

"After the beginning?"

"Yes. Where the English starts."

"Because, sir, that's not how the song was written."

Frowns all around. I might have said that a little too pointedly. Maybe.

"The film is themed around African animals and culture. It is at the core of the song."

There. That's better.

Oh, wait, no. They're frowning even more.

"Then why not select a song from a film that's set in America, Mrs. Larson? You're a patriotic American, aren't you?"

Oh, boy. I wasn't too far off about this being a witch-hunt, it seems.

"I am immensely fond of the U.S. Constitution, sir. Especially the First Amendment."

OK. That's not making it better, even though it's true.

There's muttering among the board members.

"Mrs. Larson, I'm afraid our concerns remain, about this song and several others you've selected, as well as the overall theme. We'd like to ask you to revisit the selections and theme, and come up with a revised lesson plan using acceptable material."

"I've already arranged for the licensing for these songs. The district has paid the licensing fees. If I change the songs, I'll have to get new licensing, pay fees for those songs."

"Then you should do that."

"My budget is already very tight, Mr. Galworth. We're hosting a fundraiser later this week just to try to raise the money for new instruments."

"You're not performing any of these songs at that event, are you Mrs. Larson?"

"Well, no — these songs were selected for teaching during the fall and performing at the winter concert."

"Good. I'd hate to have to suggest at this late date that we cancel your fundraiser over inappropriate material."

There's a flash of lighting so bright it overcomes the illumination in the room. It's followed immediately by a boom of thunder so loud I clap my hands over my ears. A few of the board members have moved to take cover under the table. Everyone else is looking worriedly at the windows. After a moment, everyone regains their composure. Everyone except me.

My hands are gripping the arms of my chair so hard that my fingers hurt. My heart is racing, my breath shallow, and I'm afraid of what might happen if I don't get myself under control. Meditation breathing. Consciously loosening my hands.

"Mrs. Larson?"

"Yes?

"I asked if you could have a list of the fundraiser songs to us by tomorrow morning, just so we can be sure there's nothing to be concerned about there."

I nod. It takes a moment longer to get my mouth working again.

"Yes. I'll email that to the board secretary as soon as I get home tonight."

"Understand, Mrs. Larson — this change of theme for the winter concert — it's a suggestion. We can't order you to make the change." A pale ray of hope. I absorb it desperately. "Until we've voted formally, that is. And we won't be doing that until the conclusion of our meeting tonight. So, if you are planning to leave after we're done speaking with you, you'll have to call the district office in the morning to confirm our vote. Though, I think I can safely say that it will be to order you to change the concert theme."

There are nods of agreement from more than half of the board members. And that ray of hope gutters out entirely.

There's more distant clap of thunder that rattles the windows, then a cascade of percussive, liquid noise as the skies open up and dump a deluge on the world around me.

And now I have to drive home.

CHAPTER 24

RAINSTORM

Rhys
Earlier that night

"That's awesome, kiddo! You've almost got it."

Aria's legs wiggle around as she tries to settle her knees on her elbows, the sofa right behind her, just in case.

"That's it! You did it!"

"But I'm not standing on my hands yet, Mr. Rhys!"

"No, but you've mastered the first part of learning how to do that. Like a lot of things, doing a handstand involves learning a lot of steps. Each one gets you closer—"

"To the top of the stairs!"

"What? No. Well, yes. But I meant it gets you closer to what you're trying to learn."

"Oh!"

The screen door slams again. I should really try to fix that, or get somebody to do it.

"It's getting windy out," I say, as much to myself as to the kids.

Tommy's lying on the floor at the back of the sofa, spinning gears. He went back there as soon as the wind started up.

"Can I go sit on the porch, Mr. Rhys? Wind's exciting."

She's not wrong. I love a good storm. Preferably not when we've got a gig or when I'm planning to jump out of a plane. But otherwise...

"Let's see if we can get your brother to come out with us."

"He won't go. He's scared of storms, like Mommy said."

Hmm... Two kids. Two very different sets of desires. One me.

Compromise.

"Let's try this... Tommy — can you come sit on the sofa instead of back there, please?"

I peek over the back of the sofa, and he's looking right at me, for a change. His eyes are like Lyric's, only lighter. A sunny summer day. Lyric's are like the sky outside now.

"Come on, buddy. You'll be safe up here, I promise. But I need to keep an eye on you while your sister is out on the porch. Can you help me out? Please?"

Tommy gets up and sits next to me on the sofa.

"We're going to be right outside. I'm not even going to shut the door, so if you need me..."

What? Shout?

Alright, this isn't a circumstance I'm used to. Think, Rhys. Outside the box.

Got it!

I go into Lyric's music room and pick up a small hand-drum that I spotted in there the other day, tucked up on a high shelf.

"If you need me, buddy, just pound on this drum, and I'll come right back in, OK?"

I pat the drum lightly. Tap, tap, tap. Tap, tap, tap. He hits it, too, mimicking me. I pat it again. He repeats it. Interesting...

"Oh, we are *so* going to work with that later, buddy. But after I take your sister out. Just drum if you need me, for right now."

Aria and I set up camp on the top step at the front of the porch. Far enough out to feel the storm coming, close enough to cover that we can dive back inside if rain or lighting start up. I can see Tommy through the screen door. Perfect.

"So you like storms, huh?" I ask her.

"I love them!"

"You know you have to be careful, right? Stay inside when there's lightning? Don't ever stand under a tree? Don't ever drive into floodwaters?"

What? That's important knowledge if you're in a storm. OK. Fine. She's 7. She'll be ready in nine years or so, when she gets her driver's license.

"You're silly, Mr. Rhys."

"So they tell me." They do. Often. And in many ways.

She just closes her eyes, and I can see her savoring the feel of the wind.

There's a pair of squirrels up in the big tree in the corner of the yard, and they seem energized by the wind, too, chasing each other around the trunk. I'm tempted to get closer and watch. I did that one time — started to get off my drum throne during a gig in the park when aMUSEd first got started, just to follow the squirrels — but Declan got so pissy with me that now it's like squirrels come with their own warning signs.

We sit there, quietly, for a half-hour or so. I check on Tommy every few minutes, but he's busy with his gears.

There's a big gust of wind, and the screen door slams again. I swear — I'm going to get that fixed for her.

"Uh-oh..." Aria says suddenly.

"'Uh-oh' what?"

She's looking around her at the wind blowing the trees.

"Mommy's angry."

"Why do you say that?"

"Look at the trees — they're blowing angry."

I look. I agree that the sky looks "angry," but trees *blowing* angry?

"The trees are angry?" I ask her.

"No — *Mommy's* angry. She's making the wind blow the trees, like a storm, only it's Mommy."

I look up at the trees around the house, then at the ones in Callie's, in Declan's, Nonna's? — oh, flibbertigibbets — the yard next door. They're getting blown around, but not nearly as hard. Down the street, the trees are even less disturbed.

Are we sitting under a mini tornado or something?

I step out onto the walk to check. There's no sign of a funnel cloud, but everything has started to feel weird... off... angry.

"Mommy's angry."

Is it possible? Could Lyric possibly be causing this crazy weather? Without even being here? I mean — she's a witch, but *Brighid's* never caused a storm, at least that I know of.

The wind picks up even more, and I catch myself looking nervously at the trees closest to the house. They're not small. Already some twigs and small branches have fallen out of a few of them. Maybe it's better if I take Aria back inside.

Lightning cracks across the sky, followed by a concussive boom that makes me duck and grab Aria in one motion, pulling her under the cover of the porch.

A monsoon-level downpour starts, instantly drenching everything in sight.

"Oh, no..."

"That's your mommy, too?" I ask Aria, nodding out toward the weather.

She nods gravely.

"She's extra-angry now?"

"No, Mr. Rhys. Mommy's sad now. Mommy's very, very sad."

She clings to my side and starts crying, too. I hold her tight, because whatever's happening to Lyric, I can't hold *her*, not until she gets home and, even then, not if I'm going to keep to my word about us being friends first. Because once I've got her in my arms, I'm not sure I'll be able to let her go.

CHAPTER 25
TWISTED

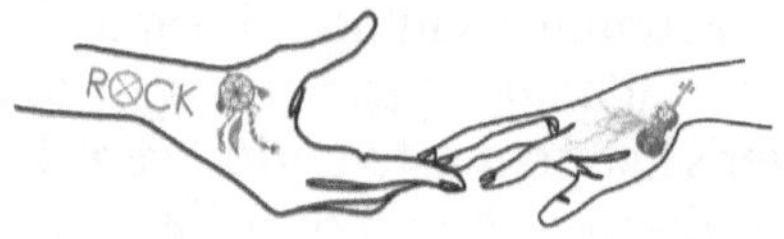

Rhys

I find Tommy inside, still on the sofa, still playing with his gears, but he's pulled the sofa blanket over his head.

"You, OK, buddy?" I ask him, my head dipped under the blanket with him.

He just looks at me. Keeps humming. No obvious distress.

She's coming home.

Maybe that's it. Maybe he's expecting her to show up any second and tell him his bedtime story. Which it's time for now, anyway.

Aria has stopped crying, but she looks exhausted, so I send them both up to get ready for bed.

The monsoon continues outside, but it's a soothing sound. Sad, maybe, but not alarming like that thunder.

As soon as they're done, I tuck each one into bed with their books, reading a few pages before they conk out.

And then I head back downstairs to wait for Lyric.

No sooner than I sit down on the sofa than she bursts through the door, soaking wet. And not all of it's rainwater. She's been crying.

She looks at me and blinks, as if she's just remembered that I was here with the kids. I've never seen her this out-of-sorts.

"Are the kids OK?" she asks, her tone wild, almost desperate.

"They're fine. Both asleep in bed. Are you OK?"

She looks at me, seeming to grasp for words.

"No. No, I'm not," she says, an angry edge to her voice.

I pull her away from the door, latch the screen door on the inside, close the wooden door and lock it.

"Tell me." I pull her over to the sofa.

"They canceled my entire winter concert! Well, no — they didn't cancel it. They canceled Disney. Or they're trying to. Or..." She's rambling. On one level, it's cute, because it's how I talk most of the time. But, really, it's a measure of how upset she is. And I don't like that. At all.

"Slow down. Take a breath. I'm listening."

She takes two deep breaths, in fact.

"The new board members seem to have built a coalition of members who are of the 'Go woke, go broke' variety. They wanted me to change all the songs, the entire theme of the winter concert, which was supposed to be Disney movie songs..."

"I love Disney movies!"

"Everyone does! That's why I picked it! That's why I spent all that time — all that money — getting the performance licenses! And now they say I can't use any of it! 'Too woke.' 'Too African.' 'Too gay!' I have to find some other theme, other songs to go with it! I spent months working on that. I'm not sure I've even got time to get anything licensed before the school year starts and I have to start teaching the kids those songs! And they questioned my *patriotism*!"

"Wait. What?"

"They suggested a patriotic theme. For a winter concert!"

"It would make more sense in the summer."

"No kidding. But they didn't like that I wasn't gung-ho about that idea. I may have said a few unwise things that may have been interpreted as being ever-so-slightly hostile."

Well, that doesn't sound good. But I don't tell her that. I'm the king of the foot-in-mouth club. The only thing I can offer is tips on how to make room for the second foot.

"And I have to do all my planning all over again!"

She bursts into tears, and I pull her into me, cradling her head against my chest, my arms wrapped around her. She wraps her arms around me, too, and I only let myself enjoy it for a moment before I focus on consoling her, rubbing her back rhythmically, kissing her hair.

Wait. I'm kissing her hair.

Uh-oh.

She doesn't seem to notice, but I do. That image of Brighid getting hair-kisses from Mace flashes back into my head.

You don't usually kiss a girl on the top of her head — not unless there's something there.

OK, Mace and Brighid didn't end up together, even after that. This doesn't have to be a thing. Friends do hair-kisses, right? I saw Hunt kiss Brighid on the hair at least a few times when they were "just friends." But they're not "just friends" anymore. And were they ever really?

But Lyric's upset. Totally different set of rules, right? Right?

Take care of her.

I set aside the issue of hair-kisses for the moment and concentrate on rubbing Lyric's back. She's stopped sobbing, and the quiet crying wanes after a few more minutes. She's silent, except for her breathing, but she's holding on to me for dear life. I like that. And I hate it. I hate that anyone could hurt her like this, and part of me wants to go find these board members and show them what "woke" really looks like. Because they've woken up a protective streak I don't think I've seen in myself since I told a bunch of people Brighid was my girlfriend.

Long story. It wasn't true.

But Lyric... Oh, who am I kidding? I told her we could be friends, and we can. But it's not what I want. And it's not what feels right to me when I look at her, when I hold her like this. And maybe she's only letting me do it because she's upset, but...

Part of her wants it, needs it, needs you.

Exactly!

Take care of her.

Yeah. And she's still pretty rain-soaked. I should get her out of these wet clothes.

Oh, really?

Not like that! Well, eventually, yes, like that, I hope. But not now. Right now, she needs someone to take care of her, be here for her.

Yes!

I'm starting to suspect I'm developing a split personality. But the other me is still right.

"Lyric, I think we should get you dried off, in warm clothes and let you get some sleep. OK?"

"Mm-hmm..." she murmurs into my chest.

I gently free myself from her grip and stand, leading her down the hallway to the bathroom.

"You want a shower?"

"Yes, please. I want to wash all this negative energy down the drain."

"Sit."

I sit her down on the closed toilet and then turn on the shower, hot, just like I like it. As soon as the water starts to steam, I look down to find her staring back up at me, her eyes huge. I have no idea what she's thinking. But I can't get hung up on that. I grab two big towels from the little linen closet inside the bathroom and hand them to her. Because I can't do what has to come next.

"I'm going to go back out and let you shower. If you need anything, just let me know."

"OK."

I retreat out into the hallway, wishing I dared help her shower, because she's still seems so vulnerable. But, no. Friends. And her friend is going to go find her some comfy pajamas and turn down her bed so she can cozy up and get some sleep.

I go into the bedroom, letting myself really look around it this time, rather than trying to keep my eyes off Lyric in various states of partial undress. It's neat, except for the pile of clothes in a chair that it looks like she discarded when she was picking out her outfit today. She went with a sexy librarian look, minus the bun and glasses. I liked it. But then I think she's sexy in her mermaid T-shirt and shorts. Very sexy in that T-shirt and panties she had on the other morning. Oh!

I move to the dresser, allowing myself a glance at the family photos on top. The kids at several different ages, Lyric with her mom, Lyric wearing... a white dress and kissing a guy who looks a few inches shorter than me, with long, light brown hair, shaved on the sides — a contrast with his suit and tie. He looks like he could be a skateboarder, or a climber, or... a musician.

Was her husband a musician? Not many of us can make a living at it. I know I'm a very rare exception to the rule. But she's got a room full of instruments in her house. It would make sense that maybe some of them aren't just hers. Or weren't.

I hear the water turn off in the bathroom, and I force myself to focus on what I'm supposed to be doing in here, which is not snooping. Mom said...

Focus on Lyric!

Right. Sleep clothes.

I pull open drawers until I find a shirt similar to the one she had on the other morning. I force myself not to look in the drawer where I found her panties, and I just stick my hand in and grab a pair, randomly, wrapping them up in the shirt. I close the drawers and head back toward the bathroom. I knock.

"I got you some clean clothes, Lyric. I'm going to leave them out here by the door."

"Thank you!" she calls back, the sound muffled, like maybe she's drying her hair with a towel.

I head back into the bedroom and pull down the comforter, fluff the pillows on the bed.

Which side of the bed does she sleep on? Which side was his?

Focus on Lyric!

Right.

I try to remember where she was when she was eating breakfast in bed. I blank, getting stuck on that image of her with her legs up in the air after Aria jumped on her. Funny and sexy all at once. I wouldn't give that sight back for anything, even though she got embarrassed about it.

In the middle, moron! She sleeps in the middle now!

Hey, voice in my head — that's not nice. We don't call people names!

Maybe I need to start going to that therapist Hunt is seeing. When my newly split personality is mean to me, it's probably a sign I need help.

I shake my head, trying to get my thoughts back in line. And I make her a small pile of pillows in the middle of the bed.

I turn around to find her standing in the doorway, dressed in her sleep shirt and... OK. Maybe I should have looked at which panties I grabbed. Because through the thin white fabric of the T-shirt, I can see the bright red color and skimpy shape of a very sexy string bikini. Now it's me blushing with embarrassment.

"I didn't — I mean, I tried not to... I didn't want to... to look in your underwear drawer, like some kind of creeper, so I just grabbed a pair with my eyes closed."

"Probably would have been better if you'd looked." She chuckles lightly.

"I realize that now. But you can get a different pair now. I'll go fix you some food, if you want."

I hold the comforter for her, and she climbs into the bed, settling down in the middle, just like the other me said.

"Not hungry."

"You need to eat."

"I had something before I left for the meeting. And I'm really, truly not hungry right now."

"Some sleep then? I'll just head back to the studio, if you're OK."

I wait for a reply, but I don't get one. I look closely at her, and I realize she's started crying again.

"Oh, god, Lyric... I'm so sorry you're going through this."

She takes a shaky breath, which comes back out as a heart-wrenching sob.

I sit down next to her on the bed and pull her back into my arms, where it feels like she belongs. Her head settles in the middle of my chest, and what little my shirt had dried from earlier, it's soon soaked again. And I just lie there, holding her, rubbing her back, and, yes, more hair kisses. She doesn't object to any of it. And when she's finally calm again and I loosen my grip on her so I can go, she pulls me tighter.

"Don't go. Please. I'm so tired of being alone."

There's not much of anything... OK, probably not anything at all... that I wouldn't do for this woman. And if all she's asking of me right now is to lie here with her and hold her, that's what I'm going to do.

Lyric

I wake up and instantly realize that something is very wrong.

Because while I'm in my bed, in the middle, where I sleep now, the arms holding me aren't my husband's. They're more muscular, longer. Every part of him is just a little bigger.

Frank snickers.

No. Not like that. Get your ghostly mind out of the gutter!

My brain finally catches up when I see the strands of curly/wavy red hair on the pillow next to me.

Rhys Madigan.

Oh, my gods. I'm in bed with Rhys Madigan.

It all comes flooding back to me. That horrible, horrible meeting with the board. Their mandate that I scrap my whole lesson plan for the fall. The threat to cancel the fundraiser. The additional costs of licensing a whole additional set of music for the winter concert. Driving home in the middle of a storm that I know I made ever so much worse when I lost control of my temper. And then collapsing on Rhys — not once, but twice. Begging him to stay.

It's demoralizing. And humiliating. And not at all like the strong single parent I pride myself on being.

You can't take care of the kids if you can't take care of yourself.

Thanks for the reminder, Vivienne.

I sigh, close my eyes, listen to Rhys breathing quietly, evenly. He doesn't snore. This is a good thing. I had so many times when Adam woke me up with his snoring. I begged him to get checked for sleep apnea. He blew it off. It was just snoring. Everybody snores, he said. I don't think either of us thought it would kill him.

A profound sense of loss. Mine, but also not mine. And a feeling of being watched.

I open my eyes, expecting to find Rhys awake and watching me.

Instead, I see a pair of summer-blue eyes staring at me from a couple feet off the floor, in the bedroom doorway.

Oh, gods.... Tommy.

He wakes up in the night sometimes. I can usually get him back to bed without an argument. Sometimes I have to bring him into bed with me, then move him back upstairs.

But he didn't wake me up this time. He came into my bedroom — his parents' bedroom — and found me asleep in another man's arms.

I've got no idea what to think. No idea what he's thinking.

But I slide quietly, gently, out of Rhys' arms, butt-first — Oh, gods above and below! — my *red satin-clad* butt-first, then one foot out and onto the floor, then the other... There. I managed it without waking up Rhys.

I walk over to Tommy, who's still watching Rhys sleep, and I offer him my hand. He looks at it like he's surprised it's there. But he takes it, stands up, and follows me back up the stairs to his bedroom, where I tuck him back in, contraption in hand, before sitting down next to him.

"Tommy — I'm sure its strange to see someone sleeping in Mommy's bed who isn't Daddy. But it's OK. Mr. Rhys was just giving Mommy hugs last night, and we fell asleep. That's all. No big deal. Right? And you like Mr. Rhys, right?"

I don't get any reaction to my babbling until I ask Tommy if he likes Rhys. Then he stops playing with his toy, reaches over and grabs my hand. And he pats it.

Is this sympathy? Reassurance?

Whatever it is, it's new. Hmm...

Pat, pat, pat. Pat, pat, pat. Pat, pat, pat.

It's a rhythm.

Oh, gods...

I close my eyes, trying not to react.

"Get some more sleep, Tommy. Mommy loves you," I tell him, kissing him on the forehead and retreating back downstairs.

I freeze in the bedroom door, watching Rhys stretched out on my bed. Above the covers. Nothing inappropriate — see!

But then I feel bad. He stayed to comfort me, and I left him sleeping in his jeans, with no blanket.

Alright, Lyric. Time to put on your big-girl panties — which are apparently red satin — and deal with an adult situation in an adult way.

"Rhys?"

I nudge him lightly.

"Hmm?" he mumbles sleepily.

"It's time to get in bed."

"I'm already in bed, Mom," he mumbles again.

I turn my head away so he doesn't hear me laugh.

"You need to take off your jeans and get under the covers, Rhys."

"Sure... Give me five minutes. I need some more sleep."

"Now, Rhys."

"Alright..."

He gets his jeans undone, his eyes still closed, and I give the pants a pull at the ankles, sliding them off and laying them over the chair.

And then I nearly fall over laughing.

"Llama boxers? *Neon* llama boxers? Neon llamas *with sunglasses* boxers?" I say it quietly, to myself, but there's no way I can keep silent in the face of this.

I'm starting to get the impression that Rhys has a vast collection of comically ridiculous boxers. And part of me can't wait to see what tomorrow's pair looks like.

Down girl!

It's just curiosity, Frank. I'm allowed to wonder.

But a huge yawn hits me, and I realize I need to get Rhys sorted and go back to bed myself.

I give the comforter a smooth, strong pull, and it gradually slides out from under gods-only-know-how-many pounds of sleeping drummer. I lay it back over him, then cross to the other side of the bed, sliding back under the covers on my side.

Dilemma.

Do I sleep on this side of the bed? Or do I snuggle back into Rhys' arms?

Girlfriend, if you have to ask that, you deserve to be single.

Shut up, Frank.

But he's right. Having a comforter between us isn't going to keep anything from happening, except keep one of us from sleeping comfortably. Fine.

I sidle back toward the middle of the bed, managing to get my head back onto one side of the pile of pillows. It's not exactly a comfortable position. Hmm... What to—

Rhys reaches out and pulls me close against him again, settling down again the moment my head rests on his chest.

"You smell good, dream-girl. Almost real..." he mumbles, then falls right back asleep.

Cradled in his arms, listening again to that steady breathing, I'm conscious just long enough to wonder who this dream-girl of his is, and if she isn't real, what is she?

CHAPTER 26

DRUM TRIP

Lyric

I wake up to...

Drumming?

Confusion. Pain. Loss. Speculation. Anger. Desperation.

Wow. That's a lot to feel in just a few seconds.

I throw the comforter off and stomp into the living room.

Rhys is sitting on the sofa, next to Tommy, a small hand drum between the two of them.

I recognize the drum. I know exactly where I last saw it. And I know Tommy didn't find it by himself, since I couldn't have reached it myself without a step-stool. Up that high on a shelf full of miscellaneous simple instruments I rarely teach, I'd forgotten it was even there. Otherwise, it wouldn't have been in that room. It would have been...

"What in the Hel do you think you're doing?" I shout over the din of the drum.

Rhys stops drumming instantly, while Tommy continues patting the drum.

I stalk over to the sofa and snatch up the drum.

Blessed silence.

"I'm... I'm sorry we woke you up," Rhys stammers. "I got into the groove, and I forgot what time it was. Things got louder."

I look at the clock on the wall. It's 9 a.m.

Normally, I'd have been up two hours ago. But Rhys let me sleep in again, taking care of the kids again.

The remnants of breakfast are still on the kitchen table, so they've been fed. Aria is sitting on the floor, headphones on, apparently listening to music while she draws on a large sketchpad. She glances up at me, frowns slightly, and goes back to her drawing.

Tommy... Tommy's reaching for the drum. When I lift it up higher, out of his reach, he whines. When I still don't give it back, he makes a growling sound that quickly turns into a full-scale wail.

"Thanks a lot," I tell Rhys. "Just perfect." I hope he picks up on the sarcasm.

I offer Tommy my arms. He stands up, sobbing, and grabs hold. I juggle the drum so I can carry them both and then head up the stairs. Putting Tommy down on his bed, I step back through the doorway, the drum behind my back, and I drop it to the floor, grateful we never took up the carpet in the hallway.

Tommy's still crying, but he's sitting down on the mattress and he's picked up a set of gears. Two fingers on one hand in his mouth, he plays with the gears with the other. Spin. Spin, spin. Spin.

"I'm sorry, buddy. I know it doesn't make sense to you. I'm not sure it really makes sense to me. He's gone. The instruments still exist. But I... Mommy just can't deal with it yet. OK?"

I'm not sure if he's listening to me or not. I'm not sure it matters. If I could change things, I would. I think. It's all a jumble right now, and I'm not even fully awake.

I brush Tommy's hair out of his eyes, giving him a kiss on the forehead.

"Mommy loves you."

He doesn't respond.

I take a step back and sigh.

"And Daddy did, too," I whisper, too low for him to hear.

Tears in my eyes, I step back out into the hallway and snatch up the drum. Approaching the door next to the bathroom, I reach up above the frame and grasp the key hidden there. I take a deep breath and unlock the door, for the first time in... a long time. And I step inside the room, closing the door behind me.

It still smells like him in here. Not as strongly. But it does. His scent is long gone from our pillowcases, our closet. Linens washed dozens of times since then, clothes donated to charity. All that's left is in here. The things I couldn't touch, let alone get rid of. This little hand drum should have been in here, but he'd loaned it to me to enhance some of my lessons, and it never made it back up. It landed on a high shelf, instead, where it sat, unnoticed by me, by anyone. Until today. And now it's back where it belongs.

That should be satisfying, but it's not. Standing in here, I feel empty, bereft.

It's all going to be fine.

That should be reassuring, as it's meant to be. But Rhys said that yesterday before that horrible meeting and look what happened.

I sigh, looking back at the room. And then I open the door just wide enough to fit myself back through — just in case one of the kids is out in the hallway. I shut it firmly, lock it and put the key away.

"You OK?"

I jump.

"Sorry," Rhys says from behind me. "I didn't mean to startle you, either. I was just worried."

"I'm fine."

That's a transparent lie.

"No, you're not."

"No kidding!" I yell at him, tears streaming down my face.

He opens his arms, and for half a second I'm torn. Then I cross the short distance between us and lean my head against his chest, my arms hanging down at my sides. He still wraps his arms around me, setting his chin on top of my hair. Gradually, my breathing slows, matching his regular, even breaths.

"Better now?" he asks after a few minutes.

Am I? I don't know.

"A little. I'm sorry I yelled."

"Want to tell me what that was about?"

"Not really."

"OK."

Well, that's surprising.

"OK?"

"Yeah," he says. "You'll tell me when you're ready. I can wait."

"You — Rhys 'The Madman' Madigan, who ran through the zoo to see prairie dogs — can wait." That doesn't sound right somehow.

He shrugs.

"I'm working on it." He gives me a sheepish smile. It gives me the perspective I think I needed.

"Thanks for staying with me last night," I tell him, speaking into his chest. "I think I was overdue for a meltdown. I'm glad you were here."

"Anytime," he says, kissing the top of my head.

And I panic. I know he did that last night when I was clinging to him like he was my life-raft, but now, in the light of day, it feels like more than friendly affection and support.

I step back out of his arms, glancing down the hall to make sure Tommy's still OK, still playing with his gears, still sucking on his fingers. Transitioning away from a pacifier was never an issue with Tommy when he was a baby, probably because he picked up this habit instead. It's almost impossible to break, but he doesn't do it often anymore. Mostly when he's stressed.

"Sorry, buddy," I say too quietly for him to hear. Rhys squeezes my shoulder.

"I — *we* — need to get ready," I tell him. "We've got a rehearsal today, and we need to get the stage setup done before the performers arrive. And we've got to drop the kids off with my mom on the way."

"Right," Rhys says. "Uh — have you seen my pants?" He looks confused. Then, somehow, even more confused. "Wait. Did my mom come over and undress me last night?"

I burst into laughter, and looking at him now, with those llama boxers, I double over, lost to mirth.

"Is that a yes?"

I manage to get control of myself.

"No. But you're a very heavy sleeper, apparently. I told you to undo your pants so you could get more comfortable, and you thought I was your mom. But you did what I told you."

"I usually do what Mom tells me. Mom's smart. She adopted me, after all."

Hmm. Rhys is adopted? That didn't make it into my fangirl knowledge base... But he just casually *told* me, like it's no big deal for him. So, I'll treat it like it's no big deal.

"That's nice to hear. Anyway — you undid your pants. I just pulled them off. I like the boxers, by the way."

"Do you? I found them in a shop during our last South America tour leg."

I'm tempted to ask him more, but time is ticking and we need to get moving.

"Your jeans are on the chair in my bedroom."

"Great. I've got a change of clothes in my car. I'll go get them."

"You have spare clothes in your car?"

"Yeah. I always keep a set in there. I never know when I might find a path to hike or a rock to climb, and that means I get dirty, sweaty. So, I like to have a change of clothes handy."

Makes sense. And it's an example of Rhys planning ahead. He's not as organizationally challenged as he thinks. But it's also a reminder of how spontaneous he is, hiking and climbing at the drop of a hat. And his South American boxers reinforce that he spends much of his life on the road.

I have no idea what that would be like. My life is planned, regimented. Kids, school, lessons, sleep if I'm lucky, writing when inspiration strikes and time allows. That's why I want — need — that fellowship, so I have real time to write, quality time to spend with the kids more than three months of the year. Freedom from this daily grind that pays the bills and not much more.

I need one more piece to complete the submission for the fellowship. Now I just need to find the time and the inspiration in the next two weeks to write it. And totally rewrite my lesson plan. Like yesterday. And...

"Oh, my gods! What time is it?"

I run back down the stairs.

Half past nine.

"Oh, Hel!"

"I thought witches don't believe in Hell," Rhys says as he reaches the bottom of the steps.

I'm scrambling to get my bag, take out my laptop and set it on the kitchen table...

"Come on! Boot!"

Rhys is still standing there, waiting for an answer.

"Witchcraft is a way of life, Rhys, not inherently a religion. Every witch has their own religious beliefs. Some of them are Pagan — worshiping gods and goddesses from any number of cultures, all of which vary in their tenets. Some of them follow other faiths, or none at all. There are even some witches who identify as Christian. So, I imagine *they* believe in Hell."

"Finally!" The computer desktop starts loading. "But I'm Pagan, an eclectic witch utilizing a variety of traditions in a way that works for me. I'm a priestess of the goddess Brighid, just like Brighid is. And that means I don't believe in the Christian devil or Hell or anything like that. The roots of my faith predate Christianity. They have nothing to do with each other, except the old faiths ended up demonized, associated with evil, when the newer faith became dominant. And a lot of what they couldn't stamp out or drive underground, they assimilated."

He looks confused.

"Remind me to tell you about the Easter Bunny sometime," I say. "But, to answer your question — when I say 'Hel,' I'm referring to the Norse goddess of the dead. Not entirely appropriate, but it's a relatively common swear substitution for those of us who are Pagans living in a Christian world. It slides under the radar without being untrue to who we are."

I start clicking around in the folders on the computer, finding the document that contains the final program for the fundraiser. I attach it to an email and send it off to the school district's main office, care of the board secretary, and CC'd to that lovely Mr. Galworth. What an utterly perfect name for him!

Ugh.

I collapse in one of the kitchen table chairs.

"You said you 'slide under the radar' in a 'Christian world.' And Aria said something about not talking to teachers or classmates about your religion."

I look over at her, now next to the TV but still with her headphones on and still drawing, like this morning's drama never happened.

"She talked to you about that?"

"She was telling me about her boyfriend, Noah."

"Oh, gods... That."

I laugh.

"It's amazing how the tiniest little perfectly normal life situation puts me, and my family, at risk. Most kids learn about Noah at home or church. I — second-gen Pagan that I am, and mostly homeschooled — learned about him in my comparative religions class in college. I wanted to explore other people's beliefs, round out my understanding. That's why I tell the kids a lot of stories from the mythology of other cultures. But the Christian stuff — it's not my comfort zone, and I've mostly left it to deal with when Aria has questions, which she does, since she's *not* homeschooled. She's learned to ask me, not her fiends or teachers. And it mostly works. But every day, we run the risk of someone finding out about my beliefs."

He looks thoughtful.

"I thought we had freedom of religion in this country."

I sigh.

"Nominally. Article VI of the Constitution states that there can be no religious requirement for serving in government office. But try getting an atheist, or a Pagan, elected to office in nearly any part of the county. It's rare that candidates don't tout their churchgoing as a reason to elect them. Many government bodies open their sessions with a Christian prayer — and they can do that, they argue, because it's optional to participate. But if you don't, all someone has to do is look around the room to take note of who doesn't. And they judge! Not only do they judge, but there have been witches who've lost custody of their kids due to their beliefs, who've lost their jobs, had crossed burned in front of their houses..."

"I though that was a racist thing."

"They often go hand-in-hand."

I sigh.

"I'm sorry — you didn't ask for a lecture on minority faiths. It's just... I live this every day. It's an extra complication to my life that I don't need or deserve. I don't bother anyone. I don't proselytize. I don't know any Pagans who *do*. I don't teach my religious beliefs to any kids except my own. I am *deeply* religious — more so than most Americans — but the details of that often lead others to conclude that I'm crazy or dangerous or immoral, just because it's not what they're familiar with. And just being myself can cause me tremendous problems if I'm not careful."

Rhys sighs.

"You told *me* just to be myself."

"I did. And I meant it. But *I* can't fully do that outside a very small circle of people I trust."

"But you're talking to me about it. Aria did, too."

"I should have a conversation with her about that... But... Rhys — I trust you. I wouldn't have let you stay with the kids if I didn't. I wouldn't have let myself... I wouldn't have let myself be vulnerable with you like I was last night. And I'm still not fully comfortable with that. But it happened, and you were there for me. And that tells me you are a true friend. It tells me I can trust you."

"Thanks," he says.

"Now — go put on some pants. We've got a rehearsal to run."

CHAPTER 27

LITTLE BLACK RAIN CLOUD

Rhys

"OK — now that the drum kit is done and in place, the piano needs to get moved... Over here, where this X is." She taps a tape mark on the stage with her toe.

"Got it."

I shift the piano across the stage, angling it toward the audience without being asked.

"Perfect. Thanks."

She checks another task off on her to-do list. A look of satisfaction on her face. She stands up a little taller. I start to get why she's so organized. It's practical. It's efficient. It keeps you from missing things, creating problems for yourself, flibberti-gibbeting up. The kind of stuff I still do way too often, even though I have Billy and the guys, and our road crew, helping me. But it's more than that — it's accomplishment made concrete. And each of those check marks is also one less thing hanging over her head. One less thing weighing her down, dragging her underwater, making her feel like she's drowning. She said she's half a mermaid, but that other half can still drown, if she's not careful. And that's just one more level of stress in her life — having to be careful.

Rory, Mom — they both told me *I* need to be *more* careful. That's because I rarely have anything to worry about. Lyric's the opposite. *She* needs to be... what's the opposite of careful?

Carefree.

Yeah. That.

And now that I know that's what she needs, I'm going to make it my job to give that to her.

W ow. I have to hand it to her — she's an amazing teacher. Seeing her former and current students come back and perform like they're doing just at this rehearsal, it's astonishing.

And half the reason it's so amazing is that each of them so clearly loves music — and loves her for the love of music she's instilled in them. Whether they're second-graders singing in a chorus or the young singer-songwriter who hasn't been in Lyric's class for years (and who I've already texted Billy about) — they light up when they perform. Like Kier, Hunt, Dave, Declan and Alex. Like I expect I do. Some of them may dream of stardom, but she's given them a love of music that will last them a lifetime, no matter what they end up doing for a living.

She's glorious.

Yeah. She really is.

The even better thing after last night's upset and this morning's drama is that her mood has visibly shifted. She's still driven — more focused now, less urgent — but she's full of that same wonderful energy as her performers. She said she's performing one piece at the fundraiser, but she's not doing it for rehearsal. I'm disappointed, but I'm trying to be patient, right?

So, they skip over her spot in the program and move on to the finale. Once more, she takes center stage, conducting the combined group of musicians and vocalists. Is it perfect? No. But these are kids. And from my spot at the back of the cafetorium — cafetorium! — they sound pretty good, even to my pro musician ears. In a decade or two, we'll have to start looking for them trying to steal our spot on the charts.

She does her conductor move to signal them to wind down the song and stop. I lift my hands to start clapping, as I've done after each part of the program. But someone else is already clapping. Slow clapping. Like the kind of slow clapping where you ask yourself if it's genuine praise or hostile sarcasm. I can't tell.

"Very nice, Mrs. Larson! Very nice," the middle-aged guy says. Squinty eyes, hair too carefully combed, a suit that looks like he's put on about twenty pounds since he bought it.

"Mr. Galworth! What a surprise! I wasn't expecting you," Lyric says from the stage.

"Thanks, everyone — you were great!" she tells the group on stage. "We'll see you back here on Thursday for one last rehearsal. Don't be late!"

She closes up her book on her music stand, smooths down her dress self-consciously, and then makes her way to Galworth.

"I'm flattered that you decided to come see a rehearsal in person, Mr. Galworth," she says.

"Yes, well... I received a copy of the program mid-morning—" I don't miss her cringe. I don't think he does, either "—and I had one concern I wanted to address."

"Alright."

"This second-to-last performance... 'Sleeping Beauty.'"

"Yes?"

"You're listed as the performer for that."

"Yes. I usually do one piece as part of the fundraiser. It's become a tradition. Is there a problem?"

"You assured the board there was no Disney material on the program for the fundraiser. 'Sleeping Beauty' is a Disney movie."

I can see Lyric thinking really hard. Trying to think of something to say, the best thing to say...

"Mr. Galworth," she says patiently, "the Disney movie from 1959 was based on a traditional fairytale from the 1500s. The music in the movie is derived from Tchaikovsky's Opus 66, completed in 1889 as the second of his three ballets. 'The Sleeping Beauty Waltz,' as I will be performing it on Friday, is directly drawn from Opus 66, which as I noted, was completed in 1889 — more than a decade before Walt Disney was even born."

Now it's Galworth trying to think what to say.

"It's a fine line you're walking there, Mrs. Larson," he says, finally. "I'll verify that information, confer with the board. I'll let you know tomorrow if we're comfortable with that song being performed."

Lyric is quiet. But her eyes are blazing, like little lightning bolts are crackling across those stormy-sky irises.

Do something!
So I do.
"Mr. Galworthy is it?"
"Galworth."
"Nice to meet you," I tell him. Wow. This lying thing isn't very hard. No wonder people do it so often. I offer him my hand.
"Is this your husband, Mrs. Larson?"
Lyric blinks. I'm kind of glad, because I don't know if anyone but me sees that fire in her eyes.
"I'm Rhys Madigan. I'm a donor to the event." He finally takes my hand. "And I'm helping out Mrs. Larson with the last-minute details, since she's handling the event alone this year."
"Yes, well. I'm sorry we couldn't provide more support — music is less in demand in the larger curricula than it once was. We've all had to adjust."
"That's a shame — the lack of appreciation of music's importance in the larger education of our children, I mean. All the studies show its value across subjects. I myself was a music major in college, and it's been a very valuable experience and a fulfilling career for me."
Wow. Lots of big words. I think I'm channeling Mom now and not that voice in my head.
"I'm sorry — what did you say your name was?"
"Rhys Madigan. I'm part of a musical group in town recording our next album. Hopefully, our fourth platinum album. It would be the fourth, right, Mrs. Larson? I lose track."
"I believe so, yes. You've reached No. 1 with every full album you've released," she supplies. There's my fangirl!
"That sounds very... successful," he replies. "And you've taken an interest in our little fundraiser here?"
"Oh, very much so. Mrs. Larson is a real inspiration, both to us and to her students. I've already referred our management to one of Friday's performers."
"You did?" she asks.
I nod, giving her a smile.
"Mrs. Larson is a real treasure. I hope you know what a lucky man you are to have her teaching your children." He looks up at me. A little higher. A little more. Way up here. Yeah.
"Yes... Of course," he says, looking a little uncomfortable. Maybe he's got a sore neck.

"I'm hoping we can fully fund the new instruments for the school with Friday's event," I tell him. "I imagine that would be a little easier if Mrs. Larson wasn't having to also re-do the licensing for the winter concert at this late date."

His jaw sets. His eyes narrow. He glances at Lyric.

"Yes, well... Seeing as the change comes so close to the start of the school year, I suppose I could argue that we should cover the additional licensing. I'll discuss it with the board and have someone get back to you tomorrow, Mrs. Larson."

"That would be very helpful, Mr. Galworth," she says. There. That's almost a smile.

"Goodnight to you both," he says with a sharp nod.

There's a moment of silence.

"Tiger, not Tigger," Lyric murmurs. I don't even get a chance to ask what she means.

"Mrs. Larson! Mrs. Larson!" a little girl shouts, running right at Lyric. "Mom wants to talk about our costumes for Friday!"

"I'll be right there, Kelly!" Lyric says.

"How was that?" I ask her, grabbing her up in a bear hug and dancing her around in my arms, grinning madly.

"That was amazing, Rhys! I wasn't even sure I was going to get past the song issue, and now at least I might get the licensing money back!"

I let her slide slowly back down to the floor, savoring the feeling of her body against mine.

She looks up at me, wonder in her eyes instead of lightning bolts. But this isn't the look of wonder fans usually give me, even if she is my fangirl. It's something more.

"Mrs. Larson — Mom says we have to go pick up my sister from camp!" Kelly runs back to say.

Lyric smiles down at her and lets her pull her to where her mother waits by the stage.

There's a squeak of shoes in the hallway behind me, and I turn around.

Mr. Galworth is there, but he's not alone. And when I recognize the person he's talking to, my blood runs cold. It's Donnie. Their attention shifts back in our direction, and that's when I know this isn't over.

Lyric

"I can't believe it's all done. All we have left is the last rehearsal on Thursday and then the event on Friday!"

"That has to be a huge relief, to nearly have it all behind you," Rhys says as he sits behind the wheel of his KITT car, ready to drive me back home.

"It is. I mean, I love doing it, or I wouldn't do it. But all the stress of making sure it'll be successful — I won't miss that at all."

"And it's going to be a huge success. All your hard work is going to pay off!"

"And now I just need to completely redo my lesson plan for the school year, which starts in two weeks." Oh, boy. Months' worth of work to do in just a few days, if I'm going to get it all handled and turned in again. "Good thing I have the day free tomorrow."

"If you have the day free, come over to the studio," Rhys says. "Bring the kids. Have a beach day. We'll have a cookout on the deck. Relax."

He's got to be joking.

"Didn't you just hear me say I have a bunch of work to do, and I'm using tomorrow to do it?"

"Then it will make it easier if you've got somebody entertaining the kids, right? And who better to help you with any music licensing issues and creative ideas than a pro musician signed to a well-connected label?"

"You think you could expedite things?" It would be a huge help if he could.

"I'll call Billy tonight. By tomorrow one of his assistants will be ready to get the ball rolling for you. You'll just have to get them a list of songs."

"Must be nice, to have managers and assistants taking care of the minutia for you." I say it with a chuckle, but it's both true and a source of frustration for me. I couldn't even get the district to find me another teacher to help with the fundraiser planning over the summer. No one else had time to do more than volunteer here and there, with their summer vacations, kids' summer camps and their own summer jobs planned months prior.

"It is! I guess that's why I never really learned to do that to-do list thing. My to-do stuff usually gets done for me. As long as I show up on time for rehearsals, publicity events and gigs — though I managed to mess that up once, because there was a fair and they had a climbing wall, and they had to use my phone to track me down..." He catches himself digressing. "Sorry. I just mean that other than showing up, there's not much else I have to worry about."

"Must be nice..."

That time, my tone is clear enough that even Rhys gets it.

"Hey," he says, grabbing my hand. "You've got lots of people who want to help you, so you don't have to worry so much — Rory, Callie, Brighid, your mom..." He squeezes my hand. "Me." Those gorgeous brown eyes of his, so warm, honest. "And I know there's more than that — that little girl..."

"Kelly," I supply.

"Yeah — Kelly. Her mom told me she'd offered to help you with the program since she does graphics for her job, and you refused."

"I had it handled."

"That's what she said you said. But you didn't have to." He gives my hand a shake, making sure he has my attention. "I know you've gotten used to handling everything in your life on your own. But you don't have to be on top of everything 24/7. You do have people who want to make your burden lighter. You've got to stop making it so hard for them."

"I'm not *trying* to make it hard for them. I just..."

But he's right. When Adam died, I'd picked up all of the things that had previously fallen on his shoulders, from some of the parenting to making sure the bills got paid, taking care of the house... I did it because it needed to be done, and it was my responsibility. And when we'd moved in with Rory, she'd been so busy with work and other things that I didn't get used to having someone else helping out again, beyond a little help around the house. And then we moved back out, and things were awkward for both of us, and she was still swamped. Callie's been busy with her restaurant since she moved back to Mystic Beach, and Brighid...

And I'm making excuses for why they can't help me. Even when they've offered.

Just like I did with Kelly's mom.

I look back and realize how many of the parents, how many of the other teachers, offered to help with the fundraiser — and how many times I turned people down, said I had it handled. And I did. But by the skin of my teeth.

"Lyric — I want you to ask yourself one thing, and really think about it, OK?"

I nod.

"Why is the time other people offer to you so much more valuable than your own? Why do you reject what they freely give, just so you can use your own time — your time that you could be spending with the kids, having fun, relaxing, writing, doing your witchy stuff..." I glance around us to make sure no one overheard that through the open car windows. No one's around, thankfully. Just us and one other car left in the parking lot. "Why do you sacrifice your time just so you can keep all of that responsibility to yourself?"

"Because when I'm the one responsible for doing it, I know it will get done! There's no one to drop the ball or make a mistake or... or delay something important until it's too late..."

"Like your husband did when he died?"

Whoa. My blood runs cold. I try jerk my hand back, but he keeps hold of it.

"How do you know about that?" I demand.

"I mean — I assume he didn't have any life insurance, or you wouldn't be giving private lessons to make ends meet, like you said..." His expression is weird, like he's guessing at something he seemed to know for sure a moment ago. It's all suspicious, and that makes me suspicious. Even with all of Brighid's and Callie's relationship drama, have I forgotten that I'm dealing with a rockstar?

"You haven't had someone checking up on me, have you?" I narrow my eyes at him. "Is that one of the things your manager does for you? Check out the women you sleep with?"

"Hey," he says quietly, holding my hand more firmly now. "I'm not sleeping with anyone these days. Including you. Unless the other night counts, which I don't think you think it does. Friends, right?"

Yeah, right. On both counts. If it had been more, I'd never have crawled back into bed with him, never have worried about pants or boxers or having his arms around me. Right?

"Right?" he asks again.

"Right. Friends."

"So, no need for my manager to check you out, right?"

"Right."

"My point — and I'm giving myself credit for even remembering I had one, so, go me! — my point is that I think you need to ask yourself why it is that you expect people to leave you hanging if you rely on them? Why is it that you expect them to fail you if you trust them to have your back? You know, Brighid and Hunter are doing this therapy thing, and maybe that's something that might help you, too."

I tried a grief-support group, right after we moved in with Rory and she could watch the kids for an hour or two a week. But it was at a church, and led by a minister, and most of the people there were churchgoers. There was lots of praying. Which is fine. I pray a lot myself. It's just... different. That's another major drawback of being part of such a small religious minority — our community, when we have one at all, is very small. Services like that often aren't available within it. That's the main reason Brighid got certified in pastoral counseling.

I never went back to the grief-support group. Instead, I spent that time in meditation or, sometimes, in talking to Brighid. Just like I think Amber should be doing. But even Brighid finds value in therapy. Maybe I should consider it. Whenever I find the time...

"Just think about it, OK?" Rhys asks. "And do us all a favor and don't make it so hard to try to help you, OK? Your time — your life — is as valuable to us as ours are to you."

I start to tear up, and Rhys reaches over and strokes his thumb across my cheek.

And then he kisses my forehead. I savor the sensation, even though it's still just a friendly gesture. Forehead kisses were something Adam did, too. And I've missed them.

But this is Rhys. And... Just friends, right?

Oh, who am I kidding? He doesn't want to just be friends. And neither do I.

I reach into his hair and pull his lips down to mine. He freezes for a second, then kisses me with an enthusiasm that tops even the other night. In my head, I see the bouncy Tigger transforming with the contained power of the tiger. And that tiger opens its mouth to consume me. But it's mutual, us tasting each other. I capture his upper lip between mine and lick at the seam of his lips. Our tongues thrust against each other, and the sensuality of it sets the rest of my body on fire. Pulse racing, breath rasping, I give into it.

Until there's a sudden noise of the heavy school doors closing and being locked.

I push Rhys away, settling back into the passenger seat, trying to look like nothing unusual was happening here. Certainly no major making out with my... friend. Right.

Rhys looks confused, but he follows my eyes, frowning when he sees Donnie headed toward the pickup truck that's the only other vehicle in the parking lot.

"This your car?" Donnie calls out as he gets closer to us.

"Yup," Rhys says.

"Pretty cool," Donnie comments. "Hey — what'd you say you do for a living?"

"I'm a musician."

"Ah, the musician and the music teacher. Makes sense." He nods. "Goodnight, folks."

And he walks over to his truck, gets in and drives away.

"That was a close one!" I tell Rhys.

"Yeah," he says. But he doesn't sound quite as relieved as I do at Donnie's nonchalant handling of what he saw the other night — and what he nearly saw more of just now. "Let's get you home."

CHAPTER 28

BACKYARD BEACH

Rhys

Y ou almost sank me there, Rhys-head-talking dude.

'He waited too long, and he died. He let her down.'
She was confused when I said it — *repeated* what I heard in my head — and I scrambled to guess at what her husband might have put off that left Lyric feeling like she had to take the world on her shoulders single-handed.

The insurance thing was a guess. I'm sure if he had any, she'd be a lot less stressed out right now.

Sadly true. But there's more.

People leave a lot of things undone when they die young and unexpectedly. I'm sure there were things left unsaid, undone. Failing to provide for his family would be right up there.

That's one of those things Billy handled for me. I've got life insurance that will take care of Mom for the rest of her life, in comfort, if I misjudge a hand-hold on a free climb. Even if she wants to go live in Fiji. My song rights revert to the band as a whole, so there's no fighting over controlling interest or who gets to perform as aMUSEd when the guys are in their 70s. I hate when bands do that. A chunk of my royalties go, in perpetuity, to a charity for foster kids that Mom supports. I try not to think beyond that. My bases are covered.

I guess his weren't.

Not even close. Idiot couldn't even make a fucking doctor's appointment.

Hey — watch the language there, Rhys-head-dude! It's *flib-bertigibbets!* And we don't call people idiots. Except Hunt. But he's being less of an idiot now than he was before he asked Brighid to marry him. I wonder if Hunt's got a will, life insurance...

Maybe I should ask Billy to set up a trust for Lyric's kids, something that'll take care of them later in life, regardless of what happens with me and Lyric. She talked about Aria having to care for Tommy when she's gone. Maybe I can make that easier for them.

That's incredibly generous. Thoughtful.

Thanks. I thought so. People don't call me "thoughtful" very often. I mean, I've got way more thoughts in my head than tend to make sense together, and that was before you, head-dude, started talking to me, which is like a whole other set of thoughts on top of the others. So, I'm super-full of thoughts these days. But "thoughtful" — as in I thought ahead to do something nice for someone? It's new. It's nice.

Sorry about calling you on the cursing, head-dude. But Mom said...

Mom!

I need to talk to Mom.

And Billy.

And I need to plan ahead for tomorrow, since Lyric is bringing the kids over for a nice family day at the beach.

Grrr...

Did you just growl at me, head-dude? Lyric said something about a tiger, but I don't remember hearing anyone growl until just now.

You kissed her.

She kissed me first! And you were the one who told me to do it!

It sounded like a better idea when I didn't have to watch it.

You gotta make up your mind, head-dude. But it's too late now, anyway. She threw herself into it this time, even after saying we'd just be friends to start. That kiss was definitely a green light.

I kind of miss having Kier as my wingman. He'd have given me a high-five for winning a girl over. Head-dude is... confusing. And confused. Does he want me to win Lyric over or not?

I'm not sure anymore.

That does *not* make you a good wingman, head-dude.

You'd think if I was going to be conjuring up — Hey! I like that! My girlfriend's a witch, and I'm conjuring shit up! — a split personality or a voice that talks to me, it'd be someone who makes a good wingman. And it seemed like he was, at first. Now...

He's conspicuously silent.

And I've got stuff to do. Maybe I should make a list. Yeah. I'll make a list.

"I 'll have Michelle call you at eleven so she can get the details, OK?" Billy says. I mark it down on my calendar, now that Alex showed me how to do that. "I swear, Rhys, when I signed on to become the band's manager, I did not foresee I'd be handling licensing rights for elementary school music department fundraisers! Getting the paperwork done to set up a trust is even outside of what most managers would be doing. And do I want to know why you're doing that? Something you need to tell me? Do we have a secret baby-mama coming out of the woodwork? You've got to tell me that kind of thing, Rhys. Otherwise, the gossip sites pick it up and I get blindsided with questions, like them asking about Declan — though that was totally his fault, since he flashed their wedding rings across the entire internet after I specifically said to keep it quiet!"

There's silence on the other end of the phone. No — near-silence. Billy's breathing heavy.

"You OK there, Billy? You're breathing awfully fast. You know — I could work up an exercise routine for you. I could even include a little time on the climbing wall..."

"Not necessary, Rhys. But no secret baby-mamas, OK?"

"Got it. No secret baby-mamas."

"Thank god. You all are going to send me to the E.R. at the rate you're coupling-up."

Oops. Probably best if I don't tell him about Lyric then, even if she's not my secret baby-mama. Give him some time to recover from Declan's marriage going viral. The second one. I haven't told anyone about the first one. Except Mom. And that doesn't count, because she's pretending Declan was never 17.

And speaking of Mom...

"What's so important about today that you needed me here, Rhys? It's not like you not to tell me what's going on..." she says as she joins me out on the deck at the studio.

"Hi, Mom!" I grab her up in another big hug, lifting her off her feet and then setting her back down as she smiles at me. That's better.

"I'd ask what has you feeling so enthusiastic, but we both know that it doesn't take much. This does seem extra-enthusiastic, though..." she looks at me carefully, scrutinizing. "Does this have to do with Lyric?" she asks.

"Did you bring the stuff I asked you to?"

"Yes. I packed for a day at the beach. I've got my swimsuit on under my cover-up, my beach shoes, sunscreen, a hat, a bottle of water. I assume you've got chairs and an umbrella?"

"Oh! I didn't think about that. Where can I get those?"

"There's a shop in town — the cutest little five-and-dime store, which I didn't think they even had anymore — but they also have a rental service right out on the beach. They put them out for you and pick them back up."

"Perfect! What's that called?"

"The rental place?"

"Yeah."

"I'm not sure. I could probably call the hotel and see if they have the number."

"Can you do that, please? I already called Callie about food, and she got the deli and bakery to send over food for everyone. She was kind of weird about me asking to make sure they had macaroni-and-cheese and chicken nuggets included, but she said they'd make it happen. And Declan showed me how to use the grill, though he seemed a little offended that I wasn't asking him to cook on it." I shrug. "So you can call about the chairs and umbrella?"

"Sure. But you still haven't told me what's going on!" She frowns slightly at me.

"Lyric's coming over for a beach day! And she's bringing the kids!"

"Oh." Mom frowns again. "Rhys — did you tell Lyric you'd invited your mother to come over today?"

"No. Why?" Mom rolls her eyes.

"Because meeting someone's parents is an important step in a relationship, and are you even in a relationship yet?"

"But I met her mom already."

"Yes, because she was somewhere when you were. Not because she'd invited her over to meet you."

"What's the difference?"

"I'm not sure how to explain it, but it's a big difference. Maybe I should go..."

"No! I want you to stay. I want to have a beach day with you, and with Lyric and the kids, and I've got half of it set up already. So, you can't leave!" I grab her arms and plead with her.

She looks uncertain.

"How are things going with Lyric?" she asks. "Is that why you're so excited today?"

"She kissed me, Mom! I mean — this time, she really kissed me! Even after we said we'd just start off as friends."

Mom looks like she's absorbing that.

"I'm still not sure this is a good idea, Rhys. But if you really want me to stay, I'll stay. I'd like to meet Lyric, and her kids. Just keep in mind that it's very early in your relationship with her, and you need—"

"—to be careful. Yeah. I know. I'm trying."

"And if your effort to show her a nice time today is any example, you're doing a good job. I'm proud of you, Rhys."

"I'm proud of me, too, Mom." I give her another hug.

She's going to make an amazing grandmother.

I know, right? No. Wait. What?

"There's a guy at the door with a fuck-ton of food, Rhys," Alex calls from the sliding glass doors. "You hosting an army today? Kier and I are the only ones here, since the guys all took the day off before we have more studio time tomorrow. I'm not sure we could eat all of this, even with your mom helping you."

"You're not invited!"

"Rhys!" Mom objects, sounding shocked.

Alex just laughs.

"It's fine, Ms. M. That confirms my theory. We'll make ourselves scarce, unless Rhys decides he needs help, or a diversion to head off disaster."

"Nope! I'm good. I've got this all planned out. At least now that Mom's getting us an umbrella. Food delivered — check."

"Did you just mark something off on a to-do list?" Alex asks, sounding astonished.

"I have the same question," Mom says.

"Yes. See!" I show them both my to-do list, with the food checked off as ordered and then delivered. "Lyric showed me how to do it!"

"The woman's a miracle-worker," Alex says, shaking his head.

"It would seem so," Mom says, sounding thoughtful. Just like me.

"I'll get the cold stuff put away for you, Rhys. And there was one box of hot food — I'll stick it in the oven on warm," Alex says.

"Thank you!"

"From sous chef to reheating mac-and-cheese. I need a new hobby," Alex mutters as he shuts the door.

"Alex seems a little... lost, Rhys. Is he doing OK?" Mom asks.

"He's fine Mom. He's always fine."

"If you're sure..."

"Yeah. Of course. Now, I'm going to get this table set. You've got the umbrella and chairs?"

"Yes. I'll call right now."

With a smile on my face and a song in my head, I can hardly wait for Lyric and the kids to get here. This is going to be a perfect day. A new best-day-ever!

Lyric

Getting the kids packed up for a day at the beach is never easy. So much stuff! But Rhys texted to say he had the umbrella and beach chairs handled. So, just me, the kids and our stuff. I packed PB&J for Tommy, even though Rhys said he'd be cooking on the grill. You learn to always have a back-up plan when your kid's as picky as my boy is. Aria will eat anything. Except raisins. Unless they're golden raisins. (Blame Auntie Callie, who confided her own dislike of regular raisins and introduced Aria to the golden variety.) But Tommy has a list of about ten foods he reliably eats. I spend a lot on multivitamins and nutritional drinks. So, it was PB&J for today.

As we pull up at the studio, Rhys leans way over the railing on the back deck and waves enthusiastically. I've picked him up or dropped him off here a few times, but I haven't been inside. Brighid and Hunter are holding their wedding here, on the beach itself, with the reception inside and a party at the Pirate's Cove afterward, so I'll be back in a month or so, since I'm doing the officiating. But it'll be nice to see the place beforehand.

At least, that's what I tell myself. It has nothing to do with spending the day with Rhys.

I can't believe I kissed him. Again!

What is he thinking? What is he thinking *I'm* thinking? Are we officially a thing now? I don't even know. And part of me wants to pull back. But Rhys keeps encouraging me to take care of myself, and I'm trying to do that. First order — a day at the beach, after I hand over my song list to his team for the licensing. Second... I enjoyed kissing him. A lot. I'd kind of like to try it again. Maybe I'll get that chance today.

"Come on up this way!" he calls as I get the kids out of the car. "I've got someone I want you to meet!"

Hmm... Maybe he's forgotten that I've met all the members of the band... Oh! I bet it's their producer, or maybe their manager. I didn't get the chance to meet them at Callie and Declan's wedding reception, since I mostly stayed with the kids.

I grab our beach bag and Tommy's hand, as Aria follows behind, looking a little overwhelmed with the giant house.

"Is this Mr. Rhys' house, Mommy?" she asks.

"No. This is the studio where they're working on their music, Aria. But it has bedrooms for all of the band members to stay while they're doing their work."

"So they get to work and play every day?"

"If they want to, yes. But today is a day for play — for Mr. Rhys and for us."

"Yay!"

"Remember, you two — we're at the beach, and even though the house is a lot closer to the beach than ours is, we still have to be safe and always stay with a grown-up, OK?"

"Yes, Mommy," Aria says, her eyes glued to the dune ahead of us. I can see she's already feeling pulled to the water. I'll have to watch extra-carefully today, because this is a private beach, with no lifeguard on duty. I'm sure the Mystic Beach Patrol would come running if we yelled loudly enough, but I'd rather not have to find out.

I let her lead the way up the stairs to the deck, so I can keep an eye on her. Which means that when I reach the top, I'm astonished to find neither of the older men I've heard about, but a woman — middle-aged, tall, with curly brown hair, and a bright smile below serious eyes. She's dressed in a cover-up, with a swimsuit beneath, and barefoot, though I see a pair of beach shoes nearby.

Is this the assistant Rhys said would be handling the licensing stuff for me? I don't know why, but I pictured a twenty-something girl, and I figured she'd be calling from New York, not here in person.

"Lyric, I'd like you to meet my mom, Sheryl Madigan."

There's a roaring in my ears. If Rhys says anything after that, I miss it. Maybe he introduces the kids. Maybe not.

His mother is here? He's introducing me to his mother? After we've kissed twice?

I have no idea what to think. I mean, I kind of gave him the green light on our relationship last night, but "Meet Mrs. Madigan" wasn't what I figured our next "date" would be.

"Lyric, it's so nice to meet you!" is the first thing I hear as she holds her hand out for me to shake. "Rhys has told me so much about you, and your lovely children."

He has?

I mean, he's told me a little about his mother, but I had no idea she even lived nearby. I figured she was in West Virginia or Virginia, since that was where he went to college. Or did she fly in. She didn't fly in just to meet me, did she?

"Call me Sheryl, please," she says, her smile genuine but a little amused.

Well, he's her kid. I'm sure nothing he does is a total surprise for her, even if it is to me.

"I'm Lyric."

She chuckles, and I realize she already knew that.

"I warned him that springing me on you was probably not a good idea, but he figured since he'd met your mother, it was only fair," she says conspiratorially. So, she knew he was springing this on me, but it sounds like he kind of sprung it on her, too. Good. I mean, as good as that can be. Oh, Rhys...

For his part, Rhys has offered the kids a spot at the dining table on the deck, complete with drinks. Is that iced tea for Tommy? And... A new contraptions set?

"I got myself a couple when I saw him having fun with it the first night we met in person," Rhys says. In person? "So, I had one handy to give him some extra options while he's here."

"That's very thoughtful of you," I tell him.

"I know!" he says, beaming. Odd.

Aria's got an erasable board and some markers at her place.

"I thought we'd have lunch first, if that works for you all. I got a lot of stuff — salads and breads and fruit and cheese..." He gestures to a spread that extends beyond the dining table and onto a second one. "And hold on one second—" He heads back inside the house and returns with... Macaroni-and-cheese and chicken nuggets?

"These are for you, buddy. I made sure they stayed warm until you got here."

"Did you cook lunch for him?"

Rhys looks surprised.

"Well, no. I didn't even think about that, since I ordered all the food. I just asked Callie to make sure they included some with the order."

Ah. This makes a little more sense now. Rhys is used to asking people to do things for him when it comes to details. It's his adaptation for his ADHD. So, he's fully capable of calling Callie to ask her to order the food — and even specify Tommy's favorites — even if he probably didn't pick out the rest. It's efficient. And the people around him love him enough that they're happy to oblige.

It's a contrast for me. Rhys asks for help when he needs it, and people give it willingly, easily. I never ask for help, and when it's given, I refuse it and handle things by myself. No wonder I'm always tired.

But speaking of asking for help...

"Thanks so much for thinking of him. And it's wonderful to meet you too, Sheryl, if unexpected." She grins back at me. Two moms on the same page. It's a start. "Rhys — I know you said you'd get the licensing expedited for me today. Do you mind if we take care of that first? I'll be able to relax more once it's off my plate."

Rhys checks his phone.

"Michelle is calling me in five minutes to do just that, Lyric. So, put down your stuff, take a seat, grab a drink, a snack, and relax... We'll have it all sorted out before we have to put on more sunscreen!"

"Every ten minutes, Rhys!" Sheryl reminds him.

"I know, Mom."

"He ended up with brown eyes, but he burns like a redhead," she says. "When he was in school, I'd remind them to put sunscreen on him whenever they went outside. They didn't always remember. He came home with some painful burns before I made sure every single teacher he had had a bottle of sunscreen with his name on it that stayed right by the classroom door."

"I do the same thing with Tommy," I tell her. "He'd never ask, so they have to make sure."

She looks over at Tommy, her expression thoughtful. I can tell what she's thinking.

"He's autistic. Non-verbal, but we're working on figuring out ways he might communicate. We just haven't had much luck yet — sign language, cards, apps on a tablet — he just hasn't taken to any of them yet."

"Rhys had mentioned he was autistic. I can see the fixation on spinning things — gears and axles — and the lack of eye contact. But he seems like he interacts pretty well. He jumped right up to the table when Rhys invited him."

"Oh, he does. He hears everything said around him — sometimes too much — and unless he's hyperfocused, he usually does what you ask when he's prompted. Sometimes, he still zones out, retreats into 'Tommy World,' but he does it a lot less than he used to. Communication — him telling *us* what *he* wants — is our big challenge these days."

"It is for a lot of kids on the spectrum. It's great that we've got so many new ways to offer them now, but not all of them work for everyone."

"You sound like you know something about that..." She has me wondering...

"Mom's a social worker!" Rhys pipes up, arriving back at the table with Aria and a plate of food.

"Oh! I didn't know that." Of course, I didn't know she'd be here, either.

"She's had lots of experience with special-needs kids. That's how she ended up with me!"

"Oh?"

Sheryl opens her mouth to speak, but just then Rhys' phone rings, and he grabs my hand and pulls me off toward the house.

"I've got her right here, Michelle. I'll put her on. Take care of my girl, OK?" He hands me the phone, beaming at me.

His girl? Maybe I should have given him the yellow light instead of the green one. Hmm...

"Mom and I can handle the kids. She's a social worker, re-member?"

He pushes me inside the sliding glass doors and closes them behind me.

I try not to worry. About any number of things.

Chapter 29

Hidden Heritage

Lyric
Three hours later

Michelle had my requests down in just a few minutes. I emailed her a copy, just to be sure. She said she'd have answers back to me by Friday, and that Rhys had arranged to cover the licensing fees. I objected. She said to take it up with him. He said I could pay him back once the money from the school district was in. For once, I didn't argue, though I suspect getting a purchase order for that is going to be a challenge.

From there... From there, it's been a fun day at the beach with the kids. We had a light lunch, with plenty left for snacking later (and probably dinner, to be honest). And then we went down to the studio's private beach, where the local beach rental company had set up not one, but two umbrellas for us, with chairs for each of us around one and some shaded space on the sand for the kids to play.

The kids had their usual wave-jumping fun, but with two grown-ups holding them up, instead of me trying to wrangle Tommy's timing while holding Aria's hand. Once Tommy was done with that, Rhys and I took Aria out in the water, while Sheryl watched Tommy play in the sand. Rhys is just as much of a fish as Aria and I are. I guess he'd have to be, with all of his adrenaline sports. But it took a load off my mind and made being out in the water a lot of fun.

Adam could swim, but he wasn't ever as much at home in the ocean as I've always been. I guess that's the half-a-mermaid thing, with learning how to swim from Mom, who is as content in the water as she is out. Even I need to take a break sometimes, though, and after a while we came back in and dried off, reapplying sunscreen, and watched the kids build sandcastles, with more than a little help from Rhys.

Sheryl and I chat a little bit while we watch them, and the stiffness created by my surprise at meeting her melts away as we share mom stories, talk about the band's music... When Rhys splashes Aria with the bucket of water he was bringing back up to the umbrella, she screeches and runs off, setting off a chase that's as much fun for the two of us watching as it is for them. Even Tommy's watching.

"I'm glad to see him like this, with you, with the kids," Sheryl says after a minute. "Other than the band, he really doesn't have many close friends."

"What about all his rock-climbing buddies? The skydiving people? His fans? He's got tons of them."

"They're people he hangs out with when he's doing those things. They don't call him to go out on a Friday night, or ask him over for dinner when he's been holed up in his apartment for a week, climbing and drumming. And his fans..." She gives me a look like I should know better. And I do, really. "It's great that he's so popular with their fans. His energy draws people to him like that. But it doesn't make for easy friendships, intimate friendships," she says, "or people who care about him, for him."

Rhys tosses Aria in the air. She screams in delight. I about have a heart attack, but he catches her. I remember this game. It's the bane of most mothers' existences, waiting for that one slip, that one lapse of attention for a fraction of a second. She's too big for this game now. Adam could never have caught her, as fit as he was. Rhys catches her easily, though I suspect Tommy's too heavy even for Rhys to toss around like that. I keep an eye out, just in case he decides to try.

"He's not as childlike as he may seem at times," Rhys' mom says. "Every once in a while, he gets in this serious mood, like maybe something's bothering him. I've never been able to get him to tell me what it is. I thought maybe he was going to tell me the other night, at dinner, but we got interrupted. Honestly, I think he's just had too many times when he was excluded — the weird kid, the one who was too much for everyone else. It's how I ended up with him, actually."

Her tone catches my attention, and I let myself look away from Rhys and Aria for a moment. What she's telling me is important. I can see that in her expression.

"He said something about that before…"

"He got returned from six foster homes in the first three years he was in the system. The foster parents — most of them have two or three fosters at a time, sometimes more if the kids are related, and not all of them are up to keeping a constant eye on a little boy who doesn't pay close enough attention not to get caught in front of the swings, or who decides the goldfish needs a bubble bath since little boys do."

I cringe. Soap and fish do not mix. That can't have ended well. And I'm all too familiar with the danger of swings when your kid is constitutionally incapable of paying attention. They're bowling balls and your kid is a pin. Boom!

"Add in getting bullied by some of the neurotypical kids, the ones who made fun of him — even hit him sometimes — because he's a 'ginger'…" She rolls her eyes, but her mouth is set in grim frown. "It wasn't easy. For him or for the foster parents. I was their last resort," she says, "the social worker with experience dealing with neurodivergent kids. So, I took him in myself. And he was the only one I kept long-term."

"Why?" I'm genuinely curious. The bond between the two of them is obvious, but how did Rhys get from foster-system problem-child to social worker's adopted son?

"At first, it was because none of the adopting families would take him. Most of them meant well, but you can't hide who he is. You have to accept him, love him, work with him, get to really understand him. And they weren't willing to do that, especially once we confirmed his ADHD and being on the spectrum."

"Wait. Rhys is autistic?"

"That part is my *unofficial* diagnosis," she says, giving a sigh. "The experts who tested him could never agree. The hyperactivity is obvious — even now, as an adult and on medication. But there's a lot of overlap between ADHD and autism spectrum disorder, as I'm sure you know." I nod. I've seen the test results, both as a parent and as a teacher. Sometimes, there are no clear answers. "And he fit in that overlap."

"Does he know that?"

"I've mentioned it to him a few times over the years, once he was old enough to understand. But it kind of ran off his back, like so much does with him. He latched on to the idea of taking his ADHD meds religiously, because he noticed the difference when he didn't take them. Taking his meds was tangible. He does well with tangible things. It's one of the reasons he loves his extreme sports — it's tangible, in the moment. He makes me crazy with worry sometimes, but he's gotten pretty good at not taking too many risks."

"Why did you decide to adopt him, rather than just fostering?"

"He was the kid who stuck. No biological parents stepping up to take him back, so we were stable. He was my constant, really. And by the time I'd had a few dozen foster kids come and go, I think I wanted that." She gives me a scrutinizing look. "I'm an old lesbian, Lyric," she finally says. "I was past my prime childbearing years, no husband, baby-daddy or even girlfriend in sight. And I wanted a family of my own. Rhys became that family, and I became his."

So, she chose to become a single parent, even knowing Rhys was "neurospicy." She took that on herself, on top of her job, on top of fostering. Rhys telling me that he gets the challenges of being a single mom — it suddenly makes sense. He watched his mom do it, just like I did. It was one reason I was glad I did the marriage and kids things in that order. Until I was suddenly a single mother anyway. And looking back at it, I have to wonder if I take on so much now because I saw Mom do it, too.

"Do you have any regrets?"

"Just that I couldn't get him connected with his heritage."

"His biological parents..."

"No — his tribal heritage."

Did she just say what I think she said? Now I feel bad. I'm just glad I didn't lecture him about telling Marian he was...

"He said he was part Native American. I..."

"You didn't believe him." She nods. "Most people don't. There's so many people yearning for something they perceive as more noble, or more connected with nature, or at least less connected with colonialism — they all have family legends of some Native American blood. And in some cases it's true. Rhys is one of them."

"You said he didn't know his biological parents."

"He didn't. His dad was never in the picture. Literally. Disappeared before he was born. I never knew who he was. His mother... She gave him up when he was 2. She tried, but she was young, wasn't equipped to take care of a child alone. I tried to help her as much as I could. But in the end, it wasn't enough. She dropped him off with me one day and disappeared herself."

"You were her case-worker."

"I was. I'd actually done my internship on the reservation where *her* mother had grown up. I knew her aunt. None of the family was willing to take him, so that was a non-starter. Beyond that, the tribal membership laws mostly measure qualification by blood quantum — how much of a person's DNA is from that tribe. And even then, when they started closing down the membership rolls, if you didn't have a parent who was already an enrolled member..." she shakes her head. "And Rhys' mother wasn't. Even back then, we always tried to place Native kids with Native families. But I couldn't find a foster for him that met that criteria."

"So he really is..."

"He's a quarter Ojibwe."

That drum. The dreamcatcher. The story his mom always told him. His tattoo. It all fits.

"His dad's Celtic ancestry showed up strong in his genes, with that red hair. Tall Nordic genes from his mother's father, too. I get it — no one who looks at him would think Native American. But he is. Just not enough to qualify for tribal membership. They're starting to change that, but..."

"But he's a grown man now, and he's lost all that culture he should have grown up with."

"I told him the stories I remembered from my brief time with the tribes. I got a few books so I could tell him others. I took him to powwows when he was younger, but no matter how much they tried to make him feel welcome, he always felt like an outsider. He stuck out even more than some of the other kids with a lot of Caucasian heritage, and he felt that. After a while, I stopped. He seemed almost relieved."

"We have powwows here. The Nanticokes have one every year. It's in a few weeks, actually. I always take the kids. I'm sure he'd be welcome there. And he's older now. And a famous drummer. They'll love him." I laugh.

"It's hard not to," she says. And I have to agree, even though I don't say it aloud.

And that's simultaneously exciting and terrifying to realize. I could very easily fall in love with Rhys Madigan. And not like I did when I was 20. Not like that at all...

"That sounds wonderful. You should take him," she says, sounding wistful as she watches her son play with the kids.

Aria is running around the beach, screaming in delight as Rhys chases her, crouched over and making "monster fingers." Tommy looks up, watching them, then focuses on his toys again. A moment later, he sets them aside and stands up, walking out into the beach. Aria blazes past him, Rhys in hot pursuit. But when he passes Tommy, he snatches him up, flipping him upside down. Tommy screeches loudly, and I start to get up to get him away from Rhys before Tommy panics or ends up in a tantrum. But Sheryl puts her hand on my arm, urging me silently to wait.

Rhys flips Tommy back onto his feet, setting him down on the sand. And Tommy... A giggling Tommy takes off after Aria, making his own version of Rhys' monster fingers. Aria squeals, and Rhys follows along behind, making silly monster sounds. Just like that, my kids are playing together, interacting. Tommy's interacting.

"He has a gift with kids," Sheryl says quietly. "Even after he went off to college, whenever he came to visit me in West Virginia, he'd help watch my fosters. The kids who struggled the most, the ones who were like him, the ones who were missing their parents — he gathered them up like the Pied Piper, and soon they were all having fun."

I'm having a hard time believing what I'm seeing.

"Tommy is entirely non-verbal," I tell her. "He rarely makes eye contact. He won't participate when the teachers try to use other communication methods. This is... This has never happened before." My eyes well up.

"Rhys doesn't carry the same expectations as you do as Tommy's mother, or as his teachers do. To him, it's just play. He goes with the flow. It's one of his best qualities. It invites people to join him. If more of his fosters had seen that in him, I don't think I'd have ended up with him. Now I'm glad they didn't. He's been the greatest joy of my life."

"I can see how he would be," I say without thinking.

"Good," she says, her smile satisfied.

I want to tell her it's not how she thinks it is, Rhys and me. But it is. I know that, even if I don't want to admit it, embrace it. It *is* thrilling. And it *is* terrifying. And I have no idea how to handle that.

Chapter 30

Holdin' Out

Rhys

I sent Lyric home with most of the leftover food, figuring it would make life easier for her. The kids were already half asleep, and it wasn't even dark out yet. It was a good day. Yeah — best day ever. For sure.

"This shrimp salad is really amazing, Rhys — where did you say you got it?" Alex asks.

"Callie said she was calling the local deli, so I'm betting that was it," I answer absently.

Mom's given me some things to think about. She waited until Lyric and the kids left, and then pulled me aside for one of our mother-son chats.

"She's lovely, your Lyric," she said. And I like hearing her called "my Lyric." It's starting to feel like she really is. "And the kids are wonderful in their own rights. And you're incredibly good with them," she adds.

"Thanks, Mom. They're fun, and they're smart, and they're interesting. I even had Tommy playing the drum the other day, until Lyric started screaming at me..."

"Why was that?" she asks, looking troubled.

"I don't know. She wasn't ready to tell me, and it seemed like I should wait until she was."

Mom does a double-take.

"You decided to wait until she was ready..."

"Yeah. She was really upset. I could tell it was important to her. She's got a room upstairs that she keeps locked. When she took the drum, she put it in there, locked it up tight again."

"Did you ask her about it?"

"No. It seemed like I—"

"Should wait until she was ready to tell you."

"Yeah. But I went up to check on her, because I was worried."

"And?

"She let me hug her."

"That's a good sign."

"It doesn't matter — it was what she needed at the time, and I'm trying to give her what she needs."

Again with the double-take.

"That's incredibly thoughtful of you, Rhys."

"I know. I told myself that... kind of." I mean, it wasn't me who said it, but it was inside my head.

She looks confused but moves on.

"You started to tell me something the other night at dinner... Did you want to talk about that now?"

"I don't know." It's an honest answer. I don't.

"You want me to wait until you're ready to tell me?"

"I think maybe, yeah," I tell her. "But I want to at least show you what got me thinking, since you're here."

I took her back inside, into my room, and it's instantly clear to her what I'm showing her.

"You got a dreamcatcher."

"Yeah. Not one of those fake-ass—"

"Rhys..." she says, warning.

"Sorry. It's not one of those fake ones that they sell at gas stations and stuff. This one's real. Ojibwe. The lady at the shop Lyric took me to said so. I don't think she believed me when I said I was part Native American. No one ever seems to."

"That doesn't change who you are, Rhys. You know that. And if you want to go talk to your relatives, I'm sure they'd welcome you, even if you're not a tribal member."

"I always told you no before — that if they didn't want me, I didn't want them."

"You did. Have you changed your mind?"

"I don't know. That's what I'm thinking about. And, it wasn't just the dreamcatcher that made me start thinking about it."

I pull the drum out from the other side of the bed and show it to her.

"What an amazing piece!" she says, taking it gently from me when I offer it to her. "I know this has to be real. And so elaborately decorated! That had to cost a pretty penny," she says.

"I'd have paid a lot more for it, Mom."

"Because it's made you think."

"Yeah. It's my heritage, and it's music. And it has all these stories in it — both the decorations from the Ojibwe stories, and the music that it can make. And I want to know those stories. I want to be able to tell them to my own kids someday. Not just the stories in the books, but the ones you learned and all the ones you didn't."

"I see," she says, looking pensive. "It sounds like it might be time for you to go visit. I can contact your aunt, if you like. As far as I know, she still lives on the reservation. She's about my age, so chances are she's still alive."

"But she didn't want me."

"I can't tell you what was in her mind or her heart when she made the decision, Rhys. She wasn't obligated to take you, just because her half-sister was your mother. They'd been estranged for most of their lives. She had three kids of her own already, and money was tight. In her shoes, I don't know what I would have done."

"You'd have taken me. That's who you are, Mom."

She thinks for a second before responding.

"Maybe. But that also means I'm not your aunt. So, we can't expect the same things from her that you do from me."

"Right. I get it."

"I know it's disappointing, Rhys, and I wish I'd been able to give you that heritage, more than anything. But if you are wanting it now, I will do everything I can to help you get it. Is that what you wanted to talk about?"

"Yeah, that's most of it."

"And you can tell me the rest — whatever it is — when you're ready."

"Just like Lyric."

"Just like Lyric." She grabs me up in a hug, pressing my head over her heart, like she always did when I was a kid. "You were an amazing boy, Rhys, and you've become an amazing man, and

any woman would be lucky to have you. I think Lyric knows that.
Just give her time to come to terms with that. Let her tell you her
story in her own time. I think that story may be as important for
you as any Ojibwe tale."

I suspect Mom is right. She always is.

"**B**and meeting!" Alex calls soon after he finishes off that
shrimp salad.

Kier takes about twenty seconds to get to the living room,
since his room is just down the hall.

Hunter and Declan are already sitting on the other end of the
sectional.

Dave trails behind Piper as they come up from the studio,
where she's been mixing Declan's vocal for his latest song. I was
starting to wonder if he'd ever finish the thing.

Piper takes a seat in the armchair across from the sectional,
and Dave sits on the arm of the chair, his own arm around her.
She looks a little less green than she did the other day. Mom said
that usually goes away after a month or so, but not always. Was
Lyric sick like this when she was pregnant? Would she be again
if...

OK. Whoa. Way too early for that.

Yeah. It is.

And head-dude has made his appearance for our band meeting, too.

You know, I need a better name to call him than just
"head-dude." Alternate-Rhys? Rhys' Alter Ego? My Brother from
Another Mother? Wait — maybe he really *is* my brother. My
half-brother, maybe? Did my bio-mom have more kids, and
we're connected by some sort of telepathy?

Not your brother, dude.

Fine, then you can stay head-dude. Head-Dude? Headdude?
HeadDude?

"OK — now, with all of us off on our own today, we've all had
time to relax, enjoy our significant others where applicable," he

says, sounding a little wistful. Maybe there is something up with Alex after all, like Mom said. "Tomorrow, we buckle back down again, because Declan's finished his second song and is ready to get that one down, too."

You can't.

"I can't."

Wait. Did I say that?

Yes. Because you can't.

Why not?

Because Lyric has her dress rehearsal, and you said you'd be there.

Right. I did. I should have put it on my calendar.

You did.

I pull up my calendar on my phone. Sure enough, it's right there. I have to be there at one, for rehearsal at two, so we can check the sound system.

"Rhys!" Kier shouts, practically in my ear.

"What?"

"We asked you why you can't record tomorrow."

"I've got a thing."

"A thing?" Kier asks, looking at me suspiciously.

"Is this a *fundraiser* thing?" Alex asks.

"Yeah. Dress rehearsal. The fundraiser is on Friday."

"What's this about a fundraiser?" Kier asks. "Did Billy book us for something and forget to tell everyone but you and Alex?"

"No. It's just me. I'm helping out."

"Wait — is this Lyric's fundraiser?" Declan asks. "Callie set her up with a caterer for that. Is that what you've been up to the last week or so? Helping Lyric with her fundraiser?"

"What fundraiser is this?" Dave asks.

"And Lyric — is that the blonde girl from the interview the other night?" Kier asks.

"No — that was Rory, her best friend."

"I know the reporter's name, ye eejit," Kier says. "I meant the one you were all gaga over, *her* friend."

"And Callie's," Declan adds.

"And Brighid's," Hunt adds.

"Piper and I have babysat for her a few times," Dave says. "But not recently. So I guess we're kind-of friends." Piper nods.

"I'm starting to feel left out here," Kier says, frowning. "Wait — this was the widow, with the two kids?"

"That's her. And she's awesome!" I smile, still full of lingering warm feelings from our family beach day. See — I told Mom it was fine to have them meet today. It all worked out great.

Lyric wasn't so sure, at first.

How do you know? She did fine. They got along like a house on fire. Wait — why is that good thing, a house on fire? *Is* it a good thing?

It's fine. But you missed the look on her face when you first told her.

Hmm... Maybe. But why did Head-Dude notice it if I didn't?

Because I did.

Not helpful.

"Rhys!" Alex smacks me on the back of the head. I didn't even see him get up off the other end of the sectional to do it. So, maybe I earned that one, even if I hate it when he does it.

Then tell him to stop doing it!

I have. I think he thinks I'm kidding.

"I asked you what time you need to be there," Alex says. Repeats, I guess.

"One."

"Can you lay down drum tracks in the morning? Or tonight?"

He looks over at Piper, who looks almost as tired as Lyric does. Kids must make you tired, even before they're born.

Piper hesitates and then nods.

"No. Not happening," Dave declares, more emphatically than I've seen him say anything in a long time. "She's exhausted. She was up half the night puking again, and she's going home right after this meeting to get some sleep."

Alex looks sympathetic.

"Tomorrow morning, then? Assuming Piper isn't puking?"

"Mom always called it 'tossing your cookies.'"

Everyone's staring at me again. I don't get it.

They're waiting for you to answer them about tomorrow morning.

Oh, right.

Dude, how do you ever get anything done if you need me to remind you about that?

What time is it?

Eight.

I'm late taking my meds. With Lyric and the kids here, it slipped my mind. I managed to lose a bottle the other day, and

I had to have Billy get me a new one early, but I only missed a dose or two. I'll take my evening dose after this.

Ah. Good for you. But they're still waiting for an answer.

Right!

"I can do them in the morning. If Declan has time to go over the arrangement with me tonight, I'll be ready to do the drum tracks in the morning. As soon as Piper gets here. Just come wake me up if I'm not up already."

"Callie won't be off work until at least ten," Declan says. "I can go over it with you now."

"Great. Because I can't miss rehearsal." And, for once, when I say "rehearsal," I'm not talking about aMUSEd.

K ier is waiting for me in the living room when I come back up from the studio.

"I meant it when I said I was feeling left out, Rhys. And I don't just mean that everybody seems to be hooking up with these Mystic Beach girls."

He nods at the sofa, and I sit down.

"What's going on with you lately? I ask because you haven't exactly kept me in the loop. You went from begging me to play wingman to sending groupies home unhappy, all in the space of a few months. And now you see a girl for the first time, and you're instantly head-over-heels for her? And a widow, a single mom? Do you have any idea what you're letting yourself in for?"

"I know exactly what I'm in for, Kier. I've been spending a lot of time with Lyric, and her kids. And they're awesome. All three of them!"

Damn straight!

Kier leans back, looking at me from a greater distance, as if that'll bring this all into focus for him.

"You're wanting to be a step-dad? Weeks after you met the girl?" He seems both skeptical and really asking me those questions.

"Yeah. It's... I feel like I've known her a lot longer than that, you know? It kind of feels like it's meant to be, that I'm supposed to be here, with her, with the kids."

Took you long enough to get here, though.

What do you mean, "took me long enough"? I got here when the band did.

Head-dude is quiet now. He seems to have all the answers, but he's not giving me this one.

"You sound like Brighid... Feckin' hell — you sound like Hunt and Declan and Dave, too. Is there something in the water here? Everybody goes all mystical as soon as they get to Mystic Beach? Hell, they go all romantic and want to settle down, too. It's feckin' strange. All of it."

"Haven't you ever wanted to find someone you could come home to, who you take care of, and they take care of you?"

He doesn't answer me, but I can see that he's thinking about it.

"Maybe," he says after a moment. "But I haven't ever heard you say *you* did. What changed?"

"I found the girl of my dreams. Literally."

"Alright — that's going to require an explanation, my man. Are you really doing a Brighid? You got a goddess you're talking to, too?"

"No. But... I've been dreaming about Lyric, Kier. Not a girl like her, but her exactly. For months. When I stopped going off with the groupies, the waitresses? It was because the only woman I see when I close my eyes — the only one I *want* to see — was coming to me in my dreams."

Not quite. But close enough.

Care to explain?

Silence.

Unreliable Head-dude.

"You're winding me up..." Ah — I know this one. He means I'm joking, pulling his leg, setting him up for a punchline.

"Nope."

"Feckin' shite..." He shakes his head. "You've all lost your marbles."

"You're the one who was talking about mermaids!"

"It's a story, Rhys. A myth. That shite isn't real. As much as I love Brighid, there's no such thing as mermaids or selkies or Druids or witches or whatever you want to call them!"

"That's not true!"

Witches, at least are very real. And mine, at least, may or may not be able to control the weather. I still have to ask her about that, now that she's feeling better. She's got her winter concert back on track, with my help. I'm a little proud of that.

Kier shakes his head at me again.

"Dream-girls... I'm starting to wonder if we're going to make it out of this town with our sanity intact. I love you like a brother, Rhys, but I'm really starting to despair for the future of this band. Especially when half of it's already moved to feckin' Delaware. After all I risked to get here..."

He stands up and walks out the sliding glass doors, down the stairs, still shaking his head, his long not-quite-as-red-as-mine hair flaring out behind him.

As long as I've known Kier, as sorry of a flibbertigibbeter as he's been for most of that time, with his secrets and his hidden past, I've never felt truly sorry for him, until right now.

I kind of hope he's right about one thing, though: that there's something in the water — or the air, or whatever — here in Mystic Beach. Because that would mean there's a chance for him to finally find his happiness, too.

Too.

Because when I'm with Lyric and her kids, I'm happy. Happier than I am on stage. Happier than I am meeting fans. Happier even than I am behind my kit. Happier than I can ever remember being. If nothing else, today proved that. And I don't know if I can have it all — the band, the touring, the fans — and still have Lyric and the kids in my life like they deserve, but if it comes down to it, I made a decision tonight that tells me where my priorities are.

Yes!

Glad to know you agree, head-dude. Glad to know you agree.

Let's just hope we can get Lyric on board. Especially after I tell her about my dreams.

CHAPTER 31

NO QUESTIONS ASKED

Lyric
The next day

I now have an email from Michelle that confirms the licensing for the winter concert has been secured. This morning, I re-did my lesson plans with the songs swapped out. I opted to do a safe seasonal theme, with a few traditional secular holiday songs that won't satisfy the preferences of Galworth and his ilk, since they're not hymns. They're mixed in with some modern songs from holiday movies and TV shows — none of which are associated with Disney, woke or otherwise.

Two hours later, I had an email that confirmed that — pending a formal vote of the board — the revised concert song list had been approved. Tentatively. Pending a formal vote. It's not a true win, which would have required the board not veto my original theme, but it's at least a draw.

In between, I had two piano lessons and a guitar lesson. And after feeding the kids lunch — yes, I did eat! — I spent half an hour on the Tchaikovsky-waltz-that-shall-not-be-named. I've played it a million times. It was my audition piece as a music major. My technique isn't a sharp as it was when I graduated, since I spend less time playing, but it's better than most people hear from a regional orchestra. New York Philharmonic-caliber, I am not. Not anymore, if I ever truly was. But I can still wow an audience at an elementary-school fundraiser.

That is both entirely true and tongue-in-cheek.

I smirk at my own humor.

Ah... When's the last time I did that? Told myself a joke, let alone laughed at it...

I have to hand it to Rhys — when he suggested I really take the day off yesterday, I just kept picturing things left undone, falling through the cracks. But not only did my work get done in an expedited fashion, Rhys had everything in hand with yesterday's plans.

And his mom... Sheryl gave me such incredible insight into the man she raised. I only hope I can do as well with my kids as she's done with him, neurospicy or otherwise.

As for *my* mom — she's going to watch the kids again today. She had to move up her "lunch date" by an hour to do it, but she agreed. And that was as much as I got out of her about who this person is that she's seeing. She's being so closed-mouth about it, I'm starting to suspect it's a man this time. She was always sneakier about her dates with men. Either that, or she's really smitten and she doesn't want to risk jinxing it. Well, if it lasts long enough for her to tell me, I'll guess I'll find out then.

I didn't tell her I'd met Rhys' mom. It was too soon in our... friendship? relationship? I'm tempted to call it that, because anything less is inaccurate. But it really is too soon... to meet his mom or call it a relationship. But we're doing both at a breakneck pace, it seems. And that leaves me wondering what previously distant milestone will turn out to be right over the horizon.

"Grandma!" Aria yells as Mom lets herself in the open front door without knocking. I can't complain. It was her house, and I've got nothing to hide. Yet.

"How're my lovebugs!" she says, intercepting with aplomb the fervent hugs of two kids who act like they haven't seen her in years, instead of the forty-eight hours it's been.

"Awesome!" Aria says. "We went to the beach at Mr. Rhys' big house yesterday and had scrimps and gooey cheese, and nuggets for Tommy, and made sandcastles, and I dove under the waves with Mr. Rhys and Mommy!"

Well, that cat's out of the bag.

"Oh, really?" Mom asks, raising an eyebrow at me. "Mr. Rhys has a big beach house? Has he already bought someplace local, looking to settle down, perhaps?"

Oh. My. Gods.

"We went to the studio just outside town, Mom. The band is staying there, with their private beach, since it's a live-in arrangement. Or they were, since half of them are living here in town now."

"Oh? Sounds promising!"

"Mom..." I say warningly.

"Fine. Fine. Message received. I'll respect your privacy." Yeah. That'll be the day. But I let it go, count my blessings.

"I should be home around five at the latest," I tell her. "They've had lunch. Go easy on the snacks. I'm having a hard enough time getting Tommy to eat anything nutritious."

"Have you considered spinach and carrot smoothies? There's a guy on the fair circuit who sells them, and they're very popular, as well as healthy. Just a little chia seed..."

"He won't drink something like that, Mom, no matter how much fruit juice goes in it."

Or how little spinach or chia seed. Chia? Not happening.

"Fine. But I worry, you know."

"I do. So do I. That's why he's got his nutritional drinks, and I'm still trying some things with his regular foods. Callie suggested carrot and cauliflower in the cheese sauce. I'm going to give that a shot next time I make it from scratch. But, right now, I've got to go. We've got to get the sound system set up before rehearsal. Have fun! Love you all!"

I do. But the few days I've had alone with Rhys have reminded me that a little time off from 24/7 mom-duty is healthy for me, and for the kids.

And that's put a whole-hearted smile on my face for the first time in I can't remember how long...

"Thank you all for such amazing work, and for volunteering your time to support the fundraiser this year! I really can't think you all enough, or your parents for making sure you got here for rehearsals and practiced at home. You're going to make us all proud. You already have, really!"

There's a short round of applause. I love seeing everyone so excited about this!

"Now — make sure you're here on time tomorrow evening, in costume and with your instruments if you play one," I remind them. "This is the real thing, with lots of people from the school and the community coming to see you perform and to help us get our new instruments. So, let's act like the pros I know you are! OK?"

Cheering is more than I hoped for, and the piercing whistles of support are more than I asked for. Thank you, Rhys... I smile at him, blushing a little. His support has been so incredibly important for the event, but his personal support for me has come at a time when I truly needed it, even if I didn't realize how badly.

Once all the kids and parents have left, he and I stack up the chairs we used during rehearsal and leave them near the door for Phil to put back in storage. Rhys shuts off the sound and lighting systems from the mixing board and control panel in the little loft at the back of the room, not even bothering to pull down the access ladder. He just jumps up, grabs hold of the railing and pulls himself right up. I shake my head in wonder. I close the curtain on the stage, checking to make sure the riser, piano and chairs for our mini-orchestra are concealed for tomorrow.

All that's left is the open, beautifully decorated (if I do say so myself) room, now dotted with little high-top tables for family-friendly mocktails and heavy hors d'oeuvres, and edged by the auction tables at the back and catering tables on the sides. Everything is in place. All of my to-dos are checked off. And all that's left is to get the food and people in here tomorrow night, and fill the room with music.

Rhys comes up from behind me and wraps his arms around me, setting his chin on my head.

Brighid didn't quite fit, he said. I do.

This time, I let myself lean back into him, relishing that feeling of being held, supported, protected. A kiss on the top of my head makes it a perfect moment. We did this, together. And now we'll get to enjoy the fruits of our labor together.

"How would you feel about a little celebratory dinner?" he asks, his deep voice sending shivers down my spine.

I sigh, turning around to face him.

"I wish I could, but I told Mom I'd be back around five. And that means leaving now."

"Call her. Ask her. I'm sure she won't mind."

I look up into those eyes of his and find the tiger, not his bouncy counterpart. This is Rhys asking me on a date, even if it's just dinner, knowing I have to get home to the kids.

"Alright. I'll ask her."

My heart pounds, just saying the words. It's my first real first-date in more than a decade. I'm suddenly nervous. I almost hope Mom says she's got plans.

"Hi, sweetie! How'd rehearsal go?"

"It went wonderfully, Mom. I was planning to come straight home, but..."

"Rhys asked you to dinner, didn't he? I knew it!"

I can't help but smile. She's enjoying this almost as much as I am. Maybe more, actually.

"He did. Would that be OK? Can you handle the kids for a few more hours, get them fed? I can order out if you're not up to making something."

"I've been eating restaurant food most of this week myself," she says. "It'll be nice to cook dinner for the kids. Have fun! No need to rush back! And just text me if you need me to stay overnight!"

"Mom!"

She just giggles.

"I'll see you in a few hours, Mom. Goodnight."

"She said yes?" Rhys asks. "I knew she would!"

"She did. You two are getting a little scary, you know?" He just smiles at me. "Where did you want to go?"

"I asked Callie to hold a table for us, just in case."

Oh, boy. A first date at my friend's restaurant. And I suspect she knew before I did. This is going to be interesting.

CHAPTER 32

ARMS WIDE OPEN

Lyric

"We have a table all set aside for you, right over here. The chef's table," the host says, leading us briskly to a corner close to the kitchen but tucked away from the walkways and other diners. It's intimate, almost private. Wait... Isn't this the table she said Declan took when he was pursuing her for a second chance? I mean, it worked, but...

Rhys walks close behind me, his hand resting in the hollow of my back. Adam used to do that, too. I still like it. But I need to stop thinking about things in terms of Adam. This is a first date. Let Rhys be Rhys.

I'd have dressed up more for a first date, or dinner at Castalia, but this is a resort town, and as nice as Callie's restaurant is, there's no dress code, and there are as many people here in T-shirts and shorts as there are in suits or dresses. I'm dressed nicely enough, though not dressy. Rhys is in a T-shirt and shorts, but they fit him so perfectly they look like they were made for him. No one would question whether he belongs here. His presence is as big as he is, and the world just seems to make way for him, no matter where he goes or what he does.

He intercepts the host when she goes to help me with my chair and scoots it in under me before taking the seat across from me. His mom certainly taught him some manners, no matter how often he sticks his foot in his mouth or makes an inattentive mistake.

We order drinks — a single glass of wine for me and another Dogfish beer for him, both agreeing that we'll stick to water after that, since both of us are driving. No sooner do our drinks arrive than Callie pops out from the kitchen, beaming a smile at us. I blush. I know what's coming.

"Well, hello, you two!" she says. "I hoped when Rhys said he wanted a table for two tonight that you'd be the other half of that pairing." She leans down close to my ear. "Not what it looks like, huh?"

"Thanks for holding it for us, Callie," I say, ignoring her reference. "I know you don't take reservations."

"This is now officially the chef's table. I can hold it for whomever I like," she says. "And I like seeing you two sitting here."

"Me, too," Rhys says, grabbing my hand across the table and squeezing it.

Callie's face lights up. Mine goes red.

"If you two are up for it, I'll be happy to devise a special menu for you. I know Lyric's preferences, and I remember what you ordered with your mom the other day, Rhys, so I can work from that."

"Wait — you knew his mom was here?" I ask her. You'd have thought she might have mentioned that to me. Maybe. If things had been what they looked like. Which is not what I told her. Oh.

"They came in for lunch the other day. She's wonderful. You'll love her!"

"Oh, they met yesterday." Rhys says.

Callie gives me a speculative look, like this tells her all she needs to know.

"And?"

"She is wonderful. We hit it off," I tell her honestly.

"Perfect!" she says. "I'll have your appetizers out to you shortly. Relax, enjoy!"

Rhys is quiet for a minute, as if he's trying to decide what to say. It's weird, for him. I almost wish he'd just say whatever he's thinking.

"You really liked Mom? 'Cause she really likes you," he says. "And the kids."

"I did. She's very smart, kind, thoughtful. And she and I have a lot in common."

"You do."

"I also realized you and I have something in common, besides being music majors."

"What's that?"

"We were both raised by single mothers."

"I know Iris said she never married, but I'd just assumed..."

"No, Mom raised me all alone from the start. I never knew my dad. I don't even know who he is. She's always been kind of hush-hush about it. I think I was an accident from a one-night stand or something."

"Does that bother you? Not knowing who he is? Not having him around?"

"No. Not really. I know — especially now — that Mom struggled sometimes to make ends meet. But she was a wonderful parent, and a wonderful teacher. I'm not sure I could have had a happier childhood, except maybe to have had more friends. I always got close with the ones I found, though."

"I didn't have a lot of friends, either. Lots of fosters, but they came and went. I always tried to make them feel like they were part of the family, but they'd go back to their parents or grandparents, or get adopted... and I learned not to get too attached."

"Was it hard? Being in foster care?"

He looks surprised.

"Mom told you some of my background, I guess..."

"I'm sorry if you didn't want me to know. I think she thought it would help me understand you, and your relationship with her."

"No — it's fine. You knew I was adopted. I've never hidden it from anyone. I told Hunter the first day we met."

"But there's a difference between being adopted and having been in foster care long-term."

"Yeah. Honestly — I don't remember most of it. I was so little when I went into foster care, and it wasn't very long before I ended up with Mom. Some of the foster homes before that... They weren't great. I mean, they tried, but... I was a literal red-haired foster-child, and one who didn't look where he was going and said odd things when people talked to me. Finding a place where I fit was always going to be a challenge."

"But you did. You ended up with your mom. And she kept you."

"Yeah. I couldn't really believe it when she told me she wanted to adopt me. Part of me was always waiting for her to say I had to go to a new foster home. But there she was, asking me to be her son, for real. Somebody finally wanted me, and best of all, it was the woman who'd made me feel like I fit, like I could be myself and still be loved."

"That really shows — in you and in your relationship with her. It's beautiful to watch. It definitely gives me mom-goals for when the kids are grown up."

"Thanks. That's nice to hear. But I don't think you have anything to worry about. Your kids are already great."

"Thanks. I think so, too. We've got some challenges, but I think they're happy and growing. That's what counts."

"It is. And you're doing a great job..."

I hear the words he leaves unspoken. He's not subtle with it, probably from lack of practice. It doesn't sit well with me, that he doesn't just speak his mind. It's contrary to his nature.

"Just say it. It's the elephant in the room."

"What happened to your husband, Lyric? No one would tell me. All I know is he passed away suddenly a few years ago, and I can't really tell if you're even ready to let anyone else in."

Callie approaches the table at exactly that moment, leaving Rhys' question hanging heavy in the air between us.

"This is a ravioli duo," she says, putting a large plate down between us. "One ravioli is a three-cheese blend with black truffle and truffle oil. The second is a sundried-tomato and goat cheese ravioli with my special sundried-tomato oil blend. Don't ask what's in it. I'm not telling."

"Thanks, Callie," we both say together. Her face lights up again. I think she's enjoying this more than I am. Especially with that question of Rhys' left unanswered.

"Here," Rhys says, cutting a piece of the truffle ravioli with his fork and raising it to my mouth. If that alone didn't make me want to melt, the flavor of the bite certainly does. Callie's done it again.

He cuts himself a second piece and tastes it, savoring it. That tigerlike sensuality is on full display.

"You'd never know it to look at you, but you love food, don't you?"

"I love to eat it. I'm not really big on gourmet cooking, not like Declan or Alex. But I enjoy the sensory experience of eating interesting flavors, whether that's the flavor combinations or the richness of it. I like my microbrews more than the average guy, but I mostly just order food that sounds good to me. I'm just lucky that I'm active enough that I burn all of it back off. Declan's always complained about extra calories. Of course, now we know he was secretly cooking when we weren't around, so maybe he had a point."

I chuckle at that. Callie had tailed Declan one night, from this very table, thinking he was up to something with another woman. She found him cooking. Now, they cook together sometimes here at Castalia, and they're planning to open a second restaurant when they get back from their culinary honeymoon. They got their happily-ever-after, over a restaurant table.

I catch Rhys looking at me, his expression warm. He offers me a piece of the tomato ravioli. It's just as wonderful as the other, but entirely different in taste. It's amazing how well these two different things go so well together.

"What were you thinking about, just now?" he asks.

"About Declan and Callie finding their happily-ever-after."

"You can see the joy on your face, how happy you are for them."

"I've seen the same look on your face when you talk about them, and your other bandmates who've found love."

"Yeah. I guess so," he says. "If you'd asked me a year ago whether I thought any of us would settle down anytime soon, I'd have laughed. But things changed in the last six months or so. Longer for Hunt, really. And Declan, too, though we were all clueless for a long time."

"And you?"

"I've been thinking about finding someone special for a while now. I didn't know until I saw you at the wedding reception that it was you."

And my heart stops. Dead. Right there.

"How is everything?" the host asks, refilling our water glasses.

"Amazing," we both say.

She smiles and walks away. We eat in silence, trading off bites of the ravioli until they're both gone.

"Sorry if that was too much, the part about finding you," Rhys finally says. "I don't know how to do this stuff. I haven't been on a real date since high school. If I ever had 'game,' I don't now."

"That's OK. I don't like games. I like honesty, communication, people being themselves, with no hidden agenda."

"About that..." he says.

"How goes it?" Callie asks, a plate in each hand. One of her staff clears away the ravioli plate and sets down two smaller plates, one in front of each of us. Callie places the two serving plates in the middle of the table between us.

"Everything is great, Callie. Thank you so much for doing this," I tell her, while simultaneously wishing she'd just leave us to talk. No offense.

"My pleasure! Now, for your entrées, I've got a twist on surf-and-turf: a petit fillet with asparagus and potatoes dauphinoise, and a seafood bouillabaisse featuring local and sustainable seafoods with a saffron-forward broth."

"I'm almost disappointed not to see a lionfish sitting on top of the dish," Rhys says. "Hunter told me that was an unbelievable meal you served that night. But no one would tell me how it tasted."

Callie splutters a little, and I don't blame her. I know what went down that night, but for reasons other than her skill with turning an invasive fish into a gourmet meal.

"Trade secret," she stammers, returning quickly to the kitchen.

"Something I said?" Rhys asks.

"Let's just say things got a little heated that night between her and Declan, and it was better for everyone that they ended up working things out alone." I chuckle. Not my secret to tell, not even to Rhys, who admittedly isn't great at keeping secrets.

We're halfway through our entrées, sharing both equally, before we start talking again. And I push myself to get back to that elephant, since he's raised the issue twice already. I can't blame him. I'm overdue to tell him.

"My husband, Adam, passed away... It'll be four years ago in January. It was sudden, unexpected and tragic. And it didn't have to happen."

"I'm sorry," he says, reaching over to squeeze my hand again. "Do you mind if I ask what happened?"

I sigh, put down my fork and finish off the last of my wine. Once I do this, I won't have to do it again, and I find myself wanting to start with a clean slate with Rhys tonight.

"Adam was a snorer. He'd snored since we'd first met, and probably before that. But once the kids were born, we had more times when one of us was up while the other was still asleep. It's just something that happens when you've got little kids.

But it meant that I noticed not just how loud his snoring had gotten, but also that there were times when it seemed like he stopped breathing, for a second sometimes and for much longer at others."

"What was wrong?"

"He had sleep apnea. Basically, his breathing got obstructed while he was sleeping, and he'd just stop breathing, briefly. He'd start again, but this would go on all night, without even waking him up."

Rhys waits for me to continue, and I appreciate that patience, knowing how much of a challenge it is for him.

"Sleep apnea is actually pretty dangerous. When people stop breathing, their brain is deprived of oxygen. The risk of a number of potentially deadly conditions increases. It's not hard to address. The most common way is for patients to wear a mask device when they sleep that forces air into their airways so they stay open and can breathe normally."

I wipe away a tear. Rhys looks like he's ready to get up and come hug me, but I shake my head, warning him off.

"Adam was... hard-headed is one word. A rebel, really. And I loved that about him. We were our own people and we never worried about what anyone else thought, at least until we had the kids. But Adam was not the type of guy who wanted to sleep every night with a mask tethered to a machine. He still considered himself immortal, even after the kids arrived and we had to start thinking about the longer-term. So, when I told him — begged him — to go to the doctor, get the apnea treated, he refused." I can see Rhys judging Adam, for nothing else than not doing what his worried wife was asking him.

But that's not how it was, not really.

"Not in so many words," I continue. "He wasn't like that. But he procrastinated making the doctor appointments I got him to agree to make. He canceled ones I made for him, saying he was too busy or too tired..."

More tears. Rhys reaches across and wipes them away for me. I give him a thin smile of thanks. But I have to get this out.

"He *was* too tired. That was true. Sleep apnea leaves people exhausted, because they never get the deep sleep people need to feel rested. And the longer it goes untreated, the more sleep-deprived they get. It's not uncommon for them to develop narcolepsy — falling asleep randomly, suddenly, even at times they'd normally be awake. I saw Adam do it a few times, and that's when I insisted he schedule a sleep study to get diagnosed and treated. And he listened. He set it up. 'Finally,' I thought."

I pick up my napkin and dab at my eyes, seeing Callie looking worriedly at me from the kitchen door. I shake my head in the tiniest of gestures, begging her not to interrupt.

"Adam's job had him working at night a lot. Late hours, coming home at three in the morning, tired and wired after a long night. But we had small kids, and my job has me up at six or seven in the morning, so he drove home alone most of those nights, while I was asleep at home with the kids. And, one night, while he was driving home, he had an episode of narcolepsy. He fell asleep behind the wheel, and the car ran off the road, into a ditch. He died instantly."

I take the deepest, slowest breath I can manage, trying to get my emotions under control, now that the worst of it is out.

When I exhale again, there's a sense of release. It's not something that I've felt on the few occasions that I've told someone this story. It feels right to be telling this to Rhys. It doesn't matter that we're in public. No one's watching. Callie's got us so tucked away that no one's noticed my crying or overheard what I've said. Except Rhys. Who stands up, walks up next to my chair, kneels down, and takes me into his arms. And we stay that way, quiet, while our food gets cold. But I don't think either of us cares about that right now.

"I'll pack up what's left and bring it over to you tomorrow morning, Lyric," Callie says quietly from behind Rhys. "Take her home, Rhys. Take care of her. I'll have Declan come get her car, bring it home for her."

She holds her hand out, and I hand her my keys.

"It's time, sweetie," she says, wiping away more tears. "You're overdue for some happiness again. Let yourself have that."

Rhys stands up and pulls me up beside him, tucking me under his arm. He pats my tears dry and sweeps me out through the door and into that amazing car of his.

He turns and looks at me, considering.

"Callie said to take you home. But I don't think that's what you need," he says.

I shake my head.

"Beach."

"Your wish is my command," he says.

Ten minutes later, Rhys and I are sitting on the beach in front of the studio, just watching the waves wash on the sand. This is something Brighid and I have in common, along with our devotion to the same goddess. The beach is our touchpoint. It's the place we go to think, to feel, and sometimes to cry.

I look over at Rhys, and he turns to meet my eyes with his own. He gives me a sad smile. It's strange to see on his face, which is so often full of mirth or joy, or even just caring. At least with me. He scoots closer and pulls my head into his chest, once again peppering my hair with gentle kisses. After a while, I'm calm enough to talk again.

"Rory was the one who told me he'd died. One of her cop friends knew we were close, so when he heard Adam's name, he woke Rory up and had her come with him to tell me what had happened. The kids slept through it all, somehow. It was a blessing. It gave me time to absorb and begin to mourn, and to regain enough composure to tell them their dad wasn't coming home."

"I can't imagine how hard that was. Or how brave you've had to be," he says, squeezing me harder against him. "You are just amazing."

"Well, thanks for listening, and letting me cry on you again," I add with a laugh. Even when I'm sad, Rhys makes me laugh.

And that seems really important all of a sudden. Maybe Callie's right. Maybe it's time to let go of the past and allow myself some happiness again.

It is time for the healing to be complete.

Rhys kisses my temple.

She's right. It is.

Rhys

I once dreamed of meeting a mermaid who'd take me with her to her secret cove full of treasure and colorful fish. Maybe even a talking crab. Though, then I'd have ended up having to apologize for eating his friends as a cheesy topping on a burger. So, maybe not that part.

Then Kieran told me about his Irish mermaids — who it seems he doesn't even believe are real — and that they keep their human mates captive under the sea. That didn't seem nearly as fun as what I'd envisioned, especially with no drums to play underwater.

Then, Lyric revealed the secret of the not-so-real mermaids I'd always thought were real, and the magic of it seemed to evaporate in an instant. Until this real-life witch and self-proclaimed "half a mermaid" reminded me that there are plenty of things in this world that can't be explained or studied with science, but that must be believed to be seen.

Are mermaids real? I don't know. But I do know now that this woman is a greater treasure than anything an actual mermaid could lead me to. And her kids along with her.

She's smart and talented, warm and passionate. She's giving to the detriment of her own well-being. But, above all else, she's incredibly strong. Literally incredible. Like, I'm having a hard time believing anyone can be as strong as I now know her to be. Forget me hanging off a cliff by my fingertips — Lyric's been holding up her entire family, hanging by her emotional fingertips, for years. It's past time someone helped her carry that weight. I just hope she'll let me do that.

She has to. Otherwise this was all for naught.

So this was what you meant by her husband waiting too long, letting her down.

Yeah.
No wonder you called him an idiot.
Hey!
You're the one who called him that.
It's fine when I say it. You don't get to.
Whatever. And that doctor appointment he didn't make?
Yeah.
How do you know all this shit?
I know people. People who know stuff.
I'd ask why you're telling *me*, but that's pretty clear now.
Is it?
She needs me.
If she's going to really heal, really move on — yeah, I think so.
And that's why I kept dreaming about her. So I'd know her when I saw her, so I'd be ready to step in to help her.
Yeah.
To love her.
Head-dude goes quiet again. I listen to Lyric breathing, and I can feel her sorrow fading, the weight of carrying all of that emotion around finally starting to slip away. If nothing else, I'm glad I could help her get to that point. But now that she has, I really hope she'll give me the chance to do more. Because I want that, for me and for her and for the kids.
Take care of them.
I will, head-dude. I will.

Chapter 33

Fresh Feeling

Lyric

Last night with Rhys, it's like a dam burst, finally relieving the pressure, letting the fresh water flow to clear away the debris of the past. No matter who I've talked to about my loss, no matter how often or how soon, it never felt like that, like I walked away from the conversation lighter, washed clean, like a pouring rain does to the air on a hot and dusty summer's day.

Is this what therapy is like? If so, maybe Brighid is onto something. Wow.

But I don't think I could have gotten this from talking to some psychologist or counselor. Not even to Rory or Callie or Brighid herself. And as much as I've tried to unload this burden on Brighid the goddess, as willing and able as She is to take it from me, it never worked.

What was missing?

Sitting in front of the statue on my altar this morning, well before the kids wake up, I see what I didn't see before — I was lacking just one thing: The drive to build a future, for myself and the kids. I was still stuck in the past, still making do with what fate had left me after destroying my dreams. There was no moving on — not until I allowed myself to start dreaming new dreams.

Building a future for me and the kids won't happen overnight. It can't, and it shouldn't. It won't mean leaving Adam behind in the past — he's too important to us all. He shaped our lives. But it's time for me to start shaping a future.

Is Rhys part of that picture? Part of those new dreams? Maybe.

But trying to imagine a future with him in it — that's what broke me out of the cage of my past. I feel... Free.

Saoirse.

It's one of the few words of Irish I know. Mostly because it's also a name. But it seems a fitting word to know now. It means "freedom."

And I'm excited to see where this newfound freedom will lead.

"**A**lright — you know where to go? You have to be there before seven, or it'll be chaos, with the performances and the auctions. Supposedly there's a buzz over Rhys' donations to the auctions, so there may be more people there than usual. Parking could be a hassle."

"I know where the school is, Lyric. I lived here well before you were born. And you work there! I've got the kids handled. I've got snacks for Tommy, just in case, and a spare set of gears in case he loses one."

"Good. Perfect."

I run into something with my foot.

"Mom, what's this bag doing here?"

"It's my overnight bag."

"Why is it in my room?"

"Because the sofa is hard on my back, like you said."

"You're not going back to the loft tonight?"

"Can't do that and watch the kids."

"I meant after the show is over."

"So did I."

She's got a mischievous tone to her voice, and I drop the towel from my still-damp hair and peer out into the living room.

"I'm coming straight home as soon as the auctions are sorted and the room is ready for the custodial staff to clear out."

"Mm-hmm..."

"Mom. Don't 'mm-hmm' me. I'm going to be sleeping in my own bed tonight. Alone."

"Right."

"Mom."

"Fine. I'll put my bag back in the car. Where it will be readily available should you decide you need your mother to stay with your children overnight. For any reason."

"Oh, for gods' sakes, Mom!"

"Well, at least I taught you how to swear properly!" she says, laughing heartily.

"I give up." I throw my hands up in the air, then finish towel-drying my hair before twisting it up into what I hope is an elegant up-do. Makeup, jewelry and a dress to match, some low heels. Nothing too overtly sexy. It may be summer and it may be a Friday night, but these are still kids and parents, co-workers, maybe a boss or two, plus Rhys... And now I'm nervous again. And not just because it all — the planning, the driving, the phone calls, the rehearsals, the consults with caterers and on and on — not just because it all comes down to this. Because part of me suspects Mom's right, and I may not be sleeping in my own bed tonight.

I realized this morning that it's all up to me now — deciding what I want, who I want in my life, what the future will hold for me and the kids. It's heady, that freedom. And I want to enjoy the sensation while it lasts. So, at least as much as a mom with two kids can, I'm taking a lesson from Rhys Madigan: I'm going with the flow. I'm letting myself play. And I'm letting my sense of adventure determine the path.

"You look beautiful, Lyric," Mom says, giving me a hug.

"You're so pretty, Mommy," Aria agrees.

Tommy looks at me like I'm a sparkly faerie or something, then his gaze slides away again. But just for a moment there...

I grab my bag and my violin case — the first time it's been out of the house in nearly a year. It's overdue for a little fresh air, too. For a night out, even.

I open the door so I can see when Rhys pulls up. And then he does.

"I'll see you all in a little bit."

"Brightest blessings, my dear," Mom says. It's formal, especially for Mom. But I'll take any blessing she offers.

"Thanks," I tell her with a smile.

I step out the door and blush furiously when Rhys wolf-whistles at me.

"I'm not sure I'm good enough to take a woman this gorgeous out," he says, opening the passenger door for me. "But maybe the car will help with my cred."

"It doesn't hurt," I tell him, teasing. "But you look very nice, Rhys."

He's wearing a beautifully tailored jacket and dress pants, with a silky-smooth T-shirt underneath. Looking at it, I expect the shirt cost more than my entire outfit, including the heels, jewelry, bag, and maybe my violin, too.

It's not a suit and tie, but it's rockstar dressy, and I think I like it better that way. I like him better this way than I would in a designer suit. Because it's true to who he is.

The next hour is all last-minute preparations and fixes, from having Rhys turn on the sound system so it's ready for our volunteer engineer to tying a few ties for the performers whose moms never learned. At six o'clock, with everything in its assigned place, including our young performers seated backstage, awaiting their turns on stage, we open the doors. Everyone gets a program, and they file into the cafetorium, immediately wandering around to see the auction items on offer. They're chatty and enthusiastic — the best response I could hope for as an indication of the night to come. And now it's time to begin.

"**T**hank you, everyone, for coming out tonight to support the music program here at Mystic Elementary," I say into the microphone. "Your donations, your time, your enthusiasm for ensuring our children enjoy the benefits of music for their minds and their souls — it is all invaluable. So, now we're going to put a value on it..."

Laughter. Good.

"The first live auction of the night will come up right after our first performance, from our chorus all-stars."

The curtain opens behind me, and I turn to face the kids on their riser, with a special smile for Aria. From second through fourth grade, each of these kids has had me for a teacher for at least a year, and they'll have me as a teacher again this year. Each of them has shown both talent and enthusiasm for singing, and music in general, and they are my favorite students each year, if only because singing is a natural thing for kids. They can learn better technique, better performance skills, but even the littlest kids sing. OK — not Tommy, who I can see sitting against a wall off to the side of the room, with Mom. But Tommy hums. He has always hummed. He's inherently musical, like his parents. And it gives him a voice when words escape him. Music does that. For everyone.

And now my students give voice to what makes them sing.

CHAPTER 34
THE MAIN EVENT

Rhys

"Wow! Thank you all once again for your incredible support of the music program! As you may have noticed, I am not Mrs. Larson." Laughter amidst the murmuring of those who hadn't yet realized I was here. Laughter is good. And they're laughing *with* me, not *at* me, which is even better. That's not always how it works with me. "My name is Rhys Madigan—" whistles, applause, an "I love you, Rhys." It's amazing how much appreciation I get just for being me. Weird.

Yeah, you are. Get on with it!

"And you may know me as the drummer for the rock band aMUSEd." More applause, etc., etc.

Yeah, yeah, you're a rockstar. We get it.

I'm getting heckled from inside my own head. Not cool, head-dude. I'm trying to focus here!

"I've been lucky enough to have helped Mrs. Larson with pulling tonight's event together. She did nearly all of it single-handed, so she gets the credit. She worked incredibly hard to give you a great time tonight, and I think she's succeeded beyond all expectations! Am I right?"

That's better. Credit where credit is due.

And she gets it, because they applaud even louder and longer than they did for me just being Rhys Madigan.

"I'm up here for two reasons. The first is to remind you that our next live auction is for a Rhys Madigan signature drum kit in my signature Madman Red. I will happily put my literal real-life signature on the kit for the winning bidder, in thanks for your generous support. And don't forget the three silent auction packages from aMUSEd, including one with a band-signed drum head and VIP tickets, with backstage passes, to the winner's choice of dates on our next tour!" More murmuring, more applause. "The second reason I'm up here is so that our next performer doesn't have to introduce herself." Laughter. "It is my honor to introduce Mrs. Lyric Larson, performing a Tchaikovsky waltz on the violin."

I step back to the wings of the stage, watching Lyric breathe slowly as the curtain opens, the spotlight highlighting her blonde hair and the shine of the violin. The piano accompanist begins a slow intro and then the rhythm of the waltz. And then Lyric begins the smooth strokes of her bow across the strings, her fingers dancing, evoking the bright sounds of the song. The audience is instantly captivated, as am I. But then, I was already captivated by her.

It's not the same as her movements through her music room the other night, when she was playing "White Bird" so beautifully that I couldn't help but join her, but she sways in time to the beat, putting more than her arm and fingers into the music. She may have told old Galworth that this was a Disney-free performance, but in my head, I see her waltzing in the woods, wild animals gleefully gathering to listen. And then, just like her prince, I step in, becoming part of the dance, part of the music. There's no drum part to this song, so I shouldn't fit here, but I do. I fit wherever Lyric is, especially when there's music on the wind. I find myself swaying on my feet, matching her movements. My physical foot steps forward, ready to join her...

Not so fast there, buddy!

Saved by the head-dude. Whew. That was close. Another second, and I'd have been standing behind her, my hands on her waist, ready to lift her into my arms. And that would have been... not cool.

I've been jarred out of the trance she conjured with her music, but the audience remains spellbound, their eyes glued to her, their ears attentive. Lyric, for her part, has her eyes closed, immersed in the music, still swaying, as if the dance isn't limited just to her imagination but has to express itself in her limbs, in her very being.

She is the song made tangible, glowing from inside, full of passion for the music. This is the woman I've seen in my dreams so many times in the last year, the spirit of her lighting my way, pulling me to her, like she did that night we first met, captivated by *my* music. I was so drawn to her that it seemed like my spirit slipped free of my body, just to be near her. I have no idea how I kept a beat when I wasn't even in my head to control my limbs, but somehow I did. And it still sounded flibbertigibbeting amazing!

That was me, dude.

Wait. Head-dude? You drum?

If I didn't, you'd have flibbertigibbeted *up an aMUSEd song for the first time in your life. As it was, Alex still noticed something was different.*

Well, huh…

Head-dude — are you a fan? Only an aMUSEd fan could have pulled that off.

Me? No. Not really. I mean, you're good, but I prefer punk to hard rock. I knew someone who was, though.

Well, I guess I got lucky, then.

You did. Luckier than I think you'll ever realize.

Head-dude sounds almost sad. I wonder…

Applause pulls me back to the scene in front of me, as Lyric bows to an enthusiastic round of applause from the audience. I pull her up to the microphone with me, my arm around her, thanking her and thanking the audience. Cameras flash, as they have every time a performer was on stage. Parental paparazzi. Fresh off her own performance, she goes stiff for a moment, then relaxes into me. I'm reluctant to let her move away again, even to introduce the auctioneer for the auction of my donated kit.

Lyric

I'm still coming out of the headspace that I find myself in when I perform. Going there is like being transported to a magical land, where everything is bright and clear, and the only thing that matters is the music itself. It reminds me strongly of how I felt after talking to Rhys last night, like the world is full of possibilities.

The feeling of Rhys' arm around my shoulders grounds me back in reality, standing on the stage in front of a room full of people who are applauding, for me this time, and not just for the kids. It almost makes me miss performing regularly. Almost. I never really liked the spotlight. That was Adam's thing, the one thing he chased aside from me. But having my performance greeted so warmly, on the heels of the high from just playing the music... That I enjoy. I let myself relax into Rhys, if just for a moment.

Then it's time to introduce the auctioneer for the live auction of Rhys' signature drum kit. I expect it will be one of our top items tonight, and my rough calculations so far suggest we're close to reaching what we need to fund the new instruments. This could put us over our goal. By Monday, I could potentially be ordering them — and none too soon. It'll be close timing to get them in before the school year starts in two weeks.

I duck backstage to put my violin away and get the kids sorted out for the finale, which will combine the chorus and mini-orchestra for one last song, with a solo by my star former pupil. We've got fifteen minutes before they'll all be on stage, and I head back out into the cafetorium, waiting by the stage steps to watch the auction of Rhys' kit.

Rhys stands on the stage, next to the auctioneer, the stage curtain opened wide to show off the kit we assembled last week. I blush at the memory, but it doesn't bring the same kind of embarrassment and fear it did then. Donnie's said nothing to anyone about what he saw, at least as far as I can tell. If he had, Patty would have heard the rumor by now and interrogated me about the "cute" drummer, who even now is sitting down at the kit, tossing off a brief drum solo that drives the bidding even higher.

Unlike me, he lights up when he's on stage, feeding off the attention, the adulation, as well as the energy of the music, which he then feeds back to the audience. It's a symbiotic relationship. But it's something more. Brighid's talked about it before — how

Hunter lights up when he's on stage, how the audience responds to him and he to them — and it never struck me as unusual. But watching Rhys now — now that I know him as a person, not just a distant rockstar on a stage or a poster — I realize what she meant. Seeing them on stage like this, even on this tiny scale, it's seeing the person you know and love come into their true glory, fulfilled in their destiny, their gift. It's like they channel the divine and become something more. Still themselves, but more. And it makes you love them even more.

Oh, gods... What did I just say?

Is it possible? Can I have already fallen in love with Rhys? That fast?

The auctioneer shouts, "Sold!" It brings me back to my duties as host of this event, everything else pushed aside for the moment. I confirm the amount of the winning bid and approach the microphone to make an announcement. Rhys slides in behind me, his arm going around my shoulders once again.

"Everyone — I have an announcement to make!" The room goes quiet, all eyes on me, and on Rhys behind me. "With the winning bid on the Rhys Madigan signature drum kit, we have officially reached our fundraising goal! We will be getting new instruments for the students for this school year!"

Applause consumes the entire room. Rhys leans down and kisses my hair. The world goes silent to my ears, and I'm half-blinded under the spotlight and the camera flashes. I can't tell if they're all excited about the fundraiser's success or speculating as to why the rockstar is kissing the music teacher.

"We'll be back with our final performance of the evening in ten minutes! Please make your final bids on the silent auctions. We'll be announcing those winners in just five minutes! Five minutes to go on the silent auctions! Get your bids in now!"

I duck out from under Rhys' arm and head out into the crowd, still deafened by the murmuring around me.

"Lyric! Wait up!" he calls from behind me. When he catches up, he puts his hand on my back, like he did last night on our date. I react instinctively to his touch, my body and mind relaxing, absorbing that feeling of being protected. My hearing slowly returns to normal. And for the next five minutes, we circulate among the attendees, accepting praise, thanks for our hard work and no few selfie requests for Rhys. Then, it's the announcement of the silent auction winners, with the auctioneer, thankfully, handling the issue of payment for those and the live auctions so I don't have to worry about it.

Rhys, it turns out, had the winning bid on Marian's basket of instruments. He immediately donates them back to the music department. I'll have to find a way to incorporate them in my lesson plan.

The finale performance is almost an anti-climax. The kids perform as beautifully as they did in rehearsal, and with final thanks to everyone involved, it's all over. Months of work. So much stress. And the unasked-for blessing of having Rhys Madigan show up to make my life easier. Has he? No question. It's also more complicated, and now, as he walks on stage to hand me a huge bouquet of red roses, more subject to speculation as to exactly how close musician and music teacher have become.

That's not a question I can answer. Yet. But I have two weeks to find out before I'm once again immersed in the routines of school and mom-life.

CHAPTER 35

BECAUSE THE NIGHT

Lyric

"**I**'m going to take the kids back to the loft with me," Mom tells me as people start filing out of the cafetorium. "I packed them both bags, and Aria will sleep on the sofa and Tommy can share the bed with me," she says.

"No! That's not necessary, Mom — I told you."

"Are you sure?"

"Very," I tell her, still overwhelmed with the added attention brought by Rhys' intimate gestures tonight, in the full view of what has to have been half the town.

"Fine," she says. "But I'm going to take them back home and bring my overnight bag in, because if you're not going to use your bed tonight for something *other than* sleeping, *I'm* going to use it for sleeping. It's more comfortable than Callie's. So, if you do decide to come home tonight, you're the one who's sleeping on the sofa," she says. I frown at her. Leave it to Iris. "Say goodnight to Mommy, you two. You're headed off to bed." I get in some hugs and kisses as the room starts to empty. "Don't come home," she urges before she steers my kids out through the masses.

"What was that about?" Rhys asks as I find the two of us standing alone for the first time since we got here.

"Nothing. Just Mom being Mom."

"They do that."

"Yeah."

"Did you get enough to eat?" he asks, nodding at the catering tables, the contents of which the caterer is starting to pack back up.

"Definitely. You?"

"Yeah. Callie gave you a good recommendation. Those little crab puffs? I think I had about thirty of those alone."

I chuckle, because I know he's probably not exaggerating. He's a big guy with a high metabolism. He probably burned them off during that brief drum solo.

"So... what else is left to do?"

I look around us. The auction items are all gone — even the second drum kit, which the winner had Rhys sign right after he handed me those roses, which are back in my classroom, along with my purse. The auctioneer will call me Monday with a final total. The caterer is in charge of cleaning up the food, the custodial staff will clear out the tables and remove the decorations. All that's left is the stage setup. The sound system is already off, and there's no reason to clear the stage right now. That can all be done a few days before school starts. I'm officially on vacation.

"Nothing. That's it. I just need to get my bag and violin, and then we can leave."

"Cool!"

Rhys follows me back to my classroom. I grab my bag out of my desk drawer and slide the strap over my shoulder. And find myself pressed up against the wall behind my desk.

"Did I tell you how gorgeous you look tonight?" Rhys asks, his lips just inches from mine.

I nod, having apparently lost the ability to speak the moment my back touched the wall.

"I undersold it," he says. "You're a goddess."

I giggle. Totally inappropriately.

"Occasionally," I tell him.

"What?" he asks, confused.

"Inside priestess joke," I explain vaguely, laughing at the double meaning even in that explanation. "I'll explain it another time."

"That works. But I had something else I wanted to ask you. Two things."

"Alright?"

"First, will you come back to the studio with me tonight?" My heart flutters again. It's the expected surprise. He's not taking me home to ravish me. He wants to bring me home with him. And part of me, at least, wants to go. "And, second, do you really make the trees blow angry?"

Whoa. This is not the time or place for either of these topics.

"Let me text Mom, and then I'll come with you to the studio. We can talk about all of this there."

"Really? You're coming with me?"

"Yes, Rhys. I'll come with you."

"Sounds like a plan, then."

Rhys

Lyric looks really uncomfortable texting her mom. I guess it comes down to basically telling Iris that we're planning to have sex tonight. I'd probably feel a little uncomfortable telling my mom that I was planning to have sex tonight. So, I get it. I guess that's one of the things you deal with when you have kids. Gotta tell the sitter if you're not coming home on time. Or until morning.

Head-dude is curiously quiet. Like dead silent. It's weird. I guess I've gotten used to sharing my brain with him. He's been a big help where Lyric is concerned. A decent wingman. A solid friend, really. I kind of wish he was an actual real person, instead of my second personality or whatever. I mean, the dude even plays drums well enough to mostly pass for me. Mostly. We'd have a blast hanging out. I wonder if he's ever been rock-climbing...

Lyric picks up her flowers, which I'd left with Iris earlier in the day so I could surprise her. It worked! She was surprised! She offers me her hand, and we walk back through the school to my car. No words. Just walking and holding hands. And my brain... for once my brain is almost as silent as we are. I've got questions, but they'll wait.

We drive back to the studio, still holding hands. I like this hand-holding thing. It's not something I've done before, but I like touching Lyric. I like the feel of her skin under my fingers. I like the reassuring warmth of her hand in mine. Yeah.

I let go long enough for us both to get out of the car, then it's right back to holding hands as we walk up the wide front stairs above the studio entrance.

She glances at me when I pull out the keys to open the door. Nervous or excited? I can't tell.

"I think I've used these keys twice," I tell her. "At first, one of the guys was always here, unless we were all going out together. Then, one by one, they started moving out. Then our producer, Malcolm, was here for a while, but he's back in D.C. this week. So, it's just me, Kier and Alex, and Kier and Alex said if I had plans tonight, they were going out for a drink. Which is good. Because I think they both need one. They're not acting like themselves these days."

"How so?" she asks as I finally get the lock open and show her through the door. The living room light is the only one on, so it's dark and quiet for a change. I gave her a brief tour the other day, when she and the kids were here. I didn't take her upstairs, though, and tonight that's where we're going.

"Kier's kind of down, I guess. He gave me a lecture about believing in magical stuff like mermaids."

"Did you tell him about the storm?"

"No. I want to ask you first."

"I appreciate that. What about Alex?"

"I dunno. He's written two songs, which is more than he usually writes for an album, but they're both... Kind of angsty, I guess? But he's been a little snappy and also a little too... interested, I guess? Invested, maybe?" I shrug. "In our love-lives. Not in general. And not his. Because I haven't seen him with a girl in months. Hey — maybe that's it! Maybe he needs to get laid!"

She laughs quietly, like she doesn't want to do it out loud.

"The house is empty — you can be as loud as you want," I tell her.

Her eyes go big.

Oh!

"I meant you can laugh as loud as you want. But, yeah, you could be loud in other ways, too."

She chuckles.

"Things do go over your head sometimes, don't they?" she says. It might be an insult, but the way she's looking at me is full of affection. If she's insulting me, she can keep doing it, as long as she looks at me like this.

"What'd I miss this time?"

"You said Alex needs to get laid, right as you're getting ready to lead me upstairs..."

Oh. See! This is the kind of stuff I miss. Not all the time. But sometimes.

"It's unrelated in my brain, because Alex's life is Alex's life, and you and me..."

She looks at me, tilting her head, like she's trying to figure out what I mean. I mean, I know what I mean, but maybe I should say it.

"You and me, together we're..."

"Special," we both say at once.

And then I can't take it anymore, I pull her against me, hard, and I kiss her just as hard. Just the one kiss. But it's firm and tangible, and it makes me want more.

"Come upstairs."

"OK," she says.

Hand-in-hand we head upstairs. With Alex and Kier both having their bedrooms downstairs since we got here, I'm the last one left upstairs. So I've taken over the best room on this floor, with its doors out onto the upper deck, the view out over the dune and then to the ocean. I try to forget that Declan was chained up to this bed, naked. But the bedding's from the room I was in before, so no Declan parts ever touched these sheets.

I open the bedroom door, and Lyric walks straight to the sliding-glass doors. It's a full moon tonight, and the moon is glowing over the ocean. She opens the doors, and the cool evening breeze off the ocean comes right in, rippling through the sheer curtains, which flow around her. She's like a vision, or something. A painting of a perfect moonlit night, with the romantic heroine alluring, striking in a way that goes beyond physical beauty. And she is.

I walk up close behind her, pulling at the pins that secure her hair, freeing it to fall to her shoulders and beyond, where the breeze ruffles through it. As pretty as she was tonight, all made up, it was her inner glow that made me call her a goddess. I think she's her prettiest in her everyday look, even with her hair rumpled from sleep and her luscious ass hanging out below her shirt.

She finally turns around to face me. Her blue irises are so big, the blue so deep that I feel like they could swallow me, and I'd go willingly, eagerly, if they did.

"You look like a dream, standing there in the moonlight like that," I tell her, sitting down on the bed.

"I'm not a dream, Rhys. I'm real." She picks up my hand and pulls it to her cheek. "See?"

Lyric

"I feel like I've got to be asleep in my bunk on the bus, dreaming dreams of this incredible woman who makes me feel things I've never felt before," he says, stepping back and sitting down on the bed. "And any minute I'm going to wake up, and she'll be gone again."

It's strange, to see Rhys so suddenly uncertain of himself. He's always so carefree and in the present. Usually, it's *me* caught up in worry about things changing, about the ground shifting under my feet.

I sit down next to him, looking at the wall behind us.

"You don't trust the dreamcatcher?" I ask him.

"What? Well, yeah, I do. It's the real thing, after all."

"And if I was a dream, what would happen?"

"If you were a bad dream, you'd get caught in the web and disappear when the sunlight hits it in the morning."

"Right. But if I was a bad dream, you wouldn't be worried about me disappearing, right?"

"No — if you're a dream, you're definitely a good one," he says, smiling. He reaches for my face and rubs his fingers along my cheek.

"And that means I can come straight through the web, to you." I press a kiss into his palm. "I'm not going anywhere, Rhys. You asked me to come, and I'm here now. I'm not a dream. You've got a real girl sitting right next to you. In your bed."

"Oh. Right." He looks around us, taking in the room, and after his talk about his bunk, I have to wonder if he's even used to having a girl in his actual bed. But I'm here, using that newfound freedom of mine. And this is where I want to be. In Rhys Madigan's bed. Wow.

"Is that what you wanted when you asked me to come back with you tonight? Or did you just want to talk?" I ask him, teasing a little, hoping it'll get him out of his head.

"No, I definitely hoped..."

Fine. Rhys requires a direct approach, apparently.

"Kiss me."

"My pleasure."

He closes the distance between us in an instant, grabbing my face between his hands, stroking my cheeks with his thumbs. And then... It's like lightning, but good lightning, like we're fused together at the lips — delightful, happy energy spreading out from there to the rest of my body. And I want more of it.

But he pulls back, looking at me carefully.

"I don't want to rush you. We haven't known each other very long. We said we'd start as friends. And you're just now getting over..."

"Rhys..."

"Yeah."

"I wouldn't be here, in your bedroom, if I didn't want this thing between us to move forward exactly as it is."

"Oh."

"Are you normally this hesitant with women?"

"No. Not at all. Before... Before, I used to pick up girls in minutes, and we'd be back in my bunk minutes after that."

"Groupies?"

"Waitresses, mostly. But yeah."

I laugh.

"Waitresses?"

He shrugs.

"Less likely they'd want to be with me just because I'm in a band. And even if they did, they weren't around just because they were looking to hook up with me or one of the other guys."

"So, still casual, but deeper, without ulterior motives."

"Exactly! I know that makes me seem a little slutty... I would understand..."

"Rhys, you're a grown man. As long as everyone involved was consenting and played safely, I'm not going to condemn you for enjoying yourself."

"Oh, definitely consensual and safe. We get tested every month, just in case. But condoms are the rule, and I never had a girl in my bunk who didn't really want to be there."

"You still don't."

"Oh. OK."

"You're still a little awkward..."

"Yeah."

"Why?"

"Because you're not a waitress and this isn't a bunk on a tour bus. You mean something to me that isn't just about getting off. That's why I've been waiting..."

"For someone who meant something to you?"

"Well, yeah, and I knew it would be you the first time I saw you. You're my dream-girl."

Oh, my gods. Even with all this talk about me being a dream, I never even asked him about that half-asleep comment he made the other night, about his dream-girl. And now he says she's me? I don't think I was even Adam's dream-girl. That's like someone you'd dream up, the perfect person, unattainable. Who you end up with, if you're lucky, is a close approximation. But then how many times did I daydream about kissing Rhys Madigan? In a lot of ways, he's my dream-guy. And this... this thing between us feels so meant, fated. Maybe that's how it was always supposed to be.

"That may be the nicest thing anyone has ever said to me," I tell him. "I used to wonder what it would be like to kiss you, be kissed by you, have you make love to me. So, this is kind of a dream come true for me, too. And now *I'm* having a hard time believing it's even real."

He kisses me again, hard, pressing his lips into mine.

"Does that feel real?"

"Definitely," I say, though, honestly, I'm a little dazed.

"How about this?"

He reaches behind my neck and angles my head to the side, licking up the side of my neck.

"Very real," I reply, my breath halting.

"And this?"

His hand trails up my thigh, bringing my dress with it.

"Super, amazingly real," I say after a second.

"Do you have those little white panties on right now?"

I stop breathing. He was looking. But he wasn't thinking about how embarrassing it was. He was thinking how much he wanted to see me in just my panties again. And not the red satin string bikini ones, either.

"They're light blue, to match the dress."

"Perfect. But you won't be matching in a minute."

"What?" I ask confused.

"Because I'm stripping you out of that dress after I kiss you again."

"All of a sudden you seem much more..."

"Focused?"

"Yeah."

"You said I'm your dream-guy. That makes this mutual. An even playing field."

"It wasn't before?"

"Not quite. Now it is. Makes me feel like I'm on solid ground again, even if it still feels like a dream. Dream ground, I guess."

"Oh. That sounds nice, actually."

"So I can kiss you again?"

"Definitely."

His hand goes behind my neck, his lips to mine. He lays me back on the bed, and I reach into his hair, pulling him against me. He nuzzles at the corner of my mouth, licking, tasting, nudging my lips open, and I open up for him to explore. It's a night for exploration. This is an adventure, after all. And now we're both taking it together.

CHAPTER 36

SKIN

Rhys

God, she tastes so good. I already love the feel of her skin under my fingers. Who could have thought she'd taste even better?

It took me too long to get out of my head and remember how sex is supposed to work. But she's so understanding. And she said the best thing she ever could have: That I'm her dream-guy. Has she been dreaming about me, too? Maybe even since she was younger and my picture was on her wall?

Doesn't matter. I've been waiting for this for months, even before I knew she was Lyric and that Lyric was real. And I want to take my time, for once. This is the night that changes everything. No quickie with a waitress, no groupie just there to do the deed and leave, never to be seen again. I'm going to make love to this woman, like she deserves, like maybe I deserve to experience at the ripe old age of 32.

I told her I'd kiss her again, and then I'd strip her out of her dress, down to her pretty little panties. But I don't want this kiss to end, not yet.

I caress her tongue with mine, and she returns the touch. Another lick, another caress. I angle her head, deepening the kiss. She's breathing hard, fast. She's enjoying this, being kissed, kissing me, exploring me.

I've kissed tons of girls. Too many to keep track of. But never has one of them explored me — not just my body, but all of me. Lyric wants to know me, and the more she knows me, the more she seems to like me. I want her to know all of me, and I want to know all of her. It's a lot easier without all that weight dragging her down. She's more open, freer now. She opened herself up to me, and I want to dive inside her and enjoy every tiny sensation, revel in her, just like my tongue is her mouth. Can we survive like this forever? Maybe stop time and just be together like this, Lyric and me, our mouths entwined, our souls finding each other in that dream space?

She moans under me, and that's it. I can't wait any longer.

"Up. That dress is coming off."

She sits up slowly, seeming just a little dazed. Good. She leaves me dazed, too.

I move behind her on the bed, running my hands over her shoulders, my thumbs pressing into the muscles of her neck.

"Oh, gods, that feels good..."

She's lived with so much stress for so long. It's no wonder her muscles are tight like this. I let her enjoy the sensation as they begin to loosen under my touch.

"You're really, really good at that. Maybe you should work as a massage therapist." She chuckles and then moans.

"You learn a few things when you do sports that leave odd spots sore and tight," I tell her. "But I only want my hands making one person feel good. This is just for you, Lyric. Only for you."

As soon as she's nice and mellow, I find the zipper on the back of her dress and slide it slowly down, until it reaches that spot on her back where my hand naturally finds itself when we walk together. Then I slide the sleeves forward, down her arms. I pull her arms free, running my fingers back up, across her shoulders, to her neck. And then I turn her head sideways, just far enough to reach her mouth for another kiss.

"Up, Lyric. Stand up for me."

She stands and turns, letting the dress fall to her feet.

There she is, in just her bra and those sweet little panties.

My mouth waters, wanting to taste her skin again.

She slides one bra strap down, then the other. More than I'd been prepared to ask her for. Then she reaches behind and unhooks it, letting it drop to the floor with her dress.

An expected surprise!

And is it glorious...

I called her a goddess, and I meant it. She's the model for any goddess I'd want to worship, full of gentle curves and soft planes, her long hair trying — and failing — to cover the most perfect pair of breasts...

I move to the edge of the bed and pull her close, burying my face in her cleavage. I reach out with my tongue and lick along the inside of one breast, up to her collarbone. She shivers. I look into her eyes to make sure it's me and not that she's getting cold. No, her eyes are blazing with heat. I pull her mouth to mine, savoring that taste again. She whimpers.

I lean back. Her nipples have tightened, hardening into sharp points. I run my fingers over them.

"Not cold, are you?"

The breeze still flows in from the ocean through the open door.

"N-no," she says. It could be her teeth chattering, but we both know it's not.

"You like that? Like me touching your breasts, your nipples?"

"Yes, very much. It feels good."

"Good. I'm going to make it feel better."

I pull one nipple into my mouth, sucking softly on it. The other I caress with my thumb, making it harder, more erect, matching the one between my lips.

"Oh, gods."

I could get used to that, hearing that sweet little voice moan, calling her gods in thanks for what I'm doing to her, how I'm making her feel.

That she's here, that we're here together, it's got to be something they've set in motion. Because what other explanation could there be?

I pull her against my mouth, my hand caressing that little hollow above her butt. She wiggles against me, visibly enjoying what I'm doing to her.

I lean back, pulling on her nipple with mouth and fingers until she's mewling with need. And then I lean down, running my lips along the front of those little blue cotton panties. Fuck the red ones, the satin. These... they smell like her, and the scent alone makes me hard. She grabs hold of the back of my head, her fingers tangling in my hair, pressing my mouth harder against the pale blue cotton.

It's time.

I open my mouth and run my tongue up the center of her, wetting her panties with my tongue, just as she's making them damp on the inside. I find the seam between her lower lips, pressing my tongue into it, diving between them, licking.

She moans.

Even through the fabric, I know I've found the center of her pleasure, a feeling she reinforces when she pulls my mouth even harder against her. She's seeking the sensations I'm giving her, the touch of my mouth, my tongue, my lips.

I reach for her hips, finding the edges of the cloth where they meet her soft, silky skin. She wiggles against me as I caress the skin there, savoring the feel of it.

"I know..." she starts.

I sit up and look at her, encouraging her to say what she's thinking.

"I know you're probably used to..."

"What?"

"I've had two kids!" she finally says. "Natural childbirth with Tommy. A C-section with Aria. I've got lumps and bumps, scars and... and stretch marks. All over."

"Like this one here?" I ask her, running my finger along one little river in the landscape of her as it curves across her hip.

"Yes."

"And this one?"

I touch my tongue to a spot on the other side, following the geography of her body like the holds in a rock face. It's a beauty I've always appreciated when I'm climbing — the dimples and crevices, the spots where the movement of water and earth have shaped the stone.

She quivers, her hands again going to the back of my head, though this time she lets me decide my own path. It takes me across her belly, rippled with little crests and valleys, accented in the center with the deeper depression of her bellybutton. I nip at the rise beneath it, causing her to jump. That distracts her, and I seize the moment, sliding my hands out across her hips again, sliding the sides of her panties down.

I don't get far with that before she's panting, my mouth still pressed to her belly. I push the panties lower and lower, until they finally fall away. I don't look at her pussy yet. That's yet to come. But I have an idea where...

There. Just below the curve of her belly, just above the top of her mound, nestled in a little crease between the two. I press my lips there, and then I turn my head to lick across the old wound.

It's a small scar, all things considered. I have no idea how you fit even a tiny baby through an incision that small. It's a miracle, really. Just like giving birth to a kid the other way. And Lyric has done it twice. Yes, a goddess incarnate.

I press a second kiss to the scar, and Lyric gives a deep exhale, tension dropping away from her. That was all the reassurance she needed to know I find her beautiful. I'm glad I could give it to her. Years of being with one man, years alone, her body reshaped by carrying two children, of course she's not a flat plain of female geography. But she's a glorious one, and one I want to get to know as well as the surfaces of my favorite climbs. Better. I want to know Lyric deep below the surface. Starting now.

Lyric

Oh, gods... Rhys Madigan just kissed my C-section scar.

Here I am feeling insecure about the stretch marks, the muffin-top, the bulges and bumps I didn't have when I met Adam, and rockstar Rhys Madigan — with his countless waitresses to help him get off — is caressing my scar with his tongue.

Goddess bless... I mean, as a goddess, Brighid has a close association with childbirth, but that didn't spare me the C-section with Aria. Sometimes you still need modern medicine, even if the surgery is ancient. But it's one scar I'm sure the majority of Rhys' partners haven't had.

And now I'm standing here, totally naked, in front of him, just the moonlight from the beachfront lighting the room. Maybe it's better that way, but Rhys acts like he doesn't even care. No — like he *treasures* me, scars and all.

And Rhys... Rhys is still wearing everything but the jacket and shoes he had on earlier tonight.

"You're still dressed."

"I am," he agrees amicably.

"I'm not."

"Thank every god in the universe for that." His smile is lascivious, but with an undercurrent of Rhys' characteristic humor.

I chuckle. It doesn't seem to matter what we're doing. Rhys finds a way to make me laugh, usually when I need it most.

I pull him back up to me, winding my arms around his neck and kissing him softly on the lips. He puts his hands on my waist, kissing me back sweetly.

"Clothes off," I tell him, picturing the leisurely strip tease I did for him.

But this is Rhys.

He jumps up to his feet, standing in the middle of the bed, his hair brushing the ceiling above him. He strips off that soft T-shirt in an instant, then undoes his belt, then his pants, dropping them to the bed.

I crack up.

The boxers of the day are music-themed, covered with anthropomorphic instruments, like saxophones playing themselves, and music notes disco-dancing. Perfect for the fundraiser, and, frankly, perfect for us, for this moment.

"You don't like them?" he asks, looking frustrated.

"I *love* them! They're perfect! So perfect I couldn't help but laugh."

"Good! Because having a girl laugh when she's standing directly in front of your crotch is usually not a good thing." He kicks his pants off the bed, in the general direction he threw the shirt before. "Now, get your naked ass up here, woman!"

"You've still got some clothes on," I remind him, since he's pointed out how naked my ass (and the rest of me) is.

"You want to do the honors?" he asks, beaming at me. "*Come on* — you only get one first time..."

I take my cue from him, and just pull them straight down in one move.

OK. The size thing — it's true. At least where Rhys is concerned. I find myself glad I had Tommy the natural way. But I had a few boyfriends before Adam, so I know it's not about size. Shape, technique, passion, how well partners read each other. But right now there's a very large penis directly in front of my face, and I'm a little intimidated. I haven't touched one in years. I'm out of practice.

Rhys drops to his knees, grabbing my chin and looking into my eyes.

"You OK, Lyric? Second thoughts?"

I take a deep breath, let it out again.

"No. It's just been a while."

"And you were with one man for a long time," he says, the sympathy pouring off of him.

I nod.

"So, we'll go slow. No — we'll go at your pace. Bring that naked ass up here."

I climb onto the bed with him. He flicks one of my nipples with his thumb. It tightens back up in an instant. OK. Maybe slow isn't my pace. It never was before.

Rhys smiles at me, sexy and mischievous all rolled into one.

"First things, first," he says. "Lie down."

I do as he says, keeping my eyes locked with his as he observes me from above. There's a hunger to him now, and I remember what he said about enjoying the sensual aspect of eating. I wonder...

He dips down and captures my mouth with his, again tasting, mouthing, licking. As soon as he's kissed me breathless, he moves downward, kissing, licking across my neck, my chest, my breasts, my belly. He moves down to the end of the bed and gently pulls my legs apart, then presses my feet upward, until my legs are bent. There's no hiding any bump, or even my arousal, from him now. He moves up slightly and pulls my legs over his shoulders, settling his face directly above my mound.

"I've been looking forward to this longer than you'll ever know," he says cryptically.

I don't get a chance to analyze his words, because his mouth is on me, kissing me between those lower lips, licking up between them. He hums, eyes closing in pleasure, and mine follow his lead there, too. He eats me with the same enthusiasm he did that burger the first day we spent together. The steaming sensuality of him that always radiated from beneath the surface is on full display. If this is what being eaten by a tiger is like, then I now know how I want to go.

He uses his fingers, his tongue, his lips, and brings me slowly to a peak, slowing down just as I'm about to topple over, and then he starts all over again. His face is coated with me, his fingers slick where they play with my G-spot.

"Please!" I beg him.

His smile as he looks up at me, his lips glistening, is carnivorous. His eyes glow with the same feral hunger. And he puts his mouth around me, working me with lips and tongue, taking me past the prior peaks, up and up, until I'm not sure how I can rise any higher. A touch inside me, another, a third, setting up a rhythm only Rhys could devise, and higher I go, until I'm hanging in mid-air and he pushes me right over the edge.

"Goddess bless!" I yell, convulsing around Rhys' shoulders and head as he licks me through the orgasm and through the ride down what feels like the world's tallest elevator, if it was equipped with a vibrator. When my sensory feet finally land back on solid ground, Rhys looks up at me, still coated in me, his face a study in delight.

I lie there, panting, while he watches me.

"Where the Hel did you learn how to do that?" I ask.

"I didn't. That's the first time I've had time to play like that, and I was just enjoying myself."

Oh, Holy Mother Goddess Brighid... What have you gotten me into?

CHAPTER 37
SAOR–FREE

Rhys

I give Lyric a few minutes to recover. Then I move up next to her, lying on my side, running my fingers along breasts, her hips, her thighs. I could spend a lifetime exploring her like this, bringing her pleasure, making her feel good, physically and emotionally, pampering her with massages and reassuring words. But, for now, we've only got tonight, and...

God, I want her. My cock's already poking her hip. If she can't feel it, I'd be surprised.

But I don't want to wear her out. If she needs a break, needs to sleep until morning, I'll let her. I'll be walking around with a baseball bat in my pants all day, but I'll let her.

"If you keep doing that, Rhys, you're going to find out what a hungry *female* tiger looks like."

"What?"

"You ate me like you were a starving tiger."

"Is that good?"

She gives me a look. That's a yes.

She leans up to kiss me, and I lean down to meet her. She kisses me slowly, like she's savoring it. And then her hand glances across my cock. No. Not glances. She's stroking me, making me harder. I wrap my hand over hers, showing her how I like to be touched. It's like the other day, when we played "White Bird" together, working together, in time, the rhythm carrying us both, like a wave... rising on the crest...

I pull her hand away, looking into those stormy-sky eyes of hers.

"I want to make love to you, Lyric. Not just a handjob. I want to be inside you, for us to be inside each other, body and soul."

"I want that, too, Rhys," she says, caressing my cheek.

I lean down and kiss her again. Soft and slow at first, then deeper, harder, faster, our tongues thrusting at each other, mirroring what's to come. I reach down between her folds, teasing her, teasing myself with how wet she is.

"Give me a sec," I tell her, going for my wallet and the condom I stashed in there, just in case. I've got more, but they're farther away, and I don't want to leave her side any longer than I have to. Something about that strikes me, but my dick's too hard to think straight.

Man, she's sexy when she comes.

I climb back into bed with her, give her another kiss and start to unwrap the condom.

"Rhys?" she says.

"I've almost got it."

I free the condom from the wrapper and raise it up to show her. She looks like she wants to say something.

"Second thoughts?" I ask her, a little worried.

"No! No second thoughts. Never," she says. "Seersha."

I cock my head at her.

"Freedom," she says. "It means 'freedom.' And I feel like a weight's been lifted off of me."

She looks like it, too.

"Good. That's what I wanted for you..."

"You're good for me."

I can't keep the smile from my face.

"You have no idea how much I wanted to hear that. And I want to hear it again when I'm done."

I roll the condom on and settle between her legs.

She sighs, but I can see the anticipation in her eyes. I fit myself to her entrance and push gently forward, savoring the feeling as I'm slowly sheathed within her. And that's what it feels like — a perfect fit, like she was made for me.

I close my eyes and take a deep breath, praying for the control I don't always have. I exhale slowly.

"OK?" I ask her.

She nods, her breath catching as my cock twitches inside her.

I lean into her again, pressing my lips to hers, and start moving — slow, at first, then speeding up gradually, building the rhythm like the intro to a song. Her arms wrap around my back, caressing the muscles, sliding over skin, grasping for hold as our movements join us together. Her thighs spread to wrap around my hips, her calves locking around my thighs, pulling me harder into her with each thrust.

I resist the urge to close my eyes and focus on my movement, instead allowing those blue irises of hers to capture me again. Our gazes locked together, just as our bodies are, the room drops away around me. It's just me and Lyric, body and soul, making love just like I wanted — like I never dared dream in all these months of dreaming about touching her, holding her, spending time with her. It all culminates here and now.

A quiet mewling escapes her throat, and I can feel her tense around me. She's getting close. Without me even touching her with my fingers, she's close. Did I mention how perfect she is for me? I pick up my pace, pressing harder inside her, hoping the friction between us will carry her over the edge like it nearly has with me. The sound gets louder, a bright keening between gasps for breath as the sensation carries her closer to the edge. I keep her eyes locked with mine, waiting for it... there... that tingle... A whimper, and she clamps down on me suddenly, her limbs wrapping tightly around me, her pussy grasping my cock, and I roar my own release, as she gasps again with each final out-of-control thrust.

I lose the battle with keeping my eyes open, allowing my lids to shut and collapsing onto my elbows over her, my hips pressed so hard against her that I worry she'll bruise. A few panting breaths later, and I open my eyes to look at her again.

Wow, she's gorgeous. Sated, content, a sheen of moisture across her skin that I want to lap away and consume. Maybe her tiger analogy isn't far-fetched.

"Let me take care of this," I tell her, withdrawing to dispose of the condom. When I return, she's pulled down the sheets and slid underneath, her body a symphony in curves and shadows under the linens, and I slide underneath with her, enjoying the ocean breeze blowing in off the porch as I take her into my arms. I press a kiss to her head, and she smiles.

"How do you feel?" I ask, wondering as much about her emotional state in this moment as about how I made her body feel.

She looks up at me and smiles again.
"Good. Really good," she says. "And..."
"What?"
"Free," she adds, snuggling into me.

CHAPTER 38
SEVEN WONDERS

Rhys
A few hours later

Normally, when I'm lying in bed — just lying there, not having sex or anything — I'm still drumming. Feet and hands moving one minute, unconscious the next. This is like the second time ever that I can remember just lying in bed, my mind quiet and my limbs with it. The first was when I consoled Lyric in her bed the other night. The second is, now, in my bed, after spending hours making love to her for the first time. Making love to *anyone* for the first time.

So much of what Hunt, Dave and Declan have been doing in the last few months suddenly makes sense. Even the crazy stupid stuff. What wouldn't you do to feel like this all the time?

Lyric idly strokes her thumb across my hand, which rests on the comforter, her naked hip below. Our other hands are latched together, fingers entwined, my hand atop hers, over the covers, over her belly. The sheet loosely covers her breasts, the natural curves of her mingling with the haphazard folds of the thin fabric. I lean over and kiss her bare shoulder. She smiles but keeps her eyes on our hands, seeming reflective.

"You wanted to know about the 'trees blowing angry,'" she says.

And I do. I want to know everything about Lyric.

"Aria said that it was you making the trees 'blow angry.'"

"I figured it was Aria," she says, sighing. "We've talked about it before. I wasn't sure she didn't inherit it, so I wanted to make sure she understood. But she isn't supposed to talk to anyone else about that stuff."

"She doesn't think of me as just 'anyone.'"

"No, she doesn't," she agrees. "Not anymore, if she ever did." I can't tell if she's good with that or not.

"So, it *was* you — the wind, the trees, the storm?"

"Not me alone. But, yes, it was me."

She looks up at me, like she's gauging my reaction to what she's about to say.

"You saw how upset I was when I got home that night."

"Angry and then sad... bereft."

"That's a good word. Poetic." She looks up at me. "You're not bad with words yourself, you know, for all that I'm the poet and you don't write songs."

"I *do* write songs. They're just usually drum solos, though, and the guys won't let me just record a drum solo for the albums."

"That's sad. And a waste. I'd bet your drum solos are incredible. I'd enjoy hearing them."

"Then I'll play one for you sometime."

She nods, thoughtful.

"When I was a kid, Mom realized that the weather seemed, at times, to be influenced by my emotions. Snowstorms when I didn't want to go to school. Winds when other kids were teasing me. Lightning when I got angry. Rain when I was sad," she sighs. "It doesn't usually happen on its own. Anytime a weather front is moving through, there's always a tipping point where it can go from mild to extreme, or shift in one direction or another. And, apparently, I am such a tipping point." She looks for my reaction, and then looks away and out the glass door toward the ocean when I don't give her one. I want to hear her whole story first.

Lyric

One of the first baby-witch things Mom taught me had to do with the weather, and with poetry, really. So it makes sense that one of the first things I teach Rhys about my witchy self is this...

"Rain, rain, go away. Come again another day," I sing-songed on a stormy late autumn day when I was barely older than Aria.

"Do you know why you always tell the rain to come back another day?" Mom asked.

"Because it rhymes?" Even then, I thought about the world in the context of poetry.

Mom shook her head sharply at me, frowning slightly.

"It's a spell, Lyric. It sends the rain away — but not forever. Just for a day or two. Put enough energy behind it, and it will shift a raincloud, push a storm off the coast. Put too much behind it, it'll twist itself into a tornado, or a hurricane. Forget to tell the rain to come back another day, and it could become a drought."

I imagine the look on my face was pretty blank.

"In a drought, the plants die because there's not enough water, witchling," she says. "The cows go hungry because the grain withers in the fields. The fish in the pond fight each other for space and oxygen so they can breathe."

"Oh."

"Yeah. 'Oh.' So, what do we do?"

"Tell the rain to come back another day."

"Yes. But, better yet, we don't mess with the weather in the first place. The only time you mess with the weather is when people are in danger. Because weather magic gets out of control very easily. And an inexperienced witch is the last person you want wishing the rain away. OK?"

"OK."

"You're telling me that kids' rhyme is a spell?" Rhys asks after I tell him the story.

"Maybe not when it was first written. But it was called a 'charm' soon after, and it works — lot of witches and Pagans have used it. It's pretty harmless."

"Because it releases the spell."

"Yeah. But not even Mom knew then just how tightly the weather and I were linked. We found out soon thereafter, when I didn't finish my science project on time and was desperate to miss school one day in December, rather than get in trouble with the teacher. And it snowed. It doesn't snow often in coastal

Delaware. A foot of snow? Really rare. We saw my 'gift' in action again when some boys on the beach were teasing me and the wind whipped up, blasting everyone on the beach with sand."

"They shouldn't have been teasing you."

"Well, boys do that. Especially to pudgy little girls on the beach."

"I wouldn't have teased you. Mom taught me better than that. And, besides, I like your curves."

I blush, and there's no question Rhys can see it, because it creeps across my chest, too, and his eyes follow it.

"Finish the story, because you're already distracting me," he says, licking his lips. That's districting enough I almost forget the rest of the story anyway. But he asked...

"It wasn't long before Mom decided her little 'weather witch' would be better off homeschooled. Then I got my heart broken the first time, and the back yard flooded in a sudden monsoon. Mom called in some of her circle, and I ended up in a weeklong "bootcamp" — witchy, pointy-toed boots, naturally — where I practiced grounding and centering and shielding until I could do it while standing on my head. Literally. While they pelted me with pillows and prodded me with every bit of magical power they could muster, from elemental magic to projective empathy."

"You can stand on your head?" He looks very excited about that. "I have no idea what the rest of that means."

"I could when I was a kid. And it's not important. The important part is that was the last time my innate weather magic got out of control. Until I lost Adam."

Rhys

I squeeze her hand to reassure her that it's OK to talk to me about this.

"The night of his funeral," she says after a minute, "after I shut myself up in the bathroom to have a little mental breakdown, a huge limb from the ancient oak tree in the front yard got caught up in a sudden gust of wind, broke clean off, and missed the house by six inches and my car by a foot. If there hadn't been a sizable birch tree between it and the driveway, shunting it aside..."

"You could have been killed." I lean down to look in her eyes, horrified by the idea that I could have lost her before I even found her.

"I usually avoid pointing that out, but yeah... If the roof had fallen in, me... the kids..."

I hug her tight against me.

"That's when I knew I needed to get us out of that house, which held too many memories for me at that point. So, we moved in with Rory. And it worked — it was enough change, enough distraction from missing Adam, that it never happened again."

"Until they took your concert theme away."

"Yeah."

"But you don't do it intentionally."

"It's not weather magic in the sense of traditional ritual magic. No walking in circles, no offerings to the gods, no channeling elemental energy. This — it's an innate part of me. Ritual weather magic is something witches sometimes do, especially if an oncoming system poses danger."

"Like a hurricane or tornado..."

"Exactly. To mitigate the danger. But the weather is finicky, fiddly. The tiniest shift in the wrong direction, and it can go from a stormy sky to a landscape torn apart by tornadoes. So, wise witches don't mess with the weather — not intentionally — unless the risk it poses on its own is dire. But the weather, when it's in a charged state like it was the other night, it's easily influenced. And my emotions, when they're extreme, are a strong influence. When I got angry with the board for censoring my lesson plans, canceling the concert theme I'd worked so hard on... The looming storm came on fast — faster than it would have otherwise. Full of wind and rain and lightning. And all of that got focused right where I was — blowing, rattling windows and then a few close lightning strikes. And then I got overwhelmed with sadness, and the rain came down in a deluge."

"Aria asked me to let her go outside to watch the storm, feel the wind."

"Even though I said not to," she reminds me.

I nod, ready to apologize.

"No — don't. I know how she is. It's hard to say no to her."

"I went out with her, kept an eye on Tommy through the screen door. And when it started to get bad, dangerous, I grabbed her and brought her back inside."

"How close was it?"

"How close was what?"

"The lightning strike. You said it got dangerous. It had to have been lightning."

"I don't know — a mile or so, maybe. Not close enough to hit us. But close enough the thunder scared the crap out of both of us. Sorry."

"But you got her inside."

"Yeah."

"Then you did fine. That was my fault. It tends to focus where I'm focused, whether it was the office during the meeting or home when I was on my way back. That's one of the reasons I try to keep her inside when it storms. Tommy won't go out willingly. But Aria... I suspect she's inherited my gift. That's why—"

"Why she wanted to be outside to feel the wind. She said it was exciting."

"She's probably feeding off the storm energy, the same way I do. I'm going to have to start working with her to keep that under control, like Mom and her friends did with me."

"But that didn't work, did it? I mean..."

"I still influenced the storm the other night." She sighs. "Yeah. I did. And it's a measure of how upset I was that it happened at all. So, now you know. Do you even believe me? I know a lot of people wouldn't. But you asked."

"I think I knew it was real when Aria said the rain was because you were sad. I knew it for sure when you got home..."

"And turned into a sad puddle in your lap. Sorry about that."

"Don't be. I want to be here for you. That was just part of the deal."

"I can't tell you how much I've appreciated it. It's been such a crazy couple of weeks."

"No — it's cool. Actually, it's really cool! My girlfriend's Storm! How great is that? I'm dating a mutant!"

Lyric

I can't decide if Rhys' take on the situation is amusing or concerning.

His willingness to accept what I've told him at face value is beyond welcome. It's rare outside the magical community. His delight in my being a "mutant"... That's a little less welcome.

"You can't tell anyone, OK? Like I said, most people, you talk to them about real magic, they think you're out of touch with reality."

"I know that feeling quite well lately," he says.

"Oh? Too much talk of witches and mermaids?"

"No, but Kier responded like that when I tried to talk to him about things."

This is one thing that has worried me, at least as much because of concerns about my friends' happiness as because I'm a fan of the band. What happens when half — well, now, more than half of the band — is on the inside of so many magical happenings and secrets, and the rest of them are left on the shores of mundane reality? I had hoped Kieran O'Connor's heritage would give him a bridge to accepting us. But it seems his murky past includes a more typically American take on magic.

"He's going to have to find his own way, Rhys. I hope it doesn't drive a wedge in the band, because I love your music. But Hunt's marrying a healer-priestess..."

I catch myself, but it's already too late. I don't know what it is about Rhys that unravels all the thoughts in my head, letting more of them come out of my mouth than I plan. But this much is done. Rhys has a hard time focusing, but he's very good at putting puzzle pieces together.

"I really shouldn't be talking out of school about the girls…"

"Brighid healed his hand, didn't she?"

"Twice." I wait for him to take it in, absorb it, maybe even question it.

"No — it makes sense. And it's not like I didn't already know she's a witch." He's letting me off the hook. "But you said 'girls' — plural?"

"Oops." I frown, not giving him any answers.

"So, what? Callie's witch, too? I'm going to assume she is unless you tell me otherwise."

Well, he's got me there. That was clever of him. I'm between a rock and a hard place — lie and tell him no, or explain. And Callie's not a religious witch, nor an intentional one, so maybe it's OK to explain.

"Not exactly. She's like I am with the weather, only it's food. Her emotions go into her food."

"No wonder it tastes so good! It's magic!"

"Well, she's an amazing chef, even without the magic. But with it…"

"Is that why you told me about your husband the other night? Because Callie wanted you to, and we were eating her food?"

Whoa. *That* I had not considered. Rhys and puzzle pieces…

"That hadn't occurred to me, actually. And now that you've said it, I suspect you're right. But she doesn't really do it on purpose, so I can't get mad at her. She wasn't manipulating us. She just gave us her hopes."

"I specialize in thinking outside the box," Rhys says, confirming my puzzle-piece observation. "I keep thinking up these amazing ideas that no one's thought of before. Only they don't always work out. Sometimes they blow up in my face. Literally. But I've got this one I'm working on… Well, the guys don't think it'll sell."

"What's that?" He's got me curious now, and a little sad that his bandmates don't support his ambitions.

"Well… maybe it's not the time to discuss it. Or maybe it's the perfect time," he says, giving me a smile as he slowly pulls the sheet down, revealing the edges of my areolas. "I call it 'The Cock Sock.' It's a… well, it's a thing for guys, who… uh… don't have girlfriends."

Oh. OK. How to respond to this…

"So, you've created something to give them a… *hand*?"

"Exactly! I knew we fit! You get it without me even having to say it!"

"I think the name says it all, if you know anything about men."

"I thought so, too! But the guys said it won't get on 'Big Fish Finds.'"

He's downcast about it. I hate seeing his enthusiasm dampened, especially after what he said about the guys and his drum solos.

"They're probably right, Rhys. But it's not because the idea's a bad one. They just won't put something like that on TV."

"That's what the guys said. They said I should just make it myself, use my rockstar money."

"You could definitely do that. It's probably the most direct way to make your idea a real product."

"Good point. I'm going to offer all kinds of colors, textures — things that feel really good, like the real thing..."

I sense a lengthy digression coming on. It might be a good time to interrupt.

"Which you have right here in your arms..." I remind him. I lift his hand up to my mouth, taking his thumb inside, sucking on it, licking...

"You really are a witch, aren't you? You make things rise into the air in an instant — no hands!"

He's looking down below the spot where his arm joins with mine on my belly. Sure enough, there's a growing bulge beneath the covers.

"Imagine what I can do when I *do* use my hands... and my mouth..."

"Magic..." he says with a groan. And I open the curtain on our own *very personal* magic show.

Chapter 39

Lazy Days

Lyric

I wake up not to drumming, but to the sound of the ocean pounding on the beach and the sun shining bright through the sheer curtains over the sliding glass doors. We never closed the doors last night, and the fresh air and Rhys' arms around me gave me the best night of sleep I've had in ages.

It's still early — a benefit of having come straight back to the studio after the fundraiser. So I've had a solid six hours of sleep, even after two lengthy rounds of pleasure with Rhys. I stretch languidly, seeing him still sleeping quietly next to me. That, I'm used to — musician hours, often leaving them sleeping well into the afternoon, just to get a normal amount of sleep. I was used to getting the kids up and ready on my own even before Adam passed.

Speaking of which... I expect my mom's doing that right about now. I'm sure she has an idea where I am, but it's an ingrained mom habit to make sure your kids' caregiver knows where you are, just in case.

My phone's still on silent from the event last night. It's set so a call from my emergency contacts will ring through, but everything else just makes the phone vibrate.

Lyric: *I'm fine. Amazing, actually. I should be home in an hour or so.*

Even if I have to call for a ride to get there. I'm not waking
Rhys up for that.

Mom: *I just woke up myself. The kids are still
asleep. Take your time. Enjoy. You're overdue. And
you're on vacation now. I can handle the kids.
Maybe we'll go to the amusement park today.*

I'm actually a little jealous. I haven't been to the amusement
park since opening weekend. I should have taken the kids again
before now. And now I'll miss out, unless I go home soon and
tell her I'm taking over.

Mom: *Just text me when you're headed home. Love
you!*

Before I can put the phone away again, it buzzes another time.
But it's not Mom.

Brighid: *Why didn't you tell me you were seeing
Rhys?*

I guess Callie spilled the beans. It's unlike her, though. She
doesn't do much "girl-talk," and when she does, it's usually with
me, or Siobhan.

Lyric: *Well, we were just working together on the
fundraiser. He was a big help in making it a success. We got the money for new instruments!*

Brighid: *Yeah. I know. It's all over the internet this
morning! The band's PR assistant sent me links
along with the usual screened mentions of me and
Hunt. I love that dress, BTW.*

Lyric: *There's pictures, of me? Online? Just the lo-
cals-only groups, right?*

Brighid: *I think that's where the photos came from,
but it's not just you conducting the chorus and stuff,
like usual. How do you think I found out about you
and Rhys?*

Why don't I like the sound of this?

Lyric: *Send me a link.*

A minute later, a link to a gossip site pops up on my phone.

Brighid: *When I saw that, I woke Hunter's ass
up to find out what's been going on. I mean —
I've been busy with the wedding, but you'd have
thought someone would have mentioned you and
Rhys were an item!*

And we are.

As in the original meaning — a line item in a gossip column.

"Falling Like Dominoes — Is yet another of the amazing men
of aMUSEd taking himself off the market? After news of Hunter
Graves' engagement and the bombshell announcement of Declan Carter's marriage (again?), photos of Rhys 'The Madman'
Madigan with a blonde woman have rumors running rampant
that the adrenaline-junkie drummer may be off on a new adventure — in love.

"Local sources say the woman is an elementary school music
teacher in the same small town of Mystic Beach, Del., where two
of Madigan's bandmates have both settled down while the band
records its next album. At this rate, will there be any eligible

bachelors left in the band by the time the album is released? Millions of fans want to know!"

The photos are of me and Rhys at the fundraiser, his arm around me, on stage and as we mingled with the crowd.

"It's too early to be up," Rhys mumbles into my shoulder before pressing a kiss there. "Are the kids OK?"

I love that he asked that first, knowing they'll always be my first concern.

"They're fine. Mom's going to take them to the amusement park today."

All of a sudden, Rhys is wide awake.

"She is? Can I go? I love that place! The Haunted Mansion is legendary among dark rides."

My head falls forward. Would that my biggest concern right now was whether Rhys got to ride the Haunted Mansion today. I mean, I love the ride myself — it's just family-friendly enough that even Tommy will ride. But Brighid's just dumped a big problem in my lap, and she, of anyone, should know what I'm potentially dealing with.

> Brighid: *You OK? Your lack of a reply is concerning.*

I wouldn't mind talking to Brighid about this. She didn't have the best experience with the paparazzi and social media when the news that she and Hunter were together as a couple first came out. That's why her news now comes via the band's PR team and is screened. But if she rushes over to my house, she's going to realize that I'm not there, and I'd rather keep that part of Rhys and me being "an item" quiet for a while, even if Mom knows. But not even Brighid can understand one aspect of how this news is affecting me.

> Lyric: *I've got kids, Brighid. All this time I was wondering how Rhys leaving on tour would impact them if we got involved. I never considered what it might be like when he was still here.*

Brighid: *Do you want me to come over so we can talk? Do you want me to put you in touch with the PR team?*

Rhys kisses my shoulder again when I don't respond to him and sits up to look over it at my phone.

"Why's Brighid getting you PR's number?"

"Because apparently I need it," I tell him, handing him the phone with the link Brighid sent pulled up.

"Ah — the parental paparazzi! We make an attractive couple," he says, smiling and pulling me into him, kissing my hair. My phone falls unnoticed to the bed, until it beeps again and I pick it up.

Brighid: *Don't panic. It's one item in a wrap-up, and they didn't include your name. The guys get photographed with random women all the time. I'm sure it'll get chalked up to a simple photo-op at a fundraiser. You're not being stalked by the paparazzi.*

The difference between her tone when she uses that word — paparazzi — and Rhys' is concerning. I'm not sure he understands why I'm a little freaked out.

Lyric: *By the time I am being stalked, it'll be too late.*

Brighid: *I'll give Billy a heads-up on your concerns and ask the PR team to get in touch, start monitoring for any reference to you or the kids. It's going to be fine.*

People keep telling me that lately, but it hasn't been the case any time they have...

Rhys

When Lyric said she had two weeks off before school starts, I decided I was going to do my utmost to spend every moment with her, and the kids, that I could. So there's no way I'm missing a trip to one of my favorite places here in Delaware with my three favorite local residents. (Iris is pretty cool, too!)

Piper has my tracks from yesterday morning to work with, so I'm good with recording duties until we move on to the next song or someone decides to change the arrangement. (Declan never changes his arrangements. It's why he takes longer to finalize his songs than Dave does.)

"I'm going to go take a shower," I tell Lyric. "Then we can go as soon as I get dressed."

"OK," she says absently.

Those photos of us showing up online have her weirded out. But I think Brighid's right — they don't have her name on them, and it's not even actual real paparazzi. If my main goal in helping with the fundraiser had really been my image, those photos would still be floating around on the internet, just with an official PR release. And Billy's always got this stuff handled.

Did he have Hunter's blackmailing ex handled? Did he have the naked photo of Declan handled? His marriage announcement?

Head-dude has a point.

You think I should be worried about Lyric and the kids because of a couple of photos?

Yes! You promised me you'd take care of them!

I am! Did you miss how relaxed Lyric was last night? Even before I made her come on my tongue?

Don't. Just don't.

Don't be a prude, head-dude! Sex is natural. It's fun.

That's when it's one-on-one. Don't pull me into this like some kind of twisted threesome!

Fine. But I didn't just *fuck* her. (Sorry, Mom.) I *made love* to her.

You love her? This fast?

Why not? She's awesome! And so are the kids!

This is all happening very fast. And you still haven't told her about the dreams.

So I'll tell her tonight, once the kids have gone to bed. She told me all that weather-witch stuff. We're still getting to know each other beneath the surface. That doesn't change how I feel about her.

Just make sure you keep them safe. I didn't think about the paparazzi when...

When what?

Nothing. She's a fan of yours. She knows what your life is like, right?

Well, I don't know. It's not exactly how people think it is. There is a lot of hassle, like Hunt had to deal with.

Yeah. Maybe...

Maybe what?

Nothing.

Head-dude goes silent, and then I realize how quiet it is in the room, since I'm still standing here and not in the shower.

Lyric's still sitting on the bed, looking at the photos of us.

"Join me?"

She looks up at me, the sheet falling lower on her breasts. No one else is upstairs, even if Alex and Kier are back. I could walk her naked down the hall and then take her up against the shower wall.

You won't have to twist her arm. She loves shower sex. Look at her.

Head-dude almost sounds jealous now. I wish he'd make up his mind... But he's right. There's a flush to her cheeks, her cleavage, that wasn't there a moment ago. Her gorgeous eyes darken. Her breathing is speeding up.

I hold my hand out to her, and she lets the sheet fall. My breath catches. I've seen her naked already, of course, but that was mostly by moonlight. Then, tangled up in my sheets. Now, with the sunlight streaming in off the deck, hitting the highlights in her pale gold hair… caressing that silky skin as it curves over her shoulders, her hips, her thighs, her ass…

Did I say she's a goddess?

I mean it.

And I want her to teach me what that means to her…

I take her hand and lead her off to the shower.

Lyric

R hys pulls me down the hall to the bathroom — me clutching the bedsheet around myself, and him stark naked. Oh, my…

As he starts the shower, letting it heat up, I can't help but take in the view. Rhys is more muscular than the other guys in the band, between drumming and his sports, his workouts. But it fits his frame so nicely, giving the impression of fitness and not bulk. The little bit of him that isn't hard muscle is still artfully carved, smooth like marble, but soft and warm to the touch. And with his back to me, that's what I see. Goddess bless…

Once we're in the shower, he washes my hair for me, his fingers — so strong when he's climbing or on his kit — incredibly gentle, attentive. I can't remember the last time someone else washed my hair. It might have been the hairdresser for my wedding.

He bends down to let me help him with his, too. It's longer than it was when they were on tour, just like Hunter's and Declan's. It looks good on him. He's practically purring when I'm done, and as the water rinses away the last of the shampoo and his eyes open again, I witness the shift from pussycat to pussy-eating tiger.

He pushes me backward until my back hits the back wall of the shower. It's an awesome shower, with steaming-hot water coming from every possible angle, in a variety of spray patterns.

Pressed back flat against the wall, it's a sheet of mist, keeping both of us warm, even though we're out of the direct spray. I put my arms around Rhys' neck, and he lifts one of my legs up around his hip. His hand dives toward my center, caressing, teasing.

"Jump up," he says, his hand on my thigh.

"No! I'm too heavy." After how he worshiped me last night, a lot of my insecurities have been assuaged. But this is simple physics.

"I hang from rocks by my fingertips. Do you have any idea how much *I* weigh?" he asks me, looking me right in the eyes.

"Well, no... Not now. You were, like, almost two hundred pounds when you joined the band."

Wait. I shouldn't know that.

Rhys' face breaks into the biggest grin. Busted!

"You are *so* my fangirl!" He shakes his head in wonder. "I don't think my *mom* knows how much I weighed when I joined the band." He slides his hands down either side of my face, holding me still, and kisses me briefly, sweetly. "And it was closer to a hundred-ninety," he adds. "I grew another inch that year. And with all the climbing and stuff — another thirty or so pounds of muscle since. Do the math, teach," he says pointedly.

OK. Fine. He weighs a good bit more than I do, even after two kids.

He rubs his thumb over my nipple, then back down to my thigh.

"Jump. Up."

I do it, grabbing around his other hip with my thigh, steadying myself with my arms around his neck.

"Crap. Forgot the condoms," he says, sighing. I can see him contemplating going back to his room for them, and... I don't want that.

"Don't need them. Assuming you're still clean after your last test... I had my tubes tied when Aria was born."

"Oh," he says. "So, no more babies?"

He's not asking me... is he? Way too early for that. But he asked.

"They can reverse it sometimes, but it's not a given."

"OK, then," he says, thinking about it for a second and then giving a nod.

"You sure?"

"Yup. I'm adopted, remember?"

"I do," I tell him with a smile. "And — if you're clean, that means no condoms, too!"

"Oh, I'm clean. Been waiting for you for a while, sexy mama."

I laugh.

"You are, you know," he says. "Sexy, and a mom."

"Thank you."

"Now, about this..." he says, nodding down at his massive hard-on, which rests between us. "I'm going to put my hands under that luscious ass of yours, and unless you tell me you want me to go easy on you, I'm going to pound you into the wall, OK?"

Going easy isn't what I want.

"Fuck me hard, Rhys..."

"So sexy..." he says, taking my mouth with his, then nuzzling into my neck. His hands grab my butt, lifting me up higher on the wall, higher on him, and then he pulls me back down on his cock.

"Goddess bless," I say, an exhale this time, instead of a shout.

"Thank you," he says. "I have a feeling I'm going to need it if I'm going to make you come before I do. Man, you feel good. Hot and wet and..."

My muscles clamp down on his dick inside me.

"Goddess bless," he exhales himself. "I've been working with a handicap all these years."

"What do you mean?"

"The condoms. Haven't had to hold off like this, with skin on skin... This is going to be fast, too, Lyric. OK?"

"Hard and fast, Rhys."

He lifts me up and slams me back down on him again, then steps forward, using the shower wall to help hold me up, pinned between it and his strong hips. He sucks my lower lip into his mouth, giving it a nip and then a nibble. And then he smashes into me, over and over again, hard and fast, just like he promised.

"Touch yourself," he says as his speed picks up. "I'm getting close, and I want to see you come on my cock with the lights on."

I grab around his neck with one hand, sliding my other down between us, and stroke my clit just as he strokes into me. We follow the same rhythm, ever increasing, both of us getting closer and closer to our climax. It's like a duet, both of us individually building our parts, but doing it together, making it more than the sum of the whole.

"Let me see," he says, pulling back to watch my fingers on my clit, his cock spearing into me over and over again. It pushes us both higher, and everything ramps up.

I close my eyes against the sensations, forget to keep touching myself, because Rhys is doing enough with just his cock. And then he kisses me, deep, wet, consuming. In that moment, it's as much about the kiss as it is about the sex, both of us focused on what the other is doing to us, how we're making each other feel. And Rhys slams into me, hard and fast, cock and tongue, and...

A whimper is all I can manage, riding out my orgasm.

Rhys gasps and groans, burying himself inside me, spasms rocking him. His release hits him, and he tucks his head into my neck, his fingers grasping my butt like it's his only defense against gravity. Keeping me pinned against the wall, he finally exhales.

"Whoa," he says. "Best high ever."

"Better than jumping out of a plane?" I can't help myself. I have to ask.

"Way better," he says, looking in my eyes. "Perfect."

He kisses me again, sweetly this time.

"Let's go ride some rides!"

I end up wearing one of Rhys' amazing soft T-shirts, after he sees me fingering the one he had on last night.

"Alex gets them for me," he says. "I've got T-shirts for everyday and the good ones like that."

"Do I want to know how much they cost?"

"No idea. They take it out of my royalties."

"Of course they do."

I shake my head.

The shirt's big on me, but it was that or wear last night's dress again and set myself up for the "walk of shame" when we get home, knowing Mom, the kids and half the internet, apparently, know what I was wearing last night. It's not long enough, though, to cover my ass, and after briefly contemplating trying a pair of Rhys' shorts, he had one of his "outside the box" ideas.

"Brighid's slept over a couple times when we were recording late. I think she left some clothes here!" he says, running off down the hall and returning with a pair of leggings. She's a little bigger than me, but they fit well enough that they don't fall off. I'll return them later. At which point I will be talking to her about how to handle this fifteen minutes of fame.

Rhys puts the cap back on his meds, walks up behind me and puts his arms around me, and I lean back into him.

"You OK with all this?" he asks. "I know it's a lot. I know *I'm* a lot."

"You're not a lot. You're Rhys. Exactly who you should be."

"You really are magic," he says. "You know exactly what I needed to hear, even when I didn't know I needed to hear it."

I turn in his arms and kiss him.

"It's just the truth. You have no idea how I needed what you've given me these last couple days, weeks. If you're a lot, a lot is exactly what *I* needed."

We head down the stairs, once again hand-in-hand, only to find not just Alex and Kieran in the living room, but the entire rest of the band.

"Hey, guys — you remember Lyric, right?"

"Good morning, Lyric," Alex says, kicking off a round of greetings.

"Nice to see you all again."

"You all look like you're headed out somewhere," Alex says.

"We're going to take the kids to the amusement park today!" Rhys says, his exuberance clear.

"I told you he'd forget," Kieran says, shaking his head.

"He must have hit his head on the shower wall this morning. Repeatedly," Declan says, snickering.

I turn bright red.

"Forget what?" Rhys asks.

"Yup, he forgot," Hunter says.

"Forgot what?" Rhys repeats.

"We're supposed to be going over the mix for Declan's song this morning — the one you did drum tracks for yesterday?" David reminds him.

"That was this morning? I thought it was Saturday."

"It *is* Saturday, Rhys," Alex says, smacking Rhys on the back of the head. Rhys says nothing. But I have to.

"Stop hitting him!" I step between them, grabbing Alex's arm and facing him down, so he knows I mean business. "I spend half my time telling little kids to keep their hands to themselves. If they can manage it, you'd think a grown adult could, too. I mean, I know the grouchy guy got away with it on that Navy cop show, but he had issues, and that's just not the way you treat co-workers. To most people, that's an assault."

Alex's blue eyes go wide, and he freezes, stunned, as if *I'd* slapped *him*. Instantly, I'm regretful, especially after I see the other four staring at us, then exchanging glances. I've over-stepped. Rhys is a grown man, and he doesn't need me to intervene on his behalf with this man he considers his brother.

Maybe that's how I should think of it — like brothers getting physical with their squabbling. I just know I wouldn't let my own kids treat each other like that, and I don't like seeing anyone treating Rhys that way, even if I get why Alex might find him annoying.

After a moment, Alex takes in a halting breath, shaking his head.

"You're right. You're totally right," he says. "I've been doing it so long I don't even think about it anymore." He turns to look at Rhys. "I'm sorry, man," he says, emotion bleeding into his voice. "I... Well, I had some bad examples as a kid, and I guess I never realized I was following the same pattern. You know I love you like a brother."

"You've always acted more like a mother," Rhys says. "And that's cool. But, yeah — I could do without the head slaps. I'm not trying to flibbertigibbet up. I'm always trying *not* to flibbertigibbet up. I'm just not very good at it."

"No — this is totally my issue, Rhys," Alex says. "I need to... I need to deal with that." He turns to look back at me. "Thanks for calling me on it, Lyric. You're totally right. I apologize. To both of you."

"I don't need an apology, Alex. Rhys does."

"I'm sorry, man," Alex says again, offering Rhys his hand. But Rhys uses it to pull him into a bro-hug, and the two bandmates hug it out.

"So, I guess I have to cancel on you, Lyric?" he looks around at the other guys, silently begging them to let him off the hook. Based on their reactions, Rhys' puppy-dog eyes work just as well on them as they do on me.

"Piper could use some more sleep," Dave says. It seems like he's trying to help Rhys as much as he is trying to get his girlfriend another morning off.

"*I* could use more sleep," Kieran says, seeming a little irritated.

"Callie's shorthanded at the restaurant," Declan adds. "I could go help her out."

"Brighid did want me to help her with the wedding stuff," Hunter says.

"Fine. Go," Alex says with a sigh. "We'll get back to it tomorrow morning. But everybody be here on time! Ten sharp!" And the guys start to disperse.

"Is it silly that I think I might kind of miss having him smack me upside the head?" Rhys asks me quietly as we head out the door.

"Not silly. It's what you're used to. You just need to get used to a different way of doing things. You and Alex both. I'd say don't let him do it again, stand up to him if he does — but I don't think he will."

"Yeah. He kinda looked a little like *you'd* smacked *him*. I didn't like seeing him that way. It makes sense that you wouldn't like seeing me that way, either."

"I didn't."

"Does that mean you care about me? A little?" He smiles, clearly willing me to say yes.

But I have no idea how to answer that question. I mean, the answer is clear to me. Yes, I care about Rhys. Do I care about Rhys as more than another human being who doesn't deserve to get hit, even if it's just a brotherly head smack?

I consider that as he waits for my answer, amazingly patient for someone as hyperactive as Rhys is. He tilts his head, curious, imploring me with those bronze eyes of his.

Oh, I am in so much trouble.

"A little, Rhys. Just a little."

"Good. 'Cause I care about you. More than a little."

CHAPTER 40

AMUSEd-MENT PARK

Rhys

"Come on! It's almost our turn!"

We've been waiting in line for the Haunted Mansion for almost an hour. It doesn't open until dusk, and there's always a line when it opens. And when I say "we" have been waiting in line, I mean me. Tommy can't wait in line that long. He'd melt down, Lyric says. So, we got special permission to have just me stand in line while she took the kids on more rides.

I love this place. Granted, I can't ride a lot of the rides, because half of them are for little kids. But I got lucky — a few of the adult rides have a maximum height of six-foot-four, and I just barely squeaked in under the wire on that one. So, I got to wave to Lyric and the kids from way the flibbertigibbets up in the air, hanging upside-down, just like when I first saw Lyric up close, with my own physical eyes.

She and I stood and watched the kids ride in circles on mini motorcycles, firetrucks, big hauler trucks (Lyric rode behind them — I didn't quite fit), and boats floating on real water. She and Tommy got the carousel carriage, while Aria and I rode the horses in front of them. Lyric and Aria loaded into a helicopter that went up in the air, while Tommy and I stayed on the ground, because he didn't want to go with them. He stood next to me and shifted back and forth on his feet, humming while he spun some of his gears.

But when they loaded up the next-to-last helicopter, there was no one left in line.

"You two want to get on?" the ride attendant asked.

"I don't know. He's..." Well, what the flibbertigibbet... Why not try? "Tommy, buddy, would you like to ride on the helicopter with me?"

He doesn't respond, and I shrug. Then he grabs my hand and pulls me through the gate with him.

"I'll get you the tickets when we get off, OK?" I tell the attendant.

"Can I get a selfie, too?" she asks.

"Sure."

And the next thing I know, Tommy and I are sitting in one of these little helicopters, rising up and down as I pull and push the little bar. I wave to Lyric and see her panic for a second, until she sees Tommy sitting next to me. Then she's all smiles. I like seeing her like that.

"How did you manage to get him on the helicopters?" she asks when the ride is over.

"I just asked him if he wanted to ride with me. I guess he did." I shrug.

She looks baffled, but happy.

We grabbed dinner on the fly, sitting on one of the benches on the boardwalk with hotdogs, fries, grilled cheese and, for me, a cheesesteak. Oh, my god. So good!

Then I made the sacrifice, agreeing to stand in the line for the Haunted Mansion. It's not a huge sacrifice. I get to chill out and digest, and then the animatronic characters on the exterior start up their bits. It's not Disney World, but it's a classic — first opened in 1979 and cutting-edge for the time — and it has an established following with dark-ride enthusiasts. Of which I am one. Everywhere aMUSEd has toured, I check for dark rides that I can get to during our touring schedule. If there's a ride and I can get to it, I do.

When Hunter told me about the Haunted Mansion here, just down the road from Mystic Beach, it topped my list of things I wanted to do. I even tagged along with him and Horrible Holly, the ex, on one of their "dates." I came back later, on my own, just to get the taste of that out of my mouth. And, now, I'll get to ride it with Lyric and the kids.

"Is that the drummer from aMUSEd?" I hear one of the people in the winding line behind me ask. I smile but don't respond. "I think it is! Oh, my god! I have to get a picture." I asked the attendant at the helicopters not to post her selfie until she got off her shift, and she agreed. That usually does the trick on keeping the fans from mobbing us when we're in public. But I can't ask people not to take pictures when I'm in public. Half the time I don't even know they're taking them. And if I do, I don't really want to make a scene. It's not usually a problem.

"Excuse us — I'm so sorry," Lyric tells the people behind me while she and the kids get escorted up from the exit to the front of the line. "He's autistic," she says, smiling, but looking out of sorts.

"Someone's getting the VIP treatment," someone farther back in the line mutters. "Rockstars...."

"He's been in the line since before I got here," someone else says. "He's waited his turn. The kid's autistic. Give 'em a break."

I see why Lyric's apologizing to people, but I hate that she feels like she needs to do it, or explain the accommodation, or that someone has to clear up the impression that I used my fame to get special treatment. We do, sometimes. But it wasn't needed here. I can wait in a line. Tommy can't.

The attendant opens the front gate and lets Lyric and the kids join me. I give her a hug, hoping it'll reassure her.

"Are you ready, Aria?"

"I sure am, Mr. Rhys!" she says enthusiastically. "This is my favorite ride, after the boats and the bumper cars!"

"We can do those next," I tell her. "Does Tommy like bumper cars?" I ask.

"He actually does," Lyric says. "He tries to drive, but he hasn't figured out the accelerator and the whole backwards thing when you turn the wheel too far."

"I can help him. You ride with Aria, and I'll work the accelerator and keep him going forward. We'll make it work."

"That would be great!"

A minute later, we're tucked into one of the Haunted Mansion cars — barely. I'm not exactly small, and Lyric has all those amazing curves, but we squeeze a slender Aria and Tommy between us. And then, it's through the doors, up-up-up past haunted portraits, out onto a deck overlooking the park, through a wall, a jump scare or three, a giant spider — Lyric shrieks, which surprises the heck out of me because she's a witch — a werewolf, banging doors, skulls and skeletons, a bat, a descent into a smooth-talking devil's lair, then a close call with an oncoming truck, only to emerge back in the park again.

"Mr. Madigan," the exit attendant says as we hop out of the car, one by one, "if you could come over here for a moment, please..." He gestures off to the side, where a booth sells ride photos and T-shirts, but he pulls us behind it. Lyric looks as confused as I feel. "I don't want to interrupt your fun, but I wanted to warn you... We — well, this doesn't happen often, if at all — but a few minutes ago, a gentleman came up to the photo booth and offered the attendant five hundred dollars for a copy of your ride photo once you and your family got off the ride."

The guy looks decidedly uncomfortable. Lyric, too. I'm not far behind.

"Of course, we refused, asked him to leave the park, made sure he left the grounds, at least... But I thought you should know that your presence didn't go unnoticed by certain elements. So, what we did was print out your ride photo, and we have that for you here, along with a few Haunted Mansion T-shirts in adult and child sizes." He glances at the kids. "We've deleted the original file of the photo, so this is the only copy. We're just really sorry this happened, and we hope you'll be back. We know you love our ride as much as we do, and we'll do our best to protect your privacy whenever you're here."

Lyric and I are both speechless, but she accepts the bag he hands her.

"Thank you," I finally tell the guy. "I can't tell you how much I appreciate your care for our privacy." I don't call them my family. Maybe they will be someday, but I can't rush Lyric that much. "You said the guy's gone? No one else like him spotted since then?"

"No. I think you'll be safe to get in a few more rides, if you'd like, but I can't say past that. A few people posted your photo on social media earlier. None of our staff, of course."

I'm relieved by that last part. I wanted that girl to have her selfie, guilt-free. The rest... It happens. I just wish it hadn't happened like this, tonight, with Lyric and the kids.

"Bumper cars?" I ask Lyric quietly, hoping she'll be game for a little more fun so that our night isn't ruined.

She thinks for a minute, looking at the kids.

"Please, Mommy!" Aria begs.

"Alright — bumper cars, and then we'll go get some ice cream and head home. OK?"

"Yes!" Aria says.

"Thank you," I tell Lyric. We're going to have to talk about this stuff, and soon.

Take care of them.

And I'm probably going to have to talk to Billy, and maybe even to Gryff, our head of security, too.

Please don't let this scare Lyric away. I can't lose her.

Especially after all it took for you to find her.

Lyric

Tommy screeches as he slams his car into ours. Rhys' long arms wrap around his shoulders, ready to correct his steering, but other than getting knocked sideways and then driving backwards for about ten feet, Tommy's actually done a very good job piloting his bumper car for the first time ever. He's a natural, waiting for his chance to hit his sister and me in our car, and then aiming right for us as Rhys hits the accelerator. We returned the favor a few times, though I was the one behind the wheel, since Aria's still a hair too short.

It puts a positive spin on the end of our night, after that unexpected wake-up call of someone — I would suspect a paparazzo or celebrity-beat journalist — trying to buy our ride photo, at a premium price.

Whether they were just after a photo of Rhys or they specifically wanted images of him with me and my kids, it's a reminder that if I pursue a relationship with Rhys, I'm putting myself, and my kids, in the spotlight, and in a way that goes beyond invasive.

"Look, Mommy! Sprinkles!" Aria says, her already-dripping cone of frozen chocolate custard covered in rainbow sprinkles.

Tommy's cup of vanilla is sprinkle-free, because he doesn't like the texture. He's also much safer with a cup than a cone, for several reasons.

"Look, Mr. Rhys!" Aria says, showing Rhys her mess in the making. This is why we brought my car, and not Rhys' show-piece, as cool as the kids think it is. "It's dripping!" she shrieks.

I growl, spotting the need for an immediate intervention. I don't particularly like chocolate custard, but a mom's got to do what a mom's got to do. But before I can grab the dripping cone to clean it up for her, Rhys swoops in and does it.

"Mr. Rhys! Don't eat all my ice cream!" she says reprovingly.

"I won't!" he says. "No — wait. That was really good. I think I will." He opens his mouth wide for a big bite right off the top. Aria shrieks. "Tricked you!" he says, laughing and handing her back a much cleaner cone. She giggles.

"Thank you," I tell him. "Chocolate is not my favorite."

"No, you like... Orange-vanilla twist," he guesses. I nod, surprised that he guessed right. "Which is why that's why I got." He shows me a waffle cone full orange and vanilla custard. "We can share." He winks at me.

"Did you ask Aria what flavors I like?"

"No! That would be cheating!" he insists. "I just guessed. Maybe I know you even better than you think."

Maybe.

R hys and I put the kids to bed, de-ice-creamed, teeth brushed and in clean pajamas. They don't even make it to a story. It was a long day, full of fun and surprises, not all of them good. Rhys and I have a few things to discuss, now that the kids aren't around to overhear.

"Look, about the photo..." he says, before I can even sit down on the sofa. "I'm going to call Billy in the morning, let him know we need some careful handling of any publicity, any social media posts, because of the kids. They sometimes offer people payment, or concert tickets, in exchange for taking down problematic posts."

Part of me wants to object to the heavy-handed maneuvers, but we're talking about my kids.

"I'm also going to call our head of security, Gryff, and see if he thinks we need security assigned for the band, and for you, as well as the other girls."

It's a reminder that I'm not the only one who's been impacted by aMUSEd's high-profile presence in Mystic Beach.

"Thank you," I tell him. "I'm going to go talk to Brighid in the morning, once her shop's open. I can leave the kids with Mom, since Callie's old loft is like two hundred yards away."

"I could watch them," he volunteers.

"No. I want you to focus on what Billy and Gryff...?" He nods. "On what they suggest we do. We can talk about it tomorrow night, once the kids are in bed."

"Does that mean I can sleep over?" he asks.

I sigh.

"Not tonight." His disappointment is obvious. "You promised the guys you'd be there in the morning. And I want to talk to the kids tomorrow, about us, about their dad. If you're going to be around, I've got to start things off right, by telling them what's going on and what they can expect to happen."

"Which is?"

"Rhys, I want to give this — us — a try. But I won't lie to you — this publicity thing is really scary for me. Brighid's had such a terrible time with the social media and the paparazzi. Callie — who never even had social media until Declan showed up here again — almost got herself in trouble, and now..." Well, that's a separate story. "But none of them have kids yet. Not only do I have kids — they're old enough to understand a lot of what might be said about you, me, us, and them. And Tommy... He can't speak for himself. *I've* got to do that."

"You had me at giving us a try," he says, running his fingers along my jaw. He leans in and gives me a sweet kiss that lasts an eternity. After that, I don't want to send him home. But I do.

CHAPTER 41
LIFE IN THE FAST LANE

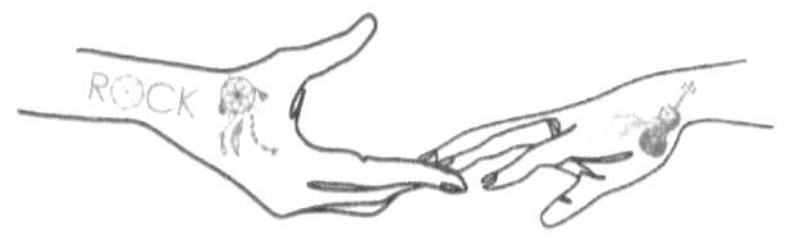

Rhys

"**B**illy, I need you to do whatever you can to get these guys off Lyric's trail. Send out a press release saying that I was just helping out with her fundraiser, deny any personal relationship..."

Wait... Hunt tried that, and it backfired. Hmm...

"You sure about that?" he asks.

"No. I'm not. I have no idea. This stuff is your specialty. Can't you just fix this?"

"Are you seeing her? Lyric? As more than a professional contact or friends?"

I hesitate, but I trust Billy to help, if I give him enough to work with.

"Fine. Yes. We're dating. But, listen, Billy — she's a widow. Her husband died in an accident almost four years ago. Her son is autistic. And she's a school teacher. I don't want my life, my fame to be the thing that causes her stress. That's why I was helping her in the first place. She's a single mom who's working her ass off for her kids."

There's a pause on the other end of the phone.

"Billy?"

"I'm sorry. Give me a second, Rhys. I'm still trying to get past 'Rhys is dating.'"

"Oh, ha-ha."

"Well, you have to admit it's a big change from drive-through-style waitress hookups."

Geez.

"It is. I know. That's why this has to be handled carefully."

"She means a lot to you, huh?" he asks.

"They do. All three of them."

"OK. Got it. Special handling, with kid gloves. You talked to Gryff about getting some bodyguards down there?"

"The guys don't want it. I don't want it. Not for me, anyway. But if things get any worse, I'm not sure I'd object to Lyric and the kids having security."

"That comes out of your share, you know."

"I figured. I can afford it. Whatever is necessary to keep them safe, I'll take care of it."

"Just like you did in setting up that trust for the kids? I assume these are the same kids, right?"

"Yeah."

"Ooh, buddy — you are in deep, aren't you?"

"The deepest."

"OK. Then we'll handle it. I'll have Ciara reach out to... Lyric?"

"Yeah. Lyric Larson."

"And she's a music teacher? That's—"

"Perfect. I know. So is she."

"Ciara will be Lyric's PR contact, and she can arrange for curated coverage updates, just like Brighid gets. If Lyric has any concerns that aren't related to security and personal safety, she can contact Ciara 24/7."

"You're paying her to be on duty 24/7?"

"Yeah. It's part of the job. What did you think *my* hours were?"

"Never thought about it."

"Because I'm always available if you need me — 24/7."

"Right. Got it. And thanks. For that and for this stuff, Billy. I need them protected."

"Call Gryff next. He'll make sure of it."

"I can have a guy there tonight, if you want," Gryff says. "He can do close protection on her and the kids, but if you're not all in the same place, I'd be better off sending you at least two guys."

"And what? Have them follow us everywhere? Watch the house 24/7?"

"And the studio, while you're there."

Oh, this is way more involved than I'd expected. We have close protection when we're on tour, but otherwise… I'm not used to having someone following me all day, every day, while I go to the gym, grab dinner, take a run… It feels almost as invasive as having paparazzi following us, which I didn't think I'd ever have to say, either.

"What kind of curtains are on the bedroom windows in her house?" Gryff asks.

"Regular curtains, I guess. I don't know."

"If they're at all sheer, you're going to want to replace them with room-darkening, and probably noise-dampening curtains, just to start."

Ugh. I haven't even gotten her screen door fixed.

"What about the studio — the curtains on my bedroom are sheer, looking out on the upper deck."

"You're in Dave's old room?"

"Yeah. How'd you know that?"

"We had a security concern there earlier in the summer, when he was first dating Piper. I'll talk to him about getting new curtains put in, since he and Piper are running the studio for now. Did he give you the wireless fob for the door lock?"

"Uh… No. There's a wireless lock?"

"I had it put in so he wasn't always leaving the deck doors unlocked while he was out surfing. Have him give it to you. Use it. Lock those doors every time you walk out of the room. Just in case."

I think back to the other night, with Lyric. We left the door open, the sheer curtains the only thing between a photographer and some steamy photos of our own.

"Right. Is there a motion sensor on that deck? Anybody could just walk up the steps, peer in the windows."

"The curtains will address that, but if you're leaving the doors open for the breeze — and I know you all do that — we may want to put something in. I'll talk to Dave. But — hey, Rhys…"

"What?"

"You didn't tell me if you want me to send my guys."

"I don't know, Gryff. I honestly don't know. I need to talk to Lyric about it. Right now, this is one incident with an unknown person wanting a picture of me, and maybe her and the kids, on a ride. The rest has just been speculation over photos some of the parents took at her fundraiser."

"I hear you. Just don't wait until something happens before you let me get you some guys, OK?"

"OK."

Lyric

The kids were surprisingly cool with the mom-talk about Mr. Rhys. Of course, I don't know what Tommy is thinking, but he usually lets us know if he's upset about something. The idea of Mr. Rhys staying at our house sometimes actually got a smile from him. Aria is all on board.

"Can Mr. Rhys and I have sleepovers, too, Mommy?" she asks. "Then he can tell me stories, and we can watch movies, and play video games after we make you breakfast in bed, and..."

OK. So maybe calling Rhys sleeping in my bed a "sleepover" wasn't the best idea. But she's only 7!

"Is Mr. Rhys your boyfriend now, Mommy? He said I had to wait until you did grown-up talk before I asked you."

"You talked to Mr. Rhys about being my boyfriend?"

"When he was making breakfast, I asked him if he was. And he said he wanted to be, but you had to decide."

Oh, boy... He'd known us for not even a week at that point. I can't imagine what he was thinking when she asked him that. Nevermind. It's Rhys. I can imagine. No filter, no hidden cards, no pretense, even with a 7-year-old.

Honestly, it's probably better that way. Things get a lot more complicated when it comes to adult conversations. Which I'm about to have with Brighid. Mom's got the kids for the morning.

I cut through the alley courtyard between Brighid's shop and Callie's restaurant. Brighid's been open for a couple hours now, but it's Sunday morning, so it's quiet inside.

"I can get you a few large pieces of black tourmaline, Mrs. Lowell, but it'll take a couple weeks to arrive," she tells the little elderly lady at the counter.

Mrs. Lowell is a regular customer since Brighid took over the yarn shop. I'm not sure what she, or her husband, maybe, did for a living in their prime years, but she's asked Brighid for a lot of large and rare crystals over the years, as well as being a regular customer for Brighid's medicinal teas, tarot readings, Reiki healing and spiritual counseling. Even her yarn. She's well-heeled.

"Getting them sustainably-sourced means it takes a little longer," Brighid tells her. "I can ask the wholesaler to expedite shipping for me, but the price will be a little higher."

"That's fine, dear," Mrs. Lowell says. "I'm in a bit of rush, but I'm happy to pay to get them here sooner."

"Alright. I'll put in the order for you today, and I'll give you a call when I have an update."

"Thanks so much, dear," Mrs. Lowell says. "And thank you for the tea! We're going stand-up paddling in the morning, and you know how my old joints are."

"Have fun, but be careful, OK? They go a ways out on the ocean in that class."

"Don't worry, dear. I swim like a fish! It keeps me young." She turns, her package in hand. "Oh, Lyric, dear! So good to see you! How are the children?"

"They're doing well, Mrs. Lowell, thank you."

"And I hear you pulled off a major success with your fundraiser the other night! A job well done! Music is so important — for children, especially. And that handsome fellow... Rice? Is that his name?"

I chuckle.

"It's Rhys, Mrs. Lowell. Like the candy, just spelled differently. The name's Welsh, though he's not, at least not directly."

"Such positive energy he has — right, Brighid?"

"That he does, Mrs. Lowell. Rhys is one of the warmest and kindest people I know," she says, giving me a look. "He's very special."

"Then he's perfect for our Lyric... Have a wonderful day, Ladies!"

The little seaglass chimes over the shop door jingle as she heads outside.

"She's so cute!" I tell Brighid. "And all of the activities she gets up to! I don't know where she gets the energy at her age."

"Probably from doing all those activities," Brighid suggests. "Plus lots of tea." She chuckles.

"Now, as for that warm, kind, handsome, special man... Spill, girl!" she insists.

I look around, making sure no one else is in the shop.

"It's clear. But we can go in the back room, if you prefer. Molly's off today, but I'll hear the chimes if someone comes in."

"Let's."

Settled in the back room, in Brighid's comfortable consultation area, cups of calming tea steaming next to us, even though it's summer... I let Brighid in on much, if not all, of what's going on.

I start by returning her leggings, freshly washed.

"I see... So you needed pants... at the studio... on short notice..." she says slowly, trying not to crack up and, ultimately, failing.

Once she gets control of herself again, I give her the upshot.

"So, you're really trying this — a relationship with Rhys?" she asks when I finish. "I wondered when he borrowed my car. I kind of expected him to come back by for some yarn, with all their downtime. Him, with you... Not what I expected."

"Yeah... He's been... Wait. Yarn?"

"You don't know?" She gives me a conspiratorial smile. "Rhys knits. He learned during college, from the ladies at Kara's shop there. He knits when they're on the road for long stretches. He usually sends me a scarf or a hat for my birthday."

Rhys... knits. OK. That's... yes, unexpected. But, then, that seems to be the rule with Rhys: Expect the unexpected. And, it's been... he's been...

"He's been such an amazing gift, on so many levels, just these past couple of weeks," I tell her in answer to her question.

"You finally decided to move forward," she says, giving me a gentle smile.

"I hadn't realized how stuck in the past I was. I was just trying to maintain the status quo, and I was barely managing that. But then, you knew that — you all knew that."

"We did. But other than giving you what help and support you'd allow us to give, there wasn't much we could do. You had to decide you were ready to let go and find a new future."

"I can't let Adam go. I won't. But the life we had — that's the past. It got us where we are now, where being with Rhys is possible, where letting him in my kids' lives is possible. I'll always be grateful to Adam for that."

"How are the kids taking it? I imagine Rhys is wonderful with them. He's so childlike and joyful himself — even Mrs. Lowell noticed his energy, and she's never met him."

"They love him! And... I can scarcely credit it, but there's something about him that draws Tommy out of his shell. He actually played with Rhys and Aria the other day, and Rhys got him on the helicopters at the amusement park when I couldn't. Rhys' mother said he's always had a way with kids, that just playing, not having expectations, helps him connect with them."

"You met Rhys' mother?" She sounds shocked. "Even when the band first started, I never got to meet her. She was always so busy! Rhys made her sound amazing, though."

"She is. She's a social worker, and a foster mom until recently. She came to visit Rhys on her vacation."

"And..."

"We got along great. She loved the kids, and they loved her. And she told me some things about Rhys that I didn't know."

"That he's adopted?"

"Well, he told me first, but she filled in the blanks. How'd you know?"

"Hunter told me a long time ago. It was literally one of the first things Rhys said to him. Rhys just seems to know who he can trust. And I couldn't think of a nicer person for you to have in your life, in the kids' lives. Just..."

"What?"

"Well, I have this theory that Rhys is part chaos elemental," she says, smirking at me. "You know about his ADHD, right?"

"It's pretty obvious. But it's part of who he is, and he wouldn't be that person without it. I wouldn't change it for a moment."

"Good. I know it means doing a little more hand-holding with practical stuff, and not everyone wants that in a partner. But you're built for that kind of stuff. You're so organized."

"He's been as much of a help to me as anything, Brighid. I showed him how to use his to-do list app, and I think he's even been trying to use his calendar app, too."

"Then he's one step ahead of Hunter," she says, laughing. "But that's part of who Hunt is, too. No detail goes unescaped. And that's what I've been trying to get Hunt to really see — that he's loved just as he is. That nothing that happened in the past has to hinder his future, because it's what got him where he is now, where he's truly happy. He still has his moments, but we're working to get through those, too."

"How's the wedding planning going?"

"Nearly done. We've had a few hiccups, a few complications. But it's all on track, and I have to thank you again for agreeing to officiate."

"I'm delighted to do it. You two deserve your happily-ever-after so much after all you've been through, finding your way back to each other. It's fate."

"I feel incredibly lucky, and I know Hunt does, too. And that's all I need. We both appreciate what we've been given."

"Even after all the..." I don't even want to bring up the paparazzi and the social media.

"I figured that's what you'd stopped by to talk about." She sighs. "We made it through that. It wasn't a big deal in the end. I got my feelings hurt a little, but I don't really care about how anyone feels about me, except Hunt. And he loves me so hard..."

I smirk at her.

"I don't mean like that," she says, rolling her eyes, "though he does that, too..." She chuckles.

"Rhys is talking to Billy and... Gryff?" I ask. Brighid nods. "He's talking to them today about the PR and security stuff, see what they suggest we do to handle any problems that might arise."

"Has something happened already?"

"Just the one story coming out. And then... someone tried to buy, of all things, the ride photo from when we rode the Haunted Mansion last night. They didn't get it. The park people were so nice about it, when it wasn't even their fault... But some of the other customers were taking photos of Rhys in line, and maybe me and the kids, too."

"I know that has to be scary. Especially with the kids."

"Yeah. I expect the one guy was a reporter or paparazzo. And that makes me think..."

"That they might show up in larger numbers, like they did with me?"

"They've mostly left Callie alone."

"Callie had a high profile already, just on a more local scale. And she and Declan are already married, so there's less of an anticipatory thing to it. And that was all before the photos..."

"I still can't believe she did that. Actually — yes, I can. It's Declan. Nothing intimidates him, and she's taken that cue from him. She even cooked Rhys and me a special dinner the other night."

"Uh-oh."

"Yeah. But she had good intentions. And I think I have her to thank for the breakthrough I had."

"It all works out fine in the end."

"People keep saying that, and then things go wrong."

Brighid looks at me, her lips pursing.

"Don't borrow trouble yet, Lyric. Better yet, get an idea of what's coming and see if you can't turn that to your advantage. I can do a reading for you, if you like. But you can do that for yourself anytime."

"I haven't been happy with my tarot lately. I was thinking about trying something else."

"I've got a new deck, 'Boadicea's Tarot of Earthly Delights.' I haven't tried it myself yet, since I just got it in, but you're welcome to borrow it. Or I've got some Ogham, or runes."

"I was thinking about trying Ogham. I'm connecting a little more with the Irish stuff these days, for some reason."

"Priestess of Brighid. It was bound to happen eventually," Brighid says with a gentle smile.

"I'll take the tarot, too, if you don't mind loaning them to me."

"Not at all. With all the wedding stuff, I won't have time to sit down with them properly for weeks."

There's that jingle of seaglass as a customer comes in.

"Perfect timing," I tell her.

"I'll wrap these up for you."

The two of us emerge from the back room to find a young woman reading through Brighid's list of herbal teas.

"I'll be right with you," she tells her. "Call me if you need anything," she says to me. "I mean it. If you don't get satisfaction from whatever Billy and Gryff have to say to Rhys, call me, text me, and I'll make sure whatever needs to happen happens. Billy still owes me, on several counts."

"I will. Thanks."

"My love and blessings to the kids. I'm going to stick a few crystals in for them, even though I know Tommy will probably just ignore them in favor of gears."

"Thanks. Aria will gladly take them all for herself. She's got quite the little collection going."

"Witchlings and their pockets full of rocks," Brighid says, smiling warmly and handing me the bag.

I head back out, ready to pick up the kids and get an update from Rhys. Then we've got some things to figure out.

"Now, what can I do to help you?" Brighid asks, the seaglass once again jingling as I open the door.

"I was mainly interested about getting a reading," the woman says. "But those teas look amazing. And such beautiful yarn!"

"That's made from local alpaca fleece..."

Sounds like Brighid may have a new regular customer.

Wait... local alpaca fleece?

CHAPTER 42

GOOD VIBRATIONS

Rhys

"Hi," I say when Lyric opens the door.

"Hi," she says back.

Conspicuous silence.

"Everything OK?" she asks.

"Well... I guess that depends on how you look at it."

"Mr. Rhys! Mr. Rhys!"

I catch Aria as she hurls herself at me.

"Well, hello, Aria! What's got you so excited?"

"Mommy says she's taking us to see the 'pacas!"

"Packas?"

"Well, it was supposed to be a surprise, but... I thought we could go out to the alpaca farm down the road."

"There's an alpaca farm down the road?" Aria's totally right to be this excited.

"Yes. Where did you think Brighid got her alpaca fleece?"

"The zoo?"

"Silly Mr. Rhys!" Aria declares me.

"There's an alpaca farm about ten minutes from here," Lyric explains. "They do tours, alpaca walks, and alpaca yoga, and sell things made from the fleece."

"Then, let's go!"

I honestly didn't know that alpacas hummed.

And now that I do, I kind of want to incorporate it in a song.
I think today established that alpacas are far superior to llamas in nearly every way. Except you can't ride them.

No, I did not attempt to ride an alpaca. I just asked whether the kids could.

The answer was no. With prejudice.

Lesson learned.

I bought a bunch of stuff. The alpaca people were happier with me after that.

We brought dinner back to the house, my treat. Lyric gave the kids their baths, and I did bedtime stories, and the kids went straight to bed.

It's all very domestic. I like it.

What I didn't like was picking up where we left off with "Hi."

"So... I talked to Billy and Gryff..."

"And what did they say?" Lyric asks.

"Billy said he'd have somebody call you."

"Ciara. Yes, she called while the kids were having lunch."

"And she told you she'd monitor PR stuff for you?"

"Yes. She said if I needed anything, just to let her know."

"Right. That's what Billy said she'd do."

"That's fine. It's fine."

She doesn't sound like it's fine.

"Are you sure?"

"Well, I don't like the idea of someone having to keep an eye on the entire internet to make sure the kids and I don't end up splashed all over gossip sites."

"It's probably nothing. They don't usually pay attention unless I jump out of a plane or have myself set on fire."

"On fire?"

"You didn't know about that?"

"Uh... no. Why did you have yourself set on fire?"

"It was a stunt for the video for our last single. You didn't see it?"

"No. I think I'd have remembered that."

She doesn't sound like she wants to watch it, either. Hmm...

"I trained to do it! I didn't just have them light me on fire!"

"I would hope so."

She still doesn't sound happy.

"It was totally safe! The label wouldn't let me do it unless it was safe."

"They let you jump out of planes."

"Also safe. They weren't OK with me running with the bulls, though."

"You asked to run with the bulls. In Spain."

"Yeah, I thought it'd make a great scene for that video, but they said we'd have to fake it if I wanted to do the stunt."

"So, you didn't run with the bulls."

"Well, not for the video, no."

She sighs in relief.

"I did it later, when we were on tour."

Yeah, she's giving me a look now.

"Why?"

"Just for fun."

"Of course..." She rolls her eyes. "Speaking of security concerns..."

"Yeah — I talked to Gryff. He said he can have security assigned for you and the kids, if you want. They can watch the house and go with you wherever you go."

"They'd follow me and the kids around all day? What about when I'm teaching? Or when the kids are in school?"

"I don't know. I guess they'd wait outside the school?"

"But Tommy goes to a special school."

"Oh. OK. Well, I can see if Gryff can get each of you a bodyguard..."

"And... you'd pay for this? For each of us to have a bodyguard?"

"Well, yeah. I want you to be safe."

"Are we not safe now?"

"Well, we only had the one issue. You're probably perfectly safe right now."

"Probably?"

"Well, I don't know who that guy was or what he wanted."

"He wanted a picture of you, me and my kids."

"Well, besides that. I mean, we don't know why he wanted it. It might have been totally harmless."

"I see…" she says.

"You know — it's never a good thing when people just say, 'I see.' They say they see, but they really don't. Or they do and they don't like what they see. Which of those is your 'I see'?"

"I don't really know."

"See — that's how it is! I don't really know what was going on, or that there's really any other reason to be concerned. But if you want security, I'll get you security — however much security you want."

"Well, no — I don't *want* security," Lyric says. "But what I really want is not to *need* security."

"I don't think you do. Need security, I mean. Not right now. But Gryff said it was up to us."

Lyric looks up the stairs toward the kids' rooms, and I know she's thinking about whether they're safe.

"I don't want to scare the kids, making them think they're not safe, when — like you said — they probably *are* safe."

I didn't think about that. Is there a correct answer for this? Bring in security and then realize we don't need it, but maybe scare the kids in the meantime? Don't bring in security but then decide we should have, but only after something scary happens?

"You're their mom. I think you have to decide that."

"Do *you* feel safe?"

"Yes."

"I'm not sure you're a good measure of what's safe. Especially after finding out you ran with bulls. For fun."

Hmm… Maybe I shouldn't have told her that.

Ya think?

Ah — head-dude. I thought you were being awfully quiet. You have any input here?

You need to make sure they're safe.

So, have Gryff get us a couple of guys?

But I also think she *has to be the one to decide.*

Right.

"I think you have to be the one to decide," I tell her. "If things change, we can do something different, but right now, it's your decision."

"Then, no. Not yet, anyway."

Alright then. That's settled.

For now.

"So, Aria said something about sleepovers?"

I waggle my eyebrows at Lyric, put on my most winning smile.

"Only if you can be quiet," she says, blushing a little. "And no walking around naked or anything."

"Is that just outside the bedroom, or all the time?" No nekkid time in the bedroom would be a major bummer.

"We'll play it by ear. For now, outside the bedroom."

Yes!

Lyric

"**G**ods, Rhys! I can't! Please! Have some mercy!"

I'm keeping my voice down, praying to every god I know to keep the kids from waking up.

Rhys lifts his head up, giving me a quizzical look.

"I didn't picture you as a quitter," he says, his smile sly.

"There's a difference between quitting and expiring under torture!"

"Torture? You're not enjoying this?"

He gives a lick directly over my clit, and my thighs clamp shut around his head.

"Or this?"

He presses against my G-spot, and my legs wrap tighter around his shoulders, pulling him toward me.

"How about this?"

He dives in again, nibbling around my clit until I'm a moaning, mewling mess desperate for release.

"Get. Up. Here," I tell him, once I catch my breath, pulling on his hair to make it clear my request is more of a demand.

"Yes, ma'am," he says, climbing up over me, wrapping his arms around my shoulders, settling his hips between my thighs. He rubs his dick against me, and my head goes back. He runs his tongue up my throat. "Anything else?"

"Fuck. Me."

"With pleasure," he says.

And he does.

Rhys puts his boxers back on once we're done. They've got bees and honey drips all over them, today, with two big beehives on the back, labeled "honey buns."

Oh, my... He does have a lovely butt. It's almost a shame to have him put them back on. Oh, well.

I grab my sleep-shirt and make sure the coast is clear before I head out to the bathroom to clean up a little.

When I glance in the mirror, I see the same dark circles under my eyes that I usually do, but maybe they're a little smaller, a little lighter. Totally unsurprising. I'm on vacation, after all. The light in my eyes — that's harder to explain. Maybe it's just knowing I've got a set of instruments on the way for the kids in a couple weeks. That's a big load off my mind.

And worry about one guy at an amusement park? It seems silly now, in retrospect. No one so much as blinked when we showed up at the alpaca farm. Not even a single selfie request when we were there, or when we picked up dinner. It looks like my fifteen minutes of fame are behind me now. And, honestly, it's a relief.

I head back into the bedroom, finding Rhys lying in my bed, the comforter pulled back invitingly. And I crawl in, resting my head on his chest, his arm around me. It's probably just the sex, the endorphins, getting a little release before bedtime... but I sleep like a baby.

Rhys
Three days later

Yeah, I think we were overreacting about the security thing. Maybe even the PR stuff, too. It's been three days, and no sign of any paps, no mentions online after some social media posts from the night at the amusement park. Other than responding to a few friendly "Hey, Rhys!" calls when I went to the climbing gym while Lyric spent some time with her mom in the mornings, it's been... well, it's been astonishingly normal. Even quieter than when I'm back in New York, just going back and forth from my apartment to grab food or go hang out with Kier.

I could get used to this. Really. I start to see why Hunt's happy to make this little town home again, and why Dave and Declan were so quick to decide to move here to be with their girls.

I've been splitting my afternoons between working in the studio with the guys — Malcolm's back for a few days, so I've had a couple drop-ins to do, and Piper's feeling better in the afternoons, so that's when we get work done — and doing beach-time with Lyric and the kids. We managed to get Tommy in the water up to his knees this time. And Aria... I think her being a quarter mermaid is underselling it. She swims as well as I do. And no fear, either. I love her spirit. But we've got to keep an eye on her, just in case.

"Are you really enjoying it here, Rhys?" Lyric asks. "I know it's probably boring compared to what you're used to..."

"Boring? No. I'm having a ball. The only thing I'm missing is that I haven't made it out kiteboarding yet, and I'd kind of like to go back to the amusement park."

"Well, I don't think you're going to get me or the kids kiteboarding, but you're welcome to do that whenever you like," she says. "The kids and I have some last-minute school shopping to do, so no need to hang out with us 24/7..."

"I like hanging out with you 24/7." And I do. I lean over and kiss her, making sure no one's watching first, including the kids. We've kept things quiet at home, other than our "sleepovers." The kids haven't said or done anything that implies they're uncomfortable with it. So far, so good.

Lyric smiles at me. I love seeing her like that. She seems so happy, so relaxed now. I'm starting to think that maybe I really am good for her.

"Still, you should go do what you want — and you've said you've been wanting to kiteboard for a while..."

"You sure you don't want to come give it a try? I'm sure your mom would watch the kids for an afternoon. Or maybe my mom could, if you're comfortable with that."

She thinks for a second.

"I'm comfortable with that. But we really do have some school shopping to do. I was so busy with the fundraiser, my lesson plan, my fellowship application, that I never got around to it, and now..."

"Now I'm monopolizing all of your time?" I suggest, giving her a smile of my own.

She shrugs, smiling again.

"We've been having fun. And I *am* on vacation. But, yes, I've got some things I need to do. Not only the shopping, but I've got to get one last piece done for the fellowship submission."

"What's this fellowship thing about?"

"I'm applying — again — for a poetry fellowship. It's very competitive. Practically every poet in the region applies for it at some point. I've applied nearly every year since before Tommy was born."

Nearly every year.

I'm not asking. I expect I know which year she didn't apply.

"What happens if you win it?"

"They offer you a mentor and publishing assistance, some appearances, and there's a big cash prize!"

"So, you buy a new car?"

She laughs.

"No, silly. The fellowship sponsors the poet to take the following year and just write — it's basically a modest salary to offset not having to work a regular job during that year."

"So, you'd take a year off teaching?"

"Yeah. At school at least. I'd probably keep my private students. It's more than I make at my school job, but not by much. The big deal is I'd be able to work from home, spend the days writing while the kids are at school and the evenings with them, instead of trying to squeeze in writing after they've gone to bed. And during the summer, I wouldn't have to worry about a lesson plan or the fundraiser."

"You'd let someone else take over?"

"The district would have to find someone to do it, which they didn't this year. And — thanks in no small part to a certain pro musician — we've got new instruments for this year, which means we won't need nearly as much next year. I could take the year off with a clear conscience."

"You won't miss it?"

"I'll miss my students. And probably miss teaching, a little. But I've been wanting to work full-time on my poetry since before I went to college."

"Why'd you major in music, then?"

"I'd had a few mentors who'd suggested I could find a spot with a regional orchestra, maybe something even bigger."

"As a violinist."

She nods.

"You're better than you let on."

"Maybe," she says shyly. "Like I said, I did some studio work back in the day."

"Like what?"

"A few solos here and there, on some folk-rock songs."

"Anything I would have heard of?"

"Meredith March's 'A Way Back Home.'"

Well, she's achieved making Rhys Madigan speechless.

"That charted."

"I know." More shy smiles.

"I'm going to have to drag you into the studio now — you know that, right?"

"Nah. I've got too much going now. I gave up on music stardom when I decided to become a teacher. Besides, violin isn't part of aMUSEd's sound."

"Alex's used keyboards instead the few times we've needed it this summer for covers. Maybe you sit in with us…"

"No, really. I'm happy with my life here. Except for having more time for poetry and the kids, and maybe not having to worry so much about bills, I'm good."

Don't push her.

Head-dude's mostly been quiet since I started spending most of my time with Lyric and the kids. I've taken that as approval of how I've been handling things with her, and with them. So, taking his advice now seems like the smart thing to do.

"So, school shopping tomorrow, while I go kiteboarding?"

"Yeah. We can catch back up after dinner."

"I like how we catch up after dinner," I tell her. The saucy smile she gives me tells me she agrees. I lean in and kiss her, not giving a flibbertigibbet who sees. She opens up to me, tangling her tongue with mine.

"Eww! Gross, Mommy!"

Lyric goes bright red.

"Aria — that was rude. Apologize to Mr. Rhys, please."

"Sorry, Mr. Rhys. I don't kiss my boyfriend like that."

"Wait — are you kissing Noah?" Lyric asks her.

"Once. Under the slide at recess. Mrs. Perry told us not to kiss at school, or we'd have to go to the principal's office next time."

"Then you should be glad she let you off with a warning, Aria. I'll have to talk to Mrs. Perry when school starts."

"No, Mommy! I won't do it again!"

I feel sorry for her. They're kids. I give Lyric a look, pleading the case for letting Aria off with that warning.

"Fine," she says. "But no more kissing at school. OK?"

"I already promised!"

"Good."

I don't remind Lyric that she and I also got caught kissing at school and didn't get punished for it. It's good karma to let Aria off.

I take Lyric's hand and give it a squeeze. She relaxes back into her beach chair and smiles, then sighs as Aria takes off for the surf again. She starts to get up, but I gesture for her to stay. I follow Aria down into the water, diving into the face of a wave and coming up on the other side with Aria there before me. A little mermaid, indeed.

CHAPTER 43
LOVE IS AN OPEN DOOR

Rhys
Four days later

It's been amazing, spending most of my nights in Lyric's bed, making love to her until we're both sated and then holding her while we sleep. Most mornings, I let her sleep in while I make breakfast for the kids, and then for the two of us. It's peaceful and domestic, and I love it. I love her. Yeah. And the kids, too.

I'm still waiting for her to feel like she can tell me why she reacted like she did to the little drum. I guess it's got some sort of sentimental value for her. Maybe her husband gave it to her and she doesn't let anyone else touch it now that he's gone? But why not Tommy? It's his dad, after all...

Head-dude is quiet. I guess I'm still doing a decent job taking care of Lyric and the kids. And I love that, too.

Lyric left mid-morning to go have lunch with her mom. She'd suggested dinner, but Iris has another date tonight. Lyric's a little bemused by that. I think it's awesome. If Mom's had a date in the last decade, she didn't tell me about it. But then she's headed home next week, so maybe she's got somebody waiting for her there and just isn't telling me.

Aria and Tommy are up in their rooms, doing what Lyric called "solo play" after they finished lunch. If it was me, at Tommy's age, I'd have been doing "solo play" on my first kit, which Mom got me for my 10th birthday. But, for Tommy, it means building a huge Lego... Well, I'm not sure if it's a contraption or not. No axles or spinning parts. But he's really into it. For Aria, it means writing her own poetry, headphones on and music playing.

So, I leave them to it and head back down the hall. I'll go back downstairs and check in with Kier, see if he's in a better mood than he's been the last week or so.

But the next thing I know, I go flying, and with my height, that's a long way from feet going out from under me to landing on my face. Lucky for me, my arms are long, too, and my hand-eye coordination is awesome. I manage to grab hold of the first thing my hand finds in reach — a doorknob. My knees will be bruised tomorrow, even with the carpet. And, what in the hell... Hel? I don't know if I'm supposed to follow Lyric's lead in swearing while I'm in her house or not... Anyway — why did I trip?

I look back behind me and find... A drumstick? It's not one of mine. A Vik Firth Nova, pro-quality, but not with my signature on it. Literally. Mine have my signature on them, because they're my signature sticks. It's closest to Tommy's room. Could it be his? Is that why Lyric freaked out like she did that morning? Because he'd gotten into trouble with his drumsticks, and she'd taken them away?

Open the door.

What door, head-dude? Is this a metaphorical door? Because the kids' doors are both open. And nobody's knocking on the front door or anything. I know I need to get the screen door fixed, still. But...

Open the door.

Wait. The door I grabbed on the way down, to keep from cracking my very hard head open?

Open it.

It's locked, dude. I saw her lock it.

There's silence, but it's silence that says, "Just flibbertigibbeting do what you're told, Rhys."

Fine.

But I don't have to open the door. It's already open. Just an inch or two, but it's open. Did Lyric decide to let me in and just didn't tell me yet?

I push the door open farther, and...

Oh, wow.

The room's full of drums. There's a kit — almost as big as mine.

Bigger, in some ways.

What are you on about, head-dude?

It's a pro-quality kit, Pearl custom shells, Zildjian cymbals... I round the back of it... double kick pedal, pro-quality throne — a little low for me, with my legs, but raised up a couple inches... Perfect. Laid across the snare, there's a single stick, a match to the one I tripped over. Did Tommy come in here, take a stick and drop it on the way back into his room?

I look around the room from the vantage point of the throne.

This is a dedicated practice room. There's acoustic foam on the walls, even the back of the door. A set of shelves holds a variety of smaller hand drums, including... yeah — that looks like the one that was in Lyric's music room. It's the same brand as the others on the shelf. A cajon in the corner, perfect for jamming without a kit. Cowbells. Cabasa. A stick case, the top open, with more of the Vik Firth sticks peeking out. Brushes.

There's a big duffle next to the cajon... Inside, a drum drop for hooking up to a sound system. A carpet remnant to go under a kit. A metal case... full of mics — drum mics. This wasn't a high-end hobby kit. This is a working musician's kit, suitable for use in a live venue, though more than most drummers would try to fit in a car. (I am not most drummers.) There are even photos on the walls — a guy with long brown hair, shaved on the sides, playing out with a band, with a smaller version of this kit, stage lights painting him with shifting colors, reflecting off the cymbals, his green eyes, or eyes closed, his mind sunk into his work, part of the music, like me playing to a crowd of thousands.

I pull off my shirt, wipe the thin layer of dust off of everything and drop it on the floor. Ah — a drum key. I pick up the key from under the throne, tune up the drums. They're in good shape, considering how much dust there was.

Thump thump-thump.

The kick drum has a great tone. Almost as good as mine. It'll cut through the noise of metal or punk... Where did I hear someone talking about playing punk recently? Can't remember. No surprise, with my Swiss-cheese brain.

I give the snare a smack, tap the cymbal, do a run across the toms. It's a solid kit. I'd play it.

I pick up a polyrhythm, then settle into my solo. Six minutes of joy on the way...

But I only know it's six minutes because I've recorded myself playing it before, trying to get the guys to let me put it on an album, on a B-side for a single — something, anything. When I'm playing it, the only thing that exists is the music. It's my heartbeat made audible to the world, elaborated upon, given a life of its own. For six minutes, my soul exists outside of my head, not tangled up in random thoughts, impulsive actions or social faux pas. My feet can't go in my mouth when they're busy telling a story in low bass beats and shimmering high-hat. For six minutes, I can't fuck anything up.

Until I do.

Lyric's standing in the doorway, white as a sheet, tears streaming down her face, staring at me in disbelief. Then she looks down, and I follow her gaze, finding Tommy sitting in the middle of the floor in front of the kit, patting away on that little hand drum, smiling.

"Get out," she says. It's quiet. So quiet. Too quiet.

"Get out," she repeats. It's less quiet. Loud enough to bring Aria out of her room.

"Lyric — I..."

"Get out!" she yells, and Tommy starts crying. She snatches him up, turns around, grabs Aria's hand and walks down the hall, slamming Tommy's bedroom door behind her.

I set down the sticks, grab my shirt and follow her.

I can hear her crying, Tommy crying, Aria's quiet voice asking questions I can't understand through the door, making soothing sounds.

My hand goes to the doorknob, ready to do anything I can to soothe her, soothe the kids...

I know I fucked up. I just don't know how.

Wedding photo, dude.

I run down the stairs and into her bedroom, looking at those photos I snooped in that first night I held her while she cried and then slept.

The guy with the long brown hair, shaved on the sides, in the tux, kissing Lyric in her beautiful white dress.

Her husband.

Her husband was a drummer.

And she locked away everything that reminded her of that fact, including the little hand drum that gives her son such joy.

Because... because... he...

Died on the way home from a gig.

Fuck. He died on the way home from a gig. The late nights she talked about, not going with him because she had the kids, had to get up early. So he drove himself home, in the wee hours of the morning, after playing for hours, doing load-out, his gig kit in the back of the car, wired and tired, and exhausted to the point of falling asleep behind the wheel, because he hadn't gone to the doctor like his wife asked him to.

Oh, geez... Lyric just walked in to find me playing her dead husband's kit.

Give the man a prize!

Shut up, asshole. The door wasn't locked. It was open. She'd left it open.

Did she?

If *she* didn't then... Tommy? Is he tall enough to have gotten that key down? Maybe.

I told her she could talk to me about the locked room when she was ready.

She'd never have been ready.

And now she's told me to get out. She's kicked me out. Kicked me to the curb. Because I fucked up. Again. Only way worse.

Are you sure?

About what, dude? You heard her — she told me to get out.

Do you always do what you're told?

Well, no. I'm no rebel, but I ran with bulls. I accidentally told Mom that Declan and Callie got married at 17. And any of about a million other things I've done that resulted in Alex smacking me on the back of the head.

If he was here now, he'd be smacking you harder than he ever has before.

For doing what she told me?

Yes. Because what she wants and what she needs aren't the same thing. Not now.

She's upstairs crying her eyes out. The kids are upset. That's my fault.

Then fix it!

I don't know how to do that.

Take care of them!

I look behind me at the bed, the bed where I've held Lyric so many times in the last couple weeks, after making love to her, after finishing breakfast, when she was so upset that night after her meeting...

That's the only thing I can think to offer to make this better. I can tell her I'm sorry until the cows come home. I can explain what I was thinking, or wasn't thinking, really. But none of that is going to make any difference for her right now. Right now, she's bereft. There's that word again. I'm not sure why she didn't tell me this one thing, this one really important thing about her husband...

She wasn't ready to let it go. Not that part. You just had to force the issue.

I know. I didn't know I was doing it. Stupid Rhys.

Not stupid, Rhys. Just what was needed, Rhys. Now go finish fixing it.

I don't know if this is going to make it better or worse. But I have to try.

CHAPTER 44
SECRET LOVE

Lyric

I rock back and forth with a crying Tommy in my lap, an arm around Aria, who seems more puzzled than distressed. In fact, she's trying to console me, and I don't think she even really knows why I'm crying like this.

I'm a horrible mother. I yelled and upset Tommy again, and now my 7-year-old is trying to make *me* feel better.

I look up at the ceiling, start counting the little glow-in-the-dark stars up there, trying to calm myself, get things back under control. I take a deep breath and... sob.

No, this is not working.

Why couldn't Rhys leave a locked door locked? Why couldn't he just wait until I was ready to talk to him about this, about Adam, about what he did for a living, about how he died? Why?

It's Rhys, sweetie. He doesn't always think things through. He never has. At times, it's one of his better qualities, along with being kind, giving, warm, supportive...

Are you a founding member of the Rhys Madigan fan club or something, Vivienne?

Maybe. I've been around a while, watching, waiting... But you're the one who had his picture on your wall.

Don't remind me. I should have left that daydream in the past, where it belonged.

Are you sure Rhys is what you should be leaving in the past, Lyric? Because he's the one who's here, now, alive and doing his best to take care of you and your kids, doing his best to love you and your kids.

I want to scream at her, rage at her, but — well, the kids would know I was off my rocker, but also... she's right. I know she's right. Rhys is doing his best for us. He's made some mistakes, but he keeps trying to take care of us. Do I just chalk this up to another mistake? Forgive him, like this wasn't an incredible invasion of my privacy?

You told him to be himself, Lyric. You told Brighid that you wouldn't change him. But here you are, ready to end things with him because he made a very Rhys-like mistake. He found a drum kit sitting abandoned—

It wasn't abandoned! It was locked safely away! On purpose!

Are you sure it was locked? Are you sure?

I locked it. He saw me put the key away. He knew where it was.

And no one else did?

I look down to where Tommy clings to me, no longer sobbing himself, but crying quietly. I remember the look on his face as he played along with Rhys... and suddenly, I'm no longer sure. But this isn't the time to interrogate him, hoping he'll somehow tell me whether he unlocked that door. I've already upset him. Maybe later, once some time has passed. And Aria... She's rubbing my back, oddly reminiscent of how Rhys soothed me... twice now, at least.

"I'm sorry, kids. Mommy got very upset, but I shouldn't have taken it out on you two, even a little."

I kiss Tommy's hair, and he settles a little more. And that just reminds me of Rhys kissing my hair when I was upset. He's tried so hard to get me through my pains and losses lately. And Vivienne was right — *I* was right — you can't take just the easy parts of someone and reject the hard ones. It's all or nothing. You either appreciate them, love them, for who they are as a whole, or you don't really... love them.

And, gods help me, I do. I love him. I love Rhys.

About damn time!

Shut up, Frank.

I love him and I just threw him out, no explanation, no giving him a chance to explain. After all he's done for us.

"Is Mr. Rhys OK, Mommy? He looked sad, too."

"Yes, he did, didn't he?"

Is he even going to want to come back after that?

There's a quiet knock at the door. It's not even locked...

"Lyric... Can I come in, please? I need to talk to you."

I look at the kids — huge, sad eyes on both of them, and probably on me, too, if I'm honest.

"Yes, come in."

Rhys opens the door, and, yes, he looks sad, and a little stunned. Not that I can blame him.

I scoot over with Tommy, and Aria moves over behind me, hugging me around my neck. Rhys sits down in the empty space on the bed.

"Lyric — I'm not sure exactly what happened, or how, but I know now that I intruded into something I shouldn't have. And I'm sorry for that. I wouldn't have done it if I'd realized. Maybe I should have, but..."

"No — it's my fault for not having told you sooner, or at least given you some explanation. You've earned that. I just... I wasn't ready."

"Are you sure you ever would have been?"

Huh. Well... He's got a point.

"That room has been locked for nearly four years," I acknowledge.

"Since he... since he passed."

"Yeah. He had the smaller kit in the car. He left that one set up here after he got it."

"And no one's touched it since that night."

"No."

"OK. That makes more sense now, with the other things I figured out."

Oh? What else did he figure out?

"Are the kids OK? Are you OK?"

"I'm OK, Mr. Rhys. Mommy was sad."

"Thank you for trying to make her feel better, Aria. That was very nice of you."

"Yes, it was," I add. "Aria — if you're feeling alright, I'd like to talk to Mr. Rhys, alone."

"Grown-up talk."

"Yes." I nod. "You can go back in your room, and in a little while, we'll have dinner, and maybe a movie."

"Yay!" She runs out of the room and back into her own.

"Hey, buddy," Rhys says, ruffling Tommy's hair. For once, Tommy doesn't object. "Sorry that Mom and I upset you. That was a grown-up mistake. And I hope Mom and I can fix that. But I need to talk to her first. Is that OK?"

Tommy just looks at Rhys with his big blue eyes then climbs out of my lap and onto his bed, picking up a big Lego construct that's new today. He's been busy.

"I think that's a yes," I tell Rhys. "Let's go downstairs and talk."

Rhys stands up and offers me his hand, and after a moment's consideration, I take it. The instinct not to is as much because I wonder if I deserve it as it is because I'm suddenly less at ease with Rhys. And I know that's as much my fault as it is his.

He leads me into the bedroom, sitting down on the bed and holding out his arms to me.

It's like there's a fork in the road ahead of me — reject him now, and know that we may never come back from it, or accept the comfort, and the apology, he's offering and see if we can't move forward, together, with this one last secret left behind us.

"Please, Lyric," he says.

Gods, those big brown eyes... Once again, I melt, folding myself into his arms. I take a deep breath and find myself sobbing again. Rhys just holds me, rubbing my back and pressing kisses to the top of my head. After a while, my tears dry, and it's just me and Rhys, lying quietly together. But the silence weighs on both of us, and eventually, I break it.

"He was a professional drummer. I don't know why I didn't tell you. I guess..."

"You weren't ready to share that part of him with me. Because we're alike in that."

I nod.

"And that's why you didn't want to consider getting involved with me."

"It was part of it, at first. And then I just tried to pretend that it wasn't a thing."

"But it was. And when you found me playing the drum with Tommy..."

"Aria doesn't remember Adam. Not well, anyway. Tommy... Tommy is his father's son."

"A natural drummer."

It steals my breath, hearing Rhys say that. Not because it's not true or because I hadn't already realized it, but because it reminds me that I've taken that from Tommy, and the guilt of that weighs especially heavy in this moment, having found him playing with Rhys the first chance he got.

"It's OK, Lyric. You're still mourning him. You're going to have things you're not ready to deal with yet."

"But I thought I was. I really did think I was letting him go, moving forward with my life... with..."

"With me."

"Yeah."

"You can't shut things away and also be letting them go."

Ouch.

"No, you can't. And I held that back."

"Until I accidentally forced the issue."

I nod.

"Why'd you go in? Why'd you open a locked door?"

"I didn't. It was open. Part of me hoped you'd unlocked it for me. Now I'm wondering if Tommy did."

"I wondered that myself. His desk chair is tall enough to reach. If he'd watched me unlock it..."

"Maybe. I don't know. It doesn't matter, I don't think. The reality is that it was open, and I didn't think. I just followed my impulses. And that was a mistake."

"It's OK, Rhys. Really. I know you didn't mean any harm."

"I didn't. I just hope I didn't *do* any lasting harm."

I sigh... I want to let him off the hook. Vivienne was right about accepting him for all of who he is. I need to walk the walk, not just talk the talk.

"I should have told you. All of this could have been avoided."

"I wish you felt you'd been able to. You can trust me, you know — anything you're thinking or feeling, you can trust me with that. I wouldn't ever willingly hurt you. Really, I just want to help you. I just want to love you."

"You do?"

"I do. I mean, I already do. I love you, love the kids so much... I couldn't leave you like that, even though you told me to. I love you too much to do it."

Did Rhys Madigan just tell me he loves me?

"Does that really surprise you?" he asks. I guess it showed on my face.

"I don't know. Does it surprise you to know I feel the same about you?"

"You love me? Really?"

I nod.

Say the words, girlfriend. He needs to hear them.

Right.

"I love you, Rhys."

I lean back to see his response, and... he's lit up, joyful, like he is when he's drumming...

He leans down and kisses me, and I kiss him back, because... I love him... and he loves me!

Rhys

"Tell me about him, about Adam." We've been sitting quietly for a while. (I know! Me, sitting quietly! Lyric's a flibbertigibbeting miracle-worker!)

"We met in college, at the conservatory in Baltimore," she explains.

"Wow. I applied there. Didn't get in. My grades weren't good enough."

They weren't. Not even close. Like I said — school and I didn't mesh well. Music was the only part of it where I didn't just barely get by.

"But you did get selected to major in music, and that led you to aMUSEd. It was where you were supposed to be," she says.

I like that idea, that fate led me there, where I ran into Hunter, into Alex... which then brought me here.

"Adam was a year behind me in school. But he wasn't happy there. He wanted to be out, gigging, making music, not in something structured like college. So, when I graduated, got the job back here, with a place waiting for us to move into..."

"He quit and came home with you."

She nods.

"He figured he could get a job playing in local bands here. And he did. It just — it isn't easy finding a year-round gig here that pays enough..."

"To support a family. Yeah. I know I got lucky. We all do." Hunt was basically homeless for a while. He was looking for a job when we met. He lived on my couch for a while. And then I lived on his and Alex's for a bit, after an... unfortunate... choice with one of my inventions.

"Adam took all the gigs he could get, a few regular ones. But that's two, three days a week. Even with my salary, it wasn't enough. And the other jobs around here — it's easy to get a job that's weekends or nights, especially during the summer. But when you're a working musician, those are hours you can't make work. And a regular 9-to-5 means no Friday-evening gigs, and being exhausted all the time. You have to choose between making ends meet and quitting music."

"And he didn't want to quit."

"No! I wouldn't *let* him quit."

That's not what I expected her to say. But it also makes total sense in the context of who Lyric is.

"Having him be happy, fulfilled — that was way more important to me than having extra money in the bank. I was more than happy to give lessons to make ends meet. I saw the light go out of him when he talked about getting a regular job. It would have destroyed him."

He ended up destroying himself instead. And nearly destroyed her with him. Selfish bastard.

Head-dude, she loved him. Still does, I think.

She just told you she loves you.

And maybe she does. But it doesn't change how she felt about *him*.

It means she has to let go of the life they had, so she can build a future that will mean she's loved, that the kids are loved, and taken care of. And you can do that for her. All that money, you can do that. You already did, and you hadn't even gone out on a date with her yet!

Dude, it's not about the money. Didn't you just hear what she said?

That's easy to say when you've got enough cash to fill a vault and swim in it. But with you, she gets the guy on her wall in college, who also loves her and the kids, and can actually take care of her. You're perfect for her. I knew you would be.

Head-dude. Maybe I'm missing something here, but I think you need to explain that.

"And we were happy. It worked," she says. "We could support the kids, even if I couldn't go to gigs like I did before we had them, even if we skimped on things like life insurance." She frowns. "And he worked his connections, picked up fill-in gigs for jazz bands, classic rock, even though punk was his first love. It was a compromise, but one we could live with..."

And the light goes out of her as she hears her own words. I hug her tighter, let her sit quietly, feeling what she needs to feel, and waiting until she feels she has more to say.

"We were happy," she says. "And I miss him. Aria misses him. Tommy misses him. He can't tell me that in words, but I see it in him. And I see it in him when he sees a drum..."

She sniffles, but it's not sobbing like it was earlier.

"Lyric... about the drums..." I hate to do it, but there's a thing we haven't addressed, and it seems like maybe it's a way of helping her let go, and maybe even of helping her and her kids miss him a little less.

"What about them?"

"I'd like to teach Tommy to play."

Clouds race over her eyes. OK. Maybe not.

"I see."

See — there's that phrase again. It does not bode well.

"I know it's a sensitive subject, but I think you've seen how he is around even that little hand drum. And if you're right and he's the one who unlocked the door, I'm not sure you're going to be able to keep him away from them. I'd like to make this a positive. Otherwise, you're looking at having to get rid of the kit, at minimum. He's got a gift. And it's a nice kit."

"I know. We scrimped and saved up for it, and then, later, we used anything extra he earned for the smaller kit, so it was easier to do load-in and load-out by himself."

She knows the right terms. She must have helped him sometimes, at least before they had kids. More reason why when and how he died would weigh on her.

"He used that hand-drum with Tommy sometimes, when he was little."

"That's why Tommy takes to it so strongly, then."

Lyric nods.

"I got my first kit when I was Tommy's age. It's a good age to start learning."

"But he doesn't communicate with us. How can he ask you if he doesn't understand something?"

"We'll figure it out. We're drummers. We don't need words to communicate."

The look she gives me now is almost hostile, and I can see the poet in her objecting to the very idea.

"No offense!" I add quickly. She quirks a smile at me. No offense taken, I guess.

"Are you prepared to deal with meltdowns? Because you'll probably be dealing with them anytime he gets frustrated, including when you're ready to take a break and he's not."

"I really think this is going to be a great outlet for him. Maybe it'll encourage him to interact, communicate a little more."

She thinks about it for a minute.

"Fine. But if it seems like it's causing problems, we'll have to stop."

"Yes!" I can't help celebrating.

She chuckles, shaking her head.

Tommy and Aria are eating their lunch in the kitchen. Lyric's working on her poetry in her altar room. And I've got that melody running through my head again. I head into Lyric's music room and pull down the acoustic guitar. I'm pretty sure I'm safe doing that. She didn't object the last two times I helped myself to it.

I close the door, too. Not because I'm worried she'll freak out about me playing, but because I don't want to risk distracting her from her writing, or having the kids leave their lunches half-finished to come listen to me play.

But, bottom line, I need to get this song out of my head. It's the first one I've had in a while that wasn't just a drum solo, and I don't want to lose it.

Instead, it's me who gets lost in it. I lose track of the time and only look up when I hear the door to the music room open.

"Hey, buddy!"

For once, Tommy is without Legos or gears or even his astronomy and bridges books. He's got this sense of anticipation about him. There's no way he knows that his mom gave me the OK to teach him to drum. Maybe I'm reading into it. Maybe it's me who wants to take a crack at it. But, either way, I put away the guitar and offer him my hand, taking him upstairs to the formerly locked room, full of the memories and spirit of his dad.

He hesitates at the door, as if he's waiting for his mom to come chew us out again.

"It's OK, Tommy. Mom said it was OK. And, if you'd like to play, I'd like to teach you."

He doesn't respond with sound or expression, but he walks straight over to the shelf and gets the little hand drum, sitting in the middle of the floor. I grab a matching one off the same shelf and sit down facing him. I pull out my phone, too, because the best way to learn to make a beat is to learn how to keep your beats regular. Like, clockwork regular. Or, in this case, metronome regular.

I don't need a metronome anymore. I'm known for being a human metronome. But it'll help Tommy hear where the beats fit. I start it up and we go from there, until he's got a solid rhythm down, perfectly in time with the metronome. He won't need it for long. A natural-born drummer if ever I've seen one.

"Adam used to play beats on my belly when I was pregnant," Lyric says from the doorway, a trail of tears running down her face. I start to get up to comfort her, but she holds her hand up, telling me to stay.

Tommy turns to look at her and then holds up the drum to her, like it's a prize he's just earned.

"I see that, buddy," she says. "Are you having fun playing with Mr. Rhys?"

Tommy puts the drum back down and taps it in a rapid rhythm, far faster than what we'd been practicing.

"I'm going to take that as a yes," she says. "That's good, Tommy. You have some fun."

"Thank you," she mouths at me. I can see the emotions threaten to overwhelm her, but she shakes her head, wipes her eyes and heads back downstairs.

Thank you.
You're welcome, Lyric. And you, too, head-dude.

CHAPTER 45

DREAMING OF ME

Lyric
Four days later

Time is running short. Shorter than I like, with just a week left of vacation. The kids are ready for school. I'm ready for school, now that my fallback lesson plan has been approved. What I'm not ready for is not having these idyllic days with Rhys, with my kids. I haven't been this happy since before Adam passed, and I don't want to lose a moment of it, let alone hours and days, which is what has to happen once school starts again.

And that's before we get back to the other bit of reality that I don't want to face — Rhys will be heading back to New York soon, and then back on the road. What will that mean for us? Even now that we've both said those three big words to each other, it's no guarantee we have a future. The odds are against us, and I know it. I suspect Rhys knows it, too, though he's doing a better job pretending that he doesn't, I think.

When he hasn't been pulled into the studio or hanging out with the kids and me on the beach, at the trampoline park, at the amusement park (thankfully, without any more incidents), he's been teaching Tommy to play. They've graduated from hand drums to playing on the snare drum, hands being replaced with a pair of his dad's drumsticks.

It's bittersweet to watch. These are moments that should have been Adam's to have.

He'd rather Rhys had them with Tommy than Tommy not get them at all, Vivienne says. *You know that, dear.*

I think I do. But having the sounds of drumming return to my house reminds me of what I've lost. I knew it when I locked that door the first time. I just spent the years since then pretending I didn't know it, not dealing with it. The empty space in my bed — that I learned to deal with. The empty space in my life was filled with taking care of my kids. Mostly. But the loss of Adam's music... That I hadn't let touch me. Until now.

The joy on Tommy's face, on Rhys' face, eases the pain, now that I'm finally letting myself feel it. Rhys still finds me crying in front of my altar some afternoons after a lesson.

"You want me to stop?" he asked the first couple times.

"No," I answered, honestly. I've realized that this, too, is like therapy for me. It's painful. It's work. But I feel a little lighter every day.

And I have Rhys to thank for that. I'm not sure if She sent him to me, or if some other benevolent entity or agent of fate decided it was past time for me to finish my healing. I'm not sure I'd ever have dared dream that the answer to my prayers would be the rockstar I'd admired before I'd even met my husband. But here he is, caring for me, my kids, and asking nothing in return but that we let him into our lives.

Rhys

"What's that you're humming, Rhys?" Kier asks me as I adjust my kit with the updated signature snare the manufacturer wants me to test out.

"Oh, nothing... just a little melody I've been playing with."

Kier gives me the most confused look he's ever given me, and he's given me a lot of confused looks over the years.

"Did you just say 'melody'? A melody you're playing with? Not another drum solo?"

"Is it so hard to believe I can write an actual song?" I sound more than a little offended, maybe even angry, and, honestly, I am. I'm not the virtuoso on guitar that Kier is, or a keyboard master like Alex, but I was a flibbertigibbeting music major! Lyric gives me props for that. Why can't the guys I've played with for more than a decade?

"Whoa, man — no need to tear his head off!" Alex says, coming in from the control room. I notice he doesn't smack me this time. Lyric was right. I should have made it clear to him before that it wasn't cool. But Alex can't not be band-mom. And, as usual, he's right.

"Sorry, dude," I tell Kier. "I'm just tired of being treated like the stupid little brother who gets the job done behind the kit but isn't a 'real musician.'"

"No one thinks that," Kier says. "Least of all me... It's just — you don't write melodies."

"He did in college," Alex says. "We all did. Couldn't graduate without being able to compose."

"Well, there's one you've got on me," Kier says. "I didn't even go to college. And it's not like I can play drums worth a damn, either."

"None of us can," Alex reminds us. "Even after all the shit we had to learn as music majors. I'm kind of at a loss if it doesn't have a keyboard. We lose Rhys, we've got a problem."

That makes me feel a little better.

"Now, what's this about a melody? You've got a song for us?" Alex asks.

"Not yet. But I think I might sometime soon."

"Well, when it's done, tell me, for feck's sake. I'm really curious to hear it," Kier says.

"I think that goes for all of us," Alex adds, clapping me on the back. Yeah, I like that way better than the head-smacks. Things seem to be looking up all around.

Later that night

"Alright, buddy — it's time to chill out and get ready for bed. We'll do more drum time tomorrow, OK?"

Tommy ignores me and keeps on working the fill pattern I taught him today. He's got it down almost perfectly already, but he doesn't want to stop.

"All done for today, Tommy. Mom said it's bedtime, and we've got to follow the rules."

No dice. I hold my hand out for the drumsticks, hoping he'll follow the physical cue. And that's a no. Finally, I snag one of the sticks out of his hand. He stops, but there's a stiffness to him that I don't like. I recall Lyric's warning of the potential for a meltdown, but it's too late. He hurls the other stick across the room, knocking one of his dad's photos off the wall. And then he starts crying, wailing.

"Oh, buddy... Come here..." I hold my arms out to him, and he lets me pick him up, carry him to his bedroom, like I've seen Lyric do. But he's not calming down. I hand him a set of gears, and he throws them to the floor.

Sing to him.

Sing what? "Cows with Guns?" Lyric'll go full-on witch and turn me *into* a cow.

Sing to him.

I can't think of anything to sing to him right now except the melody I've been working on, and that doesn't even have lyrics yet.

Sing it.

So I do. Wordlessly, just humming the melody.

I'm barely through the first phrase when Tommy finally starts to calm down, listening closely. Well, what do you know — it's a magic calming song! Tommy settles down on his bed as I continue through the verse. By the time I've hit the little break, his eyes are closed and it looks like... yeah — he's asleep.

Seriously — a magical calming song. I could create world peace with this thing if everyone responds to it like Tommy does.

But not everyone does.

Because Lyric is standing in the doorway, mouth tight, eyes wide in disbelief.

"I'm sorry — he didn't want to stop," I tell her quietly. She gestures for me to follow her out of the room, so I do. She shuts the door behind me, leaving a sleeping Tommy in bed.

"Maybe I should have come and gotten you when he refused—"

"Where did you learn that song?" she demands.

"I've been working on it at the studio mostly."

"No — where did you *learn* it? Where did you *hear* it?"

"In my head. It's been popping into my head for a while now. Since the night we first met, actually. In person, anyway."

"That's the second time you've suggested we'd met before that night at Callie and Declan's wedding reception," she says. "I think I need you to explain that now. And about that song."

OK. So, the time to explain the dreams has come. Good. I've been waiting for that.

"Let me get Aria to bed, and then I think we need to talk."

And suddenly things sound less good. I don't have much experience at this relationship stuff, but I know "We need to talk" is rarely a good thing.

I go down to the bedroom, in case she wants to shut the door against eavesdropping little ears, and wait for her on the bed.

"I'm not sure this is the best spot to do this," she says.

"Why not? We talk in bed all the time," I say, hopeful. She gives me a dubious look, but she sits down next to me.

"Explain — why do you think we'd met before?"

"Well, not 'met' so much as..." How do I explain this? She's going to believe this supernatural dream stuff, right? She's a witch.

Just spit it out. Let her decide.

Right. Good advice, head-dude. I hope.

"I had a dream." She rolls her eyes.

Dude — you sound like a historical speech.

I try again.

"We were on tour, about six months ago — I think it was the night of the Baltimore gig, actually. How coincidental is that?"

Not at all.

I want to ask, but Lyric is waiting for me to continue.

"After the show, I crashed out in my bunk on the bus, because we were heading straight out for Richmond. And, at some point, I must have started dreaming, because all of a sudden, I'm seeing this beautiful girl, smiling at me, with these incredible blue eyes. And it just struck me. She struck me. It was a dream, but she was so real..."

I can't read the expression on Lyric's face, so I keep going.

"After that, nearly every night, I dreamed about the same girl — woman, really, because that's respectful when talking about an adult female, right?" No change in her expression. OK.

Keep going. She needs to hear the whole thing.

"Anyway — I kept dreaming about her, only some nights it was just waking up with her face in my head, but others, we'd be walking, holding hands. There were a few kisses." She frowns slightly. "Very respectful, sweet kisses," I emphasize. "Nothing more than that. I promise."

I take her hand, and she lets me, and I think that's a good sign.

"But the whole time I'm dreaming of her — like I said, most nights, basically all the nights I can remember dreaming from that night onward — it doesn't matter how many groupies, or waitresses, throw themselves at me, I've got no interest. I mean *none*. I'll happily sign an autograph, but I can't even find enough interest to make small-talk with these chicks. Uh — women. And it all feels like it's really important, you know?"

She nods, like maybe she might understand. Cool. This is good.

"So then we get here, and it keeps on going — all the dreams. Right up until that night — at Declan and Callie's party. And we're finally allowed to perform our own stuff, and I'm getting into the groove on 'Fire in the Head,' and I look out into the crowd and see this woman — and I can't really believe it, because this kind of thing isn't real, right? But there she is — the woman I've been dreaming about for months and months! Right there, on the dance floor, watching me like I'm watching her. And then some weird shit — sorry — some weird stuff happened, like I was..."

"Floating over the crowd, part of the music, but above it, like you were—"

"Connected," we both say.

"See! I knew you'd get it!"

"And the woman you were dreaming about — she was me."

"Yeah. So, when Rory brought you backstage, I was like, 'Finally! I know who she is! I can talk to her, and kiss her for real, and...'"

"And that's why you treated me like we were a foregone conclusion..."

"Yes!" She frowns. "Well, no — not like that! But I knew we had a connection, and I knew you had to feel it, too, because when I was floating over that dance floor, you looked up and you saw me! Really saw me! The real me. Like, my soul."

"I did," she says.

"Were you dreaming about me all that time, too?"

"No," she says. "I didn't see you coming at all. You were a total surprise. Naturally."

Naturally.

"And then head-dude, he kept telling me to take care of you..."

Uh-oh.

"Head-dude?"

Uh-oh.

"Well, yeah — since we got to Mystic Beach, I've had this voice in my head. And, at first, I thought maybe I was losing it, developing a split personality or something, but head-dude gives good advice, so I decided to go with it."

OK. Now Lyric looks alarmed. Maybe I was right about head-dude being a new personality.

"Did you tell anyone about this... this 'head-dude'?" she asks.

"Well, no. Because... the whole losing-it thing seemed like a problem, but he wasn't causing any problems himself."

"And the song — you heard it in your head, like you do his voice?" I nod. Absently, she spins the rings on her left ring finger. "Did he tell you his name?" she asks, looking almost afraid of the answer.

"Well, no. I'm not sure if I even asked him, actually."

You didn't. It was kind of rude, but I wouldn't have answered you then anyway.

"Ask him now," she says.

OK, head-dude. Introduce yourself. Lyric wants to know.

Silence in my head. Silence in the room.
Adam. My name is Adam.

CHAPTER 46

LULLABY

Lyric

Rhys is quiet. Too quiet. For that matter, so are all the various dearly-departed spirits who've been talking to me for the last three years. Not a word from one of them. And now it all begins to make sense.

"It's Adam, isn't it?" I ask Rhys, unable to wait a moment longer for confirmation.

He nods.

"Oh, gods... Why? Why, when I've got all these dead people talking to me, did my husband end up haunting a rockstar?"

"We're both drummers?"

"That's not enough. You weren't even close by — and it was years after he passed."

"Wait — go back. You hear dead people?"

"I have since Adam died. But never once did *he* speak to *me*."

Rhys is quiet, introspective. Except I recognize that look on his face. We're now having a three-way conversation, with Rhys serving as interpreter.

"He says he tried, but you couldn't hear him. He doesn't know why. He says he's sorry he didn't go to the doctor, sorry he left you to deal with everything on your own. If he could go back and change it, he would. But he can't. So, he did the next best thing... What? Dude... I appreciate the vote of confidence, but she's right — why me?"

"He remembered that I had a crush on you when he and I first met."

Rhys looks a little shaken.

"Yeah," he confirms. "He knew you'd be more likely to talk to me than just some guy off the street. And you needed someone to talk to, someone who'd take care of you and the kids, since he couldn't."

"So, he haunted you, gave you dreams of me, advised you on how to seduce me..."

I'm working up a good, solid mad with both of them.

"Whoa! No," Rhys objects. "At least not much, anyway. You know me — I've got no game, no filter. Could any ghost... Holy shit, I have a ghost haunting my head... Head-dude, you suck! ... No, *you* suck! ... *You* do. Times infinity!"

I can't believe it. My dead husband and my boyfriend are arguing with each other like a pair of children.

And that's when the absurdity of this whole thing catches up with me. And I crack up.

Rhys stares at me.

"I don't know, man. I think maybe we broke her brain. She's laughing like she's lost it herself, instead of it just being *me* who's nuts. Oh, right. I'm not nuts. I'm just haunted."

"Possessed."

That stops us both cold, and the word came out of my mouth.

"He didn't just talk to you, right? He took over that night we met, took over your body."

"Well, yeah. He said he was doing the drumming while I was doing the floaty thing."

"Just like Herself was piloting my body while I was watching you, connecting to you."

"What? Is that what you meant by 'inside priestess joke' when I called you a goddess? You said you were 'occasionally.'"

"Yeah. That's what I meant."

The realization hits us at the same moment.

"We were set up!"

"If that wasn't the most bizarre blind-date setup in the history of the universe, I'd be surprised," I say.

"No kidding. We'll never be able to tell anyone how we really met," Rhys says.

"Well, Brighid would probably understand. She and Hunt first met and got married at least two hundred years ago."

"Oh. OK," he says, before my words catch up. "Oh! *That's* what they meant by 'again'! *Now* I get it! Wait... What?"

"Ask Hunter or Brighid. If you ever feel compelled to tell either of them about this."

"About us."

"Yeah. Us."

And that's when it hits me. Is there even an "us"? Really? Because none of this was spontaneous, natural, normal — not once it got started like it did. Everything resulted from being pointed at each other, from inside information. How much of "us" is really us? And is there enough "us" in us for this to be a real relationship?

Rhys

I don't like the look on Lyric's face.

You shouldn't.

Dude — you don't get to have an opinion on this. You could have told me from the start. You could have just had me talk to her for you! She'd have believed it. She's got dead people talking to her, too!

I couldn't take that chance. I couldn't risk her shutting you out when what she needed most was to let you in!

I can't argue that. But right now... right now, she looks like she might shut me out after all.

"Lyric, talk to me."

"Is that Rhys talking or Adam?" she asks, an edge of hysteria to her voice.

No. No! Don't do that, Lyric.

"It's me — Rhys. He hasn't said a single word to you directly. Not one. I'm not sure he can. I think the drumming thing was a fluke."

I wait for confirmation of that, and his silence is enough.

"Fine. But how much of this — of us — was him? Are we who I thought we were, or do we find out in a month or a year, once he's faded, that we never really worked on our own, that it was Adam smoothing the way that made us work?"

"He's going to fade away?"

"They all do, once they've finished what they stuck around to do. And it seems like he has, if his whole plan was to get us together, so you could take care of me. That was his plan, right? To make sure I had someone to take care of me?"

"Yeah, I think so. It was the one thing he kept telling me to do. But, Lyric — I didn't need him to tell me to do that. I wanted to, all on my own. The only thing he did was make me realize that *I* actually *wanted* to take care of someone, that I was done with one-night stands, that I wanted a family of my own."

I'm practically begging her, and there aren't even any question words in there.

"His family."

Ouch. OK.

"He gave you his family."

OK. My bad. I see that now. But my intentions were good.

"I think he's apologizing for that. He's not very good at it. Worse than I am, really."

Hey!

"Oh, Adam... Why'd you have to push? Me or Rhys? Why couldn't you just let things happen naturally?"

If she could have seen herself through my eyes, seen how she was struggling, she wouldn't have to ask that.

I know. But she won't like us telling her that.

"What?" she demands. "I know you two are talking. Just say it."

"He couldn't — *we* couldn't — watch you struggle like you were. And, Lyric, I think you know that now. We talked about this."

"Yeah. We did." She doesn't sound like that makes it any better. "Gods, I am so tired..."

She puts her head down in her hands. I reach over and rub her back, and she leans into it. I don't even notice I'm humming until she turns and stares.

"What?"

"He didn't tell you?"

Yeah, I might maybe should have done that. In my defense, I didn't realize at first that you were hearing it.

"No. What?"

"That's the song he used to sing the kids when he put them to bed. A song he wrote. That's how I knew something was off, that your 'head-dude' was Adam."

Oh.

"So, I didn't come up with that on my own?" Well, that's almost as disappointing as Lyric second-guessing *us*.

"No. You didn't."

She grabs my hand and pulls me through the living room and into her music room. She sits down on the piano bench and opens up the keyboard. She takes a deep breath and lets it out. She begins to play a slow arpeggio on the piano. Then another deep breath. And she sings.

> Settle my child
> Into a world of enchantment
> Where gossamer wings
> Shine bright by the moon
> It's a world you will find
> On the other side
> Of a night that will surely
> Be ending too soon
> In a world of your making
> There's nothing forsaken
> All you need is the yearning
> For learning anew
> When you open your eyes
> Will you be surprised
> When the morning sun
> Comes to fill the room?

She hums a little break, but in my head I can hear head-dude — Adam — join in, whistling, pure and clear, so sweetly that a nightingale would surely be envious.

> So bundle up tight
> And kiss me good night
> For the night
> Will surely be good to you.

She plays it perfectly, just like it sounded in my head, but with words. And, yeah, I'm a little gutted that it's not actually my song. It's a good song. Better than good. *Dude...*

Thanks. That's a high compliment coming from a guy with a couple of Grammys on his mantle.

They're on Mom's mantle, actually. But the platinum albums are on the wall in my apartment, so...

You have no idea how lucky you are.

I think I do. If I didn't before, I do now, now that she and the kids are in my life.

You really do love her.

Yeah, I do. You shouldn't have to ask.

I wasn't asking. It was a statement. It's obvious. Just like it's obvious that she loves you.

I'm not sure it's obvious to her anymore.

Give her time. She's a smart witch. She'll get it figured out.

I hope so. Because I'm not giving her up without a fight.

Good. Because we already talked about how hard-headed she can be.

"I don't play it as well as he does... did," she corrects herself.

It was written for guitar. But she's always been more comfortable with the piano.

"It's a guitar song," I tell her.

"He told you that," she says.

I nod. "Yeah."

"Did I mention that I'm tired?"

I move closer and go to pull her into my arms. But she pulls away.

"Not right now, Rhys." She sighs. "See — I keep wanting to ask if it's really you, or if Adam's taken over again."

Sorry, dude. I thought she'd take this in stride, since she's got her chorus of ghosts following her around.

"He says he's sorry." I don't specify who he's apologizing to. I think we're both owed an apology. And I'm probably owed a second one, since this is going to complicate things for me going forward. If there even is a forward.

Give her time.

"I get that," she says. "And I'll take it under advisement. But right now... Right now, I need to be alone."

Did I say I was gutted about the song not being mine? I'm *completely* gutted hearing those words come out of Lyric's mouth.

The song's yours. Record it. I won't object to a credit. But it's the least I owe you. Just... She'll figure it out. Give her some time.

"OK. But if you need me — if you need anything — you call me, text me, hire a banner plane, whatever. Promise me."

"I promise, Rhys. Thank you." She grabs my hand and gives it a squeeze. At least she's still willing to touch me. "I — I know you didn't do this on purpose. It took you nearly as much by surprise as it did me."

"Yeah, it did. But I'm not going to say I regret where it brought me. I love you, Lyric. Me — Rhys. I've never said that to another woman, and I don't think I ever will, not after you."

I kiss her on the head. Because that's a thing you do when there's something there. And that something is love.

Lyric

Watching Rhys walk out the door is hard. Part of me wants to bury myself in his arms and pretend none of these revelations ever came to light. Another part of me wants to beg him to let Adam possess him again so I can finally talk to my husband directly. My late husband.

I don't know why this is so hard for me to absorb. I've got other people's wives, husbands, mothers, grandmothers, sons... talking to me. But when Adam didn't show up soon after the others, I figured he never would.

Why it is that he couldn't, that he ended up haunting Rhys instead of me... Well, if I had to hazard a guess, it's because Adam's unfinished business was making sure I was taken care of by someone he thought I could love, and because the situation got a little special attention from Herself. How poor of a priestess must I have been that She felt it necessary to arrange for my husband to haunt my college crush?

Not poor at all. And you know that. But you needed healing, and so did your husband's soul. And the other... He is special. He was brought here for you.

Why do I get a new boyfriend, by special delivery?

I didn't say he was brought here to be yours. I said he was brought here for *you. Words have meaning, priestess, poet. In this case, in both senses of the words. Larger things are at work than you can yet see.*

Puzzle pieces.

Yes.

So much to think through, to try to grasp. The breadth of the goddess' understanding is limitless, by Her very nature. Her human servant... It'll take time, and effort, to puzzle this all out. And I was already short on time before this day began.

CHAPTER 47
MANEATER

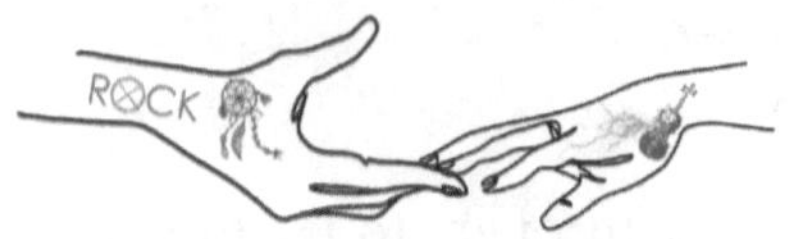

Lyric
The next morning

Rhys: *Are you OK?*

Rhys: *Can I come over?*

Rhys: *School starts in a week, right?*

Rhys: *I love you.*

Oh, gods... What am I going to do?

Jump his bones.

Annie!

What? I find sex always helps resolve unresolved situations.

Me, too.

Frank!

Hey, I'm not the one whose mind keeps drifting back to the man's glorious ass! Not that I can blame you. I always was an ass-man, myself.

Oh, gods... Why, oh why, must I be plagued with these two at a time like this?

Because you need a reminder that sometimes things are simpler than you want to make them.

Oh, yeah — simple! My dead husband is haunting my boyfriend, whom he specifically guided to find and seduce me so he — my boyfriend — could take over where my husband left off. Yeah. Simple. Why didn't I realize that?

Because you'd only barely started to truly let Adam go. And now he's back, but you know if you get your happily-ever-after with Rhys, Adam will move on. You're back to being stuck between the past and the future. And letting go of the past still scares you.

I guess I should be glad that Vivienne's sticking to her "wise mom" role and not fixating on Rhys' butt. And that Nonna's finally passed on and isn't encouraging ogling like she did with that naked picture of Declan. Which I cannot tell Callie about. Or Rhys. Of whom I do not have any naked pictures. Thankfully. Because then I might cave and tell him to come over.

He is *handsome. But he reminds me of my son, so... No.*

Well, that's interesting. Vivienne's never specifically mentioned her kids before. I wonder if she's close to getting her unfinished business done. I helped Nonna. But then I knew Nonna when she was alive. I have no idea who Vivienne was, and she hasn't exactly told me what she's waiting on.

It's close. And you're already doing your part.

Well, that's intriguing.

Girl — you're distracting yourself with other people's problems again. You did that with Callie and Declan, too.

Frank always calls me out when I'm not being honest with myself.

You're a priestess. You should know better. But even priestesses are human. So, I give you a little help sometimes. You help everyone else...

It's my job. Priestess, mom, teacher...

Lover.

Geez, Annie. One-track mind much?

Hey, when you've been dead for a couple decades, see how much you're *missing getting your hands on a posterior like that one!*

Sigh.

He does have a lovely butt...

And all the rest of him has been pretty great, too...

And I need to get that final fellowship submission done. If I can get my brain to stick to poetry instead of fixating on... other things.

An hour later

I crumple up the sixth piece of paper I've started writing on in the last sixty minutes. Ten minutes per page. Six abandoned poems that just weren't working. And I'm still distracted. Yes, by Rhys and his butt.

So run with it! Write an ode.

An ode to Rhys?

Or his butt.

Annie!

It's not a bad idea. Maybe it'll get things out of your system, let you concentrate on something else once it's done.

I know I must be stuck when Vivienne's encouraging me to write a poem about Rhys' backside.

Oh, what the Hel...

Twenty minutes later

<u>Poem for a Posterior
(Or: Ode to an Asshole</u>

Yes, indeed, I was looking at
your rump
That cushy, mushy useful
bump
I really couldn't help it
I sometimes wish I'd felt it
But you should know that it's
pleasing to the eye
That I've admired it is no lie
Soft and smooth and nicely
curved
Not too hard or muscular —
oh, I'm losing my nerve
But delicate and almost fem-
inine
How I'd love to touch it again
It's nearly as enticing as your
hair
Like shining copper spun in
air
But that glorious expanse of
skin
Is something that I'd like to
invite in
Along with the rest of you
It's something I most strongly

wish to do
And lest you think I view you
as a sex object
Let me remind you I think all
of you is perfect
Eyes and ears and chin and
nose
Mind and humor and even
your toes
So here's this silly little note
A poem that sets my thoughts
afloat
On an ocean of appreciation
A lovely little mental vacation
It's nearly as fun as time spent
with you
Your friendship, talent, car-
ing, and your butt, too.

O h, gods... it's awful.
But delightfully awful.
Thanks, Annie. I think.
I kind of like it.
You would, Frank.
If voices in my head can convey sticking their tongues out at
me, his does.
Did it free up your mind to write your submission piece?
Did it?
My eyes shift over to my phone, still on silent.
No, Vivienne. It didn't. I still can't get my mind off of Rhys.
Then I think you know what you have to do.

Rhys

The sense of relief when that text came through... Lyric telling me to come over. I can't describe how much I needed that.

Head-dude — *Adam* — has been quiet since we left Lyric's house last night. *His* house. Man, this is flibbertigibbeting weird.

I cut out of the studio so fast that I left Dave and Piper goggling at me. Fortunately, we were just listening to the playback on my final take. Because nothing would have kept me from Lyric right then.

But now... Now I'm worried about what she'll say when she opens that door, which is why I'm just standing on her front porch.

"Rhys? What the fuck are you doing over there?"

Declan's coming up his — Callie's? — driveway, clearly returning from a run.

"Uh... Trying to get myself to knock on the door?"

"You manage to piss the girl off already? Man, you're coming up on my record!" He chuckles.

"No! I mean, she's not pissed off exactly... And not at me exactly. It's just... It's complicated, OK?"

"So, uncomplicate it!"

"How?"

"Knock on the fucking door!"

Right.

"Thanks!"

I take a deep breath, and I knock.

The door opens.

"Hi," Lyric says, wearing only a silky little slip of nothingness.

"Hi." I'm tongue-tied just from the sight of her, so that's all I can think to say.

"What took you so long?" she demands.

I don't get the chance to answer.

She grabs me by my shirt and drags me into the house, straight into her bedroom, and right on top of her, on her bed.

OK, then...

She kisses me, hard.

"The kids?" I ask.

"With my mom."

"Good. That's good."

"Yeah... So get to work!"

"Right." My brain is still catching up with this unexpected turn of events.

"Rhys?"

"Hmm?"

Lyric grabs my face, those stormy blue eyes of hers burrowing into mine.

"Make love to me..."

"My pleasure."

Always has been. Always will be.

I think this is the man-eating female tiger she talked about before, because as enthusiastic as Lyric has been during our prior lovemaking, she's aggressive now, pushing me over on my back, stripping my shirt off me. She nips at my nipples, sinks her teeth lightly into my shoulder, grabs my ass hard through my shorts, then strips them, and my boxers — happy-faces today — straight off me.

As happy as I am at the idea she's gotten past the weirdness of how we got together, this feels a lot more like fucking than making love. So when she climbs on top of me, not so much as those red string bikinis between her pussy and my very, very happy dick, I reach up and grab her face between my hands.

"Lyric — are you really OK with things? We haven't even talked."

"I've had too much talking," she says, almost desperate. "Is he watching? Is he telling you what to do to me?"

"No! He was never in my head when we were together. Except he did say you like shower sex."

Maybe I shouldn't be that honest with her, but hey — it's me. Famously no-filter me.

The smile that steals over her face is... enchanting. She's a witch. Of course it is.

"He wasn't lying. And I think you know that firsthand now."

She slides up, rubbing her slit across my dick.

Sexy mama, indeed.

"I do." I rub my thumb across her perfectly nibbleable bottom lip. "And I need you to know that — that this is me. It's always been me. I got a little advice, a little encouragement. But I'm here because I fell for you. *I* did. Not because he had. I'd have fallen for you the first time we talked, or touched. It was always going to be you. We were meant to be. From the moment you stuck my picture to your wall, and the moment I realized you — you, and the kids — are exactly what I need."

The tiger fades from her eyes as they fill with tears.

"Oh, Rhys... However you got here — you were exactly what I needed, too."

I sit up and slide my hand behind her neck, pulling her to me, her lips against mine. The kiss is sweet, slow, sensual. I open my eyes to look at her, take her in, and I find her doing the same. There it is — that sense of connection, of being seen, all of me, all of who I am. And, now, of being loved.

I lie back down, settling her over my hips.

"Make love to me, Lyric," I tell her.

"My pleasure."

And mine.

She slides up over my cock again, then down on it, slowly, teasing us both. I've gotten used to feeling her bare like this, but it's no less erotic, especially when she curves her spine, writhing on top of me. Instinct says to flip her over and take her hard and fast. But we both want one thing right now — lovemaking, not fucking. So I take a deep breath and focus on the sensuality of her, her movements, the expression on her face, the feelings for me that she's expressed and expresses now in how she carefully moves over me.

This is making love.

I move my hands to her hips, caressing her, cradling her, supporting her in giving us both pleasure. We move together now, neither of us leading or following, perfectly in sync, like the voices in our duet. Distinct but perfect in combination. Great individually, but even better joined together.

It's a slow rise, each movement building toward the peak, one note after the next, each just a little higher, a little more intense, until we're both panting, tension holding us up high and also keeping us from falling over. It's the most exquisite thing I've ever felt. No moment of jumping out of a plane or hanging from a rock by my fingertips, or even hitting that first beat on my snare in front of an audience of a hundred thousand screaming fans — none of that matches the perfection of this moment, watching Lyric hover over me, her face alight with pleasure and joy, and knowing we're both feeling it, both making love to each other, body and soul.

She moans, and the sound goes straight to my dick. I don't think I've ever been harder. Delaying my release has never been harder. But I want to share this moment with her, want to watch her as she comes with my cock buried in her, watch her take her pleasure while I take mine. I want to give her the world, starting with this moment.

I slip my hand between her lower lips, gathering up the moisture there, rubbing it across her clit, then settling my thumb over it, using our combined movements to ratchet up her pleasure, which pulls mine with it. The rhythm is perfection, the two of us in perfect synchrony.

I've set the pace for a lot of award-winning songs, but this is the best song I've ever written, this duet of ours, Lyric and me. So what if it all started with a prompt? How many masterpieces of art start with a prompt or a spark of inspiration from someone else? Tons. That doesn't make them less. It doesn't make them imperfect. And this — us — is perfect.

And... and... there — oh, god, there.

"Rhys..." she moans. "I love you, Rhys."

Our bodies are smacking together, their rhythm audible now, and speeding up. Utter perfection. That tingle in my spine, intensifying as she rides me...

"I love you, Lyric."

She cries out, and I grab her hips, pulling her hard against me, her pussy contracting around my cock as I pump rapidly into her, giving her not just my cum, but all of me, body and soul.

I'm utterly bewitched by her. And I'm totally OK with that.

CHAPTER 48

MAGIC-CARPET RIDE

Lyric

In my belief system, all acts of love and pleasure qualify as sacred. Sex is a sacrament, not a sin. Giving myself to Rhys like this — eyes open, knowing how we were led to each other — it's symbolic. It's a concrete way of moving forward, committing to my future, whatever that might look like, and leaving the past behind.

I don't know if Adam is watching us now, but I know he saw this coming. He saw it, and when he did, he encouraged Rhys to follow this path to me, to bring us both here to this point. It was what he wanted. Does that mean his unfinished business is complete? Is he gone forever?

"Rhys?" I ask as I lie in his very human, very corporeal, very strong arms.

"Yes..." he says slowly, like he suspects he may not like what I'm about to ask.

"Was he... was he watching?"

"Not as far as I know. But he's been quiet since last night."

"Oh."

The silence lingers.

"Do you... do you think he's gone?"

"I have no idea. I don't even know if he just hangs out in my head or if he's floating around, taking over other drummers when I'm not playing."

"You sound almost jealous."

"Well, he and I have business to conclude. Including this idea of his — that I record that song..." He looks at me, hesitant. "Would that be OK with you if I did? I kind of told the guys I was working on something. And he — I — well, both of us, I guess, feel like it's worth recording. Maybe releasing. But the guys will have to decide that."

All acts of love and pleasure...

"I think that would be lovely."

I — Rhys and I — Adam, Rhys and I — know better than most that making music is an act of love and pleasure. Sharing it just amplifies that.

"I'll need the lyrics, Lyric," he says, chuckling.

"I can write them down. Or, better yet, ask Adam for them. If he wants the song recorded, he'll give them to you."

"If he's still around."

"Yes."

"Then I guess we'll have to see if he's still around."

I nod.

"You want to talk to him?" Rhys asks.

"Can I?"

"I have no idea. You're the one who's been dealing with the dead for years."

"I've been possessed just once, Rhys — and it wasn't by a ghost."

"Right. Any ideas?"

"Try what you were doing last time?"

"Drumming."

"Yeah."

"**W**ow. You've gone all-out for this... ritual," Rhys says, taking a guess at the proper word.

And he's right. It *is* a ritual.

I've got candles lit in a circle around the drum kit, crystals on either side of the kick drum, incense burning in a little burner on a shelf.

"If I didn't know better, I'd say you were worried something might go wrong," he says, looking a little concerned himself. "Why all this... stuff?" he asks, sitting down on the drum throne.

"Just hedging my bets," I tell him, trying to keep things as light as I can.

The look he gives me conveys concerns of his own.

I sigh.

"Fine." I force myself to come clean with him. "Last time, we didn't do this on purpose. And there was a goddess directly involved. That offers a degree of protection, of guidance, that we don't have now. I'd rather not invite Adam to take over your body and then find out something — or someone — else took advantage, and maybe doesn't want to give you your body back."

That would be highly unethical.

Don't think I don't know you're tempted, Frank. Rhys isn't gay. Chances are he'd boot you out before your first hook-up got past second base.

Fine. I wouldn't really have done it. It's just tempting to wonder. Personally, I'd be more worried about Annie.

Hey!

Oh, stop it, you two.

"You giving a lecture in there?" Rhys asks.

"Sort of. But it's moot — the circle will take care of that. It'll also keep you from floating out into the universe and getting lost." He looks even more concerned at that idea. "You won't. Don't worry."

"He won't try to keep my body?"

"He didn't before. And he could have, I think. He knows his time has passed. He's only here to make sure his family is taken care of when he's gone."

"Don't you want to be in here with us?"

"Better if I don't — two spirits with one body is complicated enough. So I'll stay out here. You'll both be able to hear me."

"Yeah. OK. So... I just start drumming? 'Fire in the Head' again?"

"Whatever seems to fit."

Rhys takes a deep breath, gives a couple kicks to the bass drum, and then loses himself in the beat.

I focus my mind on prayer, carried on the rhythm Rhys is setting. Prayers for his safety, his return to his body when this is done, for Adam to come to us when he's been silent since last night.

"Hey, babe."

My eyes open, focusing on the man behind the kit. It looks like Rhys, but there's a subtle difference in how he holds his head, how he looks at me... and... just a hint of green overlaying Rhys' bronze-brown irises.

"Hey."

"Long time no talk."

There's that crooked grin of his, strange on Rhys' face.

"You'll let him go once we've talked?"

"Yeah, babe. You know me. It wasn't easy accepting that I'd fucked up so bad, that I couldn't come back to you. Pissed me off even more than realizing you had all these other dead people talking to you, but you couldn't hear me."

"It would have made things easier."

"But it wouldn't have let you move on. You needed him for that. I know that now. I knew it when I found myself floating around backstage at the concert in Baltimore. How many times did I do road-crew there during college?"

"Enough. I wondered if that was when you latched onto him."

"He's so focused when he's drumming. It's the only time his brain is quiet, outside of doing some crazy stunt... or when he's with you."

Rhys' expression turns sad.

"I miss you, babe. I miss the kids. You've done such a good job. You've worked so hard. Too hard. I should have stuck with the old kit, spent the money on life insurance. Made sure you were taken care of."

"We made that decision together. Other than the apnea, you were in perfect health. We were investing in our future, just like you did with the piano."

"I know... I just..."

"I know. What's done is done. You've been gone almost four years. I've learned to accept it, adapt."

"And now I stir all this shit up again for you. I'm sorry. I figured he'd fall for you, the girl of his dreams, just like I did a dozen years ago, and he'd run with it from there. I didn't count on his quirks, that he'd treat me like a friend who lived in his head, that he'd sing Tommy my song."

"Which is how we got here."

"Yeah. I want him to record it. It's something lasting of mine. Take the royalties, use them for the kids. Did he tell you he set up a trust for them?"

"Uh... no. He forgot to mention that."

"I'm not sure he wanted you to know. He'd known you for like a week at that point."

"Holy fuck."

"Yeah."

"And that's him? Not you?"

"Yeah. That's him. He was right — I just opened his mind up to the idea of finding someone he could really love, who would love him back. All of him — not just the groupies who wanted to brag about bagging the rockstar or the waitresses who were swept off their feet for an hour. And he's a good guy. He deserves that. He's just... a little weird."

"He's wonderful, in his own unique way."

"And that's why I know this will work, once I'm gone. Which probably won't be long now. I'm already feeling... thinner?"

"Yeah. You've done what you set out to do."

I fight back the tears forming in my eyes.

"I couldn't have taken over again, not without your help and his invitation," he says.

"I figured that might be the case."

The tears spill over.

"It'll be OK, babe. *I'll* be OK," he says. "I'm not sure if I'll end up in your Summerlands or Heaven or whatever. But I'll be watching you and the kids, and if I'm still hanging out there on the day — a long, long time from now — when you, or the kids, or this big fuzzball..." He shakes his head, Rhys' overgrown hair falling around his shoulders and out of his eyes. "When the day comes that you all show up, I'll happily greet the four of you — the love of my life, my precious kids and one of the best friends I've ever had."

I lift my hand, wanting desperately to touch him, but I catch myself before I touch the perimeter of the circle. I won't risk letting Rhys' spirit fly too far afield.

"You really love him, don't you?"

"I do. I'm sorry if that hurts you. I never saw it coming."

"Even after crushing on him so hard all those years ago?"

"Even then. I'm a different person now."

"You are. You're still amazing, though. I picked good. With you and with him. You're good together. Maybe even better than we were."

I start to object.

"No — I know I screwed up. That's why I had to make it right." He runs his fingers through Rhys' hair, an odd imitation of his old habit of pushing the longer bits of his own hair away from the shaved sides. Not feeling that stubble seems to remind him of where he is. "And, no — it doesn't hurt me to see you fall in love again. I want you to be happy. I want the kids to be happy. And he makes them happy. He makes you happy. That's all I need. I can move on now, too. I wish it had been different. But I can't undo what happened. All I can do is hope for your happiness now — all of you. Him included."

He looks down, taking in Rhys' hands, his arms, his chest.

"It's weird, being behind my kit and seeing someone else playing it. Though, I have to say — playing with aMUSEd is a memory I'll brag about when I run into all the other dead musicians. I get why you love them so much. Good music. Good people. Especially Rhys."

"I know."

"And they're a family. I like the idea of you and the kids becoming part of that family. I know they'll take care of you. And that's what I stuck around to do."

"Thank you, Adam. Thank you for bringing him here for me, for us. I love you. I'll always love you."

"And I'll always love you. You and the kids. I'd tell you to take care of them, but you always have. I know you always will. Now you just get the help and love that you deserve."

He tilts his head, considering me.

"Bye, babe..."

"Adam? Adam?"

I knew it was coming, and it's still too soon.

Rhys' head lolls forward, and I have to stop myself from rushing to him.

"Rhys? Rhys? Goddess bless! You come back right now! Back where you belong! Rhys!"

CHAPTER 49

MADNESS

Rhys

"R hys? Rhys? Goddess bless! You come back right now! Back where you belong! Rhys!"

I'm floating somewhere near the ceiling. It's not nearly as pretty as the deck by the bay, with the sun setting off to one side. Someone needs to dust this ceiling fan.

"Rhys!"

Hmm?

"Rhys Madigan!"

There's a pretty girl calling my name. Maybe I should write a song about her. And her name. What was her name?

"Gods blast it, Rhys! Come home!"

Home. This is her home. Maybe my home now. Because she's my home, her and the kids.

Right. Lyric. That's her name. A music name. Like Aria, her little mini-me. And... Tommy, like... like... toms. Drums. He needs me to teach him, since his dad can't. They're awesome. All three of them. I love them.

"Rhys — I love you. I need you. The kids need you. Come back to us!" she yells, sounding closer.

Suddenly I'm catapulted back. Back where I belong. Fingers, toes, lungs taking in breath through lips she's kissed. My eyes open, blinded by sunlight glinting off a pretty decent set of cymbals. A kit. Not my kit. His kit. And he's... Silence. Nothing. No sense of anyone at home in this body besides me. If he's still here, he's not making his presence known. Did he do what he needed to do? Did he... did he say goodbye to her? To...

Lyric!

I look over toward the voice that's still calling my name, begging me to come home to her.

And I smile. She's crying, and I hate that. But I smile. Because I'm back here with her, in a body that craves her as much as my soul does her own.

And there she is, right next to me. Not where I left her. I lift my arms, opening them to her. She dives for me — this time on purpose — landing in my lap, in the cradle of my arms.

"Hi," I tell her.

She smiles, the joy radiating through the tears on her face.

"Hi," she says.

"I'm back."

"I see that. You OK?"

"Yeah. Think I got a little scattered there for a second. But then that's kind of who I am, right?"

"It is," she says. "And as long as you're not going to float away on me, that's exactly how I like you. Love you, even."

"Love you, too," I tell her.

I lean down and kiss her. Slow and sweet again, then harder, as she pulls my face against her own.

"Is it really you? You're back? Rhys?"

"Like the candy bar, but twice as nutty!"

She laughs, breathing deep in relief.

"Did you talk to him? Did he talk to you?"

She nods.

"We said what we needed to say. We said goodbye. Thank you for giving us that."

"So he's gone now?"

"I don't know. If he isn't, I don't think he'll be here much longer. And maybe not attached to you anymore, even if he is still here."

"Is it weird that I'll miss him?"

"No. He called you his friend." She starts tearing up again. "One of his best friends."

I nod, taking that in.

"I like — liked — him. We'd have been friends if he'd been here in person and not just cohabitating in my brain."

"He felt the same."

"Good. I was afraid he'd be pissed off that I fell in love with his wife."

We both chuckle.

"That's exactly what he wanted most in the world. Well, that and me falling in love with you."

"Did it work?"

She laughs.

"Of course it did, you madman, you."

She kisses me again.

"Crazy about you, about the kids."

"Good. Because we're crazy about you, too."

"Awesome."

I blink, breathe, look around the room.

"I think the ceiling fan needs to be dusted."

She looks confused, looks up, then back at me. And we both laugh.

"I'll put it on my to-do list."

"No need. I'll put it on mine. Along with fixing that storm door."

Lyric

Mom said she'd keep the kids overnight, but as much as I'd like some more time alone with Rhys, right now, I want my kids here with us, as a family.

I want to cook dinner with Rhys, put on a movie, sit on the sofa — all four of us — and just chill out in each other's arms.

So that's what we do. I go pick up the kids, while Rhys runs back to the studio for a change of clothes. I don't answer Mom's questions about what's going on. She won't tell me anything about who she's dating. Two can play at that game.

We arrive home, with Aria shouting "Mr. Rhys! Mr. Rhys!" and hurling herself at him as he kneels on the front porch... doing... what is he doing?

"Good evening to you, ma'am," he says, returning the hug.

"Whatcha doin', Mr. Rhys?"

"I am checking an item off my to-do list. I said I'd fix the storm door, and that's what I'm doing."

"You are?" I ask.

"I am. Apparently, Gryff knows about this stuff, as well as about keeping people safe. He told me I needed to adjust the closer and add a chain so the door can't open too far or close too fast. So, while you were gone, I stopped at the hardware store, got a chain and..." He stands up, gesturing to the door. "Voila! A storm door that won't fly open or slam shut, even if your mom works up a good solid mad!"

"Yay!" Aria says.

I look at him, shaking my head.

"Did I tell you I love you?"

"You did. But I won't ever object to hearing it again. Or saying it back." He loops his arm around my waist and pulls me close. And he kisses me.

"Mommy! Mr. Rhys!" Aria complains, rolling her eyes at us.

"Go wash your hands — we're going to cook dinner together," I tell her, and Tommy. "She'll get used to it," I tell Rhys, enjoying kissing him some more now that the kids are out of the room.

"I know," he says. "I'm not going anywhere. She'll have to."

Does he... Could he mean... I mean, obviously, he can't mean he won't leave Mystic Beach. He's got to tour. Right?

"I'm ready!" Aria declares.

So we go start cooking dinner, as a family, and I leave the biggest remaining question of my life unanswered.

Rhys

"**W**hat's this here on the table?" I ask Lyric. "All this paper."

"Oh... I was just trying to finish up my fellowship application. It's due in a couple days."

"Trying?"

"And failing, yes."

She seems bummed about it, but like she doesn't want to let it show, maybe doesn't event want to admit it to herself.

"What's left to do on it?"

"Just one last poem. I could dig one out from a few years ago, but they want something new for this last one, to show them we're still actively writing."

"You think they'd know if you dug up an old one?"

"No. But I'd know. So, I'll keep trying."

"And if you don't write one?"

"Then maybe I skip applying this year. Maybe I send it in one short and hope they overlook it when they read my other amazing work."

She's being sarcastic there. I can see it's another of her coping mechanisms, not getting her hopes up. I clear off the crumpled pages, along with the pristine application materials.

"Where do you want these?"

"Oh — just put them on my altar, in the room off the bedroom."

"Got it."

I walk through the bedroom and through the doorway I haven't yet been through, into what looks like a sunroom. I find a familiar face there. Brighid — Hunt's girl, not the goddess — has a statue just like this one. She had it in Hunt's room for a while during college, while she and I were both crashing with him and Alex. I always found it — Her — comforting.

I lay the papers down on the trunk, next to the statue. One of the crumpled ones falls to the floor.

Pick it up.

Adam, dude, is that you?

Amusement.

Yeah, the voice was way too feminine to be my old buddy Head-dude.

So... Brighid?

Warmth.

Pick it up.

Yes, ma'am.

I pick it up. I guess "Herself" doesn't like litter around her altar.

Open it.

I really shouldn't.

Open it.

Fine. But I'm not taking the hit if she finds me in here like this. That's on you. You're a goddess. You can handle it.

I uncrumple the paper, smooth it out with my hands.

This isn't an unfinished poem, left abandoned. It's a full-on ode. It says so right in the title.

Glancing through the other poems Lyric has gathered with her application, I can see there's a difference. This one's light, almost comical, and it's... It's about me. About my butt. It's an ode to my butt. But also to me. The defining clue? The line about the copper hair. Not even Kier's is copper, and she didn't have her fingers dug into his ass a few hours ago, either. So, yeah... Lyric wrote an ode to me.

And I love it.

This maybe the best piece of poetry ever written.

Granted, I'm a musician, not a poet. But lyrics are — aptly — poetry, and I work with a bunch of award-winning lyricists. So, this isn't totally outside my frame of reference. And this poem — it's not staid, boring. It's amusing. Yeah. Best poem ever written.

Mail it.

Whoa. Wait a minute. She said she's not done yet. She's got a couple days left.

Mail it.

OK. Decision time: Piss off my storm-calling witch of a girlfriend (and I say "witch" in the best and most literal of senses), or piss off a goddess who just decided to start talking to me?

Hunter yelled at me once.

Huh. Well, I remember Dave mentioning that. Hunt never explained. That was the night he broke his hand. "Yelled at a goddess and punched a house," they said.

Apparently, gods can smirk silently at you and still get their messages across.

Mail it.

I really, really hope I don't regret this.

"Hey, Lyric — I know Brighid is a healer goddess, because she fixed Hunt's hand, right? With our human Brighid."

"Yeah. Why?"

"What else does She do?"

"Well, anything She wants. But She's known as a goddess of healing, poetry and smithcraft."

"Like a blacksmith?"

"Well, yeah. Blacksmith, swordsmith, jewelsmith — anything involving working hot metal."

"Cool. And poetry?"

"She's a goddess of inspiration. Did Hunter never tell you about 'Fire in the Head'?"

"What about it?"

"It's a line from the Irish poet Yeats. He talks about leaving the ordinary world on a journey of enchantment, and the drive afterwards to capture that magic and what it inspires in you, in something tangible."

"Like a poem or a song."

"Yeah. Exactly. Many followers of Brighid liken Her to the fire in the head, because She gives inspiration. That's why She's a matron goddess of poets. I think Hunter heard about it from our Brighid."

Ah. This makes more sense now. I still think I may end up with Lyric throwing lightning bolts at my ass, but maybe this is a time to take a leap of faith...

The next morning

I keep having that song run through my head. Even lying in bed with Lyric, I can't keep my focus on her deep, even breaths. Instead, it's the melody, the gentle whistle of the break, the guitar riffs I'm now hearing in my head. Forget drumming in my sleep. I'm now playing guitar when I'm half-awake.

OK. It's making me crazy. Yes, "The Madman." Even I can be driven crazy. It's not even an earworm, because there's this compulsion to write it, create it, make it real.

I slide out of bed, tucking the blanket in around Lyric again and kissing her hair. She stirs but settles right back into sleep. And half of me wants to just stand here and watch her sleep. I get the feeling she didn't sleep like this before she spent most of her nights in my arms... But no — that compulsion...

I head into the music room and pull the acoustic guitar off the wall, sitting down in the chair by the window. I can hear it now — that opening arpeggio. I heard Lyric play it, just once, on the piano. But it wasn't quite right. He was right — it's meant to be a guitar song. Maybe two acoustic guitars, doubled over top of each other? Yeah.

The fifth time through, I've got the guitar part down. The melody's never left my head. What I need now is words. Lyrics.

"That's what it sounded like when he played it," she says suddenly from the doorway.

"Sorry — I didn't mean to wake you. It just wouldn't let me sleep."

"Then it's probably time to give you the lyrics."

And she does, singing them in her soft, quiet voice while I type them into my phone, line by line. When I've got them down, I run through the song again, vocalizing them myself this time, rather than humming the melody. Lyric's voice joins in again, providing sweet harmonies. It's exactly what the song needs.

And I want to hear more of her voice. She's so focused on instruments — why has no one talked about how wonderfully she sings?

As the lullaby drifts away, I shift into our other song... about the white bird that needs to fly. Lyric picks up her violin and bow, and weaves the smooth, rich tones of her instrument with the sharper, lighter ones of my guitar, and then comes the ex-pected surprise — she joins her voice with mine, playing and singing at the same time.

It's a challenge for any violinist, but she does it like it's second nature. Maybe it's just this song, played so many times solo, inviting her to sing for herself. But today, we sing for each other and for ourselves, too. This woman opening herself up to a new way of living, new possibilities, a new future, undreamt of until now, marrying her voice and her gift, while I put these many years of background vocals and percussion aside and let my own voice speak for me, the calluses on my fingers beginning to build again after so long pretending I know nothing but my drums.

It's a duet, in the deepest sense of the word. The two parts making a whole that is more than the sum of the parts, instrumental and vocal, playing off each other, spinning the threads of song into something expansive and freeing, shedding the limitations of the past for a limitless future, together.

But not alone.

There's a clapping sound from the doorway now, as Aria and Tommy both applaud us. I grab Lyric's hand and stand, turning to bow for our appreciative audience. Lyric giggles and then joins me in a bow.

"That was awesome, Mommy, Mr. Rhys! Can you teach me to play that song, Mommy? Then we can all play it together!"

Lyric looks to me, as if my approval is needed here, and I shrug. Why not?

"And Tommy, too, Mr. Rhys! Tommy can play the drums, and I'll play the violin!"

"It's a hard song to learn on the violin, Aria. Maybe a little easier on the drums?"

I nod. "It's within Tommy's reach, as fast as he learns, as much as he practices. And maybe we try the tambourine for you, Aria? Would you like that?"

"Oh, yeah! Or piano — Mommy's teaching me piano."

Lyric smiles.

"Let's try tambourine first, Aria. Then you'll also be a percussionist, like Daddy."

"And Tommy and Mr. Rhys!"

I pull Lyric closer to me, kissing her hair. I'm not sure I've ever been happier than I am right now, in this room full of music and... family.

Two hours later

"Do the kids have scarfs? Hats?" I ask Lyric.

"Like, for winter?"

"Yeah."

"Aria does. Tommy won't wear them. I think they're too scratchy, with his sensory triggers."

"Wool? Acrylic?"

"Whatever they had at the store. Kids grow fast. I couldn't afford to spend a lot on high-end stuff."

"Of course. Makes sense."

"Why?"

"I thought maybe I'd run down to Brighid's shop, pick up a couple of patterns, needles."

"Rhys? Are you going to make my kids hats and scarfs? You know it's still August, right?"

"Not for long, as you and I are all too well aware."

She frowns. Yeah, it's time for a little outing.

"Get the kids ready. We can all go. Brighid has rocks, too!"

CHAPTER 50

BLACK LIGHT TRAP

Lyric

"Look, Mommy! Auntie Bridge has more of the pretty pink rocks!"

Brighid smiles at me.

"And what are the pink rocks called, Aria?" she asks.

"Flower something..."

"Close! They're rose quartz."

"And what do we use them for?" I ask her.

"Love," she says. "They're soft and warm."

"The rocks are soft and warm?" Rhys asks, looking genuinely confused.

"Here," I tell him, putting a rock in his palm. "Close your eyes and just feel. Not with your fingers, but with your spirit."

"Hmm..." he says. He pulls on my hand with his other one, pulling me closer to him. His hand rests on my hip. "OK — now I'm feeling it... warm and soft." His hand slides around to my butt. "Very warm and soft," he says, giving my ass a squeeze. "And full of love," he adds, pulling me in for a kiss.

I blush, but I let him do it. No one's looking, including the kids. OK — Brighid's trying to pretend she's not looking, but I see that pleased smirk on her face.

"Now, Rhys — you said you need something super-soft? And I don't mean Lyric's ass," she adds under her breath.

I roll my eyes and move back over to the kids. Tommy's doing his usual back-and-forth dance, stimming, humming, waiting for us to get done so we can stop in the toy store and then grab popcorn for tonight's family movie. Can I say I love that? I wish Adam could be here with us, but I feel like we've got his blessing on this Family 2.0 unit, and it truly feels like a fresh start for all of us.

"How are you liking the tarot and the Ogham, Lyric?" Brighid asks while Rhys browses through her yarns and patterns.

"The Ogham is a challenge to memorize," I tell her. It's going to take me a while to feel like I've got a handle on it. "The tarot — I love the imagery. I'm starting to connect with it. Do you mind if I hold onto it?"

"Consider it a gift," she says. "I'll order a few more decks, since you like it so much. Looks like it'll be a hit."

"Thanks," I tell her.

"The smile on your face is enough thanks for one day," she says. "I'm so happy for you two — you four."

Brighid steps back behind the counter.

"Did you find everything you needed today?" she asks her customer.

"Yes — the tea I got the other day was amazing. I wanted to get some for a friend, too."

"That's great. Just remember what I said about the maximum of two cups a day."

"I'll make sure she reads the package."

"Great!"

The woman turns and gives me a smile, then heads out with her package.

"She's been in four times now. I think she's on track to beat Mrs. Lowell as a regular customer. She's expressed a keen interest in something every time she's been in."

"I'm glad the shop is doing so well."

"Me, too. It gives me hope Molly will be able to run it successfully when I'm out on the road with Hunter."

My smile falters a little.

"It will be fine, Lyric," she says quietly, glancing at Rhys, who's checking out some wooden knitting needles. "I'm certain of it."

"I hope so. We've been so happy these last few weeks, a few glitches aside."

I don't tell her about Adam. There are at least two other customers in here. It'll wait.

"Just enjoy each other. It's almost Labor Day..."

"And then back to school."

She squeezes my hand.

"Let it all unfold," she says. "Let the pieces fall into place."

"I love puzzles!" Rhys says. "We should get one at the toy shop."

I smile at him. Just because I'm happy.

Five minutes later, we're checked out, with Rhys' knitting supplies, a few vials of essential oils for me and more rocks for Aria.

"Have fun!" Brighid tells us as we head for the door, visions of family puzzle time in our heads.

"Rhys! Rhys! Is this your girlfriend, Rhys?"

We step out into a huddle of photographers and reporters on the sidewalk, all of them shouting at Rhys, at me.

"Are these your kids, Lyric?"

Rhys steps between me and the reporter, looking as menacing as I've ever seen him.

I grab the kids close and back up, pulling at the door to the shop.

"What's your name, sweetie?" one of the reporters leans around us both to ask Tommy, who wails in distress.

"Leave him alone. Leave us alone!" I tell her, only then recognizing her as the repeat customer in Brighid's shop.

"Mommy? What's going on?" Aria asks, sounding as frightened as I feel.

The door finally opens, with Brighid pushing on it from the other side.

"What is going on here?" she demands. "You're harassing my customers. Leave, before I call the police," she says.

"Public property!" one of them shouts.

"So, are you and Lyric both witches? What about Callie? Are all the members of aMUSEd bewitched?"

Oh, gods...

"No comment!" Brighid yells, dragging me, and the kids with me, back into her shop.

Rhys stands in front of the door until he's sure we're all safely inside, ignoring the continued questions being hurled at him, most of which have to do with him dating a witch.

Finally, he pulls the door open and comes back inside, holding the door closed. Showing some small degree of wisdom, none of them try to follow us into the shop.

"I'm afraid we're closing early today!" Brighid announces, encouraging the remaining two customers out the front door, where the reporters and photographers step aside just long enough to let them through. And then she locks the door, flips the open/closed sign over.

"I'd hoped I'd never need to move this weaving again, but here we are," she says, grabbing one of her woven sample pieces off the wall and taping it over the glass door. She pulls curtains over the display windows and then scrawls a hasty, "Closed due to personal emergency" sign, taping it to the door under the weaving.

"So... who's calling Gryffin? You or me?" she asks.

There's silence as Rhys and I catch up with what's just happened, including Brighid's efficient handling of the situation.

"Mommy, who were all those people?" Aria asks.

Tommy's back to his stimming, except he's shifting back and forth faster, humming louder, clearly still distressed. Rhys stands close by, stretching his hands reflexively,

"They're reporters, Aria," I tell her.

"Like Auntie Rory?" she asks.

"No. Nothing like Auntie Rory."

"I'll call Gryff," Rhys says. "He'll get this sorted out."

I wish Rhys sounded more confident of that than he does, but it seems like maybe this is as new to him as it is to us.

He moves off to the side to make his call.

"Lyric — where *is* Rory?" Brighid asks. "She helped out the last time this happened."

"The last communication I got from her said something about being out of touch and a swamp monster."

"Mother of twelve gods!" Brighid says. "If she's out in the Great Cypress Swamp, chances are she's off the grid. The cell service out there is terrible."

I don't ask her how she knows that. Given all the things I know that I've never told anyone, most of them under sworn oath to Rory, Brighid's knowledge of the swamp could mean anything. Even the impossible.

"We're on our own, then," she says.

"Not entirely," Rhys says. "Gryff's sending down four guys on the corporate jet. They'll be here in an hour or so, depending on traffic."

"Wow. That's fast," Brighid says.

"He's treating it as an emergency. And Billy's coming with them."

"Uh-oh," Brighid says.

"Why uh-oh?" I ask.

"Because if we weren't in big trouble, Billy wouldn't be coming with them. I need to call Hunt."

She steps away.

Rhys steps in behind me, hugging me close to his chest and Aria with me. We both watch Tommy stimming, though he's a little slower and quieter now.

"You OK?" Rhys asks.

"No. Not really," I admit. "They tried to talk to the kids, to Tommy! That is *so* far out of line!"

I drop down to look Aria in the eyes.

"I know that was kind of scary, guys," I tell her and Tommy. "But none of those people would ever hurt you. They just want-ed to ask Mommy and Mr. Rhys some questions, and take some photographs. We don't have to answer them just because they ask something."

"Isn't that rude, Mommy?"

I exchange a look with Rhys. Leave it to a kid...

"It's rude for them to follow us, Aria. It's rude — probably against the law — for them to bother you or Tommy. So if that ever happens again, if anyone you don't know ever tries to ask you questions, you don't have to answer, OK?"

"OK, Mommy. I didn't like that, with them all around us like that."

"Yeah. It was scary. But we're going to have some friends of Mr. Rhys come help keep them away from us, keep us safe. OK?"

"Like superheroes, Mommy?"

I exchange a smile with Rhys.

"Yeah, like superheroes, Aria," he says. "My friend Gryffin is going to make sure we keep you and your brother and your mom safe."

"Mom!" I suddenly remember. "Oh, gods... I've got to tell her to stay inside until we know they aren't following her, too!"

"How did they find us in the first place?" he asks.

"That reporter — she's been coming into the shop, like a regular customer. Brighid said four times in the last week or so."

"And I think she kept coming back hoping you'd be here, Lyric," Brighid says, ending her call with Hunter. "I'm so sorry

— I should have been more careful. But she seemed genuinely interested in the shop, what we offer. Now... Well, in hindsight, I think she was snooping so she could scoop the competition on a juicy tabloid story..."

"What story?"

"I just got a text from Melanie, my PR contact. This story just posted."

She hands me her phone.

"The Bewitching Women of aMUSEd."

The photo is one taken just minutes ago, as Brighid emerged from the shop to try to chase the reporters off of us. I look stunned, the kids frightened, Brighid like an avenging angel, and Rhys like a large, protective but happy-go-lucky golden retriever. Scratch that — Irish setter. Can't forget the red hair.

"CelebrityGossipCentral has confirmed that at least two of the women with whom members of chart-topping rock band aMUSEd have recently been associated may identify as witches. Our reporter, on the scene in the tiny resort town of Mystic Beach, Del., personally witnessed Mystic Beach residents Brighid Weaver, fiancée of aMUSEd rhythm guitarist Hunter Graves, and Lyric Larson, believed to be dating aMUSEd drummer Rhys Madigan, discussing such matters as magical crystals and exchanging divinatory devices, including tarot cards.

"Weaver, owner of a shop named Dream Weaver, sells a variety of crystals and herbs, as well as handmade yarns and other needlecraft materials. A sign posted behind the counter also offers such items as 'spiritual counseling,' Reiki healing and tarot readings. Requesting spiritual counseling, our reporter was led to a back room in the shop, where she found not only a counseling area, but a wide array of candles, oils, incense, tarot decks, and books on a variety of arcane, esoteric and occult topics, ranging from Irish mythology and herbal healing to modern Wiccan religion and candle magic."

"Holy Mother Goddess Brighid."

That's all I've got. I hand Rhys her phone, the rest of the article unread.

"This is my fault, guys," Brighid says. "I let that girl in the back room. She had me fooled. And I just let her in."

"It's not your fault, Brighid," I tell her. "She came in under false pretenses. She would have said anything she needed to. And it wasn't the guy who'd tried to get the ride photo the other night, obviously, so even watching out for him wouldn't have helped."

"No — it's *my* fault," Rhys says. "If I hadn't decided to force my way into your lives, let people take photos of us together at the fundraiser, none of this would have happened."

"Rhys — you can't blame yourself for this, either. You didn't do anything to point them at this story. You barely did anything to point them at us having a relationship." I pull his face between my hands, kissing him, hoping it'll reassure him. Because right now, I'm not finding much of anything reassuring.

CHAPTER 51

SMALL TOWN TRAP

Lyric

"I'm sure it'll be fine, dear," Mom says on the other end of the phone. "These things blow over. Just wait for these security people to arrive, then head home and hide out for a couple days. It'll be nothing by the time the weekend is over."

"And then I have to start back to work. With the whole world thinking I'm a witch!"

"You are a witch, dear. So am I. So is Brighid, whether she calls herself priestess first or not. Maybe it's time we're all out of the broom closet. We could be the next vanguard in diversity awareness."

"Mom — the school board canceled my winter concert theme because it was Disney! You really think they're going to welcome a teacher who identifies as a witch, as a polytheist? They'll fire me!"

"They can't. It would be overt religious discrimination. You could sue!"

"They'd find some other excuse."

"Then let them try! I'm tired of these petty dictators thinking that the only religion covered under the First Amendment is their own!"

"It's my job, Mom. I can't afford to lose it."

She sighs.

"Can Rhys help? Can his people? Maybe you just deny everything, tell them you were shopping for tea and candles."

"And the tarot?"

"For a friend."

This doesn't sit any better with me, for the same reasons she argued I should come out.

"Just sit tight, Mom. If I need you to watch the kids again, I'll call."

"OK. I had a date tonight, but I can cancel."

"No — don't do that. Just be careful when you go out, don't talk about this situation, about me or Rhys."

"I haven't so far. Just that I have a daughter and two grandkids."

"OK. Thanks. Love you!"

"Love you, too, honey. Hug those kids for me!"

I'll be hugging them for myself. Because I need the hugs. Aria's been playing games on Rhys' phone, Tommy on Brighid's. It's kept them busy, calm.

There's a knock at the door, only it's not the front door, where we can still see feet moving about. Brighid hops up and runs to the back of the shop.

She emerges moments later with Hunter and a wolfhound in tow.

"Greetings fellow hostages of the paparazzi!" Hunter says, far too chipper for my mood.

"Fellow?" I ask.

"They've got Brighid's house surrounded, too. I didn't like her being stuck here. So, I put this big guy on a leash, walked out the back door and down the path to the beach. I told the couple of paps out back 'No comment,' but that they were welcome to follow us on our ten-mile run down to Fenwick and back, on the beach, and see if they still had enough breath to ask me questions I wasn't going to answer. Then we outran them to the dunes, crossed over the next crossing and came up the back way to the shop, which they don't seem to have discovered yet, because the coast was clear."

"So we can leave out the back?" I ask.

"I wouldn't," he says, shaking his head. "I was counting on the dog and the sand to intimidate them. You've got the kids... At this point, I'd just wait it out until reinforcements arrive. It won't be long now."

Brighid walks into his arms, and he hugs her, murmuring quietly into her hair.

I finally sit down on the floor next to Aria, and Rhys sits down next to me, pulling me back to lean on him. Maybe I wouldn't be in this mess without Rhys in my life. I just know that I wouldn't want to be in it without him.

"We've got a couple cars out back, ready to roll, and I've got a couple guys out front, making like we're going to herd you out that way," Gryffin says. "We can take you back home, or to the studio. It's up to you. We'll set up outside whichever locations you go to."

Gryffin has the tough, no-nonsense look of someone who's served in the military and hasn't gone far afield now that he's a nominal civilian. I wouldn't want to cross him. Good.

"Where's Billy?" Rhys asks.

"At the studio, conferencing with the other guys and with the label."

"I think Rhys and I should be there, then," Hunter says. "I fucked up the last paparazzi disaster, and I learned my lesson about having a PR plan. I want us on the same page with this, since it affects so many more people."

"Right." Rhys agrees.

"Right now, Lyric and I are the most affected," Brighid says. "We have to be in on any discussion."

"I don't want the kids in the middle of this, in any way," I tell them, keeping my voice low.

"Why don't you leave them with your mom?" Rhys suggests. "She's a few hundred yards away. So long as we keep the paps in the dark, they should be safe there, right?"

I don't like the idea of not having the kids nearby, either. But it's the better alternative.

"Let me call her. She had a date tonight."

"We'll assign the kids one man for close protection, just to be safe, ma'am," Gryffin says. "Just tell me where he needs to be."

"She's staying in Callie's old loft apartment."

"Just back behind here?" he asks.

I nod.

"Roger that. Let me get Kirk in here. He's good with kids. We can make an introduction and go from there."

"OK."

I say it, but I'm not exactly comfortable with any of this.

G ryffin was right. Kirk's great with kids. He's got nieces about Tommy and Aria's ages, and he's got her talking about her favorite TV characters like she's having a chat with one of her friends at school. Gryffin had him stop at the toy store on the way over, and Tommy now has two new sets of Legos to play with, and Aria has a bunch of coloring books and markers.

"If they need to stay with your mother overnight, Lyric, we can take you back to your house and let you pack bags for them. But I'll warn you — there are at least two photographers and reporter there now, in front of your house. We can keep them off the studio property, but your house is a lot closer to public property than the studio is. It's going to be intrusive unless they get bored and leave. You may want to consider relocating to the studio for a week or two, limiting your outings to urgent needs. Right now would be an excellent time for a destination vacation, if you prefer. Someplace out of the way...."

"Mystic Beach *was* out of the way!"

All of this has me a little hysterical, and I shout that way louder than necessary.

"I'm sorry, Gryffin," I add, letting out a breath. "I know you're trying to help. But I go back to work in less than a week. The kids go back to school in less than a week. And there are photographers waiting outside my house to follow me and my kids, just because..."

"Because you're dating me," Rhys says, his voice full of regret.

He looks the most dejected I've ever seen him.

"Folks, this is just par for the course," Gryffin says. "Chances are this will blow over like the last incident did. Don't let emotions run away with you, as hard as that may be to do right now. We're going to keep you safe and as far away from the press as we reasonably can. Then it's up to the PR staff to handle things as efficiently as possible, so that, ideally, you don't need us here at all."

"OK, Aria, Tommy — you're going to go with Mr. Kirk. I'm going to be right behind you, and I'll watch you go right up the stairs to visit Grandma. You're going to stay with her, watch some movies, play with your toys..."

"A sleepover!" Aria says, already excited.

"We'll see. I'll call Grandma later, and we'll talk about that."

"Can we take Crógan with us? Please?"

That makes everyone laugh, including the security guys.

"Crógan is going to be helping Uncle Hunter take care of Auntie Bridge. But Mr. Kirk is going to be with you two and Grandma, and he's much more fun to talk to, right?"

"Yeah. I guess," she says, sounding unconvinced.

"I'll take good care of them, and your mother, ma'am," Kirk says.

"Thank you."

He gives me a nod and corrals the kids, their toys in bags, toward the back door.

"You ready?" Rhys asks me.

I nod. But I'm not ready for any of this. I just don't have any choice.

Rhys

Lyric's suffering, buried under worry about the kids, about her job, her privacy. All I can think is that maybe Adam was wrong. Maybe I'm the wrong man for this job, for taking care of her and the kids. Maybe she was better off before I made her let me help...

"Ladies — our recommendation is that you ignore this story," Billy says. "Don't confirm. Don't deny. If they ask questions about it, it maybe tempting to laugh it off, hope they'll realize it's a silly story to begin with..."

"But they *are* witches. Both of them," I object. "It's not silly. It's very serious. It's like someone attacking an actor's wife because she's a Buddhist or a pop star's husband because he's a Quaker."

Lyric squeezes my arm, thankful for the understanding.

"The reality is that we don't get the same respect for our beliefs that larger minority faiths do," she says. "That's why I fly under the radar, why Brighid is so low-key. Or part of the reason, anyway," she says when Brighid looks poised to object.

"The reality is that this story does a lot less damage to me than it does to Lyric," Brighid says. "Worst case, I lose a few customers. Maybe someone graffities my storefront..."

"Or burns a cross in your yard," I add. Yeah, I was listening when Lyric talked about this shit.

Brighid stops short, swallows.

"We can't let Crógan outside on his own, Hunt."

"I'll take him out myself. Every time," he assures her, hugging her close. "Even at six in the morning."

Yeah. All of a sudden this got really serious. The dog's not safe. Maybe we aren't either. And Tommy doesn't talk.

"I'm going to loop local law-enforcement in, get them to step up patrols in your neighborhoods, at Brighid's shop," Gryffin says. "We'll station men at each house, in rotating shifts. None of you leave to go anywhere without protection, OK?"

"What about Callie and me?" Declan asks.

"You're close enough for the guys at Lyric's house to keep an eye out for anything. If there are any issues, I'll bring in more personnel."

Everyone seems satisfied with that. At least in the short term.

"Our crisis management consultants insist that the best thing to do here is to say nothing," Billy says. "Acknowledge nothing. Ignore the media entirely. Let this blow over. They've seen it time and time again — don't feed the fire and it'll blow itself out."

"So that's the plan?" Lyric asks. "Stay quiet, hide behind body-guards and wait for the media to go away?"

"That's the core of it, yes," Billy says. "It works."

"No press releases?"

"No. It's inadvisable. At most, we'd end up telling them that the private lives of the band members and their families are just that — private — and that prying into matters of personal faith is tantamount to harassment, refer them to our lawyers regarding possible restraining orders. The same goes with the kids — they're protected from harassment. We've already had them remove the photo they'd posted earlier, reminded them, quite pointedly, of the law."

Lyric relaxes a fraction.

"What'd they put up in its place?" Brighid asks.

Billy flushes.

"It's a photo from inside the shop — of Rhys and Lyric."

"Let me guess — he's got his hand on her ass."

Billy nods.

Yeah... maybe I'm not the best guy for the job after all.

"It's fine. It's fine," Lyric says. "As long as the kids aren't in them."

"They're not."

"Alright. That's a start."

Chapter 52

Home

Lyric

Rhys, and Gryffin — and pretty much everyone else involved — wanted me to stay at the studio, even if the kids and I had to stay there overnight to wait for the press attention to die down. But as darkness begins to fall, it's not dying down.

"How bad is it out there?" Rhys asks as Declan comes back from checking in on Callie at her restaurant.

"It's not good," Declan says. "There's at least a half-dozen reporters and photographers standing at the end of the driveway."

"Flibbertigibbets!" Rhys says.

None of his bandmates reacts. I guess they're used to his alternative swearing.

Right now, I'm tempted to swear up a blue streak, myself. I guess it's good that Mom could take the kids when things blew up like that. But how is she going to get them home if the paparazzi are at my house? How am *I* going to get home?

"There's no one over at the restaurant," Declan says, "but they may be keeping an eye on it while they're staking out Brighid's shop, just in case you all come in for dinner."

"Dinner out is the last of my worries right now," Hunter says. "I couldn't even get my fiancée to stay *here* for dinner."

"You can't blame her for wanting to check on the shop after Molly re-opened it this afternoon. She's already had to shut down the shop twice this summer," I remind him.

Hunter looks a little guilty, which makes sense considering his involvement in those episodes.

"I'm calling Marina Matthews," David says. "Maybe she can twist some arms, get these publications and sites to recall their people. This isn't workable for you all, and it's not workable for the band, or the studio. And I don't like adding any stress to what Piper's already dealing with — and having a gaggle of media at the end of the driveway is stressful. I've already gotten a complaint from the neighbors, too."

I can't imagine what a community with its own private beach is thinking with paparazzi camped out practically at their gate.

"What about the police? Can't we get them to clear these guys out?"

"I already asked Gryff about that. They're on public property," Alex says. "The only thing the police can do is make sure they stay off private property and don't block the roadway."

"They're a safety hazard now, even if they're not in the roadway. No one's driving highway speeds past here with that scene to look at."

"Good point," Alex says. "I'll remind Gryff about that. Maybe they can get an officer over here to clear them out, even if it's temporary." He goes off to make a call.

"Until things calm down again, we need security on-site and probably with any of us when we go out," Hunter says. "And that includes Lyric and her kids."

He looks nervously over at me, as if I'm going to refuse. Not after this morning, I'm not. But I also don't like the idea of my kids and I living life like we're in prison.

"So, we just go home and stay inside, and the security guys stand around outside, keeping the photographers off our lawn?"

"Basically, yeah," Hunter says. "They went away after a couple days when they were first after Brighid. I'm not sure what they'll do this time. But it'll blow over at some point. And we'll need them over at Brighid's. Fuck... we may have to postpone the wedding if this doesn't blow over quickly. Brighid's going to kill me."

"No, she's going to kill Rhys," Kieran says, shaking his head.

Now it's Rhys looking guilty.

"I don't think we can assign blame here, unless it's on the invasive celebrity media." I don't like them blaming Rhys, even though it's his presence that seems to have invited this.

"Lyric's right — this is the price of fame. For us, and for the people in our lives. As much as that sucks. And it sucks big-time right now," Hunter says.

"I need to get home. I need to get the kids and get us all home." I don't like leaving them with my mom this long with all of this looming over us. I'll feel better when my family is safe at home.

"I'll get Gryff to sort out getting you all back, with security," David says.

Five minutes later, Gryffin is ready to drive me home himself so he can check the house, while Kirk and Roger are bringing the kids home. Thankfully, Aria's just over the size where a booster seat is required. Griffin assures me all his people are trained in defensive driving and that I can trust them to drive with my kids in the car. It's a bit of a weight off my mind, but I won't fully relax until I'm actually at home with the kids tucked safely into bed.

"Let's go," Rhys says.

"Better if you don't," Gryffin tells him. "Let the paps think there's less to see at Lyric's, and maybe they'll back off faster."

"No! I'm not leaving Lyric and the kids alone."

"We won't be alone, Rhys." I squeeze his hand to reassure him. "We're going to have security with us. And Gryffin's right. You pay him to know this stuff."

Rhys sighs.

"Fine. But I'm coming over in the morning. I'll make you breakfast."

"I'll see you in the morning, then," I tell him. I give him a quick peck on the lips, not wanting to do major PDA in front of the band and Gryffin.

There's only one photographer in front of my house when we get there.

"Where's Rhys, Lyric? Trouble in paradise?"

"No comment," I reply.

He looks so disappointed that Rhys isn't with me that I wonder if he'll just leave once I'm back in the house. I can only hope, I guess.

"Let me check inside the house before you settle in," Gryffin says as we open the front door. He walks briskly through the house, opening doors, peering into vents, checking window locks, closing curtains, scanning with a little box he pulls from his pocket. "Everything checks out," he says. "We'll be doing regular checks while the media interest remains. We don't want someone breaking in while you're out and planting cameras or listening devices."

"They do that?"

"It's been known to happen," he says. "You're going to want to put room-darkening curtains up in that sunroom off the bedroom, move anything personal or private out of the range of long lenses on their cameras," he adds.

"You mean my altar."

"Yes, ma'am."

I sigh.

"Lyric — it's not any of my business, but you've made an effort to keep your beliefs quiet. I think if you continue to respond like you did outside just now — always saying, 'No comment,' regardless of what they ask — chances are they'll eventually go away. I know it's a hassle right now, and it has to feel incredibly invasive and even frightening, but your best way of handling it is going to be not giving them anything to feed on."

"That's easy to say when you're Mr. ex-..." I don't want to guess what his branch of service was and guess wrong. But he knows what I'm asking.

"SEAL, ma'am — I'm a former Navy SEAL. There are no 'ex-' SEALs — not unless they got dishonorably discharged."

"Gotcha. Sorry. Anyway — you're the tough-guy, the upstanding veteran. They're not digging into your faith, looking to paint you as strange or dangerous."

"All due respect, ma'am, I wasn't raised as conventionally as you might assume. My paternal grandmother is a native Hawaiian. I spent my summers with her when I was a kid. I know it's not the same, but don't think I'm unaware of how earnest faith can be labeled as superstition."

"Understood. And appreciated." I give him a smile and a nod.

"I'm going to ask you for a house key — do you have a spare?"

I look over at the hooks by the door, where Adam's keys have rested since we got his personnel effects back. I take them off the hook, remove the house key and hand it to Gryffin.

"From this point on, we'll have Roger and Kirk stationed outside the house when you're home. If you need to go out, they'll drive. This is standard with close protection," he adds when I start to object. "If you need to separate from the children for any reason, one of them will go with you and one with the children. Plan ahead for any outings, because I'll need to ensure they can get their sleep in shifts. I can bring in another man to spell them, but I'm hoping this will be over before that becomes an issue."

"I'm really sorry about this," I tell him. All this fuss, just to keep a few reporters from asking us questions...

"No apologies needed, ma'am," he says. "This is your current reality. We can hope it passes. Chances are it will. If it doesn't..." He frowns. "If it doesn't, we'll all adapt. It will become a new normal, just like the guys have had to deal with when they're on tour. They've been lucky so far that, as famous as they are, they've been able to avoid this level of interest in their personal lives. But things are changing rapidly right now, and the need for security is something that has to change with it. That's what we're here for — me and my guys."

"No female... bodyguards? Agents?"

"I call them operatives," he says. "And I have a few who work with us when they're on the road — most of them honorably discharged military, like the rest of my people. Would you prefer a female operative was assigned to you? All of my operatives are highly capable, extensively trained, certified in everything they can be."

"No. That's not necessary. The kids seem to like Kirk already. I don't want to shake things up if you're going to be here just for a short while."

"If you change your mind, just let me know. Here's my card — it's got my direct number on it. Call me anytime, day or night, 24/7. That's what I'm here for."

"Thank you. Again."

"Goodnight, ma'am."

Five minutes later, the kids burst through the door.

"Mommy! Mommy!" Aria shouts. "Grandma ordered fish and nuggets with french fries and applesauce! Then we watched a movie, and we played Go Fish!"

"Oh? Was grandma's friend nice?" Yes, I'm pumping my kid for information.

"We had three kinds of ice cream for dessert! Meopelican!"

"Neapolitan?" I ask. Aria nods. "That sounds amazing! I'm glad you had so much fun."

I am not going to ask Aria whether Grandma's friend was a lady or a man. It doesn't matter, as much as my curiosity is eating at me.

"It's bedtime, you two," I tell her and Tommy. "Go up and get ready for bed, and then I'll come read with you."

"I want Mr. Rhys to read my story!" Aria says. Tommy gives me a look that says he wants that, too.

"Mr. Rhys isn't here tonight, Aria. He's back at the studio."

"Aww... But I wanted a story!"

"Another night, honey. Head on up to bed, and I'll be up in a minute."

I watch them walk up the stairs. Aria heads straight into the bathroom. Tommy lingers outside the practice room for a moment. I get it, but Gryffin was right — it was easier without Rhys here to interest the paparazzi. Hopefully, this will all be over soon.

CHAPTER 53
BOYS OF SUMMER

Lyric

It's been a week since everything blew up. Nothing much has changed. The paparazzi linger in front of my house in twos and threes most days. The same at Brighid's shop. The only fall-off has been at the studio, where the local cops informed them their cluster was impeding traffic and causing a safety hazard. They still stand out there — it's just fewer of them.

The Labor Day holiday? Normally, it's a final beach day for me and the kids before school starts the next day. This year, Rhys invites us over for a low-key party with the band and their significant others, potluck-style. Declan mans the grill. Callie and Alex prepare the other hot foods. The rest of us bring the cold stuff. I fall back on chips and dip, since I can get them delivered and that saves me the time and energy of making something.

The paparazzi haven't taken a holiday, and Roger drives us into the studio compound through the break in a line of unco-operative bodies armed with cameras.

One of the things I've learned this week? Those cameras can't see through the tinted windows of the car. Until the doors open, we have privacy. Roger pulls up close to the studio door just above the ground floor and we get out the passenger door closest to it, visible for just a moment as one of the other security "operatives" holds it open. From there, it's almost a normal social event with my friends and their boyfriends/husbands/fiancés. Piper is a new friend, too, (and very quiet). Rhys' mom arrives shortly after we do, getting warm hugs from everyone (including my kids). She seems to hit it off with my mom once Kirk arrives with her, and the two of them hang out while the rest of us go down to the beach.

That lasts right until we spot the paparazzo at the very edge of the neighboring state park beach with a long lens pointed at me and Rhys. No PDA on the beach today. And I'm glad I'm wearing my usual "mom" swimsuit and sarong, and not some skimpy thing that might end up on the front page of a tabloid. We corral the kids and head back up to the deck, spending the rest of the day playing games and relaxing.

"You ready for tomorrow?" Callie asks me.

"No," I answer honestly. "I mean, I'm ready for my classes. But..."

"You worried about what the other teachers are going to say? About..."

"Me being a witch? Yeah, a little. Most everyone is pretty laid-back about politics, but the few who aren't... They tend to be more... vocal. I'm actually more worried about the parents."

"Yikes. I didn't even think about that. You think they're going to cause problems?"

"I have no idea. Most of my parents love me. Or they did. I don't know."

"You call me if you need anything, OK? I'm still on the kids' pickup list, right?"

"Yeah. But the security guys are driving — me and Aria in one car, and Tommy to his school in the other. If something happens, I should be covered. Thank you, though."

"No thanks necessary. Things have been crazy, but I know Rory's not available right now. So, I'll drop things if you need me. Really."

"Thanks. Honestly, I've been missing her. I wish I knew what was going on, but it's some hush-hush investigative reporter deal. You know how that is: 'I can't reveal my sources' and such." While that's nominally true, I suspect this has less to do with her actual job than the responsibilities she's taken on with Rónan gone. That's the kind of stuff she doesn't talk about, even with me. And I'm almost relieved about that. What I've got going on these days is crazy. What she's got going on is sometimes dangerous and frequently literally unbelievable. If I hadn't seen it myself, I know I wouldn't have believed it.

"How's the honeymoon planning going?" I ask her.

"Good. It's more a matter of deciding where we can go inside a month, rather picking one spot over another."

"What's your top pick?"

"Italy. I want to get back to some of the roots of my recipes, the ones Nonna taught me."

"What about relaxing? Spending time together, just the two of you?"

"I think we are going to take that week in Fiji."

"Now, that sounds amazing!" Assuming the paparazzi don't follow them there. Especially since Callie's swimsuits are smaller than mine. But then she doesn't seem to have a problem with showing some skin in public...

"Yeah — I don't know what Brighid and Hunter are doing for theirs, but good, authentic food, and a little time alone... that's a recipe for a perfect honeymoon."

I chuckle a little. Only Callie — and Declan, apparently — would prioritize food over private time on their honeymoon.

"You think..." She gives me a look. "You think you might be headed in that direction?"

"What? Fiji? Not with two kids and a school year ahead of me." Yeah, I know that's not what she's asking. But it's too soon, and with things as they stand now, I'd be stupid not to be thinking twice about planning a future with Rhys.

"Girl... You know what I mean."

"Yeah. Too soon to even be talking about it."

"By which you mean you don't want to talk about it. I get it. But give him — give yourself — a chance. OK?"

She squeezes my hand. It's out-of-character for Callie. But she's softened up a lot since Declan came back into her life. I'd say it's ironic, considering his reputation for being a jackass, but it's easy to see that they'd both suffered during their time apart, and it had hardened them. Once they were back together, that had started to reverse itself. It's good to see it. They'd have been my only handfasting failure. Can't say I didn't warn them all those years ago that it would stick. I just wish they hadn't been forced apart in the meantime.

That brings my attention back to Rhys, who's standing on his head while Aria tries to mimic him, Tommy staring wide-eyed at him, trying to turn his own head upside down even though he's still otherwise upright. I can't help but laugh. But it's also evidence that the kids have really bonded with Rhys, and whether he leaves to go on tour or we break up after one too many run-ins with the press, they're going to suffer. Is it even worth trying? I start to see why so many rockstar marriages fail, and often quickly. Gods... Marriage? What am I even thinking? Way too soon. And things are so uncertain right now. No. Not in the cards now. Maybe ever.

Rhys comes down from his headstand, ruffling Tommy's hair (with no complaints) and helping Aria with her own headstand. He glances over at me and smiles. I smile back.

How can you even be thinking of letting that gorgeous hunk of man go?

Not now, Annie. This is about more than sex.

I never said it wasn't. You, girl, spend way too much time looking for problems to prevent or solve, and not nearly enough enjoying the blessings you've been given.

Ouch.

She's not wrong. Look at all of them, enjoying being with the people they love. Getting married, going on honeymoons, living their lives with joy, even after heartache and struggle.

Not to put too fine of a point on it, eh, Vivienne?

And now I've made her sad, wistful.

I miss him, Lyric. But things are good. I'll be ready to move on soon.

Him? A husband? A son? Who is she missing?

She doesn't answer.

Brighid smiles as Hunter leans around her from behind and kisses her hair. She's radiant, despite the chaos and worry caused by this second round of press attention. Could she be pregnant already? Or is this just a bride-to-be glow?

She catches me watching and smiles at me, too, looking over at Rhys where he's playing Legos with Tommy. Rhys' mom was right — he has a gift for pulling Tommy out of his shell. Brighid stands up and comes to sit next to me.

"How're you doing, Lyric?"

"It's nice getting to just relax with the kids, with everyone..."

"With Rhys?"

I nod. She looks back at Hunter, who's joking with David. Her expression is warm, adoring. Something strikes me...

"Brighid?"

"Yeah?"

"What was Hunter's mom's name?"

"Everyone always called her 'Vi.' I guess it was short for Violet? Honestly, she's been gone so long, I never really thought about it. I guess I should... It goes on the marriage license doesn't it?"

"Yeah."

Puzzle pieces...

"Lyric?"

"Hmm?"

"I asked if the new instruments had come in for the school."

"Oh. Yes. They came in on Thursday. The music store even unpacked them and set everything up for me. They're all ready for the kids."

"Try not to stick any of them with boring instruments they don't like, OK? I desperately wanted the xylophone when we had music in first grade, but I got stuck with a slap stick. It's how Hunt and I got to be friends, actually." She pauses. "Second thought, let fate fall out how it wants. I wouldn't undo that for the world..."

There's that warm smile again, on top of the glow. I remember feeling like that. And then the loss, the desperation, the loneliness... And then came Rhys...

I don't know if I can keep him. But I don't know if I can give him up, either.

I arrive at work early the next day. There are only a handful of teachers and staff in the building when I come in. Aria comes to my classroom with me to wait until her teacher arrives. I get everything all set. Thankfully, no thick packet of forms, since I don't have students assigned to me. Just an instrument contract and info sheet. Most of the younger kids won't even leave the building with their instruments.

"Mommy? What instrument do I get this year?"

"I don't know, honey. I'll have to see what the other kids think they want, and then I'll make some choices. Hopefully, you all end up with something you like. What do you think you want to play?"

"Violin."

Wow. Well, I wasn't expecting that. It's not even on the list of options. But I could work with her at home, integrate it with the planned ensemble, get her a starter instrument. I think I can stretch the budget for that. This is where that fellowship would come in handy, for one thing. Wait... What did I do with the application? The deadline is... was... Friday. I forgot all about it. Oh, well... I was a poem short anyway. It would have been a waste of a stamp.

"Let me look into it, OK? But think of a second choice, just in case."

"OK. I like the xylophone, too. It's kind of like drums and a piano had a baby."

I chuckle at her analogy. She's not wrong.

"I mean, you play piano, and Daddy played drums. Mr. Rhys plays drums. Tommy plays drums now, too. So, if I can't do violin, xylophone is OK. Or tambourine."

Before she adds to her list, I check the clock. It's time for her to go to class.

"Grab your bag, kiddo! It's that time!" She grabs her Little Mermaid backpack and takes my hand to walk back to the second-grade hall.

"Lyric! Are you and Rhys getting married, too?" There's a clicking noise, a flash of light.

There's a man I don't recognize standing in the hall, taking pictures and shouting. He's not one of the usual crew outside my house or the studio.

"What's your name, honey?" he asks Aria, who looks at me uncertainly but seems to remember that I told her she didn't have to talk to these people.

"You don't belong in this building! How did you get in here?"

"Aww, come on, Lyric — this is big news. An exclusive will net me a huge payday! I've got my ways... Just give me something — are you pregnant? Rumors are Brighid's pregnant."

If witches were actually like we're so often portrayed, he'd be ash on the floor the moment Brighid heard him ask that. She and Hunter are hoping, but it's a sensitive subject. I have yet to hit anyone with a lightning bolt, but this guy might be near the top of my list if I ever do.

"No comment. And you're in violation of school security protocols — you don't have a visitor pass, which means you don't belong here, and I'm going to call the constable to escort you out, see if the police will charge you with trespassing and whatever other charges they can throw at you!"

"No need to get witchy, Lyric!" That casual switch-up of "witchy" for "bitchy" makes me even angrier. The word witch derives from the term for "wise one." It should be a term of respect. If this guy was smart, he'd say it like that, but he isn't smart. He's clever — not smart.

"Mommy?"

"Come on, Aria — run with me."

"I'm not supposed to run in the halls, Mommy!"

"I'm giving you permission — run!"

Aria and I fly back down the hallway, clicking noises filling the hall behind us. One turn, and a second, and we're in the central hallway.

"Jimmy — there's a photographer back by my classroom. He's not authorized to be in the building..."

"I'm on it, Mrs. Larson!"

As Jimmy takes off down the hall, I breathe a sigh of relief.

Then I look down at Aria. She's wide-eyed, on edge.

"Are you OK, baby? Everything is fine now. We're safe."

"I don't like that man, Mommy. I saw him at the 'musement park. He kept watching Mr. Rhys."

Well, that explains some things...

"I don't like that either, Aria — he's breaking some big rules. And we need to tell Mrs. Frostberg that right now. And then I'll take you to class, and it'll all be back to normal, OK?"

"OK, Mommy."

As soon as I tell Carla what happened, she's on the phone with the police department, though Jimmy quickly reports that the man was nowhere to be found when he got to my classroom. I can't decide if I'm relieved or not.

"Why don't you let Patty take Aria to class, and we'll deal with this? You don't have a class first period, so we can get everything sorted out before you miss a class."

"How's that sound, Aria? Can Mrs. Jergens take you to class?"

"I like Mrs. Jergens," she says, smiling. "She's funny."

Patty smiles back.

"I like you, too, Aria," she says, leading her off down the hallway.

The police arrive, followed by Roger, who's extremely concerned and not inclined to be left out of this conversation.

"I've cleared my presence here with the school district," he insists. "I stayed outside out of courtesy and a desire to be discreet, and you see what happened! I'm assigned to Mrs. Larson's close-protection detail, and I need to be in on any security discussions."

"I'm fine, Roger. Aria's fine." I wonder... "Can you check on Tommy? Make sure no one showed up at his school?"

"I'll do that right now, while you're printing out one of those visitor badges for me," he says to Carla. "Call the district office if you don't believe I've got clearance."

Carla shakes her head at him but has him sign in and prints a visitor badge.

"You've got eyes on him? Good. Thanks," Roger says into his phone.

"Tommy's fine," Roger tells me. "No sign of anyone there. Kirk will stay within visual range, just to be safe."

My slight edge of panic recedes.

"Thank you."

"How did that guy even get in here?" I ask. "You wouldn't even let Roger in without questioning him. How did a total stranger get in the building with a camera and no visitor badge?"

"I'm pulling up the security video right now," Jimmy says.

Five minutes later, we're watching the paparazzo enter the building a full twenty minutes before he accosted me and Aria.

"He waited until your custodian walked outside and just grabbed the door, tucked himself in with the flow of staff entering the building," Roger says. "Easy. Too easy. I'm going to have to be inside the building with Mrs. Larson until this security threat is resolved."

Carla exchanges a look with me, then with Jimmy, who shrugs. The police officer adds a shrug of his own.

And just like that, I've got a security operative in my classroom, all day, every day.

T his fact does not go unnoticed, especially by my students, nor my fellow staff members. The teacher's lounge goes silent when Roger and I enter at lunchtime. A few whispers as I get my lunch out of the staff refrigerator. The looks I'm getting make me change my mind about eating in the lounge. I return to my desk and offer Roger half my turkey wrap.

"No, thank you, ma'am," he says, shaking his head. "I'm fine."

I find myself glad I tend to overpack lunches, due to Tommy being finicky and Aria being as hearty an eater as her mother. I hand him my apple and put half the sandwich in his other hand.

"Can't have my security operative passing out from low blood sugar and unable to protect me from a simple photographer," I tell him with a smirk. I grab two nutrition bars out of my desk and hand him one.

"Not bad," he says after his first bite of sliced turkey on a spinach wrap with Havarti, spring greens and avocado, with green goddess dressing. My favorite. Made special for the first day of the school year, to get things off to a symbolic positive start.

"I'll pack for two tomorrow," I tell him. The smile I give him is feeble, but when he objects, I reject his objection. It's the least I can do.

CHAPTER 54

INDIAN SUMMER SKY

Rhys

“He did what?”

I cannot believe this. After the warning from Billy and the label about media invading the kids’ privacy, one of them snuck into Lyric’s school.

“It’s fine. They’re going to pay closer attention going forward, even during busy entry times, make sure no one sneaks in. I’m sure everyone just thought he was a new staff member or something.”

I thought Lyric said the staff worked those half-days last week so they were all familiar with the building and procedures. How did some strange guy not get recognized by someone as not belonging?

“And Roger’s going to stay with me during school now.”

That makes me feel a little better. A little.

“And Tommy?”

“No one showed up at his school. At least they took that part of the warning seriously.”

“Is Aria OK?”

Both the kids are upstairs, unwinding after school. Lyric sent them up with snacks so we could talk, breaking her own rule about food in their bedrooms when they’re not sick.

“She’s fine. But she said she recognized the guy from the amusement park — I think he was the one that tried to get the ride photo. She said he’d been watching you.”

"I didn't even notice." And I didn't. Which isn't unusual with my attention span. And I was so excited over rides, I probably wouldn't have noticed even if I had been watching out for him. I am a shitty boyfriend.

"It's fine. We have a picture of him from the security video now. It's posted at the desk so they know to call the police if they see him again."

It's not fine. Not with me. But I don't want to stress her out even more. I'll have another talk with Gryff about making sure she and the kids are safe.

I walk around behind her where she's standing by the counter, pulling out ingredients for dinner. I wrap my arms around her, pulling her close. She leans back into me, relaxes, and I feel a little better, knowing I've helped that much, at least.

"We'll get through this," I tell her, even though I'm not really sure about that.

I'm starting to think maybe my lack of lying to this point in my life has been because I never worried so much about what someone else was thinking or feeling as I do when it's Lyric, or the kids. Because I want her to feel like this will all work out OK, even though today's incident has me on edge. And I'm never on edge. I jump out of planes, climb sheer cliffs and get set on fire, and none of that puts me on edge. This — having her and the kids constantly confronted by paparazzi — that puts me on edge. Even more when I consider that any one of these incidents could make her decide to call it quits. I don't like how this feels. At all.

"I love you," I tell her. That's the truth, and I need her to hear it, just in case she has second thoughts.

"I love you, too, Rhys." She sighs. "It's been a long day."

"Let me make dinner, then," I tell her. "I can handle it."

"That would be wonderful, actually. I'd like to spend some time meditating, but kids to feed..."

"Then go do that. I've got this."

She turns in my arms and hugs me, her head pressed over my heart. She kisses me there.

"Thank you."

She heads toward her altar room, and I start working on... I check the recipe.

"Easy Spinach Lasagna Rolls with Turkey Meatballs — quick, healthy and family-pleasing." Perfect. And I get to use a cupcake pan! Haven't used one of those since I tried to invent a super-relaxing bath-bomb. Which turned out to be more bomb than relaxing...

"Rhys?" Lyric calls from across the house.

"Yeah, babe..." I call back to her.

"What happened to the rest of my fellowship paperwork? I know I told you to put it in here, but all I found when I looked the other day was the discarded poetry scraps. I'm past the deadline at this point, but I wanted to file the submissions for next year."

Uh-oh.

"About that..."

She emerges in the bedroom doorway, looking concerned.

"Rhys?"

"OK. I... uh... I mailed them in."

"You... you mailed them in. The application, the dozen pages of poetry I had with it?"

"Yeah. All the uncrumpled pages." Including the one I un-crumpled.

"Oh. I wish you would have asked me first. They'll just dis-qualify it. I still had one more poem to write. They require at least fifteen pages of work."

"About that..."

"Rhys..." Her voice is tight.

"Yeah, babe." Maybe if I distract her. "Sorry — I'm working on these delicious-looking lasagna rolls..."

"Put down the cupcake pan." Yeah. Tight voice, tight expres-sion. She's not distracted.

I put down the cupcake pan.

I turn and look at her directly.

"What did you do?" she asks.

"I mailed the application."

"The incomplete application."

I bite the bullet. This is one of the scariest moments of my life, aside from telling her that her dead husband was haunting me and my dreams.

"No. You had that one finished poem in there, and you'd said you needed one more poem. So, I put it in with the others."

"What finished poem?"

"You know — the one about my butt."

Silence. Dead silence. Hopefully, that's not an omen for my future state of being...

"Oh. My. Gods. Tell me you're joking," she says, her eyes wide, her hand going to her mouth. "Tell me this is an attempt to lighten my mood after a hard day."

"Uh... no."

"Oh. My. Gods. My poetry career is over."

She's got her hand over her entire face now, like she's mortified.

"Why would you say that? It was good! I liked it! I think it might be the best poem ever written! Shakespeare would be jealous. But then he didn't get to look at my butt. Maybe he could have done better if he had. But I doubt it."

"Oh. My. Gods! Rhys! *You* weren't even supposed to read that poem. Now, I'm humiliated because you read it, and I'm mortified that anyone associated with something as serious as this fellowship might read it. I've got to call them and tell them to tear it up before it goes to the judges. If it's not already too late."

She starts pacing, pulling out her phone, even though it's got to be after office hours. Do poets have office hours?

"No! You can't have them tear up that poem! I love that poem!"

"You don't get it, Rhys. The rest of what I sent in was serious, thoughtful work, full of philosophy and analogies, lyrical word choices, carefully measured meter and poetic styles... That poem was... it was..."

"Sexy as hell. And a little goofy. Kind of like me. And my butt."

She sputters, and I can't tell if it's a laugh or she's just at a loss for words.

"No! It was unprofessional!" Nope, she's not at a loss for words. "It was me trying to shake myself out of writer's block by writing something totally silly that I knew I'd just throw away later. It was private and not suitable for public consumption. I'd never have shown anyone that poem!"

"Not even me?"

"No! It was... I... I crumpled it for a reason!"

"Then I'm glad I uncrumpled it. And I'm glad I mailed it, too."

"Rhys! Don't you understand what you've done?"

Apparently not.

"These poetry competitions — fellowships, grants, contests — they use a very limited pool of judges. Chances are the judges this year will judge again in the future, and most of them will judge for anything else I might apply for. That poem — it's going to stand out from everything else submitted, including the rest of what I was going to submit. They're going to remember it for years to come!"

"Exactly! Because it's perfect!"

She growls, sounding frustrated and not like the man-eating lady-tiger I'd hoped to have consuming me sometime after dinner. In fact, I'm starting to suspect I'm not getting lucky tonight. But, even worse, I'm starting to suspect I've really pissed her off.

"It's not real poetry, Rhys! I'm going to be remembered forever by these people as the woman who submitted a poem about ogling her boyfriend's butt. Moreover, now that I'm famous — also thanks to you — they're going to know that I'm the rockstar's girlfriend who was ogling her boyfriend's butt in poetic form!"

"But it didn't have your name on the submissions! It said that right in the instructions! You're totally anonymous!"

Ha — I've got her there.

"If you think that's going to hold up once they read that poem, you're very naive," she says.

And maybe I am. Maybe she's right. But I did it for the right reasons. I think. I hope.

I walk over to her, grab her hands in mine, look her right in those stormy blue eyes, and I speak from the heart.

"Lyric — it's an awesome poem. I may not write many words for aMUSEd's music, but I've watched Dave and Declan and Hunt do it — and they've all won awards for their writing. And when I tell you it's an awesome poem, it is. Trust me."

"I can't."

What?

"What?"

"Rhys — I asked you to put some papers away for me so I could serve my kids dinner. You took it upon yourself to not only send in the application I hadn't yet finished, but to select a poem I had no intention of ever showing anyone and add it to the submission packet! You didn't opt to just remind me of the deadline before it passed. You didn't even ask me if I wanted it mailed! You just did whatever you felt was best, without consulting me at all. And I can't let you do that where my life is concerned, where my kids' lives are concerned. I can't let *anyone* do that!"

"But, Lyric—"

"No. I can't do this right now, Rhys. I'm emotional over what happened at school today. I've still got to feed the kids dinner tonight, fill out their paperwork for school tomorrow, go over my lesson plan for tomorrow, make lunch for the three of us — and Roger now, too. I was just looking forward to a little meditation time, and instead I find out that you — however well-meaning — sabotaged my submission and maybe my entire reputation as a poet. I may not have ever gotten that fellowship, but it was the one thing I was hoping for to make my life easier. And, instead, it's just gotten harder and harder. And I can't do this! Please go. I... I need some time to think."

"Lyric — I need to tell you—"

"I need you to leave, Rhys."

She walks to the front door and holds it open.

Roger, standing on the front porch, looks surprised to see me. At least our voices didn't carry enough for him and... Oh — one... two... three... reporters and... two photographers to overhear.

"Rhys! Rhys! Are you going to propose to Lyric?"

I might have, maybe, eventually. Oh, who am I kidding? Definitely eventually. But right now, she'd refuse. My face falls even further. Flashes catch the expression. And that... that makes me mad.

"Rhys! Are you going to adopt her kids? Are you moving to Mystic Beach?"

Lyric shuts the door behind me.

All of this — all of it — comes back to this voracious media attention she never wanted and that never occurred to me would even touch her or the kids. I just wanted to have a relationship! For once in my life, I wanted a relationship! And now these assholes are stalking her, the kids, me. They're relentless, and they won't stop unless I make them.

"Rhys! It is true a coven of witches is working dark magic on the members of aMUSEd to make them fall in love with them?"

"What? No! That's ridiculous!"

Roger tries to shove me toward my car.

"So Lyric's not a witch?"

"Rhys..." Roger mutters under his breath, his voice full of urgency, warning. But I'm the guy with no filter, and now, for like the first time ever, I'm angry, my relationship threatened by these... these... vultures.

"Of course she's a witch! I'm 'The Madman.' Why wouldn't I be dating a witch? She's an utterly enchanting woman, and I would have to be stupid not to fall for her! No magic spell even needed, despite her being a witch. But you all have made her life a living hell! And I need you to stop! Just do me a favor — leave Lyric, and her kids, alone! Please!"

Roger drags me off the porch and into the passenger seat of his car. He gets behind the wheel, and then he just looks at me. And he keeps looking at me.

And then it sinks in...

I just confirmed to the media that Lyric's a witch.

Uh-oh.

"What happened to 'No comment'?" Roger asks, shaking his head at me. He leans over the steering wheel and puts his head down.

"I've got to call Kirk," he says.

"Why?"

"Because somebody's got to watch the house while I drive you back to the studio."

"I can drive myself."

"Maybe," he says. "But I don't trust you to get out of this car and into your own without saying something else that's unbelievably stupid, with cameras rolling."

"They got that on video?" I watch the group chatting excitedly on their phones, with each other.

"I'm pretty sure, yeah. The reporters, at least, were shooting video. They do that now. Especially for the tabloids."

"I've got to go back in, talk to Lyric, tell her I'm sorry, that I flibbertigibbeted up."

Roger looks at me like I've lost my mind, for real.

"Uh... No. You're going back to the studio to talk to Gryffin and Billy. This little unintentional press conference of yours changes the whole ballgame, for everyone."

CHAPTER 55

THUNDER WHEN IT'S RAINING

Lyric

My phone beeps.

Rhys: *I'm so sorry. I flibbertigibbeted it all up. Please forgive me.*

I put the phone on silent. Then I decide that's not enough. Not with Rhys. I turn it off.

And I go back to cooking dinner. So much for meditation. So much for putting aside my concerns of the day. Now I've got so much more to deal with, wondering if anyone will ever take me seriously as a poet after this disaster. Why does this all have to be so hard? Adam went to such great lengths to bring me and Rhys together, and we've already gotten past so many little hiccups, along with that revelation.

I never thought I'd look back at my life as a single mom and consider it simple, easy. But I never dreamed I'd end up in a relationship with Rhys "The Madman" Madigan, or all the changes in my life that would bring with it. It just feels like everything is piling on right now. And I'm not sure I can keep going if one more thing happens.

The next morning

"Finish up your breakfast, kids! We need to get ready to go!"

I don't want to be late today. There was enough of a scandal from the paparazzo invasion yesterday, on top of all the rumors. I want to get Aria to class, get Roger ensconced in a corner of my classroom and pretend life is just like it was this time last year. Thankfully, it looks like the media is going to leave Tommy alone. Especially with Kirk there.

"Go brush your teeth and be ready to walk out the door in five minutes!"

They both run off, and I start putting the dishes in the sink for later.

There's a knock at the door. Roger's early. Hopefully, that's a good sign. I open the door.

"Good—"

"Lyric — any comment on your life as a witch?"

"Can we take Rhys calling you 'bewitching' as confirmation that there's a larger plot involving magic and the members of aMUSEd?"

"Rhys calls living with you 'hell' — is that a statement on your involvement in Satanism?"

"What?"

Gryffin — not Roger — pushes me back inside, shutting the door firmly behind him.

"I tried to reach you last night to warn you, but I didn't want to stir them up by showing up unexpectedly in person when I couldn't get you on the phone. So, our time is limited right now. And I need you to listen to me, very carefully. OK, Lyric?"

He's not calling me ma'am. That's almost as concerning as... whatever that was outside.

I nod.

"Rhys... Well, last night Rhys did what Rhys does, and he talked off the top of his head. Unfortunately, he was upset about a number of things, including the media harassing you, and he blew up at them. In the process, he managed to confirm that you are a witch, though he denied any magical influence on him or the other band members. That 'Satanism' thing was totally out of context — he said they were making your life a living hell and begged them to leave you and the kids alone."

OK, then.

"So the entire world now knows I'm a witch. And a subset of them now believes I'm also a Satanist."

I guess I should be glad that he didn't also tell them I'm a weather-controlling mutant...

"That's about the size of it, yes."

I said something about one more thing, right? Sometimes the universe takes pessimistic thinking as a dare.

"I need to call out sick. Call the kids out sick."

"That's not advisable."

"Oh?"

"The crisis management consultants' recommendation is to act as if nothing has happened."

"Crisis management?"

"We've elevated this from a PR concern."

"To a crisis."

"Yes."

"And still their recommendation is that we pretend there's nothing going on that's at all unusual?"

"It is. This is the same set of rumors, just ramped up."

"Well, thank the gods Rhys didn't spout off about hearing voices, too. Then we'd be in real trouble!"

"Pardon?"

"Nothing. Nevermind."

"I'm not going to pretend that this is going to be easy, not for a while. But the consultants think this will blow over with time. In the meantime, I've given full autonomy to Kirk and Roger to handle any issues as they deem necessary, even if that means calling in the police. If one of these guys steps a toe on your lawn, they've got the green light to put them on the ground and have them arrested for trespassing. The entire property is now a secure zone, with Roger and Kirk under your direct command as to what can and cannot take place here."

"OK."

"It doesn't matter if an old school friend shows up and wants to talk to you about buying cookies for a scout troop — they won't make it a step onto your property until after you've told Roger or Kirk to let them. I've got a third operative ready to spell them, too. So, they will be on close protection with you 24/7, and with Tommy at school. We figured Aria was safe with Roger in the same building, since she's under a teacher's supervision."

"Wow. OK. What about Brighid?"

"I've got a guy on her house and one on her shop."

"My mother?"

"They don't seem to be aware that she's here, but the operative assigned to Brighid's shop is also checking in on her."

"The studio?" I ask, even though I don't want to worry about Rhys right now, not since this is all his...

"About the same as before. Rhys gave them what they wanted. The story is now here with you."

"And I need to pretend there is no story."

"Exactly."

"OK, then. Can we send that memo out to all my co-workers, my students' parents, the judgmental busybodies who'll be picketing in the street by this afternoon?"

"We're not going to let that happen — the last part, anyway. But their advice holds across interaction with your co-workers and anyone else you may talk to. If pressed, you might laugh and chalk it up to tabloid journalism taking a joke out of context. But they think even that would be a mistake."

"Great. Sounds like it's going to be a low-stress day!" Yes, that was sarcasm.

"I've told Rhys to stay at the studio."

"But we both know how Rhys is..."

"Yes, we do. Roger had to talk him out of coming straight back in here last night."

"That would have been a disaster, especially since I would have thrown him out."

"He was afraid of that. That's why told I the guys that if he shows up, they should keep him in his car."

Yeah. That's probably for the best. Right now, I'm not sure we wouldn't end up with Rhys frizzled on my front lawn if he showed up. If he does it after the day I now expect to have, he might not survive. And I don't want him dead. Not literally, anyway.

As if my words were instantly enacted, there's a crack of thunder outside.

"There's a storm moving in. We should get going. Roger and Kirk are waiting in the cars. We'll run you and the kids straight to the vehicles. Just remember — ignore them, or say 'No comment.' Nothing else. And you might want to tell Aria that, too."

"I already did, mostly. I'll remind her before we go out."

"For what it's worth — Rhys says he's sorry. And we both know he didn't mean to do this."

"The problem is what Rhys intends and what actually happens are frequently not the same thing. And I don't need that kind of chaos in my life."

A few hours later

"I don't understand, Aria — why on earth would you push Noah?"

"He said you were evil, Mommy, that you make people do things they don't want to do and that you work for some bad guy who has goat horns."

Oh, gods...

I thought it was bad when we drove past a half-dozen paparazzi on the nearest public property to the school. I thought it was terrible when the other teachers whispered and then stopped talking as I came down the hall after dropping Aria at her classroom. But this... now it's directly impacting my kids. I'll have to check on Tommy as soon as I deal with this...

"Aria, we talked about this. People misunderstood something someone said, and they're making some mistakes because they don't understand the truth. The way to fix that is not to push your friends on the playground."

"I know, Mommy — but he was being so mean! It made me mad. And I lost my temper."

It's not like I've been a great example of keeping hold of my temper lately. But I'd hoped this would go right over the heads of the students, including Aria's classmates.

I exchange a look with Roger.

"I can have Gryff bring in another man to do close protection on Aria," he suggests.

"I don't think having a bodyguard looming over them is the answer to a bunch of second-graders teasing my daughter," I tell him. "Having you in the classroom is intimidating enough."

"I have to agree," Carla says. "This situation is already creating a distraction, and while it's nice that you all have private security to handle some of it, I can't condone Aria's behavior. She has to be subject to the same kind of punishment any other child would get for pushing another child on the playground."

"Which would be?"

"Two days in-school suspension. She can sit in the office with me, or with Patty if I have to go out or take a meeting. She'll have her class assignments, and I'll go over anything she doesn't understand."

"But she'll be missing two days of instruction in the first week of school!"

"It's not anything she can't catch up with. She's bright. A lot of this will be review of things she learned last year. The academic teachers are just warming the kids' brains up after the summer."

I sigh in defeat. She's right. Aria's earned the punishment. I can't ask Carla to give her a pass.

"OK. Fine. But something needs to be done about Noah, too. Otherwise, this is only going to continue."

"I've got a call in to his parents, asking them to come in for a conference before the end of the day. It's not the same degree of a problem. But it is a violation of our anti-bullying policies."

Well, I'm glad she recognizes that. I'm not sure the whisper campaign I've endured all day violates those policies, since I'm an adult staff member and not a student, but I'll have to deal with that later. Right now, Aria's what's important.

"Aria — you owe Noah an apology."

"He owes me one, too! And you!"

"That may be, but whether he apologizes or not, you have to do the honorable thing and apologize for pushing him."

"Fine. But I won't like it."

The adults in the room all suppress smiles.

"Lyric — get back to your class. Aria will stay here with me. Let's try to get this day back on track."

Somehow, I doubt "on track" is anything this day has been or will ever be.

R hys' car is parked in front of my house when we get back from school. It's surrounded by a half-dozen members of the media, who are all shouting questions at him through the closed windows.

"I'll talk to him," Roger says. "You two stay in the car until I come back for you."

I watch as Roger walks back to Rhys' car, knocks on the passenger-side window and gets into the car.

Two minutes later, he gets out of the car and slams the door shut. I cringe for poor KITT, wondering what's got the oh-so-professional Roger so emotional. He comes back to our car, gets back in the driver's seat and turns to look at me. He takes a glance into the rearview mirror at Aria, who's got her headphones on, listening to music on my phone.

"He wants to come in, to talk to you. I told him that's a bad idea and he shouldn't even be here, because he's stirring things up again. He said he's staying here until you talk to him."

"I don't want to talk to him right now. I'd told him that *before* he blew up at the paparazzi. And now everything has just gotten worse."

"I understand. And if you don't want to talk to him, we'll keep him off the property, just like Gryff said. It's your call."

I take a deep breath, steeling myself to say something I don't want to have to say, but know I really do.

"Keep him away. Until I tell you otherwise. He should have listened to Gryffin about staying at the studio. If he gets out of the car, if he won't leave after a while, tell him that. Tell him he should listen to Gryffin and stay at the studio."

"That's basically what I just told him. But I'll tell him the message is from you if he won't take no for an answer."

"Thank you. I hate putting you all in the middle of this."

"Comes with the job, ma'am. We've been tasked with protecting you both at one point or another. Right now, you and the kids are my priority, and that should be his priority now, too."

Hearing Roger say it makes me feel less bad for thinking it myself.

Because I don't have any choice in this. The kids have to be my top priority. All the time.

CHAPTER 56
WIDDERS DUMP

Rhys

It's officially driving me crazy. I need to talk this out with Lyric. But she won't hear me. She won't answer her phone. And she's got Roger and Kirk keeping me away from the house. I'm ignoring Gryff's calls myself. I know what he's going to say. But if she'll just hear me out, at least about why I sent the fellowship application in, then maybe I can fix this. The paps will go away at some point. We can't be a top story for months on end.

Even now, they've dwindled, with me now parked on the back side of the block. Just one of them left right now as full dark closes in. The lights in the kids' bedroom windows are off. The light in the living room went out ten minutes ago. Lyric's probably in her bedroom or her altar room — I'm guessing the latter, if her day has been anything like what I've feared. I just have to get to the back of the house without security seeing me. The new guy on her detail — Geordi, who was assigned to Kier for a while at the end of the tour — is supposed to relieve them overnight. I just have to wait for that to happen, and then, boom! I'm knocking on Lyric's window and hitting her with the smolder. She won't be able to resist.

Then it'll be OK. Once I can explain about the goddess and remind her that I'm neuro-spicy, too. I messed up. But it wasn't on purpose. She'll know that once she gets over the other thing.

I see Kirk and Roger drive off, and I hop out of my car. A quick hop over the fence, and I'm in the back yard. I make for her bedroom window. The light's off, but I can see a faint glow from her altar room. See — I was right.

"Hold it right there!"

Flibbertigibbets!

Geordi's got me on the ground in a second.

"Hey, dude! Long time no see!"

"Rhys... Aww, come on, man! Gryff's going to kill me, missing a six-foot-four ginger hopping the fence long enough to get almost to the house!"

"I won't tell him if you won't!"

The look he gives me is weary. Kind of like Lyric looked earlier.

But this covert op is a bust, unless I can get Geordi on my side.

"This will all be fine if I can just talk to Lyric, explain things," I tell him. "This is all a big misunderstanding. Once I explain, everything will get better, and I'll be around to keep an eye on them myself. You can go back to whatever you were doing before."

"Keeping people from stealing Ms. K's dogs? No thank you," he says.

"You were bodyguarding a pop star's dogs?"

"After the Gaga thing? Yes. But this is a better gig. Days on the beach, cool sea breezes at night when I'm on duty. It's a nice little town."

"I know, right? I love this place almost as much as I do Lyric and the kids..."

He sighs, shakes his head.

"I feel for you, man. But this is a no-go. If you don't go back to the studio on your own, I'll have to call Gryff to come get you himself, and you do not want that, man. I promise."

No, probably not. I'm probably already going to be in trouble with Marina Matthews. Getting her pet security guy pissed off at me when he's supposed to be protecting me, the guys and Lyric and the kids — not a place I want to be. I'm toeing the line on that already.

"Fine. I'll go back. But if you see Lyric, tell her I need her to let me explain, that she'll understand once I explain."

"If I see her, I'll pass along the message. But, honestly, man — give the woman some time. She's in a pressure-cooker right now, and her kids with her. In her shoes — pointy or otherwise — I'd be hurling some major juju your way."

"You do magic?"

"Nah, but my auntie — she's a manbo, a voudu priestess. You don't mess with those ladies. They're under the protection of entities much larger and more powerful than you or me."

"Yeah. I know what you mean." I just wish Lyric's goddess would wave her hand or whatever and send these media people to Nova Scotia, Antarctica, Peru... anywhere but here.

"So let the woman take care of her kids the way she knows how," Geordi says. "We'll take care of her. Fate will take care of the rest. Have some faith, man. I'm sure she does."

Right. Yeah. Faith. I've had her dead husband talking to me, and then her goddess. Both seem to be in my corner. Maybe I just have to wait this all out, be patient. I can do that. It'll all be fine. Yeah.

Lyric
A minute later

"**M**other Goddess Brighid, hear my prayer. My life has turned to chaos, despite following what seems to be the path You intended for me. My children are suffering, my work is in turmoil — both at school and as a poet. And this chaos leaves me sorely tested as Your priestess."

Honestly, I'm glad people usually go to Brighid's shop for spiritual counseling, because I'd be a terrible counselor right now.

My standard altar blend of incense burns in a censor on the altar. My blessed candle glows strongly beside it and the statue of Herself. The candle was first lit with the flame from Brighid's blessed candle, which she first lit in the sacred flame at Kildare in Ireland, and it's precious to me. I've cleared off the altar the remnants of my fellowship application and the poems I tried to create for it. Now, it's just me, the flame, wisps of cinnamon, vanilla and white willow, and Herself.

"Please — if nothing else — protect my children. I've withstood challenging times before, but they are so young, so vulnerable. You are a protectress of children. And I need them kept safe, away from the glare—"

A flash of light illuminates the altar, and I wait for the concussive boom of thunder, counting the seconds to track an approaching storm, but there's no sound. Instead, another flash.

I stand up, move the curtains aside to look at the sky, finding instead a man with a camera peering in the window. I scream.

And then I run for the front door. I'm going to beat this man within an inch of his life with my own bare hands! How dare he! I don't care that it makes me a tremendous hypocrite considering the lecture I delivered to Aria this afternoon. I run around the side of the house, ready to throw myself at him and beat him to a pulp in the dirt.

"I've got him ma'am," Geordi says, already sitting on top of the guy, his camera in hand. "I'm going to turn him over to the police, have him charged with trespassing. Please go back inside while I do that. I've already had one too many distractions tonight, or this guy never would have gotten close to the window. And I'll erase any photos he took."

"You can't do that! That camera is private property! Those images are my property!"

"And you're literally sitting on private property," Geordi reminds him. "And I can guarantee a trespassing charge is going to outrank that claim when you had to trespass to get the photos. Class B misdemeanors carry a penalty of up to six months in jail. I'm not sure how many photos you'll lose out on during that time, but I'm betting it's not worth a photo of some rockstar's ex-girlfriend."

Ex?

Geordi turns to look at me and winks with his eye farthest from the paparazzo.

"Aww, man! I missed the whole relationship?" he whines. "These rockstars are too fucking fickle. From one girl to the next, even when she's got kids. Why not just stick with groupies?" He sighs. "Alright — let me up. You've deleted the photos — which were pretty boring, honestly. I'd expected tits, ass, a knife, a blood sacrifice — not sitting quietly and..."

"Praying. I was praying," I supply.

"I'd rather call my editor, get my lawyer in here to bail me out and get back to civilization if that's all that's involved in this big 'scandal.'"

"Go on back inside, ma'am. I'll let you know when I've got this guy off my hands. Keep the door locked until then."

I nod and go back inside.

I collapse on the sofa, glad the kids sleep like logs. That scream would've woken me up in a heartbeat. And then I get up, trudge upstairs and make sure they're still asleep in their beds.

OK. Now I can collapse.

After I order some heavy curtains for my altar room. Next-day delivery.

I'm exhausted. Discovering a man peering into my window last night hasn't done wonders for my sleep. I'm going to have to re-do my house-cleansing ritual this weekend just to feel safe in my own house.

It doesn't matter that Geordi seemed to get the better of the guy. It still chills me to the bone when I think about it.

And, as it turns out, it was apparently Rhys who distracted Geordi and gave the paparazzo the chance to get up close to my altar-room window.

Geordi said Rhys had agreed to leave, but he'd asked Geordi to give me a message — that if I'd just let him explain, everything would be OK. I don't even have the energy to wonder what explanation he thinks is going to erase both having taken my application out of my hands and having outed me to the... well, the world.

And that's today's other big problem. Aria's in Carla's office, suspended. Roger's watching my back, should someone manage to get into the building to threaten or harass me. But that's not the problem. I've had four students pulled from my classes, even though music is a mandatory enrichment class for every grade. Carla's been fielding calls left and right, full of concern about the

"Satanist" teacher corrupting children — nevermind that Satan doesn't even exist in my belief system — and about my needing a bodyguard within the school.

I'm the one being harassed, libeled, slandered, having my privacy invaded, but I'm perceived as a threat. Of course.

During my lunch period, I decide I need some caffeine to help make up for lost sleep, and I head for the lounge to get a cola, Roger in tow. Once again, an enthusiastic discussion goes silent the moment everyone in the lounge sees me. I do as advised — I ignore it. I get my soda, drop money in the cup in the fridge and turn to leave. I hear more whispering behind me, and a laugh. I turn back to confront whoever it is but instead end up bumping into someone coming into the room.

"Sorry," I say, though the only damage is me dropping both my soda and my purse. The contents of my bag is sprawled across the floor, and I scramble to stuff it back inside. It's been too long since I cleaned it out and... Whoever I bumped into is helping me pick up items and stuff them back inside. Their hand grabs onto something cylindrical. A pause. I look up. Donnie has a pill bottle in his hand. He hands it to me, and I stuff it back in my purse without looking. Whatever it is, it shouldn't be in my purse, not while I'm in school. I'll have to take it out to the car before I do anything else.

Roger hands me the last of the items from the floor, and I stuff them inside my bag, along with the soda, which I can't even drink now, since it hit the floor pretty hard. I walk out of the lounge and down the hall, and out the front door.

"You OK, ma'am?" Roger asks, hurrying along behind me.

"Yes, fine. I just need to put something back in the car." It's only now that I remember that I don't have my car with me. Roger has to unlock his car for me. I climb into the passenger seat and sit, stunned, for a moment.

"You need a minute, ma'am?"

"Yes, Roger, I do."

"Promise me you'll stay in the car, with the doors locked, and I'll go walk over to that little coffee shop across the street and get you some caffeine."

"That sounds divine, Roger."

Satisfied when the doors lock with me inside, he heads off.

And I dive into my purse, looking for the unexpected pill bottle.

I was right. It's not mine. It belongs to Rhys. And then I remember — he'd put it in there the second day we'd spent time together, when we took the kids to the trampoline park. I'd forgotten about that. But here they are — nearly a full bottle of Adderall, for Rhys' ADHD. Categorically not allowed to be in my purse when I'm at school, and yet I've had them in there for a month. Has it really been a month since I met my college crush in person? Has it only been a month? And most of that time, we've been living in each other's pockets, either working together, side by side, or spending most of our time together as a couple.

And in that month, my life has been turned upside-down. There's no way I could have dreamed that, a month later, I'd be outed as a witch, stalked by paparazzi and getting driven around by my personal bodyguard. Or that I'd have pushed Rhys Madigan away, no longer sure that I trust him to share my life, my kids' lives.

What a flibbertigibbeting mess!

Yeah. He's gotten that far under my skin. And still I can't help but miss him. But I may have to learn to live with that.

By the weekend, we've established a routine, even if it's not as routine as I'd like. Carla's been forced to offer an alternative activity for the students whose parents demanded they be removed from my music classes. The joy of all these new instruments is doused by having to reconfigure the ensemble with fewer students. I've also had two cancellations for private lessons.

My mother has demanded I let her come over on Saturday to spend time with the kids. Maybe because of Geordi's misinformation, we're down to a single photographer again, even during the day, so it seems like less of a risk to have her come over. While she's been kept clear of the media frenzy, she's angry with Rhys over his being so careless, and she's in agreement that I should keep him at a distance, at least for now.

"You've got to protect these kids!" she says. "I mean — Aria getting suspended, even if it was in-school — that's too much."

"He's stayed away since the incident with the photographer," I tell her. "He keeps asking the security guys to give me messages, but it's always the same thing: 'If you let me explain, it'll be OK.'"

"I'm not sure what there is to explain, Lyric. I doubt he meant to out you like that, but the damage is done. And you wouldn't have been in that position in the first place if it wasn't for him being famous."

"I know. I just... The kids miss him, you know? He'd just started teaching Tommy to play the drums, and now... Tommy goes up there, and he plays — he'd play 24/7 if I let him — but it's just noise. Whatever Rhys was doing, it was bringing him out of his shell, and now he's all the way back in again. And Aria's been short-tempered with me. She doesn't want me to read her bedtime stories anymore."

"They've gotten used to having him around. It's going to be an adjustment. All of this is. How about I take them today — we can go to the zoo."

"Are you sure? They're a handful for one person. Take Kirk with you, just to be safe."

"There's one photographer out there, who won't leave here just to follow the kids. We'll be fine. The zoo's quiet."

Yes, the zoo is quiet, when Rhys isn't there, running around like a madman, bouncing around like a cartoon tiger, gleefully looking at alpacas and prairie dogs.

Yeah, probably better if Mom takes them to the zoo and I stay home, try to make a decision about me and Rhys. For the best interest of my kids.

Besides, I'm not sure the zoo is ever going to be the same.

CHAPTER 57
BREATHE (IN THE AIR)

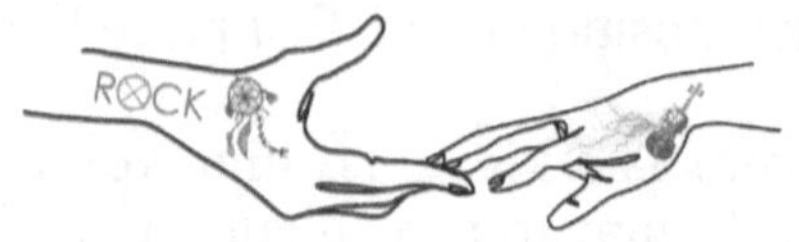

Rhys
Two hours later

"Are you sure about this? We don't usually allow people to jump from our banner planes."

"If I restricted myself to doing things that were usual, I wouldn't do much of anything," I reply to the pilot. "I need to get in close, and I need it not to look like anything out of the ordinary. Your plane is already flying over the same area. I just need you to let me jump."

"And you've done this before?"

"I've completed nearly three hundred jumps. I have a Level C license. I've jumped out of planes on four continents. I've done HALO jumps on three of them. I've done BASE jumps with parachutes and wingsuits. If it's up in the air and I've got a way to slow the fall, I can do it."

"And I'm not going to in trouble with the FAA?"

"As long as you tell air-traffic control you're dropping me, you shouldn't, no. And if you do… I think I've covered any legal fees."

"Right. Well, it's your ass on the line."

"Yup. And my girl loves my ass. She even wrote a poem about it! So you can bet I'm going to make sure it stays intact."

He just shakes his head and climbs into the plane. I do my final parachute check, gear up and climb in beside him, right in the open door. Five minutes later, we take off, then make a swooping dive down to an open field, where the plane snags one end of a long banner advertising a seafood restaurant and then rises back up. We fly over some farm fields, then a long stretch of beach full of tourists, then turn around to go back and change out the banner. But as he flies over the houses a few blocks inland, I wait for Lyric's house to come into view. And then I do a hop-n-pop — jumping and immediately deploying my chute.

This is my favorite part of a jump anyway — steering myself in for a pinpoint landing. I aced that part of my license qualification. I barely skated by on the written test. But there's no writing today, just a narrow open strip of back yard behind the house to land in, and a roof not to hit. That last part — close call. And... Touchdown.

I unhook my chute, drop my helmet and head for the back door.

Lyric's sitting at her kitchen table, her head in her hand, her posture pensive, troubled. I've got to fix this. I've got to explain, get her to understand why I sent the application in for her. We can go from there. I reach for the doorknob.

Kirk and Roger grab me by the arms.

"Mr. Madigan — you have to leave. She doesn't want you here. And we're here to protect her."

"Lyric!"

She turns and looks at me, her expression stricken.

"Come on, Lyric — I didn't do it on purpose! You know that. You know me! Please. At least let me in so we can talk!"

She walks up to the door.

"I can't, Rhys," she says through the glass. She won't even open the door. "This isn't working. And I've got to put the kids first. I'm sorry. Please — stay away."

"Lyric!"

Kirk and Roger drag me out through the gate from the back yard and to Roger's car.

"I'm sorry about that, Mr. Madigan. But you know the rules," Roger says, putting the car in gear to, presumably, drive me back to the studio.

"Yeah. No hard feelings, dude. I had to try, though."

"That was a stellar landing. Couldn't have done better myself."

Ah. He's got that look about him.

"Special forces?"

"Yeah," he confirms. "But can't say I ever dropped in on an old girlfriend like that. If I had, maybe I'd be married by now instead of hanging out with your girlfriend and her kids."

"It didn't work."

He shrugs.

"It didn't work *today*. Who's to say it won't make the difference tomorrow, or next week?"

"I can only hope." And maybe pray a little. Yeah. It might be time to get a little spiritual consultation. "Actually, can you drop me off downtown?"

"H ello, Rhys."

Brighid sounds tired. No — weary. Maybe it's Lyric's influence, but those little variations between the words make a difference. Lyric — she's tired, *and* weary. And that was before I started helping. Now...

"I need your help. Her help."

"Lyric doesn't want to talk to you right now, Rhys."

"I know that — she just had the security guys haul my ass out of her back yard. I didn't even get my parachute back."

"Para— Oh, nevermind." She rolls her eyes.

"But she's not the Her whose help I need. I mean Herself."

"Oh. Oh!" she says, her eyes going wide. "You want to... what? Talk to a goddess? Request prayer on your behalf?"

"Well, Lyric's behalf, mine — whatever. I need help. Like, divine intervention-level help. And I've got nowhere else to go."

"Lucky for you, having the security guy out front seems to be deterring the lookie-loos who've been plaguing me all week. Either that or Molly's been reading my books and has gotten really good at protective magic all of a sudden."

She flips the sign on the door to "Closed."

"Come into my office," she says, gesturing toward the back room I've never actually been in.

I'm not sure what I expected, but it wasn't this...

No five-pointed star on the floor, no black candles dripping wax everywhere — more like a rainbow of candles, interspersed with colorful rocks. There are a handful of statues on top of the highest shelves, but no menacing evil-looking dudes — just a couple anatomically-correct, buff guys with deer antlers, sitting on rocks and tree stumps, looking calm and wise, and a few pretty ladies with different animals around them... One even has antlers of her own. Cool. And ah — yeah, this one I recognize.

"That's Her!"

Brighid smiles.

The human one, not the statue.

"Yes, that's Brighid."

I look back and forth between them. There's not a lot of resemblance. Our Brighid is blonde, curvy, with violet eyes and a boho style. The goddess is a redhead — actually not much different in color from my hair — with emerald-green eyes, tall like our Brighid, but more statuesque. No pun intended. There's a certain feel to both of them, though — warm and wise, and strong.

"She talked to me."

Brighid looks surprised, seeing where my gaze is pointed. She gestures for me to sit down in one of the two armchairs in the corner of the room and takes the other herself.

"She's talked to Hunt a few times, too," she says.

This is both surprising and completely unsurprising.

"Did She tell him to do something he thought you might not like?"

"No... She told him he was stupid." She tries not to smile about it.

"Well, honestly — he was being pretty stupid where you were concerned."

"Thank you," she says, smiling. "Again. But he's figured things out now. What'd She tell you to do?"

"Mail Lyric's fellowship application for her."

"Well, that sounds pretty harmless. Why wouldn't Lyric want you to do that?"

"She wasn't finished with it yet. But she ended up not being ready on time anyway, so if I hadn't mailed it, she wouldn't have gotten it in at all."

"And she wasn't ready because of all the stuff that's going on?"

"Yeah. Which is my fault. So, I guess me mailing it in doesn't really hurt. Unless they don't like poems about my butt."

Brighid cracks up.

"Explain, please."

"Lyric had one more poem to write for the application, but she couldn't get any of them to work. Except she wrote this one..."

"Let me guess — about your butt."

"Yeah! Exactly! See, I knew you'd get it."

"And, if I know how these things go, Brighid — the goddess — told you to mail it with the poem about your butt included."

"Yeah! Does She do that kind of stuff often?"

"Rhys — She's a goddess of poetry and inspiration. If She thought Lyric's poem should be submitted, then there's a good chance there was a reason for it. What that reason might be, however, is something I can't answer for you."

"Huh. Then it was probably OK that I mailed it, right?"

"Did you tell Lyric you mailed it?"

"Yes, and that's what got her really pissed off at me, that I hadn't asked her first. But what was I supposed to do? I have a goddess telling me to mail it, and a priestess telling me I shouldn't have. Only the priestess is my girlfriend, and she gets mad, and then she kicks me out. And I say something stupid to a bunch of reporters because I don't like that they've been hassling her and caused this giant mess."

"Ah, so that's why no-filter Rhys made his unfortunate reappearance," she says, nodding in that wise way of hers. "To answer your question, Rhys — I've found that when the divine doesn't make sense to humans, it's almost always a lack of understanding on the human's part. And sometimes it's just because They see a much bigger picture than we ever can. You have to wait for fate to play out, for the puzzle pieces to start falling into place. Then it'll all make sense."

"That's it? I did what I was supposed to do, and I just have to deal with Lyric being mad at me for doing it?"

"Pretty much. For now."

"That sucks."

"It can. But..." She sighs. "Rhys — you're one of the most outside-the-box thinkers I know. And you tend to take things happening around you that don't make total sense and just accept them, even if you ask a lot of questions. But you're also impatient. You demand answers to those questions, even if the universe doesn't want to give them up right then."

"I kept asking you and Hunt about the 'again' thing, when you told him you'd marry him. And you wouldn't tell me."

"No. It was private."

"And now I know you were married two hundred years ago..." Her jaw drops.

"Lyric doesn't spill secrets easily," she says after a minute, looking closely at me, like there's a new layer to me she hadn't noticed before.

"She trusts me."

Now she smiles, widely, as if that's the answer to everything. Oh, wait...

"She trusts me," I repeat. "She trusts me!"

But then I remember why I'm here and not at Lyric's.

"And I fucked up again, and I let slip something she'd trusted me with. So, now... Now she doesn't trust me anymore."

"Rhys — that level of trust, that early in a relationship... It's instinctive. Especially for a priestess. Lyric... Lyric doesn't trust easily. She's had too much she's had to protect. But she trusts you instinctively. In my experience, that's a measure of your inner goodness — your soul. And that fits with everything I know of you myself. You would never hurt anyone on purpose. And there aren't a lot of people who can honestly say that."

"Maybe... but the fact is I did hurt her. I did betray her trust."

"No, Rhys — you made a mistake. Because you're human. Just like Lyric. And she knows that. But she's protecting her kids. And she's protecting herself."

"All I've wanted is to protect her and the kids, to take care of them."

"And she knows that, too."

"Then why won't she let me?"

"Because right now, she's scared. She'd just started giving herself the freedom to create a new future, for her and the kids. She stepped outside her carefully-controlled box. And then all this happened. She's feeling vulnerable, so she wants back inside that safe, comfortable box, where she's in control. She's never had to deal with the kind of public scrutiny she's been under since you started dating. Hunt and I were barely dating when we blew up on social media. I can tell you firsthand — it's pretty terrifying. And that was before Lyric and I got outed from the broom closet. And I don't have kids, either!"

"Then I need to fix it so the media don't care about us anymore. Make it safe for her to step back outside that box of hers, that cage."

"How are you going to do that?"

Brighid looks concerned. She's probably right to be.

"I'm going to quit the band."

CHAPTER 58

I'm Gonna Be

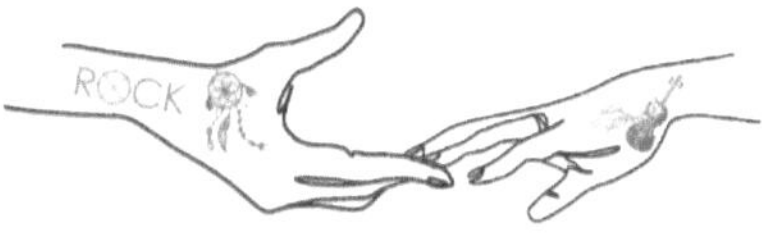

Rhys
An hour later

"Dearly beloved — I've gathered you here today to make an announcement."

"You're giving up on the drum solo!" Alex guesses.

"You've decided to take up the saxophone!" Kier says.

"You're not a natural ginger!" Hunt says.

"No — that's not it. I know for a fact that he is," Kier says.

"You've been recruited for the next moon mission!" Dave says.

"You wear lifts in your shoes!" Declan says.

"Come on guys — this is serious!"

"Well, that's a first. Rhys, being serious," Declan says. "I'm a little disturbed."

"Me, too," Dave says.

"That's three," Kieran adds. "Show of hands?"

They all raise a hand.

OK. I realize I've set the bar high for goofy, ridiculous and totally not-serious, but them not taking me seriously about this announcement — it's serious!

"Guys! I mean it! I need you to listen."

They all go quiet and, yes, serious.

"Thank you."

"Sorry," Alex says. "We're just not used to this kind of thing from you."

Lots of nodding and apologies. At least they're listening now.

"I'm quitting the band."

"You're not serious!" Kieran says.

"I totally am."

Well, the guys are all serious now. Seriously bummed.

"I'm sorry, guys. I've got to do this, for Lyric, the kids, myself. I'll finish the album. But after that..."

"It'll never stick," Kier says. "You can't quit music. You can't not play. You can't not perform. Me — I could do it. I have. You, never."

"I get why you'd want to quit, Rhys, but I think that's a very drastic move when things are so emotional," Hunt says. "Don't you want to think about it? Maybe decide when the album's done? At this rate, it'll be another month or two."

"And then what? Go off on tour when the woman I love is here with her kids, being persecuted and harassed by the media? You tell me — Hunt, Dec, Dave — would you leave if it was your girl who had to stay behind and deal with this alone?"

"I think you know my answer to that, Rhys," Dave says. He's already talked about not touring anymore so he can stay here with Piper and the baby.

"As far as I know, Brighid's coming on the road with us, at least for a while," Hunt says.

"Callie and I haven't talked about the tour yet. But she isn't being harassed, either," Declan says.

Alex is very quiet. Unusually quiet.

"You're going to have a hard time getting the label to let you out of your contract," he finally says.

It's weird. Alex is our second-hand romantic. He's practical, responsible, but given a choice between an emotional response and a practical one, he can be counted on to champion the emotional response every time. Something is definitely off with him.

"No, he won't," Dave says. "Marina Matthews has told both me and Dec that she'd make things work for us, with our personal lives. Even pissed off at Hunt, she's on board with a modified touring schedule and families going on the road."

"Why don't you do that, then?" Alex suggests. "Bring Lyric and the kids on the road."

"She'll never agree to it. She's got her job, the kids are in school."

"She's a teacher, Rhys — she could teach them herself," he says.

"She won't go for it. It doesn't get them out of the media spotlight. It takes all the predictability out of their lives."

"She did that the moment she got involved with you," he says. "Heck — even just being friends with you invites total chaos."

"Thanks. I think."

"Personally, I kind of enjoy it. At times," Kier says.

"There you go — maybe she will, too," Alex says.

"No. It's bad enough just with me, on my own. Adding the media in ramps it all up, like cranking up the mains at a show. I've got to unplug, get myself out of the mix, put up a drum shield — whatever I need to do to quiet things down so she feels safe."

The guys get it when I talk in music metaphors. That's good. I think Lyric would get it, too, if she'd let me talk to her. But since she won't, I'll talk to her through the media instead.

I t's hot out, but I put on one of Alex's fancy T-shirts and my dress pants, and throw my jacket over my arm. I'm going to do this with style, even if I can't get the other guys, Billy and the label on board.

"No. Categorically not," Billy said after Dave called to tell him what I had planned. "The crisis-management team is adamant that the best way to handle this is to not feed the media frenzy. I am not calling another press conference just for you to announce you're quitting the band because the paps won't leave your girlfriend alone! Especially when we know you're not really going to quit!"

"I'm serious — I'm quitting! Start looking for a touring drummer who'll stay with the band."

"You're going to make right bags of this, Rhys," Kier said. He made it sound like a warning, but I have no idea what any of that actually means.

Everyone is just shaking their heads at me and looking skeptical. What did they not get about me being serious about this?

It's time to go.

Except my phone rings.

"Mr. Madigan." Uh-oh. Hearing that voice on my phone, calling me "Mr. Madigan" — that's almost as terrifying as the idea of losing Lyric. Honestly, quitting the band is less frightening than facing Marina Matthews, even when I'm not actually facing her, since it's a phone call.

"Mr. Neal has informed me that you intend to announce you are leaving aMUSEd — and the music business."

"Yeah." I've got nothing else to say. Which is kind of strange. But, yeah, that's the bottom line.

"I beg you to reconsider doing this."

Wow. Well... Huh. I never thought I'd be in a position where Marina Matthews was begging me for anything. It's weird.

"I have to take care of Lyric and her kids. That's my priority. And if it means leaving music behind so I can get the media away from them, that's what I'm going to do."

"A noble motivation, Mr. Madigan. But I truly implore you to reconsider acting so rashly right now. We need time for the furor to die down, to show you that the PR plan we have decided upon will work. Just give me a little more time. Please. I am very concerned that this will just serve to aggravate the situation."

"How much more aggravating can it get? Because I'm really, really aggravated right now. And Lyric is really, really aggravated with me. And that's aggravating."

"I understand that, Rhys," she says, and somehow, it makes me feel better that she's calling me Rhys. "But I need you to trust me that I have your best interests at heart — including where Lyric and her children are concerned."

"I can't."

"You can't trust me?"

"No. And I'm sorry about that, but Lyric trusted me, and I flibbertigibbeted that up, so I can't rely on anyone to fix this but me. And this is the only way I can do that."

"Flibbertigibbeted?" I can hear the smile in her voice.

"Mom told me I should watch my language more, use fewer F-bombs."

"Your mother's a wise woman, Rhys. Have you talked to her about this decision?"

"No. Because she'll talk me out of it."

"I'm trying to talk you out of it, too. Isn't that enough to tell you you shouldn't do it?"

"No. This is the logical solution. If the media are harassing Lyric because she's the girlfriend of a rockstar, then to fix it, either she needs to not be my girlfriend or I need not to be a rockstar. And if I have to choose, then I choose Lyric. We're supposed to be together."

"I don't disagree, Rhys, but I think you're oversimplifying the problem. We need a more thoughtful solution for a more complex problem."

"But I am thoughtful. Everyone keeps telling me that! And calling me a god when they see me. But that doesn't seem to come with any supernatural powers, so I'm sticking with being thoughtful."

"Right." Again that smiley voice. "Rhys — I need you to stay at the studio right now. You're planning to cause an issue with the band's public perception, and that falls under the promotional clause of your contract with the label."

"The same one that made Hunt do a reality dating show, even though he was in love with Brighid? Even though he didn't realize it at the time."

"Yes."

"Then, too bad. You can sue me. But I'm quitting."

"That clause also says the label can make arrangements for yours and the band's security when necessary to prevent public relations problems."

"Which means what?"

"Right now? That I'm calling Mr. Gryffin to have him ensure you remain at the studio."

"He'll have to catch me first."

Gryffin's not at the studio. If I move fast, I can get this done before he can stop me.

Except his "operatives" won't let me get my car out of the driveway.

Fine. I'll walk. I'd jog if it wouldn't make me all sweaty on camera when I do this.

"Who wants a story?" I ask the small cluster of media people at the end of the driveway. "If you want a story, follow me." And Gryff's guys can't even get to me now, because there are too many people between us.

You know that song about walking five hundred miles for your girl, and then another five hundred, so you can be that guy for her? I'm going to be that guy. So, with that song setting the rhythm of our march, I lead a bunch of out-of-shape photographers and reporters on a one-mile hike down the highway. Fine — it's not five hundred miles, let alone a thousand. They chatter excitedly amongst themselves, making calls to their editors. But I don't really listen to what they're saying. No — the conversation I'm listening to is all in my head...

You're fucking nuts. She's not going to let you quit.

Head-dude! You're back!

Yeah. Because you're fucking shit up again! After all I went through to fix things for you all. Dude — don't fuck this up even more.

You think it's OK that she's being harassed? Your kids?

No, I don't. But I don't think the answer is you quitting the band. And she's not going to let you.

What's she going to do to stop me? Break up with me? She already did that.

No, she didn't. She just told you to stay away while she thinks.

She's had plenty of time to think. It's time somebody did something to stop this. You told me to take care of them. That's what I'm doing.

You think they're going to leave her alone just because you quit the band? They're going to go nuts. You quitting is a huge story. And the fans are going to blame her. She'll be the Yoko Ono of aMUSEd.

No, they're not. Yoko was a scapegoat. But I'm going to make it clear to them that it's the media to blame, not Lyric.

That doesn't solve the problems she's got here now. She's losing students.

Her lessons? I'll make sure she's got enough money to make ends meet, even if I have to recruit students for her.

Even if she'd let you do that, it's not just them — kids are being pulled out of her class at school.

Crap. I can't fix that.

See — you quitting doesn't solve all the problems she's dealing with.

But it fixes most of them. Maybe once the media coverage dies down, everyone else will just chill out. And the only way I can make that happen is to quit.

What about 'She won't let you' are you not getting, dude?

I'm not giving her a choice.

I didn't give her a choice about me quitting music to get a regular job. You know what happened.

She insisted you stick with music.

Yeah. She did. She's hard-headed. Everyone's told you that. You know that firsthand now. She doesn't like things not being under her control. That's why you sending in her application freaked her out. She's used to being in charge of everything, especially anything that touches the kids. That's why this is getting to her so much — the media, the public, none of that response is under her control.

So I'll get it back under control!

Rhys, she shaped a very regimented life for herself, for the kids, to make things work as much like they did when I was here as she could make them. It feels safe to her. She wants that back. But she can't get it back — the lid's off that box now. And the life she's living, it doesn't fit that space anymore. She's going to have to adapt. She's going to have to learn how to finally be free of what's holding her back. That's why you're here, Rhys. Don't fuck it up now. Help her!

I am! That's why I'm quitting.

God, you're stupid.

I lead the media pack through the middle of town, and then across the highway and down a side street. There are a few more of their brethren waiting for us there, along with Kirk and Roger, who block them from stepping onto Lyric's property. But they don't stop me when I stand just inside the front yard. They look confused when I stop, rather than approaching the front door, but they let me get that far. Good.

Once everyone is in place, I slide on my jacket and raise my hands to get their attention.

"Thank you all for coming here to hear what I have to say. Even though this is all your fault anyway."

A few laughs, some muttering of disagreement. Yeah, yeah, whatever. It's true.

"I've come here to publicly announce my resignation as drummer for aMUSEd."

Too much shouting for me to even hear what they're saying. Then they settle down a little.

"Are you quitting the band because your Satanist girlfriend reflects badly on the band as a whole?"

"What the flibbertigibbet, dude? Lyric is not a Satanist. She doesn't even believe that stuff is real. Respectfully, of course."

"Then you deny she and her coven are using magical means to ensorcel members of aMUSEd into marriage?"

"Dude — do you even hear yourself?"

"If that's not true, why are you quitting the band?"

"Honestly? You guys are terrorizing the woman I love and her two young children. I want it to stop. If I have to quit music to make my life boring enough that you'll leave them in peace, that's what I'll do."

"No! No, you won't, Rhys Madigan! Don't you even use me or my kids as justification to quit the band! I want nothing to do with your drama!"

I guess Lyric was listening from inside, because she comes flying at me at full speed, pounding her fists on my chest as I turn around to face her.

The photographers are going crazy, snapping photos of me holding a very angry witch as tight as I can, half because I want to hold her close and half to protect myself. I guess I'm lucky she's not a female tiger after all, because I'd be dead right about now.

Told you! You've really done it now!

Roger comes down from the porch and says her name.

She turns and looks at him, as if waking from a spell herself.

He takes her arm and pulls her back up on the porch and into the house, shutting the door behind her.

"Rhys — are you still quitting the band after Lyric rejected you like that?"

She did?

No. But you've just made it ten times harder for her to let herself have you. Especially if you quit. She'll never forgive herself or you.

I can't win. I'm starting to think I should have listened to Marina Matthews.

"I'll tell you what — if aMUSEd's fans want me to stay in the band, the best thing they can do is persuade you assholes to leave my girl and her kids alone. If you can't do that, I'm done with music. If your editors tell you to go home because our fans are boycotting your sites and social media, then I'll consider staying on. But you are not going to have any more say in my personal life, one way or the other. I'm done with the drama."

And that's the first smart thing you've done today. Maybe you're not stupid after all.

Lyric

H oly Mother Goddess Brighid!

I scream in frustration.

What on earth was Rhys thinking? Of all the stupid...

He wasn't thinking. He was acting on his feelings, which are very strong where you and the kids are concerned. It's exactly how I wanted him to feel, and the last way I wanted him to act.

Adam? You're still here? And in *my* head now?

Yup. Free-ranging spirit, for the moment. Seems my work wasn't entirely done.

Did you at least tell him how stupid he's being? Quitting the band? If I wasn't furious with him before, I am now!

I told him. Warned him, in fact. But he's head-over-heels, Lyr. It's exactly what I wanted for you, but he's...

Unpredictable? Impulsive?

Chaotic. He's an agent of chaos. I kind of like that about him. It forces you to get outside your comfy little box and take risks.

Me?

Well... you, yeah. But everyone who's around him. I like that about him. And face it, babe, you needed someone to drag you out of your comfort zone. Without me around, you'd have kept doing everything just like you have been, and you'd have withered away.

He's not like you. You...

Were a rebel, yeah. He's — he's just himself, which is even more awesome, you have to admit.

Do I?

Yes.

I wasn't asking you. Man, this having people in my head is a pain sometimes.

You not getting good advice from your "I hear dead people" chorus?

After Nonna faded, all I've got left is a gay playboy, a party girl and... gods help me — I think she's Hunter's mother!

Whoa.

Yeah. Whoa. I'm not sure if she's waiting for the wedding or something else before she goes. But she's been waiting, watching, for fifteen years. And she hasn't asked for my help. So whatever it is she's waiting for — she thinks it's on track.

Unlike what you've got going on right now.

I don't even know what to do anymore.

What do you want, Lyr? If there were no concerns about money, other people's opinions and social pressures, the media... What would you want in your life?

I don't know!

Yes, you do. You're too self-aware not to. What's your gut tell you belongs in your life?

Kids. Faith. Music. Poetry. Beach. And...

And?

He knows — knew? — me so well. Always knew when I was refusing to face something.

Fine. Someone to take care of me. Love me. Be part of my family.

I can't do that for you anymore, Lyr. My time is past. I'm only here now to help you two figure this out. What do you want?

I want Rhys.

Smugness.

I knew you would. I'm glad I was right.

But I can't have him — he's quitting music just to be with me. I can't let him do that. I have to make it clear that quitting won't change anything. And it's not like that's the only thing keeping us apart.

The application? The poem? Lyr, stop being stupid. He was trying to help, just like he has been all along. You forgave him for his mistakes before. Why not now?

Because it's all gotten too complicated.

Bullshit, woman! You mean it's gotten too far out of your control.

Ouch. OK.

That's what all of this has been about, Lyric — to get you to see that your life has changed.

I know that. All too well.

But you see it as a challenge — something to get back in control, back to the way it was, no matter how hard that is. It's hard because that old life no longer fits. The challenge now is to see that change opens up a world of possibilities for you, for the kids. That's where Rhys comes in. He doesn't see limits, restrictions, a past turned into a cage with you locked safely inside. He sees open skies, cliffs to dive off, planes to jump out of, music to create — not just replicate.

So, you're sticking around to insult me into making changes in my life — our lives — that I never asked for and don't know that I even want.

No. You always talked about fate, about what the gods had planned... I'm sticking around so that you see what fate has offered you is a chance to be truly happy. That isn't all about Rhys, but Rhys is the missing piece — the one that makes the picture of your possible future come into focus. Right now, you're determined to keep your eyes closed, your vision stuck in the past. And that'll never make you happy, because you want a past where I'm here, with you and the kids. And I won't be here much longer. I'm not even really here now. Rhys is. If you'll just let him in. No — not let him in... If you let him open the door to a future for you and our kids.

Rhys Madigan, in the present, has me and our kids living like we're in prison, surrounded by guards and people stalking us, judgmental co-workers and strangers. There's no open door, no freedom, no future. Not with Rhys.

In my head, the sound of sighing.

You just want me stuck here forever, don't you?

CHAPTER 59

IT TAKES TIME

Rhys

"Rhys Lars Madigan! What on earth are you thinking!"

Uh-oh.

That whole thing Marina Matthews said about me talking to Mom before I decided to quit the band? Maybe I should have done that.

"Honestly? Until you called me by my full name, nothing. The ceiling is blank, and so was my mind. Now all I can think about is that I'm just young enough that I hope I didn't get my middle name from my dad, unless you know for sure he wasn't a drummer."

Mom looks up at the ceiling, where I'm still looking.

"You're too tall."

This is a point I'd never thought of before. It's kind of a relief.

I look down at my feet, my legs stretched out to the very end of my bed, which is way emptier than I'd like it to be.

Mom sits down.

Totally not what I meant.

"You're quitting the band?"

"You're following tabloid journalists now?"

"No. But the room-service guy at the hotel figured out I'm your mom, and he brought me cheesecake, hoping I'd deny the rumor."

"Well, I hope the cheesecake was good. Because it's not a rumor. I quit."

She ignores the comment about the cheesecake.

"Why?" she asks instead.

"So they'd leave Lyric and the kids alone."

"How's that working out?"

"No idea yet. Hasn't been long enough. Besides, I told them if the fans pressure their bosses to leave us alone, I'd reconsider quitting. Gotta give them time to do that."

"That... that was actually kind of clever."

"Thanks."

"It would have been more clever not to have told them your girlfriend is a witch."

"No kidding."

"Rhys..." she chastises.

"Sorry. I'm grouchy."

"That's not like you."

"I know, right?" I sigh. "Me saying something stupid — that's totally like me. Me getting angry at reporters — totally not me. What is wrong with me?"

"If I had to hazard a guess, I'd say you're in love. And you're being protective of the woman you love, and her kids."

"But what kind of idiot protects his woman by outing her as a witch in front of a pack of reporters?"

"You are not an idiot, Rhys. And I think I taught you to think better of yourself than that."

She's right. She did. I may have executive function issues, but I'm smart. If I'm lucky, maybe appealing to aMUSEd's fans is the way out of this. At least this part of it.

"She told me how hard she works to keep that part of her life quiet. And I still messed things up for her."

"Not on purpose. We both know better than that."

"She said people lose their jobs, their kids, over stuff like this. And I'm really afraid something like that could happen to her."

"They can't fire her over her religious beliefs. And there's no one to contest custody, right? Her husband's passed. Any disgruntled grandparents?"

"No, not that I know of."

"Then there shouldn't be an issue. And if there is, you've got a licensed clinical social worker and experienced foster parent to testify as to her fitness as a parent."

"You'd do that?"

"Of course I would, Rhys! She's a lovely girl, and a good parent. You can tell how hard she works to give those kids a good life.

Even if I didn't know how much you care about her, I'd have to say that."

"Thanks, Mom."

I sit up and give her a hug. I feel a little better knowing that, worst case, Mom has Lyric's back.

"Why don't you go play, Rhys? Give this some time to settle down. You always feel better after you play."

"Just not feeling it, Mom. Honestly, if I can't find a way to fix this for her, I'm not sure I'm ever going to feel like playing again. Maybe it's a good thing that I quit."

"You don't believe that any more than you believe Lyric won't forgive you eventually."

"I dunno, Mom. She's really mad at me. First I send in her poem about my butt—"

"Do I want to know?"

"Honestly? Probably not. But she's an amazing poet, and I had a good reason for doing it."

"OK. I'll take your word for it."

"But then I outed her. And now that I said I'm quitting, she's mad about that, too."

"Good for her!"

"Mom!"

"You already know I don't agree with you quitting like this. You'll regret it if you do. And I suspect she knows that, too. And she cares about you, whether she's mad at you right now or not."

"You really think so?"

"What'd she do when she heard you were quitting?"

"Threw herself at me and pounded on me."

"Yeah. That's not angry. That's disappointed. And I'm in agreement with her on that."

"Ow."

It's not often Mom says she's disappointed in me.

"I'm sorry, honey. But you're made of tougher stuff than this. And so is she. So, you'd better hope that this secondary move to get the fans behind you works."

"As long as the press leaves Lyric and the kids alone, it doesn't matter to me."

"Rhys! Don't you start lying now. To me or yourself!"

Right.

"OK. Fine. Maybe the band does matter. But it matters less than Lyric and the kids being safe and happy."

"There. Now that's the truth."
"I still don't feel like playing."
"Give it some time, then."

CHAPTER 60
SET FIRE TO THE RAIN

Lyric

Patty: *Carla just got a call from the district office. They have you on their agenda for personnel issues at tonight's meeting. Are you on your way? She asked me to have you come to her office when you got in.*

Lyric: *We were just leaving. I'll be there in ten.*

Patty: *For what it's worth, I haven't talked to anybody about all the rumors, other than to point out that your rockstar is hot and that you're a great teacher.*

Lyric: *Thanks.*

I think.

Patty certainly hasn't been her usual ebullient self with me since all of this hit the media. But then, hardly anyone has. They're either whispering behind my back, avoiding making eye contact or, in a few rare cases, reassuring me that they don't believe a word of it. Maybe the band's crisis management team was right about just ignoring it. But we'll never know, since Rhys had to go and confirm the secret I've kept from nearly everyone for the last decade.

"I'm sure it'll just be the board members asking some questions about the impacts of the media frenzy on the school, Lyric," Carla says when I get in to the office, having let Roger take Aria to her classroom. "You have to admit that calling in the police for a security violation and having to have a bodyguard on-site during the school day is a little concerning."

"I would hope they could see that it's about keeping the kids, and myself, safe."

"Of course. I'm sure they just want to hear that from you, instead of me and Jimmy."

"Of course. Should I contact the union, just in case?"

"The union? Wow. No, I wouldn't think it's that serious, even if they have concerns."

Can't say I would blame them if they had concerns. The gods know I do.

And, right now, one of those concerns is whether Mom can watch the kids tonight.

Rhys

"Thanks for coming over, Mom."

"I'll always come when you need me, Rhys. You know that."

"Yeah... It's just — I know this is your vacation. And you've already had lunch with me twice this week."

"That was half the reason I came here for my vacation, Rhys. And things have been a little unusual anyway. If you need to talk, I'm glad to be here. Anything else comes in second."

"Exactly! That's my problem. Right there."

Mom gives me an understanding smile.

"More words, Rhys... What's the problem?"

"Anything else comes second, including music."

"Oh — you mean Lyric."

"Yeah, and the kids. Nothing else seems to matter until I can get things fixed between us."

"Have you tried drumming? That usually makes you feel better. Even when you were little, half an hour on your kit was better than therapy."

I give her a smile. I owe her a lot for getting me that kit.

"Yeah... But I keep trying to play and end up throwing my sticks across the room. Not even my drum solo holds my attention right now."

She frowns.

"You're taking your meds?"

"Yeah. I missed a few doses a while back when I lost the bottle, but I'm like clockwork otherwise. You know me. That's why I carry them on me, just in case I'm out somewhere when the next dose is due."

"I remember..." She sighs. "I don't know, Rhys. The best thing I can suggest is to find something else to focus on. How's the album coming?"

"It's good — I mean, the guys are still kind of pissed at me..."

I look up and see that patient-yet-irritated look she always gets when I swear.

"Sorry. I mean — they understand why I want to quit, but they're not happy about it. At all."

"How about the label?"

"The same. Marina Matthews told me not to talk to the media, and she hasn't called me again since I did. But she hasn't sicced the lawyers on me yet, even though my contract says I owe them this album and one more."

"Plus tours."

"Right."

"Rhys — have you thought about what you want to do if you do quit music? I know you don't need a job per se, but I can't imagine you just sitting around in your apartment or even traveling to climb or what have you."

"I really haven't thought about it."

"Rhys..." she chides me.

"Mom — the whole point of quitting was to get Lyric and the kids out of the media spotlight. If it works, and if I can get her to forgive me, then all I care about is spending time with them."

"So you're going to move here? Move into her house?"

"Declan will be thrilled! We'll be next-door neighbors!"

Mom knows better. The look she gives me is dry.

"Mom — I'm happy to spend my days bringing Lyric tea while she writes, making macaroni-and-cheese for Tommy, telling Aria bedtime stories, playing music for fun... I'll set up my kit next to the other one, and Tommy and I can have drum-offs. Family days at the beach, a run up to the climbing gym or to go kiteboarding, the amusement parks, maybe hearing some local live music... I'll have plenty to keep me occupied. And I'll fall asleep every night, content, with my arms around the woman I love."

"You're certain? About her, about this life without music?"

"It won't be without music, Mom. It'll just be making music for a different reason — just for fun. And, yes, I am certain about Lyric, about the kids. That's the life I want. I know it's been really fast, but I can't imagine life without them now."

"Oh, Rhys..." Mom's eyes are watery. "What if you can't change her mind?"

"That's not an option. I just have to figure out a way to do it."

H unt and Brighid are sitting in the living room when I come back in from walking Mom out to her car.

"Hi, Rhys," she says, looking a little glum.

"What's wrong? Are the reporters back harassing you at the shop again? I thought Gryff's guys had them under control."

"They mostly do. Especially now that they're focused on you again..." She looks up at me, and her eyes are sad. "Are you really quitting the band?"

"Yes. Unless we somehow get the paps to leave Lyric alone."

"According to Billy, the fans have been putting the screws to the gossip site editors all weekend," Hunt says. "They've got #LeaveLyricAlone, #WitchPower and #WeAreNotaMUSEd trending across social media."

"Can't say I foresaw #WitchPower being a thing among the band's fans," Brighid says, chuckling.

Hunt squeezes her shoulders in a hug, kisses her hair.

Man, I miss hair-kisses.

"But to answer your question... I got a group text from Lyric this morning," Brighid says.

Why don't I like where this is headed?

"She said she's been called in for a personnel-related discussion with the school board tonight."

"Is she in trouble? Are they upset about all the media attention?"

"She doesn't know. The principal told her it's probably just the board wanting to hear from her about what's been going on."

"I've got to be there."

"No. No, you don't, Rhys. She was very clear with us — she doesn't want *anyone* showing up at that meeting. She said it should be just a low-key private discussion between her and the board after the main meeting."

Maybe she said that, but when they called her in for a private discussion before, she came away so upset by their attacks on her that she called a storm. With all she has on the line now, with all the media and public scrutiny, without anyone there to support her, how badly could tonight go?

I can't risk it. I won't.

Lyric

The last time I was called before the school board, I had to sit through an entire meeting before I was subject to scrutiny over my morals. Tonight, not so much.

"As a parent of a child in this school district, I demand the district fire Mrs. Larson immediately," a woman I've never seen before says to kick off the public comment section of the meeting. "This woman is in league with the Devil, and we cannot allow our children to be influenced by evil."

Kelly's mom, so soon after enthusiastically praising my work on the fundraiser that her daughter participated in, has changed her tune entirely.

"I don't enjoy having to come up here before the board and everyone in this room, but I am a mother, and I have to protect my daughter from the dangers of this world," she says. "Mrs. Larson is a good teacher, but her personal life has created complications inside and outside the classroom. My daughter has for the last few weeks had to endure the presence of private security personnel inside her school, during her music class and otherwise, just to protect her teacher from personal threats and the media that have also overrun the school.

"Even if I didn't have concerns about Mrs. Larson's religious practices — and I do — I have concerns about the kind of role model she is. I feel very sorry for her, for the loss of her husband a few years ago, but the kind of people she's associating with recently — and most particularly her new boyfriend — have a reputation for, among other things, drug and alcohol use, wild parties, a variety of dangerous activities, and casual, promiscu-ous..." she pauses, as if we don't all know the word is coming, "sex." There's murmuring, but much of it is accompanied by nodding heads.

Nevermind that almost none of that is true, and what of it was true isn't something any of the band members seem to engage in anymore. They're a rock band — a hard rock band, at that, dipping into heavy metal, even — so, therefore, as far as these people are concerned, their life is all about sex, drugs and rock. With a side of Satanism, apparently.

The next twenty minutes go by in a blur of comments along the same lines, with a few rare exceptions.

"Mrs. Larson is one of the best teachers this district has ever had!" one of my former students' fathers tells the board. "I don't know anything about her religious beliefs, but to my knowledge she has never expressed a single religious thought in school or with any of her students, let alone during class. This situation has become a literal witchhunt and overt religious persecution. And I, for one, don't want my tax dollars being spent to defend against the lawsuit Mrs. Larson will very rightfully file against the district should you choose to dismiss her over these rumors."

Jennie's mom — who already called to tell me she would be continuing Jennie's lessons, despite the rumors and the presence of security outside my home — is unusually well-informed.

"Before anyone in this room — or outside it — judges Mrs. Larson, I think we could all benefit from a little religious education, of the comparative variety," she says. "Mrs. Larson, if the rumors are even true, is of a modern Pagan faith, meaning she worships more than one god or goddess. That's foreign to most of us, but I would remind people that Hinduism is a polytheistic faith, and it's one of the oldest and largest in the world. In fact, we have long used in our classrooms the mythology of ancient Greece and Rome, both of which are involved not only in historical Pagan belief systems but modern faiths, many of which revere the planet as sacred and most of which reject any notion of harm to others."

She scans the room, looking people in the eyes as she does, waiting until they're all paying close attention.

"Avoiding harm to others is an aim that many in this room would do well to have for themselves, as they intend irreparable harm to Mrs. Larson, her children and her students, by depriving her of the ability to do the job she has done so well for more than a decade. It would be not only an incredible loss to our children but a gross miscarriage of justice based on nothing more than rumor, misinformation and prejudice about a very personal matter. On a moral basis, it is not only unjustifiable but repugnant, as well as illegal."

She gives me a quick smile, but it's almost apologetic. She seems to know as well as I do that calls for logic, respect and compassion are lost among the many calls for my dismissal.

The board finally curtails further comment to begin their regular meeting. They won't comment on the topic, as it's a personnel matter. I also knew that going in. Many of those who turned out in hopes they'd announce my firing now leave, unsatisfied, before the core of the meeting even begins.

It's all I can do to sit still while the board discusses field trips, enrollment data, maintenance issues, upgrades to sports fields... The audience dwindles further as the meeting progresses, until it's just me and a handful of other employees, a few parents accompanying students for disciplinary hearings and a couple of local reporters, none of whom is Rory. I didn't expect her here. I know there's something huge keeping her away right now, and I've purposefully kept her out of the loop. She can't cover the story anyway, due to conflict of interest. And I asked all my other friends to stay home and let me deal with this alone. I'm used to handling things by myself. I'm more comfortable this way. Chances are if I had people here holding my hand through this, I'd end up in tears. I'll also stand a better chance of not sparking a storm if I'm here alone.

When it comes time to face the board, though, I have a surprise awaiting me.

"Mrs. Larson," the board's attorney says, "despite the commentary earlier tonight, the board wants to make it very clear that you are not here as a result of your rumored religious beliefs. Regardless of what the public discourse might favor, dismissing you on grounds of your religion would be a flagrant violation of the First Amendment, and the board has no interest in being party to that." There is some fervent nodding across the board, as if they want to make sure that I know they all agree that this isn't a matter of my religious beliefs.

"If that's the case, why am I being called into a disciplinary hearing?" I ask, genuinely confused. "I addressed the board's prior concerns about the winter concert and my related lesson plans. And Mr. Galworth's privately expressed concerns about the Tchaikovsky waltz I played at the fundraiser a few weeks ago were cleared by the board, or so I was told."

They can't possibly fire me for dating a rockstar, can they?

"Mrs. Larson," Galworth says, "we've had a disturbing report of a violation of the section of your contract regarding behavior while on school grounds."

"What kind of report?"

"We have a witness who's come forward who says they personally witnessed you engaged in an inappropriate display of... affection... while inside the school building, as well as on a second occasion in the school parking lot. Do you have any response to those allegations?"

Crap. Donnie. They're going to use Donnie against me. Someone was biding their time.

"I'm aware that one of the school custodial staff walked into the cafetorium after school hours, when no students were present, and witnessed a kiss between myself and my boyfriend. But I'm hardly the first teacher at the school to kiss her significant other on school grounds."

"This witness indicated there was more to it than a brief, chaste kiss," Galworth says. "He indicated that there was touching beneath your clothing in the one incident, and that the other was... passionate, to put it politely. Definitely not something suitable for the workplace, let alone a workplace designed for the education of children. Do you dispute that account?"

My choices right now: Lie, hedge or admit the truth.

If I'm going down, I'm going down righteously.

"I don't deny either kiss. But no students were present at the school at either point, including my own, nor, to my knowledge, were there any other staff members present other than the one who witnessed them. I believed at the time that my boyfriend and I were alone, and when things moved beyond a spontaneous kiss, they ceased."

"So you agree that the witness was accurate in their depiction of the events?"

"I can't say one way or the other, since I haven't seen the exact allegations made."

"That is your right, should things proceed in a legal setting," Galworth says. "For the board's purposes, all that's required right now is your agreement that a kiss occurred on school grounds."

He waits for a reply. I don't give him one. I've already confirmed it.

"The district has also received a report that you had in your possession, on school grounds, during the school day, with students present, a controlled substance — one that was not prescribed to you."

"What?"

"Did you or did you not have a prescription bottle of the stimulant drug Adderall in your purse while you were in school during the school day?"

"Well, yes. But it was just an oversight. It's my boyfriend's medication, prescribed for his attention-deficit disorder. He'd had me hold onto it for him when we were out at the trampoline park one day. I put it inside my purse, which was stored in a locker. And we simply forgot it was in there. It got buried in my purse, until I dropped my purse and the contents spilled out."

"I see," he says. "You are aware that Adderall is a Schedule II controlled substance?"

"I was aware that it has potential for abuse, but not the legal details."

"And you are aware of the district policy that does not allow prescription medications to be stored inside the school unless they are in the secure medication storage in the nurse's office?"

"Well, yes... But, as I said, it was an oversight. I didn't intentionally bring it into the building."

"Nonetheless, it is a violation of policy, owing to the danger it poses to students to have an unsecured supply of a medication, let alone an addictive stimulant drug, within their reach."

"I removed it from my purse and returned it to my boyfriend as soon as I realized it was in there. At no time did any students have access to it."

"Where do you store your purse during school hours?" he asks.

"In a drawer in my desk."

The board members exchange looks. Looks that don't bode well.

"Mrs. Larson, you have admitted to — in just the last few weeks alone — having violated the district policy against staff engaging in sexual behavior on school grounds and against having unsecured medications on school grounds. Both of these are serious violations that could, separately, result in your dismissal. With that established, I move that the board implement disciplinary action against Mrs. Lyric Larson for violation of the behavioral clauses of her employment contract, the form of that disciplinary action being her dismissal, effective immediately."

"All those in favor, say 'Aye,'" the board president says.

There's a chorus of "ayes" across the majority of the board.

"All those opposed, say 'Nay.'"

Just two board members vote in opposition, both of them looking highly uncomfortable with the result.

"Mrs. Larson, you have been dismissed from employment with the school district," the board attorney says. "You can return to the school at 7 a.m. tomorrow to collect personal items from your classroom, with district security staff present. You will need to be out of the building before classes begin at 8 a.m. Any remaining personal items will be mailed to you. Your final paycheck will be mailed to you as well."

There's a fugue in my head. I came into the room prepared to be fired, and to defend myself against their obvious religious grounds for doing so. Instead, one tiny mistake and two spontaneous kisses are enough to end a career of more than a decade. And I don't stand much of a chance in any lawsuit I might file to contend I was fired for my religious beliefs. They'll just deny it. It's over. It's all over.

I pick up my bag and walk out of the room.

The look on my face is enough to tell the few remaining people in the room that I've been fired.

"Mrs. Larson — do you have any comment on the board's actions tonight?"

"Lyric — did they fire you because you're a witch?"

"Are you planning to file suit against the district on the grounds of religious discrimination?"

I look at them, at a loss as to what to say. Even though disciplinary hearings are confidential, there's no doubt that word will soon spread that I've been fired, if not why.

"No comment."

See — if nothing else, my recent experience has taught me how to say "No comment" to a reporter, no matter how upset I am. Would that Rhys had been able to do the same...

I make it as far as the doors to the meeting room before I hear Donnie behind me, talking to the reporters.

"I knew something immoral was going on with her a month ago. I was walking down the hall and heard her swear. 'Goddess bless,' she said." I stop and turn on my heel, in utter shock. "So I kept an eye on her — her and that degenerate boyfriend of hers," he tells the reporters. "And then I walked in on them about to have sex on the stage at school. It was just sickening..."

I can hear the wind building outside. I've got to get home, get away from all of this, from everything that reminds me how horribly wrong my life has gone. I blow through the outer doors, into the parking lot.

"You OK, Mrs. Larson? Lyric?" Roger asks.

I ignore him, walk past, to my car, my hands shaking as I pull my keys out of my purse.

I unlock the door with the remote, my vision tunneling as I try to keep control. The wind blows my hair across my face, then out of my eyes, and I look up to see Rhys leaning on my car.

"Lyric — are you OK? What happened? I know you told everyone not to come tonight, but I couldn't just sit around at the studio, not knowing whether you were OK."

The pained expression in those brown eyes of his is almost enough to break me on the spot. Almost. I hold onto control by the tips of my fingernails, which are digging into my palm.

"Just leave me alone, Rhys. Just... Just leave me alone, please!" I beg him.

I open the door and get into the car, but Rhys grabs the door before I can shut it and drive away.

"Mr. Madigan — you need to let go of the door," Roger tells him. "She asked you to leave her alone, and I'm here to protect her, no matter who's bothering her, no matter who's paying my salary."

All the fight goes out of Rhys in an instant, faced with opposition from the bodyguard he himself had assigned to me. He steps back, his hands raised in submission.

"Mrs. Larson — I think maybe I should drive you home," Roger says through the now-closed door.

But there was a reason I refused to let Roger drive me here tonight, and this was it. I start the car and pull out, careful not to hit either of them. I don't make it clear of the parking lot before the rain begins. By the time I reach home, it's a deluge, with lightning on the horizon. Kirk has taken refuge on the porch, but he looks miserable. I walk inside and drop my bag by the door, step out of my shoes.

"Lyric? What happened?" Mom asks, drying her hands on a dishtowel. "Are you OK?"

"Tell Kirk to come in out of the rain," I tell her. She looks up as thunder rumbles through the house, shaking the glasses in the kitchen cupboard.

"Oh, honey..."

"I need to be left alone, Mom. You can sleep on the sofa or take the kids back to the loft, but I need some time alone. OK?"

"OK, honey. I'm here if you want to talk."

I nod and head into my bedroom, closing the door behind me, locking it.

I can see the lightning flashing between the sections of heavy curtains that now cover my altar room. The light sheers that were once there, letting in sunlight and the sea breeze, are a symbolic loss. I don't even want to go into the room right now. I curl up in a ball in the dead center of the bed, trying to pretend this is where I've always slept.

Warm arms wrap around me. They're not tangible, but that's the most I could handle right now anyway. No hair-kisses, no muse inked into a strong arm, no dreamcatcher tattoo to help fend off a nightmare. It's a waking nightmare now. I close my eyes and just breathe. And then it all catches up to me, and I dissolve into a puddle of tears.

CHAPTER 61
BLUES THIS MORNING

Rhys

I barely made it home in the raging storm.

Home.

No, not home. I know where — who — my home is now. And I can't go there. Lyric doesn't want me there. Because I ruined her life.

When she refused to talk to me at the meeting, I went inside. I'd kept my word — to Brighid and to myself — that I wouldn't go to the meeting. I let her sit in that room by herself while I stood in the hallway, out of sight, and listened to so many people tear her down, accuse her of things I know have nothing to do with her and everything to do with their own prejudices and ignorance. And I forced myself to do nothing.

Would Adam have told me to go to her? To sit with her? Maybe even defend her publicly?

I don't know. But he's not here to tell me one way or the other, either.

So, I did as she asked. Did as she asked Brighid. Did as she apparently wanted me to do, based on her reaction to seeing me. Aside from not being there at all, I mean.

Roger reminded me not to go over to the house, in case I'd forgotten. I hadn't. Hard to forget when the woman you love tells you to leave her alone. Can't say I wasn't tempted to go to her anyway. Again. But making a scene with my own bodyguards isn't going to help Lyric, and I don't want to upset the kids.

There's a blinding flash, a concussive boom. I'm used to some pretty loud noises but, instinctively, I throw my hands over my ears and duck. I look out at the flat patch of sand that is the studio's driveway. There's a small shiny, dark spot next to my car. And it's not a rain puddle.

Huh... Maybe I should get inside.

"What the ever-lovin' hell is going on with this weather?" Kieran asks when I walk back in the front door.

What do I tell him? My girlfriend got fired and she's unintentionally called in a major storm? She might maybe have just almost accidentally killed me?

I'm thinking that's not going to go over well with Kier. He's still kind of pissed about the witch story and the havoc it's caused. Telling him Lyric's also capable of raising a dangerous storm and hurling lightning bolts at me? Nope.

"I heard there was a tropical depression forming off the coast," Alex says. "It must have shifted much faster than they predicted. They were even talking about it possibly becoming a hurricane in the next few days."

Uh-oh. If Lyric doesn't get things under control soon, I may have to go over there and see if I can help. Maybe if I can just get her to let me hug her again... before I get zapped.

Alex is checking the weather on his phone. It beeps with an incoming text.

"Hey — Rhys... Have you heard from Lyric at all?" he asks. "Wasn't her school board thing tonight?"

"Where do you think he was?" Kier asks him. "Just look at him. Have you ever seen such a sorry look on a fella?"

"You didn't go to the meeting, did you?" Alex asks. "Brighid said Lyric didn't want anyone there."

"No, I didn't go to the meeting."

"Let me guess — you waited outside instead," Alex says.

I shrug.

"They fired her, didn't they?" Kier asks.

I just nod.

"We'll get the lawyers on it. They only targeted her because of the band. The religious discrimination is obvious — they'll end up owing her millions," Kier says, like it's that easy.

"Maybe. If that was why they fired her," Alex says.

"Why wouldn't it be?" Kier asks.

"Brighid says the board flatly denied any religious element to why they fired her," Alex says, looking at his phone. "The rumor mill at Callie's restaurant said it was due to violations of the terms of her contract."

Why does that sound familiar? Didn't she say something about the terms of her contract?

Flibbertigibbets. Oh, screw it. Fuck! The kiss.

"Donnie! Donnie ratted us out!" I smack myself this time. I've more than earned it.

"OK — you're going to have to explain that," Alex says.

"I kissed her. While we were working on the fundraiser, she fell, and I caught her, and I kissed her — right on the fucking stage. We didn't think anyone else was there. But then this custodian guy showed up, interrupted us. She freaked out, said it was a violation of her contract to be kissing someone at school. But then nothing happened, and I figured Donnie hadn't said anything. It was just a kiss, man! But — I should have known..." I smack myself again. "I saw him with that asshole Gallbladder or whatever his name is — the one who had it in for Lyric."

"So, they sat on a reason they could use to justify firing her and then waited to use it until she got outed as a witch," Alex says. "So they could cover their asses against a discrimination suit... It's ingenious."

"It's diabolical!" Kier says. "Which is ironic, considering what they're accusing her of."

"I still think we need to get the lawyers involved," Alex says. "She's in this mess because of us, one way or the other. Either because we got her outed or because Rhys couldn't keep his hands off her."

I want to object. But I can't. I couldn't keep my hands off of her. Then, or later. Now... Now she doesn't want them on her, and I have to respect that. Even if I think both of our souls are crying out for a nightlong hug and a million hair-kisses right now.

"She'd have to agree to it," Alex says. "We can't just sic the lawyers on them on her behalf."

"I don't think she'd let us help her. Maybe for the kids. But just for her?"

"I'll ask Brighid to suggest it," Alex says. "It'll be better coming from her. If she doesn't agree, we can have Billy reach out."

"She told me to leave her alone."

"Wish I could say I'm surprised, boyo," Kier says, "but if they really did use that kiss as grounds for firing her..."

"But she's so upset! She needs me. And I can't go near her because our own security takes her orders over mine."

"Talk to Gryff," Kier says. "But I doubt that will change. Maybe just give her some time to calm down. And it's not like you're going anywhere in this weather!"

I look back out on the deck, where the rain is ponding even with the space between the boards and the tall pine trees are whipping in the wind. The waves are crashing on the shore hard enough to be heard even with the doors closed.

"That wouldn't keep me away from her if I thought she'd let me in. Nothing would."

The next day

A lex looks at me, pity pouring off of him.

"You check in with your mom today?"

"No. I've been a little distracted."

Kier smirks, and I realize me being distracted is kind of the norm.

"You've been distracted since you first saw the girl," he says. "It's a wonder you've managed to get any recording done."

Recording! That's it!

"Hey, guys... Are you up for a little spontaneous recording session?"

They exchange a look.

"Not to look a gift drummer in the mouth after your sudden decision to quit the band, but we've got keyboards, guitar and drums between the three of us," Alex says. "What are you going to do for bass and lead vocals with Dec and Dave gone for the night?"

"And this crazy weather keeping them there," Kier points out. A slap of thunder echoes outside, as if to prove his point.

"We don't need them."

"An instrumental?" Alex asks. "Tell me it's not another drum solo."

"No." They both look confused. "I'm going to do lead vocals. And guitar. Kier — you up for doubling on guitar?"

"Why not?" he says, shrugging. "Might be fun, playing a riff I didn't write. And this is where I say, 'I told you so!' You can't not do music."

I ignore the "I told you so."

"Alex, can you play engineer?"

"Piper'll be irked with me, but, yeah, I can run the board."

"Then let's go record a song."

"You still haven't told us what kind of song," Kier says.

"A lullaby."

In the isolation of the studio, we can't hear the storm raging outside, but I can feel it. Maybe it's Lyric I'm feeling, but it really doesn't matter — she and this storm are inseparable. And as I introduce Alex and Kier to the song, to Adam's song, I'm singing and playing it for her. It's oil on turbulent waters to calm the storm. It's the support and reassurance that she needs, even though she can't hear the notes with her ears. It's the sweet dream the dreamcatcher lets through, filtering away the things that scare her, that worry her, that upset her.

And after just the first run-through, Alex and Kier get it.

"You wrote this?" Kier asks, marveling.

"Lyric's husband did."

"And you've got permission to record it?" Alex asks, just as practical about business matters as he's been since the day he joined the band.

"Hers *and* his."

They give me a funny look. Yeah, I know how it sounds. But it's the truth.

"My royalties will go to the trust fund I set up for the kids."

"You set up a trust fund for her kids?" Alex asks. He actually looks impressed.

Kier shakes his head.

"In for a penny, in for a pound," he says. "Put mine in there, too."

"And mine," Alex says.

"Alright — then let's get this recorded."

It's dawn when we finish, but you wouldn't know it to look outside. The sky is dark, nearly black, with almost a green tinge to it. The wind continues to roar, and while the rain has let up, the waves are huge, pounding hard on the sand. The beach has started to erode a little.

But beyond the physical storm, something feels off. It's not the same feeling of sadness, worry and desperation that poured off Lyric last night. I can't put my finger on it, but something's not right, like there's something out of place, something dangling over the edge of a precipice, waiting to fall.

"You're not going out there, are you?" Alex asks, seeing me looking out the glass door from the studio level and onto the beach.

"Just for a little while," I tell him. "I need to check on something."

"Don't go bothering Lyric," he advises. "Let her have a day to wrap her head around things. Brighid'll let you know if she wants to see you."

"Yeah. OK."

I don't know if I'm headed over to Lyric's or not, but I feel like I need to be out there. So I grab my windbreaker, open the door and step out, walking down to the beach. I ignore my ingrained habit of following the rules, pull a Hunt and ignore the signs for the private beach, walking toward Mystic Beach proper along the sand, just above the edge of the raging waters.

I got tossed out of my raft while whitewater rafting once. Level IV and V rapids. I got distracted and let loose of the safety rope just enough that a bump sent me flying. Everyone in the raft thought I was dead, held underwater longer than most of them would have survived. Honestly, for a second, I thought maybe I was dead, too. But, nope — I popped up a moment later and swam to safety. I got right back on the raft at the next waypoint, too. But these waves — they remind me of that. I don't ever underestimate the ocean, but with things like they are right now, it gives even me pause.

The beach is basically deserted, just a few bystanders taking in the storm-tossed ocean from the safety of the boardwalk. I'm the only one walking on the sand. And I have no idea what I'm out here for, what I'm looking for... Until I see a flash of gold amidst the seafoam and dark water.

My phone rings right as I dump my windbreaker onto the sand. Whoever's calling, it'll have to wait.

I run for the breaking waves and dive under one before the one right behind it slams into me. I drag a breath in before I get smashed into again and then dive for the spot where I saw that bit of gold.

Underwater, between the shifting wafts of sand stirred up by the waves, I can see it's not metal. It's far more precious.

Aria!

I don't know how she got down here, alone. But if she was in over her head on a normal beach day, she's in serious danger now. I see a hand, an arm, flail in the water in front of me, her long blonde hair — almost the same color as Lyric's — flowing past, but I can't grab hold. As soon as my arm shoots out for her, she's washed away again. I can see her paddling, a strong swimming stroke like she demonstrated on our beach days, rather than the listlessness or desperation of someone who's drowning, but she's overwhelmed by the storm. I'm not sure how much longer she'll last if I don't get her to safety.

She goes under as a huge set of waves looms over us, one after the other. I dive under, as much to avoid a pounding as to try to find her. I can see flashes of her hair, but she's being pulled out farther and farther. Could she be swimming out, away from land? She has the confidence of a swimmer three times her age, and then some. No one in their right mind would be out here to swim. Even the surfers are avoiding the water today. But yet here I am, "The Madman," swimming farther out, too.

"Aria!" I call out, hoping she can hear me, but knowing it's unlikely she will over the noise of the waves.

I dive under again, going deep enough to find some clear water between the sandy bottom and the churning wash on top. I can see her now. She smiles at me and waves, and swims away. I do a double-take, because I'm expecting a half-drowned child, and instead I'm seeing a little girl comfortably swimming in the depths of a raging sea, as at home as she is on land.

I come up for a breath and then dive under once more, kicking for all I'm worth, trying to get within arm's reach of Aria. But she's pulled away. Pulled away by another set of arms. Did someone else see her and come to the rescue, manage to beat me to her? Who cares? If they've got her, we can get her back to shore, between the two of us.

But Aria doesn't surface. Have I lost my mind? I dive down again, looking around for any sign of anyone at all. I see an arm flash by me. I grab for it. My hand slides off, getting no purchase like I would on flesh, but instead slipping off a scaly surface. I grab another breath and go back, grabbing instead for a foot this time. Again, my hand slides off. What the flibbertigibbets is going on here?

Finally, I see a small expanse of flesh below that blonde hair trailing through the water. I kick for all I'm worth and grab her around the waist, pulling her to the surface.

"Mr. Rhys!" she yells over the storm. "Did you see the storm? Did you see the water? How fun is this?"

"Aria — what are you thinking? It's dangerous out here! We've got to get back to land!"

"I'm fine, Mr. Rhys! I'm a quarter mermaid, remember! See!"

She wiggles out of my grasp and dives back under.

I can't believe it, but I dive in after her. And come face-to-face with a stern-faced man, bearded, shirtless, who grabs her around the waist and takes off for shore with a speed I can't even comprehend.

I'm half-exhausted, half-drowned myself, but I make my way back to land, hauling my ass onto the sand, where Aria sits, shrouded in my discarded jacket, staring at her own hands, the webbing between her fingers... What?

I look closer at her as I approach. Little fins on the sides of her legs, disappearing as I watch.

That's it. I've finally lost my mind. I'm truly a madman now.

"See, Mr. Rhys! I'm fine! Grandpa said I'd be fine, but he told me not to swim in storms anymore."

Grandpa?

"Where'd he go? The man who rescued you?"

"He didn't rescue me, silly Mr. Rhys! He came to introduce himself and tell me not to swim without Mommy or Grandma until I'm older, because they'll worry. Once I'm older, I can go visit Grandpa under the water. I'll have my big-girl fins by then!"

"Right..."

My phone rings again from the pocket in my jacket. Aria fishes it out and hands it to me.

"It's Grandma, Mr. Rhys! Answer it!"

I do. Because what else am I going to do?

"Rhys? Have you seen Aria? We've been looking for her all over the house, the neighborhood. We thought maybe she'd tried to come find you down at the studio, since she hadn't seen you in a while."

"I just found her. On the beach." Because what else am I going to tell Iris about how I found Aria?

"Oh, thank the gods!" she says. "We'll be right down there to get her."

She hangs up without another word.

"You warm enough, kiddo?" I ask Aria.

"I'm fine, Mr. Rhys! That was fun! I came out to feel the storm, and the water looked so exciting! So, I went for a swim!"

"Without a swimsuit?"

"Mommy said never go to in the water in my regular clothes, because they're too heavy. So I took them off. And Grandpa said I can't get my fins if I've got my swimsuit on — that's why I didn't get my fins before now!"

"I see." See — it even sounds judgy when *I* say it.

"Thanks for coming swimming with me, Mr. Rhys. I missed you. Mommy's been really sad. Especially last night."

"I know. And I missed you, too — you and your mommy and Tommy. I missed you all."

"You should come for a sleepover, then, Mr. Rhys! That'll make everyone happy."

Somehow, I doubt that.

"We'll have to talk to Mommy about that."

"Aww! My fins are going away, Mr. Rhys! I wanted to show Mommy, too!"

Sure enough, she's right. The webbing between her fingers is almost gone, and the little fins along the sides of her legs look like just a rough patch of skin now. I'm not sure if I should bring it up with Lyric when she gets here, or if I should let Aria talk to her about whatever it is that this is...

No. I know what this is. As much weird shit as has happened in the last few months, I know what I saw.

Aria is a mermaid.

CHAPTER 62

THE DREAM

Lyric
A half-hour earlier

I sit bolt upright in bed.

Something's wrong.

And it's not just that Rhys isn't here, holding me in his arms.

Right. I got fired. For kissing Rhys and having his meds in my purse.

No. That's not it, either.

I get up. No need to get dressed. I fell asleep in my clothes, worn out from crying. It's not even full dawn yet. Still dark, even without the storm that I have no doubt I made worse. I hope no one got hurt. I'm going to have to get Mom to put a binding spell on me or something. Whatever it takes to keep the weather magic in check.

Mom. Mom's on the sofa. Sorry, Mom. I should have let you sleep in the bed. I just didn't want the kids waking up to find me a red-eyed mess.

The kids!

I fling open the bedroom door and race up the stairs.

Tommy's asleep in his bed, a perfect angel, or the Pagan child equivalent thereof.

Aria... Aria is not.

I try not to panic. The last time something like this happened, they were with Rhys, making me breakfast in bed.

But Rhys isn't here.

I ignore the pang that hits my heart at the reminder.

I look back down the stairs. Mom's as soundly asleep on the sofa as Tommy is in his bed. I race from room to room.

Aria's not in either bathroom. Not in the kitchen. Not in the practice room or the music room. Not in the back yard. Not in Nonna's garden picking flowers.

Holy Mother Goddess Brighid!

"Mom! Wake up! Aria's gone!"

"Hmm? What?"

"I can't find Aria anywhere."

"She was in bed the last I saw her. Sound asleep."

"She's not there now. Nowhere in the house. Not in the yard."

"See if Kirk or Roger have seen her!"

Of course! Why didn't I think of that?

Because I'm not used to having 24/7 bodyguards. That's why. I fling open the front door.

Kirk is sitting on the porch swing with a cup of coffee.

"Have you seen Aria?"

"No. She's not in the house?"

"No. Not inside or in the yard. Not in Callie and Declan's back yard."

"I'll get Roger started on a search, and I'll go check with Declan and Callie to make sure she's not over there."

He runs off, his phone in hand.

How did I manage to lose one of my kids, with a pair of bodyguards watching the house?

They can keep Rhys from coming in, but they can't keep one little girl from sneaking out?

She did sneak out, right? No one broke in and took her, right?

No. I know Aria. She's snuck off for some reason.

The storm.

Of course. Rhys said it — she couldn't be kept inside during that storm. But she's not on the porch like she was then.

Horror as I remember the other place she can't be kept away from — the water, the ocean. And in a storm...

"I'm going to head down to the beach, make sure she's not down there."

"Wait for Kirk and Roger!" Mom says. "We need as many people looking for her as we can get."

"Right." I know what she's going to say. I don't like it. But she's right even before she's said it.

"We should call Rhys. He'll want to help look for her. Maybe... maybe she decided to go find him, since he hasn't been around lately."

As if I didn't already feel guilty enough. She's out there chasing my storm, or she's wandered off looking for the first father figure she's had in her memory, after I pushed him out of our lives again.

"Fine. Call him."

Roger runs up.

"I've checked the exterior of the house for evidence of a break-in. There's no indication anyone got in. But..."

"But what?"

"She's small. She could have snuck past Kirk and me while one of us was on a break. If that's the case, we apologize, but we planned for protecting your family from outsiders, not for keeping the kids inside when they didn't want to be."

"It's not your fault. She's sneaky. Determined. And if she's snuck off, that's on me."

Especially if she's run off to find Rhys.

"Rhys has her!" Mom yells from inside. "Oh, thank the gods. She's down on the beach."

My worst-case scenario, with tragedy narrowly averted. If she'd made it into the water...

I shudder.

"We'll take you down, ma'am," Roger says.

"No. It's just as fast to walk. Not that I'll be walking... Stay with Tommy, please. He's still asleep..."

"Yes, ma'am."

"Mom..."

"I'm right behind you!"

Mom and I take off for the beach at a run. A few minutes later, we're on the sand, scanning the shoreline for...

"Mommy! Grandma!" Aria calls.

She's all the way at the end of the beach, well out of sight of the boardwalk and any passers-by. How did Rhys even find her? And what is she wearing?

I scoop her up at a full run, holding her to me so tight it's a wonder either of us can breathe.

"Mr. Rhys came swimming with me, Mommy!" she says. "And I asked him to come for a sleepover, too!"

I ignore the last part of that.

"Hi," he says, like taking my kid swimming in the ocean during a storm is no big deal.

"You went swimming with her?" I yell at him, skipping our usual one-word preamble. "In this weather? Are you insane?"

Then I remember who I'm talking to. I suppose I should be glad he didn't take her cliffdiving.

"It wasn't like that!" he says, looking around, as if he's trying to pull answers from the air.

"Then how was it?"

"Grandma!" Aria yells excitedly. "Grandpa said to tell you he's sorry he had to leave, but he hopes he'll see you again now that he's back."

What?

I look over at Mom. She's stunned.

"Was she in the water?" I ask Rhys. "Did she drown? Hit her head?"

He shakes his head no.

"I saw her in the water. I went in after her. I kept missing her. She kept diving back under, swimming farther out. I'd grab hold of her and she'd slip out of my hands. She was under longer than I was, but she seemed fine. I was just trying to get her out of the water. And then... Then..."

"Then Grandpa told me I had to come back on land, Mommy!"

I look from her to Rhys, waiting for him to offer an explanation that makes sense.

He shrugs.

"There was a guy — older than me, but not, like, grandpa-age. He was in the water with her. And he brought her out. When I made it back in, she was wearing my jacket and he was gone. And she... she..."

"She had fins..." Mom says, making it sound like a guess.

"What?" Everyone's gone mad. I call storms. I talk to dead people and goddesses. But this is true madness.

"I had fins, Mommy! I wanted to show you, but they went away when I got dried off on the beach. I can go back in and then you'll see!"

"No! No more swimming today, or ever by yourself. Especially in a storm!"

"But I was fine, Mommy! I can breathe under the water just fine."

I look back at Rhys, who just shrugs again.

"She didn't seem to be having any issues breathing. Not when she was in the water, under the water or once she got out."

"It's 'cause I'm a mermaid, Mommy! Just like Grandma!"

"No, honey — not like me," Mom says. "I was a pretend mermaid... You..." She looks at me helplessly. "Well... it's a long story."

"Then I think you'd better tell me." I shake my head at her, no idea what to think.

"Let's get her home, get her dressed," Mom says. "Then we can talk."

"Fine," I tell her. "I'll have Roger bring you back your jacket, Rhys. I... I guess I owe you my thanks. You found her. You went in after her. You could have been killed yourself." I start to tear up. As horrifying as the idea of Aria drowning is, knowing Rhys risked his life for her on top of that is overwhelming.

"I'm fine," he says. "I did what I needed to do to protect her."

"Why were you even down here?"

"Something felt wrong. I had to see what it was. And then I saw her in the water."

"Not Adam? He didn't tell you to go look for her?"

Rhys shakes his head.

"I just had this feeling that I needed to check on something. It felt too important to ignore. Even if there'd been a tornado or a man-eating tiger, I'd have gone out to look. And I'd have pulled her from the jaws of a shark if there'd been one. Instead..."

"I think Rhys is owed an explanation, too," Mom says.

And, as usual, she's right.

I nod.

We head back up the beach, Rhys following behind. I see him almost put his hand in the small of my back again, but he catches himself. It feels wrong.

Roger sighs in relief as we come into view down the street. When we come in through the door, Kirk gives a smile from the upstairs landing, where he'd clearly been watching Tommy sleep. Both of them are a little too pleased when they see Rhys with us, invited into the house. But too much has happened to object to any cheerleading on their parts.

"We'll be right outside," Kirk says, shutting the door behind him.

"I'll be right back," I tell Mom and Rhys.

"You, young lady, are going to get on some clean pajamas and then go back to bed," I tell Aria, guiding her back up to her room.

Dressed for bed once again, she yawns widely.

"We are going to have a long discussion about what happened today once you've gotten some more sleep, Aria. But I want you to promise me you'll never leave the house without telling me or one of the other grown-ups, and that you'll never go in the water alone again."

"But I wasn't alone, Mommy! Grandpa was there! And then Mr. Rhys!"

I sigh. Too many unknowns to even address right now.

"Going into the water by yourself, when there's no grown-up right there with you — that's going swimming alone, Aria. And I need you to promise me you won't do that again."

"Or leave the house without telling you."

"Right."

"I promise, Mommy. Can Mr. Rhys stay for a sleepover now?"

"Mommy and Mr. Rhys are going to have a talk. We'll talk about that, too."

"OK. G'night, Mommy," she says, snuggling down under the covers and falling instantly asleep. I envy her that ability.

But right now, I have a mystery to unravel and a boyfriend... an ex-... a Rhys to deal with.

CHAPTER 63

DEAR OL DAD

Lyric

"**O**K. Explain."

That's all I know to say to Mom, who seems to hold the answers to a mystery that's not hers, or mine, alone.

"I never told you who your father was."

"No, you didn't. I assumed it was a one-night stand. Maybe even an on-purpose 'oopsie.'"

I glance over at Rhys, who doesn't seem entirely comfortable with the conversation but who's clearly curious as to what all of this means.

"It wasn't," she says. "It wasn't exactly on purpose, either. But it wasn't a one-night stand."

She sighs.

"I lifeguarded here every summer from 16 to 22. And then I went to Florida and played mermaid for a few more years. I was too wild for your grandparents, too free-spirited, too prone to losing myself in magic."

"There's no such thing," I tell her. And I mean it.

"Well, your grandparents disagreed. If I wanted to stay with them after college, I had to go to church every Sunday."

I cringe. I can't imagine being stuck attending another faith's weekly services, just to keep a roof over my head.

"And you already know I wasn't inclined to agree to that. So, I went off and did my mermaid thing. I came back when your grandfather got sick. He regretted driving me away and left me enough in his will that I could afford half the rent for an apartment here for the summer. Your grandmother... Well, she never mellowed like he did. And after the funeral, we never spoke again. So, I went back to lifeguarding, figuring I'd find a regular job before the fall. What I didn't count on was swimming directly into someone while I was doing my regular morning ocean swims."

She smiles, and it lights up her face like I've never seen it before.

"Oh, Lyric — he was so handsome... Long brown hair, a beard, fit..." She glances over at Rhys, and I roll my eyes. "And he swam like a fish. From that day on, he joined me for my swims, every morning. We talked. We got to know each other. He didn't tell me much about his family, his past, but then I didn't tell him much about mine. He knew I was a lifeguard, that I'd been a mermaid. He thought that was both hilarious and amazing. And I loved that, because it was. After a while, he started coming to find me in the evenings, once I was off-duty. And..."

"You fell in love, fell into bed and ended up with a belly full of Lyric."

"No need to be rude, Lyric," she says, shaking her head. "But, in essence, yes. Only..." she hesitates, glancing at Rhys again. "Fins?" she asks him. He nods. "I always told you you were half a mermaid. The truth is you are. Literally. I found out shortly before I realized I was pregnant. Your father... Well, he is one of the merfolk. A merman. A prince, in fact. Though I found that out too late, too."

She's solemn now, wistful.

I'm still digesting the fact that she's telling me my father's a merman.

Rhys... Rhys seems to be taking this in stride. I guess it's just one more thing to absorb, on top of witches, goddesses and ghosts. He's already been on a high learning curve.

"I was still absorbing what he'd told me about his nature when he came to me one day to tell me he had to leave. Some kind of infighting amongst factions of his people. He was needed at home. And he wasn't sure when, or if, he'd be back. I'd like to think I took it in stride. He left me with a gold medallion, said it was an emblem of his people, and he'd find me again someday if he could come back. A month later, I realized I was pregnant, but he was gone. I had no way to reach him. So I sold the medallion. It turned out it was incredibly valuable, ancient. I got enough for it to put a downpayment on this house, and from there I made every craft I could, did every odd job, whatever it took to ensure you had a roof over your head and food to eat, even after we had to take you out of school."

"Because of the weather magic."

"Yes. I suspect it's something you inherited from your father. Certainly, I could never do it. But once he revealed his nature to me, he showed me some things he could do — with water, rain, wind... Nothing like what you did, even as a child. But I doubt I saw the full breadth of what he could do."

"So, my father..."

"He called himself Niall."

"He's a merman. I'm half mermaid. Aria is a quarter mermaid. Why is it she suddenly has fins after swimming in a storm and meeting her grandfather?"

"She said he told her she won't get fins if she's wearing clothes," Rhys says.

"Great! I'm going to have a beachgoing nudist child who thinks she can't drown."

"I'm not sure she can," Mom says. "If she's inherited his nature, she can likely breathe underwater."

"I'm pretty sure that's what I saw," Rhys says. "If anyone was going to drown today, it was me."

The thought steals my breath. It takes me a moment to pull myself together enough to speak.

"Thank you again for going in after her. Even if it may not have been as dangerous for her as it looked," I tell him. "I'm grateful. Really."

"Anytime," he gives me a gentle smile. "She also said he told her that she'd get her grown-up fins later."

"What did you see, exactly?"

"When I came out of the water, she had on my jacket, and he was gone. But her fingers were webbed, and there were little fins along the sides of her legs. The longer she was out of the water, the more she went back to normal — the webbing shrank, the fins disappeared."

"So, I guess I need to go swimming naked and see if I get fins..."

"You may not," Mom says. "You know how DNA works — characteristics can skip a generation and then show up again. It may be her mermaid DNA is more dominant than it is in you.

It may be the DNA for weather magic showed up more strongly in you than it does in her."

"I'm not so sure about that," I say. "She went down there because of the storm. She loves storms."

"I think you may be right," Rhys adds. "I've seen her chasing that feeling. I haven't seen her cause anything to happen, though."

"Something else we'll have to wait and see… Speaking of which…"

"He told her he'd be back to see me," Mom says.

"Does he… does he come on land — I mean, farther inland than the beach?"

"He can. I never saw him out of the water longer than a day or two. But he breathes air, has legs — no fins — when he's on land. He spoke English, though with a slight accent."

"So, we just wait for a naked man to show up on our doorstep?"

"I really don't know. He said when he left that he'd find me. But he never has. As far as I know, he's never been back here until today, when Aria went into the ocean, naked."

"Why'd she do that? I mean, kids run around naked all the time when they're little. I couldn't keep a diaper on her or Tommy when they were toddlers. But why today?"

"She said you told her not to swim in her regular clothes because they're too heavy," Rhys says.

I chuckle.

"Well, that's true. I meant that she needed to change into her swimsuit before she went swimming. But I guess she figured naked was the next best thing." Too many unknowns. I'll have to discuss all of this with her later. We'll have a whole new set of things she's not allowed to discuss with her classmates and teachers.

And that's when it hits me…

"I don't have a job."

"Oh, honey." Mom pulls me into a hug. "We'll figure something out."

I pull away before I lose control again, whether that results in tears or a tornado.

Rhys

"We can get you a lawyer. You can sue. The guys and I talked about this last night. I can call Billy..."

"They didn't fire me over my religion, Rhys. At least not openly. I don't have a First Amendment case."

"Then how did they justify letting you go?" Mom asks.

I look over at Rhys, feeling guilty myself knowing how guilty he's going to feel when I say it.

"I kissed her on school property. Twice," he says before I can say anything.

"No — just once. I kissed you the second time, in the parking lot. And I kissed you back on the stage..."

Mom gives me a look.

"I fell. Rhys caught me. Things got... heated."

"And that asshole — sorry — Donnie saw us," Rhys says.

"Both times, apparently," I clarify.

"I knew it!" Rhys says. "I saw him talking to that Gallbladder guy at the rehearsal..."

"Galworth."

"Right. But I knew something not-cool was going on. I should have done something."

"There's nothing you could have done. They had it in for me. Donnie overheard me say, 'Goddess bless.' From then on, any mistake I made was being scrutinized. Including having a bottle of prescription medication in my purse in school, during school hours..."

"*My* meds. *That's* where they were!"

"Yeah. And don't blame yourself for that, either. If I'd just cleaned my purse out before the school year started... If I'd been less clumsy that one day..."

"They're firing you over a bottle of your boyfriend's medication that got left in your purse?" Mom asks.

"Adderall is a Schedule II controlled substance. It gets abused by people who don't need it. It's fine for Rhys to carry his own medication, but even having his meds in my purse could cause problems if someone were to question me about it. I just forgot they were in there. We both did."

Rhys reaches over and squeezes my hand. I let him.

"So, chances are that no lawsuit I could file claiming religious persecution would be successful. It'd be their word against mine, and all the tangible evidence goes against me. I technically violated both school district policy and my employment contract. They have every right to fire me, even if they've overlooked the same violations in other cases. With both things happening in a matter of weeks, they could just say it was a pattern of behavior or a second and final strike. A third, if we count both kisses separately. But that leaves me without a job, and with fewer private students than I had before."

"I'll make sure you and the kids are provided for. This really is my fault," Rhys says.

"I can't let you do that. We're... we're not even..." I can't even finish the sentence. He knows what I mean. Mom knows.

"I'm going to head back to the loft," she says. "I could use a nap. And I have a date tonight..."

"With your existing paramour or with the merman?" I ask, unable to hide my smile.

"Wouldn't you love to know," she says, sticking her tongue out at me. "But in all seriousness, if he shows up, I'll let you know. I'm sorry I kept it from you all these years, but it sounds unbelievable even to me, in hindsight. And aside from the weather magic, you've had a very normal life. No fins, no gills."

Mom is clueless about the full extent of how not-normal my life has been of late. But, for now, I'll keep that to myself. And Rhys.

"If you need me, just call," she says. "I'll drop whatever if you need me. OK?"

She gives me a kiss on the cheek and tweaks Rhys' chin. And out the door she goes.

"We need to talk," Rhys says.

And he's right. We do.

"Lyric, life's got enough storms of its own without you making them literal ones, too."

Wow. In all the time I've been dealing with this power of mine, no one's ever said that to me before. I've always thought of it as the storms being an extension of my emotions and just tried to keep my emotions in check. Looking at them as a literal storm on top of an emotional storm makes it seem like I'm just multiplying my problems. And that's not going to calm things down — for me or the weather. Or the people around me.

"Your lightning bolt missed my car by about a foot that night, after the school board meeting."

My heart stutters, my blood pounding in my ears.

"Oh, my gods! KITT! You weren't in it, were you?"

"No. I'd made it as far as the front door to the studio. But it was close."

To my knowledge, no one has ever been injured by one of my storms, no property damaged aside from that one tree. But knowing that I could have killed Rhys, and done it on the night before he rescued Aria...

"It's OK, babe." I cringe at how easily he uses that term of endearment, after all we've been through, everything that's still unresolved. "No harm done. And — hey — it's ironic, isn't it? That the poet can't make words when she's upset but makes storms instead..."

Yeah. Ironic. It makes me wonder whether I'm asking too much of myself, trying to be in a relationship at all.

CHAPTER 64

TALK TO ME

Rhys

The blood drains from Lyric's face.

I get it. This "We need to talk" stuff is scary. But there's no denying it. I have no idea where Lyric and I stand now, other than in her living room. I'm on the inside on this incredible secret about Aria, about Lyric's father. But does that mean I'm back on the inside of Lyric's life, the kids' lives? She's trusting me with this secret, but does she trust me enough to have me in her life, in her heart?

Maybe she needs to know that it's not just me she's trusting.

"I need to explain to you why I mailed the poem."

"I know — you thought I'd miss the deadline if you didn't, and you liked the poem, as ridiculous as it was." That explanation doesn't satisfy her. I know that now.

"I need you to know I wouldn't do anything that I thought would hurt you or the kids — ever."

"It's not about what you thought would hurt, Rhys. You are so impulsive — mailing that without telling me, spouting off at the press about me being a witch, telling them you're quitting the band."

"I *am* quitting the band."

"See! This is what I mean! You can't quit. I won't let you."

"I'll tell you same thing I told the guys — how are you going to make me not quit? You already broke things off with me!"

She frowns, because she knows I'm right.

"I'll come back to that," I say, "because nothing is getting me off track from telling you why I mailed them your ode to my butt. Because I know you won't forgive me until you understand why. I know you won't trust me again until you know I had a better reason than just being impulsive!"

"Fine. What was your reason? Why should I trust you again after that?" Her arms are crossed. Mom said that's a sign she's closed off, that she's already made up her mind.

"Because you trust your goddess, and She's why I mailed it."

"What?"

Tell her.

It's not Adam. It's Her again. I trusted Her once, and it got me in huge trouble. My girlfriend is still upset with me. For doing what this goddess told me. Do I trust her again, or is Lyric going to think I'm making things up when I tell her what actually happened?

"I asked you what She was in charge of, remember? And you told me She was a goddess of poetry. And the poem was sitting right there, next to that statue on your altar, and it seemed like I should make sure it got seen. So I mailed it."

"You shouldn't have done that. Not without asking me first."

Ordinarily, she'd have a point. But I had divine instructions to follow.

"I was acting on orders."

"What? What are you talking about, Rhys? Whose orders?"

"Hers."

Lyric

"Hers' who? Mom?" It would be just like Iris to interfere like that. She still thinks I should have taken a spot with the philharmonic or become a studio musician.

"No — Hers!" he says again, like that explains anything better than it did a minute ago. "Brighid's," he says when I don't respond.

Well, Brighid is wise, and a fellow priestess, but I'm not sure I like her overriding what I would have wanted if Rhys had just asked me.

"You texted her when all you had to do was ask me from the next room?"

"What?" Now Rhys looks confused. "Oh! No! I don't mean Hunt's Brighid. I mean yours!"

My Brighid... Oh!

"Rhys — tell me what you mean. Exactly."

"She spoke to me, when I was in your altar room."

"She spoke to you... Like Adam did?"

"Exactly! Except it wasn't head-dude's 'voice' — it was warm and female and... very insistent."

Huh. Well, that's a first. She never spoke to Adam. Though I guess She has spoken to Hunter... Maybe not a first, then.

What is going on here? And why is it creating so much chaos in my life, in our lives?

"I just did what She told me to," he says.

I want to stay mad at him, but I find my anger slipping away. I'm not sure what I'd have done in his shoes, with a strange voice inside my head insisting I do something I wasn't sure was a good idea. If I'd let him explain that night, would it have changed things?

And then I remember what happened after I kicked him out.

He's asked Roger and Kirk several times to deliver me messages on his behalf, to say he'd never have purposefully hurt me or the kids. But the reality is that his lack of a filter is why I no longer have a job, regardless of what the board would admit. His instinct is to throw himself into a stormy sea to save my child from drowning, without a second thought as to his own safety. But left to his own devices with a posse of paparazzi, he destroys the only security I had to keep us all safe and comfortable. And then he'll take off on tour, and I'll be left here, alone again, to figure out how to make my life work again. I... I can't do this.

"Do you forgive me, now that you know?" he asks, the look on his face so simultaneously hopeful and fearful that I nearly break.

But I'm the mom here. I've got two kids to take care of. Not just me. And not just a rockstar who'll find a new girl at the first truck stop their tour bus stops at.

That's not fair, Lyric.

Maybe Vivienne's right. But the facts remain. I'm the one who has to rebuild a life for me and my kids.

"I do forgive you for mailing the poem, Rhys. But I can't ignore what's happened since then. I can't have someone in our lives who creates chaos like this. I have no idea how I'm going to pay for our groceries next week, or the electric bill the week after that…"

"I told you I'd take care of that."

"I know. But I can't let you. I need stability, for me and the kids. And it's been anything but stable around here since you showed up. I can't rely on you for that stability. That's not who you are. You're like a storm, Rhys — a storm blowing through my ordered life."

"Lyric… Please."

"Rhys — I need some time to think. Can you give me that, please?"

His face falls, and again I'm tempted to just put this all behind us. But I've got more to worry about than just him and me.

"Sure, Lyric. I'll wait for you," he says with a sigh, looking deep in my eyes. "I'll wait until you're ready. But there's one thing I want you to think about, while you're thinking: Storms don't just disrupt — sometimes they clear away obstacles."

He leans in and kisses my hair. And then he gets up and walks out the door, closing it gently behind him.

For once, there's silence in my head. No ghosts, no spirit of my late husband, no goddess. Just me and my thoughts. Only now that I've asked for time to think, my mind is blank. And for just a moment, in that silence, I find myself missing the storm that is Rhys "The Madman" Madigan.

CHAPTER 65

SISTERS OF THE MOON

Lyric
The next day

There's a fervent knocking on the front door. For a moment, I panic, wondering what has stirred up our security team enough that they're pounding on the door like that. I'm just glad the kids are upstairs playing, so I don't have to keep them out of the chaos.

"Lyric — open up!" Brighid shouts urgently.

I jump up and open the door for her.

"Some weather, huh? A nor'easter during hurricane season? Weird," she says, apparently none the wiser that I've probably had a hand in making this storm worse than it otherwise would have been. Fine — not *probably*. But she doesn't know that. "They said the system's stalled just off the coast, so it just keeps pushing the water into the bay, eating up the beach and dumping water everywhere."

Stalled. Just like I am. Trying to make decisions that will impact all of our lives. And making a mess of everything until I do.

"I had to wade through a foot of water to get over here," she says. "The street was too flooded to take the car out, so I just hiked up my skirt..." She drops her sandals into the tray by the door. While her feet are wet, the shoes are dry. "And hoofed it. The only thing that's passable right now is the highway. I just had Molly close up shop for the day. It's crazy out there! I'm starting to wonder if we should get the circle together to try to break it up a bit."

I dodge eye contact, hoping it doesn't come off as a sign of my guilt.

"Is that why you came over? To talk to me about the weather?" I ask, hoping it doesn't come off as hostile.

Defensive much?

Not now, Annie.

"What?" Brighid looks confused. Did I say that out loud? "No," she says, shaking her head. "Siren's Song called a press conference." She pulls her tablet from the bag she's got stashed under her poncho and holding it up. "Melanie just messaged me with a heads-up. I guess it was spur-of-the-moment."

I glance back outside, expecting to see at least Hunter, and maybe Rhys.

"The guys are hunkered down at the studio," she says, her look reproving, "so you're probably safe if you're still dodging Rhys. I sent Hunt a text about the press conference. But if they're recording, they probably won't know for a while. The security guys will only interrupt them in the studio if it's an emergency."

She hangs up her poncho and sits down on the sofa, and I join her. What exactly does their label CEO have in mind to say, given Rhys' threat to quit the band? Please don't let it be that she's letting him quit because he's caused too much trouble. I could never forgive myself.

The rain pours down harder outside, and I'm ready to invite Roger in, even though he keeps telling me he's fine on the porch.

But Brighid clicks on the play button for what's listed as an upcoming live event, and a pre-recorded intro starts playing, displaying still images with a reporter's voiceover.

"The latest news coming out of the little town of Mystic Beach, Delaware, has the music world in an uproar, as aMUSEd drummer Rhys Madigan says he'll quit the band unless the media backs off its intense coverage of his relationship with local music teacher Lyric Larson, whose religious beliefs — and those of his aMUSEd bandmate Hunter Graves' fiancée, Brighid Weaver — have been at the center of this local and international firestorm."

Brighid and I exchange a look and a frown.

"And now we'll take you live to New York, where the band's label has called a press conference."

Then the pre-recorded footage cuts to live video of a podium with the Siren's Song Records logo behind it. There's a murmur of noise as the reporters talk to each other, but no sign of anyone else in the room. Then, a door opens and Marina Matthews walks in, stepping up behind the podium, with Gryffin and another man flanking her on either side.

"Siren's Song Records wants to make it very clear that we stand behind aMUSEd and its members, and their families," she says. No preamble, no introduction. Not that she needs one. "That includes Rhys and Lyric, as well as Hunter and Brighid," she says, her tone matter-of-fact. "We have no desire to have any of the band's members quit over how the media has handled coverage of their personal lives. We stood behind Hunter and Brighid when Hunter revealed some deeply personal information about his childhood, as well as when Brighid was targeted in social media. And we stand behind all of them now, with this strange fixation on the ladies' religious beliefs."

A look of consternation crosses her face.

"Based on the information we have, we suspect Lyric was targeted for persecution over her beliefs, and we have offered to cover the cost of litigation should she choose to pursue a legal avenue with her employer."

Brighid glances over at me, but I just shake my head.

"You don't have any concerns about your artists being involved with witches?" someone shouts at the label CEO from behind the camera. Light from camera flashes glares in her reading glasses.

"Siren's Song was founded in the United States, and we, in turn, have a deep allegiance to the founding principles of this nation — particularly the First Amendment. That amendment not only guarantees our artists the right to record the music they create, but also their significant others, and everyone else, the right to their religious beliefs. We trust in our artists' fans to agree with those principles, and based on their response to Rhys' request, the vast bulk of them do. And if any of them do not, we'd suggest they may want to listen to another band, because the band, their management and this label are in absolute agreement on this point."

"Marina — are you a witch?"

There's stunned silence in the room, followed by a low rumble of murmuring that grows and then fades when there's no reply.

Marina takes off her glasses, her expression icy.

"If I was, do you really think your best move would be calling me out during a press conference?" she asks pointedly. "Best case, if I were to answer your question, you'd have lost any exclusivity, wouldn't you? And worst case, Andrew..." she adds, drawling the name slowly. "If I was the thing so many people claim to fear in persecuting these two women, you'd be a prime target for a pin in a poppet, wouldn't you?"

The murmuring in the press room erupts again.

"Did she just threaten that guy with a voodoo doll?" I ask Brighid. She nods eagerly.

"As it stands... Mr. Gryffin, if you'd reclaim Andrew's press credentials, please."

Gryff moves from her side and into the crowd of reporters.

"Since it's obvious that some of you haven't yet fully understood my position on this issue, I'll make it very clear: From this point forward, any publication or member of the media who feels it necessary to raise in a negative manner the issue of the faith of any artist on my label, or their family members, will have their access to our artists withdrawn. If your position is that they are not entitled to practice their faith in peace, then Siren's Song's position will be that you're not entitled to your position as a member of the free press."

And Marina Matthews turns and walks out the door.

"Whoa," Brighid says.

"Yeah," I agree. "The woman is a force of nature." And I think I have the right to be the judge of that. "Are you sure she isn't one of us?"

"I don't think so," Brighid says, "but I'm glad she's at least on our side." She looks over at me, acting hesitant. "So, are you going to sue the school district? The band will pay for the lawyers."

"No. There's no point. They've covered their asses sufficiently to get away with it, even if we all know it was discrimination."

"Part of me wants you to sue their asses off anyway, but I get why you wouldn't want to."

"It won't do any good. I'm just going to have to find another job."

"You think you can do that now?"

"I have no idea. I'm going to have to find some more students, find some way to make ends meet. Somehow."

The next day

Brighid: *Meet me at the shop in an hour.*

Lyric: *Why?*

Brighid: *Because I said so?*

Lyric: *Bridge — I'm not really in the mood. I don't want to leave the house. And you're not my mother or my high-priestess, so you can't make me.*

Brighid: *It was worth a shot. Why didn't I agree to make it official when you and Amber refused to take the lead?*

Lyric: *Because you like a challenge, and there's nothing more challenging than herding cats — unless it's managing a circle of miscellaneous solitary witches after you've purposefully rejected a central leadership model.*

Brighid: *Right. Remind me to talk to my therapist about that.*

Lyric: *You're seeing a therapist?*

Brighid: *Long story. Indirectly Hunter-related. Let me try again: Because She said so?*

Lyric: *Did She?*

Brighid: *Yeah, I think She did.*

I stomp my feet on the mat at the back door to Brighid's shop and drop my umbrella in the stand with several others. Witches don't really melt when we get wet — especially not weather-witches — but it's pouring cats and dogs out, still mirroring my mood two days after I got fired.

"Where's your detail?" Brighid asks.

"Roger agreed to stay in the car, since he could see me from his parking spot." Nevermind that the only reason he got a spot that close was because downtown is deserted with all this rain. Another wave of guilt washes over me. "So what's the big rush in me getting over here?" I ask as she re-locks the back door behind me. "I had to have Mom come over to watch the kids. Not that she'd complain. Except she did. I interrupted her date."

"Iris is dating?" Brighid asks, looking a little dumbfounded.

"She won't tell me who. But I told her you wanted me down here, and she dropped everything. So why did you need me down here?"

"Come with me," she says, dragging me toward the front of the shop.

She pulls me into the back room, where I realize she's managed to, somehow, on this short a notice, assemble most of our informal circle. Amber is notably absent, and I glance in the direction of her shop, even though I can't see it from inside.

"She didn't answer my texts," Brighid says, sighing and answering the question I didn't ask out loud. "It's late enough she should be closed, but..."

"She's been staying open late for a month now," Siobhan says. "She's been open every night I've had a late client, but she's usually gone before I close up, or I'd have talked to her about it already."

"Cam said things are tight, since she hasn't been making as many of her custom pieces and the shop was closed so far into the season..." Brighid adds. "I think she's trying to catch any late tourist traffic. Not that there's much tonight anyway..."

"Is the shop in trouble?" I ask. I haven't talked to Amber in weeks, and it's been a month or two since I last saw her. If life wasn't as crazy as it is right now, I'd be planning an intervention. Wait — is that what this is? Is this my intervention?

"I'm not sure how bad it is," Brighid says. "Maybe. Cam was reluctant to tell me anything at all."

I file that away. If I can get through this upheaval in my own life, Amber is first on my list of things that need attention.

"So, why are we here?"

"Because we're witches, and there's no reason things should be as messed up in our lives as they are right now while we've got a breath left to chant a word or a candle left to burn. Or so Mrs. Lowell reminded me earlier."

"Mrs. Lowell?"

"Weirdest thing. She took her package, said goodbye and started to leave, then turned back around, patted me on the hand and gave me a stern look. She reminded me that, as much as I'm a priestess first, I'm still a witch, and that I need to either take matters into my capable hands 'or hand off the broom to someone who'll fly it up those haters' posteriors.' Her words, not mine." She chuckles.

Well, that's unexpected.

"I'm starting to wonder if she's a little more witchy than she's let on," Brighid says. "Usually, it's just yarn, tea and crystals with her... maybe a tarot reading... Hmm... Anyway — she was right, and I was also reminded recently that Herself takes an active hand in the lives of Her priestesses. So, it's about time we asked Her for help, with some extra umph," she adds, gesturing at our assembled friends and the center of the room, where the table has been cleared away and candles placed at four compass points.

Alrighty, then. Magic it is.

Even with nearly a dozen of us involved, ritual still amounts mostly to lighting candles, chanting, walking in a circle, invoking a god or two, then some singing... You get the idea. No demons appearing in a cloud of smoke, asking me to sign a contract in blood. No human or animal sacrifices. (Yuck!) And the only darkness invoked is the tray of dark-chocolate brownies someone brought to help every ground themselves back in physical reality after we we're done.

"We've got your backs, you two," Stevie says, gathering up her purse and her camera bag. I guess Brighid caught her on the way to, or from, a shoot. "Anything you need, just ask. We can't let this kind of bigotry go unchallenged."

I think that's more than Stevie's said at any of our circles in the last year. She's normally quite shy, reserved. I guess she's pretty indignant about all of what's happened to us. Either that, or the fuss over Declan and Callie's second infamous photo has forced her, as the photographer, to come out of her shell.

She looks thoughtful, as if she's debating something, then snatches up one of the remaining brownies.

"Thanks, Stevie. We appreciate it!" I tell her.

Brighid lets her out through the back door, giving Roger a nod as she relocks it with just the two of us inside.

Everyone else left in ones and twos, spaced out across half an hour, like a reverse Noah's ark, while those who remained cleaned up and set the back room to rights as Brighid's counseling and tarot reading space. Now, the two of us take one last look around the room, my glance catching on the statue of the goddess that's nearly identical to the one on my altar at home. Her namesake's eyes rest on the statue as well, before turning to meet mine.

"She'll make it right. There's no telling how, but She won't let her priestesses struggle alone. There's a purpose to things. There always is," she says, sounding quite confident.

I'm inclined to believe her, though there's no concrete reason why I should. It's just knowing how reliable Brighid's intuition has been since the day we met. Amber and I have come to rely on it. Or, we had. I glance back in the direction of the jewelry shop.

"There's more going on with her than she's let anyone know," Brighid says. "It's not just you or me, or the Circle. But something's got to break soon."

"I just hope it isn't Amber," I tell her. "She's been through enough already."

"I think we all have," Brighid says, squeezing my hand. "But it'll all work out in the end."

Somehow, I can almost believe that when she says it, too.

CHAPTER 66
BIRD IN FLIGHT

Lyric
The next morning

The phone rings. I don't even get the chance to say, "Hello."

"Meet me at the coffee shop across from the school."

"Brighid? Why? What's going on?"

"You have to see it to believe it. I'm not sure I do, and I'm standing here, with a croissant in one hand and Hunt's hot chocolate, which I'm drinking, for some unknown reason. I'm going to have to buy him another. Just get over here!"

Kirk and Roger left ten minutes ago to take the kids to school. Aria probably just got to the cafetorium, with Roger in tow. Kirk and Tommy won't be at Tommy's school for another ten minutes at least.

I quickly change out of my pajamas and into a clean tank top and a skirt just short of knee-length — neither of which I could ever have worn to work. But I'm unemployed now. I can wear whatever I like. I grin wryly, full of gallows humor, but it's a grin. That's progress, right there, that I can grin at all. I'm sure it's a coincidence that the rain's finally stopped.

Ten minutes later, I hit slow traffic that's more than the usual morning drop-off line impacting the main street in front of the school. I pull into the coffeeshop parking lot and spot Brighid standing on the sidewalk, leaning back on the hood of her old SUV. Before I can even get to her, I see exactly what's causing the traffic slowdown. It's not a pack of paparazzi, though I can see the photographer from the Mystic Beacon shooting photos.

His nominal peers seem to have abandoned their station at the school, now that I've been fired.

And that... that seems to be the root cause of this disturbance. Me. Because there's a protest going on in front of the school. My jaw drops as I recognize Patty and about a dozen of my other now-former co-workers, all dressed up with pointy witch hats, like it's Halloween. Only it's weeks early for that.

Patty waves exuberantly at me as I come up alongside Brighid, who hands me half a croissant.

"Justice for Lyric! Save the First Amendment!" Patty chants, encouraging everyone else in the group to join her. Soon, the sound drowns out the noise of passing cars.

"Holy Mother Goddess Brighid!" That's all I've got. Brighid chuckles at me as a marvel at the scene in front of us.

"You want to go join them?" she asks.

"I can't. I'm not permitted on school property except as relates to Aria."

"Right." Brighid chuckles. "You think we should tell them that we don't divide ourselves up into houses?" she asks, nodding at the crested robes a few of them are wearing. Not at all something I'd sport.

"I'm more worried that they're going to get themselves fired than about inaccurate representation."

"They can't fire them," she says. "I asked while I was waiting for you to get here. The ringleader there—"

"Patty."

"Patty said they checked with the district and they're allowed to protest out front as long as it's before school starts and their duties are covered."

Wow. They actually organized a protest on my behalf.

Those last few days at work, it was so easy to focus on the people laughing at my beliefs or hostile because of their misconceptions about them. I seem to have missed the supporters I did have, until it was too late.

Lyric: *You didn't have to do this. It won't change anything, except get you in trouble with the district.*

Patty stops and pulls out her phone, glancing at me across the busy street.

Patty: *We more than owed it to you. If we'd spoken up sooner, maybe we could have prevented this. Either way, it was a matter of principle. And there would be more of us out here, except somebody had to answer the phone in the office and keep an eye on the kids. We all want you to come back. Most of the parents, too.*

Lyric: *But not all of them.*

Patty: *No. But most. We've delivered a petition to the district, to have you reinstated.*

Lyric: *Wow. Thank you. But I think we all know it's too late. They wanted me gone. And they had their excuses to blame it on. Even the union lawyer told me they couldn't do much.*

Patty's shoulders visibly slump.

Patty: *We could still try.*

I sigh, thinking about all that's happened before I reply.

Lyric: *I'm not sure anymore that I'd want to come back, knowing that some people don't want me there. I'd be watching myself every moment, scrutinizing every word people said to me. It would take a lot of the joy out of the job.*

Patty: *So, what are you going to do? Run off with your rockstar?*

That's the thing. I don't know. I have no idea what I'm going to do. For the first time that I can recall, I have no idea what I'm going to do. My life, while stressful in recent years, has been so carefully ordered. It's the only way I could make it all work. But now, that life I've been clinging to since Adam died — it's been completely upended, the pieces swept from the game board. Am I even still playing with the same rules?

Storms don't just disrupt — sometimes they clear away obstacles.

It's Rhys' voice in my head this time, not Adam or even one of the others. But there's a gravity laid over it, a familiar sense of calm certainty. And they all seem to have been telling me the same thing, now that I think about it: From this moment onward, there's nothing holding me back. All the choices are mine to make.

Rhys
Later that night

I'm standing on Lyric's porch, once again hesitating to knock. Geordi's trying really hard to pretend he's not watching me do it, but I catch him looking when I glance over, hoping for... what? Encouragement? Permission?

I have permission. Lyric invited me over to finish our "talk." Yeah, I still don't like that. There needs to be a better word for "I have something important to say to you" versus "I'm going to rip your heart out using words." But I guess if anyone's going to use words to rip my heart out, it's probably better if it's a poet

— the word-user's equivalent of a surgeon, as opposed to some unqualified stranger trying to do it with a spoon.

The door suddenly opens in front of me, and I'm caught up in a whirlwind of trepidation and relief.

"Hi," Lyric says.

"Hi," I repeat, still frozen in my Chucks.

"Come in, Rhys," she says. "The kids are with Mom."

Part of my brain instantly wonders whether Iris is keeping Tommy and Aria overnight. But that's too much to hope for, I know. I've experienced a lot of unbelievable things in the last few weeks, but sweeping all of this mess behind us in one evening and waking up with Lyric in my arms would be more of a miracle than I can even ask for. Even if what started it all was me following the bad advice of a goddess.

You kind of owe me a favor, you know? I think at Her, just in case She's listening.

Lyric gestures at the sofa, and I sit down, counting every millimeter between us as she sits carefully on the other end. My arms are long. I could reach her across that space, pull her in for the hug I feel like we both need. But I don't. I promised I'd wait. The only reason I've managed it this long is because I've been playing Adam's "Lullaby" and my drum solo on constant repeat whenever I'm awake. The guys are getting a little irked about it, actually.

"Rhys?"

"Hmm?"

"I asked if you wanted something to drink."

She did?

"Uh, no. I'm fine. Sorry — I got caught up in an inner dialogue."

"Adam?"

"Oh — no. Sorry. Haven't heard from him since the other day. No — I just meant thinking. There's usually six or eight trains of thought running in my brain at any given moment, you know."

She smiles gently.

"I do."

Yeah. I like that about her, that she gets me like that, doesn't seem to judge me for it. Just for telling everyone she's a witch, and mailing her poetry in...

"Rhys, you apologized the other day. And I have to apologize to you, too — I'm really sorry I almost electrocuted you."

Her expression is serious, but I can't help it. I laugh.

"Just don't it again," I tell her. "Once might be accidental, but the next time, I'm going to take it personally."

Now *she* laughs. Good.

"And I forgive you — for mailing in the fellowship application with the extra poem, I mean."

"Oh, thank god! Uh... goddess... Um..."

She chuckles.

"It's fine. You're fine," she says. "I know that had to have been a really strange experience for you."

"Strange? No, not really. I mean, I already had a ghost hanging out in my head."

"True."

"I just want you to know I didn't mean to take that out of your hands, that decision. I just..."

"You just had someone else take it out of your hands first."

"Yeah. Exactly."

The silence stretches uncomfortably. I'm not sure what to do about it. Silence isn't my natural environment. Is that it? Are we all fixed now? Is she really forgiving me for outing her, too?

I stretch my arms out to hug her, and she leans in, letting me, but not settling into my arms like before. It makes me nervous. Maybe I need to assure her what I did also won't happen again.

"How about this: next time something like that happens, I'll ask you before I mail the sexy poem about my butt." I smile at her, pressing my lips to her forehead and praying really hard at whichever god, goddess, spirit or ghost cares to listen, that she's truly forgiven me.

"You really liked it?" she asks, seeming a little unsure of herself.

"I loved it. I think you've got an amazing ass, too." I smirk at her, sliding my hands down to cup said ass.

"Yours is better."

"Maybe. But I climb a lot. It's hard to beat that."

She chuckles. She smiles. That's better. She rolls her eyes. Less better, but not bad.

"Fine. But don't do it again, OK? Don't do or say anything that's going to end up with me getting humiliated more than I already am. Even if it is anonymous. OK?"

"I'll do my best," I assure her. "I'm..."

"Neuro-spicy. I know," she says, scooting closer. She takes a deep breath. "Rhys — I know you didn't mean to cause problems, with the poem or with the media. And I'd like to just put it all behind us and move forward. That's been my goal lately — really, finally, moving forward. But I can't deal with this negative, invasive media attention — and I can't put the kids through that, either."

"I know. And I meant it — I'm quitting if things don't change with how they're treating you and the kids. If I have to choose between you three and the band, there's no contest."

Lyric

"**I** can't let you do that. And I mean *that*." I'm not sure how I'll keep him from quitting, but that's a non-starter. If I have to kick him out now, just to show him I mean it, I'll do it.

"What if we can find a compromise?" he suggests. "I mean, it seems like the press backed off after my appeal to the fans."

"And Marina's threats..." I remind him. I'm guessing it was probably more that than sweet Rhys trying to leverage the band's fans.

"Maybe we promise them an interview — just one, with you and me, or just me, if you want?"

The mere idea of sitting in a room with a reporter, a TV camera... I shudder.

"I'm not really comfortable in the spotlight."

"Then that's fine. I'll do it myself, and they have to agree to leave you alone. Maybe I give them an exclusive on the Cock Sock..."

Well, I'm doubtful they'll take him up on that exclusive. Otherwise, that doesn't sound too bad, but I'm not sure Rhys can make it happen.

"Best-case scenario: What happens if they do back off and leave us alone? You're still leaving in a month or two, and I'm going to have to find another job."

It's going to be weird taking Aria to school when I'm no longer a teacher there. I've been spared that so far, just because the kids and I have bodyguards who have been doing it. And that's not going to continue after Rhys leaves Mystic Beach, I'm sure.

Of course, this all assumes I can make ends meet somehow without selling the house and moving us into an apartment. Rory spends so much time at Rónan's now. I wonder if she'd let us move back in with rent at less than market value...

"I'm working on getting some income for you and the kids, from Adam's song."

Well, that's a nice thought. But I know song royalties are minuscule these days, especially for streaming. Even if a major artist picked up Adam's song, those royalties might cover our monthly internet bill.

"Thank you, but I doubt that'll make ends meet, even if I keep teaching private students."

Rhys takes my hands in his, shaking them to get my attention.

"Lyric — you don't have to work. I'll take care of you and the kids."

Even the idea of not working, of letting Rhys take care of the bills... No. Just no. It feels wrong. The only person I know I can rely on is me. I learned that the hard way.

"I can't do that. They're my kids, and I have to take care of them."

"I was hoping you were open to letting me be part of your family, too."

My breath catches. Not too long ago the idea of us as Family Unit 2.0 was at the forefront of my mind. Then our lives got turned upside-down. And nothing was certain anymore.

"I am... I'm trying, at least."

"Are you so determined to take care of the kids by yourself that you won't let me help? Money is the easy part. I've got tons of it."

"I don't want your money, Rhys. I just want to be able to provide for my kids."

"And it's my fault you can't do that. So I'm going to take responsibility for that. Until you get another job, I'll make up the difference."

"It's not your fault, Rhys. I made the decisions I made, the mistakes I made. They didn't fire me because I'm dating a rockstar.

They didn't even fire me because I'm a witch. They fired me because I slipped and broke rules."

"We both know that's not true." He flaps his hands in frustration, frowning at me. "It may be what they said. And it may be what they'll tell the judge when you sue them for religious discrimination, but it's not the truth."

"I don't even know anymore. And I'm not sure I even care. It's not like I could go back even if I got reinstated. Half the board's hostile toward me. I'd be watching my back every minute of every day. And some of the parents aren't comfortable with me teaching their kids."

"They're idiots. You're a wonderful teacher, and they all knew that, until I gave them a reason to show their bigotry. So, yes, I'm going to help you out. But, really..." He takes my hands between his again. "What I'd like to have happen is you and the kids come on the road with us."

"That's crazy. Two kids — one autistic — on the road with a rock band?"

"Hunt's already planning on getting a custom tour bus so Brighid can come on the road with us, and their kids when they have them. He showed me some of the designs they have — it's like a giant RV, with multiple bedrooms, living room, kitchen. Basically, an apartment on wheels. Dave's warming up to the idea, too. We could have three, four buses, with all our families with us, and the single guys can have more room and privacy on their own bus."

Rhys is offering us a life with him — but is it a kind of life I want for me and the kids?

"Come on, Lyric — give this a chance. This way, I can keep touring, making music, and we can all be together. And we set boundaries — the press leaves us alone when we're here, at home."

Home? Here? Rhys is already calling Mystic Beach — this house — home?

When I opened the door tonight, to my home, I was prepared to welcome Rhys back into my life, if we can just find a way to make it work for all of us. But getting down to the nuts and bolts of it... It's more than I can handle thinking about right now.

"I need to think about it, Rhys. This isn't something I was even contemplating when I asked you over tonight. This is a huge decision, and it doesn't just affect me. The kids..."

"You and the kids are my top priority, whatever you decide, Lyric. I need you to understand that. But I think we have some room for compromise — a middle road where we can be a family, here and on the road. And that's what I want — for the four of us to be a family."

"You're not... You're not going to..." I can't even say the words. Even with everything else we're discussing, it's too soon for that.

"Ask you to marry me? No." He gives me a wry grin. "Not yet, anyway. Can't say I dislike the idea, though," he says, pulling me close and kissing my forehead. "Does that bother you? I know it's too soon."

"It is," I agree, sighing in relief. With Rhys' impulsiveness, you never know.

"We're on the same page, then. Good," he says. "Unless you don't like the idea at all."

He looks uncertain now. But this is one thing I am certain about.

"I don't dislike the idea, either," I tell him with a smile. "I just need more time to figure things out."

"I'm working on being patient," he says. "You've been pretty patient with me. I figure I owe you that much."

"It's not a matter of being patient with you, Rhys. It's just getting used to you, and all the things that have changed in my life."

"We can make this work, Lyric. I know we can. We'll find a way. Love always finds a way."

CHAPTER 67
MY BODY

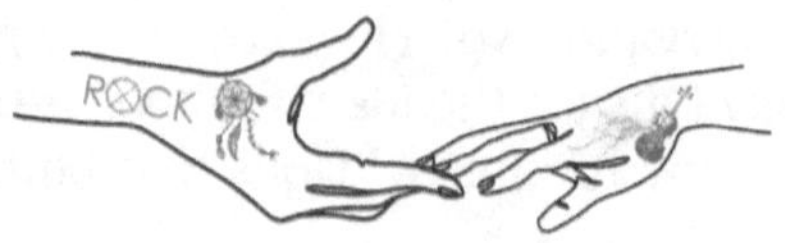

Rhys

Lyric's expression gets serious. Did I ruin things already? Did I push her too hard, too fast, by talking about love? I thought we were both on the same page there, but maybe not...

"Rhys?" she asks. "What you said the other night, about storms clearing obstacles?"

"I said that? Sounds amazingly profound for a goofy drummer-type whose brain doesn't always stay on track."

"Rhys — don't knock yourself. Even in jest. We both know better than that," she says, cupping my cheek with her hand.

I lay my hand over hers, enjoying the feeling of skin on skin. I've missed this, too.

"I have my moments," I admit.

"Well, that was one of them. It stuck with me. And it made me realize that I've been holding myself back. I took the life I had, and I made it into a cage — a cage that kept me safe, kept the kids safe... but..."

"The white bird needs to fly?"

"Yeah. I've been withering away, without even realizing it. Until you came around."

"And blew your cage door right off the hinges."

"And then some," she agrees.

"Is that a good thing?"

She's thoughtful, like I try to be these days.

"Let me get my wings under me. Once I do that, I'll know if it's time for me to fly."

"I can do that." I kiss her on her hair again. Man, I missed those hair-kisses. And the others... Speaking of which... "I know I'm pushing the envelope here, right after I said I'd be patient... But... I've really missed you. And uh... the kids..." I give Lyric a hopeful grin.

"Staying at the loft with Mom tonight," she replies, giving me a grin of her own that's more seductive than hopeful.

"Do I thank Brighid for that? Either of them?"

"No. Thank me, and Mom. Especially after I already interrupted one of her dates this week so she could watch the kids for me."

"I'll have Billy send her a gift basket. No, two. One for her date."

Lyric chuckles. It's the best thing I've ever heard.

I pull her hard against me, tipping her head back to taste her mouth. I lick at the seam of her lips, and she opens to me, our tongues tangling together.

"There's my hungry girl."

She pauses, for just a second, a bit of mischief glinting in her eyes. I recognize that expression. The face I usually see it on is my own. I like seeing her let go enough to feel mischievous.

She drops down, undoing my shorts, yanking them and my boxers straight to my feet.

"You don't have to do that, Lyric — I'm the one who needs to make up for flibberti—" The word turns into a moan as she envelops me with her warm mouth, coating me in saliva. "Oh, god... Yessss..."

I grasp her head gently between my hands, guiding her as she wraps a hand around the root of me, pulling me tight with an arm around my thigh. She works me hard, licking at my head, sucking as she pulls back along my length.

In the short time we've been together, she's learned my body well. She knows the little touches that drive me crazy. I find myself clamping my hands harder around her head and force myself to relax, let her set the pace. I don't want to fuck her face, as tempting as it is. I want this to be her show, where I follow along with her rhythm for once, rather than leading. I settle in for the ride.

It's a short one, but better than any rollercoaster or parachute ride I've ever had. She teases me, bringing me to the edge. The tingling in my spine threatens to break like a wave on the beach. She pulls back, running her tongue along the ridge on the underside of my cock. I relax for a moment, until she dips her tongue into the hollow at the tip.

"Fuucckk."

She pulls off again, sitting back on her heels and looking up at me, her expression amused.

"Flibbertigibbets," I correct myself.

"I think you had it right the first time," she says.

She sucks me back in, stroking along my root again, reaching back to press into that one amazing spot right behind it.

"Fuuucckk."

I can feel her smile around me, but she doesn't let up with the suction or stroking, and the pressure only increases. That tingle ramps up higher than I can ever remember it getting. My knees bend just a fraction.

"Lyr — careful... I..."

She sucks harder, presses harder, and I have no choice but to let go, pouring out my release into her mouth.

I'm blind with the sensations, overwhelmed. I can feel her soft hair tangled in my fingers, her lips sealed around me, the pull of her mouth, and... a swallow. She's swallowed me down.

My eyes peek open, looking down at her head still cradled in my hands as she releases me and leans back again. The finger that was pressed into my perineum swipes across her lips and catches a stray dab of semen. She licks it off her fingertip, looking satisfied.

Holy... flibbertigibbets.

And that's it. I can't take it, standing there, looking down at her, her sweet, sexy face having just sucked me off like a champ.

"Sexy mama," I tell her, grabbing her under her arms and lifting her up. She wraps her legs around my waist, like she did that day in the shower, now clearly more confident that I can pick her curvy ass up. I step free of my shorts and boxers, and carry her into her bedroom, dropping her down on the edge of the bed.

"Rhys — you can't be ready to... I mean..."

"Give me ten. In the meantime, turnabout is fair play, and I'm overdue for some playtime with you, Lyric."

Lyric

Rhys wastes no time, pushing my skirts up around my thighs and then sliding my panties off, settling on his knees at the end of the bed. He pulls me close to the edge of the mattress and leans in, setting his cheek atop my mound, dropping kisses along the flesh of my inner thigh, inhaling deeply.

I practically come on the spot, watching his expression as he savors the scent of me.

His tongue darts out between his lips, tracing a path back along my thigh to the center of me.

"Mmmm..." he moans, setting off a chain of shivers that runs up my spine. "The only thing sexier than you swallowing my cum is the way you smell, my goddess," he says. "Like flowers and lava and rain on the ocean..."

I chuckle.

"You should take up poetry yourself, Rhys."

"Maybe I will. 'An Ode to Lyric's Sexy Scent,' by Rhys 'The Madman' Madigan."

He takes a deep breath, like he's preparing for oratory, then looks down at my mound, considering.

"Nope. I've got a better use for my mouth than that."

And he dives face-first into my slit, licking me from opening to clit, then sucking that little bundle of nerves into his mouth, just as promised. A moan erupts from me as he flicks it with his tongue while applying suction with his lips. I was already highly aroused from sucking him off. There's little effort needed on his part to send me over the edge. And he knows that, once again backing off as soon as I near the peak.

"Rhys!"

"Hey — I've got to give myself time to build back up again!" he says, licking his lips. "If I let you go too quickly, I won't be able to slide inside you while you're still coming. And that's what I'm doing this time."

The visual sends another ripple of arousal through me, threatening to tip me over the edge all on its own.

"You like that, huh?" he says, smiling like the cat that ate the canary, or rather the tiger that ate the witch. "Good... We'll get there. In a few minutes..."

He tears his shirt off and tosses it aside, then slides his hands under my ass, pulling my mound to his mouth. He suckles and licks me into a frenzy, so close to coming that I can taste it. My hands contort on the comforter, holding on for dear life as he takes me on this ride, up and down from the peak of perfection. Finally, when frustration and arousal blend into a feeling I can't even put a name to, Rhys slips two fingers inside me, pressing against that spot. I wail as the sensation pushes me over, a careening ride into orgasmic delirium.

It's then that Rhys presses his cock inside, his callused fingers replaced with silky firmness. My muscles clamp down on him in rhythm — a rhythm he mimics with his thrusts. As my spasms begin to slow, he strokes my clit again, and my arousal begins to build once more, watching him, feeling him moving across me, inside me... It translates into a greater need for him.

"Rhys, please!"

"That feel good as good to you as it does to me? You want more?"

I nod fervently, unable to put what I need from him into words.

He strokes inside me, strokes my clit, reaches up for my breast and gives it a squeeze, then the other.

"Oh, yeah. That's it, Lyric. Come for me..."

I'm so close... I can feel my core tightening again, coiling in on itself.

Rhys leans forward, shifting his weight to his hips, pressing himself harder into me, his cock now stroking my G-spot with every movement in and out, faster and faster. His thumb rubs across my clit, and his lips join his other hand on my breasts, leaving little imprints in my flesh. He sucks one nipple into his mouth, squeezing the other breast hard. Then his teeth grab hold, biting lightly. The sensation concentrates in my nipple and in my clit, making me feel like I'm being split in two, erupting in the space between.

For a moment, all I can see is light, behind my eyes, then around Rhys, as he drives himself into me, panting, focused. Then, he freezes, pouring himself inside me. His eyes, closed, slide open again a moment later, lighting on my face. A smile spreads across his visage — warm and sweet, like honey. And he crawls, exhausted, up on the bed, wrapping me in his arms.

"God, you're perfect..." he says on an exhale, snuggling in and kissing my hair. His eyes close again, and he seems to drift off instantly, peacefully asleep.

"You're pretty prefect, too, Rhys... You're pretty perfect, too."

I let my eyes close, pushing away thoughts of important decisions yet to be made, and shroud myself in the peacefulness of Rhys' expression.

CHAPTER 68

MORNING SONG

Lyric
The next morning

We spend the morning together — a leisurely breakfast, a relaxing shower, a couple of hours watching a sweet romcom, followed by making love until both of us pass out from exhaustion.

"I can't wait to wake up with you like this every day," Rhys says when we wake up, snuggling into the pillow and settling me into his arms.

Every day? Isn't he forgetting something? Just like that, it all comes roaring back — the decision I have to make before we can even really decide if we have a future together.

"That's going to be a challenge when you're on the road for nine or ten months..."

He sighs, kisses the top of my head.

"I was hoping you'd decided to come with me."

"You said you would give me some time."

"I did."

I roll my eyes at him, hard.

"What? I just really want you to come with us!"

"On the road?" I scoff. "With two kids? And no job?"

"I thought I was clear that you didn't need to worry about having a job."

"I'm not the sit-at-home and spend-hubby's-money type. If you thought I was, this is definitely moving too fast."

My tone doesn't escape him. He lets go of me, settling one arm behind his head and looking at me askance.

"I never for a moment thought you were, Lyric. But I'm inviting you — you and the kids — to join us on the road. Losing your job wasn't fair, but since you won't let me sic the lawyers on the Gallbladder and his buddies..."

"Galworth," I correct, still put out about his assumption that I'd be willing to live off his money.

"Whatever. The point is you won't let me pay for the lawyers to get you your job back, so I figured we could look at it as a blessing in disguise and plan some time together. Unless you changed your mind and want me to quit the band after all, that means going on the road eventually. And I thought it might be fun, for you and the kids. You talked about not holding yourself back anymore."

"I meant about having a relationship, not going on tour with a rock band!"

"With me, that's kind of the same thing. Or I can quit." He shrugs, like it's no big deal.

"No!" I'm horrified at the idea. But he's right. Unless we're going to accept a relationship that's long-distance more often than it's in-person, either he quits the band or the kids and I go on the road, at least some of the time.

"Lyric — you're going to have to make a decision here. If you won't come on the road with us, I'm going to have to go the alternative-Dave route and find someone to replace me when the guys tour, and that's going to take some time. But I won't leave you here by yourself for most of the year."

"I can handle being on my own! I've been doing it for years!"

"Yes, and you've done an amazing job." He weaves the fingers of his free hand with mine, raising it up to his mouth and kissing it. "But you don't have to do that anymore. It's not what Adam wanted for you and the kids, and it's not what I want for you, and — honestly — I don't think it's what you want for yourself now, is it?"

In my head, I see the open door of a gilded cage, and I imagine that door swinging closed again. It was one thing when the cage was all I had. I'd grown comfortable in its safe confines. But now... now, it feels... confining. But what Rhys is asking me to do... going on the road... It's like taking a step outside the cage and then having the door slam shut behind me. No more safety, no more comfortable norm in easy reach. And that's as terrifying as the idea of having the media constantly peering into my life and that of my kids, as they surely will be if we went on the road with aMUSEd. Panic begins to set in. My pulse roars in my ears. I focus on breathing, trying to slow everything down.

"Lyric — why'd you invite me over here last night?" Rhys asks when his last question goes unanswered. "I mean, if you just missed sexy times, I totally get it. But I'm feeling a little used right now..."

Whoa. Wait. What?

Can't say I blame him, but can't say I blame you, either, girlfriend... Annie's lascivious tone carries over even inside my head.

"No! I... I mean... I guess..."

"Kidding," he says, quirking a smile at me. "Mostly," he adds. "But I was kind of hoping you'd decided to really give us a shot."

"I need more time." That's all I can think to say.

"And I'm rushing you."

"Yeah. You are."

Ouch. Cut the hunk straight to the quick, why don't you?

Not now, Frank!

"Sorry," Rhys says, kissing me on top of my head again. "I'm really not trying to rush you. It's just..."

Patience, child, Vivienne says in my head. *Take a breath. Give yourself a moment, and him. Don't let this become an argument.*

"You need an answer — sooner, rather than later."

"Yeah. I mean, I'm not good with this patience stuff, but I'm trying. The problem is that either way you decide, I've got stuff I need to do. I'd either have to find a replacement drummer so I can stay here or get a bus customized for us. That'll take months."

It's not just neuro-spicy impatience. He's got a practical reason for wanting an answer. I just don't have one to give him.

There's a cloud hanging over us now. It's not his fault, but the mood is ruined. Every time I look at him, every time he touches me, I'm reminded that he's waiting for an answer. And not just an answer, but the one he wants.

"Do you want me to leave? I kind of feel like me hanging out here just feels like I'm pressuring you."

And he's right.

"I think I need some time alone to just think things through."

It was his idea, but his expression falls just the same.

"I'm sorry," I tell him.

"No," he says, shaking his head. "I offered, and I meant it. I don't want you to feel like I'm pressuring you. It's a big decision — one that affects you and the kids. So, I'm going to give you some time, OK?"

I nod, but I'm not sure I'm liking it, now that he's agreed. I missed him. But Mom's got the kids and said she'd keep them for a few days if I wanted. If I'm ever going to have the time to think all of this through, and maybe make some life-altering decisions, it's now.

"You call me if you want to talk or want me to come over — sexy-time or to talk," he says, and the smirk on his face when he says it makes me melt. He kisses my hair again, and then dives in for my lips, in a long, slow, sensuous kiss that makes the melting a bit more literal. His hand travels up my thigh, bunching my skirt up and trailing his rough fingers along the soft skin. "You sure you want me to go?" he says as he finally pulls away, leaving me breathless.

"Not fair," I manage to say after a moment.

"Nope." He grins, unrepentant.

"I'll call you when I have an answer for you." My tone is firm. It has to be. Otherwise, both of us are going to cave.

He sighs.

"I love you, Lyric. Just remember that. While you're thinking, keep that in your heart."

"I will, Rhys. I promise."

Rhys

I double up on beats with my right hand, picking up the missing left-hand beats as I raise my left arm to drag it across my brow, keeping the sweat from dripping into my eyes. I've been drumming for hours now. No idea how many. But it's the best solution I have to keep my mind off Lyric.

OK. Well, that didn't work. Clearly.

Ugh.

"You OK there, Rhys?" Alex asks, leaning back on the open door to the live room.

I look over at the clock. It's late, too late for me to be drumming with the door open if the guys are home. Even if it's just the two of them, now. Kier's super-grumpy even without me keeping him awake. He probably sent Alex down to tell me to knock it off.

"Yeah. I guess. I mean, I'm fine. I just..." I sigh, not knowing where to even begin, except to do the polite thing. "Sorry about keeping you guys up."

"What's up with Lyric?" he asks, not even acknowledging my apology.

"She's thinking."

"About what?"

I hesitate. I haven't even dared ask the guys, even though Hunt and I talked about custom buses.

"About her and the kids coming on the road with us."

Alex tilts his head to one side. Maybe he's doing some thinking himself. Maybe he just thinks I'm nuts and is offended I'd even consider the idea without asking him and the others first.

"Things that serious already?"

"I threatened to quit the band. Well, no — I actually decided to quit. You didn't think I was serious about the girl when I was ready to quit over how she was being treated?"

"It's a different level of serious between you being ready to quit the band and you deciding to co-parent two kids on the road."

Hmm... He might be right about that. It would probably be easier to just hang at Lyric's house with her and the kids, doing fun stuff, knowing I don't have to worry about money. Dealing with the kids on the road, in transit, never sleeping in the same place more than a night or two, Tommy's schedule and his eating habits, Aria's precociousness and her love of the ocean — it reminds me of how Dave's talked about staying here instead of touring — doctors, school... OK. Maybe it's not as simple of a decision as I've been thinking it is. No wonder Lyric needs more time to think it all through. This is a serious decision.

"I guess it is."

"You ready to make that level of commitment to her, and the kids?"

"Yes."

Not a single moment of thought to that answer.

"Then, there you go. But is *she*?"

"I don't know. That's what she's thinking about." I sigh, because now I'm back feeling impatient. I snap out a couple beats on the snare, then cringe. "Sorry — I know I'm probably annoying the shit out of you and Kier."

"Kier's out."

"He is? This late? Looking for a hook-up?" I instantly feel guilty. I've kind of left my best friend hanging since that night Lyric and I met in person. He's overdue for a hook-up, but he's been so off lately, I just assumed he'd be holed up in his room.

"Ink," Alex says, giving a little shrug.

"Ah..." Well, Kier's overdue to for that, too — new ink. He doesn't often go more than a few months without a little something new inked into his skin.

"Oh. OK. You didn't go with him?"

"Wasn't in the mood. And I don't think he wanted me tagging along, either."

"He's been kind of grouchy lately, hasn't he?" But then so has Alex.

"Lots of changes happening. It makes a guy think."

"What's it making you think?"

"That I need a new hobby," he says, grinning wryly.

I open my mouth to suggest a few, but he waves me off.

"So what's Lyric's big objection to going on tour?" he asks, changing the subject pretty firmly. OK.

"She said she wants to earn a living for herself and the kids. She doesn't want to just be there as my girlfriend, in the back of tour photos."

"So, put her in the front of the photos," Alex suggests.

"Well — she's shorter than me, so she'd have to be in front of me in photos... Otherwise, you wouldn't see her at all."

"No — I don't mean literally. I mean, put her work in the forefront — find her a job she can do while we're on tour."

"What kind of job?"

"What's she do? Besides teaching, I mean?"

And a lightbulb goes on over my head.

"Is there a lightbulb over my head?" I ask Alex.

"No. But your eyes just lit up."

"Cool! Must be a good idea, then. I've got to make a call."

"It's 4 a.m., Rhys."

"Yeah... But I've got somebody who takes care of stuff for me 24/7!"

Later that morning

"Y ou want to do this project outside the confines of aMUSEd, Mr. Madigan?"

She sounds skeptical. But I know this will work.

"Yes. I want this to be my project. The guys can play on it if they want. But I want this to be mine."

"And you have all the permissions you need?"

"For the one part, yes. I'll need a little help with the other. But for the first part, I've got a contact who can make things happen."

"Soon?"

"Today."

"Alright, then. I'll leave things in your hands. Let Billy know about anything else you need. I don't want this to interfere with the album, or the tour. Am I understood?"

"Understood. I just need to make one call, and I'll get it in motion."

"Then I'll look forward to hearing the results. I hope they prove as promising as you've suggested."

She hangs up. But that's fine. I need to make that other call. Here's hoping this call goes as smoothly as the last one... A lot rides on all these pieces coming together. Like the parts of a chart-topping song.

CHAPTER 69

SONG OF THE CAGED BIRD

Lyric
Two days later

Mom's had the kids for four days. I'm expecting a call any minute, begging me for mercy. But every time I've called to check in on them, they've been having a great time.

"We're working on some projects," Mom says cryptically.

"Grandma says I can't talk about it, because it's a secret!" Aria chimes in over the speakerphone.

"Are you doing art projects?" I ask, my curiosity getting the better of me.

"Of a sort," Mom says, shushing Aria when she starts to talk. "You'll have to wait."

I chuckle. Mom relishes her reputation for being unpredictable and creative, so there's no telling what she's up to or had the kids up to. I'll find out when they're ready to reveal the big secret, I guess.

"How's your thinking going?" she asks, all subtlety gone as the takes the phone off the speaker.

"It's going."

I can practically hear her roll her eyes.

"This isn't a hard decision, Lyric. Really. I expected you to be a little more outgoing, having me as a mother!"

"I don't want to be the rockstar's girlfriend in the back of every tour photo, Mom. That's a hard-no condition for me, especially with the kids."

"So, tell Rhys that, tell the management that — no interviews, no photos of you or the kids."

"I'm not sure that's an option if we're on the tour, Mom."

"Then stay home. Let Rhys come back to you between tour legs. Teach piano lessons. Play it safe. Or, better yet — take a risk! Go outside the box!"

"This coming from someone who's been living in a trailer, driving from town to town, for the last twelve years!"

"Exactly! I've set a solid example for you, daughter. It's past time you gave life a chance to surprise you, in all the best ways!"

"You sound like Rory."

"Have you talked to her?"

"No. As far as I know, she's still off exploring the swamp for this story of hers."

Besides, I've already had to tell my ghostly chorus to buzz off, just so I can hear myself think. Is more input really what I want right now?

"Have you tried contacting her? I'm sure she'd be back here in a heartbeat if she knew what was going on with you."

"Probably. And that's half the reason I haven't tried to contact her. She's got this story... and it seems like it's important to her. More than usual."

"That may be, but she's your best friend, and in her shoes, I'd have wanted to be here for you. Your mother can only do so much, you know."

"You've been plenty of help, Mom. I'm still astonished you haven't dropped the kids off and run away screaming."

We both chuckle.

"We're having a blast," she says. "I'm storing up grandma moments before I have to get back out on the circuit again. So, until you ask for them back, I'm keeping them!"

"It won't be much longer. I promise."

"Take as long as you need. And call Rory. Give her a chance to be there for you like I know she'd want to be."

Her tone reminds me of Adam's comments on my excessive independence, and Brighid's, and Rhys... Well, everyone, really, including the chorus of dearly departed, who thankfully, have left me in peace for the last few days, after I yelled at them. But that cements it. Mom's right. The advice I need right now is from my best friend, who set all of this in motion.

Lyric: *I need some advice. I've got a big decision to make. If you get this, give me a call. I hope everything's OK.*

Ten minutes later, U2's "Mysterious Ways" erupts from my phone — Rory's ringtone, a song from her favorite band and one of mine. I snatch it up and hit the answer button.

"Rory?"

There's some crackling on the other end, like old-fashioned landline static, which I'm not sure is normal on a cell phone in this age.

"I'm here," she says, breathless. "Sorry — I had to find a spot where I could get enough signal. I swear — my next story is going to be about dead spots in Sussex County cell phone service..." There's a smacking sound, skin on skin.

"You OK?"

"Yeah — just... it's a swamp, and there are mosquitoes, and they consider me a rare delicacy, apparently. I dropped my bug spray in an unfortunate knee-on-knee run-in between *my* knee and that of a bald cypress. Literal run-in, in this case. Ow."

"But you're OK?"

"For the moment, yeah. Sorry I've been out of touch, but like I said — next to no cell service. I wouldn't even have tried if you hadn't made it clear something big was up. So, what's up?"

"You've missed a lot."

"I figured. I'm sorry if the rockstar annoyed you. You didn't blow him up or anything, did you? Do I need to come bail you out?"

For a minute, I wonder how she knows about that stray lightning bolt, but then it's Rory. She's even more scarily intuitive sometimes than Brighid is.

"No. No one's dead or in jail. It's just..."

"What?"

"He wants me and the kids to go on tour with them."

"That's awesome! But what about your job?"

"What job? I got fired!"

"What?" she screeches.

"You've been out of touch. It was big news. Rhys told everyone I'm a witch. It was all over the news."

"They fired you because Rhys told everyone you're a witch?"

"Not really. It's complicated."

"I'll be there in an hour. Call a lawyer, because you're going to need to bail *me* out."

"No! No — it's fine. He didn't do it on purpose. He just slipped up."

"I told him to be careful!"

"He was. As careful as he knows how to be."

Her sigh, even over the phone, is big.

"I'm sorry, Lyr. This is all my fault."

"Then I owe you my thanks."

"You do? For getting you involved with a guy who got you fired?"

"Yeah... Things... progressed."

"Progressed in a good way?"

"Mostly, yeah."

"Well, huh... So you have a big decision to make, then?"

"Yeah. We can go out on tour with the band, me and the kids, or Rhys says he'll quit the band and stay here with us."

"Whoa. OK. That's... unexpected."

"I told him I won't let him do that."

"And that's *not* unexpected, after your history with Adam..."

"Adam..." I sigh, not knowing where to start, knowing I have to keep this conversation short in case Rory loses signal. "Adam would have liked Rhys. He would have..."

"What, honey? What would Adam have done?"

"Told me to go out on the road."

"Then what's stopping you?"

"I haven't liked being in the spotlight. The paparazzi, the reporters, all these invasive questions, worrying about the kids..."

"The paps came back? Why didn't you call me? Then or when you got fired? I would have come back."

"I know this assignment is important to you."

"More than you could possibly imagine," she says so quietly that I'm not sure she meant for me to hear it.

"What's going on, Rory? Why are you out there?"

"There's too much to tell you right now, and I'm not sure how it's all going to work out. But know that it's important, or I'd have come back already. I've been such a terrible friend."

"No! You've got to take care of your stuff. I'm fine. I mean, I'm unemployed and trying to decide whether to go on the road and deal with the press, let Rhys quit... or..." I swallow hard. "Or break things off with him."

"You'd break up with him, rather than go on the road?"

Hearing her repeat the idea back to me, when I haven't even said it aloud to myself, or to Rhys, strikes me hard. Would I really break things off, just to avoid the potential pitfalls of going on the road? Would I break things off before I let him quit touring, or the band? Would I really willingly give up a relationship with a man I...

"Lyr... You sure you want to give up on love that easily, when you're lucky to have found it a second time?"

The tension in her voice carries over the line, the emotion hitting me straight in the heart.

She and I both have loved, and then lost the men we loved, suddenly, tragically. I was lucky enough to get the chance to finally tell Adam goodbye. Rory didn't get that chance. And she, more than anyone, knows how it might feel to go through that, only to get a second chance at love.

And that's when I know what I have to do.

"Thanks, Rory! I knew you'd be able to help!"

"What? Lyric? You're cutting out! Let me—"

There's a deep growling noise and a clatter on the other end of the line.

"Rory! Are you OK?"

Silence. Then heavy breathing. I'm torn between ending the call to dial 911 and waiting to see if she's still there, still... alive.

"I'm OK, Lyric. But I've got to go. Do you have your answer?"

"Yeah, Rory. I do. Thanks! Stay safe, please!"

"You know me better than that!"

The line cuts out, and the phone beeps with the lost call.

Yeah, I do know her better than that. There's no point in telling her to stay safe. Whether it's a story or something more personal, Aurora Carmichael is going to do what she needs to do, especially when others' lives are on the line. I shake my head, sending up a prayer to Herself to keep my best friend safe, despite herself.

"So, did you call him?"

"No, Mom. Just because I decided I want to try this doesn't mean I'm ready to tell him. That'd make it real. And I've still got so much to figure out before it's real! The house, the utilities... Am I renting it out again? Do I need to find a job I can do remotely? Can I teach lessons remotely? And the daily basics for me and the kids — like how I'm paying for our food..."

"Lyric, honey — I think Rhys will have food covered. Don't they feed the tour staff on a daily basis?"

"Yeah, probably." I sigh. This is all foreign to me. Maybe she's right. I should call Rhys, see if we can work this stuff out together. But the big issue still remains. "However, I'm not staff, and I won't be a tour employee. I won't even be background dressing in photos, because..."

"You don't want to be in the spotlight as Rhys' girlfriend. Yes, you said that. So, I say again — talk to Rhys! You can't figure all of this out on your own, as much as you're used to doing that."

"I just need another day or two to really absorb what this means, Mom."

"I think you're making too big of a deal out of this need for self-sufficiency, Lyric. Love always finds a way," she says.

"Now you sound like Rhys."

"Good. I like Rhys. He's special," she says. "Don't let him slip away, just because you're afraid of change, or of not calling all the shots."

"That's not what this is, Mom."

"Isn't it? You forget — I was a single mom for much longer than you've been one. I know that, in your shoes, I'd be leery of letting anyone start making decisions that impacted me and my children. But Rhys is handing you everything on a silver platter!"

"That's not what I want, Mom! I want to work! I want to support my kids! And I don't want to be in the spotlight as some rockstar's girlfriend! I need to be my own person."

"Well, isn't that up to you? It's not like being on tour with the band would erase that. It's not like Rhys is trying to erase that. It's up to you to figure out how all the pieces fit, for you and the kids. And since it's Rhys' life, too, don't you think you should figure this out with him?"

I want to argue. But I can't.

"Fine. I'll call him. Tomorrow."

"That's fine. He's got a gig tonight."

He does?

"How do you know that?"

"A little birdie told me."

"Rhys? Why'd he call you and not me?"

"Because you told him you wanted time to think, and he agreed to wait until you called him?"

"True... It's just..."

"You wanted him to invite you? And he invited me instead?"

"Well... yeah. But he *didn't* invite me. And... if the band's playing out tonight, I can't be there. Everyone knows who they are now, with these supposedly incognito gigs! Everyone with a phone will be recording, looking to shoot viral video! I can't come within a mile of the Pirate's Cove."

"That's your choice, witchling. Make it a wise one."

CHAPTER 70
LIGHTNING STRIKES TWICE

Lyric
Two hours later

Mom: *You sure you want to miss this? There's something special in the air tonight.*

Lyric: *Are you trying to tell me something? Are the kids OK? Do you need me to come get them?*

Mom: *Are you implying that I've been drinking? I'll have you know I've got a designated driver.*

Lyric: *Who? This mysterious friend of yours?*

Mom: *You'll have to come if you want to find out. ;-)*

Lyric: *Mom! Come on. You can't be that desperate*
to get me out there tonight.

Mom: *;-D*

Apparently, she is. But am I desperate enough to let the answer to that question to risk putting every camera in the place on me?

"Why am I here, Mom?" I demand as she meets me on the walk between the parking lot and the restaurant, Roger trailing behind. "Didn't we agree that me staying out of the spotlight was the goal?"

"It may have been your goal, honey, but it wasn't mine," she says. "Besides, right now, you're not the one in the spotlight. If you are, it'll be your choice."

"What are you talking about? And where are the kids?"

"They're with my friend — the one I've been seeing while I've been back here."

She nods across the deck, at a small table where I can now see Aria and Tommy sitting, Kirk watching them all from a spot near the bar. Aria's chattering excitedly with a brown-haired woman who has her back to me.

Ah! So Mom *has* been seeing a woman. One she likes and trusts enough to leave my kids with. Interesting...

Oh. More than interesting, once I get close enough to see her face.

"Hello, Lyric. I'm so glad to see you."

"Sheryl! I'm glad to see you, too, though I can't say I was expecting it to be in this context."

"Your mother's a private person. It's taken a while to get to know her well enough that we put things together," she says, her smile warm.

"That your kids were dating."

"Yes."

"Does Rhys know?"

"Yes. We figured it out when he called your mom to ask about the kids coming over to the studio, so Tommy could practice drums."

I look to Mom.

"And you didn't feel it necessary to tell me that? This was your big secret?"

"You told me to enjoy my time with the kids. That's what I did. Sheryl and I watched the kids, spent time on the beach, watched Tommy progress on the drums, watched him and Aria enjoy their time with Rhys... who they missed immensely, as you well know."

"Yes. That doesn't change the fact that you should have told me."

"That I was spending time with a woman I was very interested in, while also spending time with my grandchildren, as she spent time with her son?"

I sound ridiculous for objecting when she puts it that way, and we all know it.

"Mommy!" Aria says, finally looking up from her pad of paper. "Mr. Rhys taught me to play the tambourine!"

"He did? So now you play three instruments?"

"Yeah! The piano, the violin and the tambourine!"

Nevermind that she can't play violin in an elementary school orchestra with no teacher who knows how to play violin. But does that even matter if she'll be touring the world with a rock band instead?

And I can't believe I even thought that.

I glance around us, looking for anyone who has their phone running to catch video of the rockstar's witchy girlfriend and her kids. So far, so good. But I don't expect it to last.

"Sit down, Lyric," Mom says, pulling out a chair for me between Sheryl and Aria.

"You aren't going to push me to go find Rhys and talk to him?"

"It's not your turn to talk," Mom says.

"What? You wanted me to—"

"Shhhh..." she says. "Just wait!"

I sputter a little, totally off my footing. First she demands I talk to Rhys, and I agree. Then she entices me out in public when I have no desire to be subjected to public scrutiny. And now... Now, she wants me to sit down and be quiet.

OK. Fine. I'm a bit of a control-freak. I can admit it. But can a control-freak handle the chaos that is an international tour? Maybe this is all a bad idea. I'll talk to Rhys, and we'll both realize this will never work.

"Folks — we're going to start tonight a little different from how we have been during our recent shows..."

I know that voice. I look up and see that face, those warm brown eyes, glancing over at me, a smile...

Rhys is sitting on a stool at center-stage, Kieran off to the side, in his usual spot, but on a stool of his own. Each of them has an acoustic guitar in their laps.

"I love you, Rhys!"

My head swivels slowly, looking for the woman who just shouted out to my boyfriend that she loves him. I spot a lithe, pretty brunette in a red dress bouncing up and down in her seat by the bar. My eyes narrow. She glances my way and visibly shrinks, looking a little embarrassed. Good.

Good? I just told myself this thing between us will never work. Too much of this rockstar kind of stuff — women hitting on him, photographers, reporters, me backstage like some pointless hanger-on, trying to wrangle kids on a tour bus. Too many things out of my control. The security guys standing to either side of the stage are a reminder of what we've already been through.

"The sun's sliding down over the horizon, and it'll soon be time for all the kids to get tucked in with a bedtime story... or a song," Rhys says into the microphone.

I glance back at the woman, jealousy and resentment rising. Rhys is *my* boyfriend! Mine. Mine, mine, mine, minety-mine. She has no right. I have every right.

Except I don't. Because I can't go on the road with him. Because I'm a control-freak. And he's going to quit the band if I don't go with him, just to stay here with me...

OK... What is wrong with me? How much of a control-freak am I that I can't consider all of this a blessing, can't just take Rhys' presence in my life as a gift? I glance back at the bar again.

How many women would see Rhys Madigan, rockstar, walk into their lives and consider it a windfall? Rich, attractive, funny, caring... And not a one of them would understand him, not like I do. Not a one of them would appreciate him like I do. Not one of them would... love him... like I do.

Yes! I knew it!

Adam? You're back?

Never left. You two came too close to screwing this up again. I had to make sure my business was really finished.

But I'm not sure.

Yeah, you are. You know exactly what to do. You just need to stop fighting fate!

Is that what I'm doing? Fighting fate?

The world goes silent around me, my mind focusing inward.

Oh, gods. Adam's right! Why am I fighting this? Do I need a bigger, more glaring sign to follow my heart than my dead husband haunting both me and Rhys, just to bring us together?

"This isn't an aMUSEd song — and I know you all know who we are," Rhys says, smiling in that wry, amused way of his, "regardless of whatever ridiculous Dave Grohl reference Declan had them put on the marquee..."

"Hey — I take offense to that! 'The Grohling Stones' is very clever!" Declan yells from offstage. "One of my best so far!"

There's laughter all around, and it makes me smile. These bandmates, their family dynamic...

"Anyway," Rhys says. "This isn't an aMUSEd song. It's not even one I wrote, though I recently recorded it with Kier on guitar, and with Alex's help. It was written by a dear friend of mine, who I didn't get nearly enough time with in-person, though it still feels like I can hear him talking to me all the time. He was an incredibly talented musician and songwriter, and I want to share with you this song he wrote for his kids."

Oh. Rhys recorded Adam's song? With all that's been going on?

Just listen, Lyr...

"With his and his wife's permission, we're going to release this song as part of an EP on Siren's Song Records in the coming weeks, with the bulk of the proceeds to benefit a trust I've established for their children, and the remaining proceeds to benefit the program for autistic kids at the local school his son attends."

He isn't!

"The song is called 'Lullaby,' because that's exactly what it is. This is for Aria and Tommy."

The last time I heard this song, I was the one who was singing it, playing it.

Rhys has transformed it, making it the guitar-centered song it was always supposed to be. Slow, gentle arpeggios from his guitar, mirrored by Kieran at his side. Then Rhys' beautiful singing voice — for the first time on a stage taking the spotlight — weaving a vision worthy of a dreamscape. And then — something else unexpected — Kieran joins in for harmonies behind Rhys' vocals.

You have to be an aMUSEd fan to know how unheard-of this — Kieran doesn't sing. Ever. Not even background vocals. I have no idea what his singing voice is like. I don't think anyone does. I think most of us assumed he was tone-deaf or something. But for this song — Adam's song, and Rhys' song now, too — Kieran O'Connor is singing harmonies. And it's beautiful. Astonishingly beautiful.

The audience is just starting to take in this extraordinary turn of events when the song reaches that little break, and my memory of Adam singing this for the kids is pulled to the front of my mind as Rhys whistles the little melody, a nightingale incarnate. What can't Rhys Madigan do? A music major — a gifted multi-instrumentalist and vocalist that no one knew existed. Until now.

"Hey, buddy," he says quietly as the break ends, and I look up to see Tommy sitting on the edge of the stage at his feet, looking up at Rhys like he sets the sun and moon in the sky. Then one last verse as the dreamscape envelops the entire audience, Rhys' voice and the sound of the guitars fading slowly into silence.

And then raucous applause, as the entire audience rises to its feet. Tommy looks up nervously, then back to the gears in his hands, spinning them rapidly. I jump to my feet to grab him, pull him back out of the overwhelming presence of the people around him, around Rhys. But Sheryl touches my arm, in that wordlessly wise way she has, and I look back up to see that Rhys has picked Tommy up, holding him in those strong arms of his, and waiting for the applause to die down.

"Thank you! Thank you all for that amazing response to that song. Please give a round of applause for my buddy Kier, who agreed to help me bring this song to life, and — most of all — to the late Adam Larson, the man behind that incredible piece of songwriting."

Wow.

The applause picks back up again, but despite the noise, Tommy settles into Rhys' arms, looking at his gears, and at Rhys.

Mom squeezes my hand, and Sheryl's on her other side. My other hand reaches for my face, wiping away the tears. They're tears for Adam, but they're also tears of joy, of happiness, that Rhys managed to bring Adam's song to life like that. But then Rhys spoke truly — he and Adam were friends. If not in life, then in the strange life-after-death that Adam used to bring Rhys and me together. And performing this song was a tribute not just to my husband, and the kids' father, but to Rhys' friend.

I knew I picked right.

"Thank you again! I want to take a moment right now to talk about another talented member of the Larson family," Rhys says, looking from Tommy to me. Is he going to talk about Tommy's natural skill as a drummer? "Lyric Larson — Adam's widow — is both an extraordinarily talented teacher and musician herself. You may have heard her play violin on Meredith March's single 'A Way Back Home.'" There's murmuring in the audience. Some of them clearly remember the song. "But Lyric is also a master poet. And while — at her request — I'm not going to embarrass her by asking her to read the poem that earned her that honor, it is my privilege to announce to you, and to her, that Lyric is the winner of this year's Mid-Atlantic Master Poet's Fellowship."

What?

I won?

Of course you did!

And how does Rhys know and I didn't?

There's another round of applause, and I'm lost in it and in the sudden rush of noise inside my mind.

I look over at Mom, who's looking both guilty and smug.

"Opening someone else's mail is a crime, Mom."

She just shrugs, looking entirely unrepentant.

"You were so upset about it, I figured you'd never even open the envelope yourself. And what a waste that would have been. You've only got another week to accept the fellowship. The award banquet is next month."

"I won? I really won?"

"You did, dear. The fellowship, and so much more, if only you'd open the door to a world of possibilities…"

She's talking about Rhys now. Rhys, who's watching me from the stage, Tommy still in his arms.

"You won, Mommy!" Aria chirps from between Mom and Sheryl. "Mr. Rhys said they loved your funny poem, and now you don't have to worry about your job!"

And Rhys's right about that. For at least the next year, it's me, my kids and poetry. And…

"And now I have one last surprise for the night," Rhys says. "Then we'll get back to our irregularly scheduled aMUSEd covers-and-more show…" He sets Tommy down on his feet and hands him a pair of drumsticks. Tommy sticks his gears in his shorts pocket and twirls one of the drumsticks between his fingers. My jaw drops. How good has Tommy gotten during these covert lessons with our moms on duty?

"Recently, I was reminded of an old song that was a favorite of my mom's — Hi, Mom!" he says, waving at Sheryl. Everyone laughs, some turning to look again at our table. "It turned out, it's also a favorite of Lyric's mom — Hi, Iris!" More laughter, more turning heads. "And, by extension, it's a favorite of mine and of Lyric's, too. It's also very symbolic for us. It's a song about the choice between staying safe and comfortable but withering away, or choosing risk and the freedom that comes with that. And, with a modified aMUSEd lineup, I'd like to perform that song for you tonight."

Kier sets aside his acoustic guitar in favor of his beautifully carved electric guitar, while the rest of the band takes their usual spots on stage. Rhys stays where he is, though, and Declan moves not to center stage, but to stand next to Rhys' drum kit, where he helps Tommy — Tommy! — onto the drum throne. Piper brings another microphone stand on stage, setting it next to Rhys' mic. Dave bends down to pick Aria up and put her on the stage, too. Declan hands her a tambourine, and she stands in front of him, next to Tommy.

"What do you say, Lyric? Would you like to join aMUSEd — and your kids — on stage? Show them all how it's done?"

What?

Mom holds out my violin, already ready to go.

And now's the moment. The moment when I make that choice Rhys talked about. Do I shrink myself, my life, and try to fit it back in a box that not only no longer seems to fit but that's been pretty much blown to smithereens? Or do I open that cage door and choose wide-open skies and endless possibilities?

Adam's quiet, but I can feel him here with me. I know what he wants me to do. I know what Rhys wants me to do. Even Mom, Sheryl... Maybe even the kids, too. But what do *I* want to do? What do I want for my life?

A bird must fly to be truly free...

Brighid. Herself. She's giving me a choice. And I choose...

Freedom. And the future.

I take the instrument from my mother's hands and walk up to the stage.

Rhys' smile as he looks down at me is breathtaking — so full of love and support. And I set one foot on the front of the stage. Rhys catches my hand and pulls me up next to him.

"Hi."

"Hi," he says back, looking nervous. "You ready for this?" he asks. "This is the moment that everything changes."

"Yes. It's time."

"I love you."

"I love *you*."

"Then let's show them what the future sounds like."

"Two... three... four..." he counts down, cuing Tommy, who settles into a metronome-perfect rhythm to guide us and the rest of the band.

I put bow to strings, and Rhys puts his fingers around the neck of the guitar, plucking out that familiar riff as I sway with the sweet sounds of the violin. Behind us, aMUSEd plays a song like they never have before — not hard rock, no edge of metal to be found, but pure retro '70s folk-pop. And yet, it all works. Even when I add my voice to Rhys' in the first verse, it all works. Our voices intertwine just as his guitar and my violin do, and then the music soars as the violin becomes the focus of the song. I sway with it, allowing myself a glance behind me, where Tommy is completely fixated on his playing, and Declan encourages Aria to play her tambourine in time.

Oh, they're so good at it!

Back into the next verse, as I settle in to performing in this new way, finally looking at Rhys as our voices blend together in a climax.

Then, the Spanish-style guitar solo, which Rhys performs to perfection, to the surprise of the audience, and, finally, to a nod of approval from Kieran — the ultimate compliment for his friend's skill. And then my turn again, carrying the song along through the break as most of the audience rises to its feet, whether for Rhys' performance, mine, or all of it. The song rises to its climax, Kieran's electric guitar peeking through, Alex's keyboards enriching the sound, Dave bridging percussion and melody, Hunter filling the space between acoustic and electric guitars, Declan's added touches of percussion a cherry on top of Tommy's extraordinary performance and Aria's sweet embellishments.

Then, it's all left to fade away, immediately lost in the response of the audience — applause, cheers, whistling.

"Take a bow, Lady... That's for you, too," Rhys whispers in my ear.

I take in the crowd, so many of these eyes on me — not because I'm the rockstar's girlfriend, not because I'm the only witch they've ever seen, but because they appreciated the music I just helped create. The feeling is... stunning. I'm stunned. It feels almost familiar, from those days in college. But this is something... new. It's new. And I... I join Rhys in a bow, his hand settled in the small of my back. It feels good, natural. I could get used to this.

Good. You deserve it — every bit of happiness and appreciation you get. I can't see Adam, not even in some kind of ghostly form, but I can hear the love in his voice. I can picture that smile of his. *And this is goodbye, babe. I'm out, for good this time. Take care of our kids, but most of all, take care of yourself. And let him help. He's a good man, and he loves you. You've got such a bright future ahead of you...*

In my mind, I blow a kiss to him. One last goodbye. My eyes well, but it's mostly happiness that fills them.

"Thank you, everyone," Rhys says. "So, you liked Lyric's performance?" Applause. "And how about Tommy and Aria taking over my spot behind the kit?" More applause.

"Hey — what about me? I played this egg thing!" Declan complains.

Laughter and more applause, a wolf-whistle. Is that Callie?

"Declan's percussion chops aside," Rhys says, "I've got an incoming phone call from a very important person that I think Lyric needs to take right now."

"What? What are you talking about?"

Dave hands him a phone, which he brings up to my microphone.

"Say, 'Hello,' Lyric. And, no, not 'Hello, Lyric.' I figured that out the hard way."

Oh, Rhys...

"Hello?"

"Mrs. Larson — this is Marina Matthews of Siren's Song Records."

The audience goes quiet as the voice carries over the sound system.

"I'd like to invite you to join aMUSEd on their next tour, as part of a unique opening act — your violin and vocals, Mr. Madigan on guitar and vocals, various members of aMUSEd as they see fit, and, if you wish, your children. I understand Tommy's quite the gifted drummer. Suitably, considering the talents of his parents."

"I... I..."

"Say yes, Mommy!" Aria shouts. "I want to ride on the big bus! Mr. Rhys said I could even have the top bunk!"

"You've got your fellowship," Rhys says. "You can spend your time writing, teaching the kids, and perform however much you want. We're going to put 'Lullaby' and 'White Bird' on an EP, and we could perform them before aMUSEd goes on, or between sets. It's all up to you."

"The band's on board with this? Having us on the road with you all? Me? The kids?"

I look around at all of them, waiting for someone, anyone — Declan — to object. But they don't.

"We're already family, Lyric," Rhys says, squeezing my hand. "We're just adopting a few more members."

Alex, David, Hunter, Declan, and, finally, Kieran — one by one, they each nod assent.

"What's your answer, Mrs. Larson?" asks the voice on the phone. "Are you on board?"

Is there any question now, really, in the face of all that's happened tonight?

"Yes. I — we're — on board."

Rhys sweeps me up in his arms, my violin and bow dangling from one hand as he pulls me hard against his chest and kisses me, long and deep.

More wolf whistles. Tommy takes off drumming again, and everyone laughs. But he's good! He's really good!

"I don't turn my kit over to just any drummer," Rhys says as I turn to watch. "Give him another few years, and he'll be drumming for his own band. And if you want to bring them on as an opening act, we will. He'll be good enough that anybody playing with him will be opening-act caliber. He's almost as good now as I was at 20, when we got our first tour opening slot."

"For Telltale Signs."

"There's my fangirl!" he says, smiling broadly. "My sexy mama."

He dips down for my lips again, tasting, nipping at my lower lip.

"Mr. Madigan — you can hand the phone back to David now," Marina Matthews' voice calls out from the phone, which is still in Rhys' hand.

And the whole band laughs. David takes the phone and hangs up. And, one by one, each of them comes by to give Rhys a high-five and grab me in a hug. Kieran, again, is last. Rhys' former wingman — the skeptic. Though I suspect he's feeling that way as much because he feels I've displaced him in Rhys' life as because he truly doesn't believe. But time will tell... If I've learned anything during all of this, it's that life surprises you. And sometimes, those surprises are the best things that could ever happen to you.

EPILOGUE

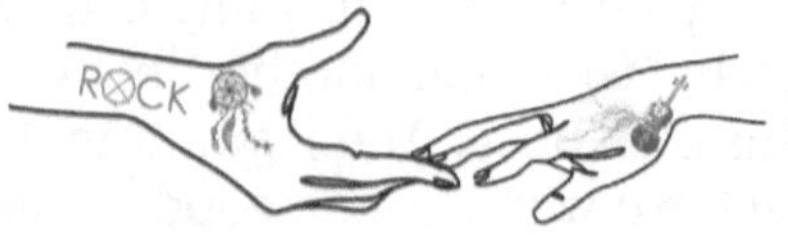

Rhys
Hours later

"So we're really going on the road with aMUSEd?" Lyric asks as we come back downstairs from putting the kids in bed.

"As our opening act — you and the kids, if you want."

"I need to talk to them about that in the morning..." she says, looking thoughtful. "I'm not sure if they're up for late nights every night, or all those people."

She seems uncertain, but I already thought about this.

"We can play it by ear. We'll have another opening act to take the pressure off. I made sure of it before I asked Marina Matthews to listen in to the show tonight."

"And you didn't pressure her to offer us this chance?"

"Nope. I made a suggestion, since I was hoping you'd be coming along anyway. And, if it worked out, it solved the problem of you having a job while we're on the road. But she remembered you from 'A Way Back Home.' She was eager to hear you play with the band. I didn't have to twist her arm. And she heard the kids playing on 'White Bird' during one of our rehearsals and thought it was great, too! She knows talent when she hears it."

"Well, yeah — that's literally her job! I just can't believe that Marina Matthews thought the kids and I are talented enough to open for aMUSEd!"

"Well, she does. Because you are." I give her a peck on the lips. "And I've got the bus contractor Hunter found calling tomorrow to help us pick out features for the tour bus. We just need to decide whether you want a dedicated bus just for us, or we can share one with Hunt and Brighid, and put the kids in bunks between the bedrooms."

"You thought of everything, didn't you?"

All the things I might possibly have forgotten start to bubble up in my brain.

"Probably not, knowing me. But I tried!"

"That's all that matters, Rhys. I was so determined to support the kids all by myself... And now I have the fellowship, thanks to you..."

"Not to me — to Herself. I just did what I was told," I point out.

"I still can't believe She talked to you."

"And I can't believe Aria's a mermaid. But I experienced both of those unbelievable things, so I can tell you for sure that they're true. No illusions this time!"

"And Adam haunting us both..." She's more somber now. "He said goodbye tonight, right before that phone call."

I feel sad for her, having had to say goodbye one last time. But I also feel a little sad for me.

"I already miss that dude. He was a good friend. Wish I'd known him longer and in person."

"I think he felt the same, Rhys. And somehow, he knew we — you and me, and the kids — he knew we'd work."

"Like I said — a good friend. He brought me the woman I love, and two amazing kids to make things even more interesting!"

"Interesting!" She chuckles. "I like that. Life with us is never going to be boring, that's for sure!"

"That's perfect for me! One adventure after another! And all the surprises we can handle!"

I pull her up against me, pressing my rising hardness into her soft center.

"Surprise!"

"Rhys!"

She's shocked, but not really, as she shows when she presses her luscious hips into mine. I grab her ass and pull her tight against me.

"Oh, that's how it is, is it?" she teases.

"With all that thinking of yours, it's been a few days, Lyric," I remind her.

"I suppose I have some lost time to make up for, then," she says.

She glances up at the stair landing, then grabs my hand to pull me into her bedroom.

Next to the bed, I grasp her face between my hands, diving in for another kiss. I lose myself in her, tasting, touching, capturing her lips between mine. She pulls back, and I take a good look, appreciating her curves, her strong shoulders, those amazing stormy-blue eyes, which are alive with passion.

The next thing I know, I'm on my back on the bed, looking up at her and enjoying that angle as much as I did seeing her from up high.

She steps back to the doorway, shutting the door and locking it with a mischievous smirk.

"Never forget those little eyes and ears!" she warns me.

"Right! Especially when we're all going to be living in close quarters on a bus!"

"The bedroom doors on the bus lock, too, right?"

"I guess so. But I'll be sure to ask tomorrow!"

"I'll remind you," she says. "Just to be sure."

She stalks slowly toward me, then climbs up on the bed, pulling her skirt up high on her thighs, straddling me.

"Yeah, wouldn't want to forget that..." I swallow. Hard.

I'm an expert at anticipation. That moment before I throw myself off a cliff, before the slack in the sail yanks me along behind, as I watch the ground loom up at me before I pull the ripcord... But watching a bull run up at me from behind has nothing on this moment, Lyric's hungry expression calling to mind that tiger she's talked about before. She could consume me whole right now, and I'd relish every instant.

Yeah. Locked doors on the bus. And at home, when it's "grown-up time." Do not want to forget that...

She grinds her crotch over mine, that thin layer of cotton doing nothing to hide the warmth and dampness of her wanting me. I get harder under her, ready to throw her over on her back and impale her on my cock. Her hand intercedes, undoing my shorts and sliding beneath the waistband of my boxers, pulling my cock free under her. She slides her panties to the side, fitting me to her opening, and settles down on me.

I gasp, loving the feel of her surrounding me after days apart. There's no way I could leave her for months at a time. I'd miss this almost as much as I'd miss hearing her voice in my ear, seeing her sexy smile with my own eyes. Thank whichever deities deserve it for bringing me here, to her.

But I want her moving freely around me. I reach down between us, running my thumb up along her seam, beneath her panties. And then I tear the crotch right open.

"Rhys! I liked these."

"So did I. But they were in the way. And they needed not to be. Problem solved."

I sweep back up between her lower lips, and she writhes atop me, moaning, then biting her lip to keep herself quiet. I love it. The restraint needed to keep from potentially waking up the kids. My adrenaline kicks up. And I can't take it anymore.

Lyric

Rhys slides his hands up along my sides, lifting me up and tossing me onto my back. He slides his shorts and boxers off in one move before pinning me to the mattress with his hips, his cock lined up with my seam. He rubs up and down against me, teasing my clit, and I moan again before I catch myself and bite down on my bottom lip again.

"God, that's sexy," he says. "Sexy mama."

He leans back, reaching down to strip off his T-shirt. I admire that draw of muscle across his chest, his shoulders.

"You're pretty sexy yourself, there, Drummer Boy."

"I love it when you call me that!"

"Or should I call you 'bae'?" I ask him, teasing.

"You call me whatever you want. I'm here for it."

He rolls his hips against me again, just to prove it. Then he dips down into my cleavage, nipping at the tops of my breasts. His hands slide down, then draw my top back up with them.

"How'd I get so lucky to end up in bed with a goddess?" he asks, marveling at me.

"How'd I get so lucky to end up with a second chance at love?" I ask him.

"About as lucky as me finally finding a woman I could love, complete with bonuses."

"Shhh…" I say, discouraging thoughts of those bonuses, for the moment. "Door's locked. Out of sight, out of mind. You've got a mostly naked woman under you."

"Right… Got distracted for a second."

I wiggle my hips against his.

"Oh! Right! That's where we were."

His smile is like sunshine. He reaches under me, undoing my bra, and slides it off my arms, tossing it away. He sucks on one nipple, pinching the other between his fingers, and I writhe against him again. He fits himself against my opening, pushing slowly inside. It's an incredible display of restraint for Rhys, and my eyes slide closed to focus on the sensation. They pop open again when he pulls back and suddenly slams home.

"Goddess bless…" I exhale.

"Totally," he says, his expression focused as he begins to move inside me, setting a fast pace that my body has no problem joining.

I wrap my legs around his hips, pulling him harder into me, turning this into a dance, tightening over him as he pulls back.

"Yeah… Keep doing that, babe… Keep doing that…"

He nuzzles into my cleavage again, nipping at a nipple before laving at it with his tongue.

"And *you* keep doing *that.*"

He looks up at me, his eyes crinkling in amusement. He nips at me again, then sucks the nipple into his mouth. The sensation drives straight between my thighs, and I grasp him even tighter. He moves faster, and we're immersed in that climbing rhythm. I can feel my core winding tighter and tighter, reaching for that peak. His hand slides between us again, rubbing my clit, as he reaches his mouth for my lips, sliding his tongue against mine.

He pulls back, his bronze irises dilated, a sheen on his skin.

"Love you, Lady," he says, panting.

My heart bursts, and that coiling tension between my legs tightens and then bursts along with it. Rhys keeps moving inside me, faster and faster, as I gasp with delight. Then a hard final plunge, spilling himself inside, before collapsing onto his elbows on either side of my head.

"Love you, too, Rhys... Love you more than I ever dreamed I could."

"Love you even more than I dreamed I might," he says, pressing a soft kiss to my mouth. "You really are my dream-girl."

A week later

"**I** can't believe they're finally gone!" I pull the curtain closed again on a decided lack of paparazzi, wondering whether it might even be safe to put the sheers back up in my altar room. Time will tell.

"See, babe — our fans love you! All it took was a little viral video of you playing with the band, the kids. You're a hit!"

"I don't know about that, Rhys — I think their main motivation was to keep you in the band, not to make me feel welcome, or even just make my life semi-normal again."

"But they are doing that! And it worked! There's nobody out there right now, right?"

I have to give him that — it was impulsive to quit the band, and it was impulsive to tell the fans they needed to get the press to leave us alone if they wanted him to stay in the band. But his impulsiveness worked. It works for him more often than not, it seems. The planner — the control-freak in me — wants to argue. But maybe now that impulsiveness works for us, too.

"No, there are no reporters, no photographers."

"See — it worked! I could walk out the door right now, and there would be no photos, no questions..."

"Rhys..."

"No — I'm going to prove it to both of us!"

"Rhys..."

He grabs the doorknob and flings open the front door, moving to stand on the front porch.

"Rhys!"

I run over behind him and stop short.

"Hi, Mrs. Lowell!" I wave to her from behind Rhys.

"Hello, Lyric, dear. Is this your young man?" she calls out, continuing her morning power-walk.

"Yes, Mrs. Lowell — this is Rhys."

"Quite the fetching outfit there, Rhys, dear," she says, still moving along down the street. "I've always been fond of mermaids myself."

Somehow, she's keeping a straight face. It's a feat I can't pull off, doubling over in laughter as she gives a glance back at Rhys, who is now standing on my front porch in just a pair of pink mermaid-print boxers.

"Thank you, Mrs. Lowell!" he calls to her. "Lyric's mom got them for me!"

"Tell Iris I said hello," she calls out.

Mrs. Lowell knows Mom? Hmm...

"Uh... Rhys — why don't we go back inside before the neighbors start taking pictures..."

"Nobody cares about me in my underwear when Declan's still naked all over the internet," he says.

And, again, he's got a point.

"Yes, but if you stand out here in your underwear, we can't leave for your surprise..."

"I have a surprise? Is it an expected surprise or an unexpected surprise?"

"Mostly unexpected, I think. Until I told you there was a surprise. So, now, more expected, I guess."

"Cool! I like surprises!"

An hour later, Rhys is dressed, and blindfolded, even.

"Come with me, Mr. Rhys," Aria says, dragging him along behind her, with Tommy and me following.

"What's that smell?"

"Food," I answer.

"Well, I knew that! What kind of food? It smells amazing!"

"Just wait until we take the blindfold off. Then you can take it all in."

Ah. There she is...

"Right this way," Marian says, taking Rhys' other arm and leading him ahead. Her regalia makes a soft jingling sound, the shimmer of the rolled tobacco can lids shining between the beats that begin reverberating through the air.

"What?" Rhys says. "What is that?"

"Drums, Mr. Rhys!"

"And now it's time for our inter-tribal dance," the announcer says over the microphone.

Marian pulls the blindfold from Rhys' eyes.

"A powwow! You brought me to a powwow!" he says, his eyes lighting up, his face overtaken by a huge smile.

"Do you remember how to dance?" Marian asks him.

Rhys nods and falls in with the beat, merging in with those already moving in a steady circle inside the arena.

"Can we dance, too, Mommy?" Aria asks.

Tommy's already dancing his side-to-side dance, but to the beat.

"Yes, honey — you're allowed to go dance right now. It's for everyone."

Aria finds her way to Marian's side and mimics her movements. Marian gives me a nod.

I stand back and watch this new part of my family reconnect, if indirectly, with his family. I take a few photos, capturing the look on his face, on Aria's face, on Tommy's face as he watches from my side.

Lyric: *You were right! He loves it*!

Sheryl: *Great! Your mom says hi. She's working on her inventory for the craft show here next week.*

Sheryl: W*hat a great photo — they seem to love him, too!*

Lyric: *It's hard not to.*

Sheryl: *I'm so glad to hear you say that.*

"Come on, Lyric — this dance is for everyone!" Rhys calls loudly. "You and Tommy, too! And then we get frybread and Indian tacos!"

Rhys picks up Tommy and pulls me with him back into the arena. Tommy drums to the beat on Rhys' shoulder, while I settle in ahead of them with Marian and Aria. I feel full of love, surrounded by love.

It's unexpected, a surprise. And yet, flying free into my future — our future — it's an entirely expected surprise.

A Note from the Author

Thank you so much for reading Mad World! I hope you enjoyed Rhys' and Lyric's story as much as I enjoyed telling it!

But we're not done yet! Keep turning the page for a few words from our reclusive aMUSEd lead guitarist, Kieran O'Connor, and a special preview of his story, Drawn to the Rhythm, coming later in 2023.

And, if you want to know Iris' story of meeting Lyric's father, you're in luck! I've written a new bonus story, An Ocean Apart, which is Iris' story of how Lyric came to be, and how Aria came to be a real-life little mermaid! An Ocean Apart is an exclusive for my newsletter subscribers, so follow that link, or the one in the aMUSEd series page on my website, to sign up and get your free bonus story and lots of other bonus material, insider info and updates! There's much more Mystic Beach to come! I look forward to having you along for the ride!

Aislinn

EPILOGUE 2

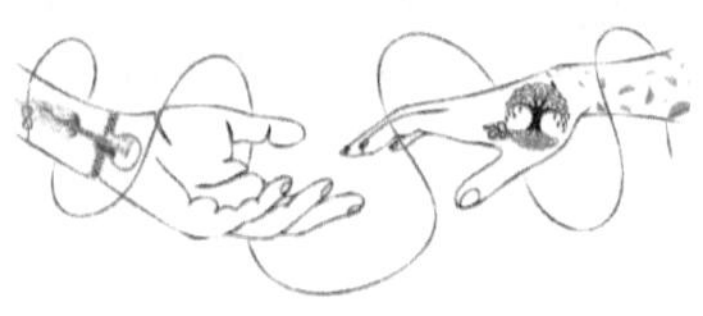

Kieran
A week ago

It's not that I don't like Lyric. Let me say that straight off. She seems to be a lovely girl, and her kids are something special, too. They'd have to be for Rhys to have gone for this family-man deal all of a sudden.

The irony is that I'm the one who kicked the groupies to the curb first. It wasn't to settle down, like Rhys seems content to do now. It was just sheer disillusionment with the whole meat-market atmosphere we always have backstage during a tour now. That's the kind of thing I never wanted any part of. It's the kind of thing that made me turn aMUSEd down when they first approached me about joining the band. Bad memories from an existence I'd tried really hard to put behind me half a lifetime ago...

And now...

My eyes rove over the crowd. I don't feel safe up here. I haven't felt safe on stage since Hunt's stupid reality show got us literally on the map, with what seems like half the planet all too well aware that we're living and working in this little beach town. Then Declan's naked photo... No — naked photo*s*, plural, now.

Feckin' eejit. I'm pretty sure if you found some grandmother riding the subway in New York and asked her where aMUSEd is right now, she'd be able to tell you we're in Mystic Beach, and also whether Declan's circumcised.

And that level of public awareness doesn't make me feel safe. Not even with Gryff's guys here to keep the media off Rhys and Lyric and the kids. Gryff was sure this little town was going to be safe for us. No need for close protection. No need for security at all. Little did he know.

Turn the page for a special preview of Drawn to the Rhythm...

A SPECIAL PREVIEW
DRAWN TO THE RHYTHM

Chapter 1
The Strange Party

Kieran
Six months ago

I haven't even taken a full step into the room and already I'm regretting it. There's too many people in here... too many random women.

I just got out of the shower, and my hair is leaving damp spots on the vintage Pogues T-shirt I threw on for the after-party backstage. I'd prefer to have on my shades, too. But people get irritated when I do that inside or at night. The female fans inevitably ask me to take them off so they can gush over the color of my eyes, and the male fans perceive it as some kind of rockstar ego trip. Even though the last thing I want is attention.

I'm not sure how many VIP backstage passes were sold for tonight or how many girls security let back for the guys to "meet," but there's just too many of them.

I told them before the start of this tour that I didn't want anyone coming backstage for me, before or after our shows. And this kind of scene was exactly why. It's like a meat market, with the only question being who's on display. By the number of scantily-clad girls, you'd assume it was them — most or all of them hoping to get picked by me or one of my bandmates for some one-on-one time. But the way they look at me, at the guys, it sure seems like what's really on the menu is *us*. And I've just had my fill of it.

This was a big part of the reason that seven years ago, when I first met aMUSEd, I'd still been determined to never join another band, never tour or even play out locally — it had made me feel cheap at 17, and these days that feeling is a lot closer to nausea. By the time I was 28, I'd already put all that a decade behind me — the groupies, the promotional appearances, the interviews, the invasive interest in my personal life, the overbearing hand of a label, manager and PR team, the resulting unhealthy relationships with my bandmates. I'd been determined to make a clean break from that kind of life, and I had.

I'd changed nearly everything about myself, except my general profession and my hair color, the day I turned 18. I moved to the States from the little town on the coast near Dublin where I'd been born and raised. I'd grown my hair out long, added a scruff of beard that was all I could manage to grow for another couple years. I got the first in my ever-growing collection of ink. I'd stopped singing — even backup vocals — and even switched from the right-handed guitar I'd learned from childhood to follow my natural left-handed tendencies instead. That had only made me a better guitarist, so I soon shopped myself out as a hired-gun for studio work in New York, and it wasn't long before I had more demand for my services than I had time for projects.

The only rules I had were no live gigs, no photos, no video from the studio and no talking about my life before I got to New York. For all intents and purposes, I was a new man, complete with a new name, so long as people didn't get too creative with a web search.

And it worked. I stayed below the radar for everyone but select industry insiders. Which is, of course, how I got myself into this mess I'm dealing with tonight. Well, that and falling prey to the powers of persuasion exerted upon me by a witch.

I barely make it ten feet into the hospitality room before a blonde in a skintight dress has attached herself to my left arm, looking up at me with starry-eyed wonder overlaying carnal interest. I'm not sure if that combination is better or worse than either of those things separately. But none of it appeals to me. And she's touching me without asking, which makes my skin crawl. I suppress an urge to flee, and then a secondary urge to rage at the girl. But she doesn't know any better. This is standard practice for backstage at a gig for a band with this kind of draw. The other guys are still all-in on groupies, except Hunter most of the time. And it's only recently that I had my fill of it and warned our security and management to ensure it didn't happen with me.

I shoot a pleading look at our manager, Billy, who's across the room, navigating a crowd of girls surrounding our drummer and my former wingman, Rhys, and our diva of a lead singer, Declan. (Feel free to call him Dick-lan. I do.) Billy excuses himself and brings Geordi, one of our security guys, with him as he heads to my rescue.

The blonde is nattering away at my elbow, her nails dug into the Celtic knotwork etched into my arm, and a little more tightly than is comfortable, like someone trying to bathe a cat who knows if they let go, the creature will be lost under a bed and scheming its revenge.

"Kier — can I borrow you for a minute, please?" Billy asks. "Sorry, darlin' — I need this guy to sign some paperwork back in the dressing room. Otherwise, he won't be able to get on stage tomorrow."

I'm torn between genuine surprise at his chosen subterfuge and avoiding showing too much relief at being freed from the clutches of the blonde.

Billy's a New Yorker born and bred, and he only slips on that good ol' boy Southern charm when he needs to make nice through a situation with a potentially negative reaction. Geordi sticks with the girl and guides her over toward Rhys while Billy and I slip out to the dressing room for real.

"What the ever-lovin' feck, Billy? I thought security was supposed to keep them from manhandling me. I really can't keep doing this. It's only gotten worse this tour."

"I'm sorry, man. I'll ask Gryffin to remind his guys to stay on you whenever there are fans around. We weren't expecting you out of the dressing room for a few more minutes, so I had Geordi helping with Rhys and Declan. We'll tighten things down. Won't happen again."

"Don't make promises you can't keep," I warn him. "You know a groupie's going to get some local crew guy to sneak her backstage at some point in time. It's inevitable. I know how this works."

"I know you do, Kier. But we'll tighten things up." Billy looks genuinely regretful, and I feel a little bad about reacting so strongly.

"Thanks, man." I slap him on the back. "No hard feelings. I just really am at my limit with the girls this tour."

"They know you're all single. It's part of the appeal." He shrugs. "And unless you're planning on settling down sometime in the near future, it's something we're just going to have to deal with. Maybe you should take a page from Hunter's book."

Our rhythm guitar player has largely opted out of the groupie scene these last two tours, in favor of a handful of high-profile "girlfriends" he's dating all at the same time. It keeps the fans from pawing him quite as much, so I can see the appeal there. But it's not much better than random hookups, and I've had my fill of those, too. I don't know what I want, but I know it's not this.

I have to admit that it's partly a side-effect of my divorcing myself from my past. I'm not fond of lying to someone I might be interested in having a relationship with, and when I can't tell them where I grew up or about my family back in Ireland, or even why I hate the spotlight so much, it doesn't exactly make for the basis for a strong relationship. That's my own fault, but I can't say I'm not chafing under the weight of this solitary existence, which has gone on, to one extent or another, for nearly half my life. At 35, I'm the oldest member of aMUSEd. I think I'd figured that by now I'd have found a nice girl I could take home to Ma, maybe have a kid with, or at least a dog.

Nevermind that I haven't been home since I left seventeen years ago, and only occasionally has my family come to visit. Da hasn't been to see me in New York in five years (when he'd accused me of getting my ears pierced just to wind him up). It's been almost two for Ma, and three for Flynn and Aoife, who'd visited after they finished at Trinity. If Ma wants grandkids, she's going to have to look to the twins at the rate things are going with me.

"You OK there, Kier?"

"Yeah, Billy. Just thinking. No — no harem for me. Just keep the groupies off of me. Please. I hate feeling like I'm at a bachelor auction every night."

"We'll do what we can, Kier. I'll try to keep your appearances down to orderly signings for a while, something we can control a little better. Take a break tonight. I'll get Gryff to get his guys sorted out on their assignment to you."

"Thanks, man."

He makes his exit and I sit back on the worn leather sofa in the dressing room, taking a deep breath. I'm not sure why I'm so on-edge lately. Just feels like I'm in a spotlight that never goes away. Someone's always watching. I slip in my earbuds, put on my bilingual Irish/English playlist for a taste of home and close my eyes, picturing the Irish Sea swishing across the beach.

The door slams shut and I jolt awake, expecting to see Billy or one of the guys coming in to disturb my rest. But there's no one there. Someone must have come in and then rushed back out upon realizing I was in here napping. I stretch and check my phone for the time. I was only out about half an hour. It's been a long tour and a short nap isn't going to make much headway in my exhaustion, but I feel better than when I closed my eyes.

Until I catch a glimpse of myself in the dressing room mirror along the wall by the door.

"Dead tired?" is scrawled across it in what looks like red lipstick.

Someone was in here. While I was asleep. And that someone seems to either be a little deranged or a sick sort of practical joker. Either way, not cool.

I use the bottom of my shirt to open the dressing room door, careful not to touch it with my bare hands, and I head back to the hospitality room, gesturing urgently at Billy, who brings Geordi with him.

"What's wrong? Tell me that girl didn't get past security and pester you," Billy says.

"Maybe. Someone did. And I think we need Gryffin for this."

"Get him," Billy tells Geordi.

Gryffin — built like a tight end on an American football team, with the unflappable, all-business attitude of a Navy SEAL (which he comes by honestly, I'm told) — rounds the corner and heads straight for me.

"What's the problem?"

"I was asleep in the dressing room and heard the door slam shut. Someone had scrawled a message on the mirror, in what looks like lipstick."

"Love notes?" Billy suggests.

"Not any kind of love I'm wantin' to be on the receiving end of, I don't think." I shake my head.

"I was careful not to touch anything when I came out here," I tell Gryffin. I get a sharp nod in return. He pulls a pair of gloves out of his pocket and slips them on before carefully opening the door and going inside. After a few minutes, during which Billy and I are staring uneasily at each other, the door opens again and Gryff gestures for Geordi to come inside.

"Don't touch anything. I've got photos, and I'll have the police come in and see if they can get any prints or DNA. No one comes in here until they've cleared the room."

Geordi gives a curt nod and pulls on the gloves Gryff gives him before ducking carefully inside.

"Kieran, I'm assigning two of our guys to you in rotation 24/7 for the duration of the tour. Make sure you don't go anywhere without one of them. If you go down the hall to Rhys' room, you take one of them with you. If you go to the gym or the pool or the bar, you take them with you. When you go into your hotel room or a restroom, you have them clear the room first. Got it?"

"Sure. But isn't that a little excessive for one message scrawled on a mirror?"

"It might be, if that was the only reason for concern."

I exchange a glance with Billy.

"What aren't you telling me?"

"We'll have a full security briefing for you in the morning," Gryffin says. "I want to get things sorted out here and see if we can resolve this incident. I'll have your security team with me then so we can set up some ground rules. Geordi will be stationed outside your room tonight."

"Alright. I guess."

Billy pulls Gryff aside and they speak in quiet tones, glancing frequently in my direction. I have no idea what's going on that has these guys on high alert, but that feeling I had before, like I was being watched? That's cranked up to 11 on the volume scale of discomfort. Is it possible that someone really has been watching me?

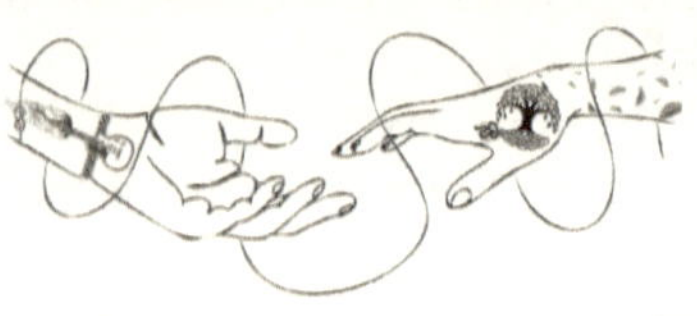

<u>Chapter 2</u>

An hour later, I'm back in my hotel room, with Geordi positioned outside the door after he's checked the room from top to bottom. I told the police what happened, and they did their thing, and I was happy to get the hell out of there.

"Don't say anything to the rest of the band," Gryffin warned. "I want this in hand before we let any information out beyond the people already involved. OK?"

I agree, though I'm not sure what I would have told the guys anyway. This can't have been the first time some groupie or joker left a message like this for one of us. Can it?

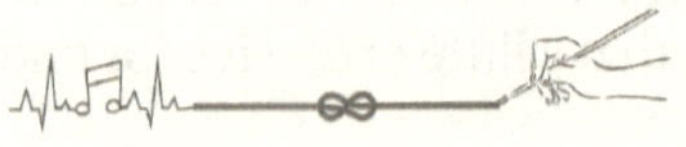

The next morning

"Kier, this is Franco and Tony," Gryffin says, gesturing to Franco, a hulking linebacker type to Gryff's tight end, with a complexion and wavy dark brown hair down to his shoulders to match his name, and then Tony, who's a total contrast, tall and rangy with broad shoulders and close-cropped black hair, reminding me of a Chinese basketball player. "They're your new security team — two of my best guys. They are on you 24/7. No one else."

"So you think this is targeted solely at me."

Gryffin gives another of his trademark curt nods.

"We've had a few concerning letters and e-mails in amongst the usual fan-mail lately, and it does seem to be focused on you. You've all gotten letters we've set aside as concerning in the past. That's not unusual. But these recent ones suggest there may be a person who's fixated on you personally. There's no imminent threat, or we'd be calling in the police for additional security at all of your shows. But there's enough to make us take a little extra care right now."

"It may be nothing, Kier," Billy says. "Last night's incident may have just been a groupie going over the top or a joke that went too far. The venue was an older one, and the security camera in that hallway wasn't pointed at the dressing room door, so we don't know who it was. But we're going to take some precautions regardless."

"What about after the tour? Am I going to have to have bodyguards 24/7 from now on?"

"We'll have to play that by ear," Gryffin says. "A lot will depend on what happens and what we find out between now and then. That's still a couple weeks away. Plus, my understanding is that you all have some time planned in the studio, as well as some vacation time coming up."

"The label is sending them down to the beach in Delaware for the summer to work on their next album and get in some R&R," Billy confirms.

"Delaware? Where the feck is Delaware?" This country is huge. After seventeen years, I'm still lost on American geography outside places like New York and L.A. Unless we tour there regularly, I have to google these places.

"Little state south of Philly. You may have heard of one of its more famous sons: Hunter Graves," Billy reminds me.

"Oh! Right. Brighid is down there, isn't she?"

"As a matter of fact, this new studio is in Hunter's hometown of Mystic Beach, where Ms. Weaver lives and has her business. It's a live-in situation with a state-of-the-art studio right on the beach. You'll get in your post-tour break while having a few months to record the next album. It's not the Caribbean, but it's a nice, quiet resort town where you'll largely be left alone. And we've arranged for some incognito performances so you can try out your new material — no aMUSEd songs except your new songs."

"Well, that sounds pretty safe."

"Nearly ideal, in fact," Gryff puts in. "The studio staff have been vetted, and the facility is on a private beach with minimal foot-traffic from outside. If need be, we can send a couple guys with you, but barring some more concerning incidents, it's likely we can send you down without any security at all."

"So I can get some fecking rest and be left alone — no groupies and no press — for a couple months?"

"Yes."

"Sounds like paradise to me."

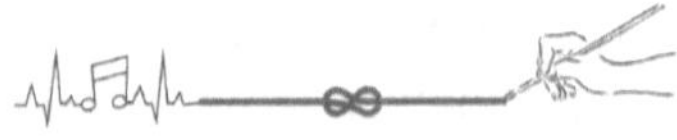

A week ago

In just over three months, Hunt, Declan and, now, Rhys have thrown away any anonymity we had here. We'd be more anonymous at home in New York, mixed in amidst the millions, than we are here, sticking out like sore thumbs. It's got me longing for home, my apartment in a secure building, the ironically quiet and meditative space of the old studio, the comforting buzz of a tattoo gun against my skin as Olivia adds more art to my canvas.

And as I scan the crowd again, for anything that might be amiss, out of place... There's an itch in my skin — not a literal one, but a yearning, a need, for more ink. Maybe it's finally time to get my right arm done. I've held off, waiting for the perfect design, the perfect time... something intangible. And maybe the guys — as much as I resent the attention they've brought to us being here — have been pointing the way.

Hunt's Brighid's cross on his hand, Dave and Declan finally getting the aMUSEd muse tattooed on their shoulders — with their girls' faces incorporated — and now Rhys idly mentioning getting Lyric's face added as the visage of the muse he's had inked on him for a decade. I'm getting to the point where I don't think there will ever be a woman in my life whose face I'll be willing to get inked on me, though there's an even deeper longing in me for that than there is for the ink.

But, for now, maybe I should pay a visit to the tattoo artist who's been doing all the guys' work. They're good, whoever they are. My bandmates' new ink is Olivia-caliber, and she's the best I've seen. The guy I visited a few weeks ago on a whim — really, more like restless desperation to get out of the house in the middle of the night when Rhys wouldn't stop drumming... Forget "artist" — he was barely more than a scratcher, despite some promising designs on his website. That was a no-go.

But this artist the guys went to — a friend of Brighid's, I think she said. Good. They'll be more willing to accommodate an ink addict with a desire for privacy. Maybe even an after-hours appointment. I'll have to check the place out tomorrow, line up a consult. Yeah. That'll get my mind off the security issues, and all the changes that seem to be coming our way.

Tomorrow is a new day, and I need some new ink.

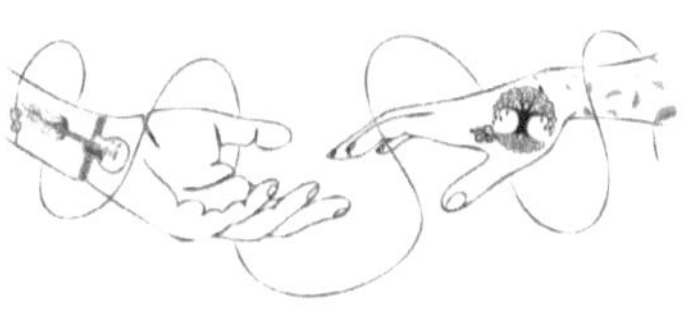

Kieran's story continues in Drawn to the Rhythm, set for release in the second half of 2023. Sign up for the Mystic Beacon newsletter at http://aislinnarcher.com/subscribe for updates on new releases, bonus material and more.

The Wedding Album

Up next in the Mystic Beach Fantasy Rockstar Romance series is the series' second interstitial novel, The Wedding Album, set for release in the late summer of 2023.

If you've been eagerly anticipating the definitive happily-ever-after for Brighid and Hunter, this is the book you've been waiting for! But there's more in store than a simple walk down the aisle. You'll find family drama, ongoing healing of wounds from the past, answers to questions previously left open in the main series arc, tension over plans for the future, a final resolution for some challenging loose ends, an appearance by the Sexiest Guy on the Planet™ and, yes, even a dragon!

In addition to the Brighid and Hunter wedding novella, The Wedding Album includes a Declan and Callie honeymoon short story in which the would-be culinary tourists find themselves getting a little more "alone-time" than they'd planned. The interstitial book also contains a Rhys and Lyric short story that explores the latest twists in their musical careers, and their lives (Is Lyric really more than half a mermaid?), as they head into the studio to record "White Bird" and produce an EP that's the first-ever aMUSEd side project. With a special guest star and true security concerns on the horizon, this story offers hints at the stories to come, both in Book 6, Drawn to the Rhythm, and in a Gryffin-centric novel that will help round out the series once the main arc is complete.

There's much more Mystic Beach yet to come! That includes Rory and Rónan's story, and the real story of what Rory was up to while her bestie's life was in turmoil, which will be part of the new Mystic Beach Mysteries contemporary/urban fantasy series.

Drawn to the Rhythm

At 18, Kieran left his entire life behind in Dublin to lose himself in New York. But the one thing he could never hide was his musical talent. Half a lifetime, one favor and one witch later, he's the lead guitarist for aMUSEd, one of the hottest rock bands on the planet. Only now the spotlight has put a bullseye on his back. Can the Druid enchantments in Siobhan's tattoos redraw their stories with a happily-ever-after, or will the tangled roots of their pasts lead them on a dangerous detour?

Kieran

I just had to listen to the witch... I'd been content hiding away in the recording studio, working with select clients. But then a favor owed came back to haunt me, and the witch said to take the risk, so I took the risk. Now, that's coming back to haunt me, too, right as I get a chance to finally create a real life for myself, with a total badass of a woman who's enchanted me from the moment I saw her. But I'm not the only one with secrets, and Siobhan's secrets are locked as tightly away as her heart.

Siobhan

Kieran's taken great pains to hide his past. Born in Ireland, his story shrouded in mystery, his soul full of music, he longs for something he can't even express — except in guitar licks and ink. During the hours I spend adding to his canvas, it's the ink that tells me his story. It intrigues me. He intrigues me. More than I want to let him. Because unearthing his past may mean unearthing my own, and doing that could destroy any chance we have at future.

Siobhan's magical gift and Kieran's musical talent merge in one extraordinary tattoo, but will the connection it creates be enough to save them from the threat that looms over them?

Drawn to the Rhythm is a spicy romance between a rockstar and a tattoo artist, with a deep current of music and magic running throughout. It is the sixth book in the Mystic Beach Fantasy Rockstar Romance series. It can be read as a standalone, but it is part of an interconnected series and is best read in series order.

Note: A content review for this and other books in the series can be found on the author's website at AislinnArcher.com. If you have concerns about content you may find disturbing, make sure to check the content review for the book before buying or reading.

RETURN TO MYSTIC BEACH

<u>The Mystic Beach Fantasy Rockstar Romance series</u>
Once Upon a Dream (Brighid & Hunter duet, Part 1)
Down to the Sea (Brighid interstitial novel, 1.5)
Dream Weaver (Brighid & Hunter duet, Part 2)
Dreams (Mystic Beach Fantasy Rockstar Romances Collection
I — Books 1, 1.5 & 2, plus bonus content)
Smoke on the Water (David & Piper, Book 3)
Remind Me (Declan & Callie, Book 4)
Mad World (Rhys & Lyric, Book 5)

<u>Coming Soon</u>
The Wedding Album: An Interstitial Novel (5.5) (Brighid &
Hunter, Callie & Declan, Lyric & Rhys)
Drawn to the Rhythm (Kieran & Siobhan, Book 6)
Carry Fire (Alex)
and more to come...

<u>Bonus Content</u>
Included in the collection Dreams,
and available **free** to newsletter subscribers:
Good Golly Miss Molly (0.5)
(Molly & Logan, series prequel novella)
Here Comes the Sun (0.25)
(Hunter & Brighid sweet pre-prequel short story)

Newsletter subscriber exclusives
(**free** to subscribers):
Spooky (2.75)
(Hunter & Brighid seasonal bonus novelette)
Remind Me bonus scene "Building a Mystery" (4.1)

Remind Me bonus story "Centerfold" (4.25)
Mad World bonus story "An Ocean Apart" (5.25) (Iris & Niall)

Visit AislinnArcher.com now to subscribe to the Mystic Beacon newsletter and get your FREE bonus content. *As a subscriber, you'll get early access to details on new releases, sales, exclusive content and more. You can unsubscribe at any time.*

Also by Aislinn Archer...
The Mystic Beach Mysteries
(Aurora Carmichael contemporary fantasy series)
Coming Soon
Safe Harbour (2024)

PLAYLIST

"Mad World" Playlist

(This playlist can be found on Apple Music at https://music.ap
ple.com/us/playlist/mad-world/pl.u-33P5FKVear)

Mad World — Tears for Fears
Dream Girl — Belouis Some (Prologue)
Drumming Song — Florence & the Machine
Meet Virginia — Train
Ghost Dance — Robbie Robertson (With the exception of
the single "Showdown at Big Sky," this album by the legendary
Robbie Robertson is little-known, but it's an amazing blend of
his rock talents with his Native American roots.)
Pick Up the Pieces — Average White Band
Running Down a Dream — Tom Petty
Careful — Horse (I love this emotional little song by an artist
almost no one has heard of.)
Give Me One Good Reason — Tracy Chapman
Sweet Child O' Mine — Luca Stricagnoli (He does these
amazing covers of rock songs on acoustic guitar, with the guitar
itself used as the percussion. This one adds even more sweet-

ness to the original, which was perfect for the scene where Rhys meets Lyric's kids.)

Taking Care of Business — Bachman-Turner Overdrive

We Can Work it Out — The Beatles

Rock a Little — Stevie Nicks (There's a lot of Fleetwood Mac and Stevie Nicks on this playlist. I've steered a bit clear of it since the schism, but Lyric has a Stevie quality to her that I just had to go with.)

Jump Start — Seven Nations

White Bird — It's a Beautiful Day. (I've loved this song for years. It's been one of my "happy place" songs since I first saw that episode of "Knight Rider" in which it appears. Yes, the Pontiac Firebird has also remained my dream car, which I handed off to Rhys, too. I will note that I consider the 2013 remaster of this song to be vastly superior to the earlier recordings. They tweaked just the right things to make it gel.)

Cows with Guns — Dana Lyons (Al gets the blame for this. Well, not blame. It's a great song. Just not entirely child-appropriate. Therefore, it had to be a song Rhys played for Lyric's kids.) See the video here: https://youtu.be/FQMbXvn2RNI.)

It's Raining Men — The Weather Girls (As soon as I realized how many moms were ending up in this book, this song came into my head, with a slightly altered lyric, just for all the moms!)

Dreamer's Chant — R. Carlos Nakai

Don't Wanna Fall in Love — Jane Child (I think a little of Jane Child has snuck into my vision of Siobhan in my head. With her funky look and earring-to-nose-ring chain from the video for this song, she's got that same kind of vibe.)

Lovely, Love My Family — The Roots

Let's Go to Bed — The Cure (Alternatively, I love the Celtic-flavored Seven Nations cover of this one from their Cure cover-song EP.)

I Believe — Robert Plant (One of my favorite songs ever.)

Zoo Station — U2

Under a Stormy Sky — Daniel Lanois (One of my favorite artists of all time. He's pretty good behind the mixing board, too.)

Riders on the Storm — The Doors

Rainstorm — Daniel Lanois

Twisted (Twister soundtrack) — Stevie Nicks & Lindsey Buckingham (A rare duet for the closing-credits song for the movie "Twister," and one that blows me away every time I hear it. Pun mostly unintended.)

Drum Trip — Rusted Root

Little Black Rain Cloud — Pooh Bear (A brief interlude of innocent childhood, where it's most needed.)

Backyard Beach — Ferb (Phineas & Ferb)

Hidden Heritage — Peter Buffett (Peter Buffett is an incredible composer and visionary of multi-media entertainment, and his turning his attention to Native American issues and the need to reconnect people with their heritage produced an amazing show, "Spirit," or "Spirit Dance," which I was lucky enough to see during its tour. It combines contemporary and Native American musicians, dancers and singers, telling a story of a man discovering and connecting with his Native American heritage. You can find a recorded version of the show on DVD, if you're curious. This idea of rediscovered heritage is a major thread of Rhys' story that we'll continue to explore in future stories.)

Holdin' Out — Indigenous (Amazing Native American musicians doing traditional blues!)

No Questions Asked — Fleetwood Mac

With Arms Wide Open — Creed (I wanted a song that encompassed the sense of Lyric opening herself up to the possibilities of a new life, as well as Rhys opening his arms to support her as she lets go of the past and looks into the future. This fit.)

Fresh Feeling (Live WNYC) — Eels (I love this goofy little song. It truly carries a feeling of freshness, especially in this live version. At this stage in their relationship, Rhys and Lyric are both finding a welcome newness in each other, and this song captures that.)

Sleeping Beauty Waltz — Tchaikovsky (The Main Event — The presence of the original Tchaikovsky waltz in Disney's "Once Upon a Dream" from "Sleeping Beauty" is clear. But Lyric salvaged her favorite performance piece from anti-"wokeness" by sheer cleverness.)

Because the Night — 10,000 Maniacs (The live performance by 10,000 Maniacs of this Patti Smith song, with contributions from Bruce Springsteen, brought it to the awareness of so many people, and deservedly so. .It's an incredible performance.)

Skin — Rag'n'Bone Man

Saor–Free — Afro Celt Sound System (Saor means "free" in Irish.)

Seven Wonders — Fleetwood Mac

Lazy Days — Robbie Williams

Grim Grinning Ghosts — The Mellomen (Because what better soundtrack for a haunted mansion dark-ride than one of the best?)

Life in the Fast Lane — The Eagles

Good Vibrations — The Beach Boys

Love Is an Open Door — Kristen Bell & Santino Fontana (One of the great ironies of "Frozen" is the fact that one of the most romantic songs Disney's put out in years is not between the eventual romantic partners, and is, in fact, darkly ironic, considering. But that doesn't make it any less romantic. Taken on its face, it's impulsive, but utterly appealing. And I picked it here not because Rhys is a deceitful snake faking a genuine connection, but because this beat in the story is one in which Rhys and Lyric are experiencing that perfect first blush of romance, with no clue that things are looming over their heads that will turn it all upside-down again.)

Secret Love — Stevie Nicks (The secret love here isn't Rhys/Lyric, but Lyric's love of her late husband, which she's finally forced to fully reveal to Rhys. But the rest of this song almost perfectly fits this moment for Rhys and Lyric.)

Dreaming of Me — Depeche Mode

Lullaby — Al Cook (Al has once again let me borrow a song of his to put in the books. In reviewing what songs of his fit with which books, this was an instant pick for Mad World, and it quickly became part of the storyline as well. Beautifully sweet and haunting! Hear it for yourself at https://on.soundcloud.com/BSMnL)

Maneater — Hall & Oates

Magic-Carpet Ride — Steppenwolf

Madness — Muse

Black Light Trap — Shreikback

Small Town Trap — Eve 6

Home — Alexi Murdoch

Boys of Summer — Don Henley

Indian Summer Sky — U2

Dreams — Fleetwood Mac

Widders Dump — King Swamp

Breathe (In the Air) — Pink Floyd

I'm Gonna Be (500 Miles) — The Proclaimers (I was struck one day by the image in my head of Rhys marching a pack of reporters down the highway to Lyric's house, and this was the song that popped into my head with it. And it's perfect!)

It Takes Time — Fleetwood Mac

Set Fire to the Rain — Adele

Blues This Morning — Indigenous

The Dream — Peter Buffett

Dear Ol Dad — Blind Melon

Talk to Me — Stevie Nicks

Sisters of the Moon — Stevie Nicks (As I've noted in previous books, Stevie Nicks has denied persistent perceptions of her being a witch or Pagan. She is reportedly part of a very old Celtic Christian sect. But it's songs like this that have given her that reputation. And this one was too perfect not to use for the first [nearly] full gathering of the circle that we've had in the books so far.)

Rhiannon — Fleetwood Mac (Chapter 66 — Bird in Flight)

My Body — Belouis Some

Cherokee Morning Song — Robbie Robertson & the Red Road Ensemble (Chapter 68 — Morning Song)

Song of the Caged Bird — Lindsey Stirling (I pulled this one for its thematic appropriateness, having totally forgotten that Lindsey Stirling is one of today's best known popular violinists. Serendipity!)

Mysterious Ways — U2

Gypsy — Fleetwood Mac (Chapter 70 — Lightning Strikes Twice) (I picked this one early on for its thematic appropriateness for Lyric. I long hesitated to use it solely because of the title word, which has become more widely recognized for the pejorative it originated as. But the song itself is too perfect for Lyric. So when it came time for the chapter title, I pulled a theme from the song, rather than the title. Times change. People learn and do better. I'm not sure what we do with a musical legacy that gets caught in between.)

Spirit Dance — Peter Buffett (Epilogue 1)

The Strange Party — The Edge (Epilogue 2 / Preview of Drawn to the Rhythm — This is from the soundtrack U2's The Edge did for a film titled "Heroine," as in female hero, or "Captive" as it got renamed in some locales to avoid confusion. It's a funky blend of atmospheric and melodic with electronica and soaring anthems, including the title track with vocals by the stellar Sinéad O'Connor, who passed away as this playlist was being finalized. Shuhada' Sadaqat, as she preferred to be known these days, is someone I have long held close to my heart — for her strength, her perseverance in the face of being so misunderstood, her passion and her raw talent. That she has left us so soon is a loss I am feeling deeply. As to the album, it is, perhaps strangely, one of my favorite beachside soundtracks. But this track is among the funkiest of the bunch, and carries that strange, overwhelmed "lost" feeling that Kieran has during this sneak peek from his book, giving you some insight as to where his head is at these days.)

ACKNOWLEDGMENTS

After six novels published, this all should start to feel like it's old-hat, right? Well, I don't think it ever will. Every book is a new experience, and one I've come to cherish, despite all the worries and stress that accompany the joy of creation and my appreciation of my readers' amazing responses to the stories and characters.

But this is the point where I say some of those thank-yous to everyone who's helped bring this story to life.

First, this time, is James "Mez" Cook, my godson, who gave me permission to share some of his experience as an autistic child who was initially non-verbal but today, at 21, spends much of his time talking to us about gears, bridges, astronomy and, most importantly of all, drumming! Mez is a big inspiration for the character of Tommy, and the joy he takes in his chosen instrument, as well as representing a different segment of the autism spectrum from David Carter. I hope I've represented our friends on the spectrum well. I'll keep trying, I promise.

Now old enough to play out in any local venue, Mez has recently been dubbed a "savant" on the drums, taking over as drummer for a longtime Ocean City, Md., hard rock band, as well as occasionally sitting in with his dad's band, the legendary Tranzfusion. He's only been playing an acoustic kit for a few years, and as much as I've tried to keep my bias in check by not calling him a "savant," I think I've finally got to acknowledge that's an appropriate term. You can find him online at https://w

ww.youtube.com/@MezCook/ to see for yourself. For my part, I can't wait to see where this talent takes him in the years to come, and I thank him for letting me share some of his experience in the form of Tommy, whom we'll see again later in the series, including in The Wedding Album later this year.

Rhys' experience with attention-deficit disorder is also drawn from my ADD/ADHD friends and family members, and I thank them for sharing their experiences with me, both in relation to this story and in their daily lives. The challenges of executive-function disorders have been pressed home to me over the years, and that's one of the things I wanted to convey with Lyric in this story — different and challenging doesn't mean less, in any way shape or form. Neurodivergence is just one of the diverse ways of being that we humans have, and it's just one more way we adapt and learn to accept, and work with, the people around us who may have differing experiences. Learning to give each other a break and be compassionate is a big item on the to-do list for pretty much every human, so keep at it!

Thanks so much to my beta readers, my ARC readers and my street team, the Mystic Beach Rockstars! I could not do this without you! You come to my rescue and ensure the ship stays afloat, even when I'm off-kilter. I have to thank Julia and Chris, in particular, for being hugely supportive, as they have been since I met them. Chris — who started off as just a reader — has helped me out at events, becoming my ersatz assistant at times when there was no way I could have done it all on my own, as well as my front-row cheerleader. My son — "the spawn," as we have come to call him — has also stepped in as PA to make things possible when I wasn't up to doing them alone, and he has my deep thanks and appreciation as well.

My author friend Jilleen Dolbeare has remained a strong presence in my corner, despite her own urban fantasy and women's paranormal fiction series having taken off, and I can always count on my amazing author friend L.A. McBride to cheer right along, even though I haven't managed to get my urban fantasy series going full-steam yet. The amazing Kaylene Winter and her PA, Willow, have also been a huge help in getting the word out about my series, even though it's fantasy, as well as being in Kaylene's own genre of rockstar romance. Thanks go, too, to all the other amazing author friends who have given me space in their newsletters, shared my books with their readers and joined in to celebrate new releases!

Lending reality to Lyric's single-mom life is some personal experience of my own, so thanks go again to the spawn, as well as to Mez's mom and fellow author Katherine "Liz" Cook, whom I watched handle the challenges of parenting an autistic child from Day 1. That brings me to my own mom, who's done a lot of smoothing of the ways for my second, simultaneous career. Without her, you might not be reading this book. Thank a mom in her honor. This book is dedicated to her.

Thanks also go to all my friends, co-workers, fellow authors and other professional contacts who have offered their support, shared word of my books or otherwise helped make all this possible. That especially includes Shaun, who served as a sensitivity reader for sections of this story that reference Native Americans. Shaun is mostly Inuit (my "in-house Eskimo," as I call him, with his blessing), as well as Athabaskan Indian, and his laidback warmth and geeky (in all the best ways) enthusiasm has long been a touchstone for me. My warmest appreciation also goes to our real-life Nanticoke Indian Tribe, which hosts such a wonderful powwow near Millsboro, Del., each September, welcoming so many to enjoy and learn about their culture and that of other tribes. (And to eat that amazing frybread!)

I also want to give a nod to the real-life Funland amusement park in Rehoboth Beach, Del. The real-life Haunted Mansion dark ride got a cameo in this story, and it's well-deserved, as it is just as much of a legend among dark-ride enthusiasts as I described it in the book. It's simpler, more retro than Disney's version, and that's one of the things that makes it the draw that it is. I have no idea what the staff would do if someone offered to buy another person's ride photo, celebrity or otherwise, but the Funland staff and owners are amazing people, so I imagine it would be a lot like what happened in this story. (Note: this element of the story was planned well before I found out Disney was making another "Haunted Mansion" movie, releasing right around when this book will be released. Another great bit of Mystic Beach serendipity.)

Finally, thanks go to my dear friend Al Cook, who once again served as my musical consultant and was generous enough to again allow me to "borrow" one of his songs to include in the book. "Lullaby" has long been one of my favorite compositions of his, and I hope you'll all love it as much as I do. When I conceived of this story, I knew that was the song that would be one of its centerpieces. I'll once again post a link to the song on my social media, so you can hear it for yourselves!

I said "finally," but this set of acknowledgments would not be complete without thanking you, the reader, for reading this, and for all of your support over the last year and a half. Literally, none of this happens without you! So, give yourself a pat on the back for me! I am endlessly grateful for you and your support, and I hope this is still just the beginning of a long and happy author-reader relationship to come! You rock!

ABOUT THE AUTHOR

Aislinn Archer is an award-winning journalist, columnist and photographer, music and tech journalist, and editor, as well as a semi-retired live sound engineer.

She is in the process of writing two interconnected series spanning the urban fantasy and rockstar romance genres, set in her personal stomping grounds in Coastal Delaware. She is a member of Mensa and the Order of Bards, Ovates & Druids.

In her free time, Aislinn is an Irish language learner, persistent advanced-beginner guitar and bass guitar player, photographer, foodie, gadget guru, jewelrymaker and lampwork glass artist. She is a voracious reader of the urban fantasy, fantasy and rockstar romance genres, and dedicated music fan across many genres. Aislinn also loves attending concerts and spending time on the beach.

For release updates, freebies, sneak peeks and inside details, sign up for her newsletter on her website at AislinnArcher.com, and follow Aislinn Archer on social media, at https://www.f acebook.com/AislinnArcher; on Twitter @AislinnArcher; and on Instagram and TikTok @aislinnarcher. Visit her websites at AislinnArcher.com and MysticBeachRocks.com.

amazon.com/Aislinn-Archer/e/B09TQP3S3Q/

goodreads.com/author/show/22271645.Aislinn_Archer

bookbub.com/authors/aislinn-archer

facebook.com/AislinnArcher

instagram.com/AislinnArcher

tiktok.com/@aislinnarcher

twitter.com/aislinnarcher